The Kreiser Affair

The Kreiser Affair

To Editha —
Thanks so much and best wishes.
[signature]
12/2/09

G.K. Sutton

Copyright © 2009 by G.K. Sutton.

Library of Congress Control Number: 2009904291
ISBN: Hardcover   978-1-4415-3399-9
              Softcover   978-1-4415-3398-2

All rights reserved. No part of this book may be reproduced or transmitted in any form or by any means, electronic or mechanical, including photocopying, recording, or by any information storage and retrieval system, without permission in writing from the copyright owner.

This is a work of fiction. Names, characters, places and incidents either are the product of the author's imagination or are used fictitiously, and any resemblance to any actual persons, living or dead, events, or locales is entirely coincidental.

Cover photo—exterior Washington National Cathedral by David Krohne. Used with permission; all rights reserved.

Author photo—author at console of Spivey Hall by J. O. Love. Used with permission; all rights reserved.

This book was printed in the United States of America.

To order additional copies of this book, contact:
Xlibris Corporation
1-888-795-4274
www.Xlibris.com
Orders@Xlibris.com

Were the whole realm of nature mine,
that were an offering far too small;
love so amazing, so divine,
demands my soul, my life, my all.

Isaac Watts (1674-1748)
excerpt, *When I survey the wondrous cross*
(preferably to the tune *Rockingham*)

Foreword

Again I begin by apologizing for writing an introduction. It is expected, and there are some people who would not read a book without the obligatory first somnolent pages. In fact, my three-and-one-half friends count on the foreword as a safe alternative to prescription sleep medications. Therefore, I put a lot of effort into this. I'm either getting better or worse—the foreword and the book are longer.

I must ask my readers' indulgence. This is a "racy" novel. There is sex, more than usual, although I hope not an overabundance in quantity or graphic detail. I don't want this to be deemed a 'trashy novel'. If you are offended, just tear those pages out and keep reading.

The setting for this novel is far removed from the world of Amanda Child's small-town fundamentalist Christian upbringing and its long and safe list of unpardonable sins. Instead we have momentarily relocated to another jurisdiction, that of the small big city, if anything about sprawling Atlanta and its 'suburbs' can be called 'small'. The protagonist Charlotte Lawson is steeped in the fondue pot of old heritage-rich Atlanta and the Southern cultural mystique, mixed with the new generation of wealthy progressive cosmopolitanites.

Never doubt there is a method to my madness. I have tried to distill within the murder plot and underlying story a snapshot of modern-day unrequited love, people's need to love and be loved, and their fixations on how they perceive the best means to achieve the end. This concept is no longer merely the favorite subject of troubadours, but fuels a multi-billion dollar media industry.

People have over the centuries thrashed about mistaking many emotions for love. In fact, the legends are legion over the ages about those artists and musicians who choose someone to adore intentionally because the latter is unattainable. The word 'love' is bandied about pretty loosely in our age, encompassing warm fuzzy feelings, a sexual encounter, an obsession or compulsion, many things mistaken for love or mixed in with love. This is the underlying theme I wanted to develop as my backdrop.

Anyway, on to other things. I was castigated for not divulging the sites pictured on the cover on my first book, *The Witherspoon Legacy*. The church was the Princeton University Chapel, built by Ralph Adams Cram in the 1920s. The angels wrapping across the top of the cover are a feature of an organ case found in the fair city of Stockholm. As of this writing the photographer Joe Routon is somewhere in mystical India, so I cannot ask him to recall the actual location. The picture of the author was taken by J.O. Love while I was sitting at the console of the Mander organ (the first one—they have two now) residing at Peachtree Road United Methodist Church, Atlanta, at its dedication service. No, I didn't play the dedication—'twould be more punishment than the world could bear. The people asking you to play dedication recitals want the instrument to sound good for some reason. I didn't grasp that concept, so I'm not asked to do those anymore.

The decision regarding the current cover pictures was made only after protracted discussion and attempts to obtain just the right photos. I of course have the final say, and take the full blame for the final product. You cannot imagine the number of times I and others took photos of Christ the King Cathedral in Atlanta, just to be disappointed in the final results. I finally took it as a sign from God that it was not meant to be, and instead was presented a gift of this wonderful exterior view of Washington National Cathedral, right after my visit there over Easter weekend. Gratefully I latched onto it with the tenacity of a kid presented with an ice cream cone. Thanks to my friend David Krohne for parting with the permission for its use.

Forgive me a moment while I digress. I must acknowledge with overwhelming gratitude the efforts of William Van Pelt. Bill is the Executive Director for the Raven recording brand, and a great photographer in his own right, known by many organists as a mighty champion for the Organ Historical Society. His knowledge and wit are vast, and he was a godsend to me. He helped me track the provenance of several potential cover photos. He even tried to make others' attempts into something I could use, and doctored a photo taken of me. That alone was a task worse than ingesting spun fiberglass, and his work is a marvel, far eclipsing deKooning's portraits of me in a former life. However, although my eyes were and are a breathtaking blue, the rest of me is such a put-off that the likeness (very realistic, I must say) frightened me as well as dogs and small children.

So again I turned to my archives to find something as inoffensive as possible. Kudos to J.O. Love again for the photo of my broad backside at the Spivey Hall console, circa 2002. This is such a lovely room, and I was grateful for the opportunity to explore the organ for myself, thanks to Larry Embury making the necessary arrangements with Richard Morris, Robert Serrendell and Sherryl Nelson.

Of course, there are many other people to thank. I'm hoping to remember most of them, and know with my premature aging I will not succeed. However, there are all those people who encouraged me, actually ordered and read my first book, and said nice things to or about me afterward. Those who sent me favorable comments have made it all worthwhile, and have created a monster, for here I am again.

There is a plethora of people from the Atlanta area who went out of their way to assist me in obtaining contacts, information and access to venues as part of my research. Among them are the members of the Atlanta Chapter of the American Guild of Organists, including but not limited to Bill Coscarelli, who actually forwarded my inquiry to the members and provided helpful suggestions; J. Franklin Clark (who contributed some of his valuable time to meet with me on a Saturday, and shared some interesting anecdotes); Sue Goddard (who has remained in touch, made inquiries for me, and has even promoted my first book!); Herb Buffington (who I accidentally stood up! what a sweetheart he is); Sarah Hawbecker (who let me sit through a wedding in the choir at her church); Jeffrey McIntyre (who showed me the 'crypt' in the basement of the Shrine); Don Land; Josh Duncan and Daisy Luckey, both who made great meal companions and provided ideas.

I must mention again with gratitude my friend Larry Embury, resident organist at the Fox Theatre, for lodgings, introductions, entertainment, wonderful food, and suggestions over several trips the last few years. Few friends would offer to be murdered to further my writing career, but he graciously proffered to allow me to kill him off at the Fox console. Thankfully, I decided the world was not ready for Larry's demise. I have not played the Fox, even though Larry has offered several times, but it is only because I quail in terror before the myriad of bells and whistles at the organist's disposal. To paraphrase the psalmist, 'such knowledge is too wonderful for me; . . . I cannot attain it.' And Larry knows how to wield them all to great effect, in an impressive room. A definite must-see is this gem of a theatre.

An overwhelming thanks goes to Frederick Swann, who not only looked up one of his Spivey Hall recital programs for me, but provided information and permission for me to include him as an actual character in this book. Fred is a phenomenal musician of international fame, who has done his time at the great Riverside Church in New York City, the Crystal Cathedral, and First Congregational Church in Los Angeles, to name a few of his illustrious 'jobs'. He has also served as former national American Guild of Organists President and one of the greatest current ambassadors for the instrument.

Not only that, but he is a charming and gracious man, never too busy to respond and assist. I am deeply indebted to him for all his help during this project. He reviewed my manuscript and provided valuable editing points and brainstorming. We debated whether the organ in Aunt Mellie's salon should have three or four manuals. I cannot thank him enough.

As always, I shall warn you that all the characters (except for Fred) are purely fictional, and not based on any actual persons. The characters are not intended to exhibit any similarities to actual persons, and I am not casting any aspersions at great Atlanta performers/teachers such Timothy Albrecht, Richard Morris and others, all of whom I admire. However, I did intersperse allusions to very real people and places in this book, and hope they are recognizable. I did not identify many of the churches and other venues, but they exist (except for the Cain residence on Lake Spivey; don't go knocking on doors asking to look in people's salons for the organ). To name a few: Abbey Simon is one of the most unforgettable interpreters of Chopin and Ravel piano repertoire. Maurice Durufle, Johann Sebastian Bach, Johannes Brahms, Sergei Rachmaninoff, Claude Debussy, Maurice Ravel, Cesar Franck and Louis Vierne composed some of the most sublime music we may enjoy today. And of course, Virgil Fox, who spent time in Atlanta, Emilie Spivey, who among many other lasting legacies left us the wonder which is Spivey Hall, E. Power Biggs, Joyce Jones, Michael Murray, and Marie Claire Alain (this list is not exhaustive) are or were real persons, great performers all.

There are those who have provided much influence in a general way. Those that I named in the foreword to the last book I again include. My college English professor Lawrence Maddock very graciously provided me comments after the first book. Although I will never be Thomas Wolfe (the dead one, or the living one for that matter), Dr. Maddock's forcing me to read much great literature and to write (at the time I thought it was emotional torture in some cases) aggravated the dilemma you face in reading my drivel today (in other words, I am passing on the favor).

In addition there is Tom Bartholomew, who built the tiny organ at St. Agatha's Episcopal Church, DeFuniak Springs, a lovely instrument deliberately reminiscent of the one found at St. James' Church, Great Packington, England, where legend has it George Frederick Handel himself was consulted as to design and stoplist. Tom allowed the tiny church to realize its dream of a pipe organ, and it is still a shining gem where I served as organist for many years.

Finding dedicated proofreaders is always a challenge, and I have been fortunate in that regard so far. Among these were Owen Burdick, Marietta Bricker, Sheri Hundley, and Fred Swann himself, as well as my husband Rick. Even though as a modern-day lawyer I draft all my own pleadings and orders on computer, I find proofreading my own stuff a difficult task, so am happy to find others ready to share that load and find my gaffes. My gratitude knows no bounds. I'm always thrilled if someone made it through one of my books.

I want to dedicate this not only to Almighty God, through and by whom all things are possible, but also to his gift of my father Aubrey Andrews, who would probably beat my butt for writing some of the scenes you will find. He was a self-educated man who worked hard to provide for us, who could pick up any string or keyboard instrument and play it very well by ear, who could listen to music and reproduce it, and who had the opportunity to become a star, but chose his family first. He arranged for my first piano lesson the day I completed first grade, and inspired me, by word and example, to always be the best I could be. He was a bright star, and I miss him.

My next release, God willing, will be a sequel to *The Witherspoon Legacy*, and we shall return to small-town Mainville to recount the trouble awaiting Amanda Childs (did you think she lived happily ever after? Pshaw! That dog ain't gonna hunt in my field).

PART ONE

I come to bury Caesar, not to praise him.
The evil that men do lives after them;
The good is oft interred with their bones;
So let it be with Caesar.

From *Julius Caesar,* Act III, Scene 2
William Shakespeare (1564-1616)

Chapter 1

The subdued light of the overcast afternoon outside filtered through the mostly azure stained glass of the immense ornate windows as the rolling measures of Cesar Franck's *Choral in A minor* roared throughout the dim cathedral, filling the room, straining to burst forth. The music pushed its way inexorably past the elaborate marble altar, then, thwarted in its attempt to escape, doubled back into the cavernous nave. The only light in the nave originated from the accent lighting throwing relief upon the carved stone reredos over the altar depicting the crucifixion, and in the loft by the two small pendant lights hanging under each organ chest flanking the organ console, itself illuminated only by the keydesk lamp.

The source of the sounds was the pipe organ housed in the rear gallery, standing as sentinel over the entrance to the nave. The stone walls of the gallery were almost oppressive, cocooning the space they surrounded. Two flanking divisions supported rows of chests, which in turned imprisoned a host of pipes, from sixteen feet to a mere inch in length, surrounding and framing an imposing rose window, in turn visually supported by two tall stained-glass windows. Twin divisions of pipes perched in formation on either side of the window, with mouths open like a divided English choir of Edvard Munch figures. They made their cries heard, their multi-frequencied pleas for release reverberating against the hard surfaces of wood, marble, and stone throughout the darkened church.

In the center of the loft rested the console, encased in matching paneling. On either side of the three stacked manuals were numerous neat if intimidating rows of round wooden drawknobs, their cheerful little white faces bearing the names of the pipe ranks they controlled. Surrounding the console were rows of oak choir chairs. Overhead pointed arches met to form an elaborate canopied ceiling over the nave of the church. The small pendant chandeliers hung under the canopy of the twin organ facades, illuminating the gallery, which lay suspended between the oaken and stone heaven and the tiled aisles and pine floors bearing pews in neat rows.

The lithe figure at the organ console in the back gallery seemed much too petite to produce such an abundance of decibels. She busily brought the piece to a thunderous if awkward and screeching close, then timidly sat, her hands folded in front of her, breathlessly awaiting the verdict, her white gauzy blouse and short denim skirt making her appear even younger.

"You never cease to amaze me, Miss Rhodes," a deep voice broke the silence. She visibly tensed as the man drew nearer. "The Franck sounds much improved. I listened downstairs. I notice you took my advice on registration changes. You perform so much better when you practice and concentrate," Professor Kreiser added, a glint in his eye.

He was tall, lean and strong, exuding a vitality adding to the indecipherability of his age, his skin handsomely tanned. His short wavy hair was carefully groomed; the gray at his temples and the severe chiseled features of his face only magnified his Greek-godlike appearance. He was dressed in pressed pleated gray trousers and a herringbone tweed jacket over a starched white oxford shirt. He loosened his inevitable tie as he shrugged off his jacket and neatly folded it, laying it over a nearby chair.

"It's warm in here," he remarked. "That's why the reeds sound out of tune. Frank the sexton must have been overruled by Gladys the secretary on the AC settings again. That's a woman who blunders where angels fear to tread."

He teasingly ran one long finger lightly along her arm, and she jumped. "Lighten up a little, Miss Rhodes. I'm not going to gore you too badly today," he smirked, as he bent forward toward the score before her. "Why are you so uptight? Relax. Your jury is complete, I've already determined your semester grade, and the term is almost over. In fact, I'm cutting your lesson short today. You'll soon have the whole summer to enjoy without me. We must give you plenty of projects."

"Yes, sir," she attempted a wary smile as he picked up a pencil and circled a measure.

"Your performance today is much improved. I only wish you had exerted as much effort earlier in the year."

He warmed to his task as he began rifling through the pages, circling a measure here, pointing out a dropped note and a rest not taken, at one point slashing the score and counting to her, playing the melody interspersed with accompaniment with his slender, strong fingers. He was precise in his remarks, one minute cold and biting, the next warm and animated, making her play back passages as he lectured her on delivery, reaching around her from time to time to demonstrate a particular fingering pattern or technique.

Taken aback at his rare compliment and galvanized by his attention, Cecelia Rhodes blushed. She was accustomed to his caustic criticism and angry scrawls on her musical scores in his illegible script, creating in her a havoc of reactions, from silent submission to flushes of temper and tears when she sensed he was baiting her, testing whether she was reading the assigned reference literature. Sometimes she was certain that he provoked her purposefully, his lectures about her practice habits and his sardonic remarks regarding deficiencies in her performance carefully honed to feint, then to wound. She took each criticism to heart. Kreiser's encomiums were too rare for her to be equipped to deal with them; she was reduced to a stammering silence, and he knew it and appeared to enjoy those infrequent moments of her discomfiture.

It was thus with all his students, she had been informed, but still she always felt singled out. He was demanding, seldom pleased, and always driving his flock of pupils relentlessly, mercilessly toward his ideal.

Yet Kreiser was touted as one of the very best organ instructors in the country. A long queue of hopefuls had auditioned, and she had been extremely fortunate to secure the slot as one of the tiny entourage of his current pupils. She knew her cousin Katharine Fellowes' influence with Kreiser had borne no small part in Cecelia's obtaining the coveted position.

But Cece, as her friends called her, didn't care how she got it. She always admired Kreiser's string of past recorded flawless performances and the adulation heaped upon him by the music and art community, both in Atlanta and elsewhere in the music world. Most of his former students had gone on to distinguish themselves, winning competitions and securing coveted positions around the world in the performing and teaching communities.

Her emotions toward the man bordered on hero-worship, and she entertained girlish fantasies, both about her teacher and her future as an organist, before each grueling session, and nursed her shredded ego after each lesson. And when her neighbor and idol Stefan Chadwick had become Kreiser's current star student, she became determined to vie for the master's attention.

Kreiser continued, methodical, his eyes on the score, oblivious to his effect on the girl. "Let me guess. You are attempting to model yourself after Michael Murray's recording."

Cecelia gasped. "How did you know?"

He waved her to silence peremptorily. "Please don't. Much as I like this instrument, it is not a Cavaille-Coll. Bring something of yourself to this music, a little less stiff, although you could certainly use some of his strictness of tempo in this last section here. You must fall in love with this piece, to make it your own. You are not there yet. It is not just some notch on your figurative gunbelt of repertoire. While it is the simplest and my least favorite of the three chorals, it is not chopped liver, and is still impressive music in the right hands."

His face softened as he continued, almost to himself, giving in momentarily to a pleasurable memory. "The *Adagio* theme is such a lovely melody, like the taste of a buttery cabernet on a beautiful woman's lips. Do you ever just listen to it? You must—let it get under your skin and seduce you. Only then can you understand it. Here, a little manipulation of the expression pedal, please."

He paused momentarily. "I recall a performance by a former student, seems like only yesterday. She was no more than a child, but so exquisite, you could taste it . . ."

He broke off abruptly, as if embarrassed. His expression became fathomless again, and his tone returned to its business-like cadence. "In other words, slow it down a bit, make it last, like a long kiss. *Legato*, Miss Rhodes. Don't you know what that means? Apparently you don't. Look it up. That's why you need to study my suggested fingerings."

He pointed. "Here at measure 142, whose notes are these?"

"Yours, Professor," she smiled tremulously at him.

"And can you read this horrible handwriting?"

"Yes, sir," she nodded, smiling more broadly at what she perceived as a joke, falling into his trap. "'Make pedal very pronounced'."

"And these exclamation points after that—did you get the impression during the last two lessons when we discussed this I meant this as a mere suggestion?"

She blanched, realizing her error. "I thought I—"

"Well, you didn't. Do you know where I came up with that idea?"

She faltered, realizing what was coming. "Tournemire?" she almost whimpered.

"You only know that because I told you last time," he accused, his voice cold. "You didn't bother to go back and read the perhaps two pages of his discussion of this piece for yourself, did you?"

Before she could answer, he continued. "And this latter," he turned a couple more pages, gesticulating with a pencil, tapping the score impatiently, "*mon Dieu*, it needs to be fast, yes, but don't make it sound like a runaway train. More of a controlled swirl. When Tournemire says Franck played it freely, he didn't give you leave to allow the music to disintegrate into cacophony. Don't throw the tempo completely out the window. It's hard, but not that hard. Work on that, please. Don't forget the accents; rein it in." Finally dropping the pencil on the music desk, he turned away, curtly dismissive.

Trembling in awe, she murmured. "I do love Franck. I thought about starting the *Priere* this summer."

He turned to her, his face hard. "No," he startled her with his vehemence. "You must play no piece before you are ready. The reach of the *Priere* is not right for you yet. That's why I give you the exercises you continue to ignore. You still have to master the *Choral.*"

Her heart caught in her throat at his words, and tears stung her eyes. She lowered her eyes. "Yes, sir. I'm sorry I'm not as good as Stefan."

"Where did that come from?" he demanded angrily. He looked at her fallen expression. "Look at me." He held her eyes in a long heart-stopping gaze, his voice reproachful. "The *A minor* is your piece. Finish what you have started—only one Franck at a time, please."

He stared beyond her into the dim church, his attention diverted momentarily by some sound. He finally turned back to her. "Miss Rhodes, you are not Stefan, nor are you Michael Murray. You are your own person, with your own strengths and weaknesses." His eyes became steely, boring into hers. "Do not be jealous of Stefan. Stefan is a natural born talent, but he drives himself and practices hard. He reads the required material, he does the exercises, he follows my advice. If you did the same, there's no telling how good you might be."

He sighed. "If I didn't think you worthy to teach, you would not be my student. You are not in competition here, something I think you keep forgetting."

He noted her downcast expression, and he turned away gruffly. "Don't rush the process, Cecelia." She started at his use of her Christian name. "You are young; there is time. If you love Franck so much, you need to start on the *Cantabile*, get some practice this summer on it. It will serve you much better in the future than the *Priere*. Work on the exercises. How many times must I preach that? What about the Rheinberger? We did not get to it today. You are working on it? Not all your repertoire needs to be *fortissimo*. I think we need to hear some of it for next Friday's lesson, so that I can give you some pointers before you're off for the summer."

"What about some Durufle?"

He turned away, hiding a grimace. "Miss Rhodes, playing Durufle requires a level of technique and commitment you have not heretofore attained." His bluntness was cutting. "Next week I'll present you a list of what I want to hear—well," he corrected himself, "what I want you to work on this summer."

He sighed again, placing his hand on the wood of the console lovingly. "I'm tired," he muttered. "I will miss you, old friend," he whispered, before turning back to his student. "That will be all today, Miss Rhodes."

The lesson concluded, Cecelia swung off the bench and moved away reluctantly, bending down to unlatch her organ shoes, her form slender and her shoulder-length auburn hair falling as a curtain over her eyes. As Kreiser took her place at the organ bench and punched a combination piston while drawing on additional stops in preparation for playing, Cecelia countered lightly, a slight tremor in her voice, "Would you just die if I told you I really don't like Rheinberger's music that much and have no desire to learn it?" Her voice echoed through the gallery eerily.

She again tensed, as though steeling herself against his angry reproof and lecture. But it didn't come. Instead, there was a loud report, a second of reverberation, then the piercing discordant shock of something heavy landing on the manuals activated for full registration. She squealed in fright. As she wheeled and saw Kreiser slumped over the console, for a split second she thought she saw a figure, all in black, standing half hidden behind a column downstairs.

A second shot, then a third, whistled above her head, and sparks flew as the pendant lights on either side of the organ console came crashing down in the sudden dimness. She covered her head and dived for the floor as the air filled with the explosion of metal and glass fragments and the gallery was plunged into darkness, one of the fixtures landing just inches from where she had been standing.

Cecelia raised up on her knees, shaking. Through the deafening thunder of the still depressed keys she thought she heard the sound of a door slamming. She stood, crouching, trying to peer over the gallery, but could see no one. Unmindful of the glass shards littering the floor and the cloud of dust and debris, she clambered back toward the organ bench, feeling her way.

"Doctor K, are you all right?" she coughed through the dark and dust as she unsuccessfully called over the sound of the organ. She reached out toward where she had last seen him sitting on the bench. "Dr. Kreiser!" she cried again, as she stood and pulled him off the console. His weight shifted and fell heavily against her. Her stockinged feet slipped on the polished wood floor. Losing her balance, she screamed out as she fell backward, unable to check the momentum of their combined fall, and landed heavily on the floor beside the bench, pinned under his inert form.

"Help!" she choked breathlessly. Stunned and winded, she lay there momentarily, passively. She finally wiggled her arms free. She gently pushed at the tall man. It took some time to maneuver herself free of him. As she bent over him and her eyes adjusted to the dimness, she turned his head to face her, thinking to feel the side of his neck for a pulse like she had seen on a television program.

The emergency lights flashed on, blinding her. She blinked. She noted a dark stain on her white blouse and saw his lifeless eyes, the exit wound of a bullet marring the center of his forehead.

Chapter 2

Chief Investigator Mark Roberts, Atlanta Police Department, arrived at the church already crawling with men in uniform. Tall and muscular, he was dressed in a dark tan suit, the jacket of which fit his shoulders perfectly and concealed his holstered handgun and badge. He made a striking figure, moving fluidly.

Roberts spoke briefly with a uniformed officer guarding the front door from a gaggle of sight-seers and the press. In response to Mark's query, the officer pointed the way to the gallery and gave directions. Thanking the officer, Roberts unconsciously ran his fingers through his dark wavy hair as he turned toward the stairs.

After passing the narrow darkened narthex dotted with people—some police, herding a few others he guessed were employees or members of the church, their demeanor ranging from confused to curious to frantic—Roberts finally jogged up the stairwell and found himself in the loft overlooking the nave of the church, where several plainclothes crime-scene operatives were already gathering evidence. Worklights had been set up in the gathering dusk of the gallery.

Walking up to a disheveled-looking man in a khaki colored suit, with salt-and-pepper military-cropped hair and furrowed expression examining the organ case, Roberts spoke. "Have you decided to take up the organ, Will?"

The older man grunted without looking around. "More like contemplating how to avoid organ destruction. I'm trying to determine where the fatal bullet ended up, and it looks like the trail ends there," he pointed to the stone wall under the large rose window, to an area between the two slim stain-glass windows, where a graze and chip in the wall could be seen, and fragments littered the floor.

"But there was apparently a second and third shot which took out the cables holding the two small lights. Hard to tell yet whether the shots were at the same or a different trajectory from the first shot," he mused aloud, walking over to the right and peering up at the pipes for signs of trauma. "The guys have brought in some lights to help. But we're still going to have to come back tomorrow during daylight for a second look.

"The prime witness is still pretty incoherent—someone heard her screaming and found him and her," he replied, pointing first toward the body on the floor, then to the corner of the gallery near the back wall. Sitting on a chair was a young woman, looking like not much older than a girl, her face tear-streaked as an EMT stood by and an officer engaged her in conversation and busily took notes.

"Is she a suspect?"

"If so, we found no weapon on her or in the building yet," Will smirked.

Approaching her, Mark noticed that her eyes were red from crying, and that her white blouse was stained with blood. Roberts caught the eye of the officer, who straightened up and addressed him.

"Captain Roberts, this is Cecelia Rhodes. She was a student of the deceased. His name was Wilhelm Kreiser, organ professor at Emory. She alleges that they were just completing a lesson when the incident occurred. She states that she can't identify the shooter."

Roberts studied the girl closely, as she turned her full gaze on him. She was petite, with luxurious chestnut hair waving around her shoulders. Her eyes were deep brown. He asked solicitously, "Are you hurt?"

She stared at him wonderingly, at first uncomprehending, then shook her head as he pointed to the blood on her clothes. "No, just cut up a little and shook up from the fall."

"Fall?" Roberts echoed, concerned.

"When I ran over to check on him, I pulled him off the console, and he fell on top of me," Cecelia explained. "We ended up on the floor. He—" she faltered, "he was already dead." Tears filled her eyes again.

Under Roberts' gentle questioning the story unfolded. He finally asked, "Were you able to see the shooter?"

She shook her head sadly, tears spilling over. "Not more than a second. I had my back to the altar, and looked over at Dr. K when I heard the shot and the sound of the organ. The only lights on were these in the gallery and those over the altar over there. I thought I saw someone all in black standing below," she pointed. "But then I heard two more shots and saw a light coming at me and dodged it. I heard a door slam. That was all."

"So you have no idea whether it was man or woman, build, shape, clothing?"

"Not really," she admitted ruefully. "Tall and thin, dressed in black, dark shortish hair. It was only a second."

"Can you tell us what time this happened?" Will asked.

"My lesson is generally from three to four," the girl sniffed. "We started late today, because I was—delayed. But he cut the lesson short. I don't know, a little after four, maybe."

"Was anyone else in the gallery with you and the Professor at any time?"

"No one to my knowledge."

"Have you seen anyone in the church while you've been here?"

She shook her head mutely.

The man referred to as Will had walked up and was listening intently to her replies. Suddenly he interrupted. "You saw the light coming at you in the dark?" he demanded.

The girl flushed. "I mean—I heard the shots whiz above me and the lights flickered off. I sort of felt or heard the 'whoosh' of it." She stammered, then was silent.

"How many shots?" Will persisted.

"Three. They were all close together," the girl supplied tremulously.

Will turned to Roberts. "Victim was shot only once—went right through the back of the deceased's neck and out his forehead. But something had to cut those lights. We're still looking for those. If nothing else, we may need to send a man into the organ to see if he can determine the path and try to locate any projectiles."

Cecelia spoke up quickly. "The ladders to the chambers are inside the doorways behind the division. It's close and dangerous in there. He must be small and careful not to dislodge the pipes. That's a million-dollar instrument."

Will looked at her quizzically. "You've been up there?"

"Once or twice. Every now and then a pipe ciphers, and it is easier to fix it myself than to call a technician. Dr. K thought we should know enough about the inner workings of the organ to keep from bothering the organ techs for piddly stuff."

"This organ tech—can you give me his name, how to contact him?"

She quickly reeled off the information. "The company services many organs in the area."

Will looked at her dubiously. He addressed Roberts, his voice lowered. "I'm not entirely sure, but the trajectory looks like the weapon could have been fired from floor level, but that would make the shooter a minimum of 75 feet away. Damn fine shot."

Roberts concurred. "Excellent. What about the others?"

"Right through the cables holding the chandeliers is my guess," Will pointed to first one, then the other dangling cable. "Need to get someone up there and examine the cable, as well as these front pipes."

Cecelia looked at the fallen twisted metal of the light fixture nearest them and shuddered dramatically.

Mark said, his voice low so that only Will could hear him, "Well, that limits the number of possible suspects."

Roberts stared at Cecelia a moment, then addressed her. "Are you aware of anyone who would have a motive to take out the professor?"

Cecelia shook her head. "He was a hard teacher. But I could not imagine someone wanting to kill him." Her eyes welled with tears again.

Will asked brusquely, "Do you own a firearm, Miss Rhodes?"

Cecelia returned his level gaze with one of her own. "Yes, I do."

Roberts started, swallowing his surprise. "And where do you keep it?"

"At home, locked in a drawer next to the bed." At his gaze, she added proudly, "My cousin is Gerard Fellowes. I'm sure you've heard of him. He's a champion sharpshooter, and owns his own series of gun clubs. I live with my cousin Kat, his sister."

"What calibre is your weapon?" Will wanted to know.

"A thirty-eight," she answered, her color rising. You don't think I—"

"Nothing personal—just following all leads, ma'am," Will broke in reassuringly.

Another plainclothes officer came up and whispered in Will's ear.

Roberts looked at the cop still taking notes. "Let the medics outside check her out. With all this broken glass around, she may have sustained other cuts. And that fall couldn't have been fun. Thank you, Miss Rhodes. I'll ask Detective Miller to take you home."

Will motioned for Roberts to follow him. Excusing himself, he watched the young woman being led away and followed Will and the other detective as they picked their way through the rubble, making their way to the body on the floor, where a photographer was finishing up, taking directions from the coroner, and the coroner's techs were patiently waiting.

"Only sign on him is the one shot," the coroner spoke, recognizing Roberts. "Through the base of the skull and out the forehead. He didn't know what hit him. I'm guessing between 3:30 and 4:30, but don't hold me to that until we do the autopsy."

"No fancy terms today, Doc?" Will quipped.

"No, Will. I tried to make my explanation simple so you'd understand it," the coroner grinned. "We've done all we can here. Load him up if you're done."

Roberts nodded. He and Will moved out of the way. Reaching the end of the gallery away from the milling group, Will said in a quiet voice, "Randy here has talked to the staff that was here at the approximate time of the shooting. No one saw or heard anything until the janitor came in and heard the girl screaming."

"You think a silencer was used?" Randy Miller asked.

Roberts responded, "Miss Rhodes said she heard the shots. That would have made quite some noise in this acoustic."

The detective named Randy nodded. "The minister was in his office about the same time as the shots, but we've not located him yet. His car is gone. I've had the church secretary page him—no response yet."

Roberts quizzed, "Did any of the staff give you any possible suspects or motives?"

Randy shrugged. "Per the church secretary, very few of the staff are here late Friday afternoons. This Kreiser fellow, the victim, gave lessons, and had the church all to himself. He would stay afterward to practice most Fridays. She said one either loved Kreiser or hated him. She's a virtual font of information. And she volunteered that this Kreiser is head of the organ department at Emory University, and somewhat famous, with an ego to match. She stated that he and the minister could barely conceal their dislike for each other."

"Sounds like some follow-up is in order. Good work, Randy," Will clapped him on the back.

Roberts queried, "I assume that's THE Gerard Fellowes she's talking about?"

Will nodded. "Yep. Most eligible and richest bachelor in these parts. One of the original families settling into Buckhead." He grinned. "Although Randy says they've now been transplanted to Lake Spivey. Real Southern blue bloods."

Roberts mused, "You should find out if Miss Rhodes can shoot as well as Cousin Gerry."

"We'll add that to Randy's list of questions when he takes the girl home," Will smiled at the third man of the team. "He ought to do well with the *femme fatale*, getting her statement and her pistol for testing." He looked quizzically at Roberts. "Mark, don't you have contacts at the university?"

"I'm on it," Roberts nodded. I'll see what information I could get about Kreiser, his students, contacts, whatever else we need."

"And Will," Roberts added with a mocking grin as he pointed to the organ, "that's a million-dollar instrument. Try not to make the police department liable for replacing it. I'd call that tech if I were you."

Chapter 3

The next morning, Mark Roberts arrived at the police department early, a list of names and a large book in hand. He was dressed casually in tan cotton twill trousers and a blue oxford shirt. At the largely empty police station's investigations office, he found only Will, in a rumpled suit that appeared to be a twin to his previous day's outfit, leafing through a sheaf of papers on an old battered massive wooden desk.

Pouring himself a cup of coffee and seating himself across the desk from Will, Roberts asked, "How's it going?"

"Randy was up most of the night going through Kreiser's house for clues. He's on his way here." Will didn't look up. "We also scoured the church and took some better pictures this morning. What's your take?"

Roberts looked at some of the photos and frowned. "We're looking at a marksman. Maybe hired? Maybe gunning for Kreiser for a personal reason? Was the gunman after the student as well? Easy to do, if he was that good a shot. Why take out the lights? I don't know."

Will pawed through his handwritten notes. "Best I can tell, the shooter did all the damage from one spot. That kind of shooting would make Annie Oakley jealous. We already have plenty of work to do. This Kreiser has two ex-wives. We are trying to get them in for interviews. The minister, or head priest, or Dean, whatever they call him, a Rev. Charles Wolverly, was pathetically fake in his sympathy, more concerned about cleaning up the blood, crime scene tape and policemen from his church before the Sunday services. He was not happy about cancelling the Saturday mass."

"Did you find out where he was during the incident?"

"He claims he had just left for the day, stopping off at the hospital downtown to see a parishioner. We checked. He was seen at the hospital. But that doesn't necessarily give him an alibi."

"You've solved the crime," Mark laughed. "The padre did it."

"Except that he's virulently anti-gun, anti-war, anti-nukes, even in the pulpit. But according to the church secretary, maybe this Wolverly would make an exception in Kreiser's case."

"What did you get from her?"

"Not me—Randy. He developed some form of bond." Will grinned. "Her name is Gladys Miller, no relation to Randy, or so he says. She apparently didn't like Kreiser or Wolverly. Kreiser was pretty exacting about the church bulletin, and they constantly had a go-round about her malaprops and misspellings. Randy was convinced, after spending some time listening to her, that she was probably passive-aggressive and did the misprints on purpose."

"Well, Randy needed himself a new girl," Mark let slip loudly as Randy sauntered into the room and plopped into the remaining chair.

Detective Miller, trying to tame his unruly sandy waves of hair as he crossed his denimed legs and examined his cowboy boots, yawned. "Not that Gladys woman, please. She was pretty vocal about her antipathy toward the whole world. Apparently Kreiser and she had just had words the day before, Kreiser spelling out 'and' and 'the' to her. When I started asking her about her alibi, what weapons did she own, and the like, I scared her."

"What did she have to say?"

"She had taken a late lunch and apparently picked up the Sunday bulletin from the printer's. She had only returned to the church about the time the first cops arrived on the scene. She didn't see anybody. The janitor and copy center confirmed her story. She told me the padre has only been here a couple of years, and he and Kreiser had an ongoing contest of wills regarding the service. Kreiser apparently won most of the battles, because he had the major money-bags of the church on his side.

"Kreiser apparently also had the run of the place because of the organ, which he managed to upgrade several years ago with the help of a wealthy member. The good reverend apparently didn't like sharing his authority, and is at odds with the traditional-minded congregation. He was trying to garner support from some of the younger parishioners, holding out for more contemporary music, that sort of thing."

"And the janitor?" Roberts asked.

"One Frank Bailey. Been there twenty years. He had already cleaned the church and was apparently at the dayschool. Said Kreiser was always nice to him. He said he always walks through the church after Kreiser's Friday lessons and locks up at night, sets the alarm. Most of the time Kreiser would still be there playing. When he walked in yesterday, the girl was screaming, and he found the two of them. He had not seen anyone around, said it was a quiet day. He said when he went from the church to the education building that afternoon he thought he saw a shiny black limousine in the staff parking lot beside the church, but then other than admiring it momentarily he didn't think it that unusual. He also saw a little silver or gray car pull into the parking lot at the end of the lot, but inasmuch as people come and go, he didn't pay the driver any mind."

"Who else?"

"We're still following leads, talking to people, but so far we haven't found anyone who saw anything. The church and office doors are normally unlocked during business hours, open to the public until around 9:00 in the evening. The alarm system had a coded password which wasn't all that secret. Vestry members, altar guild, church staff, Kreiser, most of his students, all had the passcode. The church hires security for scheduled events."

"What did you find at Kreiser's place?" Roberts switched subjects.

"We're still checking it out and managed to secure it to do some more work. We're trying to finish up at the church; the padre is breathing down our necks."

"Speaking of students earlier, have you run into any of Kreiser's?" Mark wanted to know.

"We hoped you might have obtained info as to them, since you were at the university yesterday. One came by the church, saw all the cop cars, and stopped. His name was Andy," Will checked his notes, "Andrei Kutuzov. He's a Russian émigré over here to study with Kreiser. He seemed to exhibit some type of adoration for the man. He described Kreiser as making a great dictator, brooking no detractors or slackers, ruling with an iron fist, a tough taskmaster. Likewise, our little eyewitness seemed a bit starry-eyed over him."

"What—this Cecelia that was at the church?" Mark was surprised.

"She kept repeating how wonderful he was, so 'sensitive to the text', whatever the hell that means. She kept crying. We couldn't get her dried up before she started all over again."

Roberts turned to Randy. "What did you think of her?"

"She's pretty slick," Randy replied.

"What do you meant?" Will demanded.

"Well, those tears turned on and off at will. And she says she doesn't know how to shoot. Yet when I accompanied her home, all she could talk about was her cousin's accomplishments, awards, gun shops, firing ranges, and money, as if she was trying to impress me. And," he paused significantly, "there's quite a collection of guns at the family estate."

"Really? Well, I guess that's to be expected," Will remarked. "Fellowes isn't a champion sharpshooter and owner of a national chain of gun stores and firing ranges for nothing. You know, there's little he doesn't know about weapons. He might be of some assistance, particularly interpreting any ballistics evidence. The guys are still crawling around the church today looking for clues, much to the padre's chagrin." He paused. "Who else lives at the family mansion?"

"Miss Rhodes' cousin Katharine Fellowes, Gerard's sister, is apparently the only other person left at the family home. Gerard is in and out, and has his own place in town, apparently."

Roberts intervened. "Did you meet this cousin Katharine?"

"Briefly," Randy responded. "She seemed awfully upset when she heard Kreiser was dead, started crying over 'dear Harry'. But Cecelia said she and Kreiser were rather close, so I guess it was understandable. There was a shiny limousine out front. I went ahead and asked where she had been all day. She seemed a little spacey, like she was on drugs, said she had been sick and home all day. Apparently she has a live-in housekeeper or nurse, who confirmed that. Ms. Fellowes retrieved the girl's gun, put in third-degreeing me about what happened, acting kind of manic. I'm glad I got the girl's statement before taking her home. Then the boyfriend showed up at the house."

"Boyfriend?" Mark echoed.

"Yeah, one Russell McCall. He showed up demanding to see Cecelia, and she clung to him and cried for a while. He seemed rather unsympathetic, described Kreiser as a 'queen asshole', I think were his words. I have him slated for more questions."

"Maybe you'd think so, too, if you were being supplanted in affection by an older dead guy," Mark smirked.

"Yeah, I guess so," Randy grinned. "What about you? What were you able to dredge up?"

Roberts, taking the cue, passed the list he brought in. "The top five names are the current students of Kreiser's. You already know about two of them, apparently. I also enlisted the music school's dean to provide me a list of all Kreiser's past students. Kreiser apparently never takes more than five or six at a time. Dean Jackson also provided us an alumni directory for us to try to track down the past students if necessary."

Will queried, "How did you get all this so easily?"

"Just happened to know the right person," Mark quipped.

Randy, scanning the list, suddenly gave a low whistle. "There are some big names from the music world on this list."

"Yes," Roberts, surprised at Randy's assessment, agreed. "Juilliard, Yale, Curtis professors, and several international recitalists; some competition winners. Dean Jackson pointed them out to me. Impressive—Kreiser was much sought after as an instructor."

"Damn," Randy remarked, "did you recognize this name? Charlotte Lawson?"

Mark nodded. "Arts editor for the *Chronicle*. If I recall the tabloids correctly, it was alleged that she and Kreiser were apparently chummy at one time. And this Stefan Chadwick, one of the current students, is her nephew. I have already left a telephone message at her office. The voice mail said she is out of town."

"Small world," Will quipped, holding up several clear plastic evidence bags.

"What's that?" Roberts reached for the first one.

"Contents of Kreiser's pockets. Usual stuff—wallet, couple of breath mints, some change. But a couple unusual items: an old, very old-looking coin, and a phone message."

"Really?" Roberts looked through the plastic at the pink message sheet, reading the message. "Charlotte Lawson called him yesterday morning, said it was urgent she speak to him. Interesting. And this coin looks pretty ancient—Latin inscription. Maybe something we can trace. What else?" Roberts was interested.

"A wadded up receipt found in the bushes outside the church, the side door just outside the staff/handicapped parking. From Gerard Fellowes' gun club just earlier that day. No name, but something to follow up on. And the weirdest thing ever—there was a book on the altar. A novel, of all things. The priest said it wasn't his, and wasn't there at the time of the Friday morning mass."

"What's the name?" Roberts was interested.

Will handed over the volume in a clear evidence bag. "*One Organist Less* by C. C. Langley. I never heard of it."

"Hmm," Roberts smiled. "Appropriate calling card to leave. Inscription inside?"

"I haven't checked," Will laughed. "I'm allergic to books. Don't destroy any prints."

Roberts pulled out a latex glove from his desk drawer and slid it on, then gingerly pulled the book out by the corner. He opened it and leafed through the first few pages.

"Here we go," he smiled with satisfaction. "'To H-K: All my best, C.L.' Nothing like an autographed first edition." Replacing the tome in the evidence bag, he nodded to Randy. "Some research is in order, maybe even some bedtime reading."

"I didn't remember that she was an organist," Randy mused aloud.

"Who?" Will's brow was wrinkled in confusion.

"Charlotte Lawson."

"Leave it to Markie to snare the looker on the list. Most of these names on the list are guys," grumbled Will good-naturedly.

"With a friend like her, who needs enemies?" muttered Randy.

"What do you mean?" Mark asked, surprised.

"Well, she reviewed one of the victim's recitals a few weeks back. It was less than glowing," Randy replied. "If they were ever 'chummy', as you say, they apparently had a falling-out."

Will jabbed him in the ribs. "I didn't know you were such an art connoisseur, Randy—reading the cultural page."

Randy flushed. "Well, I like classical music, and there are some good recital programs in the city. I try to take them in. And I happen to like this Charlotte Lawson's writing. It's conversational, not stilted or uppity. Besides, she is a looker, as you say."

"Easy on the eyes, huh? Guess we know why you go to the recitals." As Will continued to tease Randy, Mark smiled distractedly.

"Apparently Kreiser must have had a thing for her too," Randy supplied. "In his bedroom was a bulletin board where he had pinned pictures and articles by and about Lawson from the time she was a child until the present. A shrine, if you will."

"Really?" Roberts was suddenly interested. "Sounds like some kind of obsession."

"Yeah," Randy nodded, throwing a photograph down in front of Roberts, who scanned it.

"A couple more items of information," Roberts added, his eyes still on the photo. "Dean Jackson agreed to leave Kreiser's office locked and off limits. But he let me take a glance around until we could get someone out there."

"And?" Will wanted to know.

"Charlotte Lawson had called the university again in the afternoon Friday—another urgent message. Around 3:00 p.m. She grilled Jackson's secretary about Kreiser's schedule. And there was a note scrawled on his desk calendar: 'Gerard Fellowes—4:00'."

Randy exclaimed, "His name keeps popping up. Some very good reasons to make contact with those two. You know it's rumored that they are engaged?"

"Really?" Roberts was thoughtful. He saw several possible leads to pursue with Charlotte Lawson and Gerard Fellowes.

PART TWO

Take me to You, imprison me, for I,
Except You enthrall me, never shall be free,
Nor ever chaste, except You ravish me.

Excerpt, 'Batter my heart', from *Holy Sonnets* (1633)
John Donne (1572-1631)

Chapter 4

Charlotte Lawson awoke with a start. Stretching, she suddenly remembered, I'm nine years old today. She hugged herself happily. That means a treasure hunt.

She loved Uncle Howard's treasure hunts, a tradition he had instituted when she turned five, only months after her parents' untimely death and her sister Amy's and her arrival to live with Melanie and Howard Cain. Melanie Lawson Cain was their father's older sister, and a bastion of Atlanta's elite society. Years ago Melanie Lawson, a Charleston heiress active in musical and artistic endeavors, and Howard Cain, of another proud old wealthy family and head of a large architectural firm who also sat on the board of directors of several other large corporations, had married and joined their fortunes in the match of the decade. The couple settled near Howard's home town of Atlanta, and they had consolidated and multiplied their wealth while also involving themselves in community and philanthropic concerns.

When the two little girls had first arrived at the Cain's estate from their home in Charleston, they had been in shock. The children did not understand the absence of their parents and why they were leaving behind everything they had known and loved. Although they had visited with their aunt and uncle several times, they had never been outside the company of their parents at those times. Then their parents had died suddenly in a plane crash, and the girls were taken in by the Cains, their closest relatives.

Howard had upon his marriage built his bride a sprawling three-story brick home on Lake Spivey, a few miles south of Atlanta, because several of Melanie's new friends in the area were also establishing mini-estates in the area, and because he enjoyed the water and loved to dabble in building small high-gloss wooden motor launches. The woodland was transformed into a large expanse of landscaped lawn, with a gated winding driveway of crape myrtles and azaleas.

Melanie's pride and joy was a formal salon, an expansively ornate room built to accommodate a pipe organ, not a small practice instrument, but a sizable one designed to allow Melanie and her organist guests to play a wide variety of major organ literature. Melanie had spent much time with a renowned organ builder designing the sizable instrument.

Howard, a lover of nature, preserved pockets of native flora, and searched for and planted all species of trees and shrubs, most native to the South and the habitat. He had a modest conservatory and greenhouse, where both he and Melanie shared their love for plants in nursing various species. He also built a capacious boathouse topped by an apartment, and, at Melanie's behest, a wing onto the home for her dear servants Jacob and Daisy to reside on the premises. To this home they brought their two orphaned nieces to live.

Amy, at eight, had been more resilient, had grasped the concept of the finality of her parents' absence, and after a period of grieving transitioned more easily to the strict regime of 'Aunt Mellie', seeing little difference from their mother's rules, the compliance with which she excelled. Amy, always seeking acceptance from her aunt as she had with her mother, quickly established herself as Melanie's favorite.

But Charlotte, four years old, always precocious, turned defiant. She constantly asked questions about her parents, why the girls were there, when were her parents returning, why did they have to follow the rules, what was the reason behind the rules. She cried herself to sleep many nights at first, and awakened screaming from nightmares, shrieking for her father.

Melanie, having had no children of her own and being several years older than her brother, was not accustomed to dealing with small children. Even with the assistance of a series of nurses and governesses, she found Charlotte to be more challenging than she had hoped. Howard, however, wisely understood the reasons behind Charlotte's confusion and revolt. He lost his heart to the younger orphan, and spent much time with her, trying in small ways to make her feel secure, slowly building a rapport with the tiny rebel.

A somewhat divided camp ensued, Melanie favoring the docile Amy, and Howard befriending the mutinous Charlotte and defending her against Melanie's fits of frustration. Melanie, long used to controlling her household with an iron thumb and little resistance, suddenly found her hands full, and relied heavily on Howard's influence with the wayward child in maintaining an uneasy truce in the family.

On Charlotte's fifth birthday, she awoke to find an old coin on the table beside her four-poster bed in her enormous bedroom. Beside it was a note. "Come see," it read. Howard had been teaching her to read a few words, and she recognized and understood them.

Jumping out of bed, she ran to Amy's room, coin in hand. But Amy wasn't there. Calling for her sister, she ran down the ornate staircase to the polished hardwood floor of the large foyer. Forgetting Aunt Mellie's maxim that children were to be seen and not heard, she ran through the house yelling for Amy. Charlotte slid into the breakfast room which opened from the kitchen, her face flushed, to find Amy, resembling an older version of herself with darker hair, also still in her pajamas, staring in wonder at the table.

Uncle Howard was standing there, casually dressed in Dockers and a shirt without tie, balloons in hand. There were presents on the table, and Daisy, a large black woman swallowed up in an enormous white apron, was cooking pancakes.

"Wow!" Charlotte's eyes shone with delight. "For me?"

"For both of you," Melanie, always impeccably dressed in suit and pearls and carefully coiffed, came up behind them, putting her hands on their shoulders. "We thought it a good time to celebrate your making your home with us. Go ahead, sit down, and open your presents."

The girls excitedly climbed in their seats, and were given their presents, which they tore open with glee. Amy received new clothes and a dancing outfit and tutu, plus a card notifying her that she would start ballet lessons. Amy squealed with delight.

Charlotte received books, new clothes and an electronic keyboard. She looked at it for a long time, expressionless. Melanie, exasperated with the child's lack of reaction, finally asked, "Well? What do you think?"

"But we have four of these in the house," she replied curiously.

"Four?" Melanie echoed, her brow furrowed.

Howard smiled, proud that his little student could count, and divining that Charlotte referred to the grand piano in the front parlor and the three-manual pipe organ in the large formal salon. He nodded at Melanie and held up four fingers, silently mouthing, "Four."

Melanie, catching Howard's eye, explained gently, "But you can't play with them until you are older."

Howard, noting the child's confusion, added quietly, "When you learn to play a tune on this, you can have piano lessons, if you wish,"

Melanie looked at Howard sharply. "Don't promise her that," she objected crisply.

"Why not?" Howard responded, his voice low. "She may be the next musician in this family. If she shows the aptitude, feed it," he added. "Did you not begin lessons at the age of five?"

Melanie frowned, not used to be bested at argument by her husband. "Besides," he remarked, a twinkle in his eye, "who knows if she will have any interest in music? Let's see what develops."

Charlotte busied herself with the keyboard, but Amy, suddenly bored, turned to her aunt. "What is this for?" she held up an antique coin.

"Where did that come from?" Melanie demanded.

Howard intervened, shaking his head at her. "When you gave them to me, you said they were mine to do with as I please, remember?" he said, his voice barely audible.

Charlotte suddenly remembered her coin, and pulled it out of her pocket. "Me, too," she chimed in. A look of realization suddenly came across her face. "I know!" she said, and ran out of the room.

Amy quickly followed after her, as Charlotte raced into the drawing room. There on the wall was the framed collection of old Roman coins. Two were missing from the collection, and a small note was taped to the bottom of the frame, with a picture of a feather.

Amy and Charlotte dashed into the hallway, both on the same wavelength. Aunt Melanie's latest fresh-flower arrangement on the console in the foyer contained peacock feathers, over which the girls had joked only the day before. At the base of the vase was another note, with an arrow pointing toward the dining hall. The girls raced into the room, looking all over for the next clue.

Amy finally found an arrow drawn on a note taped to the french doors, pointing to the doorknob. She excitedly pulled the door open. Outside on the spacious patio were two bicycles, both with training wheels, sized perfectly for the girls.

The girls bounded outside, Charlotte admiring hers and jumping on, Amy looking fondly but apprehensively at hers. Charlotte started immediately trying to ride the bike. "Amy, c'mon," she called joyously. Amy followed her lead, and the two girls busied themselves trying to learn, as Howard supervised.

Several minutes later, Daisy appeared, hands on hips. "Is anyone going to eat my pancakes? Those toys can wait, but my cooking can't," she lamented, her jaw set.

Howard advised the girls, "She's right. Let's go. We've got the rest of the day to play."

Later Charlotte surprised her aunt, and even Uncle Howard, by working hard on her keyboard, and within only a couple of weeks had taught herself, with Howard's secret coaching, several melodies, performing a mini-recital including 'Mary had a little lamb', 'Happy birthday', with chords, and with her neighbor and new friend Gerard Fellowe's mentorship, the melody line of 'Heart and soul'. Then she pulled out an old tattered book, which Melanie recognized as her first piano book, and began playing through the book.

Melanie, amazed beyond belief, was reminded by the proud budding musician of Uncle Howard's promise, and Charlotte wheedled her daily until Melanie made arrangements for Charlotte to begin piano lessons.

Charlotte zipped through her lessons, amazing and outstripping her teacher, until after the first year the teacher was recommending to Melanie a more advanced instructor for the child. Since then she had progressed at an amazing pace, frustrating and outgrowing two other teachers.

Since that day, on every birthday and Easter, as well as random holidays and rainy days, Howard had used the antique coins to set up treasure hunts for the girls and their friends. And each year the girls became more and more competitive.

Aunt Mellie even entered into the excitement, by telling the girls and their friends a ghost story that the coins were deemed the 'coins of death' from ancient times, in that the early Roman families that later formed the Mafioso had sent the coins to those they marked for vengeance. Howard, delighted at Melanie's enthusiasm but frowning at the darkness of her story about the coins, ended up modifying the story to relate that pirates had later determined that receipt of one coin was a curse, and that it took the whole group of pirates to search for and find the treasure and share the spoils in order to lift the curse. Then he would turn them loose to scour the household for the clues to find the 'treasure', usually a cornucopia of games, toys and treats.

This day was Charlotte's ninth birthday. She was generally frustrated because in the past Amy and her friends had managed to find the treasure before she and her buddy Gerry Fellowes, but she was determined that today was the day she broke her older sister's chain of victories.

So she was disappointed to find no coin on the bedside table. Flinging herself out of bed and running down the stairs, she breathlessly arrived at the breakfast room, but no one was there. She looked lost, confused that there was no surprise, no greeting, no pancakes cooking, no Uncle Howard. She turned dispiritedly, and saw Aunt Mellie standing in the doorway, studying her silently.

"Where is everyone?" she demanded plaintively. "It's my birthday," she reminded her aunt, tears in her eyes.

"Your Uncle Howard is not feeling well," Melanie said, somewhat severely. "We mustn't overexcite him." There was a gleam in her eye. "Go shower and get dressed," she commanded. "I have an errand to run, and I want you to accompany me. I have laid out a new outfit on your bed."

"Yes, ma'am," Charlotte replied meekly, to Melanie's utter shock, as the child, her shoulders slumped, sadly slinked out of the breakfast room.

Daisy was upstairs, and helped the girl bathe and dress, toweling dry her page-cropped curly golden hair. Taking the child's hand, she brought her downstairs and prepared breakfast. As Charlotte sat alone eating in the breakfast room, she asked, "Where's Amy?"

"She was allowed to go with some friends," Daisy answered her, ruffling her hair in sympathy.

Melanie appeared. "Are you finished with breakfast? Go brush your teeth. We need to go," she demanded impatiently.

Charlotte hung her head, again to Melanie's surprise. "Yes, ma'am," she remarked as she left the room.

She appeared soon, and Melanie took her hand. Jacob was waiting at the front door with the car, a long black imposing Lincoln town car.

He drove them to a neighborhood Charlotte had never seen. She looked out the window curiously, but said nothing, knowing that too many questions aggravated her aunt, and feeling too dispirited about the lack of fanfare over her birthday to make the effort.

The car stopped before a brick home in a neat suburb of majestic homes with tidy lawns. Jacob held the door, and Melanie disembarked, holding out her hand peremptorily to the young girl, who solemnly took it. They walked up the sidewalk, and Melanie rang the doorbell, which was promptly opened by a pleasant-looking young woman.

"Mrs. Cain, please do come in," she remarked congenially, ushering them in the home. In the large handsomely furnished living room was a large Steinway grand piano. Charlotte looked with interest at the piano.

"Charlotte, this is Dr. Christine Hodges," Melanie introduced the woman, who took Charlotte's hand. "She is to be your new piano teacher."

Charlotte's eyes grew large. "Really?" she asked, incredulous. "I thought you said I couldn't have any more."

Melanie smiled slightly. "You do need to learn to treat your teachers more gently, my dear. You are running through them at a prodigious rate."

Dr. Hodges smiled as well. "I think we can strive to find a common ground, as long as you are as good as I've heard you are and promise to work hard." Pointing to the piano, she asked, "Do you want to show me?"

Charlotte started, but then turned and looked for permission at Aunt Mellie, who nodded. She hurried to the large piano and seated herself. Momentarily from the piano came sounds of Prelude XVII in A-flat from Bach's *Well-Tempered Clavier*, then a set of theme and variations from Beethoven. It was Dr. Hodges's turn to look wide-eyed at Melanie, who smiled tentatively back.

The girl completed her selections, then looked at her aunt, her hands poised as if to proceed with playing, but Aunt Mellie shook her head and put her finger to her lips. Charlotte sat very still, waiting for a response. Dr. Hodges knelt beside her and asked, "Do you already know your keys and scales?"

"Yes, ma'am," Charlotte replied politely.

"Where did you learn fingering like that?"

"I taught myself from Aunt Mellie's book—she had the numbers over the notes," the girl explained proudly.

"How quickly did she pick this up and learn it from memory?" Dr. Hodges asked Melanie.

"She found my music three weeks ago, and has been playing her way through it," Melanie answered, nodding at the woman's small gasp. "She has a phenomenal memory. However, I must warn you that she is a challenging child, and previous teachers have stated they cannot keep her on task, because she constantly wants to play music above her level. She has in the past also refused to play certain music she decides she doesn't like."

"I'm sold," Dr. Hodges breathed. "When can she start? I have an opening tomorrow and every Thursday at 3:00 in the afternoon."

Charlotte's eyes were shining. "You mean I can start lessons tomorrow?"

"Yes, but you need to bring your aunt's book and one of your own." Dr. Hodges gave instructions to Melanie as to the desired edition. "We're going to teach her to work out her own fingering as well, to think it through," she explained.

Melanie nodded. Dr. Hodges bent down and took Charlotte's hands in hers. "We are going to work hard, you and I. You show great promise."

"Cool," Charlotte breathed, then started as Melanie cleared her throat. "Yes, ma'am," she added meekly.

They were soon back in the car, and Charlotte glowed with delight. Melanie was amazed at the transformation in the child. She gave instructions to Jacob, and soon they stopped in front of a music store. She gave a note to him and sent him in, and in a few minutes he returned with a brown paper bag which he handed to his employer. She in turn proffered it to the child. "Your own music book," she intoned solemnly.

Charlotte held it to her, as Melanie swallowed a smile. "Home, Jacob," she commanded, as she and Jacob exchanged knowing looks at the girl's reaction.

Charlotte quickly took out the book, sitting quietly and reading the notes as if she was reading words in a novel. She hardly realized it when they arrived home.

"We're back," Melanie prompted her. The girl seemed reluctant to leave the car. But she hugged her book and followed Melanie into the home. As they walked into the foyer, Melanie ordered, "Put your book on the piano and come with me."

Charlotte went into the parlor to comply, reluctant to relinquish her newest possession. There on the piano bench were a Roman coin and note.

Excited, she carefully laid her book on the bench and picked them up. The note read, "Come into the breakfast room."

She ran into the foyer, but her aunt had disappeared. She ran past the stairwell and pantry into the kitchen to the breakfast nook. There to her surprise was Uncle Howard, Aunt Mellie, Amy, Amy's friend Mike Chadwick, Mike's younger siblings Matt and Alicia, and Katharine, George and Gerard Fellowes, plus a few friends from her church and preschool.

"Surprise!" they shouted.

She squealed. "Oh, you remembered!" she shouted, her eyes wide with wonder.

Howard knelt before her. "Of course we remembered, dear," he hugged her.

Amy laughed. "We fooled you." She ran up and turned the girl around. "Look at your cake."

Charlotte happily joined in the celebration, as she blew out the lit candles, and cake was passed around to the children. They laughed and talked and stuffed their mouths with cake, as Daisy bustled around them plying them with hot dogs and ice cream and party favors.

After a while, Howard nudged Charlotte. "Haven't you forgotten something?" he laughed as he held up the coin.

All the children immediately stopped, suddenly all their attention on the coin. "Where's the clue? Where's the clue?" they all clamored.

But Amy looked knowingly at Charlotte, as Charlotte raced out of the room.

"This one is especially for her. Let her win," Howard whispered to them, as they hurriedly left their seats to follow her.

Charlotte made her way to the coin collection in the dining hall. There was the note taped to the frame. A riddle? "Now I lay me down to ____."

"Sleep?" she asked. "My bedroom," she whispered, and up the stairs she flew. The others followed Amy, read the note, and trailed in her wake.

She ran into her room breathlessly. She looked around, and finally found a note with an arrow on her bed pointing downward. At first she looked under the bed, then thought a minute. She rummaged under her mattress, where she kept her journal. Instead, she found a brand new journal with a lock on it, and a note stating, "To help you keep your secrets safe. Love, Melanie and Howard."

Charlotte did not notice that George was behind her, until he knelt beside her and rummaged between the mattress and bedsprings, finding her current journal. "Ah-ha," he called triumphantly, holding it aloft.

Charlotte suddenly realized that George had possession of her secret diary. Enraged, she dropped the new journal. "Give me that," she cried desperately. "That's mine." She grabbed him, trying to reach the diary he held above his head.

George laughed at her. "Not any more. Your secrets are mine." He broke free of her, only to be tackled by his younger brother Gerry.

"Leave her alone," he yelled, but George pushed him down and ran off with her diary.

She screamed. "No!" as she ran after him, her new journal abandoned. He, being older and faster, soon disappeared. She raced throughout the house, frantically looking for him, but he was nowhere to be found.

Pandemonium ensued, as the other children were chasing after her. Everything was forgotten, as she ran into the library, where Howard was reclining on the couch, Melanie nearby. "Uncle Howard, George has stolen my diary. Oh, please, do something," she whined.

She did not notice that her uncle was white, and that Melanie was also pale and hovering over him. He patted Charlotte's head fondly. "Dear one," he whispered weakly.

Melanie spoke, her voice gentle but hardly masking her irritation. "Charlotte, please not right now. Uncle Howard is sick. Oh, thank goodness, Dr. Bennett, you're here." She looked anxiously at Howard, who shook his head at her, as the doctor made his way into the room and knelt before the ailing man. She frowned, took Charlotte's hand and led her out of the room.

The others sans George were in the hallway, Amy looking frightened. Melanie smiled bravely. "It's nothing serious. I've called your mother, Katharine, and she said you all could continue the festivities at your house. We've ordered some pizza and movies. You can invite some of your friends. Jacob will drive you over, and Greta and Daisy will help supervise."

"But my diary!" Charlotte wailed, but Melanie shushed her, pulling her quickly into the parlor and pulling the pocket door shut.

"Charlotte, my dear, your Uncle cannot help you right now," Melanie, her eyes full of tears, remarked gently to the girl, hugging her roughly. "Please try to understand."

Charlotte blinked, surprised by her aunt's tears and Melanie's uncharacteristic affection. "Is Uncle going to die?" she asked in her characteristic frankness.

Melanie gasped. "Don't say that, child," she objected, her face flushed, angry in denial. "He's just not feeling well."

Charlotte broke free of her aunt, snatched the door open and ran into the library, where the doctor was attending to her uncle. She flung herself at his feet, agitated and desperate. "Please, Uncle," she cried brokenly, "don't leave me like Daddy did. Don't die."

Howard, in intense pain but feeling the child's terror, laid his hand feebly on her head. "I'm not gone yet," he answered her, his voice low.

Melanie was behind her, and Daisy came in and tenderly pulled the girl away. She notified Jacob and Katharine, "Take the others to your home, and we'll be there t'reckly."

Daisy guided the child upstairs to her bedroom, the girl sobbing inconsolably. Daisy sat her down on the bed, sat down beside her, and pulled the girl to her. "Listen, girl," she began. "You must be strong for Miss Mellie. It's hard on her seeing Mr. Howard under the weather. They need our support, Little Miss. Will you promise me to be strong and help? Don't be giving them any grief."

She held the girl and rocked her, wiping her eyes and shushing her. Charlotte, comforted by the woman, nodded as the woman continued to soothe her. Soon the girl was calmed, and Daisy helped her wash her face.

"Now come downstairs with me," Daisy ordered.

Charlotte took her hand, and Daisy marched her into the kitchen. "Sit there at the table," Daisy gently pushed her into a chair, and momentarily placed before her a glass of buttermilk and a piece of warm cornbread.

"That will cure what ails you, and nightmares, and bad luck," Daisy informed her matter-of-factly. "Don't give me no lip—just eat it."

Charlotte gazed at her with large eyes, then inhaled the food and drink before her. Daisy then hustled the child off to the Fellowes' estate.

A week later, Uncle Howard, looking older and feebler, but having refused to remain at the hospital, walked into the parlor where Charlotte was practicing Chopin waltzes, having run through her new book already. She immediately stopped and ran to him, embracing him. He took her hand. "Come with me," he said simply. "I have something to show you."

He led her outside and down the lawn to the boathouse, walking slowly, with her hand in his and her skipping alongside him. Under the steps near the dock beside his prized wooden speedboat, he stopped. Kneeling down with some effort, he pulled something toward him from under the steps.

"Come here," he rasped quietly, his face pale. She obeyed. He showed her a lockbox with an old well-oiled combination lock. "This is your secret hiding spot," he told her, his voice a whisper. "Share only with whom you trust implicitly. This is our secret place for you to hide your most valuable possessions, such as your diaries."

He told her the secret combination. "Never forget that number." He showed her how to open the lock, and then showed her inside. There lay her diary George had stolen. She smiled and hugged him impulsively.

"I love you, Uncle Howard," she whispered in his ear. "I don't want you to be sick again. I'm sorry I caused you grief."

"Where did you get that idea?" he stroked her hair affectionately.

"Daisy said I shouldn't cause you and Aunt Mellie any more grief," she was solemn. "I didn't mean to."

He laughed weakly. "Dear one, you are the joy of my life. Don't mind what the womenfolk say around here." He kissed her forehead, then rose heavily, taking her hand. "Now come on. Let me hear you practice some more."

Chapter 5

It was Sunday morning, and Charlotte, now ten, came bounding down the stairs dressed for church. Uncle Howard, in suit and tie, stood at the base of the stairs.

"How would you like to go to church with me?" he asked, a twinkle in his eye.

"Aren't Aunt Mellie and Amy coming?" Charlotte was surprised.

"Yes, but I thought you might be up for a change in scenery," Uncle Howard grinned. "And I need a Roman fix."

Charlotte's eyes glowed. She loved their little private excursions, where Uncle Howard, an architect himself, took her to various places of architectural, historical or artistic interest. Nodding, she took her Uncle's hand, as he led her out to his polished gray square Mercedes sedan.

Settling herself into the passenger seat and buckling her seat belt, she waited until Uncle Howard pulled out from the driveway and into the street. "What is a 'Roman fix'?" she asked curiously.

"Well, you see, I was raised Roman Catholic. Even though I go to church with Aunt Mellie now, every now and then I like to go back to my old church, the cathedral," Uncle Howard explained as he maneuvered through the light morning traffic. "It's within sight of St. Philip's. You know, I met your Aunt Mellie at the church we're going to this morning."

"Really?" Charlotte smiled.

"She was raised in Charleston. Her dad sent her to Wesleyan College in Macon, a women's college, then she persuaded him to let her finish her degree at Rollins College, studying under Catharine Crozier, an illustrious organist. Your Aunt Mellie was the assistant cathedral organist here when I met her, a young college student, and a born musician, like you," Howard replied. "Then she came back here from Rollins and played again. She could have gone on anywhere she wanted to get her master's and to continue her performance, but I asked her to marry me, and she said yes. After that she decided to champion the cause of music in other ways."

"So she wasn't old then?"

"She's not old now," Howard laughed. "But she was younger. I had heard of Melanie from my aunt, who met her at some women's functions, but I never met her. I heard her play before I ever laid eyes on her. I just assumed the organist was a man, until the pastor introduced me to her. She was good. I was hooked."

Momentarily they pulled into a parking lot, and walked hand in hand into a rather large church building made of stone and concrete. Charlotte thought it not as grand as their church, St. Philip's Episcopal Cathedral, which was located just a block away. However, when they walked in, she peered at the altar area.

"Uncle Howard," she shook his arm. "Is the organ hidden like at our church?"

He bit his lip as he put his finger to his lips and greeted a priest and some parishioners, introducing her. After they were alone again, he pulled her into a pew, then made her turn around.

"Wow!" she whispered, when she saw the organ in the gallery. She stared, transfixed. "All that is the organ?" she asked in wonder.

"Yes," he nodded.

"Can we go see it?" she was excited.

"After church, I'll take you up," he promised. "But for now you're going to have to face front and behave."

Charlotte fidgeted, trying to be still but wanting to turn around and see the instrument behind her. During the hymns when the congregation stood, she would quickly take a peek behind her at the organ as it sounded forth. Howard watched but pretended not to notice.

After what seemed like an eternity to Charlotte, the service was over, and as the organ pealed forth on the *Final* from Louis Vierne's Symphony No. 1, she impatiently tugged at his hand as he spoke to people and they made their way to the back and up the stairs to the gallery. She all but dragged him up to the console, as the organist was busily thundering to a close his postlude.

"Peter, you have a fan," Howard spoke as the organist turned to face them.

"Is this the young whiz kid?" he inquired, gazing at the young girl, the corners of his mouth turning into a smile. "Dr. Hodges has told me all about you, young Miss Lawson," he addressed her.

"Charlotte, this is Dr. Peter Conrad, the artistic director of the Atlanta Symphony, and lately organist of the cathedral," Howard introduced the young musician to her older colleague.

Charlotte smiled her winning smile. "You are the one who sends us the Christmas cards from different places."

"That's me," Conrad laughed. "You know, your mother and I were distant cousins and playmates. I called her Peggy, and she hated it. I miss her."

"You knew my mom?" Charlotte was curious. "Did you know my dad?"

"Yes," he smiled. "I played for their wedding. Matthew was a fine young man. Your mom was so much like your Aunt Melanie they were more like blood sisters. Matthew was easygoing, fun-loving, and witty. Melanie has always been so anal." He and Howard laughed together.

"You got that right," Howard chimed in. He pointed to Charlotte, his tone conspiratorial. "Don't you tell her I said that," he warned good-naturedly.

"What do you think of this instrument?" Conrad waved his arm at the organ.

"That is so cool," she breathed, in awe.

"Would you like to try it?"

She shrank back, suddenly shy. "It's so . . . big," she finished.

"But the keys aren't much different in size from your piano at home, I'll bet," he answered her. "I'll also bet you know some Bach."

She nodded vigorously, words failing her. "Yes, sir," she finally croaked.

"Sit here," he coaxed her, getting up from the bench and indicating for her to take his place, drawing two knobs. "Let's put on something sparkly here, and you play me something. Does Dr. Hodges make you play from memory?"

"Yes, sir," she answered meekly. "Is this the same size at Aunt Mellie's?"

"Melanie's is a little larger," he smiled at her, amused.

"You've played it?" her eyes grew wide.

"Yes," he nodded. "A wonderful instrument. Why don't you try this manual?" he suggested, pointing to the middle one.

She looked pensive one moment, then launched into the first movement of the second English Suite. Dr. Conrad drew his breath in sharply as she masterfully played the entire first movement without error from memory.

As she drew to a close, she slowly came out of her cocoon. She turned to the organist, and saw tears in his eyes. "Have I done something wrong?" she asked, suddenly frightened.

"My God, Howard," Dr. Conrad whispered. "I didn't believe you."

He knelt down and took her hand. "Have you ever played any Mozart on the piano?"

"Yes, sir," she answered him politely.

"Do you think you might want to try playing with an orchestra?"

"Orchestra?" she echoed, confused. "You mean, like a roomful of violins and flutes and stuff?"

"Yes, like a roomful of violins and flutes and stuff," he laughed.

"Cool," she beamed. "I've never done that before."

"Not many have," he agreed, smiling at her precociousness. "I'll talk to Dr. Hodges about it." Standing up, he shook Howard's hand. "Thanks for bringing her by to see me. We'll be in touch," he said.

"Come on, Charlotte," Howard beckoned to the little girl, who obediently climbed down.

She turned back, reluctant to leave. "It was nice meeting you, Dr. Conrad," she curtsied politely.

The next Thursday Dr. Hodges had a score on the piano when she arrived. "Dr. Conrad informed me that he has met you," she explained. "He wants to see how well you might do with this piece."

She looked with interest at the music, one of the Rondos. Her teacher had her sight-read portions, and was amazed at Charlotte's proficiency at playing the music without ever having heard it. Her excitement grew, as did Charlotte's at the prospect of a new and long musical selection which provided a challenge for her.

However, knowing Charlotte's propensity to become easily bored with one piece, her teacher inundated her with other music which the teacher knew complemented the skills necessary to successfully execute the Mozart.

After a few weeks of practicing, when Charlotte exceeded her expectations and was in the process of memorizing the movements, Dr. Hodges provided her a tape. When she looked at it inquiringly, Hodges smirked. "Your fan Dr. Conrad has sent you a recording of the symphony's part for you to practice with. He apparently has big plans for you."

Charlotte's eyes lit up. "For me? Cool."

After her lesson, she arrived home, bounding into the house excitedly with her tape in hand. The pocket doors to the library were closed, and she could hear Melanie's and Howard's voices raised in discussion. Amy was at the closed door, trying to listen.

Charlotte walked up. "What's up?" she asked innocently.

"Shh," Amy whispered. "They're arguing about you," she continued.

"Why?" Charlotte whispered back. She strained to overhear also.

Melanie was saying, "I don't want her to become some little performing monkey on a stage. Peter has gone too far."

Howard's voice was low, but as Amy cracked the pocket door a bit, they could see his jaw was set ominously. "That's awfully hypocritical of you, dear. You played with the orchestra at twelve, if I recall the story correctly."

"Charlotte is only ten, and Peter is wanting to launch her as some prodigy, sending her all over the country performing. I won't have it." Melanie's tone brooked no dissension.

"No, he's not," Howard was equally firm. "But he recognizes true talent, and he wants to see her progress. He also wants to use her as a vehicle to reach other young talented musicians and give them a chance to hone their skills and perform in public."

He went up to Melanie and took her hand. "Melanie, this isn't about you, dear. But because of your one bad experience as a child, you have made it about you."

"I don't want anyone, least of all our two girls, to go through the humiliation and pain I suffered. If raising them means anything, it means protecting them," Melanie whispered.

"What you went through was a case of stage fright, a natural part of public performance, and hardly anyone noticed it except for that ass of a critic. However, you almost let it destroy you," Howard spoke gently. "Messing up in public can happen to anyone, and is a natural part of being human. But it is no reason to deny Charlotte the opportunity to nurture her ability, to see if she has what it takes. We cannot always protect them from life, and from the media with its salacious appetite for gossip. We can't keep them cloistered forever."

He took her in his arms. "Melanie Anne, it's one performance of one movement of a Mozart concerto. Charlotte has been practicing more in the last weeks and glowing like never before. She's eating the music up like it's cotton candy. Let's just see where it leads. Peter was so mesmerized when she played the organ for him."

"She played the organ?" Melanie's eyes grew wide, as she stared at Howard accusingly.

"Yes. She was so excited to see the organ, and insisted we go up to the gallery. Then he had her sit at the console and play for him."

Melanie frowned. "You went behind my back," she complained. She sniffed, "You only call me by my middle name when you want something."

"I'm only trying to keep peace in my happy Lawson-Cain Christmas home full of overbearing females," he murmured as he kissed her.

"OK, but just this one time," Melanie relented reluctantly. "I'm not agreeing to anything else for now."

"OK," Howard assented as he kissed her again.

"And she's not performing unless I'm convinced she's ready," Melanie asserted.

"OK," Howard repeated and kissed her again.

"And you two can quit spying on us now," Melanie's voice thundered through the room. The two girls jumped. Charlotte flew up the stairs in fright, Amy right behind her.

Charlotte practiced hard every day, excelling in her other studies as well. She was happier than she could remember.

A few weeks later, she arrived at Dr. Hodges', to find Dr. Conrad there. His eyes glowed as he shook her hand. "Well, my little star, are you working hard on the music?"

"Yes, sir," she answered smilingly.

"Could I hear some of it?" he asked, with a look at Dr. Hodges.

Dr. Hodges nodded to the girl, who pulled out some music and placed it on the music desk. Dr. Hodges interrupted, "I thought you had this memorized."

"I—uh—feel more comfortable today with it in front of me," she faltered.

Dr. Hodges looked at Conrad and shrugged. "OK."

The child launched into the music. Dr. Hodges, surprised, started, "That's not—" but Conrad placed his hand on her arm, silencing her. He listened intently as the child played through the entire movement.

The child sat very still, biting her lip, anticipating their disapproval. Conrad broke the silence. "Where did you find this music?"

"I—uh—I ordered it," she replied, her voice small. "Aunt Mellie doesn't know," she whispered, hanging her head.

"That is not the Rondo," he said simply.

"No, sir," she wouldn't meet his eyes.

"That is the D-minor Concerto. Why did you pick this?" he continued, his face a mask.

"I just like it so much better. It reminds me of *Don Giovanni*. Aunt Mellie took us to the Met to see it earlier this year. I like this music so much." Her chin tilted upward in a small gesture of defiance.

"You know this is more difficult than the rondo you were working on?" Dr. Hodges interjected.

"It's more fun to play," Charlotte argued precociously. "I know the rondo, and I was ready for something new."

"Jesus, Christine," Conrad turned to Dr. Hodges. "You have a monster on your hands." He shook his head in wonder. "I cannot get over you, little Charlotte. I know adult concert pianists who would hesitate to play that piece for me."

"You do?" Charlotte asked. She bit her lip in embarrassment. "I'm sorry if I did wrong."

He laughed loudly. "No, I'm glad you did. I have underestimated you. Now I guess I need to prepare the orchestra for the KV 466 instead."

"Then it's OK?" Charlotte was confused.

"Yes, as long as you don't change pieces on me again," Conrad remarked with a grin. "Let's stick with one at a time, OK?"

"Do you want me to learn the whole thing?" Charlotte asked hopefully.

"No," he was firm. "I don't want to run afoul of any child labor laws for having you on stage too long," he winked at Dr. Hodges. "Besides, your aunt is going to be the major hurdle. Let's not complicate matters any further. You've done enough. She will be tanning my hide when I break the news."

A couple months later, Charlotte made her debut at the beginning of the Atlanta Symphony's Mostly Mozart Festival, to the ovation of the audience and critics. Howard beamed as she made her bows, and she glowed in the knowledge that he was proud of her, and basked in the adulation of the public clamor over her.

The next week Howard died from a sudden massive heart attack. Charlotte, stunned then brokenhearted, withdrew silently, isolating herself in her room and crying alone. She was convinced her world was ending, and that she had lost her closest friend.

The night before the funeral she quietly stole down to the drawing room. She took three of the Roman coins from the collection, and before the funeral secreted one in his hand in the coffin with a note saying simply "Come back to me. You know where."

After the funeral Melanie discovered that the three coins were missing, and could not pry out of the girl their location. The remainder of the collection disappeared into her safe for safekeeping.

The day after the funeral, Gerard Fellowes went looking for his friend. He finally found her, crying and morose, at the boathouse, sitting on the steps by the dock where Uncle Howard's speedboat was berthed.

"Everyone is looking for you," he announced.

"I don't care," she cried petulantly, her face streaked with tears.

"Charl," he sat down beside her. "Don't cry," he begged.

"Uncle Howard was supposed to come back. I gave him the coin and a clue to come back to me," she wailed. "I just knew he would be here, but he's not. What's going to happen to me? Nobody loves me."

Gerry took her hand and held it. "Mom says that Uncle Howard has gone where your daddy's gone. They're not coming back, Charl," he whispered solemnly. "But I'm here. I'll share my Dad with you. I'm not going to leave you."

"Oh, Gerry," she sniffed. "Do you promise?"

"I promise," he nodded, putting his arm around her awkwardly.

They sat there side by side for several minutes, comfortable in each other's company. Then Charlotte whispered, "I have something to show you."

She looked around to make sure no one was around, then knelt by the steps and pulled out the lockbox. Gerry's eyes grew wide.

"What's this?" he asked, full of awe.

"Uncle Howard showed this to me. It's my secret place. He told me to share it only with someone I trust."

She pulled him down to kneel beside her. She whispered the combination to him as she dialed it, and opened the box. Inside were her diary, two of the Roman coins, and a butcher knife from Daisy's kitchen.

She pulled one of the coins out and held it up for him. "I took these. If ever you need me, send me one of these. I'll do the same. That means we meet here."

Gerry nodded mutely. She put the coin back and took out the knife. She pricked her index finger, and ordered, "Hold out your finger."

He did so, and she pricked it. They touched fingers blood-brother style, and she intoned melodramatically, "Repeat after me: May we die a horrible death if ever we reveal this secret place."

He repeated her words somberly. Then she put everything away, closed the lockbox and put it away. They knelt there gravely for several minutes as if in prayer.

As they stood up together, Gerard's older sister Katharine suddenly appeared. "What are you doing out here? Miss Mellie will kill you. And what is this?" She grabbed each one of them, turning them around and seeing the blood on their hands. "Looks like you two will be candidates for tetanus shots."

Katharine grabbed each one of them by the ear. Charlotte screamed, and Amy appeared. "Let her go, Kat," Amy ordered.

"But they've cut themselves. We need to take them to Miss Mellie right away. She's looking for Charlotte."

Amy looked down at Charlotte's hand, which was bleeding. "Goodness, Charl." Grabbing her by the arm and wresting her away from Katharine, Amy dragged her sister thrashing and yelling up the hill to the big house, Katharine following with Gerry in tow.

The two were grilled by Melanie about their injuries and the missing coins, as Daisy busily washed their wounds and fussed over them. Then they were hustled off in the custody of Daisy to the doctor's office, where they received tetanus shots. But they both refused to disclose the secret, their friendship sealed.

Chapter 6

Katharine Fellowes, sixteen, was asked to babysit Charlotte, eleven, and her brother Gerry, twelve, at the Cain residence one evening so that Melanie and Katharine's mother Agatha Williams Fellowes could attend the opera. Drafted into service, Katharine, dressed all in Goth black, in true teenaged fashion, arrogantly ordered them to not bother her as she propped on the sofa and watched television in the large den.

Charlotte and Gerry played together until they grew bored, then Gerry worked with his construction set while Charlotte played piano in the parlor. Thus they entertained themselves for a period of time.

Finally tired of practicing, Charlotte wandered into the salon, to see Katharine sitting in a club chair staring at her arm. As Charlotte drew nearer, she could see that Katharine was carefully slicing herself on the arm with a pen knife, staring at the bloody parallel lines she had made.

"No!" Charlotte cried, and ran out of the room. A few minutes later, she reappeared with a kitchen towel and a bottle of Stolichnaya in her hands. Before Katharine could react, she poured vodka on the towel and covered the wound with the alcohol-soaked cloth.

"Yeowch!" Katharine roared, jumping up from her seat. "What the hell are you doing?"

"I'm saving you," Charlotte said excitedly. "Why would you hurt yourself? You want to kill yourself?"

"N-no," Katharine's eyes smarted with tears, as Charlotte wrapped the towel tighter. "It actually makes me feel better."

Charlotte stared at her. "It doesn't hurt?" she was incredulous.

"Not really, not as much as I hurt inside sometimes," Katharine whispered, slumping back into her chair, embarrassed at the girl's questions. "It's complicated. Why should I tell you?"

"Why not?" Charlotte was direct. "I like you. Otherwise, I wouldn't have asked Aunt Mellie to get you to babysit."

"You asked for me? Why?"

"I said I liked you," Charlotte was exasperated.

Katharine suddenly grabbed her by both arms. "You know, I don't like you. I bet you join Gerry in calling me 'Hell-Kat' behind my back."

Instead of cringing in fear as Katharine expected, Charlotte giggled. Katharine, exasperated, shook her. "Well?" she demanded severely.

Charlotte laughed. "I came up with the name. Don't you think it's cool?" she giggled again.

Katharine was trying to look ferocious, but at the girl's continued hilarity the corners of her mouth turned up, and she let the girl go.

"Well, no," she answered loftily. "It's insulting."

But Charlotte pointed at her as she started smiling in spite of herself. "Hell-Kat," she laughed at her. "You need a leather jacket to go with the name."

"Stop it," Kat commanded, but she was smiling too.

"Why are you mean to Gerry?" Charlotte asked precociously.

"I'm not mean to him; I just ignore him," Katharine looked at her curiously.

"Don't you know he worships you? That he would do anything to get you to notice him? Ignoring him is mean," Charlotte's eyes bored through her.

"Because he was a mistake," Katharine's tone turned nasty. "I heard Agatha and Dad talk about it. They didn't mean to have him. He was an accident, and is always in the way."

Charlotte's face grew somber. "No one is an accident," she proclaimed. "He loves you, and would do anything for you if you would just be nice to him."

"Anything?" Katharine asked, glints in her eyes.

Charlotte pinched her arm. "Don't be mean," she cried.

"Ow, you little twerp!" Katharine yelped, as she pinched Charlotte back.

"Why do you call your mom Agatha?" Charlotte steered her to another subject.

"'Cause that's her name, and she says she feels younger if we don't call her 'Mom'," Katharine suddenly laughed, diverted by the child's question. "But Dad makes up for it by calling her 'Mom'. She hates that. And he told us he would cane us if we called him by his first name."

"Weird," Charlotte breathed. "I called Auntie just 'Melanie' once, and she locked me in my room without supper."

"Grownups are crazy," Katharine agreed.

"Now why would you cut yourself?" Charlotte demanded, again changing the subject.

Caught off guard, Katharine just stared at Charlotte. She sneered, "Because your sister stole my boyfriend, the man I love."

"No, she didn't," Charlotte was matter-of-fact. "Why would you moon over a guy who doesn't notice you? You're pretty, except when you're slicing yourself, and there are 'other fish in the sea', as Aunt Mellie says. No one, even Mike, is worth you hurting yourself."

"Because, you simpleton, I don't have anyone to take me to my Sweet 16 coming-out party, and nowhere to go tonight," Katharine replied bitterly.

"Why not Toby Fitzpatrick? He looks at you funny like guys do at girls they like. He'd say yes in a minute. He would look good in his dress military outfit from prep school," Charlotte suggested slyly. "And everyone would be jealous. Or how about that new organ professor? He's cute."

"He's old," Katharine retorted, grimacing.

"He's not all that old," Charlotte countered.

"What's his name?"

"Something with a K. Mellie calls him Harry. He's staying at our boathouse right now while the school is courting him."

"How do you know he's cute?" Katharine was interested.

"Well, because I've seen him once or twice. He practices on the organ. And I've seen his picture and bio on Mellie's desk," Charlotte sounded worldly. "Go check it out. Just leave everything like you found it, or she'll accuse me."

"You've been snooping at your aunt's desk?" Katharine smirked.

"How else can I keep up with what the teachers are saying about me?" Charlotte grinned.

Katharine suddenly smiled with her. "You're not so bad, Charlotte. I like you. Mind you, you're just a kid. I can't be seen hanging with a baby."

"Oh, you're a snob?" Charlotte stuck out her tongue and laughed at her.

"Yes," Katharine laughed too.

"Promise me you're not going to do that any more," Charlotte whispered, pulling the towel off and looking at Katharine's arm. Her eyes grew bright with tears as she dabbed at a couple of cuts that were still bleeding slightly.

Katharine, touched, whispered back, "OK."

Charlotte ran off. A few minutes later she came back with some bandages and antibiotic ointment. "We mustn't let it get infected," she tried to sound grown-up.

Katharine watched as Charlotte put the bandages on. "That is the nicest thing anyone other than my dad has done for me in a long time." Suddenly feeling more congenial, she asked, "Would you and Gerry like to watch a movie? I'll make popcorn."

The next day an engraved invitation for Charlotte arrived. It was to Katharine's party, and on it was written, "You and Gerry will have to behave—this is a grown-up affair. I've chosen Toby to escort me. Hell-Kat."

She showed the invitation to her aunt. "That means you and Gerry need to go to some charm classes," Melanie was thoughtful.

"What's that?" Charlotte was dubious.

"If you're going to a grown-up function you need to know how to carry yourself, how to speak to others, the correct etiquette, and how to dance," Melanie answered the girl.

"Ugh!" Charlotte replied with disgust.

"That means we have to rearrange your schedule for the lessons. Don't worry. Agatha will send Gerry too, I'm sure."

That Saturday morning, Mellie received a call. After some discussion, she replaced the receiver. "Girls," she announced at breakfast, "you are invited to go water skiing with the Fellowes. Mr. Fellowes has promised to make sure the two of you can swim properly and will wear protective gear."

"Aw, Uncle Howard taught us how to swim," Charlotte drawled, but despite her outward nonchalance she was excited.

Then began a pattern of activities on weekends, where Louis Fellowes regularly took the young ones skiing or sculling or sailing, teaching them the intricacies of his favorite water sports. Many Saturday afternoons when the older teenagers were otherwise occupied, Gerard and Charlotte would spend the weekend afternoons swimming, skiing, boating or rowing under the tutelage of the older Fellowes, who helped fill some of the void left by Howard's death. Katharine, an excellent water-skier who shared a special bond with her father and was often jealous of the attention he gave to her siblings, more often than not joined them on the excursions.

In the meantime Dr. Conrad was filling much of Charlotte's free time, enlisting Dr. Hodges' help and engaging the child in learning additional piano music for trios and quartets with stringed instruments, and Charlotte was happily soaking up the music and instruction from Dr. Hodges and Conrad. Conrad was amazed and excited at her effortless technique and attention to detail, and her tireless desire to learn more repertoire, as well as her interest in playing in ensemble. She clamored for, and was granted, the opportunity to play a Beethoven piano concerto with the orchestra.

She was unknowingly garnering a fan club, people clamoring to know when she was performing again with the symphony, was she going on tour, what was next for the young girl. Charlotte was oblivious to this attention focused on her, her aunt insistent that the girl was not to become some circus performer, and quietly but firmly controlling Charlotte's public appearances. Conrad acted as liaison, quietly keeping public interest in the young prodigy alive while respecting Melanie's wishes to preserve the girl's privacy and to keep her childhood as normal as was possible for a young wealthy musical prodigy already subject to potential intense media attention. He procured for her occasional slots where she could play solo piano music.

The young piano quartet was working hard, and Conrad made sure that they had regular opportunities to perform. Thrown together for constant rehearsal, Charlotte and Erik Eliot, the first violinist, became close friends, and the two of them rehearsed and played regularly with Boris Marshall, a cellist. From time to time Alison Paulsen, another violist, would join the group, and other young musicians would come and go. Conrad would constantly feed their musical appetites, suggesting and supplying repertoire to the prodigies. Erik proved to be an exceptional instrumentalist, and he and Charlotte would often do duet music if the others were otherwise occupied. The two were much in demand for small events in the city.

In addition, Charlotte accompanied Daisy to church a few Sundays when Melanie would allow. She marched up after church and introduced herself to the church musician, Darrell Lamont. She marveled at how effortlessly he played classical preludes, accompanied the gospel choir and the minister's exhortations on organ and piano. He smiled as she watched him do the postlude, a piano improvisation on 'When the Roll is Called Up Yonder'.

"I want to learn how to do that," she laughed admiringly when he finished.

"It helps to take lessons," he responded flippantly.

"Oh, she's already done that," Daisy replied, appearing behind Charlotte.

"Miss Daisy, how you doin'?" he said warmly, standing up and hugging Daisy. "Who is this with you?"

"This is Miss Charlotte Lawson, my charge," Daisy beamed as she placed her hand on Charlotte's shoulder. "She is a pianist, Darrell. She's played with the Atlanta Symphony."

"Has she now?" he asked quizzically, looking Charlotte up and down critically.

"But I can't play like that," Charlotte added, smiling. "That was wow. Could you show me?"

"It could happen," Darryl nodded. "But you don't learn it from just reading music. I watched someone else and learned what I know, listened and wrote down the chording. You know what blue notes or blue chords are?"

Charlotte shook her head.

"Well, then, your education is seriously lacking," he laughed. "Sit down here and let me show you a few things."

Daisy interrupted. "Now, Darrell, you know your momma ain't gonna wait Sunday dinner for you."

He laughed. "No ma'am, she's not. But if you go on ahead, you can tell her to save this here girl and me a piece of chicken and a biscuit and we'll be there 'to-reckly', as they say around here. We have work to do."

Daisy looked at Charlotte. "You sure, girl?"

Charlotte nodded excitedly.

Daisy bustled off as Charlotte took a seat next to Darrell and he began playing chords, showing her at each step what he was doing and explaining to her the progressions, as he improvised on old well-known hymns. He also discussed with her some of his inspiration for improvisation, referencing as some of his mentors Duke Ellington, Oscar Peterson, and Billy Preston.

"So you rely on jazz and rock sometimes?" she asked in wonder.

"And classical music as well, such as Beethoven, Bach or even Debussy," he grinned. "When the juices get flowing, you don't really know what motifs may come to mind that fit in with your theme."

"Cool," she breathed.

"That's why it's good to have taken piano lessons," he reminded her.

"Who did you have lessons with?" she asked.

"Dr. Christine Hodges," he answered her.

"No!" she cried. "My Dr. Hodges? Here in Atlanta?"

"Yep," he laughed. "Small world, isn't it? Although I started out with her at Juilliard before she came back here a couple years."

"Juilliard?" Charlotte was confused. "But that's where she went back to," she mused.

"Yes. Her mother was dying, and she took a sabbatical to care for her mom just as I graduated. She has returned to Juilliard."

"You graduated from Juilliard?" Charlotte's eyes were round and wide.

"Yep again," he smiled. "Surprised?"

"Why did you come back?" she asked precociously.

"Well, I wanted to bring back all I learned to teach others who couldn't make it there," he explained. "I teach music at Morehouse College."

"Cool," she smiled. "That is a neat thing. And you've taught me a lot. Could I have another lesson if I get to come back with Daisy?"

"I don't see why not," Darrell laughed. "If you are a star, we'll have to arrange a concert right here some time, just you and me."

"That'd be fun," she glowed.

Her face suddenly wrinkled in a frown. He noted it. "What is it?"

"Why do you talk two different ways—one way to me, another to Miss Daisy?" she stared at him.

He laughed. "Well, little Miss Charlotte, I was raised in this neighborhood, and Miss Daisy and some of the others don't like it when I talk 'uppity'."

"But which is the real you?" she insisted.

"Which, indeed?" he smiled.

Later, he drove her to his home, a pretty brownstone home, where she met his mother and they ate leftover fried chicken and talked about music.

Charlotte tried to accompany Daisy to church every time Melanie would allow, so that she could have the opportunity to turn pages and watch Lamont accompany the Sunday services.

Furthermore, she remained involved with her piano lessons and the work with the trio/quartet, as Conrad kept the young kids involved in providing pre-concert music for the audience and sharpened their performing abilities.

One day Gerard showed up at the end of one of their rehearsals, dressed in a suit. Erik nudged Charlotte, also dressed up in a dress and tights. "There's your boyfriend waiting on you," he remarked, teasing.

She laughed. "Gerry's not my boyfriend," she declared. "He's my best friend."

"Who's your boyfriend?" Erik demanded.

"I don't need one of those. I'm too young," Charlotte giggled. "Why, do you have a girlfriend, Erik?"

"No, but I kinda like Alison," he admitted sheepishly. "But she doesn't come around as much. I even offer to play second fiddle or viola if she'd play with us, but she seems to be more interested in solo stuff."

"We can fix that," Charlotte suggested. "We give her an offer she can't refuse. I'll ask Dr. Conrad what he would suggest as quartet music. Or," she added, "you could form a string quartet. Maybe Alison doesn't like to compete with the piano."

"Naw," he smiled. "I like playing off you. We click. If Alison doesn't like that, well, good riddance."

"Never let it be said I stood in the way of true love," Charlotte stated, standing. "I gotta go. Gerry and I are going to the opera with Aunt Mellie and his mom. It's the first time they've let us tag along with them on one of their 'girls' night' outings. We have to be on our best behavior."

The night's offering was Puccini's *Tosca*, and Charlotte was rapt with attention, even shushing Gerry when he grew tired during the middle. Afterward she peppered her aunt with questions about the opera and requests to study foreign languages so that she could understand the words for herself.

As they stopped at the Varsity to let Gerry and Charlotte out to get ice cream, Melanie looked at her friend Agatha and shook her head. "See what life with Charlotte is like," she lamented. "She is insatiable, and I can never keep up with her. She makes me miss Howard even more. He had a true gift with her, and she responds to a father figure."

Agatha laid her hand on her friend's arm. "You mustn't discount what you give her, Melanie."

"No, see how Peter Conrad has her eating out of his hand, and even your Louis gets more feedback from her than I do. My talking to her is like having a discussion with a brick wall. I worry about her, that she will be ever susceptible to male influence as she gets older. I keep a close eye on her."

"You've taught her to be a good girl," Agatha objected. "The Good Book says to teach a child in the way she should go, and she will not depart from it."

"No," Melanie laughed at her friend. "You've missed a few Sunday School lessons, my dear. "It states that when the child is OLD, he or she will not depart from it. There's no mention about the time period between childhood and old age."

Agatha smiled at her friend. "OK, so you got me. But we can only do so much for our children, then trust God or fate that they will take to heart our lessons. Look at the grief Katharine and George serve up, Katharine with her adolescent blues and emotional ups-and-downs that scare me and have me rushing her to psychotherapists, and George with his fast crowd and the media attention on his escapades. My hairdresser is becoming rich just keeping my gray hair concealed."

Melanie nodded, her eyes scanning out the car window at the two adolescents waiting for their ice cream. "But at least these two are staying busy. In fact, their agendas are more crowded than ours these days. Perhaps that will help them keep out of the troubles we have with the older ones."

"But you don't have any trouble with Amy," Agatha pointed out exasperatedly.

"You just don't know," Melanie retorted. "She is crazy about this Michael Chadwick, yes, the same guy your Kat made moon-eyes over. He comes from a good family, but not a lot of money there. I think they are more serious than they are letting on. I want to get Amy out of college before she marries, but I worry about getting her past her debutante ball next year before she loses her virginity."

"Amy is a good girl, and she is not likely to defy you if you lay down the law," Agatha remarked reassuringly. "But when Charlotte gets her age . . ." she left the sentence unfinished.

"Don't remind me," Mellie grimaced as the children came bounding back toward the car with their ice cream cones in hand.

Chapter 7

"Charlotte, come here," she heard her aunt's peremptory summons. Reluctantly she entered the library, where Melanie held forth sitting at the massive carved mahogany desk. The woman, always elegant, was wearing a pink boucle-knit suit, pearls around her neck, as usual the epitome of Southern gentility. Although only in her forties, she exhibited the reminders of a beauty and grace from a former time.

The tousled-haired twelve-year old, dressed in school uniform of white shirt, navy vest emblazoned with the parochial school crest, and green and blue plaid pleated skirt, knee socks and loafers, plopped down in one of the heavily ornate carved chairs facing the desk. The girl gazed restlessly out the window at the daffodils and blossoms of the huge Japanese magnolia and the dogwoods.

Her aunt was reviewing some papers on her desk and did not look up. "Please sit up straight. My God, girl, I taught you better than that."

Charlotte squirmed around in her chair. Suddenly she was aware of her aunt's eyes upon her. She looked directly into the cold blue eyes of the matriarch.

"I received a call from Miss Dorian just now. Seems you missed another piano lesson."

Charlotte was silent, aware of the mounting storm. Melanie sighed. "Charlotte, you told me you want to be a concert pianist. How do you intend to accomplish that if you won't practice and you miss lessons?"

"She's a dork," Charlotte protested. "I'm way past her. I'm tired of sitting through *Fur Elise* recitations. I miss Dr. Hodges."

"I can't help that. Dr. Hodges has returned to her permanent position at Juilliard. That's too far for you to travel for weekly lessons, don't you think? Perhaps if you practice hard, you could get into Juilliard later. In the meantime, Miss Dorian is a fine teacher, and a sitting member of the competition committee, Charlotte. It pays to cultivate the right people if you are serious about the business," Melanie repeated her lecture to the defiant girl.

Amy walked in behind Charlotte. "She's too busy mooning over Sammy Fellowes again," she tattled, Charlotte's journal in her hand.

"His name is George, and you have no business reading my diaries," Charlotte jumped out of the chair and snatched the book out of Amy's hand.

"Charlotte!" Melanie's voice rang out angrily. "Sit down. Amelia Grace Lawson, this is a private discussion. I don't notice that you are excelling at your ballet lessons. Go do your homework, or next we'll be discussing curtailing your extra-curricular activities."

Amy smirked at Charlotte and left the room. Charlotte stuck out her tongue at her sister's retreating form.

"Charlotte, face me please," Melanie scolded the girl.

Charlotte whined. "I need a new teacher. Can't you get me an audition with that college instructor Ms. Harmon?" Charlotte pleaded yet again. "Or how about that hunk organ professor you like so much? What's his name? Kreiser? The one who's staying at the boathouse and playing your organ?

"You know," she gushed on, "Uncle Howard would want you to find another husband. Dr. Hunk is hanging around here all the time, and eats dinner with us and goes with you to stuff in town. And while he is a lot younger than you, I think you'd make a great couple, no matter what others may think."

"Enough!" Melanie's voice rang out authoritatively. "I know you are trying to divert my attention. I also know Howard and I were too old to bring you up as we should. I should have beaten you as a child." She paused, trying to look stern. "I wish Howard were still here."

Charlotte's face grew cloudy at the mention of her uncle and she looked away. Melanie stared at her silently for several minutes.

She finally ordered, "Go into the parlor and practice. I want to hear the sound of that piano being played for the next two hours, or no more lessons at all."

Charlotte shrugged, getting up and sauntering out, to Melanie's utter fury.

She wandered into the salon and toward the organ, noticing the musical score on the stand, the *Prelude and Fugue in E-flat major* by J.S. Bach. Sitting down at the organ, she pushed a combination piston and studied the notes on the page. She struck the first chord, thrilling to the sound of the organ. She studied the music. Satisfied, she started the piece over, deftly feeling her way through the patterns of the Bach. She never noticed the handsome man who had come up behind her and was studying her with bemused expression.

"I think it would sound better with perhaps this diapason pulled," he remarked, startling her. She stiffened. "And I'm particularly fond of this mixture." He reached around her and pulled the two stops. "Try it again," he suggested, smiling at her.

She froze at the sight of him, recognizing him as Professor Wilhelm Kreiser from the university, whom she had just referred to as "Dr. Hunk". He was young, only in his mid-twenties, his blonde hair waving at his temples. He was dressed in black slacks and white starched shirt, the sleeves rolled up and showing suntanned sinewy forearms. His black tie was loosened and his collar button undone. He peered at her through round wire-framed glasses, and showed his white teeth as he briefly smiled.

She had overheard several discussions about him when he was hired at the university just the previous year. Melanie, upon Howard's death, had thrown herself even more into community activities, was an active supporter of the music and arts departments at the university, and followed the interview process avidly. She was a vocal supporter of Kreiser, despite his young age.

Wilhelm Kreiser was a child prodigy in organ and piano. He had grown up in West Germany, his family being refugees from Thuringia during World War II, before his parents moved to the United States for him to study. He had studied at the Juilliard School with Vernon de Tar and privately with Alec Wyton, then organist at St. John the Divine and adjunct professor at Union Theological Seminary in New York City, which was subsequently taken over by Yale. Kreiser had taken top honors at several international competitions, including the most coveted Chartres competition. He had spent several years in Paris studying with Maurice Durufle, Pierre Cochereau and Daniel Roth. He was highly sought after until the local university managed to woo him.

"But I can't really play the organ," she protested, embarrassed at Kreiser's proximity.

"The young star concert pianist and protégée of Peter Conrad? What would he think if he heard you shrinking from his second favorite instrument?"

She started to retort, but he insisted gently, "But you were playing the organ. Let's try this beginning passage again."

"But what about the pedal part?" she demurred, suddenly fearful of playing for him.

"Forget it for now. We can add it later," urged the young man. "Please—just for me."

Mesmerized by his smile, Charlotte again began, hesitantly at first, trying to concentrate on the music before her.

"Make this chord very strong and majestic, a real statement, despite the mordent. They are played together, distinguished from grace notes," he commanded quietly, as she began. They slowly proceeded, he demonstrating to her or placing his hand over hers to show her the fingering he wanted. As she began playing, he murmured, "Good, but this fingering would be more practical, for you're going to run right into this next chord and have to be ready for it." He reached around her and demonstrated.

She followed his instructions carefully as the music began to come alive before her. She remembered hearing him play this selection earlier in the week, and now she tried to mimic what she recalled as he continued to tutor her, measure by measure, then backed her up to play the passage before progressing. She finished the first two pages, completely entranced.

"Cool!" she cried. "That was bitching. But it will sound better with the pedals."

"Does your aunt realize you talk like that?" he pursed his lips as he tried not to laugh.

"Couldn't you take me as a student? I've heard you're a hard teacher," she ignored his question, the excitement in her face infectious.

"Charlotte, I do not tell you to do things merely for the sake of hearing my voice. Go!" There was no mistaking the anger in Melanie's tone as she glowered from the doorway.

Charlotte slid off the bench, hanging her head. "Yes, ma'am. Sorry," she whispered to Kreiser, as she slinked out of the room.

"I'm sorry, Harry," she heard Melanie state to Kreiser. "I'm afraid Charlotte's chief talent is in defying me and trying my patience, particularly with Howard gone. He was one of the few who were able to exercise any influence over her. I'm sorry if she disturbed your practice."

"Nonsense," she heard him reply. "She's a gifted musician, and you know it. I saw the spark in her. She's a phenomenally quick study. I've heard her tackling every piece of music she can find. She craves constant challenge. You should let her study organ."

"She's too young. Her teacher will not begin organ lessons until she is fourteen."

"I generally have no use for child prodigies, but I think she is ready now," he asserted, so quietly Charlotte could barely hear him. "How long has she studied piano?"

"Since she was five, but she claims she's outgrown her teacher. She's been through five instructors already. I despair of her progressing any further."

"All she needs is the right inspiration, the right guide, someone who is accomplished enough to give her the continuity she needs. My God, Melanie, she's having to teach herself. That talent shouldn't go to waste."

Melanie laughed. "With Christine Hodges having left our fair city, who else is there?"

"Ms. Harmon has completed her doctorate in performance except for submission of her final thesis. She's really very good. And I'm not chopped liver," he winked.

"Really, Harry, you're not saying you are interested in taking her as a student?"

Charlotte could not hear his reply, for suddenly the organ pealed forth, Kreiser playing the Bach. She was hypnotized by the power, the sound, the precision as he played the music she had just attempted.

She was rooted to the spot just outside the doorway. The music flowed around her, filling her as he continued inexorably to perform and she to listen. She subconsciously drew ever closer to the instrument and performer.

When the music died away, she was standing next to Kreiser, her face rapturous, tears in her eyes. He turned to her, captivated by her expression. She whispered, "I want to play like that." She clasped his arm and pleaded, "Please."

"Charlotte!" Melanie's voice was full of exasperation.

"I'll consider teaching you," he replied gravely, unable to resist touching her face gently. "But you must audition for me, on piano. What can you play?"

"What do you want me to play?" she countered precociously.

Melanie started to interrupt, but he held up his hand, silencing her. "Do you do Beethoven?"

"Yes, sir. Do you have a favorite piano sonata?"

"Chopin?"

"Yes, sir."

"Debussy? Ravel?"

"I've doodled with them, but Ms. Dorian doesn't teach the French guys."

Kreiser looked at Melanie, his manner mocking. "Tut, tut, Melanie, you are neglecting this child's musical education. No French guys?"

Charlotte looked at them, her eyes pleading. Melanie pursed her lips, looking at Kreiser, then nodded ever so slightly.

Kreiser was crisp, businesslike. "Two weeks from today, at 3:00, the college auditorium Steinway 9-foot will be set up for auditions. You'll play for Ms. Harmon and me. One Bach, one movement from a Beethoven piano sonata or Chopin polonaise, waltz or etude, and/or your best attempt at a 'French guy piece' of your choosing. Make it good. The competition will be keen."

Charlotte looked at both of them, her eyes shining. "Really?"

He smiled ever so slightly. "Really. Now go practice and leave me alone."

Her resolve renewed, she applied herself with a vengeance, and earned her slot to study with both the piano teacher and Kreiser. She was now an organ student.

Melanie was amazed at the transformation in the girl as she tackled both piano and organ with gusto, inhaling the instruction given her by Dr. Harmon and Dr. Kreiser. Her memory, always prodigious, soaked up the music, and she spent most of her time at an instrument while managing to complete her other school subjects as well.

Melanie surprised her one day by asking Charlotte to accompany her to a weekend reunion at Rollins College, where she was introduced to Melanie's teacher Dr. Catharine Crozier, and had the opportunity to tour the school and play the organ at the chapel. Melanie was persuaded to sit at the console and play as well, and for an incredible moment the two were tied to each other, united in their love for music.

Chapter 8

Charlotte, just turned thirteen, walked in to the salon early for her lesson, to find that Kreiser had inadvertently left a score on the music desk. Reviewing it, she realized it was the Mozart organ sonata she had heard him perform the week before in recital. I can do this, she thought, climbing onto the bench. She tried her hand at the first movement. Challenging, but nothing I can't handle, she told herself.

Suddenly she had an idea. I'll learn this for next week's lesson and surprise Kreiser. Besides, maybe he left it here for me. The anticipation of his pleasure at hearing her play it was delicious. So she secreted the Mozart in the organ bench and carefully practiced her assigned music, sneaking down every night after Melanie had gone to bed to work on the Mozart.

The day of the next lesson she was warming up on the Mozart, when Kreiser walked in. She turned around to catch his reaction, but was not prepared for the perturbation she saw on his face.

"Who gave you permission to start the Mozart?" he demanded testily.

"Permission?" Charlotte laughed, but the laughter died as she saw his jaw tighten.

He strode across to her, ripping the music off the desk and throwing it on the floor. She stiffened, suddenly frightened, as he said icily, "You are not ready." His face was suffused with color.

"Of course, it's not ready yet, but I'm getting there. That's where you come in," Charlotte stammered. "Why are you so mad? I didn't sound all that bad."

"What is it you young people say—you suck!" he exclaimed hotly. He shook her by the shoulders none too gently. "Little Carlota, you asked me to teach you. If I do so, you will listen and obey."

Charlotte's chin remained defiant, but her eyes shone with sudden tears. He saw it and became angrier.

"I do not teach little girls," his voice rose exasperatedly. "Do not cry, or you are no student of mine."

"I'm not crying," she replied, her icy tone matching his, although her lower lip was trembling. "I wouldn't waste tears on you," she continued, biting her lip proudly.

Despite his anger, he could not help but smile at her childish insolence. He cupped her chin in his hand, turning her to face him. "And why is that, *cara mia?*" his tone softened.

His amusement only infuriated her more, as she wriggled, trying to extricate herself from his grasp. "None of your business," she muttered, her eyes flashing fire as she tried to slide off the bench away from him.

"Oh, but you can certainly come up with a better reply than that," he crooned, his hold on her tightening. "Be still," he commanded her, his tone brooking no opposition.

She became still, her eyes locked on his in a battle of wills. He moved his face to within inches of hers.

"You are a spitfire, and I like that. Your potential and your memory are amazing. You play with fire and ice, with passion, and you have great potential. But you are like a young Liszt, totally lacking in discipline. You need that discipline, to feel the silences and manipulate them, to become precise in your delivery. You must learn to control the keys in a different manner from the piano, *cara*. The organ is a different instrument entirely. There is music in the spaces between the notes, in the chiff, in the attack and release, and in the dynamics."

She continued to stare at him, but he had her attention. He released her, bent down and picked up the music from the floor, arranging it on the music desk in front of her.

"Scoot over," he demanded, and she complied. "Now, I want you to listen carefully. I will walk you through the Mozart. Have you played Mozart before? I mean," he added mockingly, "other than your piano concerto with the Atlanta Symphony?"

Her jaw tightened with anger. "Yes. Dr. Harmon makes me play the sonatas from time to time," she spat.

"Do you know anything about Mozart?" he persisted.

She sighed, still angry. "Yes. Child prodigy, prolific composer, fell on hard times, buried in a common grave."

"In what period does he belong?" Kreiser baited her.

She paused, suddenly diverted. "The schoolbooks place him in the classical period, along with Haydn. But he defies classification, doesn't he? I mean, he has broken free of the baroque and sounds a lot like Haydn, even though there are baroquisms still in his music. He is pre-Romantic, but there's definitely a romantic bent in some of his music. So what do we call him?"

"Baroquisms?" Kreiser smiled. "Did you just make that up?"

Slowly he began to play, accentuating the notes and pauses, speaking softly. "Mozart embodies classicism. Do not over-romanticize him. This was supposedly written for musical clock, but little is known about the commission for this particular work. The beginning is *Maestoso*, a typical Mozart flourish, with hints of romance but requiring the precision of the classical. Hear the attack and release of this chord; there, the slight break; now, the trill must be precise, all the harmonies as one voice. Watch the fingering here; see what I'm doing. Hear the tiny breaths, almost military in nature, the pickup and downward movement, the tiny spaces. Hear the crispness of this dotted note. That all points to the classical bent. They are important, my dear. With them you are singing." He stopped playing and sang the phrase. "Do you hear?" he asked her.

She nodded dumbly.

"Now, close your eyes and just listen to the music." He played on for several minutes, watching her reaction. Her breathing began to match his, in time with the pulse of the music.

"Precise. Very stylistic. Now the *Andante*. We don't play musical clocks nowadays, and this was meant to be more warm. Not Beethoven, mind you." He played some more, through the flourish to the return of the *Maestoso*. When he stopped, she remained perfectly still.

Kreiser whispered, "Do you see the music in your head differently now?"

Charlotte nodded again, opening her eyes.

"And you see how the voices play off each other? The left hand has to sing it just as well as the right hand—it's like they are competing. Have you already memorized the notes?"

Again she nodded.

"How long have you been looking at this?"

"A week."

He shook his head in disbelief. "My God. Well, never mind. Take my place on the bench." He slid off. She started to speak, but he cut her off. "No talking. I want you to play what I just did."

Without preamble she launched in, perfectly mimicking his performance. Before she made it to the point at which he had concluded, he stopped her.

"That's enough Mozart for today," he voiced curtly. When she looked at him, her eyes questioning, he coldly turned away from her. "Now back to the Bach."

That evening she attended a rehearsal arranged by Dr. Conrad. Spying him in the wings of the concert hall, she ran up to him. "Dr. Conrad, I want to do something big," she announced, her eyes sparkling. "I want to play the Brahms Piano Concerto Number 1 in D minor."

"Wow! Where did this come from?" he laughed, putting his arm around her.

"I just finished listening to a recording of it, and it is so great," she gushed. "If I learn it, can I play it with the orchestra?" she asked, suddenly shy.

"Well, if you learn that, I will pull out all the stops," he grinned. "But I need your help as well. I'm actually auditioning musicians for a young persons' orchestra," he explained to her through the din of string players warming up. "I would like for you to consider being the resident pianist. Challenging music—I expect you to do the standard rep plus a few concertos, and might feature the group from time to time at symphony performances."

"That would be great!" Charlotte's eyes shone. "You know I would love to do it."

"I know," he laughed. "We have to convince Aunt Melanie, particularly with our champion Howard gone."

Charlotte's smile faded. "I'm sorry, Charlotte," he murmured as he noted her change of features.

"I miss him," she stated simply, looking away.

"I do, too," Conrad squeezed her arm. "He was my biggest fan." Changing the subject, he continued. "Speaking of biggest fans, how are lessons going with Melanie's new star Dr. Kreiser?"

"He's insufferable," Charlotte remarked plaintively. "But he's a good teacher. I know Aunt Mellie will always take his side. And he's so much in demand. I try to keep my mouth shut, because he could always kick me to the curb as a student."

Conrad suppressed a smile at the girl's response. "You know I've recommended that he take my place as organist at the Cathedral," he mentioned.

"Then I won't ever get to play there," she lamented.

"Don't sell yourself short," he smiled. "Kreiser is just as impressed with your abilities as I am. He's just used to being a prodigy himself, stealing the limelight. He's still young, so hasn't tasted the vicarious joy in another's art yet. And he was raised in a culture that doesn't give lavish praise. You have to earn it and then some."

She took his arm. "I like you so much better than him. Why aren't you married, Dr. Conrad?"

He laughed, surprised at her question. "I've tried that. Didn't take. My first love was music. Still is. Now let's get to work and make some."

He paused, rapping his baton to restore order. "Welcome to the auditions for young orchestra," he announced to the milling group of young people. "I want to introduce you to Miss Charlotte Lawson, a gifted musician who has already debuted with the Symphony earlier this year."

The young musicians peered at her and applauded. Her friend Erik blew her a kiss.

"Miss Lawson is going to assist me with these, by listening to you all, and by playing the accompaniment for auditions for those of you who don't have an accompanist," he announced. Charlotte looked at him in surprise. He winked at her. "Sight reading is good for you," he told her, his voice low.

He started out by having them organized into groups and having them sight read some scores as a group, with principal members of the symphony present as section leaders. By the end of the session, he had provided a schedule for auditions on the next Saturday, and told those needing an accompanist to provide the music to Charlotte.

As a result, after a couple of weeks Conrad selected a young symphony, selecting Charlotte as pianist and Erik as first violinist and concertmaster, with rehearsals on Saturday mornings.

When Gerry Fellowes heard that Charlotte had rehearsals every Saturday morning, he was livid.

"What about our Saturday water-skiing with Dad?" he complained the next afternoon, as they were sculling together on the lake.

"What about it?" she argued. "You don't get out of bed until ten or later anyway. By the time you've had breakfast, I'll be through with practice," she pointed out.

"We'll see," he sulked, but was mollified.

"Besides, you're too lazy," she added mischievously. "We should be pulling twice this fast."

"I'm just being kind to you," he sneered. "Now you've asked for it." He started rowing harder, as she matched him stroke for stroke. After a while, he shipped the oars, signaling surrender, breathing heavier.

"OK, you win," he panted. "I'm going shooting after this, and I want to be able to hold the shotgun."

"Shooting? That sounds like fun," Charlotte remarked.

"You want to come? I'll have to get Dad to talk Melanie into it," Gerry smiled slyly. "But it will cost you."

"What?" her eyes danced. "How about a kiss? I saw you kissing Priscilla after church the other day."

"Aw," he drawled. "Kissing you would be like kissing my rugby team, or Toby's Irish setter."

She swung the oar at his head, but he caught it, grinning. "Actually, kissing Priscilla was like kissing Toby's dog."

"What if I told Agatha you were kissing a girl in church?"

Gerry glowered. "Don't even think about it. I'd have to do double penance, and you'd be on my black list." His eyes twinkled. "And I'd have to tell Melanie about you and that Evan boy."

Charlotte hooted. "That would be rich. Evan likes guys. In fact, just that morning at church he stated you had a cute butt."

Gerry's eyes grew dark. "I'll thrash him," he muttered.

"No, you won't," Charlotte laughed. "He isn't going to come on to you. That is, unless you want him to. I could put in a good word for you."

It was his time to swing the oar and splash her. "I'll think of some suitable payback."

Several months later, she performed the Brahms in concert with the orchestra, to standing ovation. Conrad himself congratulated Melanie on her allowing the young girl to perform publicly, as Charlotte listened, half-ecstatic, half-anxious, for Melanie's reaction. But Melanie smiled in her enigmatic way and acknowledged Conrad's effusive praise of her niece, saying nothing.

Likewise, Kreiser's praise was forthcoming but not as warm as she had hoped. She was disappointed.

Chapter 9

Charlotte rushed into the salon, late and flustered, wearing short shorts and a tank top over a swimsuit. Kreiser was sitting in a club chair near the organ reading the newspaper, dressed as usual in pressed trousers and tweed jacket over a starched white shirt, his tie loosened. He examined her appearance over the newspaper. Charlotte was now fourteen and in high school, and her tomboyish figure was developing curves, a fact which was accentuated by her skimpy clothes.

"That is not proper attire for organ lessons with me," he observed severely.

"But we're going skiing afterward," she protested. "Gerry has a new motor launch, and he's picking us up at the boathouse."

"That's fine, but no lesson in that outfit," he countered stubbornly.

"Oh, please go with us," she coaxed. "It's so much fun."

"Charlotte, I don't have the time to deal with your adolescent behaviors. I'm not your babysitter, and you will follow my rules. Now I'll give you five minutes to change clothes or else."

She started to argue, but her attention was arrested by a couple of colorful silk scarves nearby on a table. "For me?" she asked excitedly, picking them up and admiring them.

"Guess you won't be finding out," Kreiser replied, taking them from her and lazily walking toward the door.

"OK, OK, I'm hurrying," she relented quickly.

"You have only four minutes left," he looked at his watch.

She ran out of the room and bounded up the stairs two at a time. Within minutes she was back, dressed in jeans and a blue pullover, her hair bound into a ponytail.

"Come here," he commanded. She walked up to him, smiling.

"Sit on the bench facing me." She complied, and he proceeded to tie a scarf around each leg just at the knee, then tied the ends of the two scarves together.

She began laughing. "If you're going to tie me up and have your way with me, why did you have me change clothes?"

"You'll see," Kreiser smiled slightly. "And you are much too provocative for your own good," he added, a gentle reproof in his voice.

Her knees bound together, he carefully spun her around to face the console. Before her a book was opened to pedal exercises.

"Ugh," she moaned.

"No 'ugh', just play," he admonished her.

She began, slowly at first, then gaining speed. "Damn," she muttered as she strained to reach an octave. "Why do I have to be a lady when I play the organ?"

"This has nothing to do with etiquette, and everything to do with technique," he replied next to her ear, making her jump. "Don't pound the pedals. The feet are supposed to remain close together whenever possible, while anticipating their next move. The knees should remain together. The feet should be positioned right over the note. Press the pedals. Follow the markings," he coached her, as she grimaced, her hands gripping either side of the bench.

He continued to grill her for an hour, one minute animated, another coaxing, another angry and reproving. Finally he laid a hand on her shoulder. "Enough for today," he announced. "I want you to spend time each day practicing this. In a few weeks this will be second nature."

She swung around the bench, only to be distracted by the sight of a young man lounging across one of the club chairs facing the organ. George Fellowes laughingly regarded her as she stood up, her face flushed. She started to flee, but stumbled, forgetting her knees were tied together. He jumped up and caught her, righting her.

She looked over at the doorway, where Kreiser had strode and was deep in conversation with a young woman, looking none too pleased. "I told you never to interrupt my lessons," he was saying, his voice raised.

"Here, lean against the bench," George smiled beguilingly, bending down and reviewing the knotted silk scarves. "Kinky," he added, smirking. "Do we sacrifice her and eat her, or just ravish her? I never thought organ lessons could be this fun."

"What are you doing here, George?" Kreiser demanded, returning to the room. "Your sister is waiting outside."

"Oh, Kat said we'd wait here for you to finish," he replied lazily. "She wanted to make sure you didn't forget that you promised to attend the exhibit at the art museum tonight with her. Now you've gone and made her mad."

He turned to Charlotte. "Gerry will be here soon. You're not going skiing like that?"

"No," she found her voice. "Are you going with us, George?" She knew he was nineteen and away at college. She still referred to him as George because that was how Gerard addressed him, although most people called him Sammy.

Sammy lazily untangled the scarves. "I haven't seen you in years, Amy's little sister. Gerry talks about you all the time. I thought you were supposed to be a skinny little ugly thing. Gerry didn't tell me you were pretty. Now I'm sorry I didn't accept his invitation."

Sammy handed her the scarves, patting her on the back, before turning away. "Gotta go," he announced. "I've done my errand, which was the price of having Kat's Porsche tonight." Turning back to give her another dazzling smile, Sammy blew her a kiss. "Later, beautiful."

Charlotte stared after his wake. Kreiser watched her, amused. "Well," he remarked, "you seem smitten."

"He's the best-looking guy I've ever seen," she breathed. "I want to marry him." Then, realizing what she had just said, she turned beet-red and ran out the door.

Later, as she was putting her skis on sitting at the dock while Gerry threw her the rope, she remarked, "I saw George today."

"So?" Gerry shrugged. "Am I supposed to be impressed?"

"You know he is so good-looking, and so much more charming than you," Charlotte retorted slyly.

"Yeah, yeah. But do you think my brother is going to notice you?" Gerry shot back.

"He did today," Charlotte smirked, as she took the grip in her hand and nodded.

"You ready?" Gerry said, then without waiting for her answer, he throttled up the engine, jerking her off the dock. Charlotte barely avoided falling over the skis as he took off without a backward glance.

"Jerk!" she yelled at him as she hung on for dear life.

Chapter 10

"OK, I'm fifteen. I've got to play piano with the symphony three times, and I'm playing with the quartet and the youth orchestra. I've even played solo at symphony events. Don't you think it's time I got to do an organ recital?"

Charlotte stood, hands on hips, haranguing Kreiser at the beginning of a lesson.

"So you think you're ready?" he raised his eyebrows.

She flushed. "You don't? As hard as I've been working? Does my playing suck that much?"

He sobered, looking at her hurt expression. "No, *cara mia*, you are coming along very well," he replied.

"Why do you call me that?" she asked, her expression still downcast.

"Because my mother always called me that," he said softly. "For some reason I feel protective toward you."

"So that's why I can't do a recital?" she sniffed. "I don't want your protection. I want to play."

"OK," he capitulated, surprising her. "We're going on a field trip. I'll give you five minutes. Bring what music you think you want to work up for a recital. Meet me out front."

She looked at his retreating form, then rushed to an ornate armoire standing beside the organ, full of music. She busily pulled some pieces and stuffed them into a book bag along with her organ shoes.

She ran out the front door and climbed into his square gray Volvo sedan. "Where are we going?" she giggled excitedly. "The cathedral? Grace? Not Spivey?"

"None of those," he smiled. "You'll see."

He drove her north of town, and they stopped at an older brick church building. "What church is this?" she asked curiously.

"A very nice church, great acoustics," he said cryptically. "We'll go meet the pastor."

They walked into a side door and into the pastor's office, where a black gentleman stood and shook Kreiser's hand gravely. "Reverend Brown, this is my newest star pupil, Charlotte Lawson. She thinks she is ready to debut on the organ. I immediately thought about your church."

Brown shook Charlotte's hand warmly. "My congregation is always ready with open arms to greet one of your stars, Dr. Kreiser. How have you been, Harry?"

"Busy but well. And you?"

"The Lord's work keeps me hopping. The congregation is flourishing, and our organ project has taken off. I think a recital would be just the thing to help us reach our goal."

"Goal?" Charlotte asked.

"A new organ for the church," Rev. Brown informed her. "Although this organ and its predecessor have served us well, and our organist has become quite fond of it."

"I can't wait to see it," Charlotte enthused.

Kreiser took her by the arm. "I'll introduce her to the instrument, then leave her to work. Maybe if you have time we can catch up."

He marched her out and down the hall, then up some steps into a doorway. They walked out into a dais with a choir loft. At the other side sat a console. Although the room was dark, Charlotte could tell the room was large.

Charlotte peered through the dimly lit room. "Where are the organ chambers?" she asked excitedly, moving quickly toward the console.

He followed her. She examined the console, then looked again around the church, staring into the cavernous space. "There are no pipes," she accused him. "This is electric. I can't believe you." She flung herself down on the bench, her back to him, as tears filled her eyes.

"Charlotte, this is how my star pupils start their careers," Kreiser spoke quietly. "Let me tell you a story."

He walked over and faced her, one hand on her shoulder. He cupped her chin in his other hand and forced her to look at him.

"When I first went over to France, I intended to enter and win the Chartres competition. But I had just begun my studies over there, and had not proved myself. I didn't have that many contacts, didn't know very many people over there. It was hard to find an organ in Paris for practice. And I didn't have any money; I had to make my fellowship funds last.

"So I practiced wherever I could, at all sorts of churches and organs, in the alleys, the suburbs, the outlying villages. I found some awful organs, but I also found some real gems that were unknown. It didn't matter, *cara mia*."

He gazed at her upturned face. "And they were not just a means to an end. I would fill in and play services in payment for my getting to practice. And people would be appreciative. I realized that no matter where I was I needed to make music as best I could, to spread my art. And in return doors began to open. Word of mouth is still the best advertisement."

He had her attention. "Yes, Carlota, this is not a pipe organ. Do you realize that somewhere, sometime in your life you will be called on to play these? They are getting more and more technical, and you need to know the ins and outs of them. There is a lot more gadgetry on these, with reversibles, extra pedals, and now the newer ones have sequencers. They will never go away. The pipe organs are borrowing technology from the digital, and the digital ones are trying to sample and emulate the pipe organs.

"But you would be surprised how sophisticated the tastes of this congregation and their organist. They bleed this instrument dry while working toward its successor. Don't underestimate them."

"Do you really have your students play on electronics?" she whispered.

"Yes, I really do," he smiled. "Now practice. I'm leaving you alone for a while, to explore. I'll be back to see what you've discovered."

After Kreiser left, she glanced at the neat stacks of music beside the organ. "Wow, that's some collection," she mused aloud. Then she looked at the organist's catalogued stack of church bulletins. "Whoa," she exclaimed. "He does all this? On this?"

She put everything back as she found it and turned to the console. "OK, my work is cut out for me," she said to it.

An hour and a half later, Kreiser walked back into the church. "Well, what do you think? Are you up to this?"

Charlotte nodded, preoccupied. "Sure. There are some things I'd like to play, but am not sure I can come up with the necessary sounds."

Kreiser walked up behind her. "Like what? Sometimes you have to improvise, fudge. However, there's a fine line in what is appropriate and *verboten, cara mia*. Show me what you're thinking."

They worked for another hour and a half, as she played through several possible selections for him, and they discussed registration problems.

"I need to get you home. I have a date," he finally looked at his watch. "I suggest that you visit a Sunday service for yourself, so that you can hear the organ in action from the congregation's vantage and with the pews filled. Then we'll come back next week and try again."

Charlotte took his advice and visited the church the next Sunday, and was blown away by the organist's music and the congregational participation. She went up after the service to introduce herself to Jayvon Jackson, the organist. He was enthusiastic about the idea of her recital, and she found herself more excited about the project. She suggested that perhaps something could be done to raise funds for the organ project in conjunction with the recital.

So she threw herself into the preparation, and mentioned the recital to her aunt. Melanie, always interested in philanthropy, was gratified to see Charlotte involving herself in a plan that benefited others, and offered to help by requesting donations from others.

So during the intermission of Charlotte's recital, an announcement was made that several generous donations had been made and that the organ fund was able to move to the next stage. She was happily surprised. The recital went well, and she was presented with a plaque.

After the recital, she walked up to Kreiser. "Well?" she demanded.

He smiled enigmatically. "You exceeded my expectations, *cara mia*."

"So can I play some pipe organs now?" she persisted.

"I will see what I can do," he promised.

Kreiser arranged for her to perform at more recitals, including Grace United Methodist and Spivey Hall. As she clamored for more opportunities, he relented and allowed her to accept other recital invitations conditioned upon Melanie's consent. But Charlotte agreed to come back every year to give a recital at the church that gave her her start.

Chapter 11

Just before her sixteenth birthday, Charlotte's 'coming out' ball was scheduled, and Melanie was pressing her to focus more on the preparations. Charlotte resisted being presented to society, but Melanie was firm that it was a necessary evil she must endure. Charlotte dutifully provided a guest list, but invited her acquaintances from the music world, determined to make it more a party of her choosing.

Gerard was getting ready to leave for college at Stanford. Charlotte was sad to see him go so far away, and made him promise he would be at the ball. "I cannot go through this without you," she told him.

She had an idea that she presented to Gerry. She had already secured his brother George as her escort, much to Melanie's chagrin and her friend Agatha's delight. But regarding whom to present her Charlotte had asked Gerry's advice, and he had advised caution in how to arrange it.

Charlotte made her way to the Fellowes' residence one evening to see Katharine. Katharine was surprised to see her, but invited her to her room while Katharine was getting ready to go out to a sorority party. Charlotte hit her with the request.

"Kat, you know my coming out party is being planned."

"Yeah, I got an invitation. Thanks. I hear my brothers are going to be there, and that Sammy will be your escort. So what's up?" Katharine turned and looked at her, hairbrush in hand.

"I need a favor."

"I can't wait," Katharine looked at her quizzically.

"Well, I don't have my Dad or Uncle Howard to present me, and I was wanting to know if you would object to your dad being the one," Charlotte was direct, looking at her hopefully. "He's been there for us ever since Uncle Howard died, and I would be honored. But I wanted you to say it's OK first."

Katharine put the hairbrush down slowly. Charlotte knew that Katharine was extremely devoted to her father, and jealous of his attentions toward anyone else. She was sensitive to Hell-Kat's bouts of depression, because Gerry had confided to her about his sister's serious mood swings and chronic periods of delusional thinking.

Katharine remained silent for a while. Charlotte finally added, "I just wanted someone I respected a lot to walk me in. I wanted to make sure it was OK with you before I asked him to do it."

"Why do you care how I feel?" Katharine was suddenly insolent.

"I always care how you feel, Hell-Kat," Charlotte replied.

"You want my whole family dancing your tune!" Katharine shot back angrily.

"No, I want you and your family included in my big moment."

She looked up at Charlotte finally, a sly look on her face. "Tell you what," she quipped. "You get Mike to take me to the ball, and I'll let you have my dad to present you."

Charlotte shook her head. "You know I can't do that, Hell-Kat. He's already asked Amy." There goes that, she thought, deflated. Now who will I get? "I thought you were dating that University of Georgia football player," Charlotte interjected desperately.

"I am, but I want Mike," Katharine's voice rose. "No Mike, no Dad. You gonna ask him anyway?"

"Not if you say no. Thanks anyway," Charlotte spoke dispiritedly.

"You want my invitation back?" Katharine smiled saccharinely.

Charlotte was surprised. "Of course not. I asked you a favor, and you said no. That's that. I am disappointed, that's all. I'll see you there."

Gerry met her outside. "Can you give me a lift back?" she asked.

"Sure," he replied. "How did it go?"

Charlotte outlined what transpired with Katharine.

He shook his head. "Kat doesn't care about anyone but Kat. You know Dad would do it in a minute."

"I know," she mused. "But Hell-Kat is your and George's sister. I want us to be friends. If I knew how she felt and asked him anyway, it would hurt her. And she might make a scene at my party."

"You're strange," Gerry laughed.

"All this debutante stuff is stupid enough without making enemies over it," she explained.

"What are you going to do?"

"I'll let Melanie sort it out," she shrugged, trying to appear nonchalant.

When she walked in the door of the Cain residence, Melanie was on the telephone. "She just walked in," she said. Melanie held out the telephone to Charlotte.

"For me?" she wondered aloud.

She took the phone. "Charlotte, it's Kat. I thought it over, and you can ask my Dad," she heard Katharine say.

"But—" Charlotte started.

"No strings attached," she replied.

"Are you sure, Kat?" Charlotte asked, surprised.

"Sure. I gotta go; I'm late."

Charlotte replaced the phone in its cradle. Melanie asked, "What did Katharine want?"

"She said it was all right to ask her father to present me at the ball," Charlotte said slowly.

Melanie gushed. "How sweet of her. That takes care of that problem. Have you asked Mr. Fellowes?"

"Not yet. I will," Charlotte promised, her mind elsewhere.

That Saturday she saw Gerry just before he left for the airport to school. "You gonna miss me?" he hugged her as he finished putting his luggage in the car.

"I'll try really hard," she teased him. "You are going to be back for this shindig?"

"I don't know," he hedged. "If there's a big party on campus—"

"If you're not there, I will have you thrown out of that school," Charlotte threatened him, a gleam in her eye.

"I'll be back," he promised as he climbed in the car.

"I'm the one you should be worried about being there. I'm your date," his father winked at her as he took his place behind the wheel.

So one Saturday morning a couple months later while she was rehearsing with the youth symphony, she was surprised when Gerard walked in. She jumped up and ran to greet her best friend, but saw his face.

"Why are you back already?" she asked. "What has happened?"

He took her arm and pulled her aside. "It's Dad," he answered in a whisper. "Charl, he's had a massive stroke."

"Oh, Gerry," she breathed, a flood of sorrow coming over her. "Have you seen him?"

"Yes. He's comatose," Gerry's voice broke.

"Let's get you out of here," she whispered. She ran to Dr. Conrad and briefly advised him, before taking Gerry by the arm and leading him out.

Gerry stopped outside before the grand sculptures on display. "I don't know what I'll do without my dad," he murmured. Charlotte's heart broke for him.

"I know, dear," she stroked his arm in sympathy. "Let's go see him, OK? Maybe it will be better when we get there."

They reached Gerry's car. "Do you want me to drive?" Charlotte asked. "Melanie finally let me have my learner's permit."

"Can you drive a stick-shift?"

"Of course I can," Charlotte spoke with confidence, although she had no idea how to drive a car with standard transmission.

"OK," he assented as they got in and he handed her the keys. She adjusted the seat then stuck the key in the ignition.

"I think it would help if the foot was on the clutch first," he suggested.

"Oh, yeah," she nodded knowingly. She looked down at the diagram on the shift lever. Piece of cake, she thought.

She managed to put the car in reverse without too much trouble, but then had trouble, grinding the gears as she looked for first. Gerry finally located it for her. "Maybe I should drive," he remarked. "This car needs to last a few weeks at least."

"Give me a chance," she retorted through gritted teeth.

"OK, it's obvious you don't know what you're doing, so let me teach you," he replied patiently. "Give it gas as you slowly let up on the clutch."

She jerkily followed his instructions as they made the rough trip to Emory Crawford Long Hospital and he directed her to the nearest parking lot. They screeched to a halt.

"Whew!" he exclaimed. "At least I'm still alive."

"OK, so I lied," Charlotte smiled.

They hurried up to the intensive care unit, only to find Agatha leading Katharine out of the room, Katharine sobbing and out of control, and George by her side.

Gerry looked anxiously at his mother. "What's the news?"

She just shook her head, tears streaming down her face. Gerry looked wildly at Charlotte and plunged through the door of the room. Charlotte hurriedly followed him.

A nurse was in the room when he flung himself inside. He went up to the bed, with Charlotte beside him. "I'm sorry," the nurse whispered. "He is gone."

Charlotte gazed at the still form of Mr. Fellowes, as Gerry dumbly stood there, tears flowing down his face. They stood there side by side for several minutes.

"I'm so sorry, Gerry," she whispered. "Come on. There's nothing we can do." She took his arm and gently led him out. As they made it to the door of the room, he threw his arms around her.

"I'm here, Gerry," she whispered. "I won't leave you. Just like you were there for me." She hugged him and pushed open the door.

Charlotte was as heartbroken as Gerry, for she had lost yet a third father-figure in her young life. She asked that Melanie cancel the ball to honor Mr. Fellowes' memory.

The funeral service was held at Peachtree Christian Church, where Mr. Fellowes had been a member for years before he married Agatha, who was Catholic and had 'converted' him. He had stipulated that his funeral would be at his family church.

The sunlight streamed through the omnipresent impressive stained glass windows surrounding the mourners in the packed church. Charlotte was surprised to see that Kreiser was playing the service instead of the regular organist. He was gazing at her as she glanced up to the rear gallery, and nodded at her.

Melanie, as Agatha's best friend, sat with her friend, with Katharine propped up weeping between them, and Charlotte was between George and Gerard. During the sermon she slipped her hand in George's and squeezed it briefly. He looked at her and winked, then put his arm around her, his hand resting on his brother's shoulder. He took her right hand and held it during the rest of the sermon. She glowed with secret delight at his show of attention, even as she held onto Gerry's arm with her left hand.

As they stood for the benediction, he leaned over and whispered to her, "Thank you, pretty Charlotte."

The graveside service was a blur, and she and Melanie accompanied the family back home after the service. Charlotte found herself helping with guests, as Gerry was called on to greet people and help host the family and friends who had come to pay their condolences.

At one time she went into the kitchen looking for more sugar for the coffee service. She bumped into George. "Hi," she breathed, suddenly embarrassed.

"Hi, yourself," he greeted her, his voice low, as he sidled next to her in the doorway, making no effort to move out of the way.

"I came to get some sugar," she blurted breathlessly, then colored as she realized what she had said.

"Oh, now, if that isn't a come-on, I don't know what is," he bent over her and lightly brushed her lips with his.

"I'm sorry, I meant—" she tried to explain, flushed, but he laughed at her.

"Do you play tennis, Charlotte?" he inquired, his mouth near her ear.

"Yes," she whispered, aware of his nearness.

"What if you and I meet up on the courts here, say, tomorrow?" he asked provocatively.

"Well, you know I am in school during the day," she said uncertainly.

"But couldn't you make some time for me afterward?" he winked at her. "I'd really like to see you in a short skirt. You could comfort me in my sorrow before I have to go back to school myself."

"I could see what I could do. Tomorrow at 3:30?" she laughed nervously, as he kissed her on the forehead.

"It's a date. Go serve your sugar," he teased her, and he was gone.

So she daydreamed all the next day at school, hurried home and quickly changed into her best tennis outfit. As she slipped out the front door, a sleek Jaguar convertible roadster pulled up. George reached over and opened the door for her.

"Wow!" she admired the car. "This is great."

"It was to be a gift from Dad for my birthday, but I got it early from Mom today," he said somberly. "So I thought we might break it in. Besides, I wouldn't make a date with my best girl and not pick her up."

"I didn't tell Aunt Mellie where I was going to be," Charlotte was dubious, but he laughed.

"I'm not going to eat you, Charlotte," he teased her. "We'll take this down the road, then you're going to give me that game you promised."

"OK," she grinned, climbing in.

So George and she rode down the nearby highway as he put the car through its paces. When they reached a point where he turned around in a parking lot, he shifted into neutral, pulled up the brake, and turned to her.

"Wanna drive it?" he asked. "Do you have a driver's license?"

"I have a learner's permit," she admitted. "I shouldn't—not your new car."

"Have you driven a stick-shift?"

"I tried to drive Gerry's—the other day," her face fell as she remembered that being the day of his father's death.

"Well, then, let's give you another lesson," he jumped out and ran around, opening her door. "Crawl over," he ordered. "Give me a thrill by letting me see those legs."

She looked at him, then slid across the gear shift panel, settling into the driver's seat. He climbed in behind her and reached under her legs. "Let's move the seat up for you," he suggested, at her surprised look.

"OK, seat belt," he ordered, reaching across her and pulling the seat belt, clicking it closed.

"You're enjoying this, aren't you?" she laughed.

"You bet," he smiled slyly. "Now left foot on the clutch, check to make sure the car is still in neutral, and unlatch the brake."

She did. The car started rolling backward. "Foot on the brake, dear," he instructed. "Now shift into first and give it a little gas as you ease slightly off the clutch."

She did and the car lurched, then went dead. He laughed as her face flamed. "No problem. I did that plenty of times while learning. Feet on the clutch and brake, and let's try again."

He worked with her until she was able to move forward without killing the engine. "OK, don't let up entirely on the clutch, because you want to shift into second as soon as you're moving well."

So she shifted into second. "Great!" he applauded her, and she beamed. "Don't move into the road yet, let's work in the parking lot a little," he suggested.

After about thirty minutes, she was feeling more comfortable with the actions of shifting, and he suggested they try to make it home. "No," she objected. "I think it's time you drive us back," she asserted.

"You sure?" he asked. She nodded. "So what do you do?"

"I put on the clutch and brake, shift it into neutral, and put on the parking brake," she stated.

He reached over and kissed her quickly on the lips. "Good girl," he whispered, jumping out before she had time to react.

She scrambled back over the console as he retook the wheel. "Now for that game," he smiled. "Are you going to let me win?"

"Hell, no," she laughed.

They made it to the Fellowes' home, and walked around to the courts. He tossed the ball to her. "You get first serve."

They played until almost dark, and George threw up his hands. "You're wicked," he shouted. "That's not fair. You wore me out. Let's get a drink."

They walked inside, George's arm around her. "Uh-oh, we have company," he whispered in her ear. "I guess I'll have to fantasize about the rest."

Charlotte stopped short as she walked into the Florida room and there was Melanie sitting with Agatha, sipping an aperitif.

"It would help my heart immensely if you would just leave a note where you are every now and then," she said placidly to her niece.

Agatha came up to Charlotte. "Thanks, my dear, for coming over and spending time with Sammy." Her eyes were sad.

Charlotte warmed to Agatha. "I'm so sorry about Mr. Fellowes," her eyes were shining with unshed tears.

Agatha put her arm around Charlotte. "Me, too, Charlotte. Katharine has taken it hard."

George leaned over and pecked Charlotte's cheek. "I'll go check on her. Thanks for the game, Charl."

"Where is Gerry?" Charlotte watched George as he left the room.

"He's kept to himself today," Agatha sniffed. "He has not said much since last night. He disappeared a little while ago."

"I think I know where he might be," Charlotte said quietly. "I'll check the boathouse, if you don't mind."

She looked at Melanie, who nodded. She slipped out and made her way down the little stone pathway to the boathouse and slipped in. There was a light just outside the boathouse that lent a few rays to show the way.

At the end of the dock she found him sitting alone staring off into the dusk. She sat down beside him. "What are you doing, Gerry?" she asked quietly.

"Has George seduced you yet?" he stared out over the black water.

"No," she replied. "But that's not what's bothering you, is it?"

"No, it's not," he agreed.

They were silent, just listening to the sounds of the night. As the song of the crickets and frogs crescendoed around them, Charlotte put her arm around Gerry, and they both wept.

Chapter 12

Charlotte turned sixteen with little fanfare. Amy called her from college.
"Did you like your gift?" she asked.
"What gift?" Charlotte asked.
"Oh, nothing," Amy replied breathlessly. "Have you checked the mail yet?"
"No, I just made it home from practice."
"I sent you a card. Happy birthday. I'll call you later." Amy hung up.
Charlotte looked at the receiver, then shook her head. The doorbell rang. When she went to answer, a delivery guy stood with roses.
"Wow! Who are they for?" she asked.
"Charlotte Lawson," the guy responded. "You gonna sign for them?"
"You bet," she signed the clipboard and took the vase. Closing the door, she placed them on the foyer table and pulled out the card. "Love to my favorite Sweet 16, Gerry."
The telephone rang, so she ran to catch it.
"Did you get your gift?" Gerry's voice greeted her.
"The roses? Yes. Sixteen, and yellow is my favorite color. You are so sweet. Thanks."
"I'm sorry I'm not there. We'd find some trouble together. Sixteen is important."
"I miss you, Gerry," she was somber. "How are you doing?"
"It's hard," he admitted. "School isn't easy, and now with Dad gone it's even more difficult. He always checked on me to see how classes were going."
"I know," she said sympathetically.
"What did Aunt Melanie get you?"
"I haven't gotten it yet," she stated. "I hope she remembered."
"Oh, I'm sure she did," Gerry laughed.
She heard the front door closing. "Someone's here. I gotta go. Call you later."

She walked into the foyer to find Kreiser standing there. "I don't know where Melanie is," she spoke impulsively.

"You guessed wrongly," he replied quietly.

She looked at him questioningly.

"I'm here to deliver a gift." He paused. "For you. From Melanie."

"Really?" she smiled happily. "Where is it?"

"Come with me," he took her arm and steered her out the door.

There in the driveway was a new silver BMW convertible.

"Oh, that is so cool!" she cried, turned and wrapped her arms around Kreiser.

"I'm glad you approve," the voice of her aunt spoke.

Charlotte released Kreiser and ran up to Melanie, engulfing her in a bear hug. "Thank you," she murmured. "This is too cool," she continued. "Can I drive it now?"

"Only with adult supervision," Melanie was stern. "You can go later this week and take the driving test. If you pass, then we'll see."

Charlotte ran to the car and opened the driver's door. "Please come with me," she asked them.

"I'll let Harry do the honors," Melanie smiled. "My heart is not strong enough."

"Oh, pooh, Aunt Mellie," she laughed. "Let's go."

"It'll be dark soon, so not far," she warned.

Charlotte turned the ignition and the vehicle sprang to life. As she carefully made her way out of the driveway, Kreiser quietly spoke. "I have a surprise for you."

"What?" she asked, looking at him.

"Watch the road and not me," he ordered. She slowly pulled out onto the avenue.

"Tell me," she begged.

"Now that you have your own wheels, I've added your name to the substitute organist list," he informed her. "Now you can get more experience playing for churches and choirs."

"Cool," she answered. "And Jacob will be thrilled that he doesn't have to shuttle me around all the time."

"But you have to remember that you must help those in need as well, even those without four-manual million-dollar pipe organs," he reminded her.

"Deal," she smiled.

Later that night the phone rang while Charlotte was practicing. She heard Melanie talking, then call to her. "It's for you," Melanie handed her the receiver.

"Hello?"

"Hi, Charlotte Lawson," she heard a familiar voice.

"George!" she cooed warmly. "What a nice surprise. How are you?"

"I'm fine. And I hear it is someone's birthday today."

Her heart beat quicker. "Yes, it is," she purred, she hoped sexily, as Melanie walked out of the room.

"Well, a birdie told me that you deserved a special birthday present in lieu of your coming-out party," George drawled.

"Which birdie? Was he named Gerry?" laughed Charlotte.

"Actually, Agatha thought it was a good idea. You don't have any plans this weekend, do you?"

"Not really," she smiled broadly. Was he going to ask her out?

"Do you know who Aerosmith is?"

"It's a what, a band. Yes, I adore Aerosmith. I also know that they are playing Atlanta this weekend, and tickets have been sold out forever. Why?" her eyes were sparkling.

"You like Aerosmith?"

"I really like Led Zeppelin, but you took Barb Carbuncle to that concert. I would have given anything to go to that one."

"It's Carpenter, not Carbuncle."

"I know, but that's what she's called."

"You constantly amaze me," George snickered. "You're not the prim and proper one at all, nothing like your sister. Anyway, Agatha has convinced the Matriarch to let me take you and Gerry to the concert Saturday night."

"That's so cool," Charlotte responded enthusiastically. "I'd love to go. So Gerry is coming too?"

"Hope that is OK," George's voice dropped. "I'd rather have you all to myself. Mom thinks Gerry is taking Dad's death badly, and wanted him included. I've still got to call him. But we have to have an escort, so I asked Kat."

Charlotte grew warm, but hooted. "Yeah, right. Like Aunt Mellie is going to let me go with you chaperoned by your sister."

"It's true," she knew he was smiling. "The Omni, front row seats, back stage passes. You're going to be sixteen in style. Kat asked your music teacher, but he said he valued his ears too much. I didn't think you'd want him around to cramp your style."

She laughed at the thought of Kreiser at a rock concert.

"What time?" she asked breathlessly.

"We'll pick you up around seven. Concert starts at eight. Do you have a sexy short skirt?"

"Sure," she blushed.

"Wear it," he demanded. "Later."

Friday night she waited anxiously. Thankfully Melanie and Agatha had gone to hear the symphony, and there were no lectures. The Fellowes limousine pulled up, and Charlotte was on the steps before George could step out.

"You should always keep the boys waiting, particularly for that sight," he admonished her good-naturedly, as she climbed in. There sat Gerry.

"Gerry!" she cried, and engulfed him in a bear hug.

"Happy birthday, Charl," he returned her hug. "You are certainly excited," he smirked, glancing at George sitting across from them.

"My first rock concert—why shouldn't I be?" she retorted gaily.

"Your education begins tonight," George's eyes traveled down her torso, as Katharine languidly applied dark lipstick and checked her matching painted nails. Charlotte admired Kat's outfit, a short leather skirt suit, fishnet stockings and high heels.

"Wow, Hell-Kat, you look great," Charlotte said with admiration.

"Thanks," Kat replied shortly without looking up. "You kids need to lay low and not embarrass me tonight. And for God's sake, don't treat me like some babysitter." She turned to George. "I'm doing my own thing after backstage, so don't wait up. What Agatha doesn't know won't hurt her."

"No problem," he drawled, his eyes still on Charlotte.

They pulled up to the back of the coliseum, and he handed them each a pass. "Here we go," he led the way.

Charlotte's heart raced, as she followed George, Gerry at her heels and Katharine sauntering behind, through a maze of hallways and into a large dressing room full of people. George took Charlotte's hand and started introducing her to the band members, as she smiled in acknowledgment. One groupie looked at her approvingly. "I like 'em young," he spoke to George.

"Don't touch her," George warned. "She's a virgin, the only one in the room."

"George!" Charlotte cried indignantly.

"And there's not to be a mark on her, for the Matriarch will have her strip searched, examined, and blood and urine tests to make sure she hasn't been contaminated," he continued.

Gerry frowned as the others laughed. George was handed a toke and inhaled, then offered it to Charlotte.

"No, thanks," she smiled. "Virgin, remember?"

"Scared?" some female dressed all in black laughed behind her.

"Only of acting like you," Charlotte retorted, piqued.

George laughed as Gerry took her arm protectively. "She has claws." Pulling them both with him, he ended up at a table where tequila was being poured in glasses. "Here, Charlotte," he handed her one.

She looked at Gerry inquiringly, before downing the liquid in one gulp. Instantly she coughed, the fiery liquid burning her throat.

"What's that?" she asked hoarsely.

Gerry smiled. "No, Charl, like this." He licked the skin of his outer hand between thumb and forefinger, then sprinkled salt on the spot. He licked the salt, downed the glass, and sucked the lime wedge in quick succession.

"I see Stanford taught you something valuable," George smirked. "Now you try it, girl," he took Charlotte's hand, licking it himself. Charlotte was transfixed as George sprinkled salt, then handed her the drink.

She followed suit, gasping again as the liquid hit the back of her throat. She grasped at the lime and sucked it, as Gerry and George laughed.

"Take it easy on those," Gerry warned her. "Next thing you know you'll be crawling on the floor and you won't be a virgin anymore."

She looked past him. George had left them and was leaning over a mirror doing a line of cocaine. He motioned for her to join him.

"I'm good," she waved him away. "Gerry," she whispered, "I think I'm out of my depth here."

"At least you're getting your wish," he remarked. "George is paying you quite a bit of attention. You're making the rest of his entourage jealous. It's said he likes to deflower sweet young things," he added wickedly.

"Where did Hell-Kat go?" Charlotte asked over the din of noise.

"I think she had a rendezvous with the drummer or something," Gerry said into her ear.

George came up. "We've got an escort to our seats," he yelled. "They're about to go on. Let's go."

He took Charlotte by the arm and half-dragged her as they made their way through the crowd and the noise to their seats. Charlotte started feeling a bit woozy from the tequila, but was too excited to care.

At one point during the applause, George crushed her to him and kissed her. She felt warm with delight, until Gerry warned, "Break it up, you two."

After the concert, George wanted to go with the crew to party, but Gerry said, "Melanie will expect Charlotte home. Remember, no marks and all that jazz?"

"Aw, Brother, c'mon," George's voice was slurred. "Let her grow up and live a little."

Charlotte took George's hand. "Thanks for a wonderful birthday gift," she rasped, her voice hoarse from cheering. "I had a great time. If I don't go home, Mellie won't ever let me out again."

He embraced her, whispering, "But I had big plans for you tonight."

She felt as though she was glowing. She lingered.

Gerry intervened, tugging at her. "Melanie said midnight, and it's almost that now."

Charlotte blushed. "I'll hold you to that one day." She reached over and kissed him quickly on the lips.

Gerry pulled her away, and they crawled in the limo as George lurched away, waving at them. Charlotte's eyes were shining, as Gerry gazed at her wearily. "I have permanent hearing loss, but that was so cool," she sighed.

Gerry yawned. "Glad you enjoyed it."

"I think I'm going to enjoy making out with George," she added wickedly.

Chapter 13

As they arrived at the Georgian Terrace, she surveyed her reflection in the mirror of the grand lobby. At sixteen Charlotte felt all grown up, but the face of a girl looked back at her. Her hair had been loosely bound, with curling tendrils around her face. Her peach-colored bridesmaid gown of chiffon boasted demure wide shoulder straps that criss-crossed in the back, leaving parts of her slim suntanned back bare.

"Are you coming?" a familiar voice asked her. "We're supposed to be in the receiving line. Aunt Mellie will be pissed that we're late."

"Sure," she replied to Gerry, dressed in a black tux, who was urging her on. Just then, she caught sight of her aunt hurrying forward, her jaw set in that familiar grim line.

"Charlotte, please just once refrain from giving me a heart attack," Melanie muttered angrily, all the while smiling at guests as they passed by. "You two are needed for photos."

"Yes, ma'am," Charlotte responded meekly. Melanie stopped dead in her tracks and examined her niece's face.

"What have you done now?" she hissed, her voice low.

"Nothing, ma'am," Charlotte smiled sunnily, taking Melanie's arm. "I'm just trying to take to heart your 'family to the end' speech of last night. I know I've been a handful, but I want you to know that just like you I want to make today fabulous for Amy and Mike."

Melanie looked at her suspiciously, but her tone softened. "Just stay out of trouble today at least," she whispered, as she led Charlotte away, Gerry trailing behind.

Inside the bride and groom were being toasted. Charlotte beamed at her sister and brother-in-law. Amy was the most beautiful bride she could ever remember.

As the dancing began, Charlotte looked around for Gerard, but saw him at the other end of the room flirting with another bridesmaid. She sauntered around the room, watching people enjoy themselves.

Suddenly she felt someone at her elbow. Turning, she saw Gerard's brother, dazzling in tuxedo, his blonde hair immaculately in place, regarding her with laughing eyes.

"George!" she cooed with pleasure, her face flushing. "How nice to see you. How is law school?"

"Boring as hell. Care to dance with me?" he asked her, smiling.

Her heart caught in her throat, as she nodded and he pulled her to follow him on the dance floor. Putting an arm around her, he gave her a heart-stopping smile. "You're the only person who calls me 'George'."

"That's not so. I know for a fact that both your mom and Gerry call you that. It's a distinguished name," she managed to say, her eyes locked in his.

"I've missed your driving lessons and my tennis lessons," he laughed in her ear. "We need to make up for my time away."

"What, you out of practice? Poor baby," she laughed at him.

"I think you're the prettiest girl here," he drawled. "Where's your boyfriend, my brother?"

"He's not my boyfriend," she retorted quickly, "and he's getting it on with Priscilla Madden over there."

George gave a hoot. "So baby brother is getting busy? Who is your boyfriend, Charlotte?"

"You could be, if you wanted," she answered impulsively, then crimsoned, almost stopping in the middle of the floor. He laughed, twirling her around, and kissed her on the cheek.

"You're funny," he remarked in her ear over the din of the music and voices. "I like you, Charlotte Lawson."

She felt light-headed as they continued to dance. He whispered, "Where were you and Gerry when rehearsal began yesterday? I thought your aunt was going to have a coronary when you weren't there on time."

"We had been skeet-shooting, after sculling early yesterday morning," Charlotte grinned. "I thought my arms were going to fall off. I couldn't very well tell Aunt Mellie that Gerry and I have been hanging out at the gun club instead of being at her fussy rehearsal. Talk about coronary!"

"Are you any good at shooting?" he smiled at her.

"I am very good at it," she beamed. "I won a ribbon last summer." She suddenly became somber. "I'm sorry, George, about Kat."

George smiled, but the smile didn't reach his eyes. "First Dad died. Then she fancied herself in love with Mike, and I guess it just became too much that he was marrying someone else." He paused. "Were you at the bridal shower when she went off?"

"Yeah," Charlotte nodded sympathetically. "Everything was going well, and suddenly she just started shouting at Amy, and collapsed. I felt so bad for her and for Amy." Charlotte glanced at him. "Is she going to be OK?"

"The doctor says she will be," George responded. Changing the subject, he flashed her another winning smile. "If I was your boyfriend, would you let me tie you up with those silk scarves?"

She blushed again prettily, but replied impishly, "That might be arranged."

The music ended, and Amy was frantically waving at her. "I have to go for now," she remarked sadly.

"Don't worry," he grinned mischievously. "I'll see you again."

She made her way across the room to where Amy and Mike were standing. She felt as though she was living a dream. Dancing with George! And he said he liked her.

Melanie kept her busy with photos and errands until Amy and Mike finally left to a fanfare of birdseed. The reception party was slowly drawing to a close. Charlotte looked around for Gerard but did not see him.

"Come with me, girlfriend," a voice said behind her.

Turning, she found George regarding her, a mischievous smile on his face. He took her hand and pulled her with him toward the front door.

"Where are we going?" she asked breathlessly.

"I have a surprise for you," he was cryptic.

Together they threaded their way through traffic, crossing the road to the historic Fox Theatre. Taking her to one of the side doors on the street, he knocked purposefully, and it opened.

"Thanks, man," he slipped a bill to the usher. "I owe you big time."

He led Charlotte down a winding hallway through an office suite, and suddenly they were in the main lobby of the theatre. "Come on," he commanded her, linking her arm in his and leading her down the aisle to the front of the darkened theatre.

"Are you sure we should be here?" Charlotte tried to mask her nervousness.

"It's OK—it's part of my surprise," he assured her smilingly.

They finally arrived to the orchestra pit, where a man in denims and navy blazer was waiting for them.

"Max, this is Charlotte. Charlotte, this is Max, the resident organist here."

"Hi," Charlotte smiled warmly at the man, who took her hand and kissed it briefly.

"*Charmant*," he murmured, as he pushed a button. The organ came out of its pit, the lights suddenly coming on and gleaming off the gilded veneer.

"Wow," whispered Charlotte. "I haven't seen it up close in years."

"And now for the *quid pro quo*," George gave her a little push. "You have to play something."

"Me? I've never played one of these—all those bells and whistles," she cried.

"Max here will help you. How about 'The Star Spangled Banner'?" George suggested, a gleam in his eye.

She hesitated a moment, then giggled. "Why not?"

He lifted her up to the console as Max climbed the small stairwell. She sat there a moment, then hiked up the folds of her gown. "What do I do next?" she turned to Max.

"Well, let's see if I have a registration here that will work—hit the No. 7 toe piston over there," he remarked, then surveyed the stops critically. "Yep, it's all yours. You can play, can't you?"

"She's one of Kreiser's organ students," George supplied, grinning.

"Well, then, that's good enough for me," Max smiled broadly. "Let 'er rip."

Charlotte stared at the console, her heart fluttering, then tentatively touched a note on the great division. She tried a chord on the swell, and the low C on the pedal. Satisfied, she launched into the music.

She felt like she was driving a Mack truck, the massive myriad of sounds swirling around the room. She lost herself in the pleasure of playing, as Max added and retired stops around her.

She almost shouted in his ear, "Can you add the piccolo part?"

He nodded and pulled on some stops, reaching above her and with one hand supplying the piccolo as she played the rest. When they finished, she was shaking with laughter.

"Oh, my, that was cool," she cried. "Thank you so much," she glowed.

"One more thing," George interjected, giving a sly look at Max. "Max, play something while I dance with my girlfriend here on the stage."

"Sure thing," Max grinned. "Ed, put a spotlight on the stage," he called up through the darkness.

George gingerly led Charlotte up a narrow flight of steps to the main stage. She almost stumbled, but he put his arm around her and helped her up the remaining steps. She felt faint being so close to him.

Max started playing 'Isn't It Romantic' as George pulled her to him and started swaying in time with the music. She laughed as Max put the organ through its paces and they danced. George pulled her closer to him until their bodies melted together and they were cheek to cheek. One hand moved up to her breast. She was afraid to breathe, suddenly frightened.

"Charlotte, have you ever been kissed?" George spoke into her ear, his breath fanning her cheek as he nuzzled her earlobe.

"Yes," she said, her heart fluttering wildly.

"I haven't," he spoke, his mouth caressing her ear. "I'm still a virgin. Would you do me the honor?"

She knew he was lying, but she didn't care. They stopped as the music drew to a close, and he cupped her chin in his hand and touched her lips with his. As she gasped, he delved deeper, his tongue parting her lips and exploring her mouth, the other hand gripping her buttocks and holding her to him. She was limp as she tried to return his kiss and mimic his movements.

"Just what is going on, Sammy?"

"Hey, Harry," Max called, as Kreiser appeared, striding across the stage. Charlotte jumped, pulling away as George muttered an oath under his breath.

"Hello, Max. I see you haven't lost your touch. Hope you were able to teach my student here a few things," Kreiser spoke pleasantly to the older gentleman, although as he came up to the couple Charlotte could see that his lips were bloodless and that he was trying to contain his rage.

His voice low, he hissed at George, "Just what do you think you're doing? She's under age, for God's sake. Melanie would have you arrested in a New York minute."

George smiled, but his nervousness showed. "It was all just harmless fun, Harry. Charlotte will tell you."

Before Charlotte could respond, Harry gripped her arm and pulled her away from George. "I promised your aunt I would see you home," he spoke calmly, but she could feel the steel in his grip. "We'll talk later," he added to George, as he half-led, half dragged Charlotte with him across the stage and down the steps, George following in their wake.

"Harry—" Charlotte began, but he cut her off. "Not a word," he warned with a quiet voice. "Do not make a scene. Do not make trouble for Max and Eddie. The manager is watching."

Chastened, she remained quiet as Kreiser called pleasantly, "Thanks again, fellows. I'm sure this will be an afternoon Ms. Lawson doesn't forget for a long time." He gripped her arm menacingly.

"Yes," her voice matched his. "I'm so thrilled to have this opportunity. Thank you so much. It was nice to meet you, Max."

He led her through a stage door, down a hall and onto the street, where a limousine was parked. Without a word, he opened the door and pushed her in, getting in behind her, George following suit.

"To the Cain residence," he told the driver curtly. Ignoring Charlotte, he spoke harshly to George. "How could you? Get your kicks with someone other than Charlotte. Just because you are rich doesn't mean you are untouchable. I wouldn't want to tangle with Melanie Cain if I were you."

George was silent, sullen. Charlotte, suddenly angry, spoke up. "How dare you!" she hissed at Kreiser. "You are not my parent."

"No, I'm not, thank God," he gritted his teeth, "or I'd thrash you to within an inch of your life. Now if you don't shut up and obey me, that's exactly what Melanie will do to you when we get you home."

Charlotte was silenced. She knew he was right. The ride home seemed interminable. As they pulled up to the front door of the residence, Kreiser's hand was already on the door handle. "Thanks for the lift," he spoke tightly. "Take Sammy home, please. Come on, Charlotte."

Harry scrambled out and offered his hand to Charlotte. Charlotte ignored it and stalked out. Harry caught up to her at the front door.

As they walked in, Melanie was standing in the hallway. "Where in God's name have you been?" she cried, dabbing at her eyes with a handkerchief.

Charlotte, shocked at seeing her aunt in tears, was speechless. But Kreiser stepped forward.

"It's all right, Melanie," he crooned soothingly. "She and Gerry had borrowed the limo to take Priscilla home. Sammy told me where they were, and gave us a lift here. I told you she was fine. She has a head on her shoulders."

Charlotte looked at Kreiser in amazement, before recovering and approaching her aunt. Hugging her, she murmured, "I'm so sorry, Auntie. I did not mean to worry you."

Melanie returned her embrace warmly. "God, Charlotte, I was so worried. First seeing Amy off today, and then you disappear without a word. I thought you might have been kidnapped. Don't scare me like that again."

Charlotte murmured her assent as she looked across toward Kreiser. But he had disappeared.

The next afternoon Charlotte was practicing in the salon. The day outside was dismal, rain pelting the landscape and casting a pall. She was dressed in jeans and a coral-colored cotton tank. She missed Amy and Mike, and had no one with whom to share her turbulent thoughts. She had called the Fellowes' residence for George, but he had already left to return to school. She knew Gerry had caught a morning flight back to California.

She suddenly threw her hands in the air. She sat for a long time just staring at the notes of the Durufle *Sicilienne*, her mind wandering, remembering George's kiss and the sensations it produced.

"Are you trying to learn it by osmosis?" she heard a voice in the doorway.

She stiffened at the sound. Kreiser, dressed in denims and a pressed chambray shirt, walked into the room and spread himself on a club chair. "Actually, that is a very good way to study Durufle—the patterns of the notes suggest the water-fountain effect he was trying to achieve."

She said nothing, her mind seething. She finally looked around to see his eyes on her. She swung around and disembarked.

"Where are you going?" he demanded.

"I'm just not interested anymore," she muttered.

"Carlota, I want to talk to you," he said quietly, authoritatively.

"I don't want to talk to you," she stated emphatically.

She expected him to argue with her, to try to stop her, to forestall her exit, but he did nothing. At the doorway she paused. "Why did you cover for me yesterday?"

He did not respond. She turned around. He was staring out the window at the rain beating against the glass panes.

Suddenly angry, she marched back and faced him. "Not that I'm not grateful to you for not blurting out everything to Aunt Mellie, but you have no right telling me what to do. I'm not a child."

"You are such a child," he spoke, almost absently. "So impulsive, so willful, so selfish." He looked at her. "Melanie was beside herself last night with worry about you. Despite how hard you think she is on you, she adores you and is more permissive than is good for you. I could not break her heart and tell her that trust was misplaced, that you indeed need a keeper."

Charlotte flushed. "Just because I kissed George?"

"You have no idea, do you?" he shook his head. "Sammy is out of your league, *cara mia*. Sammy was wanting more than a kiss, much more. I interrupted something that could have turned out badly, very badly. Not only is he too old for you, but he is dangerous, a playboy hanging with the wrong crowd."

"No!" cried Charlotte. "I'm in love with him. I am going to marry him one day."

Kreiser stood suddenly, standing only inches from her. "Damn it, Carlota. He's no good for you. Stay away from him!" he shouted, pushing the chair over as he turned away and strode angrily out of the room, leaving her shaking with rage.

Chapter 14

Crying and angry from her confrontation with Kreiser, Charlotte ran out of the room and headlong into a young man her age, with dark hair and large brown eyes.

"Whoa," he said, reaching out and grabbing her quickly. "Charlotte? What's wrong?"

Looking up through tears, she recognized Evan Bartlett, a classmate and fellow organ student of Kreiser's. "Oh, hi, Evan," she sniffed, trying to smile through her tears.

"Is it a bad time?" he asked, concern written on his face.

"No, it's OK," she wiped her cheek. "What can I do for you?"

"Miss Daisy let me in," he replied. "I know the weather's awful, but why don't we go out for a sundae? My treat," he added, smiling.

"Sure," Charlotte smiled back. "I just need to wash my face."

Minutes later they were in Evan's Volkswagen hurtling through the patches of remaining rain. They said little as Evan pulled into the parking lot next to a chic little eatery.

"This looks nice," Charlotte gazed at the façade.

"Best ice cream in town," Evan told her. "Race you in."

They both exited the car and ran through the rain, laughing as they reached the door where an attendant was waiting to show them in.

Soon they were seated at tall barstools at a counter. The waitress looked at them quizzically.

"We're here for two chocolate sundaes with the works," Evan stated, smiling at Charlotte.

Charlotte surveyed the room. "This is cute," she replied.

"Now tell me why you were running out the door crying," he looked at her pointedly.

"I had just had words with Harry," she confessed soberly. "It was pretty nasty. I don't know where he gets off bossing me about my personal life."

"He's that way to a certain extent with everyone, I think," Evan offered. "But I have noticed that he seems especially tough on you." He paused, looking away. "I think he sees something special in you, and wants to drive you to achieve it."

"I just think he feels he can do what he wants to me, with my aunt wrapped around his finger," Charlotte retorted sharply.

The waitress brought their sundaes and left them. Evan plopped a mouthful of ice cream into his mouth and swallowed. "Umm, that's good," he intoned. "No, Charlotte, I don't think you get it. I've listened in on your lessons, and he spends all this time and extra energy on you that I don't see with even his college students. He's a perfectionist, and he is trying to make you one."

As Charlotte looked at him with surprise, Evan smiled wistfully. "I wish I had someone that cared that much about how I do," he added. "Of course, I don't have half the talent you have."

"That's not true," Charlotte protested. "You have a way of playing that makes it look so easy and effortless. And you can improvise like no one I've ever heard."

Evan smiled. "Thanks. I work at it. You won't laugh?" he asked suddenly.

"At what?" Charlotte asked, her mouth full.

"You spur me on to do my best. I keep wanting to do as well or better than you," he admitted, flushing.

She laughed. "And I am always trying to one-up you," she confessed sheepishly. They both laughed.

They ate in silence for a few minutes. She suddenly asked, "What are you going to do after graduation next year?"

"I'm applying to Stanford, to the music program," he remarked confidently.

"Wow! California," she replied. "I wish I could do that."

"Why not?" he looked at her quizzically. "My dad lives out there. He's got a nice big place. You and I could both apply and audition out there. If you get in, you could stay with us. Professor Zell out there seems really hot right now."

"I doubt Aunt Mellie would allow me to go to college so far from home," she began doubtfully.

"Ask her," Evan was enthusiastic. "In fact, I got some admissions information just the other day. I'll bring it to you to read. And isn't your friend Gerry going to Stanford?"

"Cool," Charlotte's eyes glowed. She thought about being out in California with Evan and Gerry, and all the fun they could have together.

The next night she called Gerry. "What are you doing?" she asked when he answered the phone grumpily.

"Hey, Charl," his tone softened. "The flight back was hell. I have a physics test tomorrow, so I couldn't party, and I'm just damn tired. I'm taking a break from studying. What's up with you?"

"I was just missing you," she crooned.

"More like missing my brother and pumping me for information," he growled good-naturedly. "I'm tired of you mooning over George. From what I hear about him, you need to be covered in latex if you even come near him."

"What do you mean?" she asked innocently.

"Charl, he hangs with a party crowd," she could hear the serious note in Gerry's voice. "There's always a buzz about him and what he's into. Mom's always upset. Just watch your step."

"It's not like I get to see him much, with him off at law school," Charlotte replied defensively.

Gerry changed the subject. "Do you have any good gossip for me?"

"What happened with you and Priscilla?" she goaded him.

"I told her I couldn't raise my arms to fondle her breasts because I had been rowing with you."

"You didn't?" she was incredulous.

"Yeah, I don't understand it," he replied with mock innocence.

"You don't talk about one girl when you're making out with another," she laughed. "It's a definite turn-off, Gerry."

"It's all your fault. I should never have taken that rowing challenge."

"You should never have called me the 'gentler sex'," she teased him.

"I'll never do so again," he groaned good-naturedly. "And I could barely hold the gun steady when we went shooting afterward. By the way, I hear you have a new rowing partner."

"Who told you that?" she was surprised.

"Katharine doesn't miss much, particularly when it comes to Kreiser, and particularly now that Mike has been snagged by your sister."

"Well, Harry claimed his doctor ordered the exercise, and I told him he'd have to keep up if he sculled with me."

"How is he?"

"He can give me a run for the money," she laughed. "I'm kinder to him than I am to you. But he's a late riser, so I generally do my rowing alone."

They giggled for the next thirty minutes, chattering about mutual friends and people they had seen at the wedding.

He surprised her. "Charlotte," he used her full name. "Can you keep a secret?"

"Sure," she replied, her tone confidential. "What is it?"

"I'm dating this girl. She's really kind of nice."

"So what's new?" Charlotte hooted. "You're always dating some girl."

"No, I think she's special."

"What about Priscilla Madden?" Charlotte unabashedly pried.

"She's OK, but a little too stiff and uppity for my taste. This girl—well, my stomach ties in knots when I'm around her."

"Tell me more," Charlotte prodded.

"There's not much to tell yet. But she's a chemistry major out here, and has pretty eyes, kind of the color of yours."

"Really?" Charlotte breathed. "That's great, Gerry. But you have plenty of time—don't start getting serious on me. It's only your first year out there."

Gerry chuckled. "You're right." He changed the subject. "OK, girl, out with it. Why are you really calling?"

Carefully she asked, "What would you think if I applied to Stanford?"

"You're kidding!" he cried enthusiastically. "That would be great. We could have such great fun. But," he asked suddenly, "what box have you stuffed Aunt Mellie in? Are you slipping her LSD or something to get her to sign the papers?"

Charlotte giggled. "No. Why?"

"Well, not to rain on your parade, but 'cold day in hell' best describes your chances of Aunt Mellie's letting you come out here unchaperoned," Gerry reminded her soberly.

"Well, I'm cooking up a plan," Charlotte murmured conspiratorially.

"It had better be good," she could picture Gerry shaking his head. "But I'm in."

Secretly she sent in an application, forging Melanie's name on the consent forms. She had provided as a return address Evan's post office address. The time dragged on while she anxiously awaited word. Evan received an invitation to audition, and she longingly awaited news, trying to weave a story to sell her aunt so that she could sneak off to Stanford.

Meanwhile, she was trying to complete her high school requirements, having opted for an accelerated program and being dually enrolled at the college. She was practicing daily, having briefly scanned Evan's list of audition requirements for piano and organ. Kreiser had signed her up for an AGO convention master class, and she was working on the Reubke *Sonata on the 94th Psalm* to present. He was pushing her to prepare repertoire for auditions at Yale and Juilliard, and grilling her in preparation for the master class. Meanwhile she was spending her nights secretly practicing audition materials for Stanford.

"You are not listening to me," Kreiser's voice was strident. "The emphasis must be just so, without it seeming just so." He laid his hand over Charlotte's on the manual, stilling her fingers. "Just stop a minute. At one level it must whirr, at another you must feel the dynamics, the in and out, the crescendo and decrescendo. It's critical that you get this right. It must be a unified whole. These registration changes are not smooth enough. You can't rely just on the crescendo pedal for this section."

"I'm trying," Charlotte, yawning, felt her temper fraying. "It just doesn't feel right yet."

"Dr. Murray will eat you alive in master class," Kreiser warned for the nth time. "You must practice. How do you expect to do this in competition if you can't get it now?"

"I'll get it," Charlotte snapped, emphatic. She rubbed her left wrist, wincing.

"What's wrong?" Kreiser asked her.

"I'm just having some pain down my thumb. It's nothing," she muttered irritably.

"Let me see," he demanded, taking her hand.

"It's nothing," she repeated, trying to wrest away as he examined her hand.

"Where does it hurt?" his voice was suddenly tender. "What do you think caused the pain?"

"Nothing," she said tightly. "I've been doing long stretches of piano practice, that's all."

"That's good," Kreiser gazed at her intently. "Any particular reason?"

"I've just been neglecting it, and had a sudden desire to work on some Rachmaninoff and Scriabin. Figured it was good for my Franck."

"Playing a lot of octaves? Stretching for all those thirds and fifths?" he nodded understandingly.

"Yes," she replied shortly, not meeting his eyes.

"Poor girl," he said sympathetically, suddenly raising her hand to his lips and kissing it.

She looked at him in surprise, but his next words took her breath away. "When's your Stanford audition?"

She reeled, her shock evident. "What?" she managed to croak.

"When were you going to tell Melanie you had applied to Stanford?"

"How did—" she began in consternation.

"For that matter, when were you going to tell me?" he demanded, dropping her hand and stalking away.

She was speechless, her mind searching for something to say. He whirled around, pain registering in his features.

"You forget I teach Evan too. I know all about the audition requirements, and I overheard him telling someone the two of you were going out to the auditions together."

"Oh, shit," she muttered under her breath.

"Oh, shit, is right," he replied, the irony in his voice evident. "Why Stanford? And if you were so hell bent on going there, why didn't you come to me?"

"I knew you'd never agree to help me," she said in a small voice.

"You could be right," he replied tersely. "And if you think Melanie will agree to your going to California at your age, I'll sign for you to be committed to the nearest insane asylum."

"But," he continued derisively, "didn't you read all the audition requirements? Didn't you realize that Stanford is going to want a letter of reference from your current instructor? That Sandy Zell would pick up the phone and call me to ask what I know about this young girl in Atlanta who had applied to her school?"

"I was going to worry about that when the time came," she murmured defensively.

"The time has come," Melanie asserted, overhearing as she glided into the room, her cheeks two spots of pink, her face carved in stone.

"That was Malcolm Jackson on the phone. He received a call from the Stanford music department, an inquiry about an applicant from here." She looked pointedly at Charlotte. Charlotte knew that look. "There's the university here, there's Juilliard, Curtis, Yale, Eastman, and even Westminster and Peabody and Oberlin. There are any number of excellent piano and organ programs on this side of the Mississippi. Why, pray tell, would you go behind my back, behind Harry's back, and apply to a school on the West Coast, so far from home?"

Charlotte just stared at her aunt, unable to speak. Melanie stared back. Neither spoke for several minutes. Finally Melanie sighed and shrugged her shoulders, resignation in her voice.

"Charlotte, you are still under age, and in the accelerated high school program, when you graduate you will still be under 18. If you will promise me to attend college here two years, or if not, to one of the schools on the East Coast I have named and that Harry approves, I will foot the bill for Stanford or wherever else you want to go after that. You will be almost 19 by then, and I won't stand in your way. I'll release the monies from your trust fund."

Charlotte was thunderstruck. Her aunt had called her bluff. But before she could react, Kreiser intervened.

"Wait just a minute, Melanie. If she doesn't think I can teach her anything else, maybe she is a candidate for Stanford after all. I think she should audition."

Now it was both Charlotte's and Melanie's turn to show amazement. "No," Melanie, recovering from her shock, replied furiously, "the deal is one of the schools on this side of the States for her first two years."

Charlotte had a sudden epiphany. If she left, she would be half a world away from George. As it was, his being at Duke seemed like a world away, and she never saw or heard from him. What if she went to California and he forgot about her? And Gerry had a girlfriend. What if he didn't have time to pal around with her?

And deep down she came to the realization that she didn't want to study under anyone other than Kreiser. As domineering as he was, he was still considered the best organ instructor in the nation by many. And she knew that Evan was right: Kreiser was hard on her because he expected her to become the best. The thought of a new teacher suddenly filled her with dread.

"I accept Aunt Mellie's deal," she interrupted suddenly. "I'll finish my degree here and study under Harry."

As Melanie gazed at her, Kreiser replied smoothly, "It's apparent you don't think much of me. I don't think I want to teach you anymore. It's time you tried your antics with someone else."

Charlotte blanched. Her knees buckled, and she collapsed onto a chair in despair. She had never considered that Kreiser might reject her as a student. She was full of panic. She swallowed as she fought the tears she felt welling up.

"I'm so sorry, Professor Kreiser," she murmured, averting her eyes. "I never meant to make you think I didn't want to be your student." She fought for control, wringing her hands. "I mean, it was all Evan's idea that we go to Stanford together. It sounded fun at the time, and Gerry is out there. I guess I—I didn't think it through, that if I went I wouldn't get to study organ with you." The tears fell down her face unheeded. "I don't really want to study anywhere else, with anyone else," she whispered piteously. "Please."

Melanie stared at her, then walked over to her, placing a hand on her shoulder. "My God, she is human after all, not some alien being," she quipped to Kreiser, shaking her head in disbelief at Charlotte's sudden uncharacteristic show of humility.

She enfolded the girl to her, as Charlotte sobbed, "I'm so sorry. I've made such a mess of things, and you and Harry have taken my crap all this time. I can understand why you don't love me."

"My God, child," Melanie breathed, her voice gruff, "where would you get the idea I don't love you? I'm hurt that you've felt you had to slip around behind my back, that you couldn't confide in me. We decided we had to confront you."

Charlotte pulled away and looked at Kreiser, whose expression she could not fathom. "I want to study with you more than anything," she stated fervently.

Kreiser nodded slightly. "I know it took a lot for you to say what you just did, Carlota. But I have to be able to trust you, and so does your aunt. I want you to be the very best, but you have to keep me in the loop, and you must listen to me. I'm grooming you for great things. I think it will soon be time for you to look elsewhere for your training, but I want to make sure you're ready."

He took a step toward her, then turned abruptly and walked to the door. "You know I hate emotional scenes," he remarked lightly, "so I shall leave you two now. Tomorrow we shall try again, shall we, Carlota?"

She nodded tremulously. "Thank you so much for giving me another chance."

He paused. "Stanford? My God—where did I go wrong with you?" he exclaimed, the hint of a smile on his face as he winked at Melanie. Then he was gone.

Chapter 15

The next Sunday Charlotte accompanied Daisy to her church, in order to hear Dr. Lamont play again. She had been absenting herself for the last few months, concentrating on her now abandoned preparations for the Stanford audition.

After the service, she appeared beside the organ console. Darrell completed his postlude, an improvisation on Martin Luther's hymn 'A mighty fortress', then looked up.

"I thought you gave me up," he remarked dolefully.

"I had a project which is now over," she explained. "I think it's time you did a recital."

"What kind of recital?"

"Right here in this community, doing classical music. The congregation has no idea how good you are at it. Only your students are aware of that, so it's time you showed everybody."

"That's funny," he laughed. "I've been thinking that a certain classical piano and organ virtuoso should be showing she can do gospel and jazz. Maybe you should do a recital."

"I'll do it if you'll do it," she challenged, her eyes sparkling.

So thus they planned a joint recital, meeting every Sunday after services to collaborate on the program.

When she broached the subject to Conrad, he was enthusiastic about the idea, and offered to help support and promote the recital. However, Kreiser raised objections.

"Carlota, you need to be focusing on your master classes and rep for upcoming auditions. You should not be wasting time on endeavors that are not going to further your applications," he stated to her one day after a lesson. They had been having lessons at the cathedral, but because he was recovering from a cold he had begged to move it to Melanie's home. He finished the sentence with a hacking cough.

"I told you we should skip the lesson today. You're still sick," Charlotte answered him, patting him on the back. "But this is not a waste of time. More and more universities are looking at what extracurricular activities students are doing. Harry, I don't have a church job, and Melanie curtails a lot of things I would like to do, saying I need to 'remember my place'."

"You have your frequent appearances with the symphony and the ensembles," he reminded her.

"But I really want to do this," she argued. "I've picked some challenging music. See?" she pulled some scores out of her bag. "Plus I'm going to improvise for the head soprano from his choir to sing. I just think this is as good a workout as a master class."

He was silent, studying the music before him, as Melanie walked in on the conversation. "I for once have to agree with Charlotte," Melanie spoke, surprising her niece. "Apparently Peter says a lot of community interest has been expressed in this recital, particularly in the area schools and independent music teachers. He thinks it will be a boon to the musical education departments, inspiring more young people to take up music."

Charlotte smiled at her aunt, thankful that Melanie had taken her side. She knew then that Harry would not actively oppose the idea, even though his support might be grudging.

The day approached, and the music was approved by the minister as appropriate. The church was packed, and the program was a mosaic of music:

> Prelude and Fugue in D minor—J. S. Bach (Darrell—organ)
> Two gospel preludes by William Bolcom (Charlotte—organ):
>   What a friend we have in Jesus
>   How firm a foundation
> Piece Heroique—Cesar Franck (Darrell—organ)
> Take the 'A' Train—Duke Ellington, improvisation (Charlotte—piano)
> Symphonie VI: Final—Louis Vierne (Darrell—organ)
> Blessed Assurance—sung by Madeline King (accomp. Charlotte—piano)
> Mouvement—Jean Beauvillier (Darrell—organ)
> Amazing Grace—George Shearing (Charlotte—organ)
> Naiades—Louis Vierne (Charlotte—organ)
> Clair de lune—Claude Debussy (Darrell—piano)
> Fantaisie in F minor—W. A. Mozart (duet at organ—Darrell and Charlotte)

They created a moment of comic relief when Lamont finished the Debussy and took his bow, then ran back up the steps, calling to Charlotte not to start the Mozart without him as she launched into the introduction. As an encore they alternated on the same piano playing their own arrangement of 'Soft Winds', a Benny Goodman number. The crowd grew more animated as they playfully pushed each other off the stool in order to take their turn, and ended up in a four-hand duet.

The recital was a great success, and a greater surprise awaited them when Peter Conrad approached and introduced them to a critic from the *New York Times* after the recital, and they were informed the recital would be covered in that periodical. Conrad stifled a grin at Lamont's shocked disbelief and Charlotte's look of delight.

As Daisy, Darrell's mother and Melanie came up, Charlotte hugged Lamont. "That was so great," she beamed, gratified by the looks of pleasure bestowed by her aunt and Daisy, joined by Lamont's mother and Kreiser. Photographs were made, and they all celebrated at a reception given by the church ladies after the recital.

At the reception she approached Conrad. "Dr. Conrad."

"Honey, you earned the right this evening to call me Peter," he smiled at her indulgently.

Charlotte blushed. "Thank you. But I want to do something crazy," she confided.

"What, my dear?" he asked. "After today, I would agree to almost anything. You and Dr. Lamont have given the cause of music a shot in the arm." He stopped. "When you say you want to do something 'crazy', it means something musical. What is it?"

She took a deep breath, then plunged in headlong, running her sentences together. "You know I only have one more semester after this before I finish my piano degree first, and I have to do a senior recital. But I really want to do something big." She paused, flushed. "I want to play the Rachmaninoff Piano Concerto No. 2. And," she stood on tiptoe and whispered in his ear.

He looked at her, astounded. "That's biting off more than a mouthful," he intoned. "I have no doubt you can pull it off, but are you sure? That's a great deal of work, and Harry is not going to be happy if it takes away from your time from completing your organ performance degree."

"You're damn right," Harry had walked up behind her, and she tensed visibly. He looked at her, his hard face softening. "But we already know you don't follow my directions all that well," he murmured.

She linked her arm in his, then around his waist. "C'mon, Harry, please don't say no," she wheedled, reaching up to kiss his cheek. "I promise I'll keep up with whatever you throw at me while I'm doing this," she added. "Besides, you have me for another year."

The photographer snapped a picture, as he gazed into her upturned face. He was gruff, uncharacteristically tender. "Carlota, I plan to throw a lot at you this year," he smiled briefly. "This is a critical time, and what we do this year you are going to carry with you the rest of your life. If you do this, I will hold you to your promise. You must excel."

Conrad looked on as she nodded. "I won't let either of you down," she said gleefully.

Conrad spoke up then. "Well, I guess we need to cut back on your ensemble work."

"No need," she retorted. "I can do this. What else do I have to do? Gerry is gone to Stanford. School is not nearly as hard now that I've finished my high school diploma and my college basic requirements. I have no one but my musical friends to pal with. I've finished all my degree requirements but my English. I almost have enough for a degree there too," she added, her eyes bright.

And she made good her word. She practiced harder than ever, pouring every spare moment into her projects. She made time for one additional duty: singing in the choir at St. Philip's when she was not subbing for a church organist. Because of that, she was not able to get away as often to see Lamont, but still showed up at least every other month. Both Conrad and Kreiser were amazed at her indefatigable energy, as she continued to work with the youth orchestra, her ensemble playing, rehearsing for the Rachmaninoff, the new difficult repertoire that Kreiser was giving her, and her studies, plus several recitals.

During this time Kreiser and his wife separated, and he again was invited to move into Melanie's boathouse apartment. Most of Charlotte's lessons ended up back at the Cain residence, with regular field trips to various organs in the city and general area. He was introducing new music to her, at unfamiliar organs, for her to sight read and register on the fly. His demeanor ran the gamut from tender to tyrannical, as he coached her and railed at her. She patiently bore his tirades at first, but would increasingly be drawn into discussions and arguments about composers' intentions, intended registrations and degrees of variance, and points of divergences in views between musicologists about the music she was studying.

In addition, Harry was meeting Charlotte several mornings early each week in order to scull at the lake, although he was not faithful to show up for her every-morning ritual. Charlotte teased him unmercifully about his late nights in the arts and social scene, which prevented his rising early regularly for exercise. He countered that it was necessary to raise funds from

Atlanta's elite to support the varied musical programs at the schools and in the community.

One morning she appeared at the boathouse at 5:30, her normal time, and Kreiser was there waiting for her. He looked haggard, unshaven, his eyes bleary, as he sipped a cup of black coffee and waited patiently for her.

"Late night last night?" she quipped.

"I haven't been home long," he replied ruefully. "I thought you were going to accompany Melanie to the museum fundraiser last night," he mumbled accusatorily.

"Yes, but you also know I have live rehearsal with the orchestra tonight, after our lesson where I'm supposed to be going through the Durufle *Suite* with you," she retorted. "Something had to give. Dr. Conrad excused me. Besides, I have been working on a surprise."

"What?" he demanded.

"If I told you, it wouldn't be a surprise. Don't worry. I won't disappoint you," she remarked mysteriously.

"I missed you last night," he muttered peevishly.

"Yeah, but you had plenty of rich women vying for your attention, including Hell-Kat Fellowes," she teased him, as he gulped the coffee and grimaced.

"We're just friends. We kind of fall in together for these events. Why, are you jealous?"

"Oh, insanely," Charlotte laughed. "You get to see her a lot more than I get to see George."

Kreiser frowned. "You know I don't approve of him for you," he spoke, his voice low.

"Yes, I know," she nodded solemnly. "I also know you need to replenish your body fluids before and during exercise," she changed the subject, throwing him a bottled Gatorade. "It's nippy for October," she added.

"Let's get started," he remarked irritably.

"Maybe you need to go back to bed," she responded, touching his arm. "You don't look so good."

"No," he shook her off gently. "We need to talk."

"But this is exercise, not chat time," she argued.

They shoved off, and in deference to him, she set a moderate pace, and they rowed in silence to the agreed point. At that point she showed no sign of slowing down. "Come on," she urged him. "A little further will do you good."

They continued until Kreiser groaned and shipped his oars. "No more," he begged, panting.

Charlotte grinned and relented, leaning back. "OK," she smirked, "what is so important that we need to talk about?"

Kreiser stared at her back. "It's time you started thinking about your future. You are trying to excel on too many fronts, Carlota. You need to make some decisions, narrow your focus."

"Why do I need to choose?" she argued. "I'm enjoying myself."

"But you are going to need to work toward some specialization. Are you going to teach, perform? Focus on early music? Bach? French romantic? Piano? Organ? Solo or ensemble performance? You are young, but cannot continue at this pace."

"Harry, I don't want to teach, at least not anytime soon," she explained patiently, as though to a child, even though they had engaged in this discussion many times before. "I want to perform. Don't make me choose," she warned. "For all you know I may choose piano."

"You wouldn't," he asserted quietly, almost sternly. "You are neglecting your pre-Bach and French classical rep."

She turned to look at him. "You know I have no interest in early music; leave that for someone else. Harry, I've paid my dues. And for your information, I also like to write and read literature. I want to focus on the French romantics."

"What do you plan to do when you graduate?" he insisted.

"I'm going to go to Paris and study, I'm going to apply to Juilliard and Yale and Curtis, and I'm going to get married," she listed flippantly.

"All in that order?" he was sardonic.

"Probably not," she turned with her back to him. "Harry, George and I are talking about announcing our engagement soon. I'm seventeen, and his mother is anxious. She doesn't want us to wait too long."

She waited, but he said nothing. She finally broke the silence. "I know you don't approve. But Melanie keeps telling me it's time I start considering my 'place in society'. She's wanting me to join the Junior League, volunteer at the hospital, and other 'good little girl' chores. I'm doing just enough to keep her off my back. She wants me to wait until I'm an adult to announce an engagement.

"I'm crazy about George. He's perfect for me, and he doesn't demand that I be at his side every minute. He's agreeable with my continuing with my music studies, which is better than a lot of the guys Melanie wants me to consider. And he's OK with a long engagement, although his mother is pushing for us to set a date when I turn eighteen."

She paused, aware that she was arguing with herself as much as with Kreiser. "I don't want to be tied down just yet. I don't want to be a dutiful society wife whose place is two steps behind her husband. And this way, I get to do what I want while making everyone else happy."

"Sounds like you have it all figured out," Kreiser's ironic tone was not lost on Charlotte. "But is that what you really want to do?"

She bit her lip, aggravated. "Let's start back."

"No, answer my question," Kreiser reached out and put his hand on her shoulder, stilling her. "What do you want, Carlota?"

She was silent for a moment. "I want to make music," she finally whispered, her voice muffled. "I want to play and play and play, with others, by myself. I want to play until I die at the bench, like Louis Vierne. I want to immerse myself in others' music, and compose my own, improvise. I want to keep that overwhelming longing and passion going, to suck the living out of life, to reach those moments of bliss when I've done well and provided extraordinary pleasure for someone else. I want to find love that feels just like that, where love-making rivals the music-making."

She broke off, shame-faced. "I know. Real life isn't like that, is it? That's why I have doubts about marriage. Married people don't seem to experience that feeling. Are George and I really going to make each other happy? I don't know. But as long as I have my music, maybe it doesn't matter."

She turned to face him, her face upturned, the question in her eyes. "Do you know what I mean, Harry? Do you?" she repeated.

Kreiser reached out and touched her face, then took her hand. "Yes, I know, my dear," he murmured. "Real love is unrequited. It never reaches that level of passion you feel for the music. You never sense that all-encompassing pain and release. You have the gift, *cara mia*. Although I'm much older than you, I still feel that passion too. It can be a curse as well."

Charlotte laughed uneasily. "Really, Harry, you're not old. Although I was worried about you when I first saw you this morning. You're really a sexy guy if you'd take better care of yourself."

She reached over and kissed him on the cheek, but he caught her as the shift in weight caused the craft to shudder. She grabbed the sides as he held on to her.

"Perhaps we should avoid capsizing this morning and head back," he suggested lightly as he released her.

A month later Charlotte performed the Rachmaninoff as her senior piano recital with the Atlanta Symphony. Surprising Kreiser and even Conrad, she finished the program with *La Valse* for solo piano by Maurice Ravel.

Again the hall was full, and she was called back for several ovations with Conrad. Flushed with excitement at her success, she blew a kiss to Kreiser and Melanie sitting in the front.

She walked backstage, still breathless, after the final bow, and there stood George, in a tuxedo, with a mass of red roses he held out to her. "Damn, Charlotte, you are a star," he laughed, as she approached him. Instead of handing her the roses, he shoved them at Conrad and took her in his arms.

"I've never heard you play like that. You are wonderful."

He took her face in his two hands and kissed her. Reeling with surprise and pleasure from his ardent show of affection, she barely noticed that he had stopped. She opened her eyes and he was on one knee. "Will you marry me?" he beamed at her.

"Quit joking," she giggled.

"No joke. I want us to schedule an engagement party. Your playing has done this to me."

Conrad intervened. "We must go," he spoke almost sternly to George. "I'm hosting a reception for Charlotte next door at the museum. Her audience is awaiting."

Conrad handed her the roses and took her arm, as George bowed and followed. She saw Kreiser standing at the back stage door, a pained expression on his face. He saw George kiss me, she thought. She noted another handsome young man standing there, staring at them.

Conrad shook his head. "What a wonderful surprise. I didn't know you were doing the Ravel tonight."

"It was meant to be a surprise for you and Harry."

They entered the museum lobby, as a wave of applause greeted her. Conrad whispered, "I'm so proud of you, my dear," as he kissed her forehead and presented her. She was mobbed by enthusiastic well wishers. She looked around for George, but he was nowhere to be seen.

After a while the hubbub died down, and she was congratulated by her aunt and Kreiser. Melanie embraced her. "That was beautiful, Charlotte. I have never been so proud."

Melanie introduced her to several community and civic leaders present. Finally she was left alone with Kreiser.

"I was really surprised," he spoke quietly, reaching over and kissing her forehead, lingering for a moment.

She gazed at him. "What did you really think?"

Kreiser's eyes met hers. "Do you remember the other morning? Talking about love-making that rivaled the music-making? I fell in love with you during your music-making."

She blushed. Kreiser asked, "How in the world did you manage to keep the Ravel a secret from me?"

Conrad walked up as she explained. "It was hard. I kept it from Dr. Conrad as well. I told him I wanted to do a solo piece following the Brahms.

I swore Dr. Harmon to secrecy, and contacted Dr. Hodges at Juilliard. She set it up, and we prevailed upon Melanie to allow me to go coach for a week with Dr. Simon while he was in Houston. I wanted it to be a surprise, so I told you and Peter I went to an American Guild of Organists' convention."

Kreiser grinned. "I knew there were no AGO conventions that time of year. I was upset that you were keeping something from me. Now I understand. That was beautiful, my Carlota. I am proud of you. Only Abbey Simon could play it better."

"I concur," Conrad spoke up. "What a wonderful performance."

She glowed from their praise.

Afterward she was inundated with invitations to perform, and was anxious to accept as many as she could. However, Melanie intervened, and she and Conrad argued over Charlotte's celebrity. Meanwhile, Charlotte completed the piano performance degree, and knew she still had only a few months to go before obtaining her organ degree and having to make decisions about her future.

Chapter 16

Charlotte walked through the Atlanta Hartsfield Airport trailing her carryon bag behind her. She felt drained; the Yale audition for a slot in the graduate program was actually more stressful than the Juilliard and Curtis tryouts in the last weeks. Part of it, she assumed, was the fact that because she was eighteen, Melanie had finally decided that for the first time she could travel alone.

Although the thought at first had exhilarated her, she found that she was anxiety-ridden from all of Melanie's directions and exhortations to exercise caution and to avoid anything that would initiate media speculation. She had in fact experienced several encounters at the airport with persons who recognized her from the newspaper accounts of her performances, and some who had read in the tabloids about her anticipated engagement to George Fellowes. She finally bought a cheap hat at one of the stores in the airport, to help provide a disguise.

She also felt more stress because she knew that although Kreiser was not there with her, he had contacts at Yale, eyes and ears ready to report to him every misdemeanor and misstep of hers during the interview and audition. She felt unusually nervous, and was not sure of her performance. In fact, one of the judges took her aside. "Miss Lawson, I've heard great things about you, but you are obviously not at your best today. What is wrong?"

She was mortified that her anxiety showed. The judge placed her arm around the girl. Sympathetically, she noted, "You're afraid of embarrassing Harry Kreiser? Don't be. You are your own person, and the committee is quite interested in you. In fact, I'm more impressed with what Peter Conrad says about you than Harry. And your resume is amazing. They are still raving about your senior recital for your piano performance degree. Rachmaninoff and Ravel? You don't do things by halves."

"I'm so sorry," Charlotte was shame-faced. "I've never been this nervous before."

"Forget Harry. In fact, forget everyone, and just play. Don't you realize it would be very hard to deny you a slot, with all your accomplishments? We just want to hear you for ourselves."

Charlotte had taken the advice to heart, and her second attempt was much better. But after the audition, she was exhausted, and had decided to take an earlier flight and come home, cancelling her sightseeing of the area.

She took a taxi from the airport, and on impulse gave George's address. She needed to talk to him. She was full of doubts about whether marriage with him was right, and she had been bothered by his evading their being alone or discussing their future together, other than his somewhat public proposal after her recital. In fact, lately he had seemed cold, distant and withdrawn, and she was wondering what she might have done to cause this change in him.

I just know we need to have it out, she thought. I cannot continue with these lingering doubts. If I have done something wrong, I need to know before I make decisions about where I'm going from here.

The cab pulled up to a well-kept multi-storied brick apartment complex in Buckhead, and she paid the driver and climbed out with her bag and purse. Greeting the doorman warmly, she made arrangements to have her bag sent on to her home. "Thanks so much, Tim. I just want to pop in on George a minute, if he's in," she informed the man.

Tim looked at her nervously. "Miss Lawson, I believe he—um—had someone with him. Some sort of business I heard them discussing," he stammered. "I should ring him first."

"Don't bother. I'll wait." Charlotte was preoccupied and didn't notice the man's discomfiture.

She sat on the leather sofa in the small lobby. Tim looked at her sympathetically and shook his head, before being called away. She sat there deep in thought for some time, until she heard a man announce, "Delivery, Room 431."

She looked up. As the food delivery guy entered the elevator, she followed him quickly. He pushed the button for the fourth floor and the doors closed.

"I'm going to 431. Want me to take it for you?"

"I don't know," the man was doubtful. "Mr. Fellowes generally tips generously."

"I'm his fiancée. How much is the tab?" she asked.

He told her, and she handed him a one-hundred dollar bill. "Will that cover it?"

He grinned. "Sure thing."

"Keep the change," she took the bag from him.

She exited the elevator, then continued on to George's flat. She started to ring the bell, and trying the knob noticed the door was unlocked.

She cracked the door open and called, "George?"

She heard George's voice: "Just put it on the table. The tip is there."

She laid the package on the table, then followed the sound of his voice to the bedroom. Entering, she was brought up short by the scene. There was George naked on top of the covers, and he wasn't alone.

"My God!" she murmured, backing up against the door jamb to steady herself.

As George turned at the sound, she saw that the other naked form under him was another man, the same man she had seen the night of the recital. She gasped again, then turned and bolted from the room. "Shit!" she heard George exclaim.

Confusedly she retraced her steps, blindly stumbling down the hallway to the front door, but as she reached for the handle a hand grasped her arm. She screamed, as the person roughly pinned her to the wall, putting his hand over her mouth.

"Charlotte!" George hissed angrily at her. "What the fuck are you doing here?"

She looked wildly at him, unable to speak. As she choked, he removed his hand from her mouth. "What, are you spying on me?" he was malevolent.

She tried to shake free. "How dare you! You're hurting me. Me spying on you? What the hell are you doing? I thought we were engaged," she managed to stammer.

He turned her loose, grasping the towel he had hurriedly wrapped around him. "Surely you are not that naïve," he sneered. "Do you think that makes any difference?"

"Yes, I guess I did," she pushed him away. "I thought maybe you loved me."

"Oh, but I do," he said mockingly. "I love your looks and your money and your goody-two-shoes appearance. Isn't that what you like about me? The fact we look good together?"

He grabbed her arms and hauled her against the wall. "I thought you knew that our union is to be one of convenience. Did you think we were going to have an old-fashioned wedding and profess undying love to each other and only each other for the rest of our lives?" He laughed harshly. "How quaint. But of course, that's what Melanie was counting on, Miss Goody-Two-Shoes herself."

He kissed her roughly, his hand around her throat, as she struggled against him. "But perhaps you're still a virgin, and was saving yourself for me," he said softly. "That's the way good girls are, isn't it?" His hand ran up her thigh.

She pushed furiously against him, and finally he released her.

"You pig," Charlotte said, slapping him full in the face.

He gingerly touched his cheek as he regarded her. She shrank, fearing he would strike her back. But he laughed. "You see, it works both ways. You can have all the affairs you want, and I won't complain. Our engagement and marriage shuts up the paparazzi about my lifestyle and the rumors about you and old Kreiser. You can even have him, if you like them a little more experienced. The papers say you already have."

"Me and Kreiser?" Charlotte echoed, stunned.

"Besides," George leered at her as his face came close again. "It might be fun to try a threesome every now and then. You wanna try it now?"

She jerked away, pushing against him with all her might. Her only thought was to put as much distance as possible between her and what she had just witnessed. She jerked the door open and ran to the elevator. However, she saw from the indicator over the door that it was on the ground floor, and flung herself through the stairwell doorway.

She ran breathlessly down all the stairs, bursting forth into the lobby flushed, wild-eyed and out of breath, her hair flying around her face. Tim the doorman saw her first. Quickly he made his way to her.

"Come with me," he whispered. "Outside the lobby the press are lining the street. Someone tipped them off that you were here and there might be a scene. Let's get you out the back way before they see you."

He quickly led her through a doorway marked "Staff Only". Moving past employees, some looking at her curiously, Tim took her through winding rooms and halls, until they made it to a side exit of the apartment building.

He beckoned a waiting taxi, and hurriedly shoved her in the back. She handed him a bill and thanked him, as Tim told the driver to get her out of there as quickly as possible.

The driver jerked into motion, and Charlotte, still dazed, had to be asked twice her destination. Even then she was unsure. Do I go home? she thought. There's no one there.

Finally she gave the driver her home address and leaned back, closing her eyes. The cab screeched to a stop, and she opened her eyes. Suddenly there was a sea of faces peering into the windows at her, calling to her, along with cameras flashing in her face.

"Miss Lawson, is it true you and Sammy Fellowes had a lover's quarrel? Did you have sex with him and his boyfriend?" she heard a woman with a microphone asking through the window.

Another man was asking, "Did you know Sammy Fellowes was a homosexual before today? Have you and Sammy had sexual relations?"

Another man queried, "Is the wedding still on? How does Dr. Kreiser feel about your engagement? Are you two still an item?"

Paralyzed with fear, she stared at the faces until the driver spoke. "Light's green; hold on." He whisked them away from the scene.

Charlotte hugged herself and rocked back and forth, petrified, her eyes wide. The driver looked at her through his rearview mirror. "You're that pianist lady, aren't you?" he asked kindly.

"What?" she at first did not understand him. "Oh, yes," she nodded, as tears filled her eyes.

"My daughter got a part in that youth orchestra," he announced. "She is so happy. I was afraid she wouldn't be able to make it in."

Looking at her again, he was alarmed at her ashen expression. "Are you going to be OK? Is there someone you could call?"

"No," she shook her head, the tears falling. "Just take me home, please."

Dark was falling as she finally made it home, thanking the driver and tipping him handsomely. She walked inside the cavernous house, knowing she was the only one there, because Daisy and Jacob were off visiting relatives, and Melanie was still out of town the rest of the week.

She sat down heavily on the bench in the foyer, and the tears fell. She felt betrayed by the one person with whom she had hoped to spend the rest of her life. The scene played itself over and over in her mind, and she could not escape the horror of seeing George, and of the press crowding her.

She staggered into the library, and saw the row of Waterford decanters and tumblers. She poured some bourbon in a glass and downed it, coughing as the liquid burned her throat.

She thought about hunting for some cola to mix with it. No, real adults drink it just like this, she told herself. So she poured another glass of it, and drank it, shuddering, grimacing as she swallowed, sinking into a chair, lost in reverie.

A lamp on a timer suddenly blinked on, and she started. She didn't know how long she had been sitting there. She finally stood up. "I can't stay here alone," she said aloud. "I'm going to Harry's."

She walked all the way to the boathouse before she looked at her watch and realized that Harry had an organ recital that night. "Oh, hell," she said aloud.

She took the key out from under the mat and opened the door, letting herself in. She wandered around the rooms in the flat, looking at the art on the walls. Walking into the kitchen, she found a large bottle of cabernet sauvignon. She rummaged through the kitchen drawers until she located a corkscrew, then managed to open the bottle.

Finding a wine glass, she sat down at the table and poured the glass full. She sat at the counter staring at the warm ruby liquid in the glass. She downed it rather quickly, pleased at the resulting flush from the alcohol she had imbibed. She rummaged through the refrigerator, finding some cheese, then through his pantry, finding some crackers. She realized that she was hungry.

So she munched on her little meal and drank more wine. "I want a man," she said aloud, the buzz taking hold. "I want a real man. It's time I knew what it's all about. I'm an adult and still a virgin. If I was a guy instead of the niece of an uptight Atlanta socialite, that wouldn't be true. Instead, my fiancé doesn't want me. He is gayer than a party hat."

She thought about what she said and giggled, the spirits making her giddy. Then she felt sad again. My life is all screwed up, she reminded herself, pouring some more wine. What am I going to do?

She began crying again, and drank down the rest of the bottle of wine. She found another bottle, but gave up after several fumbled attempts to uncork the bottle. As she stood from the table, she staggered. Ooh, she thought. So this is what it's like to be tipsy.

As she walked to the bathroom, she looked in at Kreiser's bed. A tiny seed of a plan formulated in her mind. She brushed her teeth with Kreiser's toothbrush, then returned to the bedroom. She began stripping off her clothes, then slipped beneath the cool cotton sheets under the downy comforter.

She felt sensuous, the wine stealing through her senses, and the cotton sheets caressing her bare skin. "I wonder how long before Harry comes home. Hope he doesn't bring someone else with him," she thought aloud, as drowsiness overtook her.

Kreiser made his way home a little before midnight. He felt good. It was a successful recital, and his hosts plied him with Courvoisier and good cigars afterward. He thought back to the discussion with Charlotte in the scull; yes, the rush from a performance done well was heady wine, hard to top.

He suddenly felt a little sad that Charlotte wasn't there, for he always loved to hear her opinions. Sweet little Charlotte, so precocious, so intuitive about music, but naive about human relationships, and engaged to that undeserving snot Sammy Fellowes. The thought angered him momentarily. She could do so much better, he thought, but deep down inside he was perceptive enough to know that he would not probably approve any mate for her. She is a remarkable talent, and needs to be free to pursue her art. She has a phenomenal future ahead of her. She will leave me soon. And God, how I love her, he thought. When I hear her perform it is as though I am performing. It's as though she's an extension of me. I feel with her what I have never felt in the bedroom.

He sighed, squelching that momentary lapse of the tight rein he held over his emotions. Switching on the lights to the small living area, he made his way past the island segregating the kitchen area from the living room.

As he rounded the corner, he noticed the empty wine bottle and glass, and another full wine bottle on the counter.

"What the hell?" he muttered. "Who was here? Probably Kat. Glad I missed her tonight."

He looked around the room, but saw nothing else out of order. He shrugged out of his tuxedo jacket and untied his tie, loosening his collar. "I'm tired," he said aloud.

He walked down the little hallway to the bedroom, and cut on the bedside lamp. Turning away, he removed his cufflinks and unbuttoned his shirtfront, pulling the shirt and his t-shirt off, rubbing his neck. Turning back, he suddenly started in surprise at the sight of the girl in his bed asleep. She looked so dreamlike he had trouble convincing himself she was real. Could it really be?

He sat on the bed and shook her gently. "Carlota, what are you doing here?"

She moaned and shifted sleepily, then opened her eyes and gazed at him confusedly.

"Harry," she said hoarsely, squinting blearily at him.

"So it's you who has been drinking my wine," he said severely. "Melanie will have a fit. But what are you doing home from Yale early?"

She stared at him uncomprehendingly, then raised herself and flung her arms around his neck. "Kiss me, Harry."

He pulled away, shocked. "My God, Charlotte, what are you thinking?" as he tried to extricate himself from the girl. He looked down at her. "My dear, you're naked."

She started crying, clinging to him. "I'm not a little girl any more. So don't treat me like one now. I want to be a desirable woman, Harry," she sobbed.

Harry, surprised at her reaction, felt his heart lurch. He held her to him and rocked the inconsolable girl. "My sweet Carlota, you are irresistible," he whispered in her ear. "What, did you and Sammy have a lover's tiff?"

She cried even harder. "He prefers guys," she murmured brokenly through her tears. "I found him with someone else. A guy, Harry. Can you believe it? He was vicious to me. We're through. Oh, Harry."

Kreiser's heart went out to her. So she's found out Sammy's dirty secret. The bastard, he thought.

Charlotte clung to Harry as he continued to hold and shush her. "It's OK, *cara mia*," he crooned, his voice husky. "I told you he was wrong for you, but the right one will come along. You are so young. There is time."

"I want you. Now. Tonight," she cried, wrapping her arms tightly around him and kissing him wildly through her tears. "Please don't say no to me, Harry. I can't handle it if you say no. I'll kill myself."

"No, you won't," he whispered gently, as he lowered her to the bed and extricated himself. He gently brushed her hair out of her face and wiped the tears from her cheek. "Oh, my sweet Carlota," he bent over, kissing her forehead.

She pulled him to her forcefully, taking his hand and placing it on her breast. "You don't understand. I'm very serious. I need you."

"We mustn't do this, my dear," he groaned, as she clung to him, kissing his neck and stroking his back. "Please don't, Carlota."

"I want you now," she demanded again, as her hand slipped down past his belted trousers. "Don't you want me? Am I not the least bit desirable?" she cried desperately.

He took her into his arms, kissing her with fervor, giving in to his feelings, his lips traveling down her neck to her breast. She sighed. "Please," she arched against him. "I want to know what it feels like with you."

"You have always been my Laura," he whispered, as he bent and traced her lips with his tongue, his hands caressing her form. "I have always loved you, Charlotte, and dreamed about you. But this is so wrong."

"No, it's not," she countered stubbornly, clinging to him. "Show me you love me," she mumbled. "I need to know. I'm not into the unrequited stuff." Her hand reached for his fly as she pulled him down with her.

Chapter 17

The next morning, Charlotte awakened early, finding herself in Kreiser's arms. He was propped against the pillows, awake, and staring into space, deep in thought. She snuggled closer as he kissed her forehead, then she met his mouth with her own.

"I never thought sex could be that great," she mumbled, embarrassed.

"Me, neither," he smiled at her as he stroked her hair and pulled her closer. "You were always a distant dream of mine, a forbidden one. They say real life is never as good as the fantasy you make. But you are so entrancing, *cara mia*."

"I love you, Harry," she declared fervently. "I never realized how much you are a part of me until last night. I don't ever want us to be apart."

"You are so young," he whispered. "I love you, my dearest Charlotte, but I won't hold you to that."

"You don't understand," she stared up at him. "You are my first, and I'm so in love with you. I think I've always loved you."

"Shh," he kissed her tenderly. "You need your morning breakfast."

"I don't do breakfast," she smiled at him.

"You do this morning," he commanded. "You get to sleep in. I'll make breakfast."

She did not realize she was so tired, but she fell asleep again, until shook awake by Kreiser, who held a tray for her. "Eat now," he coaxed her.

She did, with the first bite realizing that she was indeed hungry, and that she had not eaten the day before except for her crackers and wine while waiting for Kreiser. "Grits?" she asked wonderingly, her mouth full.

"Yes, I have worshiped at the oracle of Miss Daisy, and she has imparted the secret of cooking grits."

He laughed at her as she stuffed food into her mouth, disappeared while she ate, then reappeared, freshly showered and buttoning a crisp shirt.

"You're leaving?" she asked, her eyes large with fear.

"I do have two classes, *cara*," he remarked, as he reached for a tie. "One of them is your class as well. But I will excuse you today."

"But I hoped you could stay," she pleaded.

"Charlotte," he sat beside her on the bed, taking her hand. "Nothing would make me leave your side, but we must be discreet. The tabloids have already stated rumors about us, and we must take care to prevent fueling them." He kissed her forehead. "I will see you at our lesson time. Tonight at the house, OK?"

"You promise?" she looked apprehensive, doubtful.

"You bet," he kissed her, silencing her. "Now finish your breakfast and get a shower. I think a short skirt might be in order for our lesson today."

She smiled slyly.

That evening Kreiser slipped in the salon as she was playing the organ, Louis Vierne's *Clair de lune*. He cut the lights out. As she stopped, surprised at the sudden darkness, he commanded, "Keep playing—you should be able to play under adversity. Think of poor Louie, virtually blind, trying to recall and imagine the beauty of the moonlight and set it to music."

Excited at his presence, she resumed, playing in the blackness of the spacious room. Suddenly she felt his hands on her, sliding underneath her top, stroking her skin. She kept playing as he had reached up and undid her bra, running his fingers around to cup her breasts. She gasped in delight as he gently stroked her nipples seductively.

He whispered, "Do you like that?" kissing her ear lobe, his breath fanning against her cheek.

She shook her head distractedly, her breathing labored. "I'm concentrating on my music."

Her breathing quickened as he ran his hands down inside her short skirt, his body molded to her back, gently rocking her back and forth. His hands kept going lower, unzipping her skirt and slipping beneath her panties, feathering against her thighs until he found what he wanted. She writhed, her music forgotten.

"I can't do it," she laughed, giving up, as he nuzzled her neck and fondled her. She turned and threw her arms around his neck, finding his mouth with hers, pulling him down on top of her on the organ bench, both of them trembling.

Suddenly he lifted her, carrying her bodily to the next room to the massive dining table. Groping in the darkness, he hauled her unceremoniously onto the large banquet table, then joined her. "I'm hungry, aren't you?" he whispered, his hands undressing her and wreaking havoc with her senses.

She murmured, "I'll never think of this table in the same way." They laughed like children, making love with wild abandon.

The Kreiser Affair

The next night Kreiser and Charlotte agreed to meet at the boathouse to go sculling in the midnight moonlight. Charlotte gingerly made her way to the boathouse, pausing at the doorway, peering through the spooky darkness, trying to get her bearings through the light from the crescent moon streaming in randomly, cutting through the inky blackness.

She made her way to the boat, checking the mooring and the oars. She heard him behind her, and felt his breath on her neck as he embraced her. "You hadn't decided to go without me?" he whispered in her ear.

She relaxed against his chest, and he enfolded her to him and caressed her neck. "No," she sighed. "I've been waiting all day for this. I missed you."

She turned and found his mouth with hers, her hands feeling his hard chest through the t-shirt. As her hands slipped further down, he grabbed them with his own. "No, *cara mia*," he crooned. "First we commune with nature. Don't incapacitate me before we get started."

They laughed together, as he helped her launch the two-man boat. He stepped in and took her hand, helping her in. They settled in, and carefully maneuvered their way away from the dock. "Not this way," he objected as she paddled the boat to face west.

"Why? You afraid Kat will see us and be jealous?" she teased him.

"No. I'm afraid Katharine will see us and tell Melanie," he retorted gently.

"You're right," she agreed. "But don't you think we need to tell Melanie?"

"I'll choose the time and place," he was momentarily stern. His voice softened. "You're my lead," he spoke softly. "Set the pace. Don't make it so fast we can't enjoy the stars."

She complied, and they were silent, concentrating on their strokes as the sound of the water lapping against the oars and the crickets on the shoreline kept accompaniment.

Reaching the point at which she knew he liked to rest, she shipped the oars, and he did likewise. She leaned backward, her head on his lap, gazing up at him. He bent down and kissed her, as she tangled her fingers in his hair.

She suddenly whipped around, her face buried in his lap, as he gripped the sides of the scull. "No, my dear," he said sternly.

"But I promise you'll like it," she whispered wickedly.

"Can't you enjoy the moment of aesthetic pleasure?" He gently pulled her up by the hair to stare at her. "All those aeons of unrequited love yearned for in the moonlight? Wordsworth, Shelley, Byron, Keats?"

She obediently turned back around and laid her head again in his lap, as he stroked her hair. They watched the stars together quietly, as he quoted poetry to her in French and German, then fell silent.

He finally broke the silence. "And the final program?"

"Yes, I've decided," she stated.

"You're not going to tell me?" he demanded authoritatively.

"Not now," she looked away. "I don't want to argue with you here."

"You need some Buxtehude or other pre-Bach," he admonished her half-sternly.

"I've had my fill of those guys. I'm into the French guys now," she murmured. "There's only room for two German guys in my rep," she added slyly. "JS Bach and you. Kiss me, Harry."

He obliged. "We need to make the return trip, *cara mia*," he murmured against her lips.

"I thought you wanted to stay here forever and contemplate the night," she teased him.

"I'm ready for sterner stuff now," his hand ran down the length of her body. She smiled in anticipation.

The next evening he was gone to an obligatory social function. She penned a poem and left it on the door to his apartment:

I sense how you hoard the taste,
sucking the lemon dry, savoring the salt,
holding the tequila against your burning tongue
and mingling it with the tears
of the unrequited dry spell to come.

I sense the pleasure you garner
at the lapping of the oars in the darkness,
and the silent rocking of the tiny waves
that churn up as you pause and gaze at the cold lady
raining cold light on the cricket's song.

But I don't want to dissolve
into just one of those myriad memories
straining against the closed covers
of your metaphorical dusty photo album.
Breathe life into me, my love.

That night he came to her in her room. "So you're a poet?" he asked, as she opened the door to his knock. He held a bottle of champagne and two fluted glasses in one hand, and a record album in the other.

"It's silly, I know," she responded, embarrassed.

"No, it's very evocative," he set the champagne and glasses down on the bedside table, placed the record on the bed and turned her to face him.

She whispered, "Melanie comes back tomorrow."

"I know." He stroked her hair. "My dear Laura," he whispered.

"Who is Laura?" she asked. "I think you've making love to someone else."

"You don't recall your Petrarch, I gather," Kreiser kissed her ear. "He wrote of his unrequited love for a Laura. It's been the subject of many art songs as well, including this one by Liszt, borrowing Victor Hugo's poem. Do you have a stereo?"

She led him to a stereo in the corner. He walked back and retrieved his record, placed it on the turntable and turned it on. In a moment the sounds of a soprano singing *Oh! quand je dors* came wafting through the room.

"Let's see if your French is good enough for your trip," he smiled. "Translate for me."

He pulled her to him, her back to him. She listened as he held her. "'When I dream, approach close to my bed, like Laura would appear to Petrarch.'"

She listened. "This is beautiful, Harry."

But he prodded her. "Continue, please."

"'Let your breath touch me as you pass . . . suddenly my lips will part.'" She paused. "How am I doing?"

"Not bad," Kreiser moved against her, his hands running down the length of her torso.

Aroused, she turned to face him. "There are better things to be doing to this music than French lessons," she reached up to kiss him.

"You are my dream, Charlotte," he murmured. "I have trouble believing you are really here with me. I always wanted to love you from afar."

"I'm really here," she said petulantly.

"But you won't always be here. You must go on to face your destiny. You are a rising star, my star."

"But there's no reason our stars cannot rise together," she put her arms around him. "You've been wanting to go to Yale to teach. I could go there as well, if I'm accepted."

"What's this 'if you're accepted'?" Kreiser looked at her sharply. "Is there something you didn't tell me?"

"I was nervous during the Yale audition. I think I did OK, but I'm just not sure. But even if I don't make it into Yale, it's not far from Manhattan. We could be together, away from all this constant rumor and speculation in the largest city in the world. Who cares what they say? You could go with me to Paris. There's nothing to stop us."

"Your aunt will have something to say about it," Kreiser reminded her.

"I'm an adult with my own trust fund. And Mellie would not deny us," Charlotte argued, although her voice held a touch of doubt. "We're in love. Are you going to tell her? Shall I?"

"Let's not discuss this right now," he whispered, drawing her to him and inching toward the bed. "We'll deal with that tomorrow. We have tonight. I want you too badly to even discuss your audition. Come, my Laura."

PART THREE

There is no greater sorrow
Than to be mindful of the happy time
In misery.

The Divine Comedy: Inferno, Canto V
Dante Alighieri (1265-1321)
(Tr. Henry Wadsworth Longfellow)

Chapter 18

"Mike, it's Charlotte."

"Hi, Sis," Michael said into the receiver of his office phone. "What are you doing?"

"Well," she paused, so long he thought she was gone.

"Charlotte? Are you there?"

"I need your help."

"All right," he laughed. "What is it?"

"I'm at the bus station," she spoke uncertainly.

"Bus station?" he was instantly alert. "Where?"

"Here in D.C.," she cleared her throat nervously.

"Charl!" he exclaimed. "What are you doing here? Why didn't you call ahead? I'd have met you. A bus?" Suddenly suspicious, he added, "Does Melanie know?"

"No," she was vehement. "I don't want to tell you over the phone," she stammered.

"OK," he was worried. "Why don't you come on over to the office?"

"Uh—I would rather not," she was clearly uncomfortable. "Can't I meet you somewhere?"

"You're scaring me now," Mike admonished her. "I'll come get you. Tell me which station."

She reeled off the station address.

"I'll be right there. Are you safe?"

"Yes," she said hoarsely. "And Mike, please don't tell Amy or Melanie I'm here."

"Why not?" he was surprised.

"I'll tell you when you get here."

Mike told the secretary he had to run an errand, asked her to make his excuses for the next scheduled meeting, and grabbed his jacket. On the way out he ran into Ben Loftin, his boss and the U.S. Representative from Georgia.

"Where are you going?" Ben exclaimed. "I need you. We're set to meet with a contributor in five minutes."

"Ben, I have an emergency," Mike spoke hurriedly. "This is one time you're going to have to schmooze him alone. I'll check in later."

Mike jogged down the hall and a couple flights of stairs to the parking garage. Soon he was speeding along a back street, thankful the traffic wasn't terribly heavy. Why was Charlotte in D.C., without notice? And why didn't she tell her sister?

He mulled the questions over in his mind. Charlotte was young and headstrong, but he'd never known her to do anything foolish like this. There had to be an explanation behind her actions.

He turned onto the avenue, saw the bus station ahead and looked for a parking spot, luckily finding one nearby. As he got out of the car, he saw a young woman walking toward him with a carryon bag. He did a double-take.

It was Charlotte, and she was dressed in denims and a sweat shirt. He had never seen her dressed so shabbily. But even more disturbing was her pale, wan appearance. She had lost weight, and was even thinner than her normal slim self. Her face, devoid of makeup, was chalky white, and her eyes were bloodshot and sunken, with dark circles under them. Her hair was stuffed into a baseball cap.

He ran to grab her bag from her and pulled her across the street, embracing her. "My heavens, Charlotte, are you ill?"

"You could say that," she laughed shakily, her voice catching in a sob. He could feel her trembling.

"Here, let's get you in the car," he opened the door for her and carefully helped her in, before placing the bag in his trunk and making his way around to the driver's side.

Once inside, he turned to her. She was sobbing.

"Charlotte, what is wrong? Please tell me," he whispered, as he took her hand clumsily.

"I'm such a mess," she blubbered. "My life is a shambles."

"When was the last time you've eaten?" he was concerned.

"Sometime yesterday, I think. I don't remember," she sobbed. "I'm sorry I had to call you."

"Nonsense," he said encouragingly. "Let's go somewhere and get you something to eat. You'll feel better."

She shook her head. "I don't want anyone to see me."

"It's OK," he assured her. "I know a pub not too far away. Good food and anonymity."

He carefully pulled out into the street. As he looked through his rearview mirror, he asked, "Tell me why you are here."

"I had to leave," she mumbled. "Melanie doesn't know where I am."

"Oh, God, Charl," he murmured. "She'll be crazy with worry."

"I couldn't face her. It's so terrible. Oh, Mike, what am I going to do?"

"You're coming home with us," he said confidently. "Amy and I will take care of you, no matter what. But it would help if we knew what was going on."

"I'm pregnant," she whispered.

Mike almost threw them both through the windshield as he hit the brakes in shock. A car horn behind them blew impatiently.

"Damn," he swore under his breath. "Sorry, Charl, you threw me for a moment."

They were both silent for the next few moments, while he negotiated traffic and finally pulled into a parking place. He shut off the car. "Here we are."

He quickly got out and ran around to her door, helping her alight from the car. Taking her arm he steered her into the small but neat little bar.

"Fred, is my favorite back booth open?" he smiled engagingly at the proprietor.

Fred craned his head toward the back. "Yep, you picked a good time to come in. Need a menu?" he gazed curiously at Charlotte.

"Yes, please," Mike gently pulled Charlotte along with him, then ensconced her in the booth.

Quickly menus appeared. Mike ordered a beer for himself and an orange juice for Charlotte. Charlotte, suddenly hungry, ordered some chicken fingers and fries, Mike favoring some popcorn shrimp.

When the waiter was out of earshot, he turned to her. "Out with it," he ordered. "What in the world has happened, that you would run away up here on a bus and not tell Aunt Mellie?"

"It's hard enough," she begged, "without you looking at me like that. Just listen to me."

So he sat impassively as she told him about her discovery about George, and the resulting affair with Kreiser. "Melanie doesn't know anything about Kreiser and me, or the pregnancy. And it needs to stay that way," she finished miserably.

The waiter brought their food. She stared at the food. Mike asked, "What is it?"

She bolted to the restroom.

Several minutes later, she emerged, and Mike was standing by the door. "Are you all right?" he was solicitous, taking her arm and supporting her.

"I've been sick for a couple of months now," she replied weakly, as he led her back to the table.

"Can you eat anything?" he sat down across from her.

She nodded mutely. Mike watched her as she picked at her food, and offered her some shrimp, which she declined. "I love them, but they're fickle," she smiled tremulously.

"We need to get you in to see a doctor," Mike asserted, "and I know just the man. And I need to take you home."

"But Amy will call Melanie!" Charlotte objected weakly.

"Firstly, she's your sister and will honor your wishes. Secondly, we have to let Melanie know something, or all sorts of law enforcement are going to descend upon you. She will have the world's best investigative minds out looking for you. We need to ease her mind and forestall all that."

"But I'm not going back," Charlotte interposed fearfully. "I need your help. I can get a job here. I have a little money from my savings, and my trust fund income if Melanie will release it to me. Dean Jackson is applying for a fellowship here for me to pursue my English degree. I'll get my teaching certificate."

"But Charlotte, you're a musician."

"Not any more," she declared, her tone flat. "You gotta help me, Mike."

"Why, Charlotte? Why would you give up your dream?"

"Because I—I can't do it anymore," she became hysterical, her eyes wild. "I can't play. What am I going to do? My life is over."

"No, it's not, dear," he squeezed her hand. "Just take a deep breath. I'll see what I can do," he promised. "Let's box this up and go home."

Later that evening, after Charlotte was put to bed, Mike and Amy were discussing the matter. Mike had Amy call Melanie with news that Charlotte was safe for the moment. But Charlotte had been adamant that she would disappear if Melanie tried to make her return, or did anything to jeopardize Kreiser's job.

"This is Aunt Mellie's worst nightmare come true," Amy whined to Mike. "That Charlotte would get into this trouble . . ."

"But for the grace of God that could be any of us, including you," Mike remonstrated. "Charlotte has always longed for her father. She has always gravitated toward older men. Haven't you noticed it? She developed a close relationship with Kreiser. I'm just surprised that she made it to adulthood before doing something like this. It was almost predestined that it would be the wrong man. Thank God it wasn't Sammy Fellowes."

Amy looked with surprise at her husband. "No, I never imagined this. Charlotte has always been so—so smart."

"You women pride yourselves on your predictive properties," he frowned, shaking his head. "Yet you and Melanie never saw this coming."

"Well, Charlotte is in terrible shape. I've never seen her so shaken and unhappy. I'm scared for her and the baby."

"I called Bob and asked him to make time to see her tomorrow," Mike confided. "So you need to take her in."

"Dr. Smythe? My doctor?" Amy sniffed. "What if he tells someone about this?"

"Amy, get over yourself," Mike said sternly. "He is bound by doctor-patient confidentiality. And Charlotte is your sister. He'll be discreet, and so will we. We'll get through this."

"What if Charlotte doesn't cooperate and Melanie cuts off my allowance?"

Mike laughed. "Amy, you might have to tighten your belt and forego a pair or two of Gucci shoes. God forbid that happen. I'll take care of us."

Amy took his hand hopefully. "Do you think Charlotte would allow us to adopt her baby?"

Mike turned away disgustedly. "Amy, please, focus on the issue. This is your only sister, and so far all you have thought about are Melanie and yourself."

Her eyes filled with tears. "I'm sorry, Mike," she flung her arms around him. "I did not mean to sound so mercenary. I love Charlotte, and I will take care of her, if she will let me. She's always been so independent and willful. I've never seen her helpless. She's never needed anyone before."

Mike enfolded her in his arms. "My pretty dingee wife," he murmured. "I've never seen her this way either. Let's take care of your baby sister for the moment, OK?" he kissed her. "For once she really needs you."

Chapter 19

Daisy timidly opened the door in response to the peremptory knocking, and Peter Conrad stormed past her and down the foyer.

"Mr. Peter, Miss Mellie isn't seeing anyone," Daisy called, running after him.

"She'll see me," he thundered, then stopped short as Melanie appeared in the doorway to the study. He was shocked by her appearance. One who normally was impeccably dressed and coiffed at all times, she looked old and haggard, in her gown, robe and slippers, her hair disheveled, no makeup, and her eyes dull and lifeless.

"Where is she? I demand to speak to her."

"She's not here, Peter," Melanie muttered, her voice low. "She has run away. She didn't even leave a note. She cleaned out her personal bank accounts and the line of credit I set up for her Paris trip."

"Where?" his voice softened, as shock registered on his face.

"She's somewhere in the D.C. area, or at least I hope she still is," Melanie replied wearily. "I've been trying to find her for two days. Amy finally called last night, and has had contact with her. I spoke to Amy again this morning—Charlotte spent the night there, but left this morning. Charlotte would not let her give me any more details, and if I try to intervene Amy's afraid she will cut off all contact. Charlotte has threatened to disappear."

"Why?" Peter insisted. "Were the tabloids true? What is going on, Melanie?"

There was a knock on the door. Melanie turned to Daisy. "That will be Malcolm Jackson. Show him in." She motioned for Peter to follow her into the study.

They took their seats as Jackson appeared. "Oh, Melanie, I am so sorry," he said, coming up to her chair and taking her hand. "I am to blame for your not knowing. But Charlotte swore me to secrecy, said she would disappear without a trace if I told you. I've applied in her name for a writing fellowship at Georgetown. I'm trying to tie her to some known location close to Amy until we can talk some sense into her."

Melanie's eyes filled with tears. Jackson knelt by her side. "She looked so sick, so frail. She had lost weight. I was afraid for her. I tried to get her to see reason. I threatened to come to you, to go to Kreiser. When I mentioned his name, she became hysterical, and was screaming and shaking."

"Kreiser?" Peter interrupted. "What does Harry have to do with this?"

"He's been having an affair with my niece," Melanie spat coldly. "I trusted him with her, and look what happened."

Conrad recoiled as if slapped. "The bastard! I will ruin him," Peter exclaimed hotly, but Melanie raised her hand, quieting him.

She took a deep breath. "I was in New York with Agatha Fellowes. The gossip columns broke with a story about Sammy and Charlotte breaking up. I wanted to come home immediately, and Agatha was crushed. But she assured me that we should not fuel the media speculation, that we should stay and sort it out when we got home, that it was probably at most a trivial quarrel. That's Agatha, always full of wishful thinking. I was secretly glad about the breakup, but worried about Charlotte's state of mind, given her impulsivity.

"I called Harry, and he told me that Charlotte was with him, and that all was well. She had discovered about George's—promiscuity, and broke with him. But Harry assured me she was fine. I knew I should have come home, but I didn't. I listened to Agatha.

"Then I returned. Charlotte was acting strangely, always running off somewhere, avoiding me. Kreiser came to me not long after I arrived home, and told me that she had come to him, almost suicidal, and that they had been—seeing each other." She paused. "A sexual liaison. God, I was sick. I told him to cease and desist, and to find another job—I wanted him out of here.

"I could not get her to talk to me. She kept refusing, running away, saying she was working hard and not sleeping well, then she was tired, then she had the flu. She denied anything was wrong. She didn't come home until late, and was gone in the mornings before I awakened. Some nights she didn't come home at all. Then she disappeared two days ago. Off the radar. I've had my investigator looking for her. She did not fly out; she must have taken a bus."

Peter whitened. "My God," he exclaimed. "A couple days after she came back from the Yale audition, she called me. I knew about the newspaper stories. She told me that George was 'so yesterday's news', and that she was seeing someone new. She asked for a few weeks off from the ensemble. She sounded so—euphoric," he concluded, almost to himself. "That it was Harry . . ."

Jackson stood and faced the mantel, not looking at them. "Charlotte took all the blame for the affair. She said it was not Harry's fault, that she threw herself at him after finding out about Sammy. She told me it was over, that Kreiser had broken it off, had pushed her away, was adamant that he was not going to ruin her life and career. She begged me not to tell you, not to blame him, to leave him be.

"Melanie, she told me she couldn't play any more, that she couldn't even sit at an instrument without overwhelming fear and nausea. She begged me to help her get away, and to keep it from you. She was so ashamed. She said she didn't want you to know she had failed you again."

Melanie sniffed. "Why could she not come to me?" she cried piteously. "What have I done that she could not trust me?"

Peter asked, "What are we going to do? We can't sit by and do nothing."

Jackson turned and looked at both of them. "I cannot fire Kreiser. We would just be confirming the media speculation about him and Charlotte. And we run the risk of her making good her threat and disappearing if Kreiser is terminated. She was clear about that. He has volunteered to leave, but I really think that can only hurt both him and her."

They both looked at Melanie. She answered slowly, "You're right. As much as I want to blame Harry for all this, I know Charlotte. She is impulsive and headstrong, and I can picture it happening just the way Harry said. He came to me right after I got home and confessed everything. He said he could not dishonor my trust by keeping it from me, professed he loves her and wants to marry her. He wanted my blessing, for God's sake." She paused, her lip trembling. "I forbade him seeing her again."

"That could be why she doesn't want to see you," Peter suggested gently.

"What else could I do? Have her committed?" Melanie retorted angrily. "She wouldn't talk to me. I was afraid she might do something if I confronted her, but I never had the chance. She may act like an adolescent, but under the law she is an adult."

Melanie buried her head in her hands. "God, if only I could trust Harry to be faithful to her. But we all know Harry's proclivities. He is constantly in and out of love, and we've had to deal with some of that fallout before. Charlotte is young and vulnerable, one to fall headlong for him and do something horrible to herself when he tires of her. If he is going to hurt her, better now than after she commits herself and does something stupid like conceive his child."

Jackson paled. "What if it's too late?"

Melanie stared at him. "What do you mean?" As his meaning dawned on her, she cried, "No, Malcolm. You don't think—?"

She buried her face in her hands. "Not little Charlotte," she moaned. "And I can't even confront her to find out. Oh, God in heaven. I have one niece dying to have a child and can't, and another who may be out there with an unwanted pregnancy. It's too much."

They were silent, Melanie in her grief, and the two men digesting this possibility.

Peter finally spoke up. "Charlotte needs our help and support somehow. She is under a great deal of stress and out there by herself, except for what help she will accept from Amy and Mike. Is there some way one of us can approach her that will not cause her to flee?"

Melanie mumbled, "Gerard."

They looked at her expectantly.

"He's her best friend. I will send him. He'll find her. Maybe she will listen to him."

Chapter 20

Charlotte Lawson sat alone in a classroom reading and grading English papers, rubbing her forehead wearily. She had covered her own class alone today and secretly substituted for another teacher as well, against school policy. The college students in the second class, a writing class, had kept clamoring to hear about her novel about to be released. She was chagrined that the professor had identified her as the author, but gratified at the students' interest in the work. It gave her a chance to focus on dealing with point of view and elements of a plot with the students.

Charlotte was working in the District of Columbia area, doing some student teaching at Georgetown while completing her teaching certificate. Her brother-in-law Mike had pulled some strings and helped her secure the post, because Charlotte insisted on trying to make her own way after abruptly running away from Atlanta without a word to her aunt.

Charlotte had thought about moving to New York City and disappearing, but she knew in her condition she would end up needing help, and she was not willing to risk Melanie's fire and brimstone. So she ran to the most obvious place: her sister's home. Despite Amy's loyalties to Melanie, she would not turn away her sister, and Charlotte's close friendship with her brother-in-law Michael meant that he could be counted on to help her.

When Charlotte absconded, Melanie had demanded explanations from Charlotte and her sister. Charlotte, ashamed and afraid of her aunt's reaction and equally stubborn, had refused all contact, even when the matriarch had threatened to cut off all financial assistance to Amy and Mike. And Charlotte had sworn Amy to secrecy, allowing her only to tell Melanie she had contact with her sister and Charlotte was all right, that she was temporarily in the area, and that otherwise Amy did not know how to reach her.

Melanie called daily and threatened to come up and drag her niece back, if she had to risk publicity and have Charlotte committed. Charlotte in turn refused to talk to Melanie directly, and threatened to disappear without a trace. Mike with unflagging patience ran interference between the women and tried to negotiate a truce. Charlotte demanded that Melanie leave her alone and not punish Amy and Mike for honoring Charlotte's demands. Melanie in turn ordered that Charlotte stay in the area close to Amy and Mike, and provided her a line of credit. Charlotte in reply insisted that Kreiser be left alone.

During this time Kreiser had also called, frantically searching for Charlotte after she had left town. Charlotte had forbidden Amy to disclose her whereabouts. Desperate, Kreiser then pleaded with Amy to have Charlotte call him, that it was urgent. At that point, Charlotte had returned Kreiser's call.

"How are you?" he had whispered over the phone. "God, I have missed you. I never realized how much you are a part of me. I am so sorry, *cara mia*. Please come home."

"What is so urgent that you need to talk to me?" she had demanded curtly, not giving in to the weakness at hearing his voice.

"Carlota, I do not want to live without you. You must believe me." He continued hurriedly. "I have to know that you are all right, and that you are going on with your organ performance. It means everything to me."

She cut him off. "That's not what you said to me the last time we met. You said I was ruining us both. Do you think I could just forget how you gutted me? How you canceled my recitals? Destroyed my dreams?" She took a deep breath, stilling the trembling in her voice. "I heard you with a woman at the boathouse," she confronted him, her voice icy.

"This is only a marriage of convenience, Carlota, to hush up the rumors about us, to protect you."

"Marriage?" she had echoed, disbelieving.

"Yes, marriage. I had to let you hear it from me. But I swear to you—I feel nothing for her. This is all for you, to protect you from the press," he was trying to explain.

Shocked and angry, Charlotte had hung up on Harry, not revealing that she was pregnant with his child. She refused to talk to him again, and would not allow Amy to reveal her address to anyone when she moved into a studio apartment near the college.

Conrad had also called demanding to speak to her, and she had reluctantly returned his call.

"Charlotte, my dear. How are you?" he exuded concern. "Can I do anything for you?"

"Peter," she choked at the sound of his voice. "I'm so—so sorry. I have let you down."

"Nonsense," she heard him say. "You could never let me down. I just want to help you." Before she could interrupt, he continued. "Darling Charlotte, you were accepted at Juilliard. Christine Hodges called me, told me they want you badly. Yale does too. The dean called me, asked why neither Kreiser nor you are returning his telephone calls."

Charlotte gasped, her heart constricting in a sharp series of pains. Tears pooled in her eyes.

"Charlotte, are you there? Are you all right?" he asked, suddenly concerned.

"Oh, God, no," she whispered brokenly, unable to contain her sorrow.

"I have contacted Dr. Hodges about the hypothetical possibility of your deferring enrollment a semester. She said you could take a year. She said that she and Melanie could make it happen. It can be arranged," he hastened to assure her. "All you have to do is say the word, my dear."

"Oh, Dr. Conrad," she sobbed uncontrollably. "I can't do that. Not now. I just can't. So much has changed. There was a time—" she fell silent, overcome.

"It's Peter, remember? And I know," he was sympathetic. "I could kill the one who did this to you."

"You know?" she cried.

"I suspect the worst," he responded.

"You must not do anything," she was beside herself. "It is all my fault. Please promise me, Peter."

He was silent a moment. "Charlotte, you know I would do anything for you," he informed her. "Do you need money? References? If you want to leave, go to Paris, disappear, I can arrange it for you. I have friends there. I can set up your continuing studies like you planned."

"No," she swallowed and forced herself to respond. "Thank you. You are so good to me, and I've been such a disappointment to you."

"Never," he was vehement. "Please let me know how you are. I love you, little Charlotte."

"I love you, too. I need to go," she said, her voice a whisper. "I promise. Thank you, Peter."

Today she had stayed behind after class reading and grading papers. She couldn't erase the memory of Conrad's call. She was distressed that others might surmise her predicament. Her fingers moved involuntarily against the desktop.

She stared blindly at a paper until a shadow fell across the desk. Looking up, she had been surprised to see Gerard Fellowes, smartly dressed in a dark Armani suit.

"Gerry, what are you doing here?" she had exclaimed with pleasure, then crimsoned as he looked at her drawn features, to her frumpy appearance, then down to her swollen belly. She was suddenly blinded by tears of shame.

Wordlessly he had swept her into his arms and hugged her close. Finally he spoke. "Good God, Charl, why didn't you call me? I was so worried about you. The engagement party was called off, suddenly I didn't hear from you, people said you left town without a word. I could have helped you."

"How did you find me?" she whispered, mortified.

"I finished up school at Stanford early and came home, expecting to find you in the middle of wedding plans or on your way to Paris. But you were gone, so I started searching. George wouldn't answer any of my questions; he just said you broke off the engagement. Melanie was beside herself. But you forget I have friends in high places. Even then it wasn't easy, and Amy wasn't talking," he said, his mouth pressed to her ear. He released her and held her at arm's length. "I knew you had to be somewhere close."

He laughed suddenly. "You look terrible," he grinned.

"Thanks. You were always such a flatterer," she smiled tremulously.

"Come on, let's get out of here. Let me take you for a bite."

He had packed her papers into her satchel, picked it up as if it was a doll, and took her arm, gently helping her and bundling her into the limousine. He had taken her to a deli down the street, where the students had looked curiously at them and the limo outside.

"Where are you staying?" he asked as she picked at a grilled chicken salad and he sipped some coffee, watching her intently. "With Amy and Mike?"

"No, I have my own place not far from here," she replied. "Just an efficiency. It's not much, but I felt Amy and Mike needed their privacy."

Gerard gazed at her over his coffee cup. "But this is not the safest of cities, Charl."

"It's fine, really," she insisted, clasping his hand momentarily to reassure him.

"Do you have any protection?" he inquired.

"Protection?" she echoed, laughing hollowly. The term had suddenly brought back to mind her illicit liaison with Harry. I'm pregnant, she thought; isn't it too late to ask about protection?

"You know, a weapon in case someone broke in on you. Here you are, alone in a big city full of crime, and pregnant. Jesus, Charl, you can shoot like a pro, and you don't even have a pistol? When you finish your salad, we're going to take care of that."

"Oh, Gerry," she exclaimed. "The students are very good to me. My neighbor checks on me regularly. He is a campus cop and a graduate student."

"Charl, this is no good for you. I can't believe my brother. If George is not going to do right by you, I will. Marry me. Let me take care of you."

"Marry you?" she echoed with a curt laugh, but the sound died as she saw the grim expression on his face. "Gerard Fellowes, I love you too much to marry you," she quipped.

He covered her hand with his. "Charl, you've always been special to me. Let me be there for you."

"I thought you had a girlfriend," she reminded him.

"Yeah, well, that's over," he said shortly. "Besides, no one holds a candle to you for finding adventure. I realized I kept looking for another girl just like you."

She blushed, not meeting his eyes. He pressed her hand. "We go back a long time. We have a history." He smiled. "Remember our secret hiding spot at the boathouse, our 'treasure chest'?"

She too smiled at the memory. "Yes. I've never told anyone about our secret. I remember us hiding my diaries, some seashells, some notes, and your cigarettes in there. Oh, and your 'F' on that science test. And our two coins."

"Remember all of Uncle Howard's treasure hunts? Those ghost stories Aunt Mellie told us? And the 'coins of death' story?"

"Those treasure hunts were the best," recalled Charlotte, joining in the reverie. "And what about the night after Amy's engagement party when you sneaked us into that wedding reception at the Georgian Terrace? You made a toast to the bride and groom. We didn't even know them."

"The hotel manager recognized you and called Aunt Mellie on us. Oh, was she mad. And how about the night you climbed in through my bedroom window and tried to seduce me?"

"I just wanted to learn how to do it, so I'd know how to with George if he asked," she blushed. "That didn't go far," she laughed. "My sex education was short-lived, thanks to you."

"Thanks to you," he laughed with her. "You couldn't leave well enough alone. I remember you licked my ear like Toby's Irish setter. You and your 'research'—that damned romance novel."

"Melanie got it from your mom, and I stole it from Amy," Charlotte teased him.

"Agatha doesn't read that trash," he was defensive.

"All women read that trash at some time," she smiled at him.

"At least you didn't decide to pick that up, or have you?" he asked her, his eyes full of concern.

She flushed and did not answer.

He took her hand. "We had some good times." He traced her lifeline with his finger. "Come back with me," he pleaded.

She gently disentangled her hand. "I'm not going back," she announced flatly. "Not ever."

"Then I'll move here. I'll take you anywhere you want to go," his brown eyes locked in hers. "I'll marry you, I'll be your baby's father, and I'll take care of you."

"No, Gerry, I'm not saddling you or anyone else with my problems," she was firm.

"But you need my help," he persisted.

"I need to grow up and make my own way," she said in a low voice. "I've made my bed, and I'm going to lie in it the best I can. I need a friend, Gerry. The rest will take care of itself."

Chapter 21

Afterward Gerard insisted on taking her home to her shabby duplex. Walking her up the steps and inside the dull brick building, he looked with distaste at the drably furnished room. "Amy allows you to live here?" he muttered angrily.

"Amy doesn't dictate to me," Charlotte replied defensively.

"Does Melanie know? Can't you do better?"

"No, she doesn't. Money is not the issue," she retorted. "Independence is. I'm trying to make it on my own. The irony is not lost on me that I had to clean out my accounts to come here, and that I'm still dependent upon Melanie."

He walked up to her refrigerator and opened it, noting its meager contents. She anticipated his reaction. "I eat out most of the time," she volunteered, suddenly uncomfortable at his accusatory eyes on her. "I do most of my work and writing elsewhere. I only sleep here."

"God, Charl," he exclaimed irritably. "I'll drag George up here myself to retrieve you and take you home."

"You'll do no such thing," she hissed impetuously. "I don't ever want to see him again. George didn't do this to me. I refused to be the cover for his harem, to expose myself to whatever communicable diseases he possesses and dishes out to his companions. Besides, George prefers his own gender."

She stopped, covering her mouth, horrified at herself. Gerard's shock was evident. "Gerry, I'm so sorry," she breathed, full of remorse. "I thought you knew."

He sat down heavily on the edge of the ugly sofa, the color drained from his face. "Geez," was all he could say.

Finally he looked at her. "Is that why you left?"

"No, that's not why I left," she murmured, her heart breaking for him.

"I thought maybe you were too ashamed to go back to George when you found out you were pregnant."

"No," she managed. "I—I didn't do it with him." She was embarrassed, and turned away.

"Listen, I have to get out of here," he said suddenly, glancing at his watch and looking about the room dismissively. "I have a dinner meeting with a lobbyist and a senator, looking for some tax incentives on a new project. It's too late to cancel. Come with me. Let me put you up in a hotel room, and we'll find you something better in the morning."

"No, it's OK. I'm safe here. You've done enough, more than enough," she took his hand. "And I've repaid your concern with terrible news." Awkwardly she kissed his cheek.

He enfolded her in his arms. "I refuse to leave you here."

"You don't have a choice," she remarked stubbornly.

He looked long and hard at her. "Melanie sent me looking for you."

Charlotte gasped, backing away. "She mustn't know, Gerry. You cannot tell her where I am, that I am pregnant."

Gerry stared at her for several moments, then shook his head. "I'll call her if you don't come with me tonight."

"You wouldn't!" She was terrified.

"I don't want to," he admitted, "but I've not come this far to leave you alone in this neighborhood. I'll get you a suite at the Ritz."

"No," she was adamant. "I don't want anyone we know seeing me like this."

Reluctantly she finally agreed to go with him, and he had put her up in a discreet suite at the Hyatt, taking an adjoining room.

The next morning he arrived along with room service, the cart filled with breakfast foods. "You're eating for two now," he told her solemnly. "We must take care of you and the baby."

As Gerry sat, sipping coffee and watching her eat, he was silent. However, she felt his eyes on her and the unspoken questions. Finally he could take it no more. "If not George, who is the father?" he demanded.

She was silent, refusing to meet his eyes.

"It is Kreiser, isn't it?" he divined, his eyes smoldering.

"How did—" Charlotte was startled, but Gerry stood, knocking the chair over in his haste.

"That bastard! I cannot believe it. I'll castrate him myself," Gerry exclaimed, his face flushed with rage. "How dare he even touch you!"

"It—it wasn't like that," Charlotte stammered, still sitting, suddenly afraid at Gerry's vehemence. "I'm the one who—I came on to him," she confessed, her face aflame.

"But he's old enough to know better," Gerry shouted, throwing the china cup against the wall, it shattering into shards.

Charlotte came up to Gerry, taking his arm. "Please, Gerry, you don't understand," she pleaded, tears running down her face.

Gerard looked at her features, his own softening. "Then tell me, Charl," he placed his hands on both her arms, gently backing her up and sitting her down, kneeling in front of her. "Tell me."

Charlotte relayed the story, haltingly at first, omitting nothing, as Gerry stared at her impassively, only interrupting to ask a question now and then.

When she finished, she was silent, drained. He stroked her hair affectionately. "You're right," he replied softly. "You don't need to go back. He had no right to treat you the way he did. Either he's an utter lame bastard, or Melanie has threatened him to get him to leave you alone. Either way, he's not good enough for you."

His words stung. Charlotte retorted, "I'm damaged goods. Who am I to sit in judgment of Harry?"

"You're not damaged to me," Gerry whispered. "You were seduced, Charl, no matter what you think. I'm just sorry I wasn't here to protect you from that slime."

He was silent for a moment. "I never for once suspected that George was—gay," he stammered. "I knew he was hanging with a partying crowd, and Mom had asked me if there was anything I could do. I never bothered reading the tabloids. But this is a shock."

Charlotte touched his cheek. "I'm sorry that I broke it to you this way. I never suspected either. And there I was, engaged to him." She faltered. "I wouldn't call you. I was mad, thinking you knew about—about George and hadn't told me."

He shook his head. "No, I never guessed that. Did you love him?" Gerry stared at her.

"I thought so at the time," Charlotte admitted. "I thought George and I would make a good match, would look good together. I knew he'd let me pursue my music. George always made me feel attractive, desirable. But love? No, I don't guess I did, even though I had a crush on him all those years ago. I always knew I couldn't keep up his pace. But I expected him to be faithful, at least at first," she looked away. "I was crushed to find out I wasn't even on his mind."

"Did you love Kreiser?" Gerry was blunt.

Charlotte caught her breath. "No—no, of course not," she stuttered. "He was just someone I ran to—to assuage my hurt feelings," she managed. "I was desperate, and he was available," she found herself saying.

Gerry stood. "I've always suspected there was more there than met the eye, Charl. I saw the way he looked at you sometimes. Are you sure you don't feel something for Harry? You can tell me."

"Gerry, I don't know," Charlotte cried, purple with shame. "That week was wonderful for me, but was it love or just infatuation? I don't know; I thought I was in love. But could I still love someone who said the vile things he said to me? He's ruined my life. I can't even bear to hear music. I just know it's over now."

"No, it isn't," Gerry reminded her, as he laid his hand gently on her abdomen. "You have a baby to think of now. Are you going to tell him?"

"No," Charlotte's jaw was set determinedly. "He rejected me, for whatever reason. I've ruined my performance career. I won't be saddling him with a child. I intend that he never find out. I'll raise my baby alone."

Gerry looked at her, his eyes sad. "Then marry me. I'll take care of you and the baby. No one ever need know any different."

Charlotte shook her head. "Gerry, you deserve so much better than to settle for me and my problems," she whispered.

He raised her to her feet and held her to him. "Remember our blood pact? You're stuck with me. I'm your best friend, remember?"

She leaned against him, grateful. "You are the very best friend anyone could have," she murmured.

Gerard suddenly pulled away, breaking the spell. "Charlotte, I have to leave later today to go out of the country for a few days on business. I'd like to take you with me. Do you have a passport?"

"No," she shook her head sadly, pulling away. "You know Aunt Mellie was adamant about that. I was invited to play with the London Symphony, and she wouldn't let me go. I had just applied for a passport for my trip to Paris when—" she stopped when all the memories came flooding back.

"If I didn't have to leave today, I could pull some strings to get you one. Well, then, that settles it. You have to stay here until I return," Gerry insisted, his voice soft. "I'll make sure you have everything you need, and when I get back, we'll discuss—other arrangements," he finished, kissing her on the forehead. "Think about what I said, will you, Charl?"

"Gerry, I'll be fine," she protested, smiling.

"Finish your breakfast and get dressed," he ordered. "You're coming with me. We have an errand to run."

She complied, and went with him, bewildered. He ordered the driver to an address across town. They pulled up to a gun club. "Come on," he said.

Inside, they were met by the manager. "Yes, Mr. Fellowes, we have everything ready as you requested." The man pulled out two boxes and placed them on the counter, opening one. "They are matches, and very lovely ones. I think you'll be pleased."

She looked inside and was suddenly faced with a shiny Sig Sauer nine-millimeter, with a birch handle. "It's beautiful," she said, running her fingers along it admiringly. "Too pretty to shoot."

"Let's see if you remember how to use it," Gerry added quietly.

"Gerry!" she protested. "Please—not a gun. Besides, this is D.C."

"Don't worry about that. I've taken care of all that. It's registered to you, and all you have to do is sign for your permit. And you'll have a membership here, so that you can stay in practice."

She had reluctantly signed the application for the license, and he took her next door to a firing range and made her fire it until he was satisfied with her proficiency. Then he chauffeured her back to the hotel suite.

"Charlotte, I have to leave, but I want you to stay here until I return," he pleaded. "I shouldn't be gone more than a week or ten days. I arranged for credit. You can have anything you want."

"Thanks for the 'protection'," she indicated the bag he was carrying.

"I know from personal experience you are not good at following directions," he smiled. "At least you can defend yourself. I'll check on you as soon as I get back to town," he said huskily, placing his hand on her cheek before abruptly turning away and striding out.

She sat down on the bed heavily. She felt drained, alone. She was sorry to see him go. She pulled out the box holding her newest possession. Opening it, she found twenty crisp one-hundred dollar bills and a book of travel checks. Putting her hand on her abdomen, she cried.

But her situation got much worse. A few days later she felt sudden, gut-wrenching pains and began bleeding. She called Mike, who found her collapsed on the floor of her flat and rushed her to the hospital.

Chapter 22

Charlotte lay unresponsive in the hospital bed. Amy anxiously hovered over her as the doctor wrote in the chart.

"Is she going to be OK?" Michael, his face haggard, quizzed the doctor.

"I told her at her last check-up I thought she was driving herself too hard, and I was worried about her anemia. I wanted to order complete bed rest, but she told me that was impossible, that she had to work. When I got the call last night, I feared the worst."

He motioned for Mike to follow him. At the door he stopped, his voice dropped to almost a whisper. "At first she was moaning, in pain, but now she says nothing. The bleeding has stopped, thankfully. Her vitals are stabilizing, and I think her prognosis is good. I can tell from her features she is still in pain.

"But after she asked about the baby and I imparted the news, she says nothing. I cannot engage her in conversation. The nurse tells me she doesn't touch her food. I think she may be sinking into post-partum depression. I am requesting a psychiatric consult."

Amy, who had come up and heard his last words, was alarmed. "Oh, Aunt Mellie will have a fit." Her eyes filled with tears, as she gazed over at Charlotte. "Oh, Charlotte, dear. Oh, sweetie. I'm so sorry."

"I have prescribed a morphine drip for now," the doctor continued. "We'll continue monitoring her. Mr. and Mrs. Chadwick, I'm very sorry. It seems that I continue to be the bearer of bad news to you and your family."

"It's all right, Doc," Mike shook his hand. "Poor Charlotte. This is a blow, after a very stressful year for her. But we got a bit of good news. We got a call this morning of a possible baby available for adoption, so keep your fingers crossed."

"I will. And I will talk to you later," the doctor promised.

Amy went back to the bed and bent over Charlotte. "Please talk to me," she begged. "I want to call Aunt Mellie and tell her. You are not well."

Charlotte muttered, "No," and turned her face into the pillow.

"Is there anything we can do for you?" Amy was insistent, stroking her hair gently.

"There's nothing anyone can do," Charlotte mumbled. "Couldn't you have just let me die too?"

Amy turned to Mike despairingly, who embraced her. She blinked back tears. "I need to let the nurses know how to contact us."

Mike looked over at Charlotte. "We cannot leave her alone like this," he whispered. "You go get some rest, and I'll stay with her for a while."

Amy looked at him anxiously. "Are you sure?" she asked quietly.

He nodded. So they agreed upon a time for her to return.

When Amy left Mike went over and took Charlotte's hand. "I know it's bad, Sis," he said, his voice low. "Everything is black right now. But it will not remain so. We love you, and we're all going to pull through this together. You are going to be OK. You'll see."

She did not move. He squeezed her hand. "I'm not leaving you alone," he whispered to her, kissing the top of her head. "I've sent Amy home. I'll be right here."

She looked at him through lifeless eyes, saying nothing. Soon the nurse walked in and added something to her IV drip, and she slipped into a blessed oblivion.

She remembered little, except that at one point she dreamed she heard Melanie's voice. She cringed in fear and shame. For a moment she was filled with panic. Tears filled her eyes, as she curled up in pain, whimpering. *I can't go on*, she thought despondently. *I have nothing left to live for.*

Mike whispered over her, "It's OK, Charlotte. I'm here."

Some time later she awakened, to see a priest standing beside her bedside. "You here to give me last rites?" she asked, looking at him blearily.

"No, I'm here to talk to you, that's all," he smiled. "Do you feel like talking?"

"Just let me die. My sins are too many to confess," she replied bitterly.

"Never," he took her hand. "I'm Father Patterson. You can call me Danny. I think you need to be saved from yourself right now, Charlotte."

"Who sent you?" she asked, her mind still foggy.

"Someone who is very concerned about you," he replied solemnly.

"You know about my baby?" she blinked, as the memories came flooding back.

He nodded. "A beautiful boy. You named him Johann? Any significance?"

"His father's grandfather's name," she whispered. "Something he let slip one day. Named after Johann Sebastian Bach." She paused, swallowing convulsively. "Did he have a funeral service?"

"A simple, very private one," the priest squeezed her hand. "If you feel up to it, we could plan a memorial service for him later."

"No," she turned her head away. "Just a Christian burial. It would have been nice to place him in the family plot in Atlanta, but it can't be helped. Too much talk."

He said nothing. She felt the unspoken question. "No, his father doesn't know, and I want it to stay that way. You won't talk me out of that one."

"I don't intend to," he smiled again. "How do you feel?"

"Hell's not so bad a place," she laughed shortly, trying to shock him. He laughed with her, which surprised her.

"But you have a ticket out," he replied tenderly.

She fell silent. He finally spoke. "Charlotte, I will drop in again, because I want to help you through your hell. Will you let me help you?"

She didn't respond, staring at the wall.

A few days later, she was released from the hospital. Amy insisted on her coming home with them, and Charlotte made no objection. Charlotte withdrew, said little, and remained in the guest room except when coaxed out by Amy and Mike. Father Patterson visited her a couple of times, which surprised her. Again, she said very little, but he appeared unruffled by her reticence.

One evening a week later Amy burst into the great room, where Charlotte was sitting passively by the fire. Mike was at a desk working.

"We've got the call! They are going to deliver the baby to us tomorrow!" she announced excitedly.

"Tomorrow?" Mike echoed dazedly. "That's wonderful news. Do we have everything we need?"

Amy ran over to him and hugged him. "I've been planning this for so long. We have more than enough," she giggled, as he picked her up and swung her around the room excitedly.

They suddenly remembered that Charlotte was sitting there looking on. Mike released Amy and Amy knelt before Charlotte. "I'm sorry," she apologized, her face flushed with embarrassment.

Charlotte squeezed her hand and smiled faintly. "I'm happy for you both," she stated quietly. "It's what you've wanted all this time."

"I will need to call Aunt Mellie," Amy said solemnly.

Charlotte nodded.

"Is it OK to tell her you're here?"

Charlotte looked away. "Sure. Why not?"

Later that evening she had a visitor. Gerard walked into the great room. She smiled sadly at him, as he knelt in front of her and took her hands in his.

"Oh, Charlotte, I'm so sorry," he was sober. "I wish I had been here for you. Is there anything I can do?"

She gazed at him sadly. "I need some help finding a place to live," she replied simply. "I can't stay here with Amy and Mike, and I don't want to go back to Atlanta."

"Did you think about what we talked about before I left? I'll marry you and provide for you," his voice was low.

"Don't ask me that," she started trembling violently. "Please."

The next day the baby was delivered to the home. Amy and Mike asked Charlotte to be present. The adoptions counselor placed the infant in Amy's arms, and Charlotte looked away, trying to swallow the hurt as the ecstatic couple gazed on the new arrival.

Amy brought him over for Charlotte to see. Charlotte felt a moment of intense pain as she looked on the sleeping form. "He's a gift from heaven," she croaked, closing her eyes, trying to smile.

Amy kissed her on the cheek. "He's yours too," she pleaded. "I can't raise a baby without my baby sister."

Later that day Melanie arrived, having broken her own moratorium on flying. She was retrieved at the airport by Gerard. Charlotte pleaded a headache and hid upstairs in her room, unwilling to face the matriarch. It was there around dusk that Melanie found her.

"Don't you need some light on in here?" she breezed into the darkened room, turning on a light switch. As the lights went on and her eyes adjusted, Melanie gazed upon her niece, and let out a gasp of surprise.

"My God, Charlotte!" she exclaimed, as she stared at the emaciated frame and dull eyes that looked back at her. "Oh, my dear," she came toward her and took the unwilling woman into her arms. "I am so sorry, my dear," she cried, taking Charlotte's face in her two hands.

Charlotte was taken aback, speechless.

Melanie continued, "I should have been home. I could have stopped all this."

Charlotte was mute, unable to look at her aunt.

Melanie cooed, again to Charlotte's surprise. "Please say you will forgive me and come home with me."

"There's nothing to forgive. I'm the one at fault. But I'm not going back to Atlanta," Charlotte asserted. "Please don't ask me."

Melanie kissed Charlotte on the cheek. "We'll talk about the future later," she took Charlotte's hand. "Come with me to admire little Stefan?"

"I—I can't," Charlotte stepped back, anxiety-ridden. "I—I will be down soon," she stammered.

Melanie gazed at her and nodded. "It's all right, my dear. Take your time. I love you, Charlotte. Never forget that."

Not waiting for a reply, Melanie swept out of the room.

Charlotte crumpled, sitting down heavily at the foot of the bed, gripping the wooden post tightly as she cried.

As the days went on, the family kept trying to draw Charlotte into the fold of activities surrounding the baby's arrival. Charlotte would participate only briefly before absenting herself, overcome with emotion.

One morning Gerry showed up early. "I'm glad to see you're up and dressed," he remarked as Charlotte met him at the door. "Would you be up to taking a ride with me, getting out a bit?"

She nodded mutely, grabbing a sweater as he took her hand and pulled her out into the cool spring day. She said very little as they sat in the back of the limo and she gazed out the tinted windows.

After a while they pulled into an exclusive gated community of large townhouses skirting the canal in Georgetown. Charlotte looked inquiringly at Gerry as the limo stopped in front of one.

He stepped out and reached for her hand. "Come on."

She allowed herself to be pulled out of the car and up the drive. "Where are we?"

"Melanie wants to see if you like this place before she buys it," Gerry answered.

"Melanie?" echoed Charlotte, confused.

"If you're not returning to Atlanta, she wants you to have a place to live that meets her approval," he grinned. "She wants you to be safe."

He produced a key and let them in. He led Charlotte through the empty rooms, waiting for her reaction.

"Well, what do you think?" Gerry asked her finally. "Your first real space."

"Does it matter? It's pretty, but still a chain holding me in my place," she retorted.

He looked at her in surprise. "Charl, I don't understand. You're an heiress with quite a hefty trust fund. You were born to a certain station. What? Do you want to turn your back on it? Live in a cardboard box? Shop at Goodwill? Eat at the soup kitchen?"

"I just wanted to be successful at something, to gain some independence, be my own person," she remarked sullenly. "I can't keep a man's interest, can't make my own living, can't practice my art, and can't even bring my baby into the world. I'm just one major fuck-up."

Gerry laughed mirthlessly, shaking his head. "OK, it is time you got off the self-pitying soapbox. You're nineteen years old, Charl. You have a lifetime ahead of you. So what if you have hit rock bottom right now on your first attempt? Get back on the horse, and try again. That's what life is—falling off the horse and getting back on."

"You've done pretty damn well, and you're only twenty," she shot back angrily.

"Yes, but I'm not where I want to be," he answered. "I'm using my inheritance for all it's worth to get me there, and working my butt off."

Charlotte felt ashamed. "I'm sorry, Gerry. You are working hard, and I'm proud of you. I am just such a failure."

"And it will turn around," he hugged her impulsively. "Enjoy the fact that you have this to fall back on," he kissed her hair. "Spend some of Melanie's money, and have a little fun with it. She's not going to say a word, because of all the guilt she is feeling over you. Hire a decorator and a pool boy."

"Yeah, right," Charlotte laughed, but she knew he was right.

After they returned, Melanie hovered around saying nothing. Charlotte finally spoke up. "Yes, the place is fine, Aunt Mellie. How soon before I can move in?"

Melanie sighed with relief. "I already have contacted my decorator, and she has recommended someone here. I think it could be done in no time. Here's her card," she rummaged in her purse and found a card and presented it to Charlotte.

"I need to get out of here soon, and give Amy and Mike some privacy to enjoy their new family," Charlotte mused. "And of course you will have your pick of places to stay when you are here, either with me or with them."

"Thank you, my dear," Melanie kissed her cheek. "I feel so much better now that I know you will be in a safe place. Why don't I contact her tomorrow and make an appointment for us to get started on your new place?"

So Melanie gently pushed Charlotte into making decisions regarding the townhouse, and the new home came together rapidly. Melanie paid handsomely to rush the decorator, so that Charlotte could move in quickly. Charlotte acquiesced passively with most of the decisions of the decorator, but recoiled in horror when she walked in one day and a Steinway grand had been delivered and was being tuned. Melanie noticed her reaction, but said nothing, and shushed the decorator who began gushing over the instrument.

Melanie surprised Charlotte by asking to stay with her once the apartment was ready for Charlotte to move in. Charlotte readily agreed.

On the big day, she and Melanie showed up at the home, a servant scurrying to bring in their bags. They found Father Patterson waiting for them at the front steps.

Melanie gave her hand to the priest. "It is good to see you, Danny," she murmured. Charlotte looked at her in surprise.

"Danny and your Uncle Howard were long-time friends," Melanie explained. "Danny is not only a priest, but a credentialed psychologist."

Charlotte was surprised, but did not ask any questions. She invited the priest in. He walked in and admired the room. "Very nice," he approved.

Melanie looked at Charlotte and said pointedly, "I'm tired, and want to check out my room a while. I will leave you two."

Charlotte offered Patterson a seat and a drink, the latter he declined. She sat down facing him. "Should I lie on the couch?" she asked mockingly. "I mean, that's why you're here, isn't it? To analyze me and make sure I don't do any more dangerous or embarrassing things?"

Patterson shook his head at her. "Charlotte, nothing of the sort. You were so depressed at the hospital that I was called in, in the hopes of keeping the staff from involuntarily committing you. I'm only here as someone for you to talk to."

"Yeah, that would have been the ultimate blow to Melanie—headlines reading that the prodigal niece ends up in the crazy house," Charlotte muttered. "Thanks so much for being there to prevent that."

"Do you always make such a practice of self-deprecation? You're quite good at it," Patterson remarked, smiling slightly. "Actually, it was your brother-in-law that called me. I met Amy and Mike when they moved here, through an introduction from Melanie. He was fearful for you, and what you might do after the death of little Johann."

"Mike?" Charlotte was astounded.

"Mike," Patterson echoed. "He is quite fond of you, Charlotte."

"And I of him," Charlotte murmured. "I'm touched. And I didn't think I could keep on living. There are times when I'm still not so sure."

"You have to allow yourself to grieve, even to be angry," Patterson stated gently. "But you must not allow the despair to win."

Charlotte was silent. He prodded her. "Charlotte, there are many people whose happiness is bound up in you, who are dependent upon you."

"Like who?" she laughed sardonically.

"Like Melanie, who is miserable at the thought she has failed you. Like Mike and Amy, whose joy with little Stefan is tempered by their sorrow over your loss. Like Gerard, who is in and out checking on you, worrying about you. Like your students, who have sent cards and made inquiries as to when you will be coming back. And you have friends and supporters back in Atlanta, silently concerned about where you are and what you are doing."

She snapped, "I cannot meet everyone's expectations and be the perfect niche-filler for them."

Patterson took her hand. She refused to meet his gaze. "It has nothing to do with expectations, and everything to do with receiving and reciprocating their love. And this constant isolation and self-destruction hurts them as much as you."

She said nothing. He continued sadly. "I know you feel like your world has come to an end. But you are young, and from the ashes of tragedy rises a new beginning. Many of us are given the opportunity to live several lives in one, rebounding from the grief of loss to start over."

He rose. "Think about it. I would like to visit you again. Could we set a time?"

To her surprise, Charlotte agreed to another meeting the next week.

Charlotte and Melanie fell into a routine. Melanie arose every morning and left early, either to meet with old friends or to visit with Amy and Stefan. At Melanie's urging, Charlotte went back to teaching, but cut her classes down to one, and struggled to start writing again. She engaged a maid and a masseuse who seconded as butler and handyman.

She tried to play the piano when no one was there, but at first was so nauseous that she would run for the bathroom at the thought of playing. She would stare at the keyboard, feeling empty and bereft, unwilling to touch the keys. After a while the feeling subsided, but she still avoided the instrument as though it was a snake. But during unguarded moments, when she was alone, she would feel the pull of the instrument, and the desire to play would flood her briefly.

One day Gerard showed up, and found her outside on the private deck, lying on her stomach on a table, naked and covered by a towel, as the masseuse performed his ministrations. "Oh, that is so good," she murmured. "Tonio, if you don't stop I'll have to—"

The maid announced, "Mr. Fellowes is here."

Charlotte turned to look toward Gerry, her face flushed.

"Am I interrupting something?" Gerry interrupted, his face a mask.

Charlotte, sat up, pulling the towel up to cover herself. "Oh, hi, Gerry," she frowned. Tonio started to withdraw, but she put out a hand to stop him.

She lay back down and indicated a chair next to the table. "Tell me what's going on, Gerry," she invited.

"If I'm going to watch, I'll need some liquid sustenance," he smirked as he disappeared briefly. He walked back out with a drink in hand, to see Charlotte in intimate embrace with the man, before Tonio withdrew, nodding at Gerry as he quickly disappeared.

Charlotte pulled the towel around her. "Give me a minute to dress," she smiled. Gerry shook his head, sitting in a deck chair and staring at the lap pool.

Charlotte soon reappeared in shorts and t-shirt, a soft drink in hand. She took a seat by Gerry.

"So you took me seriously about the pool boy?" he laughed at her bemused expression.

"Tonio was actually Melanie's idea, but she wanted some big swarthy German woman with a mustache. I instead asked for and got an Antonio Banderas look-alike. His name is Miguel, but I call him Tonio."

"He doesn't seem to mind," Gerry shook his head. "Are you sure it's a good idea?"

"In what way?" Charlotte laughed shortly. "After my running away from Atlanta and all the massive gossip that generated? I'm amazed that no one has broken the story of my failed pregnancy. I asked Mike to seal the records if possible.

"Tonio is totally discreet—nothing leaked to the tabloids. He has great hands. He makes me feel good. And I—" she stopped.

"What?" Gerry looked at her as she looked away.

"I can't go all the way," she looked down at her hands. "I can only get so far before I—I see—" she didn't finish.

"What? Kreiser?" he asked softly.

She nodded wordlessly.

"That son of a bitch," Gerry muttered. "What about your music?"

"I just can't," she stared out at the bubbling brook at the end of the lap pool. "I can't believe I can't shake him, that I lost everything, and that my new life with little Johann is over before it began. Will it ever get better?"

Chapter 23

Charlotte reluctantly agreed to attend church with the family, inasmuch as she and Gerard were asked to be godparents to the infant Stefan at his baptism. Amy and Michael had agreed to wait for the baby's baptism until Charlotte was physically and emotionally up to attending. Therefore the baptism had been put off for several months.

Charlotte, now ensconced in her own place, was still a regular visitor to the Chadwick home. However, she had resisted attempts by the family to have her hold and cuddle the infant. She pleaded that she was afraid of 'breaking' him, but Amy discerned that Charlotte was still mourning her loss and not equal to the task of giving her heart to another at the moment.

Charlotte had avoided being in public as much as possible during the pregnancy, fearing that she might be recognized by the press. She had even gone so far as to cut her hair into a bob and have it darkened, and wore wire-rimmed glasses, all in an effort to change her appearance as much as possible. After the miscarriage, she still avoided public appearance, favoring her cloistered life of school and family.

She had hoped that Aunt Mellie would insist on an intimate closed baptismal ceremony to preserve the family's privacy. But Melanie was in agreement with Michael that Michael's and Amy's church family should share in their joy, and therefore the baptism was part of the regular Sunday service.

So Charlotte was sitting in the old church for the first time in over a year, numb to everything around her, trying to ignore the organ prelude played by a faceless figure from the back gallery. She refused to look behind her at the impressive organ with divided case surrounding the beautiful stained glass, the console sitting in the center. She unconsciously kept rubbing her hands against her simple Dior burgundy drape-collar crepe dress, her face half-hidden by the brim of a hat with matching bow.

Gerry, sitting beside her, was dressed in a dark tailored Armani suit and Ferragamo dress loafers. He took her hand in his, squeezing it tightly, divining her thoughts. She glanced at him thankfully.

They stood and sang the processional hymn, 'Praise, my soul, the King of heaven', Charlotte looking ahead, seeing nothing, hearing nothing, as the choir and clergy processed up the aisle, the cross passing by and others showing obeisance.

During the homily she desultorily read through the bulletin. On the back page she noted the church staff. "Evan Bartlett," she whispered. "Evan is here?"

Suddenly she grew more interested. As the minister invited them to stand before the baptismal font for the ceremony, she looked up at the gallery, but could not catch the organist's eye, his back to her. They recited their vows dutifully.

Then, as the priest baptized the child and patted his head dry, Amy started sobbing, turning to Michael and burying her head on his shoulder. He embraced her as she cried, "I thought this day would never happen."

The rector looked inquiringly at Charlotte, as her eyes shined with new tears in sympathy for her sister. Wordlessly she took the whimpering infant in her arms from the priest, feeling faint and trembling slightly as the baby squirmed, looked up at her, quit crying and started gurgling. "Shh, Stefan Mark," she whispered. "Welcome to our family, little one."

She continued to hold the infant and comfort him while Amy tried to compose herself and the priest made the sign of the cross over the infant's forehead with oil, stating, "Stefan Mark, you are sealed by the Holy Spirit in Baptism and marked as Christ's own forever. Amen."

Then Amy took over, gently reclaiming the child from her sister, murmuring, "Thank you, Charl," gratefully.

Gerry put his arm around Charlotte as they recited the words of reception together. When the priest invited the congregation to exchange the Peace, she turned to Gerry, who embraced her. "Congratulations, Godmother," he whispered in her ear.

She turned and at her elbow was Amy with the baby. Amy kissed her cheek. "You did it," she said. "You held him."

Charlotte smiled. "Yes," she replied simply, as Michael came up to her and hugged her, and Melanie put her arm on her two nieces' shoulders.

"My dears," she sniffed. "I do love you both so much."

The choir sang an anthem during the offertory, *O sacrum convivium*, the setting by Olivier Messiaen. As Charlotte listened to the ethereal music by the trained choir wafting over them, the words pierced her consciousness: *mens impletur gratia; et futurae gloriae nobis pignus datur*. 'The mind with grace is filled; and a measure of future glory is given us,' her mind echoed. "It's a sign," she whispered. Gerry looked at her, puzzled.

After the service, the organ burst forth with the *Fugue in E-flat major* by J. S. Bach. Charlotte smiled. "It IS Evan," she said out loud. Gerry looked at her quizzically.

"An old friend from Atlanta," she explained. "Do you mind if I go up and say hello?"

He shook his head, watching her as she walked out of sight.

She made her way up to the gallery as the organist finished the postlude. He turned to slide off the bench and caught sight of her.

"Charlotte," he said warmly, jumping up and coming quickly up to her.

She hugged him. "I can't believe it's you," she laughed self-consciously. "What are you doing in D.C.?"

"This opportunity just presented itself, and I couldn't help myself," he grinned. "I hoped you would hear the postlude and come up," he added.

"How could I not? When I saw your name on the bulletin and then heard the Bach, I had no doubt," she giggled.

"Yeah, I remember when I learned that, and you were arrogant enough to tell me all the things I was doing wrong," he laughed.

"I was arrogant, wasn't I?" she joined in.

"What else should I have expected from Kreiser's star pupil?" he asked.

At Kreiser's name, she sobered, her smile fading. He noted it. "What? What's happened?" He saw her stricken features. "What have I said?"

"Nothing, Evan. It's a long story."

"How is Kreiser these days?" he demanded.

"I wouldn't know," she looked away. "I haven't been back to Atlanta in almost two years."

"What?" he was thunderstruck. "You didn't finish your degrees?"

"I got my piano degree, but didn't finish the organ degree," she said desperately, her voice low.

"I know something bad must have happened," he was sympathetic. "Are you living here now?" he asked.

"Yes," she nodded.

"Here," he walked back to the bench, snatched up a bulletin and a pencil, and hurriedly wrote his number on it, pushing it into her hand. "I'd like to have lunch with you and talk about it sometime, if you feel up to it."

Gerard came up behind her. "Melanie is looking for you," he said quietly.

Charlotte introduced the two men. "Evan and I were organ students together before he went off to Stanford to study."

"Stanford?" Gerry was interested. "I was there as well."

"I know," Evan smiled. "Charlotte told me when we were hoping she'd go there too. Nice to meet you."

"How about tomorrow?" Charlotte asked Evan.

"Great. There's a place not far from here, in fact, if that's convenient."

They made a date to meet the next day for lunch, and she was whisked away by Gerry.

The next day Evan and Charlotte met for lunch at a small bistro not far from the church. He was already there when she arrived, and motioned her over to a table in the corner where they could talk undisturbed. They ordered their meal, then when finally alone, he leaned back.

"I want to know everything," he began the conversation. "Where are you living? So you're not still in Atlanta?"

"I'm close to Amy and Mike and Stefan. I teach some here at the college."

"No one in town has mentioned your name. I figured I would know if you were in the area. What do you teach—piano? organ?" he inquired.

"No, English and writing," she supplied, nervous about his reaction.

"English? Where did that come from?"

"I changed fields," she supplied.

"But why?" he persisted. "Charlotte, you were the best pianist and organist I've heard anywhere. Are you still playing?"

She gazed at him, biting her lip. "No, Evan. I've given it all up. I can't do it any more."

He laughed. "Yeah, sure. Like Professor K would allow that to happen." He stared at her white face. "You're not serious?"

She nodded, fingering her coffee cup as the waiter brought their food and left them alone again.

"But why?" he echoed.

"I don't want to talk about it," she whispered.

"This is Evan, remember? Charlotte, this is serious shit. What would cause you to give up your dream? You were born to make music."

He reached over and took her hand. "You can tell me. You know it will go no further."

She sat there, very still, her eyes closed. He thought she was going to refuse.

"Evan, you mustn't tell anyone," she leaned forward, tears in her eyes.

"My lips are sealed," he returned her gaze solemnly.

"I got pregnant," she whispered, her voice barely audible.

"I'm sorry," he said sympathetically, squeezing her hand. "So you have a baby?"

"Not any more," her voice trembled. "I miscarried."

"Oh," he replied. "I thought for a moment you were going to tell me the baby yesterday was actually yours."

He paused as she shook her head, blushing, not meeting his eyes. "So you left Atlanta to avoid scandal. But why would you give up music?"

"I had a terrible row with Kreiser. He cancelled my final recitals. I couldn't play anymore. He told me I was a disgrace, that I was ruining both my name and his. I was a wreck. I couldn't function. I was physically sick. Then I found out I was pregnant. I ran away. No one knows this. Very few people even know where I am."

"Oh, my God," Evan murmured, squeezing her hand. "Oh, dear Charlotte. I'm so sorry."

He handed her a handkerchief. She took a deep breath, trying to compose herself. "Was this guy George you were engaged to the father?"

She shook her head. "I broke up with him before this happened."

"That must have caused a headline or two," he smiled. "But I'm still trying to figure this out. Who?" he looked at her searchingly.

"I—oh, please Evan, don't ask," she mumbled.

He squeezed her hand again. "No matter. Have you tried playing since—since all this?"

"No," she shook her head. "It's all been so terrible, and still fresh in my mind. I have a horror of even sitting down at an instrument. Melanie had a piano installed in the apartment, and I start shaking if I even try. I go blank."

"Have you talked to someone about it? A professional?"

"Only some combination priest psychologist a few sessions," Charlotte smiled tremulously. "Melanie would have a cow if the scandal sheets printed that someone in the family was seeing a shrink."

"So I guess you haven't been in communication with Kreiser?" Evan asked.

"No way in hell," she laughed bitterly. "I don't ever want to see him again."

"I just can't believe it," he said, his voice low. "Professor K worshipped you. You were being groomed to be his star, his successor on the performance stage. What would cause him to turn on you?" he mused.

She looked away. "I don't want to even think of him," she declared fervently.

"Well, that's fine, but something has to be done about this," Evan announced. "Firstly, I'm going to get you access and a key to the organ at the church."

"No," she objected, but he held up his hand, silencing her.

"You can't do this, Charlotte. You have a gift. You have to keep trying. There's generally nothing going on Mondays, so the day is yours. You will have the church to yourself, with no one listening in. You've got to try again.

"Secondly, my partner is a clinical psychologist, and I think it would do you some good to have a professional to talk to. Jon's discreet, and bound by psychotherapist-patient privilege, so everything would be completely confidential. I'll even bet we could set it up around your schedule at our house. No one need ever know."

"Your partner?" Charlotte smiled. "You haven't told me about him."

"Well, I think you'll like him," Evan smiled slyly. "I will schedule dinner this week. You'll come over, we'll drink a little wine, and we'll see what you two come up with." He smiled at her. "I'm so glad you're here in D.C.," he said fervently. "It brightens up the whole town for me."

"I'm so happy to see you again, Evan," she agreed. "You are a good friend."

"You know Erik and Alicia are here?" he asked her.

"No, I didn't," she said slowly. "I don't get out in public much still."

"It's time you did," he said. "Your old friends would be glad to see you again."

"I do a lot of writing now," she smiled. "When I'm not teaching. I have published a novel," she added shyly.

"You have?" his eyes shone with delight. "That's fabulous. What's the title?"

"*One Organist Less*," she responded.

"I've read that!" he cried. "I had no idea that you were the author. That was a barn-burner. So I guess the victim was Kreiser?"

She pursed her lips. "At the time I was so angry with him it was actually catharsis to write and 'murder' him by pen."

"Damn, you must have sold a bundle of books. I told all my friends and the AGO chapter about that book. So you are C. C. Langley?"

"Yes," she admitted.

"I would never have guessed. There's been a lot of speculation about the author. Organists all over have been wanting to know if you're going to write another. You've kept your identity a closely guarded secret."

"You must keep it so. I enjoy my privacy," she smiled.

"Well, then, you must give me an autographed copy," he laughed. "I can at least tell everyone I've met the author."

Later that week she met by prearrangement for dinner at Evan's flat and was introduced to his partner Jonathan Sanders. Evan was right, and she immediately liked Jonathan. They made a date for the following week to meet for a session. She left feeling more cheered and happy than she had been in a long time.

She started volunteering one night per week to babysit Stefan for Mike and Amy to go out. Amy at first demurred, not wanting to be away from the baby. But when she and Mike realized that Charlotte was gradually forming an attachment to Stefan, and that around the infant she began opening up, becoming more like her old self, Michael persuaded Amy to give Charlotte the chance.

Still Amy fussed and pestered Charlotte about child care, diaper changing, feeding, bottle temperature, and other minutiae until Charlotte and Mike laughed her to shame. Amy relented, and Charlotte became babysitter. She played music CDs for the baby and indulged the child, losing her heart over and over to the tiny solemn-eyed boy with wavy blonde hair.

Gerard stopped over one night at Charlotte's apartment. She let him in, Stefan in her arms. "He has just stopped fussing," she whispered. "I'm hoping bedtime is here."

"Here, what if I hold him?" Gerry offered, shrugging out of his suit jacket.

"That would be great. I'm going to mix a little formula for him, and we'll see if he nods off," Charlotte gently handed the baby over.

Gerard stared at the cherub-faced child. "You know, he looks so much like you," he declared.

Charlotte laughed. "Yeah, right. Melanie said the same thing." She sobered. "I wonder if Johann would have looked like him."

"But of course," Gerry murmured to the little boy who stared up at him. "But Baby Stefan, like his aunt, needs a little steak."

Charlotte smiled at Gerry's attempt to lighten the subject. "I'm sorry that I can't go anywhere with you tonight," she headed toward the kitchen.

"If you don't mind, I'd prefer hanging out here with you and Stefan," Gerry surprised her.

"Of course I don't mind," she disappeared.

He followed her. "I can order in, if you like. Steak or seafood? What would you like?"

"I'm not very hungry," she answered distractedly.

"Charl, you need to eat. You're so thin. I'm worried about you."

"I'm actually feeling better than I have in some time. But I promise to eat whatever you order."

"Even escargot?" he laughed.

"Let's keep the slugs off my plate, please," she grimaced.

"C'mon, Stefan, let's order us some shrimp scampi and some veal parmigiana. Need to fatten your aunt up," Gerry left the room with the baby reaching out, trying to grasp his cell phone.

Charlotte hummed to herself. She thought about how—domestic—Gerry looked with a baby in his arms. He needs to be a dad, she thought.

At first Charlotte made good her threat, and would not visit Atlanta except for Christmas holidays, and only long enough to participate in the family festivities before returning to D.C. But when she started noticing that Melanie's health seemed not as robust, she resolved to spend more time with her.

Aunt Melanie in turn had often thrown Charlotte and Gerry together socially in her push to set them up for their eventual engagement. The stage was being set.

One day while Melanie was in D.C. for a visit, she called Charlotte to come downstairs. Charlotte was surprised, but complied. Melanie wore a self-satisfied look on her face.

"I have been told by one of my old sorority sisters of an event you might be interested in," she informed her niece.

"Yes?" Charlotte's heart sank. Some other society event, she thought. She smiled politely.

Melanie thrust an announcement into Charlotte's hand. Charlotte looked at it, disinterested at first, but then she became more animated. "Herbie Hancock and—Oscar Peterson? At Avery Fisher Hall?" she was incredulous. "But Aunt—"

"I can get advance tickets for you and Gerry," Melanie gazed at her. "I think you would enjoy it."

"Darrell!" Charlotte cried. "He would love this. A dream come true." She grabbed Melanie's arm. "Could we not invite him and Delores? He provided many hours of instruction to me for free."

Melanie was inwardly thrilled to see Charlotte's excitement, even if it was directed at turning her surprise into a gift for someone else. "Of course, dear," she smiled. "We could invite them here, then arrange for rooms in the city that night."

So Charlotte called Darrell. "So you see, it's perfect," she laughed. "I'd love for Delores and you to be my guests."

Darrell paused. "This is too good to be true," he admitted. "But I'm afraid Delores won't be joining us."

"Why?" Charlotte was surprised. "I thought you were getting married."

"An old college boyfriend intervened," Darrell replied.

"I'm sorry," Charlotte was contrite. "You could ask anyone you like. There is plenty of room."

"Charlotte, would you go with me?" he asked teasingly.

"You know I'm not letting you go without me. Gerry and maybe even Melanie will be there as well."

"It's a date."

Melanie did join them, and to Charlotte's surprise enjoyed it immensely. "Howard adored Oscar Peterson, and of course he tried to convert me."

"But you didn't like it?" Charlotte interrogated her.

"It was actually quite good," Melanie admitted sheepishly. "Thank you, my dear, for including me. One of my best memories."

Charlotte and her aunt locked eyes briefly.

Chapter 24

Charlotte arrived at the Chadwick home. Melanie had come up to see Stefan, and Amy invited Charlotte to join them for dinner at home. The door was answered by a young man about her age looking a lot like Michael.

"Hello, Matt," Charlotte smiled, as he kissed her cheek. "Haven't seen you in a while."

"You know how it goes—we all stay so busy," he smiled. "Come in out of the cold. Your aunt is already grilling me about my prospects."

"It must be match-making time in Chevy Chase," Charlotte whispered.

As they entered the drawing room, Melanie caught Charlotte's eye. "Did you know Matt is completing medical school now?" Melanie asked, looking at Charlotte meaningfully. Charlotte rolled her eyes. She realized that this was yet another of Mike's and Amy's attempts to pair her off with someone, to have her dating, getting out in public.

"Dinner will be ready soon," Amy announced, coming to the door and taking Charlotte's coat.

"Well, we'll leave and come back later," Charlotte retorted.

Amy frowned. "Don't be mean. You'll be pleasantly surprised."

As Charlotte expected, she was seated beside Matt at dinner, with Melanie facing her, Mike at the end at her right, and Amy and the baby in a high chair at the other end. Mike carved the turkey.

"This actually looks good," Charlotte enthused. "Who is the caterer again?"

Amy pouted. "Don't you think I can handle cooking a meal like this?"

Charlotte looked at Mike and they both shook their heads, laughing.

Just then Stefan started crying. "Oh, don't listen to them," she cooed. "Mommy is good at taking care of the little baby Steffie, yes, she is."

They passed around serving bowls of food and engaged in small chatter. Matt turned to Charlotte during the banter and said quietly, "So you're living in the area now?"

"Yes," she replied. "And you?"

"I'm actually in Baltimore at Johns Hopkins," he smiled.

"Wow! I'm impressed," she laughed.

"But it is close enough to visit regularly," he said, gazing at her warmly. "I was wondering, Charlotte. Would it be possible to call on you?"

Charlotte knew the rest of the family, while pretending to carry on conversation, was intent upon her answer. "Sure, Matt. I mean, the sooner I say yes, the sooner everyone else at the table can relax."

They all laughed.

After dinner, Charlotte was helping clear the table, but Amy announced loudly, "Why don't you and Matt go for a walk?"

"I thought I would ask him to help me wash the dishes," Charlotte purred.

Amy pushed her out of the kitchen. "I have a cleaning woman for that," she announced.

Matt rolled his eyes as well. "I guess a walk it is," he sighed dramatically. Charlotte smiled.

They put on their coats and stepped outside in the crisp night air. Mark took her hand. "Just in case there are any slippery spots on the sidewalk," he interjected.

She smirked. "Of course."

They walked down the steps and followed the sidewalk down the block together. "OK, are you part of this conspiracy, Matt?"

"I guess so," he grinned. "Mike asked me to come down and have dinner. He mentioned that you were going to be here."

"And you still came?"

"Well, I already know you, so it's not like a blind date."

She whooped, and he joined in. They walked on hand in hand, silent, smiling, Charlotte suddenly shy.

"I never thanked you," Matt drawled, after a few minutes.

She started. "What for?"

"For your being my date at the high school senior prom," he squeezed her hand. "You on my arm boosted my self-confidence and my status in the community."

"Ah, quit teasing me," she giggled. "It was a lot of fun."

"No, it's true," he insisted. "I don't know how Mike got your aunt to agree. Then we walked into the hotel ballroom, all those girls in Gunny-Sax dresses looking on, and you were in some elegant gown dressed like a supermodel. What kind of dress was that?"

She colored with embarrassment. "Dior. The sales lady said it would be perfect for the event. Instead, I stuck out like a sore thumb. I never bought anything at her shop again."

"You were gorgeous, and I was the envy of every guy there," Matt gazed at her. "Everyone thought you were some princess, but you joined in and made everyone feel at ease, as though you all knew each other forever."

She bit her lip. "I was afraid I had embarrassed you."

"Never," he declared fervently. "And then that kiss good night—wow! I was hooked. Always wanted a repeat of that."

She pushed him playfully. "Stop it, Matt," she laughed at him. They walked on, talking desultorily.

"Do you remember our skiing trips out to Utah?" she asked him.

"How could I forget? Those were the highlights of my life. It wasn't as if my family could afford a week each year at a posh ski resort. I was grateful to your aunt."

"Remember the time I twisted my ankle on the big slope?" she smiled.

"Yeah, and I came to your rescue," he gazed at her.

"Hell, you're the one who tripped me!" she bumped into him playfully. "You were trying to beat me down the slope."

"Not me," he rejoined, grinning slyly.

"Yes, you." She shook her head at him.

"How long are you here?" she asked suddenly.

"I am crashing at a nearby hotel. Thought I'd hang around. I got tickets to see Georgetown and Duke play tomorrow evening. You want to come along?"

"That sounds like a date to me," Charlotte beamed. "Sure."

So the next evening he showed up at her place on time.

"Any problems finding me?" she asked upon opening the door.

"No, your directions were good," he smiled. "Ready?"

After he settled her in the car and maneuvered them out of the complex, he said, his eyes on the road, "You know, Charlotte, we don't have to go to the game if you don't want."

"What? This is just a ploy? You don't really have tickets?" she asked accusingly.

He pulled tickets out of his jacket pocket. "Right here. It's just that I didn't know if you still enjoyed basketball."

"Not still enjoy basketball?" she echoed. "I love basketball," she retorted. "I'm so relieved. I thought I was going to have to beat your butt for asking me out under false pretenses."

"To the game it is," he laughed.

Surprisingly for both of them, they had a great time. Charlotte introduced Matt to some of her students at the game, and they nodded knowingly. She cheered for Georgetown, and Matt chose Duke, and they bantered back and forth.

Afterward, he walked her to the car and opened her door. On the way home she asked, "How is your sister Alisha?"

"She's in college, wants to be a lawyer. She's going to University of Georgia."

"Traitor!" Charlotte giggled. "That probably doesn't sit well with your dad."

"Yeah, he's a Rambling Wreck through and through," Matt laughed. "Do you want to stop off for a drink?"

"Actually, we can do that at my place, if you like," she said, looking straight ahead.

"Sure," he replied slowly, raising his eyebrows.

"Matt, I'm not propositioning you," she laughed shortly. "Much as I might like to," she added, blushing. "I—I was in a bad relationship, and I'm not sure I can try again."

"It's all right. You don't have to explain," he stated. "Besides, Charlotte, you're not the only one who has had to recover from a broken heart."

"Not you?" she joked, then sobered as she looked in his eyes.

"Sometimes you can only worship from afar," he stared at her. "That's the way it has been for me with you."

"Don't tease me," she warned.

"I'm not," he was earnest, turning his attention again to the road.

Quickly covering her embarrassment, she continued, "I mean, I just thought it might be nice not to end the date so quickly. I can make coffee and we can get the other scores before you have to leave," she added nervously. "That's all—just the scores."

"OK, if you're sure," Matt said, pulling up to her place.

She let him in, and he walked around admiring the room while she cut on the television. "Make yourself at home, while I get the coffee going." She disappeared.

"Beautiful place," he remarked as she reappeared.

"Drink?" she pointed toward the bar.

"Coffee is fine," he replied, sitting down at the piano.

She froze momentarily. Trying to recover her composure, she walked to the bar and poured herself a drink. She approached the piano warily.

Matt stood, took her hand and pulled her toward him. "Play for me," he spoke quietly.

"No," she shuddered. "I can't do that."

"Come on," he pleaded. "I remember from when we were kids. You are so phenomenal."

She wrenched away violently. "No, I can't," she cried, walking away, placing her drink on a nearby table, and burying her head in her hands.

"What is it?" Matt followed her. "I'm sorry. What did I say?"

"I just can't play any more. Please don't ask me," she turned away from him.

"Whoa, Charlotte," he turned her back around. She buried her head in his shoulder. "It's OK," he murmured. "I didn't mean anything by it."

"I'm sorry," she mumbled. "I have not been able to play for other people since—since I left Atlanta."

"OK, OK," he murmured. "I'm sorry, Charlotte. I didn't know." He took her chin in his hand, and brought her eyes to look at him.

Without thinking, he kissed her. She was quiescent, but then pulled away.

"I'm sorry," he apologized, releasing her.

"No, it was very nice," she smiled, her eyes bathing him in a warm glow. "But this is beyond the scope of our date. Find the scores on TV and I'll get the coffee."

He complied, and she returned momentarily with a coffee service. "Matt," she said carefully as she poured and handed him a cup, "I thought about getting season tickets to the Georgetown games. Would you be interested in attending some with me? It would be—fun to go with someone."

"Sure," his response was measured. "But I won't be treading on some boyfriend's toes?"

"No. Why do you ask?"

"I mean, what happened to Fellowes?"

"Well, I broke up with George some time ago."

"Not George," he looked at her over the rim of his cup.

"Gerry?" she was surprised. "Gerry and I are just friends. He stays busy, but comes by every now and then."

"He isn't going to insist on pistols at dawn or something over you?"

"No," she laughed merrily. "He would be happy if I have someone to pal around with. He's worried about me."

"What if I want to do more than pal around?" Matt asked her. She flushed under his scrutiny.

"Don't count your chickens before they hatch," Charlotte retorted, as she turned her attention to the sports announcer. They remarked about the game highlights, laughing and chatting.

After a while, he looked at his watch. "I need to be getting back to my hotel. Got to get an early start back to Baltimore."

She stood and accompanied him to the door. "Matt," she asked shyly as he turned toward her, "you know hanging with me has consequences. I mean, when the tabloids run out of subjects they could always come back to me. Do you think you're going to be able to handle that publicity if they tag you in a story?"

"I can handle myself, that is, if you can stand having your name linked with a Georgia nonentity like me," he assured her.

"I like you," she laughed.

"I like you too," he pulled her to him. "I always have. You were always out of my league."

"That's not true," she protested.

"It was nothing short of a miracle that kept your aunt from breaking Mike and Amy up," Matt remarked. "What happened that she would smile on your going out with Mike's brother?"

"She adores Michael," Charlotte retorted. "He's the best thing since sliced bread. And he and Gerry were the brothers I never had. She apparently likes you," she nudged him in the ribs playfully.

"I need to leave before I do something to make you chase me away," he murmured, his eyes lingering on her.

Without warning she wrapped her arms around his neck and kissed him, pulling him to her as she clung to him. He responded, enfolding her to him as he backed her to the door, enjoying her nearness.

"You must really like me," he mumbled against her mouth as she slipped her hands inside his jacket. "And to think I was going to settle for only a peck on the cheek."

She froze. "Oh, God, what you must think," she muttered as she pulled away.

"Charlotte, we're two consenting adults," he murmured as he stroked her hair. "I'm thrilled. I've been coming on to you since dinner last night, but was afraid of stepping over the line."

"I'm sorry," her face was aflame. "I just suddenly didn't want the night to end. I had such a good time. I don't want to be alone. But then I'm not sure I could—and—and I would really be embarrassed—" she left the sentence unfinished.

"Mike said something about you were recovering from a relationship gone south. He didn't elaborate, and I know the mags always get it wrong. But for you to be available, instead of beating men off with a stick—"

She smiled tremulously. "I've never had many admirers."

"You've just not let any of them get close," he whispered. Matt pulled her close. "Charlotte, I'll stay if you like. It's up to you."

"I'm—I'm not sure if I'm ready to sleep with someone, Matt." She took his hand and stared at it. "I'm scared. But would you stay anyway?"

"What will I tell Mike tomorrow when he insists on knowing how things went?" He kissed her ear.

"I don't want them to know. We'll think of something," she pulled him back into the room.

Chapter 25

Then began a series of secret liaisons between Charlotte and Matt. He would arrive when he could get away from Johns Hopkins, and they would go to the basketball game or out to eat, or just watch television. He would spend the night.

Amy was insistent on knowing what was going on, but Charlotte kept telling her they were just friends. She was terror-stricken at the thought of her family finding out that Matt was staying over.

One day about three months into the relationship, Matt was at a high school gymnasium near the hospital with some of his colleagues engaging in their regular pick-up game of basketball. They were just getting into the heat of battle, when one of the guys tapped Matt on the arm.

"That guy over there is asking for you."

Matt, dressed in gray T-shirt and shorts, turned around, ball in hand, to see the man, dressed in a suit, moving fluidly toward him. He tossed the ball to the guy next to him and jogged out to the edge of the court in the huge gymnasium.

"Hi, Gerry," Matt said quietly. "Fancy seeing you here. Wondered when I was going to run into you."

"Long time no see. I had a meeting, and was in the neighborhood," Gerry regarded him, the vestige of a smile on his face.

"Are you here to kick my ass?" Matt laughed uneasily.

"Why? Does it need kicking?" Gerry's face broke into a grin.

"Not in those shoes," Matt laughed again, pointing to his Italian uppers.

"I have gym clothes, if I can change here," Gerry gestured toward the locker room.

"Sure," Matt said, looking at him quizzically.

Gerry disappeared, appearing later dressed like Matt. The crowd of players had dwindled down to two other men, who Matt introduced to Gerry as fellow residents at the hospital. They paired off, Matt and Gerry against the other two, winning handily.

After one game, the two residents begged off, and Matt and Gerry were left alone on one half-court as a game ensued on the other. "Some one-on-one?" Gerry suggested.

"I'm game," Matt wiped his forehead on his sleeve. He threw the ball to Gerry. "I'm generous—you first."

They concentrated on playing and one-upping each other for some time. As Matt elbowed Gerry, stealing the ball and heading up for a layup, Gerry asked, "Are you sleeping with her?"

Matt, caught off-guard, missed the shot, as Gerry grabbed the rebound. "That was unfair," Matt called, as he let Gerry make the next shot unmolested.

Gerry threw the ball to Matt, but Matt cradled it under his arm. "Charlotte said you wouldn't mind us seeing each other, that you two were just friends," Matt was defensive as he approached Gerry.

"She's right. I'm happy for both of you," Gerry replied, walking up to him. "I just can't help being curious. But Amy has ordered me hands-off. She is afraid I might scare you away."

"Is that why you haven't called her? Charlotte says it is unlike you. Why don't you ask her?"

Gerry frowned. "Amy again. Hey, don't worry. I'm not crowding you. I just want to check on her."

"Do you love her?"

Gerry frowned. "Charlotte and I go way back. We've been best friends since before elementary school. I've been worried about her since—since she left Atlanta. She was in—bad shape for a while." He paused. "I guess I just want to know that everything's all right. So is it?"

"I don't know," Matt started dribbling toward the net, as Gerry feinted toward the ball.

"What do you mean, you don't know?" Gerry demanded, as Mark turned his back to Gerry and drove for the basket.

"She's not the same Charlotte, that's for sure," Mark shot and ringed the basket. Gerry grabbed the ball. "Remember those Georgia Tech basketball games where she stuffed her hair in her cap to keep anyone from recognizing her?"

Gerry guffawed. "Remember how she almost mooned the Georgia team at the playoffs? The TV cameras were all over her. Oh, was she grounded for that. I didn't think Melanie was going to ever let her out of the house again."

"I am afraid those days are gone," Matt replied glumly.

Gerry stopped. "In what way?"

Matt walked up to him. "There's a line in the sand that we do not cross," he replied. "Unspoken ground rules—heavy petting, but no going all the way, no talking about what happened, and only a tiptoe around the past. She's still quite the basketball fan. But the spark is not there, the old fun-loving, 'go-to-hell' Charlotte that was the life of the party."

"You're spending the nights at her place, aren't you?" Gerry was dubious.

Matt was surprised. "How did you know? Charlotte didn't want us to tell anyone."

"You think Mike and I don't keep tabs on her?" Gerry frowned. "Didn't he tell you to go slow?"

"Whatever happened must have been really bad," Matt whistled, "if you are checking up on her."

"It was devastating," Gerry stared at him. "She doesn't play the piano, does she?"

"No, she doesn't," Matt nodded somberly. "She was almost hysterical when I asked her once." He stopped, his brow furrowed. "What happened, Gerry? What, who screwed her up so badly?"

"She'd never forgive me if I told you," Gerry's eyes narrowed. "And she would be horrified and angry if she knew we were watching her."

"How else am I going to know?" Matt countered angrily. "It's not like she is going to talk about it."

"How do you feel about her? Is it serious?" Gerry unabashedly pried.

"It could be," Matt admitted. "I'm crazy about her. But I don't know how she feels about me."

"I could break silence and ask her," Gerry grinned as he started dribbling again, and aimed for a three-pointer. The ball hugged the rim and bounced back out, but he caught the rebound.

"I'm not one to ask for help in matters involving females," Matt rejoined, chasing down the ball after Gerry rang another two points. Matt retained possession of the ball, then approached Gerry. "But I've not had this problem before. She's a tough sell. It might not be a bad idea. But I'm not into a *ménage a trois*, and not sure I trust you not to break us up."

"If I was going to do that, I would have already made my move," Gerry poked the ball out from under Matt's arm and retrieved it, driving toward the basket again. "Are you going to play ball or moon over some girl?" he demanded.

Matt blocked the shot, and they again concentrated on the game, until Gerry finally waved him off, panting, bending down and placing his hands on his knees. "Enough for today," he choked. "That was a good workout, most fun I've had in a while."

Matt, also breathing heavily, nodded. "I'm here most days when I work off a shift, unless I have the time off to make it up to Charlotte's. You're welcome any time. Want to go for a drink?"

"I'd love to, but I can't," Gerry smiled, pointing to his watch. "There's always work waiting for me. I'll take a raincheck, though. Maybe one evening we could all go out to dinner. I can find a date," he winked.

As they headed back to the dressing room, Gerry was solemn. "You're right. Charlotte is different. She's never been fragile before. I think she's getting better. But don't hurt her."

"I'll try," Matt intoned. "Am I going to get this same lecture from Mike?"

"Probably," Gerry laughed. "Does he have as hard a time kicking your ass as I do?"

Charlotte still thought constantly of Kreiser, what he was doing, whether he thought of her. She knew that his second marriage had ended. She was filled with self-loathing. *Why can't I leave well enough alone?* she thought crossly.

She picked up the phone and dialed information, obtaining a number for Kreiser's home in Atlanta. She stared at the number, longing to call, but set it aside.

Then one day as she was about to leave for class, the phone rang.

"Hello?" she answered.

"Hello?" Kreiser's voice responded tentatively.

"H-Harry?" she stuttered.

"Charlotte? I wasn't sure if this would be the right number. I just wanted to hear your voice."

"Yes. How did you manage to find me? Harry, are you all right?" she was astounded by the weakness in his voice.

"I'm fine, my dear Carlota." She thrilled to his voice still. "You could say I stole this number in a moment of weakness."

She closed her eyes. "I'm glad you did," she breathed. "I miss you, Harry."

"I miss you too, *cara mia*. I had hoped you wouldn't hate me forever. I had a nagging sense of urgency to talk to you. Are you playing?" his voice was anxious.

"No, I can't anymore. You've taken that from me. I can't do it without you. I need you, Harry," she whispered, tears filling her eyes. "Please come to me. I can't go on without you."

"Oh, *cara mia*, please don't say that," he begged her hoarsely. "You know I cannot. All those hateful things I said to you—they were lies. I wanted to make you forget me. But I never meant to chase you away from your art. It was cruel of me. I want you to return to it. You were my very best, Carlota."

"I can't, Harry," she cried. "Please tell me you love me."

"Oh, my Carlota, you know I do," he replied, his voice a whisper. "More than life. And if I could—"

"But you can," she insisted. "If you will just tell me you want me, I will come back to Atlanta, to you."

"I must go now," he panted, and the line clicked dead.

She stared at the phone. "Harry," she cried impotently.

A few days later Mike asked Matt to stop by the Chadwick home. Matt did so, a little troubled. Mike met him at the door.

"Amy has gone shopping, so I'm the babysitter," he explained as he ushered Matt in the home.

"Great. We can show Stefan some basketball moves," Matt smiled nervously.

"He's asleep right now. Have a seat," Mike ordered.

As Matt took a seat, Mike was direct. "What are you and my sister-in-law doing?"

Matt's eyebrows raised at his brother's tone. "What, have you and Gerry been comparing notes?"

"Gerry?" Mike looked at him confusedly.

"Yeah. I figured he told you he looked me up not too long ago, checking up on Charlotte and me."

"He calls me to find out about her from time to time," Mike smiled. "Amy told him he was *persona non grata* right now." Mike disappeared for a moment, then appeared with a bottle of beer in each hand. He handed one to Matt.

"So?" Mike persisted as Matt took a drink. "What are you two doing?"

"Not much," Matt confessed. "I'm making it down to see her when I can get away. We go to the games." He looked away. "I'm sleeping over at her place." He didn't meet his brother's gaze.

"You're already sleeping with her? I told you to go slow," Mike said accusingly.

"It's not like that," Matt looked down at his hands. "I mean—we kiss and make out, but we're not—doing anything. She is carrying some heavy baggage, Mike. And she has nightmares, wakes up screaming. I'm worried about her."

"I'm worried, too," Mike admitted. "Where do you see this going?"

Matt laughed harshly. "Your guess is as good as mine. She is not the Charlotte I remember, full of devilment, confident. She makes no demands on me whatsoever. She acts happy to see me, she understands when I say I have to leave. There's never a cross word. She shows little emotion. I think I'd like it more if we argued sometimes.

"There's a part of her that is closed off to the rest of the world. Sometimes it's like her zest for life has been sucked out of her. I despair of ever seeing that again. Meanwhile, she jokes that we'll have nothing to do after the Final Four. I wonder if she's serious." He paused. "Mike, I like her a lot."

Mike nodded. "Yeah, only in rare moments do we glimpse the old Charlotte. She seems to open up every now and then with Stefan. Otherwise, there's just this empty façade, where she smiles and says the right words. I hoped you might be the catalyst."

"I don't think it's going to happen. Is she seeking professional help?"

"When she first arrived in D.C. I had Father Danny dropping in on her. Since then she is secretly seeing some psychologist referred by a friend. She keeps things close to the chest."

"Well, you know, as I complete my residency, there's going to be less and less time, and I won't even know exactly where I'll be going from here," Matt said slowly. "I would be lying if I said I didn't want something more."

"I'm sorry if Amy and I landed you in a difficult situation," Mike clapped Matt on the back.

"Don't be. I'm in love with her, Mike. I just don't think she feels the same way. She's any guy's dream. I try to talk to her about us, but she seems to always divert the subject to other things."

Matt stood. "I'm having dinner with her tonight. I need to get going."

"Be gentle with her."

"You bet."

Matt wrestled with his thoughts on the drive to Charlotte's. *What is she wanting?* He thought. *There has to be something more than what we are doing. How do I reach her? I wish I knew.*

He arrived, and knocked on the door.

In the meantime Charlotte had been struggling with the same thoughts. *I don't know what I'm doing,* she thought. *I like Matt, and I want Matt, but I just cannot turn loose.*

She thought of Kreiser, and their time together, of their last night together with the Liszt art songs singing in her head. Then she reminded herself of his cruel rejection, and of his latest phone call. *I hate him so much,* she said to herself. *Life has to go on. I need to exorcise Harry from my life.*

So Charlotte had ordered dinner delivered, and had lit candles throughout the room. She had bought herself a sexy fitted strappy black dress and matching lingerie. *It's now or never,* she said to herself.

So when she opened the door, Matt was stunned. He let out a low whistle. "Oh, Charlotte, you look good enough to eat," he whispered as she pulled him in the door and he kicked it closed.

"Dinner is served," she laughed shakily. She turned around for him. "Do you really like it?"

"I really like it," he said, pulling her to him. He kissed her lingeringly, and she responded eagerly, not pulling away.

"Are you hungry?" she whispered.

"I can skip to dessert if you can," Matt murmured.

"I want to," she whispered.

In response, he took her hand and led her upstairs to the bedroom.

A few hours later Matt stirred against her, waking when he felt her presence. He found her awake, head propped on one arm, watching him.

"What are you thinking?" he stretched, before pulling her toward him.

"About how good last night was," she whispered before covering his mouth with hers.

His hands slid over her back to her butt, hauling her on top of him. "I like you here," he smiled wickedly.

"So do I," she closed her eyes, leaning over him.

They made love again, unhurriedly, taking their time. As he brought her to release, he looked at her, and noticed the tears in her eyes.

"Don't leave me," she whispered, as she clung to him, causing him to climax as well.

He held her closely as she cried silently. "What is it, Charlotte?" he asked in her ear. "Please tell me."

"Do you have to go?" she complained piteously. "I know you have to get back for your shift. I shouldn't ask . . ."

"You really want me to stay?" he replied wonderingly.

She wouldn't meet his eyes. "I know you can't," her voice was barely audible.

"I have a fellow resident who owes me big time," he took her face into his hands. "Let me make a call."

He gently disentangled himself from her and left the bed, looking for his pants and his cell phone. Hitting a speed dial, he soon had a sleepy-sounding voice on the other end. "Ralph? Matt here. I'm calling in that favor. You have got to cover my shift this afternoon." He paused. "Yeah, it's life or death," he smiled at Charlotte, who was sitting up watching him. "No, I'm not giving you details. Just do it."

He hung up and gazed at her naked form, her hair framing her face in disheveled curls. "What about you? Don't you have work today?"

"I don't teach today," she smiled pensively.

He jumped back on the bed next to her and pulled her close. "Now what do you want us to do with our day off together?"

"I want to stay right here with you," she purred. "No clothes, no phones."

"Suddenly you're insatiable," he laughed at her.

So they spent the day together, in bed for most of the morning, then watching reruns of basketball games and movies on television, ordering in pizza, showering together, then back in bed together. They told jokes, reminisced about Atlanta, and kept their chatter light.

After another period of lovemaking, Matt snuggled to her back, nuzzling her neck. "Charl," he spoke quietly, slowly, "what happened in Atlanta? Is it something you can talk about?"

She stiffened, and he felt it. "You don't have to tell me, but I'd like to be here for you. I have sensed the difference in you. I know it must have been traumatic." He trailed kisses down her shoulder. "I'm falling for you, Charlotte. It's none of my business, but I want to share everything with you, be there for you."

She pulled away, but he turned her to face him. "Forget I said anything," he whispered, suddenly anxious. "I didn't mean to mess up our glorious day together."

"You didn't," she smiled, but the smile didn't reach her eyes. "It's time for that backrub I promised you."

Early the next morning, she awoke screaming. Matt was instantly beside her. "What is it, Charlotte?" he put his arms around her, as she awoke, disoriented and panting with fear.

"No," she shuddered, pulling away, sitting up, her head in her hands, shaking violently.

"It's me, Matt," he said reassuringly, as she sat there unresponsive. He picked up her robe and wrapped her in it, putting his arms around her and rocking her. "It's OK," he crooned to her, as she sat passively.

"I need a drink," she finally muttered, pulling away and walking out of the bedroom, dragging her arms through the sleeves and belting the robe.

He pulled on his shorts and followed her downstairs. He watched as she poured a large measure of whiskey into a tumbler and downed it, then poured more.

He went up to her. "Slow down, Charlotte. Tell me what is wrong."

"I can't explain what is wrong with me," she spoke through clenched teeth. "That's the irony of it all," she laughed mirthlessly. "What might have been a major breakthrough in a relationship with you has left me dumb. I cannot tell you, cannot form the words to tell you, about the mess I've made with my life, cannot stand to see the horror on your face. But maybe Mike has already told you all about my history."

"No, he just said you had been in a rough relationship, and to go slow with you."

"I didn't let that happen, did I?" she turned away, laughing harshly.

"It's OK. It will happen in its own good time. Don't rush it," Matt started, but she interrupted.

"No, it's not happening. For you and me to evolve into 'we' I need to bury the past. I should be at a point where I can make a clean breast of it. But I can't do it. I keep making a fool out of myself. And I'm just using you, Matt."

He looked dumbly at her.

"I have used you to try to exorcise those demons, Matt. Because I want to have a normal relationship. It isn't going to happen. You're wasting your time."

"Shouldn't I have some say in this?" he demanded. "I think it can happen with us. I want it to happen. I love you, Charlotte."

"Don't say that," she commanded quietly. "Haven't you already wondered what a future with me would be like? What have you gotten yourself into with me? How long do you have to deal with a woman who can't make love?"

Matt grabbed her by both arms. "Why are you doing this?" he whispered to her. "We've not been seeing each other that long. This is not a race; we can take our time." He stared at her. "What is it, Charlotte?"

Suddenly it dawned on him. "Do you want to break up with me? Are you trying to drive me away?"

"Yes," she looked into his eyes. "Yes, Matt. That's exactly what I'm doing."

He gaped at her mutely.

"Matt, if it was going to work, it would have worked by now."

"Don't," he pleaded, still holding her. "I love you, Charlotte. I know you feel something for me. I'm not letting you do this."

They gazed at each other, neither wanting to look away. He pulled her to him and kissed her deeply, and she responded momentarily, before stiffening and pulling away from him.

Charlotte broke the silence. "Matt, you are going to make a wonderful doctor. You deserve more than I can give you. I'd like us to remain friends. But it needs to end now, before it gets more complicated than it is, before I really hurt you."

"Damn, Charlotte, you can't deny the last two days have been good," he pleaded.

"You were great," she smiled, kissing him quickly, then pulling away.

"Then why are you giving up?" he demanded. "I can wait, forever if necessary."

She looked away, shook free, and picked up her glass. "I'm not letting you. I'm calling the game. You should go now." She walked into the kitchen without a backward glance.

She stayed, gripping the counter, staring out the window into the blackness. After what seemed an eternity, she heard the front door close.

After sunrise that morning she made some calls to the school, telling them she had the flu and would be out the next couple days. She called Amy and gave her the same story. She made a few additional calls, making a credit card order and giving the house staff the rest of the week off. Then she locked the front door, took the phone off the hook, and cradled the decanter in her arms.

It was the afternoon of the next day that there was a knocking on the door. "Charlotte, open up. It's Gerry."

Hearing no answer, he used the key and alarm code given him by Amy. Striding through the entry into the living room, he was brought up short by the sight of Charlotte lying on the sofa, unconscious.

"Oh, God, Charl," he went up to her, noting the empty bottles of alcohol littering the floor and coffee table. He sat down beside her, gently shaking her. "Please, Charlotte, wake up," he pleaded.

She didn't respond. He pulled her to a sitting position. "Charl?" he was insistent.

She stirred, mumbling incoherently. He slapped her gently on the face. She opened her eyes, unfocused. "Go away," she muttered groggily.

"Have you done anything other than drink yourself into oblivion?" Gerry demanded tenderly, shaking her again. "Do I need to call an ambulance? Charl, please speak to me."

She looked blearily at him. "Can't you all just leave me be?"

He gathered her up in his arms and carried her out of the house, loading her into the back seat of the limousine, giving an address to Tom. He pulled out his cell phone. "Esme, I have a big favor to ask. It's urgent. Discretion is critical. I'll be there with a friend of mine shortly. Tell Joe I'd really appreciate it if he'd examine her." He gazed at Charlotte, who was again unconscious.

Soon they pulled up to the service entrance of a small private hospital, and again Gerry gathered her up and took her in, being met at the door by a nurse. Quickly they had Charlotte in a bed, and a doctor came striding in.

"One of your celeb girlfriends, Gerry?" he asked, glancing at Charlotte's face curiously as he took her wrist and checked her pulse. "Slow."

"No. Joe, this is Charlotte Lawson."

"Ooh, now I know why the hush-hush," Dr. Joseph Holmes remarked, suddenly all seriousness. "One of Atlanta's own. Symptoms?" He put his stethoscope to her chest.

"I found her like this. I'm hoping she's just drunk, but I have no idea what she might have done to herself, and I can't get her to tell me."

"Blood draw will tell us," the doctor raised her eyelids and flashed a light into her pupils. As he examined her, he asked, "Why?"

"My source says she broke up with a guy yesterday. She's had a history of a serious break-up. Joe, it was really bad for her. She's never gotten over it."

"I've heard the scuttlebutt. I'll see what I can do," Joe slapped him on the shoulder, then turned to Charlotte. "Charlotte, I'm Dr. Holmes."

She did not respond. He turned to the nurse. "I need that blood now. Tell the tech yesterday." He turned to Gerry. "I'll be right back. Had an emergency surgery in the next room this morning." He gave terse directions to the nurse as he walked out.

Gerry sat beside her bed, waiting anxiously. A nurse came in and drew blood.

After what seemed a lifetime, Charlotte stirred and opened her eyes. Gerry went to the door. "Get Joe," he said simply.

The doctor strode in to the bed. He leaned over. "Charlotte, can you hear me?"

She was slow to open her eyes. "Yes," she replied foggily.

"Can you tell me what you've ingested over the last two days?" he asked her urgently. "And give me the truth."

"All the liquor I could find," she responded, turning her head away. She recognized Gerry. "Where am I?"

"A private hospital, one of the best," Gerry told her, taking her hand.

"Oh, God," she grimaced. "Melanie will die."

"Doctor, the toxicologist is on the phone," the nurse interrupted.

After several tense minutes, the doctor came back into the room. "Well, she's right. Nothing else in the bloodstream, but she didn't leave room for much else. Looks like she tried to drink herself to death. It's a wonder she didn't kill herself."

"Is she going to be OK?" Gerry asked, his eyes not leaving the stricken woman.

"Charlotte, you need help," Holmes told her. "I want to admit you to a detox facility."

"Gerry, I can't," she looked at him, her eyes suddenly wide, hysteria close to the surface. "Please don't do this." She started shaking, struggling drunkenly to sit up.

"Lay back. It's all right," Gerry cooed to her, gently pushing her back against the pillows. "I'll take care of her, Joe," Gerry informed the doctor. "I'll stay with her."

"Gerry, I don't think you realize what she needs."

"Joe, I don't think you realize that Charlotte and I go way back. There's no way she could make it through detox without it leaking out to the press and hurting her and her family." Gerry was firm. "I'll do what it takes. I'll hire nurses if necessary, and I will handle the situation."

"Are you sure that's in her best interests?"

"No, but I made a promise many years ago. I intend to keep it."

"Well, I'm keeping her overnight for observation. I'll give you a list of what you need to think about. You can let me know your plan for her care tomorrow."

Charlotte drifted back to oblivion, waking several hours later. She found Gerry sitting in a chair beside her bed, tie undone, jacket off.

"You look awful," she whispered hoarsely. He looked at her and smiled.

"So do you, Charl."

"Why did you show up?"

"Mike called me. He's on some fact-finding trip with his boss. Seems he got a call from his brother that you broke it off, threw him out. You called Amy and told her you had the flu. Then Matt got a delivery at work this morning—Final Four tickets. He and Amy couldn't find you, couldn't raise you on the phone. Scared the hell out of him. So Mike asked me to check on you."

"Where have you been?" she asked wearily. "I haven't seen you in months."

Gerry shrugged. "Finishing up my doctorate. Amy thought it was a good idea for me to be scarce, that if I was around I might somehow keep you from seeing Matt Chadwick. I was happy to oblige."

"Oh, Gerry," she moaned. "That was a bad idea. I'm sorry."

"I'm not," he said. "You got back on the horse. What—he wasn't good in bed? He was gay? He was boring? He snored? Why did you break up?"

"No, he is a great guy," Charlotte's eyes filled with tears. "It was all my fault. I didn't want him wasting time hoping for something I couldn't give him."

"Is that why you called Kreiser?" Gerry asked her.

"He called me," Charlotte gasped. "How—how did you know?" Charlotte faltered.

"Charl, I just happened to guess, and you just confirmed my suspicions," Gerry smiled grimly. "And Kreiser left you hanging yet again?"

She nodded wordlessly.

"You need a keeper," he sighed. "And you decided to drink as much as you could hold, all over Kreiser?"

"I am damaged, and I don't seem to be able to repair myself," she answered.

"And killing brain cells is part of the repair?" he interposed wryly.

The next day Gerry took her home. He brought her in and gently laid her on the couch. He busied himself turning the guest room into an office so that he could work while watching over her.

She shook her head at him. "I promise I won't do it again," she smiled.

"You probably won't, but I just want to reassure myself you're OK," he retorted. He moved over to the empty bar. "Want something to drink?"

She laughed, and he smiled. "No, thank you."

Tom walked in with an ice chest and a package. "Fresh from Miss Daisy."

Charlotte's eyes grew wide. "Do they—know?" she stuttered.

"No," Gerry countered gently. "I told Miss Daisy you had a bug of some sort, and that I thought some of her hand-churned buttermilk and cornbread might be the cure."

In a few minutes Tom brought her a plate with a piece of cornbread, still warm, and a glass of the cold thick liquid. "She said I was to stand over you and make you take it," he grinned.

"Thanks, Tom, for taking the trouble to do this," Charlotte murmured appreciatively.

Over the next three weeks Charlotte slowly picked up the threads and began her regular activities again. Gerry kept a close eye on her, did all his work at the makeshift office, and took her out or cooked dinner for her, and they fell into an easy routine.

One afternoon she walked in the hallway to see Tom taking Gerry's luggage out.

"Where are you going?" she asked Gerry, surprised.

"Got to take care of some business," he smiled. "Besides, Melanie is on her way here. I didn't think she'd be too happy to see us *en famille*, even if she has designs for us."

He hugged her. "I won't ever be far away, Charl. Call me." He paused. "In fact, I've got a bit of business in Paris. Let's plan a trip to Europe together, three weeks, just the two of us. It's time you saw the other side of the pond."

"Call my assistant Della," he pulled out a business card and handed her. "Tell her what you're interested in seeing, and she'll make the reservations for us."

Charlotte looked at the card, then shrugged. "Why not?" she smiled.

He kissed her cheek. "Get a passport. No, on second thought, I will take care of that too."

Chapter 26

"I don't know why I said I would do this," Charlotte muttered to Gerry as they pulled up to the museum.

"It's just a party, and you used to always love parties," he retorted. "And no one will recognize you. That is some costume. I'm not sure why you chose Elizabeth I. Should I bow, Your Majesty?"

"It might help your chances," she laughed. "And which knight are you?"

"Parsifal," he said ruefully. "Although perhaps I should have chosen Lancelot, so I could have the queen."

"No one at this party will know the difference," Charlotte laughed, although she was inwardly uneasy.

She had on an impulse accepted Gerry's invitation to the fund-raising New Year's costume party at the High Museum while they were both in Atlanta for the holidays. He had coaxed her. "Some little old lady donor wanted a fancy costume masked ball. A roomful of celebrities and who's who will be there. Elton John and Bruce Hornsby will make an appearance. And your buddy Dr. Lamont will be there as well; they've asked his combo to play."

Charlotte at the time was happy at the thought of seeing Darrell Lamont again. But now, as they were heading up Peachtree Street to the museum, she was regretting her decision. She had renounced the Atlanta society scene, and had absented herself from it for several years since she ran away to Washington. Now she was heading right back into the thick of it.

Sensing her trepidation, Gerry reassured her. "We'll make the rounds. When you're ready to leave, Tom will take you home. He is only a buzz away."

"And you?" she asked. "Are you going to get busy with one of the current debs? I heard the crop was particularly lovely this year."

"It could happen," he smiled slyly. "We'll see if there's a damsel in distress tonight. Don't wait up."

"You'd better check her ID," Charlotte guffawed.

"We're here," he announced. "Glad the weather turned cold. I don't know if I could stand all this get-up otherwise. Masks on, milady."

"It's Atlanta," she reminded him. "The air conditioning will be on inside. And Gerry," she added suddenly, "I'd prefer that less people rather than more know I'm here tonight. Aunt Mellie will be here, and it'll be bad enough."

They pulled up, and Tom opened the door. Gerry was out first, and offered his hand to Charlotte. They walked inside separately, the room already filled with costumed persons milling around. Her aunt, in evening wear but wearing a mask, soon caught sight of her, but did not recognize her, walking up to Gerry and hissing, "Where is Charlotte? I thought you were escorting her tonight."

Gerry, his face a mask, merely winked at Charlotte and stated, "Oh, she's around here somewhere. You haven't seen her?"

Melanie turned to Charlotte. "I'm Melanie Cain. How do you do?"

"Very well, thank you," Charlotte tried to disguise her voice. "Nice to meet you."

Melanie turned to Gerry and demanded, "Aren't you going to introduce us?"

Charlotte smiled. "I must be going. Later."

She fled as gracefully as she could, biting her lip to keep from laughing. Somehow she had managed to fool Aunt Mellie. She suddenly felt freer than she had in years.

She mingled with the guests, danced with Gerry once or twice, and was whisked away by others to dance. She felt like Cinderella at the ball.

Finally, she picked up two flutes of champagne and wandered over to the combo. Leaning against the piano, she placed one beside the music desk.

"Thanks," Darrell said gratefully, continuing to play. "Although I would do better with punch."

"You deserve champagne for the wonderful music you are giving this group of drunken louts," she retorted.

"That's very flattering, especially coming from a queen," he grinned. "To whom do I owe this honor?"

She lifted up her mask for a moment. "It's me—Charlotte Lawson," she said.

He faltered a moment at the keys, then resumed, the combo staring at him. "Dang it, Charlotte, I didn't even recognize you."

"Really?"

"I'm glad to see you, girl," he spoke warmly. "You're so beautiful. I still remember our date with Herbie and Oscar."

"I'm glad to see you too. That was so much fun." She replaced her mask. "I'm *incognito* tonight. No one knows who I am, so I'm getting to enjoy myself."

"You still remember our lessons?"

"Some of the happiest moments of my life," she responded. "Your playing brings them all back."

"That's good," he ended with a flourish, to general applause. He stood and bowed. "Because you can do the next piece while I get some punch."

"No, I'll get the punch," she started.

He turned to the combo. "'Satin Doll'—make it in C. We'll make it easy on her."

He pushed her to the bench and walked off, as the band looked on. "Really, it's been too long," she protested.

The drummer remarked, "We ain't getting paid for looking pretty."

She looked frantically around for Lamont, but he had disappeared. She sat down tentatively. "Remember, no one knows who you are," she said aloud. She started hesitantly, a little run she remembered Lamont teaching her, then delved into the theme tentatively, trying to keep her mind from freezing up, as the band joined in. She knew that Lamont started out conservatively, slowly building into a swing, and she tried to focus on matching his strategy as she improvised, mimicking some of what she remembered from Oscar Peterson's recordings in Uncle Howard's collection, knowing that Peterson was Lamont's idol.

A couple of minutes into the selection, she felt as though she and the combo hit a groove together, and everything clicked into place. She forgot where she was, enjoying the moment of musical collaboration.

After a few minutes she nodded at the group, signaling that they would wind it down. When they finished, a group had gathered and applauded. She embarrassedly took a bow, as Lamont returned with punch for everyone.

"You abandoned me," she hissed at him, but he shrugged.

"Dr. Conrad told me you had given up music, little girl of mine. That is crazy. Music flows in your veins, and you need to incorporate the pain into the music, not give up the music. See how you can still mesmerize a crowd."

She kissed his cheek. He spoke gruffly, "Go dance with the mayor here and let me do my job. I might let you play again later."

"Who is this vixen who can play as well as you?" the mayor sidled up smilingly to Charlotte.

"A former student of mine, long gone from these parts. She's not likely to tell you her name, but I'll bet she'll dance with you, and even make a generous contribution," Darrell smiled as he sat down at the piano again.

Charlotte whirled around with the mayor for a dance, then made her excuses and drifted away. She ran into Gerry. "Any luck?" she asked him.

"Several nibbles, but I'm suddenly bored with it all. You have certainly been a social butterfly tonight," he remarked.

She blushed. "I found that it's fun when no one knows who I am," she confessed.

"There are certain advantages, but then again there are perks to being known as well," he agreed. "Do you want to stay for the stroke of midnight?"

"Not necessarily, but Dr. Lamont held out the promise of another chance to play. That was such a rush."

"Yeah, you sounded good there," he nodded. "Charl, you come alive when you play, and I'm always in awe. I'm telling you. You need to get back on the horse. You've still got it."

Charlotte continued hurriedly, "But you don't have to stay on my account. Besides, there's that sweet young redhead eying you from the bar."

"Yeah," he grinned. "I've been eying her too, but didn't want to shirk my chivalric duties to my date."

"Go for it," Charlotte pushed him playfully. "I'm a big girl."

"I'll send the car back for you," he promised.

She wandered back toward the piano, but was accosted by a handsome young black man without costume, dressed in tuxedo. "Care to dance?" he asked.

Before she could make an excuse, he cut her off. "I know who you are, but I'm also willing to keep it a secret, if you will dance with me."

Charlotte unsmilingly acceded. As they walked out on the dance floor, he noticed her sudden tension. "Don't worry, Charlotte," he whispered as he put his arm around her. "You don't recognize me, do you?"

"Should I know you?" she was surprised.

"It's been a while, but when I heard you play piano I put two and two together. I'm Boris Marshall. Remember our youth ensemble, all that quartet music?"

"Oh, my God!" she exclaimed, pinching him on the arm. "How the heck are you? I did not recognize you. You're so different."

"So are you," he mused aloud. "Well, I slimmed down, and I do a little jazz bass on the side when I'm not playing cello for the symphony," he smiled. "I saw Dr. Lamont's reaction when you came up, and I knew he would not relinquish the piano to just anyone." He looked at her, suddenly understanding. "You were scared I was about to blow your cover, weren't you?"

"Yes," she admitted sheepishly. "I left all this behind, and tonight was more fun than I remembered, because no one knew me. I was afraid that was about to end."

"My lips are sealed," he laughed. "It's obvious you are still playing, but where?"

"No, I'm not," she confessed. "I developed performance anxiety, and just couldn't do it anymore. That's what made it so amazing tonight, like a new lease on life."

"Well, you need to sip from that cup again tonight," he said. Boris stopped dancing, and she stumbled from the suddenness. He took her by the arm and led her toward the piano.

"Hey, Doc," he spoke when they arrived, "do you think Sleeping Beauty here could get another crack at the keyboard?"

"Next thing she'll be wanting part of my pay for the night," Lamont complained good-naturedly. "I'll let her have it right after midnight, say in about ten minutes."

Lamont suddenly launched into a countdown with the band, and from there into 'Auld Lang Syne' as people laughed, hugged, drank, kissed and applauded and balloons and confetti fell. Then he launched into 'On a clear day' with the band, and Charlotte and Boris danced again.

Before she knew it, the number was over and she was handed by Boris over to the piano. "No requests?" she asked Lamont.

"Time for something less hectic—maybe 'Tenderly'?" he suggested.

"OK," she started an intro, moving it from something slow and simple to a slower swing with the band. When they finished, her eyes were bright with excitement.

"What about that Benny Goodman number that Peterson did and you used to like—'Soft winds'? Remember we used to make that a duet?"

"I haven't played in a long time; I don't know—" she protested, but he waved away her words, sitting down beside her.

The next thing she knew they were laughingly meshing together the arrangement they had worked out when she was only a teenager, as the band fell in easily with them. She was out of breath when they drew to a resounding close, and people were applauding loudly.

"That was cool," she breathed. "I've missed it so much."

"Remember what I said," Dr. Lamont kissed her on the cheek. "And don't be a stranger."

She was turning around from thanking Lamont and Boris, when she drew up short. Standing leaning against the end of the grand was Wilhelm Kreiser, dressed in tuxedo. She stiffened in sudden fear. She had not seen him face to face since she left Atlanta.

He swaggered up to her. "Good evening, mademoiselle," he slurred. "I am in awe of your performance tonight. Might I ask your name?"

She caught her breath. Was he joking? Did he not recognize her? But he looked at her earnestly over a champagne flute he was downing.

"On a night like this, it is almost as rude to ask one's name as it is to ask a woman her age," she quipped, trying to disguise her trembling voice.

"Then please forgive my presumption," he took her hand and kissed it. "It's just that a woman of your apparent beauty and talent has stolen my heart.

I say 'apparent' because you are the only one still wearing a mask tonight. May I have this dance?"

She nodded wordlessly. Much as she didn't want to stand out by continuing to wear the mask, she was now suddenly fearful of being recognized, particularly by Harry.

He held her as Lamont launched into a slow number. She could tell that Kreiser was inebriated, and she was paralyzed with fear as she danced with him. Old feelings came back to haunt her. God, she thought with disgust, I still want him. She knew that she could not hold on to the charade much longer, and needed to make her escape.

"I feel that I must take my leave," she murmured as the number ended. "My carriage is turning into a pumpkin," she tried to make a joke as she gently pushed away.

"Please don't leave me, Laura," Kreiser muttered under his breath. Charlotte's breath caught in her throat. "Take me home before I become a spectacle."

She slowly took off her mask, watching his face to see if there was any sign of recognition. He gazed at her. "I know those eyes anywhere," he whispered. "I don't know what witch you are, and I really don't care, but don't wake me up from the dream."

"I need to call for my car," she trembled slightly.

"I'll go with you," he insisted, drawing himself up and exhibiting that arrogant bearing she knew so well.

Chapter 27

Kreiser and Charlotte walked outside into the crisp night air, and suddenly Tom and the limo were in front of her. Tom appeared and opened the door for her, looking inquiringly at Kreiser.

"I'm dropping him off at his home," she explained. Tom nodded, his face a mask.

"Harry, where do you live now?" she helped him into the car.

"Druid Hills," he muttered, rattling off an address near the golf club. She gave the address to Tom. He leaned forward, reaching for a bottle of alcohol in the bar.

She grabbed his hand firmly. "You've had enough."

He turned to her and cupped her chin in his hand. "You are so beautiful," he crooned. "My queen, my Carlota . . ." he whispered as he kissed her.

Charlotte shocked, tried to push him away, but as his kiss deepened she found that she wanted to respond to him. She hated herself for suddenly wanting him all over again. "You are such a bastard," she whispered with loathing. "Do you think I could love you after what you've done to me?"

"Don't I know it?" he laughed harshly. "Aren't you aware I think of you, my Charlotte, each and every night? Why did you come back? Why are you here tonight with me? It is such sweet torture."

He pulled her to him, and she kissed him wildly. "Oh, Harry, why did you leave me out there all alone?"

"What else could I do?" he muttered against her lips. "I had nothing to offer you, and still don't. You know this. I ruined you, and can only have you in my dreams, like now."

They came to a halt. Tom's voice was heard. "We've arrived."

"Thanks, Tom," she responded. "Can you help me get him inside?"

She fumbled in Harry's pockets for his keys, as he tried to grasp her and she wriggled away. The door opened and she climbed out. Together she and Tom managed to get the man up the steps to the door, which Charlotte opened.

"Let's get him to the bed," she ordered. "I know I can't handle him alone."

Finally he was stretched out on the bed, asleep. She loosened his tie. She looked down at him in sympathy, then turned to Tom. "I'm almost afraid to leave him like this, Tom."

"I think it's not an uncommon occurrence," he responded, waving at the bottles of vodka, some empty, some partially empty, beside the bed.

She looked at Harry one last time, then nodded. "You're right. He'll be OK. Let's go."

She turned, and her eyes widened in disbelief. There on the wall of the bedroom were pinned or taped a collage of articles and pictures. Looking closer, she saw that they were all about her. There were photos of her at consoles playing, tabloid shots of her, articles and reviews of her playing, and even her articles from the *Post*. She reeled in shock.

As she turned to leave, suddenly his eyes opened, he sat up and grasped her wrist. "My beautiful Laura, don't leave just yet," he cried brokenly.

She felt a moment of weakness, but fought it. "Harry, I can't do this with you," she whispered. "The hurt is still there. I can't forgive you."

At his pained expression, she touched his cheek, almost involuntarily.

"Please," he looked at her pleadingly.

She looked at Tom, embarrassed. "I—"

"I understand," Tom handed her a card. "Here's my number. Call me when you're ready."

"You need to go home, Tom. It's not right for you to be up all night. I can call a cab."

"You don't understand," Tom looked intently at her. "Mr. Fellowes has entrusted you to my care. I want to be able to report I delivered you safely home."

"You have," Charlotte insisted. "Now please go, before I go with you."

"Call me," he said stubbornly as he exited.

She heard the door close, and she turned back to look at Kreiser. He was staring at her. "You're going to stay?" his eyes were wide like a little boy.

"I'm here," she nodded, suddenly very afraid.

He pulled her to him, and she sat down beside him. "Oh, Charlotte, I'm not sure if I can stand this dream."

"I hate you," she whispered brokenly. "You abandoned me. You were so vile. You destroyed me. I cannot function normally. I can't—be with a man. I can't have a meaningful relationship." Their eyes locked together. "I can't play, Harry. I'm a wreck."

"I hate myself," he cupped her chin with his hand. "I love you so much, and I cannot erase the past and my words to you. Yet you are here."

Before she could respond, he pulled her to him and kissed her. She responded, kissing him passionately, forgetting her hatred as he rolled her over him and beside him on the bed.

"How does one get you out of this garb?" he muttered.

"There's a modern-day marvel called a zipper in the back," she whispered as she unbuttoned his shirt.

Afterward, she watched as he slept. "Call me," she whispered to him.

"Always," he muttered sleepily.

She struggled silently back into the costume, picked up her things, and turned off the lamp, leaving him, laying his keys and her phone numbers written out on a piece of paper on the dresser as she walked out.

She quietly let herself out, pulling the door closed. Only then did she notice the limo out front. "Damn, Tom," she murmured, as she walked to the car. Tom appeared and opened the door for her.

"You don't take directions well, do you?" she smiled tightly as she climbed in.

She suddenly froze. Gerry, sans his costume and in denims and casual dark button-down shirt, was sitting in the limo.

"He always does what I tell him," Gerry replied wryly.

She swallowed. "Checking up on me?"

"Someone has to protect you from yourself," Gerry spoke calmly, although she knew he was angry.

"How was your evening with the redhead?"

"Like you, I follow the maxim 'always end up at their place'. That way you don't overstay your welcome and they don't overstay theirs." He stared at her. "Was Kreiser as good as you remembered?"

She turned scarlet with shame. "Not really," she made light of it. "But at least we used protection this time."

"Good," he surprised her with his ferocity. "Charlotte, after all you've been through, you would go back to that slime?"

"It's a test," she spouted angrily. "I want to give him another chance. I left my numbers. I want to see if he follows up."

He looked at her, shaking his head. "He hasn't in all this time. Why would he change now?"

"I have to know," she whispered tremulously.

"OK, OK," he held up his hands in surrender. "What if we go back to Melanie's so that you can change? You can tell me about it, that is, if you want to."

"OK," she agreed. He gave instructions to Tom. They sat in silence for the rest of the ride, Charlotte reclining on one seat, her mind far away, as

Gerry sat across from her, looked at the morning papers and glanced over them at her from time to time.

"The *Atlanta Watch* didn't recognize you either," he stated neutrally, "but spoke about the 'mystery woman' and offered a reward for identifying her."

"Oh, great," she muttered.

They finally pulled into the driveway at Melanie's, and made their way inside. It was early, but Stefan was up and waiting for her on the steps, still in his pajamas.

"Aunt Charl," he cried, as he ran to her. She bent over him and tried to shush him. "How was the party? Tell me all about it."

"Let's go upstairs, and I'll tell you," she whispered, then started as she stood up. Melanie was standing in the doorway of the library.

"So you were the one dressed as Elizabeth," she noted, taking her glasses off as she reviewed her niece critically. "Why didn't you tell me?"

"I just wanted to see if I could get away with being unrecognized in Atlanta," Charlotte was defensive. "And it worked."

"And why do you feel it necessary to fool people as to your identity?"

"I don't know," Charlotte responded, tears suddenly in her eyes. "I just think it is easier to be anonymous instead of constantly raining shame onto the family name as your niece."

She took Stefan by the hand and fled up the stairs, leaving Gerry alone with Melanie. In front of Stefan's room, she whispered to him, "You know it's awfully early for you to be up. Don't you want to sleep a little more?"

He shook his head solemnly. "I've been waiting for you, so you can tell me about the party," he repeated stubbornly.

"OK," she acceded. "I've got to change clothes, so let's be quiet."

She led him into her room. He crawled up on her bed, his eyes wide. She opened some drawers, grabbing some shorts and t-shirt and lingerie. "OK," she ordered. "Close your eyes while I take off this dress."

He obediently covered his eyes, while she struggled out of the costume and walked into the bathroom. "You can sit by the door and talk to me while I take a shower," she called, as she ran the water and stepped in.

He called. "Well? Were there lots of kings and queens?"

"Quite a few, and lots of all sorts of characters," she answered him. She entertained him by describing the costumes and people.

"Was there lots of music?"

"There was lots of music," she laughed, mimicking his grammar.

"Did you play?" he asked with interest.

"Actually, I did," she answered him. "And it was fun."

"Will you play for me what you played?" he asked her.

"Maybe," she laughed again. "Didn't you sleep any?"

"No, I was too excited. I knew you were going to play."

Surprised, she called over the noise of the shower, "How did you know that?"

"I just felt it in my bones," he said.

"You and your bones," she giggled at him.

"But I know things," he insisted. "Did Gerry find a girlfriend?"

"I'm not sure, but he tried," Charlotte smiled.

"What about you?" Stefan asked.

"Well, not really," she replied, the thought of Kreiser suddenly filling her mind.

"You did or you didn't," the boy said, a remark he had borrowed from her badgering him about washing behind his ears in the past.

"I saw some people I hadn't seen in a long time," she replied.

"Did you fall in love?" he asked.

"Where do you get this stuff?" she completed her shower, cut the water off and grabbed a towel.

"I'm really smart," he smirked.

"Too smart," she retorted, as she dried herself and stepped out, dressing quickly. She brushed her teeth and toweled her wet hair, fluffing it. "OK," she pushed at the door, where he was sitting in a chair. He moved the chair, and she walked over to the closet, pulling out athletic shoes.

"Aunt Mellie was there. Didn't you ask her what happened?"

"Yeah, but she said it was a bunch of rich people acting silly," he intoned solemnly.

"Well, she's right," Charlotte ruffled the boy's hair.

She looked out the window, and the eastern sky was just beginning to lighten up. "Too early for breakfast," she observed. "You wanna go sculling with Gerry and me?"

"Cool," his eyes shined.

"We'll have to see if Gerry wants to go. You need to get dressed in some pants and a sweatshirt, and brush your teeth."

"But you have shorts on," the boy pointed to her.

"But I'm going to be rowing. You are just going to be sitting there in the cold," she explained.

She deposited the boy at the door of his room and made her way downstairs. When she arrived, she found Gerry already in gear resembling hers.

"You must have been thinking what I was thinking," he smiled.

"Yes, but we have a passenger," she informed him. "Where's Melanie?"

"She boiled over fire and brimstone at me, then we kissed and made up," he noted wryly. "After all, I'm her great white hope for saving you."

"Duly noted, except that you haven't succeeded yet," Charlotte grinned.

"I know," he nodded, as Stefan bounded down the stairs.

"Are we ready?" he asked excitedly.

"I bought a new life vest for him the other day," Gerry noted. "Let's go, before Daisy starts breakfast and prevents our getting our exercise."

With Stefan along bubbling and asking questions, they spoke no more of Kreiser.

Later, after breakfast, Gerry walked into the parlor, to find Charlotte and Stefan curled up together side by side, both asleep on the sofa, Charlotte's arm protectively thrown over the boy.

"It's uncanny, isn't it?" Amy came up behind him, following his gaze. "The resemblance is so strong. It frightens me. I worry so much about her."

"I do, too," Gerry murmured.

"Can't you do anything? Get her to marry you? Have children with her? You both could do worse."

"I know, but Charlotte is her own boss," Gerry responded. "If it's not her idea, it isn't going to happen. You know this, Amy. You tried to push her at Matt, and as you see, that ended up hurting them both."

"I want her to be happy," Amy was defensive. "She's not going to go out and find someone on her own. I'm just glad she's over Kreiser."

"Who said she is?"

"What do you mean? What do you know that you aren't telling me?"

Gerry just looked at the two sleeping forms, shook his head, and walked out.

Chapter 28

When Charlotte made it home to D.C., she called Jonathan. "Do you have some time to talk?" she wanted to know.

"Wow! You sound excited. What's going on?"

"I'd rather talk about it in person," she demurred.

"Well, I'm through about 4:30. Why don't you just come over for dinner? It's pot roast," he laughed.

"That would be great," she agreed.

When she walked in, both Jonathan and Evan were waiting for her.

"It smells so good. I'm famished," she laughed, embarrassed, as they both gazed at her intently.

Evan pulled out a chair at the kitchen island counter. "Here, while I serve it up, you can tell us what is going on."

She started. "But I can set the table or something," but Evan waved her away, pouring her a glass of red wine.

"Do you want me to disappear while you talk to Jonathan?" he asked her.

"No, I want you to hear this too," she shook her head.

She told them about the New Year's party and her playing. She omitted her reunion with Kreiser. "I found as long as I was disguised and no one knew me, I could play again. I was back in the zone again," she exclaimed. "It was the most exhilarating experience."

She saw they were both studying her. "Well," she demanded. "What do you think?"

Evan was enthusiastic. "God, that's great, Charlotte. To get back where you used to be, and play again, is wonderful. You may have something here."

She turned to Jonathan, whose expression she could not fathom. "Well?" she asked.

"I have mixed feelings," he stated. "I think it is a good experiment and one way for you to work through the anxiety of performing in public. But it should not become a crutch for you, and you are only treating the symptoms. You need to work through the cause for your loss of self-esteem."

"But you do agree this is sort of a breakthrough?" Charlotte demanded, her face anxious.

"Yes, dear," Jonathan agreed. "It is most definitely a breakthrough, but we've a long way to go."

"But this is wonderful," Evan insisted. "You must set up time to practice organ regularly, plus a regular piano regimen. You have left off your work long enough, and you don't need to let your technique slip any further."

"I agree," Jonathan concurred. "I think that the constant work helps to build on the esteem. The better you are, the more comfortable you are going to feel in public."

She smiled with relief. "OK. Now where's that pot roast?"

Charlotte did establish a regimen of practicing organ and piano, and found that she did feel stronger and more secure, as long as there was no one around to hear her. Whenever she realized that someone was listening, she would still freeze up, which frustrated her. But Jonathan continued to encourage her to keep trying.

The next week in session she confided in Jonathan about her tryst with Kreiser. He was instantly concerned. "Charlotte, every time you allow the wounds to start healing, you open yourself up again."

"I have to know if he loves me like he claims. I need to know if Melanie has forced him to stay away," Charlotte's jaw jutted out stubbornly.

"Do you really think your future is in that direction?"

Charlotte had no answer for him.

Meanwhile, she waited for Kreiser to call her, but in vain. *If he loves me so much and thinks of me daily, why can't he pick up the phone?* she fumed silently. She tried to banish him from her mind, because her mulling over his lack of contact reinforced in her mind feelings of worthlessness, which interfered with her concentration and caused her practice to founder hopelessly.

One evening Evan called her. "Are you free to run somewhere with me?" he asked.

"Sure. Gerry is out of town, and Amy doesn't need me to babysit. What's up?"

"You'll find out when we get there," Evan said mysteriously.

"You know I'm not great on surprises," Charlotte reminded him.

"This one you will like."

He picked her up promptly, and they set out. "It's not far," he told her, heading to the campus of American University and finally pulling up to a parking lot near the Katzen Center.

"Have you ever been here?" he asked her.

"No. I don't get out much," she stared out the windshield. "Am I dressed appropriately?" she looked down at her casual pantsuit.

"Probably more dressed up than those you're going to see," he smiled, gesturing at his own jeans and sweatshirt.

Evan steered them through the entrance and down a series of hallways to a pair of double doors. Trying them, he found one unlocked. "C'mon," he pulled her inside with him.

They walked down an aisle in the performance hall as a quartet was rehearsing on stage. Charlotte recognized the music of Camille Saint-Saens as Evan pulled her nearer the group, until he was dragging her up some steps onto the stage.

A woman, first violinist, saw them first. "Evan!" she called, and came toward them, abandoning the others in mid-stream. She came up and kissed him on the cheek. "And who have you brought?" she peered at Charlotte.

"Damn it, I don't believe it," a man had followed her over, and walked straight up to Charlotte.

"Erik?" Charlotte said tentatively, as he threw his arms around her, viola still in one hand, bow in the other. "Then this must be Alison. Oh, my, this is a pleasant surprise."

Alison walked up to her. "Charlotte Lawson?" she looked at her closely, then kissed her on the cheek, grasping her hands warmly. "I cannot believe it. You disappeared from the face of the earth. Evan, where on earth did you find her?"

"At a baptism," Evan grinned. "She's living here now."

"No way," Erik countered. "Surely we'd have heard of her performing."

"I'm not into music anymore," Charlotte smiled, trying to hide her embarrassment. "I am an English professor at Georgetown."

"Not in music?" Alison cried. "That can't be. We've never found a pianist to match you. In fact, we need one right now, and Evan refuses to help us out."

"See, now I have resolved your problem," Evan laughed.

"No, I can't," Charlotte pulled back, her eyes wide in sudden fear. "Evan, is that why you brought me here? You know I can't do this."

Erik, alarmed at Charlotte's reaction, exclaimed, "What is it? Charlotte, you cannot be serious. We'd be honored to have you do chamber music with us."

Evan put his arm around Charlotte's shoulders, pulling her back toward the group. "Charlotte developed a case of performance anxiety," he explained in low terms. "She is working through it, and had a breakthrough not long ago. I think it would be good for her, if she will consent, to rehearse with you. If it doesn't work out, it wasn't meant to be. But, Charlotte, remember how exhilarated you said it felt to play again in public?"

"But no one knew me," Charlotte protested.

"Listen," Erik took her hand. "Alison has been dying to do the Beethoven, but we weren't happy with the pianists we auditioned. You know that—we did it in Atlanta."

Alison looked at her with concern. "I really would love to do that again, and no one plays it like you. Please consider it."

Erik continued, "Just consider rehearsing it with us. We'll figure out something, even if we have to hire a big-wig from New York to actually do the performance."

Alison smiled. "We play the Saint-Saens this weekend. We rehearse here together every Tuesday evening, sometimes in a practice room. I'm on staff here, so I can always secure a room. How about next Tuesday?"

Charlotte hesitated, but Evan squeezed her hand. "I just happen to have the score at home," he coaxed. "You'd be doing me a big favor, because I have youth choir practice on Tuesdays, and cannot help them out."

"I just don't want to be a big disappointment to you, and slow you down," Charlotte was doubtful.

"We'll give it a couple weeks, and if it isn't working, I'll be the first to tell you," Erik promised.

"And you would too," Charlotte laughed. "OK, I will try."

"And while you are at it, give her the Schumann," Alison added. "We might as well work on two while we're at it."

"Good idea," Erik was enthusiastic. "And it's not like you haven't played these before. And the Turina trio—I still like to play the lead every now and then." He grinned at Alison.

They introduced her to the other members of the quartet. Before she knew it, she was walking back to the car with Evan, several scores in her hands.

"I don't know if this will work," she was still doubtful.

Evan countered, "But the idea is exciting to you, isn't it?"

"Yes," she agreed. "It's just been—how long—Stefan is six, so perhaps seven years or more since I have played with them."

"But you enjoyed it?"

"I loved it," she breathed. "Dr. Conrad filled my teenage years full of music. I haven't talked to him in a while."

"Maybe you should give him a call," Evan suggested.

Charlotte threw herself into practicing the music scores. At first rusty, the tactile memory from her youth soon came back, and she remembered the Beethoven and Schumann. The Turina she did not know, but found it to be intriguing and exotic, faintly reminiscent of the first movement of the Dvorak *Dumky* Trio.

The first session, she was nervous, but the group made her feel at home, and fairly soon they were in serious rehearsal, only stopping to discuss points of coordination in the score.

At one point, a man came on stage, intently listening. Charlotte did not notice him at first, but when she did, she suddenly froze, her mind going blank.

"What is it?" Alison asked. Turning, she noticed the man also. "That is Professor Kinaston, the marching band director."

Charlotte stammered, "I'm so sorry. It's just—" she began shaking.

Erik went up to her and put his arm around her. "I'm sorry," she stammered. "It happens. If someone listens to me, I freeze. See, I'm not cut out for this."

Alison came up also. "It's OK, Charlotte," she said soothingly. "You are doing great. I'm so happy. I wanted to do this music for a long time, and you are a godsend."

"I tell you what," Erik said. "We can do most of the sessions in a practice room, and there won't be as much chance of people wandering around, unless an occasional student walks in. We would only need to do this in the hall a few times prior to actual performance."

"I'll arrange that," Alison promised, giving Charlotte a squeeze. "Jim has already wandered off again," she noted. "What say we try again?"

Charlotte took a deep breath, and nodded.

The next week, there was an addition to the rehearsal. Alison was apologetic. "Our babysitter had an emergency tonight, so I had to bring Carly with me," she explained as she settled the half-asleep little girl in a child carrier.

"Oh, she's lovely," Charlotte bent over the little child. "How old is she?"

"Almost three, and a handful," Alison laughed. "Erik can tell you—he has to help with a lot of childcare activities."

"Good for him," Charlotte grinned. "But you know, you can bring her any time."

"You wouldn't mind? She can be a handful and quite a distraction."

"No. I play for Stefan all the time, and he is already taking lessons and begging for more. I babysit for him at least once per week, so that Amy can get out. I'd be glad to help you as well."

So started another routine for Charlotte, with every Tuesday in rehearsal with the group, and Carly generally asleep in her seat. Carly also became a regular visitor to Charlotte's apartment, Charlotte sometimes having two active children to watch, and enlisting Gerry's help from time to time when he was not otherwise engaged.

Erik began enthusing about playing violin solos again, now that Charlotte was slowly being coaxed out of her retirement from playing, albeit she was still not agreeing to public performance.

Chapter 29

One evening, Erik and Alison came by with Carly, Charlotte having agreed to babysit. Erik brought in a strange box, and a stranger, a young female student, which they introduced as Soon Yung. He handed the box to Charlotte.

"What is this?" she asked, curious.

"Your old friend Dr. Conrad has sent you a gift," he explained cryptically.

Charlotte opened the box and inside were a wig and a makeup kit. She looked blankly at them. "OK. What do I do with this?"

Alison smiled and took Charlotte's hand. "We thought a little experiment might be in order. Evan told us about your 'breakthrough' at the New Year's party. Dr. Conrad wasn't there—he was out of town—but heard a lot of buzz about an unknown woman at the party, who played the piano and danced divinely. No one apparently knew who she was. But Dr. Lamont did, and Dr. Conrad wangled it out of him.

"So when Erik mentioned that you were here and rehearsing with us, Dr. Conrad came up with the idea. If you feel freer knowing that no one recognizes you, maybe a disguise would work for you to perform with us."

Charlotte lifted out the black page-cut wig and looked at it.

"Soon Yung is from the theatre department, a master of makeup. So we thought perhaps . . ."

Charlotte's mind was whirring. "Wow, this might work."

Alison and Erik exchanged knowing looks, relieved that Charlotte was willing to try the subterfuge.

"That's good, because we want to do a dry run at the student recital next week, if you're up to it," Erik suggested.

Charlotte turned frightened eyes toward them. "So soon?"

"No one will know you anyway. It's just a student recital. We want to see how you feel doing it. If so, you might want to perform with us when we program this material," Alison suggested gently.

"Erik just put on the program 'TBA', so there's no pressure," she added.

"In fact, when anyone asks, we've just been calling our pianist 'TBA'," he laughed.

"I like it," Charlotte said slowly. "I will need a name."

"We'll work on that," Eric promised. "But for now, we're going to order in pizza and let Soon work her magic."

"You don't want me to babysit?"

"That was just a ruse. We want to watch," Alison laughed.

After Soon gave some instructions and applied some makeup, Charlotte looked at herself in a mirror. "Damn!" she exclaimed. "Who is that?"

Erik and Alison, the latter holding Carly, peered at her. "Soon, that is miraculous," Erik murmured. "I cannot believe it. I would never recognize you."

Charlotte looked at Alison, as Carly took one look at Charlotte and began to cry, clinging to her mother. "I'm sold," Alison breathed.

Charlotte readily agreed to the student recital. Erik had mischievously come up with the name Tabitha Auberge. "Get it—'T—B—A'. And Auberge—I thought you should have a French-sounding name, although we may place you as Eastern European. We'll leave all that as part of the mystery of your identity," he grinned.

Charlotte laughed. "I even sound itinerant—'auberge' meaning a hostel."

The recital went very well. Charlotte again, comfortable with her anonymity, performed well, and was shining with exhilaration at the end. Afterward, Evan and Jonathan came up to her.

Evan stared at her. "If I didn't know it was you, I'd never guess," he whispered.

Jonathan embraced her. "You did so well," he stated. "But you still need to work past this need for disguise, Charlotte."

"I am," she told him. "But you have no idea how good it felt to be back, to be playing like I used to."

He smiled, but she could read the concern in his eyes.

Alison then hit her with thunderous news. "We want to perform the Schumann and Beethoven at the Center here next month," she announced. "It's time."

Charlotte felt a stab of fear, but she smiled, the adrenalin still flowing. "Let's do it."

Charlotte carefully kept the news from Gerry. She wanted to surprise him, so invited him to attend the performance with her.

"How are you going to keep it from him?" Evan demanded.

"I'm just going to call him and tell him I'm delayed, and for him to wait for me," she explained.

The performance went stunningly well, and she had Evan bring Gerry back to the makeshift dressing room after the performance. She met him as he came in, his face anxious.

"Hello," she said in her best estimate of a European accent. "Miss Lawson has told me so much about you."

"Charlotte? You know her?" Gerry was thunderstruck.

"Yes. She left word that she wanted me to come to her apartment afterward, that she was sorry she missed the performance," Charlotte watched carefully for any sign of recognition from Gerry. "She said that you would take me there to meet her."

"I'd be honored," Gerry was polite. "Are you ready now?"

"Yes," she took his arm. "Miss Lawson did not tell me my escort would be so handsome."

"She told me even less about you," Gerry responded, as he steered her toward the side door and his limo.

She seated herself, and Gerry sat across from her. She patted the seat next to her. "Please to not be so cold and distant," she stated in broken English, drawing her brows up in a frown.

He obliged, sitting beside her. "Where are you from, Ms. Auberge?"

She slipped her hand onto his leg. "Why should we waste time with trivialities, Monsieur Fellowes? I am attracted to you, and I believe you want me. Is there anything more to discuss?"

He smiled provocatively. "I'm not used to moving quite that fast, Ms. Auberge," he remarked as he took her hand in his.

"Tabitha, please," she pleaded, as she moved toward him, ruffling his hair with her left hand, and pulling him toward her, kissing him full on the mouth.

He responded with pleasure, finally pulling himself away. "Please call me Gerry. I think it is called for, at the pace you're setting."

"I know what I want, and I take it," she murmured, enjoying the charade she was playing.

"We are here," Tom's voice announced.

"What a shame," Gerry announced. He got out and helped her out, his hand lingering on her waist.

"Thank you," she laughed throatily, as he walked her up the steps, his hand remaining firmly at her waist. She let her hand slip to his groin area.

"Whoa," he whispered.

He let her in. "Charlotte, are you here?" he called. "I've brought Ms. Auberge as you wanted."

She walked in before him. As she turned to face him, she removed the wig. He gasped.

"Who are you?" he demanded. As he came up, he said incredulously, "Is that you, Charl?"

She laughed heartily then.

"Why, you!" he exclaimed hotly. "Why didn't you tell me?"

"It was an experiment, to see if I could play in public. I wanted to see if you would be fooled as well."

"Damn, Charl, why did you feel the need to do all this?" he was irritable.

"You don't understand, Gerry," she went up to him, contrite. "Ever since—Harry, I've not been able to do what I did tonight. I realized the night of the New Year's party that when I was anonymous I could play again."

She placed her hand on his arm. "Please don't be mad. I know—you were attracted to Tabitha, weren't you?" she teased him. "She was more your type—strong and confident, very aggressive."

"I did like that come-on," he turned to her, grinning. "Do you think you could put the wig back on?"

She pushed him playfully. "I'm exhilarated and hungry," she announced. "I'm changing clothes, and you can take me out."

Afterward she called Dr. Conrad. "Thanks for the gift," she told him.

"It was worth a shot," he replied. "Anything to get you back on the stage where you should be. I wish you had come to me in the beginning."

"It was a bad time," she said somberly. "I couldn't tell anyone."

"Can I come hear you perform?" he asked.

"As long as I'm someone else," she chuckled. Suddenly sober, she asked, "How is Harry?"

"I wouldn't know," Conrad replied. "I keep away from him."

"Why?" she was surprised.

"Charlotte, have you forgiven him? Because I haven't. I have no desire to work with him ever again."

Charlotte was shaken. "Doc," she stuttered, "this is my problem. I am the one who seduced him. I was in the wrong, not him. That should not affect your working relationship with him."

Conrad spoke hotly, "Then tell me why it is you aren't pursuing your future as a premiere performer, Charlotte? Why the only way you can play in public is when no one can recognize you? Kreiser isn't the only one who had high hopes for you, who wanted and still wants you to shine."

He lowered his voice, as though he realized he had lost control. "I hate him as much as I have ever loved and aspired for you, girl. If not for him you would be a star, basking in your art."

Charlotte was stunned. "I—I'm sorry, Peter. I never knew." She took a deep breath. "I would hate to think that my bad decisions in life have ruined your professional relationship with Harry. You are both fabulous musicians, and no one can play the Poulenc or the Jongen better than Harry. So you would wipe those off the repertoire just because of me?"

"Why don't you bring your wig and come play them yourself?" he answered. "There's nothing Harry can do that you can't do better."

He sighed. "I'm sorry. Charlotte, please get better. I miss you. I want you back."

Charlotte, buoyed by the successful experiment, felt secure in her 'Tabitha Auberge' *persona*, and soon was persuaded to more regular appearances in the D.C. area. Furthermore, Evan had persuaded her to take his place one night per week playing at a jazz club, giving her a red wig and another persona. She met with the drummer and bass player, and they found some repertoire they could agree upon.

So Charlotte found her plate full, with rehearsals and performances and babysitting, plus the day job teaching. Stefan had started piano lessons at the age of five, and was clamoring to learn more and more music. She smiled with empathy, remembering her own burning desire to play whatever she could find. So she spent more and more time with him, providing him new music approved by his teacher and admonishing him to work on his exercises and hone his technique. He in turn insisted on accompanying her at times when she would go alone to the church to practice organ or to rehearsals with the quartet, or when Erik and Alison would come over to play with her. He would sometimes spend the night with her, and would not go to bed until she played him to sleep. She knew she had fallen for the young boy, and was gratified that people would sometimes mistake him for her son.

But she still found time to write, and was submitting short stories while working on another novel. So she was beginning to find a peace within herself. Sometimes she looked at Stefan and felt jealousy for Amy and Mike, wanting to complete a family herself.

But although Mike was quick to 'fix her up' with men on dates, she could not shake her horror of intimacy with a man. She felt the panic closing in on her—remembering how Kreiser turned on her, remembering her aborted relationship with Matt—and was therefore careful not to let any relationship become serious.

She confided her fears to Jonathan, and they again discussed her tryst with Kreiser the night of the New Year's party. She begged him not to let Evan know about Kreiser's liaison with her. Jonathan encouraged her to keep dating, telling her that it would improve her esteem, and that her chances of feeling comfortable with someone else would increase. She was again disappointed that Kreiser did not attempt to contact her, and shut her heart against him.

And although Gerry continued to date other women, fueling speculation in the media about him, he always seemed to show back up at her door. They regularly appeared together in public.

"We must be a couple of misfits," she teased him.

"We deserve each other," he agreed.

"Our biological clocks are ticking," she stated. "Sooner or later one of us needs to take the plunge."

"You first," he winked at her.

Chapter 30

Mike, Amy, Stefan, Gerry and she had joined Melanie at Martha's Vineyard for a week at the close of the summer season. The breezes were already getting nippy in the evenings.

Mike and Charlotte took a walk down to the beach while the others were drowsing before tea time. They were silent, both soaking in the sun and enjoying the silence, broken only by the surf and the cawing of the occasional gull.

Mike finally spoke as they were standing side by side looking out over the water. "Matt gets married next week," he announced gravely. "I wasn't sure if you knew."

She nodded, not looking at Mike. "Matt called me just before they announced the engagement," she replied, her voice low.

"He did?" Mike was surprised. "He always asks about you. He really cares for you."

"I know," she was solemn. "I care for him too. That's why I pushed him away. I was touched that he wanted me to know before the news went public," she smiled sadly. "He is a great guy, and apparently she is a doctor too. I asked if she liked basketball. She does. I promised him Final Four tickets for a belated wedding gift. I hope they will be happy."

"She's a nice girl, but she's not you," Mike put his arm around Charlotte. "I always hoped you'd be my sister-in-law twice."

"What—you haven't had enough grief from me?" she teased him. "Mike, you're the best brother anyone could ever ask for. I think I love you more than I do Amy."

"But you love Stefan best of all," he laughed.

"Well, he is a gift from heaven," she remarked, as they turned and walked hand-in-hand back to the house.

Gerry had borrowed a friend's sailboat to take her and Stefan out for a jaunt. As they were getting ready to go, Stefan ran around excitedly. He was nine and a prodigious piano student already, playing everything he could get his hands on.

Charlotte and Daisy were packing a picnic basket. Amy and Mike were sunning out by the pool of the spacious home rented from an old friend of Melanie's, and Melanie had left to join some old friends to play bridge.

Gerry walked in, dressed in white with a sweater tied around his neck. Charlotte smiled. "You look like you just walked out of a *GQ* photo shoot."

She looked at his face and gasped at the tears in his eyes. "What is it, Gerry?" she instinctively walked up to him.

He sat down heavily. "I just got word George died," he said brokenly.

Charlotte's voice caught in her throat. "I'm sorry," she whispered hoarsely.

"He's been so sick, and I haven't been home much," Gerry sniffed. "We haven't been as close, so I didn't know. Now it's too late."

"It's OK," Charlotte cradled his head against her, trying to comfort him.

Stefan ran in. "Are we going or what?" he demanded precociously.

Charlotte started, "Stefan, something has come up," but Gerry stood and put a hand on her shoulder.

"No, we've planned this, and we're not going to spoil Stefan's island picnic." He looked at her. "I'll have to fly back in the morning."

"I'll go with you," Charlotte took his hand.

"Thanks."

In the end it was decided that the entire family should go back, inasmuch as the Fellows and Cains were neighbors and friends.

The funeral was held at Christ the King Cathedral. And Kreiser had of course played. He had chosen conservatively, his choice of music including Barber's *Adagio for Strings*, several of Liszt's *Consolations* which had also seen service by Liszt as music for Mass, and a transcription of Ravel's *Pavane for a Dead Princess*, a piece she found incongruously appropriate. She had glanced at Gerry sitting beside her during the latter, and although he was somber she could see the corners of his mouth curve into a slight smile as he nudged her.

"Stop it," he whispered to her. "He was my brother, and if I recall correctly, your fiancé at one time."

She nodded soberly, squeezing his hand. Memories of Louis Fellowes' funeral, and of her time with George then, came flooding back, bittersweet reminders of the one to whom she was once almost engaged. She remembered holding George's hand at the funeral then, and of her girlish hopes that did not come to pass.

She had seen Kreiser only from a distance, and after the first fluttering of nerves had felt herself safe in the crush of people at the funeral and at the visitation at the Fellowes' home afterward.

During the visitation, Charlotte went looking for a missing Stefan. As she rounded a corner in the library, she came face to face with Kreiser. He reached out a hand to steady her as she stopped suddenly.

"Carlota," she heard his familiar voice.

She could not find her voice, but looked at him dumbly, as Stefan suddenly appeared. "Ah, there you are," she coughed as Stefan took her hand and looked up at Kreiser.

"I know you," he told the man. "You're Willy Kreiser, the organist."

"Willy?" Kreiser smiled at the youth.

"Yes, I've heard your records. Aunt Charl has them."

Kreiser was captivated by the youth. "She does? Did you know that she was one of my students?"

"Yes, but she won't talk about it," the child replied precociously.

"Stefan," Charlotte gripped the boy's hand warningly.

"Does Aunt Charlotte still play organ?"

"Not very much," Stefan looked solemnly at the big man.

"Do you play organ?" Kreiser looked at Charlotte, who flushed.

"Sometimes my teacher allows me. I intend to, as soon as Aunt Charl will allow it," the boy beamed. Spying someone, he relinquished Charlotte's hand. "There's Cece—gotta go."

Charlotte, uncomfortable at being alone with Kreiser, watched the child disappear. "Is he—your child?" she heard Kreiser ask.

Suddenly the memory of their liaison and its consequences floated up, and she blinked back tears. "No, he is Mike's and Amy's," she heard herself reply.

"He looks so much like you. You should let him play, if he is any good at piano," Kreiser said, his voice low, melodious.

"He's just turned nine. There's time," she said defensively, her voice small.

"You started at twelve," he reminded her.

"How is Katharine?" she asked, changing the subject.

"She has taken George's death very hard. I believe the doctors have given her sedatives," he remarked gravely. "Carlota, you must not give up your music."

"Don't call me that," she whispered sharply, looking around them. Suddenly spying Gerry, she sputtered, "I must go," and fled.

She walked up to Gerry quickly, and he took her arm. "What did he say to you?" he whispered to her angrily.

"Nothing. I was asking about Kat," she told him, although she was trembling. Trying to cover her discomfort, she asked, "How is she?"

"She's upstairs, and still very upset."

"I will go up and see if I can help," Charlotte whispered, still agitated.

"Do you think that's a good idea?" Gerry asked her, concern in his eyes.

"I don't know, but I need to show her somehow that I care."

"I'm not sure she wants to see you," Gerry turned to her. "I mean, George and she were extremely close. She wasn't fond of you for leaving her favorite brother."

"It doesn't matter. If she says to get out, I will get out," Charlotte headed toward the stairs.

Pausing in front of the bedroom door, she stood, her hand on the doorknob. Steeling herself for an angry reproof, she walked in. Agatha Fellowes was standing by the bed looking over Katharine, who was sniffling into a tissue. Katharine saw her first.

"Charlotte," Agatha came forward. "How good of you to come up, but Kat is not doing well."

"I want to talk to Charlotte," Katharine interrupted her mother. "Alone."

"I don't think that's a good idea. You need to rest."

"Don't worry," Katharine sniffed. "I'll be a zombie in about thirty minutes anyway. Go on, Mother."

Agatha squeezed Charlotte's arm and left. Charlotte slowly approached.

"Come to gloat about George's death?" Katharine sneered.

"No, Kat. I'm very sorry he's gone," Charlotte responded quietly.

"Why? He wasn't good enough for you to marry?" Katharine cried.

"Kat, it wasn't like that," Charlotte came up to the bed. "I—I can't tell you what happened."

"Why? I want to know. You were engaged to him, then you were gone. What happened?" Katharine's voice rose. She grabbed Charlotte's wrist, jerking her toward her, until they were staring at each other.

"I—I found him with someone else," Charlotte confessed. She saw the pain and the curiosity in Katharine's eyes. "He was angry with me and told me he didn't love me, accused me of spying on him." Tears filled her eyes as she remembered the event.

"Who was it?" Katharine's voice softened.

"I don't know who he was," Charlotte's voice was muffled as she turned away.

"Liar!" Katharine accused her, hissing angrily, tears in her eyes as she jerked Charlotte back to face her.

"I swear to you, Kat. It's all true," Charlotte was crying too.

"He died of AIDs," Katharine whispered. Charlotte gasped in shock. "Have you been checked?"

"We nev—we never did it together," Charlotte stared at her. "Oh, Kat, I'm so sorry," she cried. "I'm so sorry. I would never wish that for George. Despite what happened, we had some really good times together that I wouldn't trade for anything."

Katharine suddenly hugged her, and they embraced each other, both crying. "I'm sorry he's gone," Katharine sniffled. "I loved him so much. No one understands."

"I know, and I wish he was here," Charlotte rocked her back and forth.

They reminisced about him, each crying and laughing together, talking about skeet shooting, tennis, all the water sports with Mr. Fellowes, and the Aerosmith concert. After a while, Katharine pushed away, snatching up the box of tissues for herself and handing some to Charlotte.

"Thanks," she said simply to Charlotte. "I really needed someone to talk to me. Mother doesn't. She tiptoes around like she's afraid to broach the subject. And Gerry, well, Gerry doesn't understand me."

"Gerry worships you, "Charlotte told her. "He still wants to be there for you."

Katharine laughed shortly. "Yeah, he is pitiful."

Charlotte, sad at her response, decided to change the subject. "Gerry tells me you and Harry are an item," Charlotte smoothed Katharine's hair away from her face.

"Harry? That's a laugh. He's not serious about anyone. I don't think Harry is cut out for one woman."

"You're probably right," Charlotte agreed quietly, turning her face away, pained.

"Did you love him?" Katharine suddenly asked.

"George? I was fond of him, and he was a flirt. He always made me feel like I was the only female in the room," she answered sadly.

"Not George," Katharine smiled tearily, blowing her nose. "Harry—did you love him?"

Charlotte reeled in shock. "Harry?"

"I know about you and Harry," Katharine smiled knowingly. "Don't you know he slips up sometimes when he's had too much to drink?"

"He's talked about me?" Charlotte was thunderstruck.

"I've put two and two together," Katharine replied. "You know Harry isn't good lover material." Katharine lay back against the pillows, spent.

"I'm sorry, Kat," Charlotte murmured quietly.

"There are other fish in the sea," Katharine retorted. "You told me that once." She paused. "Gerry says you don't play any more. That's a shame. You were good. He mentioned you are an author."

Charlotte was surprised, still shocked over Katharine's revelation. "I published a novel while student teaching. Why?"

"I could never find it," Katharine smiled weakly. "I want to read it. Tell me—what's it about?"

"An organist killed in an organ gallery," Charlotte smiled back.

"Ah," Katharine remarked, her voice slurring. "I want to buy a copy."

"I'll just send you one," Charlotte promised as Katharine yawned. "Get some rest, Hell-Kat."

"Nobody has called me that in years," she laughed, yawning again.

"You are still Hell-Kat to me," Charlotte smiled at her.

"I want it autographed," Katharine mumbled sleepily.

Chapter 31

Charlotte stood in front of the private entrance to the large building and pressed a buzzer before her. "It's Charl," she called into the intercom.

"Come on up," Gerry's voice responded, as she heard the lock click on the heavy double doors before her.

She stepped inside, walked into the elevator and pushed '20'.

Stepping out of the elevator, she admired the spacious foyer as she slipped past, and found herself in a tastefully appointed great room. Gerard was standing before a gilt mirror tying his tie, sans jacket.

"How was the Thanksgiving happy family meal?" he asked.

"Not bad. Stefan discovered cranberry sauce. He never would try it before; suddenly this year Daisy apparently didn't make enough. He's growing so fast, ten already. Yours?"

"Sad. Kat is a zombie since George died. Mom is always worried about her. I sit there wondering what to do, but I feel in the way. As long as I make money for them and make an occasional appearance, they are content."

"I'm sorry, Gerry," Charlotte murmured.

"I've tried all my life to get my sister to love me, to notice me, just anything. I should have figured it out by now. Even with George gone I'm non-existent in her book."

"You've said it yourself," Charlotte was sympathetic. "She is ill. That's her way. Don't give up."

Charlotte moved away, suddenly hesitant. "I took Kat shopping the other day."

"You what?" Gerry's voice rose. "She's run through all her trust fund income, and left debts all over town for me to pick up."

Charlotte nodded. "I know. She told me. But Agatha was beside herself, and I offered. It's OK; I cleared it with Melanie, and I footed the bill.

"She was angry at you for fouling up her 'love life'. But she admitted that this guy she has been seeing asks more questions about her money than about her. She made the comment that you were keeping her money from her."

Gerry grit his teeth. "She has very little money left. She has run through the inheritance Dad settled on her. Mom and I set up the trust to keep her from going broke." He took a deep breath. "I'm the only one in the family making any money. And I pay my accountants a fortune to keep up with Kat. But I don't know what to do. She of course doesn't acknowledge my existence." Charlotte could tell Gerry's anger was simmering under the surface.

"I had to chase off another money grubbing boyfriend the other day," he spat suddenly.

"What happened?" Charlotte was curious.

"He showed up at the gun club saying he was going to propose to Kat and demanding that I give her control over her money. I had to inform him that all Kat had was in permanent trust which could not be invaded, particularly by any greedy spouse. I have already bought the home from Mom. Kat's inheritance will by terms of Mom's will be rolled over into the trust, with income to her, and of course she'll live in the house."

"'Another'? How often does this happen?" Charlotte was shocked.

"You would not believe the number of men who think she is an easy rich target," Gerry was white. "At one time I thought about cutting a deal with your beloved Kreiser."

"What?" she looked at him sharply.

"Kat is fond of him. The thought crossed my mind that it would better to match them up than have her constantly in this up-and-down state over a guy." But he stared at Charlotte. "She always spirals downward after a break-up, and has had to be committed privately a few times."

He paused. "But we both know Kreiser cannot be trusted to be faithful, don't we? And I'm not willing to trust the happiness of my sister to the slime. Furthermore, she informed me she was not interested in marrying him. She is apparently aware of his history with you, probably from him."

Charlotte made no reply, turning away.

"What do you think about my new digs?" he changed the subject, glancing toward her.

"Cool," she looked around her admiringly, happy to change the subject. "I thought you were going to buy something in Buckhead."

"Well, I decided to be closer to my business interests. And I bought the building for its commercial appeal—might as well live upstairs."

"Looks like the little brunette girlfriend can actually decorate a room," she teased.

"Hell, I chose this," he grumbled. "I can entertain down here, and there are a couple guestrooms if needed. But I live and work upstairs," he strided toward her.

"Do I get a tour? In fact, now that you have your own place, we should order in and break the place in. Or," she paused, a wicked grin on her face, "are you anxious to see and be seen by the lovely Miss Connally?"

He feigned a frown. "Really, Charl."

"You know, if you want to advertise your availability, you shouldn't have me tagging along," Charlotte teased.

He laughed. "But what if she doesn't dance as well as you?" He took her hand and twirled her around.

Charlotte grew serious. "You know any woman is going to be jealous of our friendship. I hate to see it change, but I guess it is inevitable."

"Not if we married each other," he rejoined with a twinkle in his eye.

"You're not serious?" she laughed.

"Why not? We'd make the couple of the year, the darlings of the media. We'd have fun, just like we always have."

He gazed at her, suddenly serious. "You know that is Aunt Mellie's scheme for us, don't you?"

"I've not fallen in with her plans so far," Charlotte countered, looking away.

"But doesn't the idea appeal to you at all?" he looked disappointed.

"Actually, the idea is very appealing," she confessed, to his amazement. "I don't ever intend to fall in love again, and I can't think of anyone with whom I'd rather spend the rest of my life. But, Gerry, it is not fair to you."

"Me?" he echoed, disbelievingly.

"You're always falling in love, and one day she is going to turn out to be Mrs. Right. Why should you tie yourself to me?"

"What if I want to tie myself to you?" he asked, his voice low. "I told you once that no one holds a candle to you for adventure."

"But is that enough?"

He turned away, walking to the other side of the room. "I think I'm already in love with you," he intoned.

Charlotte hooted. "Yeah, right, Mr. Casanova."

When he didn't join in her laughter, she stopped. "You are not serious, Gerry? This is not a joking matter."

"No, it's not," he agreed soberly.

"Well, if you're not sure, it's not real," she argued, "just one of your passing fancies."

"You see," he looked at her through the large ornate mirror over the fireplace, "I never let myself 'explore my feelings'—isn't that the term?—for this very reason. I don't want you to reject me out of hand, and I don't want to mess up what we have."

Charlotte was silent, her eyes roaming the room, avoiding his eyes as he studied her. She could sense his tension. She finally spoke. "Gerry, I love you like no one else. You've always been there for me. I'm flattered, but—"

"But horrified?" he supplied.

"No, I'm so afraid you'd be disappointed and unhappy," she finished. "I could not bear to lose you, and I would hate myself if I trapped you in a loveless marriage."

"But I can make you happy. I think you could learn to love again," he insisted. "Why not me?"

"Because Harry cut me so deeply," she spat, suddenly white-hot with anger. "Even now, when I see him, I hate him, but a part of me still clings to him, wanting him, loving him. I cannot turn loose."

"The bastard seduced you," Gerry's voice rang out in anger. "He knew better. You were too young to understand. I would gladly kill him for what he did to you. Now you're letting the past rob you of happiness. Let it go, Charl," he pleaded.

"Don't you think I'm trying?" her rage matched his. "I thought I had exorcised all thought of him. I keep thinking I can build a callous over the hurt. And then out of the blue it all comes back to me, and I'm back where I started."

She laughed bitterly. "Now Stefan wants us to move here to Atlanta so that he can study with Kreiser. The ultimate irony—back under Mellie's roof with Harry in and out under my nose, and Stefan following in my footsteps. It's just too rich." Her voice ended in a small sob.

"Do not put yourself through that," Gerard argued. "Marry me. We can live anywhere you want. Stefan can study anywhere."

She shook her head. "Gerry, you're just as tied to Atlanta. You keep saying you're going to leave, yet you always end up back here. Why? Is it your tie to your family? That Atlanta is just the right size pond?"

"I don't know," he muttered. "You're right. I could make a life anywhere, but then there's Kat and Mom. And with all my networks, I still always end up here."

She walked up to him and put her hand on his arm. "You are so tempting, however," she reached up to kiss his cheek.

"You are so tempting," he pulled her to him. "I don't want to be just your friend right this minute," he mumbled as he claimed her mouth.

Taken off guard, she responded to him, kissing him back. His kiss deepened. She finally pulled away.

"Gerry, you're a great kisser," she whispered, her face flushed.

He laughed, and she giggled too. "I'd like to resume those love-making lessons from adolescence," he grinned. "I might have a few new moves to show you."

Embarrassed, she moved away. "I'm sure you do," she murmured. "Maybe it's not such a good idea to eat in after all."

"You don't want to see the master bedroom?" he teased her. "You wanted a tour."

"On second thought, not tonight," she answered lightly. "You're rich; take me out somewhere fancy."

He fished something out of his jacket pocket and handed it to her. She looked at it.

"It's a key to the place, with the security codes," he said. "I want you to feel free to come and go whenever you feel like it."

"Gerry, this is your dream come true, your own private space," she objected.

"But Charl, what's mine is yours," he replied earnestly. "I can see what's coming. You're going to move back to Atlanta, whether next year or the next, it doesn't matter. And you're going to need to get away from it from time to time."

He gestured around the room. "This is a big place, plenty of space. Even room for a piano for you to practice. Pick out one and I'll buy it for you."

She smiled. "You are too good to be true."

"I know," he smiled back. "And you're welcome upstairs."

He laughed as she blushed and pinched his arm.

"You're incorrigible," she whispered.

"And besides, you're going to need a place to change into your disguises," he added. "You know, you need psychiatric help."

Charlotte's smile faded. "Really, Gerry, it is just a way to play my music without being hounded by the press and without everyone knowing that Melanie's precious niece is a lowly musician playing in a piano bar."

"Or doing chamber music?" he added. "How do you keep up with which *persona* you are at a given moment?"

Charlotte smiled, then sobered as she regarded his serious face. "I schedule it carefully. Gerry, you know why I do this."

"Because Kreiser messed up your mind so bad," Gerard said through clenched teeth. "That's why you need a psychiatrist. You deserve credit for your accomplishments."

"I've been seeing Jonathan regularly, and he doesn't approve. But I can't go out there and play without the security that no one knows my true identity," Charlotte argued desperately. "I know who I am at all times, Gerry. But I cannot face the public as me. It hurts too badly. I start shaking and I can't go on." She turned away. "It took a lot just to go on stage in disguise with the trio the first time. I need you to understand, to support me. It's important to me."

She turned back around, a forced smile on her lips. "And you know Melanie would never approve of my playing, even the classical music, much less the jazz. She always resisted my performing publicly."

She walked up and took Gerry's hand. "Let's not argue. Let's celebrate your new pad. Take me out. Let's just do Maggiano's, nice and simple comfort food."

"I need to ask you something first," he stopped. "I want to have a small dinner party, just a few people. Would you be my hostess?"

She paused. "You know I'd do anything for you, Gerry. But won't that give them the idea we are a couple?"

"Would you mind?"

"The question is whether you would mind," she retorted. "You're the most eligible bachelor on the East Coast."

"No. No, I wouldn't mind," he looked at her. She found she couldn't return his gaze, and looked away.

Chapter 32

Charlotte was summoned home suddenly by Melanie's doctor, to find that Melanie had suffered a series of mini-strokes. Although the doctor felt she would recover, he did not advise her living alone.

Shaken, Charlotte stayed with her until she was discharged from the hospital, and obtained the doctor's permission to fly her to D.C. so that Charlotte could care for her.

Melanie's health bounced back, much to Charlotte's and Amy's relief. Melanie at first agreed and stayed with Charlotte for three months, delighting in her family, especially Stefan, who was twelve and taking organ lessons while continuing piano studies. However, Melanie became deeply unhappy away from her Atlanta environs. At that time she began to put pressure on her nieces to return to Atlanta.

Her first efforts were concentrated on Amy. Melanie had no qualms about enlisting Stefan's enthusiastic assistance to lobby his parents to move to Atlanta. However, Amy's center of affection had become her husband and son, and she was happy in their comfortable home just outside D.C. on the Maryland side in Chevy Chase, and in supporting her husband in his task as an up-and-coming political staffer with aspirations of his own. Michael was not ready to settle back in Atlanta, and Amy wished to remain at his side. Even with Stefan's continued pleas to come back to Atlanta and study organ with Wilhelm Kreiser, Amy was resistant to the idea of being separated from her husband.

Therefore, Melanie turned her attention upon Charlotte. Charlotte, too, had forged ties with the area, many about which she had kept Melanie in the dark. Charlotte had not confided to any of the family her now regular performances under assumed identities, except one day a few years earlier, when Stefan found the wigs.

She had walked into her bedroom and found Stefan, at that time nine years old, on the floor in front of the open closet doors. "What are these for?"

he pointed, pulling aside her clothes and gesturing to some items hidden behind them.

"Stefan!" she choked. "Don't you know you aren't supposed to go through other people's closets?"

"I'm sorry. Are these Christmas presents? For who?" he persisted, taking a wig off its holder.

She was too agitated to correct his grammar. "Stefan, please," she pried the wig from his hands. "This is a secret. It's a—a costume, dear."

"Like the night of the party in Atlanta?" he asked precociously.

"Yes, like that," she sputtered, nodding.

"When do you wear them?" he demanded.

"There—oh, Stefan—sometimes there are times when I don't want people to recognize me," she was distracted, trying to determine how to extricate herself from the possible damage due to his discovery. Melanie will have me locked up, she thought crossly.

"Do you play music in these?" he asked.

She gasped again at his surmise. "Stefan, this is none of your business." Flustered, she dropped to her knees. "Now what am I going to do?" she said to herself.

He stood up and put his hands on her shoulders. "You can tell me, Aunt Charl. I can keep a secret. I won't tell anyone, not even Mom and Dad."

"But I don't want you to have secrets from your parents," she whispered, frowning.

"But they don't know 'bout this?" he looked at her penetratingly.

Charlotte sighed, and sat on the floor, taking Stefan gently by the arms and meeting his gaze. "No, dear, they don't. I really don't want them or Aunt Mellie to know. You see, I'm really scared when others hear me play. When they don't know who I am, for some reason I feel safe and can play in public."

"I promise I won't tell," he gazed at her solemnly. He carefully put the wig back on its holder and placed it back in the closet. At the sound of someone coming down the hall, he hurriedly closed the closet doors and sat on the floor beside his aunt.

"What are you two doing?" Amy asked as she walked into the room.

"We're just sitting on the floor talking," Stefan laughed, tickling his aunt under the arms.

She felt guilty about Stefan's keeping secrets from his parents. She feared he would accidentally divulge her subterfuge, but he was loyal and had leaked no information.

Now in the wake of Melanie's failure to lure Amy and Mike back to Atlanta, Melanie resorted with all her force and charm to pull Charlotte back to Atlanta, and to cement the ties between Charlotte and Gerard. Charlotte had at first resisted, but she knew that sooner or later she would lose the battle. She felt love and responsibility for the woman who had taken her and Amy in and raised them.

Gerry helped her out by making good his promise to her that she could maintain her ties somewhat to D.C. He offered use of his jet, which he kept at the ready for his ever-widening circle of business interests. He informed her that within a couple hours Charlotte could make it to D.C. for various functions.

Then out of the blue Charlotte was offered a job at the Atlanta *Chronicle*. Although she was initially flattered, she smelled Melanie's influence being behind the offer. She had been making regular submissions to the *Post* and enjoyed her teaching job, but found that teaching full-time was eating into all her other obligations. So she had cut down to one writing class per semester, and realized that if she returned with Melanie to Atlanta that would have to go as well.

Charlotte was finally persuaded by ultimatum, Melanie insisting that she was returning home, with or without her niece. Charlotte negotiated for and won certain concessions from Melanie as to nursing help to assist Charlotte, Daisy and Jacob with Melanie's care so that Charlotte could continue some activities. Melanie kept insisting to know what Charlotte found so riveting she couldn't give up in D.C., but Charlotte reminded Melanie that Charlotte was an adult with her own life.

Charlotte's biggest regret was in leaving Stefan behind. They had developed an attachment so strong that they saw or spoke to each other daily. She followed his development avidly, and was pleased in his proficiency in music as well as his burning desire to share all his accomplishments with her. She felt with her leaving as though a part of her was being ripped from her. And Stefan did not help, with his constant pleading to accompany his aunt to Atlanta. Charlotte finally had to promise him that they would see each other often, and that when he finished his high school studies they 'would see' about his studying in Atlanta.

So Charlotte returned to Atlanta, feeling sad and a little resentful. She, though, had been frightened at Melanie's sudden ill health, and knew that she must do what she could for the family matriarch.

Melanie had insisted on having a small dinner party only a month after Charlotte had come back and her aunt was well enough to make an appearance.

Kreiser was there. Charlotte had managed to place herself and him at opposite ends of the table. However, following dinner, he had followed her back to the kitchen as she busied herself arranging for coffee on a silver tray to be served the guests.

"Carlota," she heard him say. Her back was to him, and she didn't turn around. Finally Kreiser had stood just behind her. He placed his hands on her shoulders.

She resisted a shudder at his touch. "It's been a while," she heard herself saying coolly. "How are you?"

"I'm in hell," he had muttered. "What have I done to you?"

She turned and saw his glittering eyes on her. Impulsively she stated, "You have nothing to worry about. I never told Aunt Mellie anything about—us," she finished lamely. "And I won't be making any embarrassment for you."

"I pretty much guessed that," he remarked dryly. "I'm still in possession of all my body parts, teaching here at the university, and sitting at Melanie's table tonight. I don't think any of those would be true otherwise. But why didn't you tell her?" he asked, his voice low.

"Just because I made a hash of things didn't mean I had to mess up your career," she replied, not looking at him. "After all, you are probably the best organ instructor in this country. And Aunt Mellie adores you."

"At one time I might have challenged that 'probably'," he remarked wryly, "but I wasn't good enough to hold on to you." He turned her to face him, and took her chin in his hand. "Look at me, Carlota," he commanded softly.

She flinched. "Please don't call me that," she warned, trying to pull away.

He held her still, forcing her to look into his cat-like eyes, her heart beating wildly. She whispered, "I waited for you twice. I even abased myself by begging you. You made it crystal clear from your silence." She swallowed. "So I got over you, Harry." She hoped she was convincing. "Isn't that what you want me to say?"

He released her suddenly. Surprised, she swayed toward him.

"Not exactly," he whispered. "Charlotte, I'm sorry. For everything. I never wanted to hurt you."

She looked away, her heart breaking. I'm sorry, too, Harry, she thought.

He asked her softly. "Please don't tell me you have given up performance, Carlota. That would make my crime unforgivable."

Just then Melanie walked into the kitchen, her eyes malevolent. Kreiser quickly took the tray with the coffee. "I just came in to help Charlotte with the tray," he remarked to Melanie, his tone defensive. Charlotte looked from him to her aunt, suddenly understanding.

Later that night, she found herself suddenly face to face with Kreiser again in the salon. "I need your help," he spoke, looking at Melanie sitting nearby. "I would like for you to sit on some of my students' juries."

"I don't know," Charlotte began doubtfully.

But Melanie interrupted. "I think it would be a very good idea, Charlotte. It would be a way for you to give back to the community."

Surprised at her aunt's response, Charlotte had agreed.

Kreiser continued, "And I've already talked to your editor Ed Kline about the paper's covering an organ recital next month. He seemed enthusiastic. Fred Swann is performing at Spivey Hall. I can secure an interview. Your editor was also positive about the paper's regular reviews of artistic events, including the organ recitals of the area."

Hearing the telephone ring, Charlotte murmured, "Excuse me," as she went into the library to answer it.

"Aunt Charl?"

"Yes, dear," Charlotte warmed to the voice of Stefan on the line.

"What 'cha doing?"

"We're having some guests over for dinner," Charlotte explained.

"Is Willy there?"

"Willy who?" Charlotte asked.

"The Kreiser guy you studied with," he explained patiently.

"Yes, as a matter of fact, he is," Charlotte frowned.

"Good. I want to study with him, because you did. I'm trying to talk Mom and Dad into it."

"But you promised to finish your studies first," Charlotte protested.

"But I'm taking accelerated courses, so I'll be finished in a year or two," he was exasperated. "Don't you want me there?"

"Dear, I want nothing more," Charlotte almost choked, tears suddenly in her eyes. "I miss you, Stefan."

"I miss you too," he said. "I'm trying to make it happen. I gotta go—they don't know I'm up."

"Go to bed, dear," Charlotte murmured.

"Play something for me when they are all gone," Stefan wheedled.

"Love you," Charlotte whispered, as she replaced the phone. She sat by the telephone several minutes, battling tears, overcome with sadness over the geographic distance between her and Stefan. Dear child, she thought.

She did not notice Melanie studying her from the doorway. "What is it, dear?" Melanie asked.

Charlotte started guiltily. "Oh, nothing," she sniffed. "I'm sorry."

"What's wrong?" Melanie came up to her and laid a hand on her shoulder.

"Nothing," Charlotte wiped her eyes with a tissue from Melanie's desk. "It was Stefan."

"Is anything the matter?" Melanie was instantly concerned.

"Oh no, they are all fine," Charlotte smiled reassuringly. "I just miss him."

Charlotte turned to go back, but Melanie restrained her. "I am so sorry if making you return with me has separated you from Stefan," she said quietly.

"It's OK," Charlotte tried to shrug it off. "I owe you so very much, and coming back here will be good for me, I'm sure. I know how much you missed home, and I'm glad I can do this."

She laughed. "Besides, Stefan is scheming about how he can move down here with us. He wants to study with Harry, God help us."

Melanie studied her intently. Charlotte moved away "I must check on our guests, Aunt Mellie. They'll wonder what has happened to us."

Chapter 33

Charlotte did review the recital of the performer, well-known international recitalist Frederick Swann. She arranged to take him and Kreiser to dinner the evening before the recital for the interview. They had an interesting conversation, sitting in the restaurant overlooking the city's twinkling lights. She asked him about what he thought of Spivey Hall, which opened up the conversation to Emilie Spivey and his long acquaintance and friendship with her.

While Kreiser and Swann reminisced about people they knew in common, Charlotte listened and made notes. She was annoyed that Kreiser was less than helpful with his constant interruptions. Kreiser kept looking at her with a sardonic smile, as though testing her, daring her to stop him. Swann looked over at the two of them, attuned to the battle of wills.

"OK, Charlotte, this is not accomplishing your goal," he drawled. "If you are going to ply me with good food and drink, I should be answering your questions. Let's send Harry off to the bar while we talk."

She smiled, grateful for his perception, while Harry rolled his eyes and hoisted himself out of his chair. Left alone, Charlotte and Swann were free to discuss his career, and why he was devoted to performing the Healey Willan *Introduction, Passacaglia and Fugue.*

"I heard my teenage idol, William Watkins, play this when I was about 15. I lived in the Shenandoah Valley of Virginia, but spent part of many summers in D.C. with my sister and got to know Bill well. In those years, he was organist of the New York Avenue Presbyterian Church, during the pastorate of the famous Peter Marshall. I fell in love with the piece, and persuaded my teacher at Northwestern University to let me learn it during my second year. I played it so often that I expected repeat audiences to start singing along with me!

"I finally put it away many years ago, but continue to resurrect it upon request, which happens almost annually. I think it's an excellent vehicle for showing off a large and colorful organ, so I often use it at new organ dedication recitals.

"Shortly after I went to New York City I played it for Dr. Willan in Toronto. He was most generous in his comments, and told me, 'I hope this little piece [he was a very modest man] will serve you well in your career.' It has."

"Any secrets, anecdotes, the like, you'd like to see in print?" she smiled slyly.

From there they shared stories about the various performers they had met, laughing merrily.

Swann looked at her as the conversation lulled. "May I ask you a question?" he asked politely.

"Sure," Charlotte responded, curious.

"If I recall correctly, you were a fabulous pianist and organist, once a star student of Harry's. But you chose this instead of a career as a performer."

Charlotte fingered her wine glass, intent upon the contents. "We all have dreams, but sometimes real life intervenes and sends us down the 'road less traveled'," she looked away. "Something happened, and I have trouble performing in public now." She smiled tightly. "Thankfully I'm not too bad at this job."

"Is that why Harry cancelled your recital at Riverside Church?" he studied her closely.

She caught her breath. "Something like that, yes," she stammered, blushing with shame. "I had forgotten you knew about that."

Swann leaned forward, his tone confidential. "I don't know what happened. It's none of my business, Charlotte. But you need to work on that poker face. I can read from your eyes that Kreiser drew blood at some time or another. I'm a pretty good judge, and I've known Harry a while, so my guess is that it was a serious blow. I hope that did not deter you from a career in performance."

She looked down at her hands, embarrassed. "I didn't know I was that transparent."

"Like I said, none of my business."

Changing the subject, she asked, more brightly than she felt, "Do you want to preview the article before it goes to print?"

"No one has asked me that before," Swann laughed. "No, I trust you. And don't let Harry read it beforehand either."

In the end, the interview and review received favorable response from the readers.

After that, with Melanie's encouragement, Charlotte became involved with the music program at the college, sponsoring Kreiser's students' participation in American Guild of Organist conventions, helping Kreiser to solicit local recital venues for the organ students to hone their skills, acting as judge in the students' juries and securing internationally known recitalists and teachers as judges for area competitions, master classes and recitals.

She renewed her close association with Dr. Conrad, and helped him with fundraising and publicity for the Symphony. She again championed the youth orchestra, helping to subsidize events for them to perform and to participate in master classes. Conrad asked her to mentor a couple of young child piano prodigies.

She also worked closely with Ed Kline, her editor at the *Chronicle*, to promote the organ through publicizing events and writing reviews. This brought her into more contact with Kreiser. However, she kept their contact professional and in the presence of others, so that they were not alone.

In return, Kreiser smoothed introductions to his colleagues coming into the city for recitals, and consulted with her on fundraising events and ways to recognize the students for achievement. They coordinated master classes and workshops, and she and Melanie subsidized the students' trips to educational events.

Charlotte was careful to involve Melanie in these activities, and Melanie was willing to act as the unspoken buffer between Charlotte and Kreiser for the purpose of promoting the projects. And Melanie involved Charlotte in more and more social causes in the city.

Although Charlotte could no longer make every-Tuesday ensemble rehearsals in D.C., she kept performing with the quartet, which in her absence was now doing more repertoire not requiring piano. Gerry installed a grand piano at his apartment, so that she could practice without the knowledge of others. So without explanation she was still leaving, flying up to D. C. and even to Boston and New York for occasional concerts. A few times Dr. Conrad would accompany her, when he was able to get away. During these excursions she would discuss with him various projects of the symphony and the possibility of future collaboration with Kreiser.

And she was keeping up a daily telephone or e-mail correspondence with Jonathan, as he kept exhorting her to rely less on her disguises and to try to play without them. She discussed her continuing involvement with Kreiser, which he applauded. "I think that you need to loosen that grip on the fantasy of the two of you together," Jonathan replied. "Familiarity may breed exposure and a building up of immunity, when you are not able to muster contempt." She had laughed at that.

Gerard was noticing her regular contact with Jonathan. One day at his apartment after she had hung up her cell phone from talking to Jonathan, she was surprised to see Gerry standing there regarding her.

"How long have you been standing there?" she asked uncomfortably.

"Not long," he admitted. "Are you seeing this guy?" he was direct.

"You might say that," she mumbled.

"Why didn't you tell me you had a new boyfriend?" he flushed.

"It's not like that," Charlotte faced him. "Gerry, Jonathan is—he's the clinical psychologist I was seeing in D.C. I've been having sessions regularly with him for a while now." She looked down at her hands. "I didn't want anyone to know," she confessed, and smiled. "Actually, Jonathan and Evan are gay. They're partners."

Gerry was contrite. "I'm sorry. Why didn't you think you could tell me?"

"What, and have you thinking like the rest of my family that I'm looney? No way," Charlotte pinched him on the arm.

One day she invited Kreiser to tea at Melanie's. When he arrived, he found Melanie, Dean Jackson, Conrad and Charlotte already there.

"Is this some sort of intervention?" he demanded, suddenly testy.

"In a sense, yes," Charlotte took the lead. "I think it's time the Symphony performed with organ again. I don't want an outsider brought in, when we have the greatest organist right here in our midst. I have asked you here for a purpose."

Peter Conrad stood, looking askance at Charlotte before plunging in. "Harry, I want to engage you to play the Poulenc."

Kreiser was taken aback. "But you haven't spoken to me in years."

"I would still not be talking to you if it wasn't for Charlotte," Conrad replied stiffly. "She wants us to set aside our differences and start anew. I'm willing for her sake to do that. I told her I wanted to program the music, and she has persuaded me the Symphony cannot do it without you."

"But I didn't have any differences with you," Kreiser retorted.

Conrad hissed angrily, "Your star pupil and mine is not enjoying a career of public performance and international stardom, and you fold your hands as if you had nothing to do with causing it? I'm supposed to just accept Charlotte's version of the 'performance anxiety' story? I know what happened, and I hold you personally responsible, Harry. I too trusted you, apparently wrongly."

Charlotte tried to intervene, but Kreiser faced Conrad, his head bowed. "You are entirely correct. I am to blame. Don't you think I pay for it daily?" his voice was low. "I have no business still being here, and should have left some time ago."

He stood to leave. Charlotte shouted, "Stop it, all of you!"

They all looked at her, speechless.

"Enough," she was vehement. "I want this stalemate between the two of you to end. Atlanta is not big enough for its two greatest artists to behave like this. And I am certainly not worth all this fuss, when the musical world is the great loser."

She could not bring herself to face Kreiser at the moment of her vulnerability, so she turned to Conrad. "Peter, please. It is me you need to forgive, for squandering your efforts with me and for disappointing you." Her voice turned to a whisper, her face flushed from embarrassment. "You, of all people, know I am trying. It would make me very happy if you and Harry can make amends."

Conrad's eyes glistened. "You know I will do anything for you, Charlotte," he murmured. He turned to Kreiser. "I want you to do the Poulenc. But I want you sober."

Kreiser pursed his lips, as Charlotte turned back to him. "I agree," she said quietly, their eyes meeting. "You are drinking too much, and your performance is slipping. You have a great gift still to share. Please do this."

Kreiser stared at her, and finally nodded. "I too will do anything for you, Charlotte. And I beg for your forgiveness. It has always been my dream that you would be the one playing it. But I will do it."

Charlotte felt faint. Thankfully Daisy walked in just at that time with a tea tray, and she helped Daisy serve tea and scones.

Before he left that evening, Kreiser whispered to her, "Come to me. Tonight."

Her heart suddenly twisted painfully.

Late that night, Kreiser, sitting in his pajamas and robe and listening to music, heard the doorbell ring at his home. Walking to the door and opening it, he saw Charlotte standing there, dressed in sweats.

"You came," he smiled at her with relief.

"I had to," she said simply.

He nodded and stood aside to let her pass.

She suddenly recognized the music. "Liszt!" she whispered. "Were you that confident I would do your bidding?"

"I knew it was inevitable that you would appear," Kreiser took her hand and kissed it. "You come to me every night in my dreams, and tonight I cannot sleep."

He pulled her to him and kissed her, a long, slow lingering kiss. Charlotte returned his kiss ardently. They remained entwined for several minutes.

The music ended. "Thank you for what you did today. I know how much it cost you," he murmured in her ear.

"I had to do it. I could not bear Peter's enmity toward you, and had to make peace between you."

He whispered to her, "Make love to me, Carlota."

"I want to so badly," she whispered, her hands moving down his torso, pulling his robe open.

"No," he demurred, pulling away and gently dragging her behind him. She followed him and he stopped at the grand piano. He pointed to the bench. "Make love to me with music," he spoke.

Tears filled her eyes. "You know I cannot do this," she croaked.

"Come to me," he demanded, sitting on the bench and indicating the space beside him.

She shrank away, but he drew her to sit beside him. "I cannot live without hearing you. I am drowning. You must save me. Play for me."

Pointing to a score on the piano's music desk, he ordered, "I have not heard this since you were playing it when you were sixteen."

She stared at the music, a book of Rachmaninoff piano preludes turned open to the fourth from Opus 23. She thought back to a rainy afternoon when she was practicing *L'Isle joyeuse* by Claude Debussy in the front parlor at Aunt Mellie's, while Kreiser reclined on the fainting couch and listened. Every now and then he would insert a suggestion, and at one time he came to sit beside her on the piano bench.

"I would not presume to tell Dr. Harmon how to do her job, but this is a proclamation before the major climactic point," he spoke, placing his hands over hers and pressing gently.

She followed his instructions without argument, backing up and beginning again. "Yes," she remembered his sigh close to her ear.

When she had finished, he took her by the arms and made her face him.

"My dearest one, I want you to play this for my memorial service," he whispered to her, his eyes brimming with tears.

She stared at him, stunned, before he quickly changed the subject. "Now I want to hear some Rachmaninoff," he placed the book, the same book, before her.

The memories came rushing over her as the present reasserted itself and Kreiser was again sitting beside her and asking her to play it for him. She demurred. "Harry, I don't think I can any more."

"Please try, *cara mia*," he crooned. "It is my favorite, and it is the easiest. I will help you."

She stared at the page, then began, very tentatively, with the *andante cantabile* in D major. She remembered working on many of the preludes, particularly when she was preparing for the Stanford audition that never came to pass.

"Wait for it," Kreiser whispered as she slowed in measure six, then resumed. She remembered having this conversation before with Kreiser and the nuances he sought, as the music flowed from her. She felt the old excitement as she hesitantly recalled the patterns in the notes. As she came to the recapitulation of the theme, he said quietly against her ear, "The lovely exercise of eighths against triplets—it's like you and me making love."

She caught her breath and continued, her heartbeat quickening. She forced her breathing to match his as he murmured agreement with her moments of *rubato*. She completed the final *diminuendo*, and he stood behind her, molding himself to her back.

She started to stand, but he placed his hands on her shoulders. "Next, please," he whispered, turning the page.

She stared at the Number 5 prelude, before launching in. At the *un poco meno mosso*, she faltered as he trailed kisses down her neck. "Continue," he commanded quietly. "Let it flow from your gut, *cara*. Fill me with your music."

Just as she reached the final bars, he walked away. She finished, almost trancelike, only to look up and see him standing at the end of the piano, drink in hand. She noted that his hand trembled.

She quickly stood and walked over to him. "Please, Harry, don't drink," she begged, taking the glass gently from him. "Please love me," she stared at him.

"You need to leave now, before I do something I shall regret," he mumbled, turning from her, snatching the glass from her and drinking deeply, downing the drink in a gulp.

"Please don't push me away," she cried, grabbing his arm. "Why did you ask me to come? I want you so badly. I'm the one who's drowning."

He set down the glass and turned, violently taking her throat in both his hands, giving her a punishing kiss. She gasped for breath as he choked air from her windpipe, grabbed her arms roughly and pushed her back, causing her to fall onto the sofa, with him immediately on top of her, pinning her down.

Surprised by his strength, she whimpered in pain as he jerked her head back by the hair, continuing his assault on her. He choked back her cry as he imprisoned her mouth, then held her immobile while undressing her, his hands ripping at her clothes, his lips moving down her body. She tasted blood on her lip. She struggled vainly against him, as he held her captive, her wrists held by one strong hand while the other stroked her savagely.

Finally she choked out, "You're hurting me."

"I intend to," he muttered darkly. "I want you to hate me."

She continued to push, to struggle against him, as he held her down, his movements savage and unrelenting. He suddenly entered her with such force she screamed.

"Please, Harry," she panted, frightened, a sob catching in her throat. "Don't do this. I love you. I'll give you anything you want. I can't live without you."

He froze. As quickly as it happened, it was over. Muttering an oath, Krieser rolled off her and stood. "Leave now, Charlotte."

He strode out of the room and she heard his bedroom door slam and lock.

Shaken and hurt, she looked around her confusedly. She rolled off the sofa onto the floor, curling into a fetal position, burying her head against her arm, too spent to cry.

She finally roused herself, before standing. She pulled her clothes back on, and noted a dark drop on the sofa, realizing that her lip was still bleeding. She licked her lip gingerly, picking up her keys and staggering out, holding her abdomen, nauseous.

Chapter 34

Somehow Charlotte made it to her car, her gut in turmoil. She stared at the dashboard blindly a long time before turning the key in the ignition. She drove aimlessly, trying to block out thoughts of Kreiser and his violence toward her, trying to stem the shaking of her limbs.

She finally made it home and slipped inside quietly, locking up behind her. She prayed that Melanie would not appear out of nowhere and demand to know where she had been. She staggered up the stairs and fell into bed in the dark without undressing, afraid to look at her reflection in a mirror, fearful of what she might see. She crawled under the covers and lay there fitfully, her body on fire aching with pain but her mind numb. Sleep eluded her for several hours.

That night she had the dream. She heard Kreiser's voice accusing her. She felt his hands closing around her throat. Charlotte tried to cry out, but no sound would come.

She woke up suddenly when she heard her name called and the lights came on. She found herself standing in the hallway outside her bedroom, pointing her Sig Sauer pistol at her aunt, who stared at her terror-stricken.

Melanie sat heavily on the bench in the hallway, clutching her chest. Charlotte blinked, bewildered. "What—?" she asked, lowering the weapon.

"My God, Charlotte," Melanie cried, her voice weak. "Can you tell me what you are doing with a gun in my house?"

Charlotte shook her head confusedly. "I don't know. I swear, Aunt Mellie, I don't know what's going on."

"Please put that down," Melanie begged. Charlotte sat down beside her and complied, laying it between them. Melanie looked at it and recoiled in horror.

"The safety is on," Charlotte whispered, putting her hand on her aunt's shoulder comfortingly.

"You have been having nightmares," Melanie informed her haltingly. "Some nights I hear you screaming. I was coming to check on you, and you've apparently taken up sleepwalking. How long has this been going on?"

Charlotte shook her head. "On and off," she was suddenly reticent.

"But—I never—Charlotte—" she dabbed her eyes with a tissue, "my God, a gun?"

"I'm sorry. Gerry gave it to me when I lived in D.C. He thought I should have protection. I always keep it in the drawer of my bedside table."

"After tonight it goes in the safe," Melanie stated emphatically, although she shuddered. "What is bothering you?"

"Nothing," Charlotte replied firmly.

"We will get a discreet referral from Dr. Amason," Melanie directed. "We can't have you walking around being a danger to yourself."

"And others," Charlotte mumbled under her breath.

"And others," Melanie echoed, to Charlotte's surprise. "Now put that—thing in the safe right now."

The next afternoon Charlotte was summoned home early from work by Melanie. When she arrived, she found Melanie and a man in the drawing room. The man she judged to be in his early forties, medium height, slim, with dark hair speckled with gray, handsome in navy suit, and wearing round spectacles. He smiled engagingly as Charlotte burst into the room, acknowledging him briefly.

"What is it?" she asked breathlessly. "You scared me. What is wrong?"

Melanie came forward and took her arm, guiding her to the man. Charlotte winced at the pressure on her bruised forearm, encased in long sleeves. "This is Dr. Foreman, Charlotte. Dr. Amason has referred him for your nightmares and sleepwalking. He's a noted neurologist."

"Hello, Dr. Foreman," she shook his hand formally. "I'm sorry Melanie has asked you here on a wild goose chase. Nothing is wrong with me," Charlotte insisted, pulling gently away from Melanie. "I've had this all my life, Aunt Mellie."

"But not to this extent," Melanie sniffed. "I want her tested, Doctor. Whatever it takes. However, you must be discreet."

Charlotte rubbed her forehead wearily. The man instantly spoke up. "Are you having headaches, Miss Lawson?"

"Please call me Charlotte. No," she replied irritably. "Yes, sometimes. It's nothing. Just stress," she muttered.

"You say you've had this 'all your life'. What do you mean?" he asked kindly.

"I'm sorry, Dr.—" she paused.

"Foreman," he repeated. "Jeff, if you like."

"I have had nightmares ever since I can remember."

"Have they worsened as you've gotten older?"

"Yes," she replied shortly.

"Do you remember them? Are you having a recurring nightmare of some sort?"

"I don't remember them," she lied, quickly looking at Melanie furtively. "I don't know."

"You don't think sleepwalking with a gun in your hand is serious?" his eyebrows lifted in inquiry.

"No—yes. I mean," she stammered, "it won't happen again."

"How do you know?" he persisted. "How can you be sure?"

"I've locked the gun up," Charlotte became testy. "What do you want me to do?" she turned to Melanie. "Tie myself to the bed every night? Let's go whole hog and have me committed."

Melanie quickly crossed over to stand beside her and took her by the arm. Charlotte bit her swollen lip in pain. "My dear, I'm concerned about you." She peered closely at her. "Have you cut your lip?"

"It's nothing," Charlotte mumbled. She self-consciously placed her fingers over the turtleneck collar, fiddling with the scarf around her neck, glad the bruising around her throat was hidden. "You, who are always worried about the press reporting dirt on us, have engaged a doctor to examine me? You think I'm crazy?" she cried.

Melanie spoke quietly. "Charlotte, I'm truly worried. This is getting worse. You are scaring me."

Dr. Foreman, also standing by this time, gestured toward the sofa. "Can't we all just sit down and discuss this rationally a moment? I assure you, Charlotte, none of this information will leave this room."

Melanie guided Charlotte firmly to the sofa and sat down, pulling her down beside her. Dr. Foreman regained his seat in the wing chair.

He smiled briefly. "This is much better. Charlotte, can you tell me about how often you have the nightmares?"

Charlotte was clearly unhappy, but Melanie patted her hand, prodding her. "I don't know, maybe once or twice per week."

"Some weeks every night," Melanie supplied. Charlotte frowned.

"What about the sleepwalking?" he added.

"I don't know. I don't think it's that often," Charlotte gazed at him, then at Melanie, as if she expected Melanie to gainsay her.

Foreman turned to Melanie. "Is it easy to wake her from the nightmares or sleepwalking?"

"Not always," Melanie confessed. "I was afraid last night she might shoot me, but I could tell she was not herself. I was more afraid what might happen when I did manage to wake her."

Foreman nodded sympathetically. "Charlotte, you mentioned stress. What sort of stress are you under right now? Do you notice any particular events or persons that occur in close proximity to the dreams, something that might act as a trigger?"

Charlotte shook her head in the negative, meeting his gaze warily.

Melanie interrupted. "But at tea yesterday, you became upset." And she stared at her niece. "And you left last night and were gone until late. Where were you? Has it anything to do with Harry?"

Charlotte's eyes grew wide with surprise that her aunt had been aware of her absence. "I just had to run to the store for—for some headache tablets," she stammered, floundering for an excuse. "After that I just drove around."

Dr. Foreman looked at her with interest, and Melanie stared at her disbelievingly. He asked, "Charlotte, have you ever had any medical testing for the headaches? Any CT scans? MRI?"

"No," Charlotte's answer was curt.

"Have you ever seen an expert, a psychiatrist or psychologist, in connection with this or any other stress you've experienced?" Foreman was direct.

Melanie sputtered, "Of course, she hasn't."

But Charlotte stopped her, holding her hand in the air to silence Melanie. "I've been in therapy with a psychologist for a few years," she replied quietly, not acknowledging Melanie's swift surprised intake of breath.

"Charlotte, darling, why didn't you tell me?" Melanie whispered, gripping Charlotte's arm. Charlotte gasped.

Charlotte and she locked gazes, and it was as if they forgot Foreman was in the room. "Probably for the very reason that you assumed I haven't seen one. We have to maintain that façade that everything is OK, that nothing is wrong. I knew you'd be horrified to know that I'm actually quite fucked up," she finished, half-hoping to shock her aunt with her language.

But she was unprepared for Melanie's reaction. Melanie threw her arms around Charlotte's neck. "What have I done to so utterly lose your trust in me?" she cried softly. "I always knew I was not equipped to be a parent, but to think there's so wide a gulf between us . . . I love you. Please forgive me, Charlotte."

Charlotte was stunned, dumbly holding her aunt as her aunt cried. She finally found her voice. "Aunt Mellie, you are not to blame," she spoke quietly, gingerly returning her aunt's embrace. "I take full responsibility for my wrong decisions. It's just that I don't seem to learn from them. I keep finding myself inside the hamster wheel, going round and round."

"I know, and I would do anything to heal your hurt," Melanie whispered brokenly.

If only you knew, Charlotte thought sadly. "Please don't cry, Melanie. You're the queen of this castle. I can't handle it if you aren't the strong one."

Melanie wiped her eyes. "Then you'll agree to undergo testing with Dr. Foreman? To rule out any physical cause?"

Charlotte smiled inwardly. So this was what the tears were about, she thought. "Yes, Auntie, I will do the tests, as long as it doesn't interfere with my job." She looked over at Foreman. "You win."

Both Conrad and Kreiser kept their word, and the Poulenc Concerto was a huge success. Charlotte felt a burden lift as the two men took their bows together before a packed audience of enthusiastic fans, Conrad blowing her a kiss. Kreiser also looked at her searchingly, his face grim, but she could not meet his gaze. She turned away, swallowing at the memory of his assault.

Chapter 35

Evan called her one day after she had been gone from D.C. for some time. "Guess what, Charlotte? I have a chance to fly to Paris for a week and to play at Notre Dame!"

"Oh, I am so jealous," she confessed. "What a wonderful opportunity."

"That's why I'm calling," he told her. "I need a substitute for that Sunday."

"Oh, Evan, no," she breathed. "I can' t do that. There are plenty of good young organists in D.C."

"But they're not you. Just wear your black wig as Tabitha, and it will go well," he coaxed her. "I promise to make it easy on you. *A capella* motet and anthem, directed by one of my choristers. I bet Erik would do it. You can choose whatever you want, and I'll give you the hymns and service music in advance. Just come in for the weekend. Don't say no."

So Charlotte found herself in a dilemma. How am I going to do this? she wondered. Could she leave Melanie alone with a nurse for the weekend? Did she ask Amy to come down? What explanation would she give? Stefan would be upset if she made an appearance in D.C. without seeing him, but she couldn't very well appear at church in disguise with Stefan in tow, or the game would be up.

But Melanie unknowingly created a solution. She decided that she would accept her friend Agatha Fellowes' invitation to go to Biloxi for the weekend. When she relayed her decision to Charlotte, Charlotte was dumbstruck.

"Biloxi? Since when have you ever wanted to gamble?" she asked, incredulous.

"I don't," Melanie answered imperiously. "But there are good food, shows, and Agatha says I will enjoy the slot machines."

"But do you feel that you should in your condition?" Charlotte could not believe her aunt.

"Charlotte, I'm not a complete invalid, and I don't intend to start being one now," Melanie sniffed. "When I die, I want to die on my feet. You aren't the only one wanting some fun time on her own."

Charlotte tried to argue with her, but Melanie was obstinate. So Charlotte gave up the fight, but bought her aunt a cell phone and programmed all the family's numbers into it, showing her how to use it.

"Thanks for your concern, Charlotte, but I'm going to be fine," Melanie insisted after Charlotte continued to ply her with information and exhortations to be careful. "Go on to D.C. and be with Stefan."

Charlotte sputtered. "How did you know?"

Melanie shook her head. "You'd be surprised. There's so much about you that you think is secret from me," she replied.

Charlotte stared at her, but Melanie placed her hand over Charlotte's. "Go. Make your plans. I'll be fine."

So Charlotte packed, and they left home at the same time, Melanie and Agatha being flown in Gerry's jet to Biloxi, and Charlotte catching a commercial flight to Dulles.

At the airport before catching her flight, she called Amy. "You are going to church Sunday?" she asked breathlessly.

"Of course," Amy said. "Why? What's up?"

"I'm on my way up for the weekend. Stefan and I have a surprise for you," Charlotte answered.

"What?" Amy began.

But Charlotte cut her off. "Just make sure you show up for the principal service on Sunday. And is it possible that Stefan spend a little time with me Saturday?"

"Of course, but what are you doing up here? Why didn't you let me know? What about Aunt Mellie?"

"Aunt Mellie is her own boss, and has gone with Agatha to Biloxi for the weekend. I have to do a favor for a friend and I wanted to see you all, so am coming up."

"Biloxi? Since when—?"

"My question exactly, but Melanie was adamant she wanted to go, that she wasn't an invalid, and that was that."

"You didn't try to talk her out of it?" Amy was insistent.

"Damn it, Sis, I'm not a moron. I used every argument against it, but Melanie gets her way, as usual. They're on Gerry's jet now." She checked her watch. "I've got to catch my plane. I will talk to you when I get there."

She had talked to Stefan by telephone the previous evening, telling him that she had him a 'gig' to play the prelude at church that Sunday. He was excited, but even more excited that she was coming. She swore him to secrecy, telling him the prelude was a surprise for his parents.

So she was elated, having a weekend all to herself. But she knew that she was happy because she was going to see Stefan again. I can't help it, she thought. I love my little boy, even though he's not my little boy.

So she secretly hugged the thought to herself on the flight up. However, the more she saw of Stefan and discerned his resemblance to her, both physically and developmentally, the more an incredible thought niggled at her. She wrestled with it at unguarded moments, part of her wanting to believe the idea, part of her telling herself it could not be true. There, stuck on the plane with nothing to do but to sort through music scores and jot notes to herself for the next weekly review in her column, the thought invaded her consciousness again.

What if Stefan was really her son? What if her child did not actually die, but some fraud or switch occurred, so that Amy and Mike could adopt him? No one in my family would do that to me, she told herself. But she had doubts: would Melanie arrange such a terrible deed? Charlotte felt that Melanie always favored Amy, and Charlotte maintained the impression that Melanie felt her to be inept. Charlotte felt herself to be a major disappointment, if not a total disgrace, to Melanie. But would Melanie have schemed to take away her child?

There was no way, she argued to herself. Melanie did not know about the pregnancy. But what if she did? Amy was known to tell her aunt everything, keeping nothing from her. But, Charlotte assured herself, I know Michael would not have allowed such a thing to happen. But, she thought, what if Mike didn't know either? No, she argued, I'm utterly crazy. She was so irritable with herself that she ordered a vodka tonic and sipped it, hoping it would drown out the direction of her mind processes.

By the time she debarked with her overnight bag, she was again calm, laughing at her paranoid tendencies. Intent only on hailing a cab, she suddenly heard her name called.

Turning, she saw Michael and Stefan coming toward her. Stefan broke into a run, as she flung open her arms and they embraced. "Oh, my God, Stefan, how you have grown in the last few weeks," she whispered, tears in her eyes as she held him tightly.

He clung to her. "Were you surprised? Dad found out which flight you were on, and I begged him to take me to meet you."

"You have one great dad," she stood and hugged Mike. "Thanks, Bro," she kissed his cheek.

"We've missed you, Sis," he squeezed her affectionately. "Some more than others," he added as Stefan looked up at her with adoring eyes.

"This is a great homecoming," she said. "It's not the same without you guys."

"You are coming to my game Saturday?" Stefan interrupted.

"What game?" she asked.

"Your nephew has taken up basketball," Michael informed her.

"My favorite!" she exclaimed.

"I knew that," Stefan grinned.

"But we have to make some time for our little project Saturday," she reminded him.

"Shh," he said. "Don't tell our secret."

Mike looked at both of them. "I heard nothing," he smiled.

They walked through the terminal, Mike taking her bag, and she and Stefan strolled hand in hand as he chattered and she listened. Mike left them to get the car.

"What about new girlfriends?" she teased Stefan.

"Aw, Aunt Charlotte, you know you're my girlfriend," he giggled.

"I don't know," she said doubtfully. "When I left here last, there was that little violinist you were sweet on."

"Aw, I was just talking," he blushed.

"What's her name again?"

"Susan," he laughed. "Yeah, she's cute. But we're just friends."

"So what are you going to play Sunday?" she asked, her tone conspiratorial. "I talked to your teacher earlier, and he says he thinks you are ready for the ones we discussed as possibilities. Some on your list seems a little ambitious for a thirteen year old."

"Almost fourteen," he interrupted.

"OK, almost fourteen. I just don't want you to bite off more than you can chew."

"Piece of cake," he said with such confidence she laughed. He added, "I've been listening to E. Power Biggs' recordings of Bach. I think I can do as well as he did."

"E. Power Biggs?" she echoed disbelievingly. "My heavens, please don't take sides in that battle."

He flashed her a grin. "My teacher says I'm a 'middle-of-the-roader', that I'm more flashy than Biggs but more straight than Virgil Fox."

She laughed. "That didn't come from Alan Meredith; that's straight from Harry." She sobered as she saw the youth regarding her intently.

"Tell me about him."

Taken aback, she was relieved when Michael's car pulled up beside them. "Later, OK?" she responded.

Michael asked as she climbed in beside him, "Are you staying with us? Stefan would be happy if you did."

"I'd like that very much, but I don't think so," Charlotte replied. "I just think it's better this way. And I really need my own set of wheels."

"Aw, Aunt Charlotte," Stefan whined.

Mike reached over and squeezed her hand. "You know you're always welcome with us."

"Thanks, but it's part of the surprise," Charlotte murmured. "If you can drop me off, I need to leave my stuff, and then I'll be happy to see you back at home and take you all out to dinner."

"I don't think so. Amy is cooking dinner," Mike laughed.

"Cooking? Oh, my God," Charlotte gasped in mock terror. "When did she pick this up?"

"She thought it would be nice to have a regular family dinner at home at least twice per week," Michael explained.

Stefan, in the back seat, made a face. "Ugh. Mom hasn't mastered the Betty Crocker thing yet," he complained. "But Dad says we must make an effort."

"It's not that bad," Michael reprimanded Stefan, then looked at Charlotte as Stefan guffawed and he joined in. "Actually, it's pretty bad," he coughed through his laughter. "It wouldn't be bad if she just heated some Stouffer's or something, but she wants to cook from scratch."

"And Dad says her successes are few and far between," Stefan confided.

"Shh," Mike looked through the rearview mirror at his son. "You're being disloyal to your mom."

"Daisy despaired of teaching Amy to cook, so I'm surprised she is reploughing that field," Charlotte smiled at the two.

"You have to save us," Stefan groaned melodramatically.

"I'll call her from my place and tell her I'm dying to go to Citronelle, and see if she won't agree to it," Charlotte promised. "I'll call first to see if I can wangle a reservation. She's going to hate me."

"You're her sister. She'll get over it," Michael laughed.

Chapter 36

Charlotte made good her promise and called her sister once she made it into the townhouse with her bag. She first dialed information and obtained the number of the restaurant, then called and made inquiry as to reservations, securing a table for four. Then she rang up Amy.

Amy answered. "Yes?" she said breathlessly, a hint of a sob in her voice.

Charlotte was surprised. "Amy? It's Charlotte. Is anything wrong?"

"Oh, Charlotte," she sniffed unhappily. "I've burned the pot roast. I was trying so hard to cook a nice dinner for you."

Charlotte smiled. "That's the sweetest thing you've ever done, Sis. I'm so grateful."

"But it's ruined," Amy wailed. "I will never hear the end of this from Mike."

"All is not lost," Charlotte broke in sympathetically. "I didn't know you were cooking," she lied, "and I thought we might go to Citronelle. It's been a while since I've been there, and it's getting rave reviews. In hopes you would say yes, I made advance reservations."

"Really?" Amy responded, hopefully, Charlotte surmised.

"Just bury the evidence," Charlotte laughed, "and get your glad rags on. I'll just meet you all there about seven."

Charlotte unpacked her small bag, taking out the black wig she had brought, as well as the makeup case. Just as she finished, she heard the front door close. A burglar? she thought.

Suddenly frightened, she made her way to the great room and peered at the doorway. There stood Gerry, a carryon bag in his hand.

"Gerry, what are you doing here?" she exclaimed with surprise, as he stood regarding her.

"I could ask the same thing," he replied. "Remember I asked to crash here this weekend?"

"Oh, I forgot," she was chagrined. "I'm sorry. I can always stay with Amy and Mike."

"No," he smiled. "I'm not having a romantic rendezvous here. I just had some business in the city." He grinned. "You aren't scared to stay here with me, are you?"

"I could take you in a fight. No, I'm not," Charlotte took the implied challenge, her chin lifted, her eyes glinting.

"Yeah, in your dreams," he laughed. "Why are you in town, or should I ask?"

"Well, your mom and Melanie are on their way to Biloxi, so I was free to come up for the weekend and cover a service for Evan," she explained.

"As yourself or someone else?" he asked sarcastically.

"Don't tease me," she turned away. "Do you have plans for tonight? I'm taking the family to Citronelle. I'd be glad to have you join us."

"Sure," he commented. "I've got to make a quick call. Which room is mine?"

"Take your pick," she taunted him.

"Don't tempt me," he flung back behind him, as he headed up the stairs toward the guestroom.

While deciding on what to wear, she decided she really needed a soda. As she walked by the guestroom door, she heard him, "I'm sorry, baby. You know I never know when business intervenes. I miss you too. I'll talk to you later."

She smiled to herself as she went to the fridge. The private housekeeping service had stocked the refrigerator, and she grabbed a cold soft drink. As she shut the refrigerator, she heard him in the living room.

She sauntered into the room to see him mixing a drink at the bar. "I didn't mean for you to break a hot date for us, Gerry," she protested.

"I had no intention of seeing her tonight," he didn't look up as he poured scotch into a tumbler. "You just provided a perfect excuse."

"Business?" she murmured. "I didn't know we had business together."

"So I lied," he walked through a door to the kitchen looking for ice.

"Who is she?" Charlotte wanted to know.

"Nobody important," he said through the door. "Just Kimmy Randolph."

"Geez, you're standing up some big guns there," Charlotte whistled as he reentered the room. "Looks and money and family, oh my."

"But she's boring. I like her dad a lot, but her . . ."

"Gerry, you need to commit sometime," Charlotte spoke. "You would make a fabulous father, and now is the time."

"You sound like Agatha," Gerry sipped his drink. "I'll pick my own wife, thank you."

"OK, OK," Charlotte retreated upstairs to her room, as he followed her, going into the guestroom.

Soon they were ready, and walked out the door together. Charlotte looked with distaste at the limousine waiting by the door. "Can't we take the Lexus?" she pleaded. "It's just been sitting in the garage. I need to use it tomorrow, so there's no time like the present to try it out."

Gerry waved Tom away. "Take the night off," he instructed the driver.

As they pulled out of the garage, Charlotte driving, Gerry looked at her admiringly. "You clean up well," he remarked.

"So do you," she retorted as she carefully eased her way into traffic.

When they arrived, Amy, Mike and Stefan were already there. Stefan ran up to her. "Thank you, thank you, thank you," he whispered, as he shook hands with Gerry, who hugged him instead.

Dinner was a light-hearted affair, and even Amy seemed more relaxed. "So you found her?" she asked Gerard.

Charlotte looked inquiringly at Gerry. "Yes, I guess I did," his expression enigmatic.

"Was this planned?" Charlotte was suspicious.

"Not really," Gerry grinned. "I was going to invite you to join me for the weekend, but didn't catch you. I called Amy. Then Agatha let slip you were coming up here anyway."

"You are really good at lying," Charlotte frowned.

"So what is this surprise on Sunday?" Amy wanted to know.

"Well, it wouldn't be a surprise if I told you," Charlotte was cryptic. "Just be there, and you'll find out. By the way, I won't be able to accompany you to church, because I have an errand I must run first." She looked at Stefan and winked, and he nodded knowingly.

"Can I spend tomorrow night with you?" Stefan asked excitedly.

"Well, now, you need to ask your folks," Charlotte gazed at him fondly. "You know I don't mind. And with Gerry there, you can entertain each other, if he stands up his latest hot date again."

"That will be cozy," Amy half-whispered to Mike. Charlotte frowned. Amy continued, "You're sure Stefan wouldn't be in the way?"

"Geez, Amy," Charlotte muttered. "It's not like Gerry and I . . ."

"One can always hope," Mike chuckled, as Charlotte glowered at him.

"Please let me," Stefan begged his mother.

"Sure," Amy relented.

After dinner they parted company, Charlotte promising to pick up Stefan in the morning. As they pulled out on the way home, Gerry and she were silent, comfortable with each other.

She pulled in to the garage and they let themselves into the house. As she pulled the door shut and started locking up, Gerry remarked, "Well, there went my plans for Saturday night."

"You don't have to stay and entertain Stefan," Charlotte looked at him curiously.

"Oh, I love Stefan, and we'll have great fun. But I think you were anxious to make sure we weren't alone," Gerry walked over to the bar.

"You had big plans with me?" Charlotte laughed at him. "I'm not scared of you, Gerry."

"Are you sure?" he looked at her, question in his eyes as he pointed to the decanters.

She nodded, and he poured some bourbon in a tumbler for her, and more scotch into a tumbler for himself. "Want something in it?"

She shook her head. She walked up to him brazenly and put her arms around his neck. "I'm not scared, Gerry," she whispered. "I'm petrified."

He put the decanter down, put his arms around her waist and pulled her to him. He kissed her long and slow, and she responded, before pulling away.

"Why are you scared?"

"Because it would be so easy to allow myself to fall for you. You're my best friend; you are perfect in every way. But I don't ever want to feel that again. It hurts too badly." She took the glass and walked away.

"You don't have to cloister yourself," he muttered. "There are other—things we could do. No strings attached."

"As long as we don't do what you're thinking right now," she said slyly.

She took his hand and led him up the stairs and into her bedroom. "Let's strip to our skivvies and watch old movies together."

They both shed their clothes and jumped in her bed. She handed him the remote. "You choose," she was gracious.

Later, he stroked her hair as she snuggled next to him sleepily and he watched television. "Who else would allow me to cuddle without wanting sex?" she mumbled.

"Who said I don't want it?" he teased her.

She was suddenly serious. "Gerry, would you think I'm crazy if I told you something?"

"I always think you're crazy," he smiled, then frowned as he saw her expression. "What is it?"

"I know it's crazy, but I sometimes think Stefan is my son," she stated solemnly.

"Well, it would be natural, because he looks like you," Gerry was indulgent.

"No, I mean, I think Stefan really is my son," she whispered.

Gerry stared at her. "But your baby died, Charl."

"Did he?" she stared back.

"Charl, what are you saying? There was some kind of 'baby-swap'? Stefan was stolen from you and given to your sister?"

She squeezed his arm. "What if Melanie found out I was having a baby? What if Amy told her? What if she arranged for Amy and Mike to have my baby?"

Gerry sat up suddenly. "My God, Charl. Melanie is capable of a lot of things, but do you really think she would do something like that to you?"

"Why not?" Charlotte also sat up. "I've been nothing but a disappointment. Amy tells Melanie everything, so it would be natural for her to blurt out my situation against my wishes. Melanie wanted a baby for Amy, and I was certainly not fit in her eyes for motherhood or anything else."

Gerry stood up, and began pacing the floor. "I know you and Melanie have had your swords crossed at times, but Melanie loves you, Charl. She would not do anything to hurt you."

"Wouldn't she?" Charlotte's eyes glittered with unshed tears. "I need to know."

"You need electric shock treatment," Gerry whispered.

"Just find out for me," she went up to him and nestled her head against his shoulder. "I need to know about his real parents, maybe get some DNA testing done. I don't know what to do. I try to banish these thoughts, but they keep coming back."

"Have you told Amy and Mike your suspicions?" he demanded.

"Of course not. They would not let me see him if they thought I suspected this," she mumbled. "I am crazy, aren't I?"

He put his arm around her. "Yes. But I'll figure it out," he promised. "Don't cry. You know I don't handle crying women well."

She smiled through her tears. He took her hand and led her to bed, pulling back the covers and settling her in. "Get some sleep," he murmured as he kissed her forehead and left the room.

The next morning she awakened, and Gerry was gone. There was a note propped up on her bedside table. "Had some errands to run. Will call you later. G."

She showered and readied herself, and made it through the lighter Saturday morning traffic to pick up Stefan. Ringing the bell, she was admitted by Mike.

"Amy's on the warpath this morning," he smiled, pecking her on the check. "Stefan is finishing his chores, and getting his gear together for his basketball game. Do you know where the gym is?"

Charlotte started to answer, but Amy showed up in the foyer. "His game is at 3:00," she said anxiously.

"I can get him back here in plenty of time," Charlotte started, but Amy shook her head.

"I know the two of you, and he'll be lucky to get to the game on time. But if he doesn't dress out early, he sits on the bench. So make sure he's there."

Charlotte promised, as Stefan came trooping down the stairs with his duffle bag and another bag in hand. "You all be careful," Amy called as they left.

They made it to the church, and Charlotte got them past the security system and finally into the organ loft.

Stefan walked up to the console. "I have always wanted to play here."

She was surprised. "But don't you ever play at St. Paul's? That is a wonderful organ and acoustic, maybe the best in town. Everyone is jealous of Alan's gig."

"Naw," Stefan replied, hanging his head. "Dr. Meredith doesn't let us play there. That's why getting to play here is so cool."

"I'm sure Evan would let you play here," Charlotte suggested gently.

"But until lately I've been afraid to ask," he responded, blushing.

"OK, let's see what you got," Charlotte said briskly. "The D major prelude."

She selected the first of the memory levels provided by Evan as Stefan quickly stepped into his organist shoes and grabbed his music, seating himself at the console and adjusting the bench.

He looked at her expectantly. "Let's start the registration at a conservative level and work our way up," she suggested.

He began playing. After a few adjustments in registration, she stood back and listened. "Slow it down," she suggested.

"Aw, you sound like Alan," he complained.

"Dr. Meredith to you," she admonished. "And you're not Joyce Jones, so take your time."

He did as she asked, and at one point she stopped him. "Your accentuation is good here, but you need to watch and continue that pattern in the left hand here," she pointed. "It helps keep the tempo even."

She walked around as he continued playing. She didn't stop him when he began the fugue, but let him continue, noting his absorption. When he exhibited some difficulty in a pedal passage, she laid a hand on his shoulder. "Slow it down and feel it," she spoke in his ear. He nodded.

She was amazed at how maturely he played for a thirteen year old boy having only begun lessons the year before and already mastering the Bach *Prelude and Fugue in D major*. She felt an overwhelming pride welling up at this boy, who was oblivious to everything around him until the last note was played. Then he turned to her, eyes dancing.

"Wasn't that a hoot?" he cried.

She laughed. "Yes, dear," she ruffled his hair, mirroring his excitement. "I'm so proud of you, Stefan."

She playfully pushed him off the bench. "Now I have work to do. Let's go through this music for church tomorrow. I need you to spot me. We'll look at Evan's hymn registrations, and I want you to tell me what it's like down in the nave."

She methodically went through hymns and service music, and she and Stefan argued over registrations. Then, having completed the music, she pulled music out of her bag and launched into some Durufle.

"What is that?" Stefan called to her, but she was busy with setting registrations as she played.

"Just listen and tell me if it is too jarring anywhere," she answered him.

She played steadily, manually changing registrations at times, only stopping every so often to set a piston.

When she finished, Stefan was standing beside her. "I've not heard that before."

"Not many play it nowadays," she smiled, as she made some notes to herself with a pencil. "They all play the choral variations, but not the prelude or adagio movements of the *Veni, Creator*."

"It doesn't sound like a postlude," he looked at her suspiciously.

"That's because it isn't," she grinned. "I thought I would give you the postlude spot. You'll do the Bach."

"Cool," he breathed. "That means we can 'pump it up'?"

"Sure," she laughed. "But you don't want to sacrifice clarity."

"I want to play over all those talkers," he guffawed.

"You know, the congregation is pretty quiet during postlude. Father Jameson encourages them to sit and listen," Charlotte reminded him.

"How are Mom and Dad going to know when I'm playing?" he demanded.

"I'm going to bribe an usher to give them a note just before the last hymn."

"You're going to be here with me, aren't you?" Stefan looked anxious.

"Of course, dear," Charlotte squeezed his arm. "Are you up for this? Now's the time to decide."

"You bet," he declared vehemently. "Can I play it again?"

"Yes, but only the prelude," Charlotte was firm. "The fugue isn't quite ready, and Harry would not allow it before its time."

He looked at her. "Are you ever going to tell me about Harry?"

"Maybe a little over lunch," she smiled cautiously. "But you'd better hurry up, or we won't have time before heading to your game."

After he finished, satisfied with his performance, they changed back into their street shoes and headed out. Stopping in at a little deli on the way to the gym, they ordered sandwiches, and sat across from each other.

"Why this interest in basketball?" Charlotte asked him.

"I started playing at school, and liked it. Then my friend Chip and I tried out for the team and made it. Dad and I have played 21 forever."

He looked at her earnestly. "Do you think I can make it in Professor Kreiser's class?"

Charlotte sipped her soda. "I don't see why not. He can be pretty tough, Stefan. I really would rather you chose another teacher."

"Why?" he stared at her. "You know I want to be in Atlanta, and he's the man, the one everyone wants to study with. You studied with him, so why wouldn't you want me to?"

"Stefan, I guess it's because I did study with him, and I know firsthand what he can be like. It was—" she struggled with the words, "it was not pleasant in the end for me." She bit her lip. "I, like your parents, want to protect you as much as possible."

"I asked Mom about what happened and why you didn't get your degree, but she wouldn't tell me," he remarked, putting his hand over hers on the table. "Aunt Charl, I'm so sorry," his eyes were sympathetic.

"Dear Stefan," Charlotte murmured. "I love you so much, like you were my own." She squeezed his hand. "I got to the point I could not play anymore, and gave it up. But I have so much else to fill my life."

"But you're playing now," he smiled at her. "So it's better?"

"I'm getting better," she agreed. "But I still get very nervous about playing in public, and that's why the disguises."

They were brought their sandwiches. "You wanted to know about Dr. Kreiser," she said as they were eating. "He was a child prodigy whose family came over from Germany so that he could study in the U.S. He went to Juilliard, then spent some time in Paris studying with Maurice Duruflé."

"The music you were playing today," Stefan broke in.

"That's right," she concurred.

"And he won Chartres," Stefan added. "That's so cool."

"Yes," Charlotte smiled. "Then Aunt Mellie decided he should be tagged to come to Atlanta, and she lobbied for him, along with Dean Jackson. And so he came. He is much sought after, and is a good but very hard instructor."

"When did you start lessons with him?"

"Not long after he started. While he was looking for a place to live, Aunt Mellie allowed him to live at the boathouse and practice at our place. I heard him play one day, and begged for lessons. But I had to audition. I was twelve when I started organ lessons."

"Same as me," Stefan laughed. "But you don't like him now, do you?"

Charlotte caught her breath. "Of course I like him. He asked me to help him with juries, I am sponsoring some students to go to AGO convention, and he has promised to get me an interview with the guest organist next week. He's asked me to help him with a project to publicize the area organ events through regular articles and reviews."

"Cool," Stefan intoned. "So then it would be all right for me to come and study with him too?"

"Don't you want to check out some other schools, Stefan?" Charlotte asked earnestly. "I mean, there is Juilliard, and I feel you would have no trouble gaining admission."

"No, this is what I want," Stefan was insistent.

"We'll see," Charlotte frowned. "Finish your sandwich. I want to get there early so that your sandwich will have digested and I can prove your mom wrong about us."

They were indeed early, and Charlotte, Mike and Amy cheered Stefan's team on to victory.

Afterward Stefan accompanied Charlotte home. That evening, Charlotte ordered in pizza and made popcorn so that they and Gerry could watch a movie before turning in.

As she made a drink and handed it to Gerry, Stefan remarked, "This is so great. You and Gerry should get married."

"Mind your own business," Charlotte told him pointedly, as he winked at Gerry.

"You know, you could sleep together. I won't tell anyone," Stefan suggested, a wicked gleam in his eye.

"Stefan!" Charlotte reprimanded him. "Since when do you talk that way?"

"I didn't mean any harm," he snickered.

"Just for that, you go to bed at ten, whether or not the movie is finished," she feigned severity.

Chapter 37

Charlotte perched in the back seat of Gerry's limousine. She surveyed her appearance critically in the small hand-held mirror. She had decided on the 'Tabitha Auberge' disguise for her church appearance that morning.

She finally stepped out of the car. Gerard was waiting for her.

"Is Stefan OK?" she was concerned.

"Excited and pumped," he answered her. "Do you really have to do this *incognito*?" Gerry asked, his voice low. "I just don't like this, especially for church."

"What, do you think God is going to strike me down for disguising myself?" Charlotte laughed shortly. "Good grief, Gerry, you know why."

"I think you need help," he muttered.

"So does Jonathan. I'm working on it. You don't have to do this," she was defensive.

"Just go on, before I change my mind and abandon you."

Charlotte quietly made her way through the narthex and up the stairs to the gallery, where she met Stefan anxiously standing beside the organ. He looked at her with relief.

"What took you so long?" he whispered.

"Ah, Miss Auberge," a familiar voice interrupted. She turned, and there were Erik and Alison. "On behalf of the choir, we are very much looking forward to having you here today."

"Hello," she spoke in her perfected fake European accent. "It is good to be here. Mr. Chadwick here is to perform the postlude for us today."

"How exciting for him and his parents," Alison enthused.

"But it is a secret," Stefan added. "We don't want them to know until the last hymn. Aun—I mean, we planned to have someone slip them a note."

"I'll be glad to carry the message," Erik smiled at Stefan. He gave Stefan's shoulder an affectionate squeeze and looked over at Charlotte. "First time you've tried this at the organ?" he asked, his voice low.

She nodded.

"How do you feel?"

"A little nervous, but OK," she replied.

"Evan asked me to direct the choir this morning. We'll run through the anthem and the gradual, if you'd like to join us in about twenty minutes," he informed her. "I got your back, Charlotte. It's all going to be smooth as glass."

She nodded assent, then turned to Stefan.

"Now's your chance to warm up," she suggested.

"I already have," he beamed. "Gerry and I got here just after the early service was over. I'm ready."

"OK," she ruffled his hair. "Then I need to get ready."

She spent a few minutes checking her registrations and organizing her music, running through phrases of the Durufle, satisfying herself that she was prepared for the service. Then she made her way to the choir room, rehearsing the psalm with the choir, happy that she had not been recognized by any of the church members.

She made her way alone back to the gallery. A moment of panic seized her, but she fought it down. I'm Tabitha, she thought to herself. She's not afraid of anything. Piece of cake, as Stefan says.

Charlotte took several deep breaths, looking at the blur of tiny notes on the page. She closed her eyes a moment, then blinked several times. She pushed a piston, took a look at the pedals, and began hesitantly.

Her hands shook convulsively as she thought of some of Kreiser's instructions, and she prayed, God, please don't let me screw this up; this is a worship service for you. She tensed up in order to make sure the trembling did not come through in her fingering. As she focused on the score before her, everything else around her began to fade.

Her fingers locked into the memory of long practice from when she had learned this music at the age of sixteen, and the instrument and the music before her became her best friends. She was one with the notes emanating from the pipes.

All too soon the music drew to a close, and she was surprised. But at a cue from the video monitor, she launched into the processional hymn, as the congregation sang and the choir eventually wound their way into the gallery to surround the organ.

Charlotte felt excitement at being a part of the service, something she had not done since she had run away from Kreiser and the organ. She felt a deep satisfaction as she accompanied the choir through the gradual and the service music, realizing that she actually missed those opportunities when she participated in worship services. She gave a quick prayer of thanks as the choir sang their anthem, thrilled that she was again sitting at the King of instruments and doing what she had loved so much and had abandoned, and grateful that her attempts at anonymity had again been successful.

All too soon the service was winding to a close. As the priest spoke the benediction, Stefan quickly took her place at the bench and silently pushed a piston, launching into the postlude. She smiled encouragement to him as he enthusiastically tackled the piece, feeling her excitement mirror his own.

Suddenly she felt a tugging at her arm. "You have to come away now," Gerry was whispering, urging her.

"But I promised to stay with Stefan," she protested, as Erik appeared, appearing flustered.

He said, his voice low. "Kreiser is here. He's on his way up."

"Harry?" Charlotte paled visibly. "What is he—?"

"I just found out he was here this weekend visiting Alan Meredith, and dropped in for the service," Erik whispered. "I didn't know, honest."

"Let's go. Do you want to test the disguise with him?" Gerry hissed, dragging her along with him.

Charlotte, suddenly frightened, hurried away with Gerry, not daring to look back. Suddenly she found herself face to face with Kreiser on the stairwell landing.

"Ah, Miss Auberge, I've heard so much about you. It is a pleasure to finally hear you today," he held out his hand to her. "You are truly gifted."

She awkwardly took his hand, feeling faint. "So you heard all the service today?" she asked.

"Yes, even the Durufle," he smiled. "Just as I would have done it myself," he added, a glint in his eye.

He looked past her to Gerry. "Ah, Mr. Fellowes, how nice to see you as well. So do you know Miss Auberge well?"

Charlotte intervened smoothly. "I met him during one of my concerts here. He has been so kind to help provide transportation for me during my short visit here this trip," she spoke in her best accent. "And you are?"

She hoped her expression conveyed innocence. His eyes bored through her. "I'm Harry Kreiser, professor of organ at Emory University in Atlanta," he smiled his most charming.

"Ah, I have heard your name. You have—what do they say—quite a reputation," she smiled inwardly at the implied snub. "It is always nice to meet a fellow musician," she purred, although inwardly she felt nauseous.

"So you did not play the postlude?" he turned to look toward the console.

"A young man is playing the Bach this morning," she answered. "He is the son of—of some church members here, and a very talented boy," she finished breathlessly. "I apologize. I must—catch an airplane, Monsieur Kreiser, but it has been nice to meet you," she continued quickly.

He took her hand and kissed it, his eyes again boring through hers. She was glad she had changed her eye color with contacts, but was not sure but what Kreiser could see through her subterfuge.

"I feel the same, *cara mia*," he spoke quietly, before taking his leave.

She whitened at his last words, watching his back as he moved up the stairs. She broke free of Gerry's hand on her arm, darting down the stairs and out the door, looking wildly around her, oblivious to parishioners milling around looking at her curiously.

Gerry caught up with her and pointed out the limo right across the avenue, to which she ran breathlessly, as Tom appeared out of nowhere and opened the door. She crawled in, shaking violently as Gerry joined her.

"I've let Stefan down," she sobbed, tears streaking her heavily made-up face. "Oh, God, you were right."

Gerry put his arm around her. "You did a fabulous job, Charlotte. And you didn't abandon Stefan. I'm sure he will understand. In fact, he is elated, and his parents are so proud."

"You must go back and check on him," Charlotte insisted, still shaking violently.

"You're crazy if you think I'm leaving you alone like this," he hugged her, suddenly anxious for her. "You're scaring me. Was it suddenly realizing Kreiser was there?"

She nodded dumbly, the tears continuing to fall.

Gerry pulled out his cell phone and dialed a number. "Mike, it's Gerry. Yeah, I had to leave to pick up Charlotte, but we'll meet up with you all later. We'll do dinner." He paused, surprise on his face. "Yes, it was," he responded somberly. "She's OK, just shook up. She's worried about Stefan. She didn't want him to think she had run out on him."

Charlotte was surprised. "OK, later," Gerry said, then hung up.

"Mike knew it was me?" she was thunderstruck.

"He knew it was you who set up for Stefan to play. Then when Kreiser showed up and the organist was gone, he put two and two together. He'll explain to Stefan, make up an excuse. It will be OK." Gerry spoke through the intercom. "Tom, please take us back to Miss Lawson's place."

She was still trembling. "He recognized me," she stuttered.

"Of course he didn't," Gerry soothed her.

"He said, '*cara mia*' as he let go my hand," she was hysterical. "He knew it was me."

"I'll bet he says that a lot," Gerry retorted, but his concerned demeanor belied his words. "And what if he did? It's over. He'll never divulge your secret. Why would he? He has no reason to hurt you further."

She was rocking back and forth, rubbing her hands together violently. "The bastard," she cried. "Why can't he leave me be? I'm trying to get back on my feet. Can't he step off a cliff?"

"Excellent suggestion," Gerry muttered, as he continued to hold her and she wept.

The intercom buzzed. "We're being followed," Tom's voice came over.

Gerry looked out the tinted back window. "May be paparazzi. We can't go straight home, Charl," he informed the distraught woman, "or your secret is out."

He flipped open his cell phone and picked a number. "Hi, is this Barb? It's Gerry. How are you?"

He listened a minute. "I got a problem. I'm helping a celeb friend do a quick-change to avoid the press, and I need your help. You still have that Dior blue two-piece dress suit I was admiring? In a size six? And some makeup as well?

"You know I hate to ask on short notice, but I'll sent Tom in shortly. Just discreetly in a bag, please. Put it on my tab. You know I owe you. Dinner next week."

He buzzed the intercom. "Tom, we have a pick-up," giving him the name of the shop.

He turned to Charlotte. "It's OK. I've done this before," he explained simply. "We dress you up and take you home, and Tom will whisk Ms. Auberge to the airport to disappear."

Charlotte's eyes grew wide. "You've done this before?"

Gerry laughed. "You don't think you're the only damsel in distress I've rescued, do you?"

She smiled wanly. "I feel honored to be a part of your list," she sniffed. "Dior? You really didn't have to go all out."

"I like to dress my women up," he teased her. "And I don't spend as much on the others," he winked.

She busied herself in removing her wig and working with her hair as she tried impatiently to tie it up into a chignon. After a moment, he stopped her. "It's damp and curly. Let it just fall down in a tumbled fashion. It's lovely like that, and it'll look like we've had a tryst. Good for the press."

She laughed nervously, as Tom pulled to a stop and disappeared. Momentarily he came back with a bag, which he discreetly slipped into the back. She gratefully looked in the bag, removed the makeup and tried to restore herself to normal, removing the contacts and slipping into the dress, as Gerry stuffed the remaining items into the large shopping bag.

His phone rang. He answered it. "Gerry here. She's OK. We're evading the press right now. What? He did what? Damn. I'll call you back."

Charlotte, trying to reach for the back zipper, turned to him. "What has happened?"

"Kreiser asked Stefan and his parents to lunch, and Stefan accepted before they could say no. What's more, Stefan has said you are in town and supposed to meet them." Gerry zipped up the dress for her.

"Oh, God," she moaned. "Now what?"

"I'm taking you home," he exclaimed.

"No. If I don't show up, Harry will suspect something," she responded distractedly. He could see the hysteria in her eyes. "I cannot face him, Gerry. I just can't."

"Then you need to make your excuses to Stefan, and let it go," Gerry said gently, holding the phone out to her.

She stared at him, then took the phone. She dialed Mike's number. "I need to speak to Stefan."

Stefan came on. "I know," he said in a grown-up voice. "You don't have to say anything. I understand."

"Understand what?" Charlotte was surprised.

"You don't want to see him," Stefan was matter-of-fact.

"Stefan, I'm so sorry," Charlotte started crying.

"It's OK. But you know I'm going to ask him during lunch if I can be one of his students."

"Stefan—" she began, but he stopped her.

"It's what I want," he replied imperiously. "I'm going to ask Aunt Mellie if I can move there to finish school."

"But your parents—" she again started.

"They will let me." He was stubbornly confident. "We'll talk later. You go home with Gerry." His voice was curiously grown-up. He hung up.

She stared at the phone.

"What did he say?" Gerry demanded.

"He understood that I didn't want to see Harry. He's going to ask to become one of his students. He wants to move to Atlanta." She handed the phone back.

They were silent the rest of the trip home, Charlotte struggling to restore her composure and appearance, mulling over Stefan's words.

When they stopped, he told her, "Now for some acting on your part. As you step out, you need to lean back into the limousine like you are saying good-bye to someone, to lend credence to the lie."

She did as he suggested, then he took her arm and led her inside, waving at the limousine as it pulled away.

Once inside, he led her upstairs to her bedroom. "Shame that this dress didn't see much daylight," he chuckled as she slipped out of the jacket.

"I'm sorry," she was shamefaced.

"It would have been fun to see Kreiser's face when you walked in knock-down drop-dead gorgeous in it," he laughed.

"Will you unzip me?" she asked distractedly.

He complied, then turned to leave the room. But she stopped him. "Don't leave me, Gerry," she pleaded, as the dress slipped to her ankles, she stepped out of the dress and took his hand. "I don't want to be alone."

"You ask for some impossible things, Charl," he murmured. "It's hard to look at you like that and turn away as it is."

"I don't want you to turn away," she whispered. "I need to feel desirable."

He turned to her. "Don't tease me if you don't mean it," he said sternly.

"You know—I don't know if I can go all the way," she mumbled.

She wrapped her arms around him. He crushed her to him. "You know, once I start..."

"You're not going to act funny about me after this?" she murmured.

Chapter 38

Stefan was fourteen and insistent on coming to Atlanta. His parents finally relented, albeit reluctantly, and he was allowed to come live with Melanie and Charlotte. He was accepted into the high school dual-enrollment program early because of his scholastic scores, his having prevailed upon Melanie to pull some strings.

Stefan and his mother arrived one summer day, so that Amy could settle him in before the fall semester started. Charlotte helped Amy unpack Stefan's clothes in his room. Amy suddenly sat on the bed, her eyes filled with tears.

Charlotte sat down beside her, placing her arm around her sister. "Oh, Amy, dear, this is too much for you. Why did you say yes to him?"

"He wants it so much," she sobbed. "And he loves you so much. He's done nothing but talk about this since you moved back to Atlanta. It's like he doesn't love me anymore."

"Nonsense," Charlotte smiled reassuringly. "Of course he loves you. But he does want to play organ. I've tried to talk him out of this. But you know Stefan."

Amy nodded wordlessly. Charlotte continued, "Amy, we're not that far away. Gerry has said any time he wants to go home or you want to come down here, the jet is yours."

Amy tried to smile through her tears.

"And you know Melanie is thrilled," Charlotte continued. "This is her way to snare you and Mike back to Atlanta. You're still Niece No. 1 to her." She leaned forward and pecked Amy on the cheek. "Give him two nights after you go back, and he'll be crying himself to sleep."

"You must make him eat right, and he needs to mind you and Aunt Mellie," Amy spoke rapidly, bravely.

"I promise," Charlotte laughed. "And to call you and Dad every night, and to brush his teeth and wash behind his ears."

"Do you really think he is a good musician?" Amy asked her anxiously.

Charlotte nodded. "He is really phenomenal, Amy. I would give anything if he had chosen Juilliard and Dr. Hodges instead of here, but he didn't. But he is that good, I am thrilled to have him here and will protect him."

Amy smiled. "I know you will. You really love him, don't you?"

Charlotte kissed her cheek. "He is a blessing from heaven."

Amy laughed. "I knew you were going to say that. He looks and acts so much like you."

Charlotte's smile faded and she said nothing. She stood up and busied herself folding clothes.

After a moment Charlotte spoke. "You really should go with Stefan tomorrow for his meeting with Kreiser."

"You know I hate the bastard," Amy fell back on the bed and looked at her sister. "Why I should trust my kid to the man who hurt you is beyond me. OK, Stefan insists. But why do I have to deal with the man?"

She reached over and took Charlotte's hand, stilling her. "Go with me," Amy begged. "I know you hate him too, but I am entrusting Stefan to your care. If you cannot deal with Harry it's all over."

"I don't hate him," Charlotte retorted, her voice barely audible.

"Well, you should," Amy pulled her closer and messed up her hair teasingly.

Stefan appeared in the bedroom. "Oh, good, a clothes fight," he screamed, and jumped in the middle of the folded clothes on the bed.

Amy and Charlotte both yelled as their work was reduced to a mass of tumbled laundry. "You little twerp," Charlotte cried, as she grabbed Stefan by the head and playfully messed his hair, and Amy started tickling his ribs. They wrestled around for several minutes, giggling and yelling.

"Charlotte!" a peremptory voice interrupted.

They all looked up as Melanie stood in the doorway. Both Stefan and Amy stared at her, then at Charlotte.

"What, why is this my fault?" Charlotte asked petulantly. She turned to Stefan accusingly. "You started it, but I notice she didn't call your name."

"That's because we all know you're the troublemaker," Amy laughed as she threw a pillow at Charlotte's head.

Melanie announced, "I have invited Dr. Kreiser for dinner this evening."

"Shit," Amy muttered under her breath, as Charlotte's face froze.

Stefan jumped up excitedly. "How cool," he shouted gleefully.

"I thought it would be a good idea to meet here in a comfortable setting, and we can set some ground rules for Stefan's educational regimen," Melanie ignored Amy's expletive. "I have also invited Dean Jackson. Dressy casual. Please let's all try to behave."

That evening Charlotte tried to seat herself as far from Kreiser as she could, but Melanie had other ideas, seating Charlotte next to Kreiser, Stefan across from him, with Amy at Stefan's side, and Jackson at the end of the table across from her. Dinner was full of chatter, and Charlotte teased young Stefan several times, directed much of her conversation to Jackson, and was careful to avoid direct contact or conversation with Kreiser.

"I'm very interested in hearing all about you, Stefan," Kreiser spoke to the young boy as dessert was being served. "I've heard that you are a very talented young man, and I was impressed with your playing at church during my visit to D.C."

"I'm looking forward to studying with you, Dr. Kreiser," Stefan said politely, looking at his Aunt Mellie for approval as Charlotte looked away, suddenly uncomfortable.

"Tell me about yourself. I've already read your *vita*. Let me hear it from you," he smiled at Stefan.

As Stefan talked about himself, Charlotte relaxed and her heart swelled with pride at the boy's maturity and demeanor. *Amy, you've done well,* she telegraphed to Amy with her eyes, and Amy smiled back.

"So you've already taken lessons with my old student, I hear?" Kreiser asked. "Alan Meredith is doing well as an instructor," he turned to Charlotte. "He's teaching at Peabody, as well as trying to revive American University's organ program. He's developing a student and teacher exchange program with the Paris Conservatoire. He's making a name for himself," he added meaningfully.

Charlotte gritted her teeth, flushing at his snub, but saying nothing.

Dean Jackson noted her reaction. "It's my understanding that Charlotte here has also been busy," he interjected. "Congratulations on the new book, my dear," he covered her hand with his. "And for the children's books and the first novel as well."

"Books?" Kreiser stared at her. "What books?"

Melanie spoke up. "Our Charlotte is a published author now," she said with evident pride, surprising Charlotte.

"I didn't know you knew," Charlotte sputtered, staring at her aunt.

"Do I have to say it again? There's little that you girls do that I don't know about," she smiled. "We really should have a celebration over your success and Stefan's coming here to study."

"I don't think so," Charlotte began doubtfully.

"Well, I think it's time I heard the young man in action," Kreiser spoke up, abruptly changing the subject.

"Shall we withdraw to the salon for coffee?" Melanie stood and led the way.

Stefan excitedly followed. "I'm so happy you moved the piano in here as well," he told his aunt excitedly as he accompanied her into the salon, and the others followed in their wake.

He marched up to the piano and sat down. Immediately he started with the *Pathetique* Sonata by Beethoven, from memory. When he finished the last movement, he stood.

"Do you want to hear me on the organ now?"

Kreiser was amused, and nodded. "Please."

The boy went to the organ, pulled a score out of the music bench, and opened it. He started playing Bach's *Prelude and Fugue in E-flat major*.

Charlotte gasped in shock. Kreiser's eyes and hers met, and he moved to Stefan's side and turned pages for him.

Before the end of the prelude she silently escaped from the room. I can't sit through this, she thought, ensconcing herself in the powder room and running cold water over her shaking hands.

There was a knock at the door. "Yes?" Charlotte called, grabbing a hand towel.

Melanie opened the door and came to her. "My dear, are you all right?"

"I'm OK," Charlotte replied, drying her hands. "It's just like history is repeating itself. And I feel helpless. I can't stop it."

She blushed at revealing so much to her aunt. But Melanie nodded understandingly, placing her hand on Charlotte's shoulder.

"I know this is hard. I'm happy you have come home to me. I'm so very proud of you," she murmured, before she turned away.

Charlotte, astonished, stared after her, before following her out.

Kreiser was still standing by the organ, his voice low, giving instruction to Stefan, who was rapt, listening to every word. Charlotte tried to squelch the memories conjured by the scene.

Amy came up to Charlotte. "How do you like that?" she whispered. "The son of a bitch has him eating out of his hand. Is this what you want?"

"You know it isn't," Charlotte shot back quietly. "But Harry is the best teacher there is. If Stefan is serious, he can't do better. At least maybe Harry won't seduce Stefan."

"Why would Melanie be OK with this?" hissed Amy.

"Ask her yourself." Charlotte walked out of the room.

A few days later, Amy left for home. Stefan hugged her at the airport, and he and Charlotte watched the plane taxi out of sight.

"It's you and me," he intoned solemnly. Charlotte laughed at him.

Stefan applied himself to his classes and his piano and organ instruction with a relentless vigor. Charlotte shook her head, remembering herself at that age, amazed at the resemblance.

Time slipped by quickly, as Charlotte began taking her job more seriously. She and the editor in chief became fast friends, as she bantered him out of his chronic gruffness, and he sliced her articles into shreds.

"You know I wouldn't have hired you if it wasn't for Melanie Cain," he spat at her one day during a heated discussion.

"Ed, you wouldn't hire Carl Bernstein unless you thought he would get you what you wanted," she shot back coldly. "Don't give me that bull."

He tore up her draft article in front of her. "Start over," he ordered, "and don't come back in here until I invite you."

"That's no problem," she flounced out.

Later that day he showed up at her desk. "Why haven't you brought me my article?" he bellowed.

"You didn't invite me," she answered ungraciously. "Here," she shoved some pages into his hand.

Stefan was always practicing when she came home. Some days he dragged her into the salon and made her play for him, or forced her to listen and critique his work. Some days they would hold mini-competitions where they each tried to out-play the other.

One day she walked in from work and found him moping on the bench out in the foyer.

"What's up?" she was instantly concerned.

Stefan frowned. She sat down beside him. "Come on, Stef, you can tell me."

He was silent a few minutes. She ruffled his hair in sympathy. He finally blurted out, "I've been harassing Dr. K. about my first recital. He's set it up on—on an old electric organ."

Charlotte smiled broadly. Harry doesn't give up, she thought.

"Where is this church?" she asked.

He told her. She nodded sympathetically. "Did he tell you why?"

"No. I was too mad. I walked out on him," he replied. "You're right. I should have applied to Juilliard."

"Let me tell you the story," she said. "Come on—this goes well with ice cream."

She took his arm and led him into the kitchen. After raiding the freezer and serving them both a bowl, she sat down next to him. She told him about her own experience and Kreiser's story to her.

"And it makes sense," she finished. "This is necessary experience. You can't avoid it. You need to embrace it. You should be able to immediately sit down at any instrument, including electronic, old and new, and make music, share the art with others."

"But what about you, Aunt Charlotte?" he asked, taking her hand. "You need to do that as well. You're not playing as much now that you're here. You are good. Kreiser says you were his best."

"Stop it!" she ordered hotly. She covered her eyes, rubbing her forehead, breathing deeply. Angry with herself at her reaction, her voice softened. "I'm sorry. I can't help it, Stefan. I keep trying."

He stood up and flung his arms around her neck. "Don't give up, Auntie," he whispered. "You're who got me interested in playing organ."

"Me?" her voice was muffled.

"I just want to make the music flow as beautifully and effortlessly as you do. I want to feel the same things you feel when you are playing and you think no one is listening. I've seen your face," he told her. "And I do—what a rush! So do what you have to do, wear a wig, whatever, but keep it up."

She started laughing, and he did too. "Stefan, under what rock did you parents find you?"

"Mom and Dad say I'm just like you, headstrong."

She nodded, sobering. "At least you are a little more charming with it. So go plan your program on the electric."

Erik called her later that week to ask her to join the trio for some concerts. With Stefan's words ringing in her ears, she agreed. And she worked even harder at the paper, bringing in more reviews of recitals, and winning her editor's grudging approval.

Gerard was working hard also, gone for long stretches. But he showed up often, and was pegged by Melanie to be Charlotte's escort at social events where Melanie or her editor mandated her appearance. Charlotte was pegged to serve as one of the hostesses for several of the seasonal balls, to which she reluctantly agreed after Melanie's prompting, and Gerry accompanied her at her request. Rumors began flowing that there was a possible engagement soon to be announced between the two.

Chapter 39

"Where are you?" Gerry's voice, almost a whisper, demanded over the phone.

"I'm at the awards dinner," Charlotte smiled and mouthed her apologies to her tablemates, as she excused herself. "Why aren't you here? Ed has already asked about you," she whispered.

"Because I had an unexpected meeting. A prospective investor allegedly sent a marketing consultant. It has turned into something else entirely. Charl, she smells like the *Atlanta Watch*. I've checked—the investor says he has done no such thing."

"That's a good nose you have, Gerry," Charlotte made it outside to the lobby. "Just show her the door."

"I've tried. She's coming on to me like Grant took Richmond. Get over here quick. You gotta help me," Gerry was urgent.

"Gerry, you eat these tabloid reporters for breakfast. What can I do?"

"You're supposed to be my fiancée to be, remember?" he hissed. "I need for you to help me chase her off."

"Gerry, just tell her you are devoted to me and can't be unfaithful, and that we intend to run away together the moment everyone least expects it."

"I've tried everything I know to get rid of her. And you know that translates in the tabloids that I'm gay," his anger was unmistakable.

"I didn't think that mattered to you?" Charlotte could not help teasing him.

"It matters, Charl. Unless you are *flagrante delicto*, get your ass over here now. No, even if you are naked, get over here. Bring your lover, your editor, I don't care," Gerard pleaded.

"But Ed will be pissed when he is presented the award and I'm not here," Charlotte argued. "No, how silly of me. My job is not important. I can give it all up for you, darling. I'll be right there."

She snapped the phone closed. Damn, she thought, now I've got to tell Ed I'm leaving. As she walked back into the ballroom, she could see his eyes on her, his jaw set ominously.

As she approached the table, Ed reached for his phone. Glancing at it, his frown deepened. As she started to take her seat beside him, he growled, "Get the hell out of here. Just got a text from Gerry. I know I'm just chopped liver."

"I'm sorry," she whispered contritely.

"Yeah, sure," he responded sharply. "You know, I'd like you by my side just once when the paper wins an award and the publicity counts, if for no other reason than to show the world I'm the boss and not you."

He scowled at the persons sitting at the next table glaring at them. "What are you looking at?" he hissed at them ungraciously. Turning back to Charlotte, he drawled, "Why don't you just marry him and give the papers something less to talk about? Squelch the rumors?"

"Later," was all she said, as she grabbed her clutch and fled.

Minutes later she was at the apartment. She buzzed the intercom. "Charl here," she said in her brightest voice.

"Come on up, darling," Gerry's voice replied.

"Twentieth floor or straight to the master bedroom?" she asked sweetly, biting back her laughter.

"Main quarters," was his curt reply, as the door clicked and she took the elevator up.

As the elevator opened, Gerry was standing there. He took her into his arms and kissed her. "What's this for?" she mumbled, playing the game, her arms around his neck.

"She's just inside there," he whispered.

"You owe me," she whispered back.

"After all the scrapes I pulled you through?" he growled.

"You want me to help you or what?" she demanded *sotto voce*, then raised her voice. "Dear, Ed was fit to be tied when you didn't show up for the awards dinner," she purred. "I was worried. Let's do this and get to the celebration, or he won't speak to either of us for a month."

She entwined her hand in his and dragged him into the room, where on the sofa lounged a beautiful young girl hurriedly slipping a small camera into her purse.

Charlotte walked straight up to her before she could react, and held out her hand. "Hello, I'm Charlotte Lawson. And you are?"

"Daphne Marlin," the young woman stood, adjusting her tight-fitting black dress before taking Charlotte's hand.

"Miss Marlin, Gerry tells me you are a marketing consultant," Charlotte said in her sweetest voice, looking back at Gerry, whose expression was fathomless.

"Yes," the woman smiled tremulously, her eyes darting from Gerry to Charlotte.

"Gerry, you didn't tell me this consultant looked like a fashion magazine cover," Charlotte raised her eyebrows at Gerry, who smiled back tightly.

"Well, I'm very interested in your proposals. Please let's see them," Charlotte pronounced, her eyes fixed on the woman. "I'm sorry I did not know you were coming this evening, or we would have scheduled a more convenient time."

"Uh—OK," Daphne stammered, moving toward the table. "I have them right here."

Charlotte reached down behind where she had been sitting and picked up her purse clumsily. The camera fell out.

"Oh, I'm so sorry," Charlotte gushed apologetically. "You know, I think these little cameras are so cute. I've been meaning to buy one myself. Let's see."

Daphne looked wildly at her and reached for the camera, but Charlotte handed her the purse as she continued to examine the camera. "Oh, yes, and here's how one views the photos taken," she mused aloud. "Hmm, looks like you have had the grand tour of Gerry's apartment."

Gerry sputtered. "When did you take these?"

Daphne spat, "Give me my camera."

Charlotte held the camera out of reach and backed her to the glass-topped table. "No, ma'am," she pushed the woman into a chair. "I believe this is trespassing at the very least. And these," she pointed to the sheaf of papers on the table, which she perused quickly, "are not a marketing plan. You have entered here under false pretenses. You're with *Atlanta Watch*, aren't you?" she asked, her voice low. "Is there a tape recorder in here as well?"

Charlotte dumped the purse contents onto the table, as both Gerry and Daphne gasped. There was a microcassette recorder on. Charlotte angrily snatched out the tape. "Tell Mr. Tadlock, or Mr. Tadpole, whatever he calls himself these days, that his ass is mine if one word is published. We will be filing a report with the police."

Daphne squirmed, tears suddenly appearing. "I didn't mean to do anything wrong," she whined. "Please, Miss Lawson, believe me."

"What's your real name?" Charlotte asked her.

She opened her eyes wide with fright. "Gilda, Gilda Martin," she stammered.

Charlotte methodically deleted the prints from the camera, as Gerry looked on, his eyes slicing through the interloper. "I'm calling the police now," he announced.

"No, we don't have time tonight," Charlotte interjected, surprising him. "Besides, they won't do anything unless you press charges, and you're too soft-hearted."

"Not tonight," he said, the anger unmistakable. Gilda whitened at his words.

Charlotte turned to the woman. "Let me give you a story," she suggested. "Gerry and I are devoted to each other. We have known each other all our lives, and all you have to do is something like this to see us join forces and kick your ass.

"Now Gerry would have already dispatched you if you were a man, but he has a chivalric bent toward women. I, on the other hand, do not."

"I'm very sorry. It won't ever happen again," the woman pleaded desperately. "He said I had to do this, to get inside and find out what the latest is with the two of you. He strongly suggested I make out with Mr. Fellowes, to entice him to say damning things about your relationship."

Charlotte studied the ashen woman. "You know, if you want a real job as a journalist, I'll give you a card, and you can send me some material. I'll make sure Ed considers it. If you want to be pond scum, please be my guest. But two can play that game, and if you smear Gerry's name in that piece of crap you call a paper, I will find you. Furthermore, you won't work for a reputable paper in this lifetime—I guarantee it."

Gilda turned frightened eyes toward Charlotte. Gerry was impressed; Charlotte was coolly and effectively dispatching the woman. The woman stammered, "I would like to do that. But I could provide a service as well."

"What service do you think we might need from you?" Gerry exploded.

Charlotte held up her hand, silencing him. The woman continued, "I have to have a job and make a living. I have a small son, and am a single mother. In the meantime, while I'm finding something to do, I could act to forewarn you when *Atlanta Watch* is about to publish dirt pertaining to you."

Gerry started to reply, but Charlotte shook her head. She stared at the young woman. "I'm not going to play blackmail games."

"I promise you—if you help me get started doing real journalism, I will do this for free. I'll be glad to tip off the *Chronicle* to major news stories as well."

"The *Chronicle* is not likely to believe you without solid sources, and Ed is not going to get into a situation that reeks. You will have to prove yourself. All I can do is try to provide you the opportunity."

"I won't disappoint you, Miss Lawson," Gilda pleaded.

"Just get out of here, and don't let me see anything in the papers from you about us," Charlotte turned away. "I'll make good my promise."

Gilda picked up the contents of her purse and the papers. But Charlotte took the papers from her, as well as the microcassette out of the recorder. "We'll keep these for evidence," she announced. "Here, let me show you out."

She walked up to Gerry and kissed him for the reporter's benefit. "Straighten your tie, darling; we have bridges to mend," she stated matter-of-factly as she took Gilda by the arm and steered her to the elevator.

They rode the elevator in silence, the woman sniffling and searching her purse for her keys. Once downstairs Charlotte turned to her. "Gilda, I'm a person of my word. I don't know if I can trust you to do what you say. But I am warning you not to mess with my man," she said shortly, as she watched the woman dart out of the elevator and flee like a gazelle.

Charlotte made it back upstairs, shaking with laughter. Gerry met her at the elevator, his face creased in a frown.

"You didn't even get the closing, where I told her 'not to mess with my man,'" she held her sides as she stepped out.

"I don't think it's funny," he retorted, as she hooted with laughter. "Why didn't you let me call the police?"

"Honey, if you were going to do that, you'd have done that before calling me," she coughed, still laughing. "But you do need to call them, and get someone to sweep your place for listening devices now."

"Now you're engaged to me whether you like it or not," Gerry stared at her. "Do you think she'll make good her promise?"

"I don't know. Does it matter? We can't stop the paper from publishing. Gerry, rumors will happen no matter what we do, and it's better that they report we're engaged than all the other things the tabloids could be saying," Charlotte wiped her eyes, pulling out a compact to powder her nose. "Isn't that what you were afraid of?"

"But I want that to be true," Gerry claimed petulantly.

"I know," she smiled, her voice low. "Now let's make an appearance at the celebration, and make it up to Ed. Maybe you can kiss me again for a bigger audience. You'll make Melanie very happy. You may think I don't need this job, but I do enjoy it and don't want to lose it."

The next morning, there was a knock on the door of Henry Tadlock, managing editor of the *Atlanta Watch*. "What is it?" he yelled in his gruff voice.

"Charlotte Lawson is here to see you," his assistant spoke excitedly.

"Really?" he was suddenly interested. "Well, send her in. She's never come on my turf before. This has to be good."

Moments later Charlotte strode into the small untidy office. She was dressed in a flowing pale colored silk suit with coordinating scarf. She stopped short in front of Tadlock's desk, gazing down at him with her vivid flashing green eyes.

"Miss Lawson, how nice to see you," he drawled, motioning toward a chair in front of him, the other chair beside it being stuffed with papers.

"I'll stand, thank you," she said coolly. "I hope your recording device is working properly this morning."

"What? Why would I do that to you?" he smiled slyly.

"Because I want you to get every word," she stated briskly. "I've been keeping a dossier on your stories regarding Gerard Fellowes, me and my family. I'm compiling evidence against you, Mr. Tadpole."

"Tadlock," he snapped.

"Whatever," she continued smoothly. "Isn't that what Melanie called you?"

His eyes widened in surprise.

"I know that you think you can get away with your constant lies and drivel, because it's not worth anyone's while to sue you. However, last night you crossed the line."

"I don't know what you're talking about," he hedged, but she cut him off.

"Sending in someone to seduce a story out of my fiancé, planting recording devices, taking pictures, and leaving bugs," she answered. "You really need to find some fresh subject matter to 'report'," she used the word derisively. "And if you unleash your dogs on Gerard Fellowes again to manufacture baseless stories, you won't be dealing just with him. I'll make it my business to hurt your business. I will sue."

"I'm so scared. That sounds like true love," he snickered. "Why don't you two just tie the knot?"

"For your information," she smiled saccharinely, "we are engaged. You just weren't invited to the party. And we are waiting until the right moment to make it public."

"That will make a nice story," he laughed unpleasantly. "Or is that off the record?"

As she flushed and started to comment, he held up his hand. "You know, I saved your life once."

"And I'm supposed to believe you?" she retorted.

"Once when covering you as a child prodigy, I discovered you had a stalker. I notified your aunt. Oh, you didn't know?" he smiled as she looked away. "Miss Melanie Cain and I had a gentleman's agreement." He leaned forward. "If you did business with me the way Melanie Cain did, you would have less unpleasantness to deal with."

She too leaned forward, her face only inches away from his. "Firstly, I don't believe you. Secondly, even assuming you were telling the truth—oh, that's so hard to imagine—her alleged 'arrangement' apparently didn't work all that well. So I'll do business with you my own way.

"I'm putting you on notice, Tadpole. My attorneys are primed and frothing at the mouth. You might want to take some lessons in telling the truth, and finding your 'news' instead of making it up."

His smile disappeared, and he stood, facing her, sneering. "I don't believe you."

She moved closer. "Try me. See how fast I move if tomorrow's edition mentions Gerard Fellowes. I have already turned over to the police the evidence of the mole you sent in to his apartment, and the bugs that were planted." She reached out to straighten his tie, whispering, "Oh, it will be so fun to put you in your place. But that's right—you've been to jail before? But not just for defending your paper's First Amendment rights. I think those love interests of yours are illegal, very illegal."

She turned on her heel and stalked out. He sat down, his face ashen. He picked up the phone. "Get me the number of our attorney. I may be in trouble."

Charlotte called the office and told them she would be late. She drove all the way home to face Melanie, who was busy at her desk.

"Did you do business with Tadlock of the *Atlanta Watch*?" she stood accusingly facing Melanie, who didn't look up.

"Good old Tadpole," Melanie spoke. "Yes, he in the old days was very faithful about calling me to relate your and Gerry's escapades."

"Did he once report to you that I was being stalked?"

"Why, yes, he did," Melanie was unperturbed at Charlotte's inquisition. "I in gratitude offered to help get him on at the *Chronicle*. But he was happy to stay where he was. Then he became rather bothersome, trying to blackmail me not to print certain stories. I had to have my lawyers threaten tit for tat, to disclose some of his more embarrassing moments, if he pushed me."

Charlotte stared at her aunt. "Did you ever pay blackmail to him?"

Melanie was silent, staring down at the papers on her desk. Charlotte snatched away the documents in front of Melanie. "Did you?"

Melanie sighed tiredly. "When you left town so precipitously, he threatened to tell all sorts of trash about you." She looked up at Charlotte. "Yes, I did. Later, when he tried the same tactic, I had gathered enough evidence on him to tell him to do his worst and expect his own indiscretions to be aired as well."

Charlotte, stunned, backed into a chair and sat down. "I didn't know," she murmured. "I just threatened him not to print any dirt on Gerry."

As Melanie looked on impassively, Charlotte haltingly related the story of the previous evening and of her resulting encounter with Tadlock.

Melanie was silent a moment. "You did right," she finally asserted. "You are, whether you want to or not, going to inherit the responsibility for this family. You need to deal with matters in your own way. The Tadpoles and other scum are out there waiting. I won't always be here to protect you."

Charlotte held up her hand, but Melanie was not deterred. "I know you are resistant to taking my place as head of this family, Charlotte. But you know Amy is blind to these matters. For all your impetuousness, you are far more intelligent and worldly-wise, and must protect Amy and Stefan."

Melanie stood and came over to Charlotte, sitting in the chair beside her. "My dear, that's why you will be the executor of the estate when I am gone. I know you will be able to handle the situation better than Amy can. And God knows whether Amy and Mike will return to Atlanta. I would love to see you all back here in this big rambling home, but know that may not happen."

Charlotte murmured, "Please, Aunt Mellie."

Melanie took her hand. "We need to talk about this. You don't want to face the future, but it is upon us, dear. I am leaving all this in your hands to do with as you will. I trust you to make the decisions that are best for you and Amy. And if you let Gerry help you, you will be OK. You can even sell the house."

Charlotte smiled, although her eyes were brilliant. "I don't think I could ever sell this house. And I cannot imagine life without you."

Melanie squeezed her hand. "I know. I want you to know that whatever you decide will be fine. But you need Gerry. He loves you, and will protect you. He understands all about dealing with the pressures you will face. Don't give him up for some daydream."

Charlotte, feeling her heart thumping against her chest, nodded dumbly.

Chapter 40

Nervously Charlotte scanned her profile in the full-length mirror. I'm not sure I am up to this, she thought. She wore a white sequined strapless fitted sheath of silk with empire waist dotted with sequins and pearls, the material cascading to the floor, a slit up the back showing the matching strappy sandals hugging her ankles. Her blond tresses were loosely coiffed, pinned up and allowed to fall back, haloing her head, her ears adorned with pearl and diamond teardrop earrings and her slim neck by a twisted multi-strand pearl choker, both gifts from Aunt Melanie. The only other jewelry was a large three-diamond ring on the finger of her left hand, given to her by Gerard only that morning.

"I am not good at proposing, Charl," he had replied to the question in her eyes. "I know Aunt Mellie's machinations, and she's not been exactly secretive with her intentions about tonight. I must admit that I'm a willing participant in her scheme."

As Charlotte started to protest, he laid his finger over her lips softly. "Don't say anything, please. Just think about it, about the possibility of us. We're good together. You know I adore you. And if the idea isn't too repugnant, I'd be honored if you wear my ring tonight."

Melanie had insisted on a large dinner party in honor of Stefan's winning his first major performance competition. Melanie had made it clear to Charlotte that she hoped for an engagement announcement to crown the evening's festivities, and to that end made sure that Charlotte was carefully groomed for the event.

Charlotte sat down at the vanity, staring unseeingly at her reflection. Why am I doing this? she wondered. Then angry at herself, she asked the woman in the mirror, "Why am I not wanting to do this? This is every girl's dream—a handsome man who is kind and dear and wealthy. I love Gerry madly. He will make a great husband."

But she knew why the gnawing in her gut persisted. Harry Kreiser's name was on the guest list tonight. She had been thrown together with him on several social occasions, and had worked with him on many projects, but she had taken care in avoiding prolonged periods of time alone in his presence. She wondered how he would react to the news. He'll probably be ecstatic that I'm otherwise occupied and no longer mooning over him, she thought unhappily. Well, it's not as though he has pursued me or shown any interest all this time. I was just a thoughtless diversion for him.

There was a light knock on the door as she was sitting, nervously smoothing on her lipstick. Mentally, she dragged herself back to the event at hand. "Come in," she called.

Stefan walked in, resplendent in black tailcoat, white waistcoat and white tie. He looked nonplussed at her scrutiny. "Aunt Mellie said this was a la-ti-da affair, very white tie," he colored slightly as he self-consciously pulled at his tie. "Even Dad has one of these on."

Charlotte stood as he walked up to her, and laughed to put him at his ease. "It's a most important occasion honoring you, and Aunt Mellie is fond of giving white-tie affairs, dear," she replied lightly, trying to appear more casual than she felt. "She is so proud. You look absolutely stunning," she added, as she smoothed his hair and straightened his tie.

He held her at arm's length. "You are beautiful, Aunt Charlotte. I've never seen you look so gorgeous."

She laughed self-consciously. "I clean up well, do I?"

Stefan regarded her soberly. "Are you announcing your engagement to Gerry tonight?"

Her smile faded, but she turned away to cover her reaction. "It could happen."

"Do you love him, Auntie?" Stefan was direct.

"He's all a girl could ask for," Charlotte answered truthfully. Hearing strains of the orchestra playing, she continued, "It's time we made it downstairs. Aunt Mellie believes in receiving lines."

Linking her arm in Stefan's, she pulled him with her out the door and down the hallway. "You go first," she commanded quietly. "You are the star attraction tonight."

She stood just outside the line of sight watching as he glided downstairs, greeting people, kissing his mother and taking his place by Aunt Melanie as she took charge of him and introduced him and his parents to her guests. Then she made her way in his wake, smiling pensively.

As Charlotte made it to the landing, there stood Gerard waiting, his suit a mirror of Stefan's. He held his hand out to her. As she took it, he pulled her slightly toward him and brushed his lips lightly against her cheek, murmuring in her ear, "My God, I think I'm in love."

She laughed. "You always know what to say to make me laugh. You're too good for me, you know."

Gerard smiled back. "You're probably right," he replied mischievously. "You know I wouldn't wear tails for just anyone. But Melanie was most insistent, and you know her—she is old school."

He tucked her hand inside his elbow and led her into the hallway, where they greeted guests. She felt her nervous jitters subsiding as they made light conversation with old friends and acquaintances, moving from room to room. She greeted Peter Conrad warmly, as he took her hand and kissed it. He noted the ring. "Good for you," he whispered, smiling broadly as she hugged him.

A waiter passed with fluted glasses filled with champagne. Gerard looked questioningly at her, but she shook her head. "Not yet—I'm saving myself," she said slyly. Noting that Dr. Jackson was present, she excused herself and made her way to him.

"My dear!" he exclaimed as he saw her. "You are a vision. It does my heart good to see you so happy."

She kissed his cheek, then pulled him into the library away from the crush of people. She held her ringed hand out. He gasped.

"Oh, my God! How utterly delightful. You are finally going to make me a happy man. Gerry must be walking on clouds."

She gazed into his eyes, her own mirroring her doubts. "Malcolm, am I doing the right thing? I just don't know."

Jackson's smile disappeared, and he enfolded her to him. "My dear, I'm worried about you. You know I cannot tell you how to be happy. Your life has been in a holding pattern for much too long. I always felt you were waiting for things that weren't meant to be. You deserve this, and Gerry will leave no stone unturned to make you happy. He will take care of you."

She pulled away, smiling wanly. "You are absolutely right. Gerry is my best friend. He will make a good husband and father."

Jackson, concerned, queried, "But surely that's not the only reason you are marrying him? My dear, you're such a passionate person—do you not love him?"

Charlotte, embarrassed at her *faux pas*, stammered, "Oh, but of course. I'm utterly crazy about him, Malcolm." Suddenly relieved at an influx of guests into the room, she turned and greeted them, engaging in small talk until she felt it safe to flee.

As she gained the doorway, she met Katharine Fellowes and her charge Cecelia Rhodes. "Kat," she exclaimed warmly. "And Cece. Thank you both for coming tonight."

"Where's Stefan?" Cecelia asked breathlessly, her eyes upon all the guests and their glitter.

"He's close at hand," Charlotte smiled at the girl. "Why don't you find him? I know he'd be thrilled to have a friend his own age to pal with."

Cecelia moved off, and Charlotte was left alone with Katharine, who was carelessly dressed in a pale pink organza confection. "You look marvelous," Charlotte squeezed her hand. "I'm very sorry about Agatha's death," she added, lowering her voice. "I wish she could have been here tonight. I'm very happy you came."

"Are you? It's just as well," Katharine replied lightly. Charlotte looked at her questioningly. "Have you begun your trousseau yet, darling?" Katharine continued, her voice carrying. "I've heard they have some fabulous gowns in off-white that you should check out."

Charlotte, caught off-guard, gasped. She suddenly felt someone at her elbow. Gerard growled, "Please, no scenes here, Kat. Can't you just once act as though you're happy I'm your brother?" He looked around quickly. "I've never asked you for anything until now. Don't spoil our night."

"Oh, dear brother Gerry," Katharine gushed saccharinely, her voice even louder, "you've spent your life playing second fiddle. Instead of marrying Priscilla Madden, you've waited in the wings behind Sammy and Harry Kreiser. Even you could do better than a used bill of goods."

"Excuse us, dear," Gerry whispered to Charlotte, who had recovered from her initial shock and was trying to smile at guests who were passing nearby. He took his sister by the arm and led her none too gently away.

Turning shakily, Charlotte bumped into someone. Her eyes widened as she recognized Kreiser. His eyes bored into hers as she smiled tremulously. "Harry, it is good to see you." She swallowed convulsively. "Are you here with Kat?"

He was rakishly encased in black cutaway with white tie, tailored to his form. She noticed that he seemed thinner. His thick hair, touched with white, was carefully groomed and waved impishly over his forehead. She was frighteningly aware of his hand, which had reached out and caught her waist to steady her and was resting there.

He smiled enigmatically. "No. I came alone. Dear Charlotte, how ravishing you look. Thank you for inviting me to such a special occasion for both Stefan and you."

Her heart caught in her throat as he dropped his hand and walked away. She stared at his retreating form as Amy came up to her, visibly relieved at having found her. Charlotte saw Gerard down the hallway, his eyes searching hers, as he made his way to her side.

"I'm so sorry," he murmured, taking her hand. "Kat's apparently not taking her medication. I've sent her home to Miss Mandy and asked Tom to ring her doctor." Miss Mandy was Katharine's personal companion.

He took her ringed hand and touched it to his lips briefly. "Thanks for wearing my ring tonight. Does it mean what I hope it means?"

Still speechless, she nodded at him. He pulled her to him. "Then I think this calls for a dance. Shall we show them how it's done?"

She dazedly allowed him to lead her into the dining room and out past the open French doors, where the ensemble was playing on the large verandah. The outdoors glowed with soft lights as couples danced and drank champagne. Even Melanie's reflecting pool gleamed with floating lights.

Gerard twirled her to him, and Charlotte laughed self-consciously. "Glad all those mandatory dance and etiquette lessons haven't gone to waste," she quipped as he caught her and held her to him.

"Aunt Mellie and Agatha knew what they were doing," he smiled. "And we've used those lessons to get us in and out of a lot of trouble over the years."

"You managed for us to crash almost every debutante ball, prom, and wedding in the area when we were kids," she reminded him.

"Hell, we were invited to most of them. You were a cheap date," he joked. "We could dance our way in, drink all the champagne and eat all the petit fours we wanted. And people said we looked divine together."

As the band played he whispered to her, "Don't worry, Charl—I'll make sure our marriage is as fun as those days were."

She gasped. "You know me too well. Does it show?"

"I can read you like a book. You're still afraid. Leave the past where it belongs. Let's start a new chapter. You know I'll be good to you, to Stefan, to Aunt Mellie."

Touched, she whispered, "I know. But what about Kat? I'm worried about her reaction."

Gerard took her chin and held it, looking down at her. "Kat never got over George's illness and death. They were close. Mom always kept close tabs on Kat, but now Mom is gone. Miss Mandy does well with her, but tonight—well, she was in rare form."

He gazed into Charlotte's eyes. "Charl, don't think twice about what she said. It's a mental illness. She wasn't right when she said what she did. And she's always had a way of sticking a knife in me. Why would she change tonight?" He kissed her lightly. "Besides, I'd wait a lifetime for you."

Charlotte blushed, feeling guilty about her earlier reaction to Kreiser.

The dance ended, and Gerard directed her attention to Melanie, who was imperiously waving for them to join her. As they made their way to her, Charlotte's heart leaped to her throat; she knew what her aunt wanted.

Melanie took each of them by an arm and said quietly, "Don't you think it is time we made an announcement?"

Gerard, seeing the panic in Charlotte's face, interposed quickly. "Aunt Mellie, nothing would give me greater pleasure, but I really think this should be Stefan's night. An announcement would be superfluous, anyway, because your niece has been sporting my ring on her finger all night. It is now pretty much all over the room, if not official."

Melanie quickly looked down at Charlotte's bejeweled hand. "My God, is it true?" she cried, her face rapturous. She gripped Charlotte's hand as she gazed upon the ring, calling attention to it as Amy and Michael came forward. As they heard Melanie's exclamations and saw the ring, they both hugged Charlotte and congratulated Gerard, their guests looking on with knowing smiles. Melanie nodded to the butler, who rang a bell and announced dinner.

Melanie, smiling broadly, took Gerard's arm and Stefan his mother's, and Charlotte was left standing with Michael. He wrapped his fingers around hers. "Is this what you want, Sis?" he said softly, watching her anxiously.

"Yes, I think so," she replied, trying to smile, to reassure him, as he led her into the dining room.

"Then I am happy for you, dear," he announced solemnly, as he helped her to her seat. "Gerry is a great guy."

Melanie was seated at one end of the long mahogany dining table, with Gerard at her left and Amy at her right. Stefan was placed at the other end, with his father at his left and Charlotte at his right. Charlotte looked quickly around to see where Kreiser was seated, but she did not immediately see him. She gave her attention to the man at her right, the current senator-hopeful, for whom Michael was currently working, an engaging man only slightly older than she, who searched her eyes soulfully while he talked about the programs he intended to promote in Washington. Her smile broadened as the young and lovely newspaper reporter across from him engaged Stefan in conversation about his future plans.

Suddenly there was a stir from the head of the table, as Miss Melanie slowly stood, raising her champagne glass. Waiters quickly scurried around filling flutes as the guests looked expectantly at her. Charlotte, suddenly feeling faint with apprehension, felt Stefan's hand squeezing hers reassuringly.

Melanie, her face encased in a broad smile, spoke. "This occasion is to celebrate my dear great-nephew's distinguishing himself in national competition. I was specifically asked not to call attention to the ring adorning my niece Charlotte's finger given her by our dear Gerry." Charlotte flushed as many of the guests looked her way, there was a loud chorus of 'oohs' and 'ahhs', and an enthusiastic spatter of applause rang out.

Melanie continued. "But I must confess to you that I am extremely proud of my family, all of them. They have made me so very happy, and I hope that tonight is only the beginning of many happy returns to them."

She paused, and Charlotte prayed irrationally, Please, Aunt Melanie. But Melanie, as if reading her mind, said only, "To family," to which all the guests raised their glasses and repeated the toast.

Dinner was an unhurried event of many courses. The combo group's music continued to waft through to the dining room as people passed in and out between courses to enjoy more champagne and dancing. Stefan stood and asked Charlotte to dance, and his mother and father followed suit outside. Stefan and Charlotte said little, for which Charlotte was grateful, as the cool air fanned her flushed cheeks. Then Gerard claimed her, and they danced quietly together.

As the dessert course was served, she suddenly sensed someone behind her chair. Looking up, she saw Kreiser there. He held his hand out to her. "May I have the honor of a dance?"

Silently she stood as he took her hand and led her outside. He drew her to him, placing his hand around her waist. "Don't worry, I have Melanie's blessing," he announced quietly. "In fact, I was ordered to make a public showing of our mutual non-romantic amicability. You are to act perfectly charming and give your old teacher one chaste dance."

She drew her breath in, the electricity of his touch going through her. "And is that what you want too?"

He unobtrusively folded her hand in his to his heart.

She opened her mouth, but he continued. "Feel my heart beating? I sometimes feel it only keeps beating until the next opportunity to see you. That is how my life is measured. And right now I can feel your heart beat throughout my whole being."

She was mesmerized. He sensed it, and smiled, a heart-melting smile. "Carlota, there are times I would do anything to re-write history, to change my lot in life, just to slay your dragons and be your Lancelot."

"Why are you telling me this now?" she breathed, wanting him and hating herself.

"I just want to make sure you know my motives are pure, and my absence from your life not just some selfish desire to expunge the memory of—what we shared," he finished lamely.

"Why didn't you come to find me?" she managed to ask, almost choking with emotion.

"Had I not hurt you enough?" he demanded huskily, smiling at her as though imparting some triviality. "Why should I prolong the agony of something that could never be?"

"Could you not allow me to make that decision?" she smiled back, although her heart was hammering in her throat.

"What could I give you?" his voice was low. "I spent my prime as nothing more than a gigolo searching for fame and fortune and a good time, then I found you. Would I, now that I've wasted myself, also waste you? I may not be much of a man, but by God, if I love anyone, it is you." At her bewildered expression, he continued, "Having said that, I wish I could go back and undo all that I've done to you."

Stunned, Charlotte reeled. He gripped her tighter. "Remember to play your part—charming and chaste," he whispered sternly. "People are watching. And if love means anything, it is not allowing you for one moment to consider throwing your life and talent away, even though you have certainly tried."

He relaxed his hold. "I'm so sorry for our last—encounter," he whispered, his eyes melting her heart. "I so wanted you to hate me, but I realize now I don't. Not at all."

She smiled tightly at another couple dancing by. His features softened. "That's better. We're just teacher and student, recalling fond memories. Speaking of which, I pray every night that you play again. Your talent was a gift from God, an extension of you. You are as fine a musician as ever I heard, certainly the best I've taught. You are not whole without it, Carlota." And he smiled slightly. "And we both know you still have it deep inside. Whether or not you wear a disguise. You proved it that evening at my home."

The picture of his assault flashed through her mind. "That's over," she was curt, wanting to lash out, to hurt him. "I can never go back. It's too late."

He looked at her sadly. "It's never too late. But if you do not, then I am truly doomed to hell."

He glanced over at the doorway, and she followed his gaze, to find Gerard watching her intently as he danced with Amy. "Fellowes seems to be a fine man, and truly devoted to you. Do you love him?"

"I love you, Harry," she said simply.

Kreiser drew in his breath sharply. "He's perfect for you," Kreiser said quickly, as though trying to ignore her statement. "He's good husband and father material. And we've established that I'm neither. I insist that you have a full life, and that means with someone other than me."

He paused. "If you will resume performance, I will do all in my power to help you. If you want to get your advanced degrees, I will work it out with whatever teacher you choose. I've talked to Malcolm about awarding you your degree. I will do all in my power to promote your playing again in public. It's late, I know. Do not deprive yourself and others of the joy of your art."

The music died away, and he released her quickly, taking her hand and leading her toward Gerard. She followed as if in a trance, as he kissed her hand and handed her over.

"Thank you for a lovely dance and for the chance to share those old memories of organ lessons, my dear. I'll take my leave now—I need to say my goodbyes to Melanie," Kreiser spoke, almost bowing to her as he turned and walked away. Charlotte stared after him impotently.

Chapter 41

The next musical number began. Gerard swept her into his arms possessively as she watched Kreiser walking away.

"What did he say?" Gerard demanded, his voice low, his grip on her unconsciously tightening.

"Oh, this and that," she heard herself saying, and she smiled calmly, even though her chest was pounding wildly and her heart was breaking. She was oblivious to everything else going on around her. As a waiter came by with more champagne, she stopped and took a glass, downing it quickly and giving the glass back.

"Are you all right?" Gerard demanded anxiously.

"Yes," she said recklessly, suddenly wrapping her arms around his neck and kissing him on the lips. "I want to go home with you tonight."

"You what?" Gerard was dumbfounded, pulling away and searching her face.

"You heard me," she replied, looking full into his amazed eyes. "I want you, Gerry. I don't intend to wait any longer. It's been a perfect evening, and I don't want it to end. I want champagne, roses, candles, and love."

She pulled away from him, full of purpose. He stared at her. "Are you sure, Charl?"

"Never more sure in my life. Aren't you?"

"What caused this?" he demanded, as he pulled her to him and they resumed dancing.

"I just had a grand epiphany," she spoke, forcing herself to sound gay.

"What did he say to you, Charl?" Gerard's voice was urgent.

"Nothing. It's just in that moment I realized how much I've been missing, and how lucky I am to have you," she remarked truthfully. "See, people are beginning to take their leave. I need to go upstairs and get a few things."

She left him, her heart fluttering as she tried to gracefully make her way through the throngs of people congratulating her. After several prolonged minutes of politely responding to persons saying their goodbyes, she was able to excuse herself and flew up the stairs. Reaching the sanctuary of her room, she locked the door, then looked quickly through the closet, finding a large black straw bag. She started filling it with small toiletries and a spare outfit, reaching into the closet for a lacy peignoir set, which she started folding.

There was a knock at the door. She heard Amy's voice whispering, "Charlotte, let me in."

Charlotte unlocked the door quickly. Amy burst in. "Are you OK? I saw you dashing through the crowd up here. What did old Kreiser have to say to you?"

Charlotte did not look at her sister. "I'm going home with Gerry tonight," she announced carefully, turning her back to Amy.

"You're what?" Amy exploded. "But Charlotte," she stammered, lowering her voice, "is that such a good idea? I mean, with all the guests here, it just doesn't look good. The paparazzi will have a field day."

"What is it with you all?" Charlotte shouted, flinging her arms out helplessly. "First you all are pushing me into Gerry's arms, and now you are questioning my decision."

Amy grabbed her and spun her around to face her, shushing her. "Charl, calm down. I'm happy for you, really I am. I want only your happiness. But what is this? You are not yourself. What did Kreiser do to put you into this state?"

Charlotte looked wildly at her sister. "What does Harry have to do with any of this?" she insisted. "I just realized tonight how stupid I've been. I've wasted my life, and now that I've made a decision to do something about it, I don't want to waste any more time. I want to begin the rest of my life tonight."

Amy sat down heavily onto the bed, staring at her long and hard. "OK, Sis, but let's at least wait until the guests go home, shall we? Let's not give Aunt Mellie a coronary. I'll help you slip out once the party is over. People are leaving. Just remain calm."

"I can't be calm," Charlotte retorted, unconsciously twisting Gerry's ring on her finger.

"Just stay here and get your things together. I'll take care of everything and come for you," Amy soothed her. "I'll make some excuse for you."

After Amy left, Charlotte locked the door back, changed out of her gown and chose a filmy black fitted sheath with spaghetti straps that fitted her form perfectly and ended six inches above her slim shapely knees, and some matching black sandals. She busied herself stuffing things into her bag.

She suddenly heard a knock. "Charlotte?" the imperious voice of her aunt demanded. Startled, she quickly hid the tote behind the bed like a child, sitting on the bed very still, barely breathing, praying.

Suddenly she heard Amy's voice through the door. "Aunt Mellie, I believe she is downstairs with Gerry saying goodnight to Dean Jackson."

"Then why is the door locked? I want to talk to her," Melanie sniffed, trying the knob. Charlotte froze.

"Auntie, you must be very tired, and I think we've all had enough excitement for the night. Surely it can wait until morning. Leave the lovebirds be."

She heard Amy coaxing Melanie down the hall to her suite, and sighed weakly with relief.

After what seemed like a small lifetime, Amy knocked again. As Charlotte unbolted the door, Amy swept past. "The coast is clear. Gerry's limo is downstairs for you. He said something about roses and candles."

Charlotte felt a moment of panic, then smiled. "He's so sweet."

Amy took Charlotte's chin in her hand and lifted her eyes to meet her own. "Make sure you know what you are doing. Don't hurt him, Charl. Gerry's the best thing that ever happened to you."

Charlotte nodded, not trusting herself to speak. She picked up her bag, squeezed Amy's hand, and walked with her to the door.

Charlotte made her way down the corridor, silently passing the door to her aunt's suite, barely daring to breathe. The hallway lights were dim as Charlotte made it down the stairs. She could hear the caterers still tidying in the kitchen as she made it to the front door. Opening the door, she saw the limousine and froze. Don't back out now, she told herself sternly as she quietly pulled the door closed behind her.

Gerry's driver appeared from nowhere and held the door for her. She murmured her thanks as she stepped inside, then stiffened in shock as she found Gerry waiting for her, a mass of white roses which he handed to her, the privacy window closed.

"You scared me," she laughed shakily. "I thought Amy said you had gone on ahead."

"I made arrangements as you ordered," he surveyed her, his face impassive. "That's a hell of a dress." He paused. "Are you still sure?"

She looked at him with a shy smile, renewing her resolve. "Yes. I'm sure."

She looked around her, seeing a bottle of champagne in an ice bucket with two glasses. "I'm a bit thirsty," she nodded toward the bottle.

He took her cue, expertly uncorking the bottle and filling the two glasses with the frothy liquid before handing her one.

She clinked glasses with him. "To us, Gerry," she said simply, before downing hers in one swallow. He followed suit. "More, please," she whispered seductively, as she held her glass to him and he refilled the glasses. Again she gulped the contents, before disentangling herself from the roses and reaching over to kiss him on the mouth, a long, lingering kiss.

Startled, he let his glass fall to the floor, wrapping his arms around her and pulling her to him. He returned her kiss tentatively, his response becoming more impassioned as she threw herself at him, embracing him with abandon.

"Whoa, Charl," he finally said, his voice ragged. "What brought this on? Why suddenly hath the ice maiden become a fire goddess?"

She faltered, ashamed of her wanton behavior. He ran his finger down her spine, and she shivered. "Not that I don't like the new Charlotte," he chuckled as he pulled her on top of him and nuzzled her neck. "I just want to know where the secret switch is," he mumbled as he found her mouth again.

"Do you want me?" she asked breathlessly, fearfully against his lips.

"Like never before," he answered her fervently, his hand running through her tresses and loosening them, her hair falling down. "I never dared to dream you might reciprocate, even after that day at your place," he continued as his finger followed her profile down to the cleft of her breast, taking the strap of her gown down her arm and stopping just above her bodice. He groaned as she ran her hand up the leg of his trousers.

"Oh, Charlotte," he whispered, one hand stroking the calf of her bare leg, moving slowly and seductively upward. "I've never met anyone who could make me forget you. I was so angry back when Mom made the decision that you should marry George, to further his image."

"Your mother? Arranging my marriage?" Charlotte paused briefly, but his hands on her skin were wreaking havoc with her senses.

"Yeah," he whispered as his hand kept moving up. "I think that's why I was so determined to be successful. Everything at home was always 'George this' and 'George that'. It was the final straw when he was going to get you too.

"I think, though, Mom would have been happy about tonight, ecstatic about finally uniting the Fellowes and the Cains." He groaned as Charlotte found his fly and pulled it down. "But Hell-Kat was livid when I told her I had given you a ring. I really thought she was OK with the idea, but my announcement seemed to resurrect all her old resentments that you had broken up with her idol George." His tongue traced her profile from her ear down her slim lovely neck, as her hand slipped inside his pants and she began stroking him.

Suddenly, the voice of the driver was heard over the intercom. "Mr. Fellowes, we've arrived at the penthouse."

"Good," Gerry murmured as his hand removed the fabric and his mouth found her breast. She arched against him, her breath coming in gasps as the fingers of her free hand raked through his hair and held him to her.

He finally pulled away reluctantly. "I need to get you upstairs in one piece, Charl, away from prying eyes, and quick. We mustn't provide more fodder for the papers."

Dazed she sat upright, pulling herself together awkwardly as he did the same. She reached for her glass, filled it with champagne and downed it again, refilling the glass.

"Slow down," he remarked, taking her glass and downing the contents himself. "We have the rest of our lives."

The driver pulled to his private entrance, and Gerry stepped out, looking around carefully, taking her hand and gently guiding her out of the car. He took her tote from her. She followed him dreamlike through the door and into the elevator. As the doors closed, he not so gently slammed her against the wall, pinning her with his body. She wrapped her arms and legs around him as he pulled her off the ground and held her to him, his hand pulling up the fabric of her dress. His fingers found the filmy material of her panties and pulled it aside. She gasped with delight as his finger stroked her. She groaned and her body tensed against his.

"Charl, don't tease me. If you are, stop me now," he whispered, his voice hoarse with emotion. "I'm quickly going over the edge."

She answered by covering his mouth with hers and raking her fingers through his hair and down his back as the doors opened. He carried her bodily through the room, finally falling with her on top of him onto a leather sofa.

She quickly undid his bow tie and collar, as he found the hidden back zipper of her dress and in one sweep pulled it, leaving her back exposed. He sat up, shrugging out of his jacket as one hand explored her curves. Her hands flew to his pants, as his mouth met her breast. Frantic, she tried to unfasten his trousers.

Suddenly he muttered an oath, stood up and whisked her into his arms, carrying her like a child through the hallway and into the bedroom. She gasped as she looked around her. Everywhere were flowers and candles, and two buckets held chilled champagne bottles.

"My God!" she exclaimed. "How did you do all this?"

"I have my ways, and some very discreet servants," he answered, as his mouth claimed hers. He dumped her on the bed, then stood and rapidly undressed himself as she watched, hypnotized.

Again she froze as she realized that she was practically naked and acting wantonly. She reached for the champagne bottle, suddenly needing a shot of courage or oblivion.

He took the bottle from her. "You're not having second thoughts?"

She felt the room slipping away. "No, Gerry, it's just that I want to keep this delicious buzz going," she lied, suddenly frightened at his nearness, as lust and disgust warred inside her woozy head.

"I should be scared of you," he spoke, his eyes searching hers as he poured champagne for both of them. He knocked his back as she watched, then refilled his as she drank hers.

"That's OK," she murmured provocatively. "Sometimes I scare myself."

As she drank, a picture of Kreiser dancing with her that night filled her thoughts. His words played over in her head. You bastard, she thought, then thought in horror, Did I say that aloud?

She looked at Gerry, who was still gazing at her. She then realized how disheveled she looked, and her dress had slipped to her waist, leaving her exposed. The champagne began its numbing effect, and she was filled with self-loathing.

"I look a mess," she mumbled, her face burning.

Gerard took her hand and kissed her palm, then sat down on the bed beside her. "You are the most beautiful woman I've ever seen," he whispered, entwining her fingers in his. "And I don't care right now whether you love me or not. Maybe you're just using me to get back at Melanie, or Kreiser, or to exorcise your demons, whatever. All I know is that I want you, Charlotte. I think I've always loved you. I try to forget that you only need me after you've been rejected by Harry Kreiser. I just want to have my way with you and forget what your eyes look like when you look at him."

Tears stung her eyes in shame as she murmured, "I'm so sorry, Gerry. You're the best thing that's ever happened to me, and I want to make you happy." She paused, grasping for words. "I want to be happy with you." As the room began to swim, she continued, "I want to live happily ever after with you."

She felt herself slipping backwards, and she pulled him to her. "Make love to me," she commanded. She closed her eyes as she felt him slipping her clothes off, and clung to him shivering as he kissed her, running his hands over her flesh, claiming her with his hands and mouth. "Oh, my God," she moaned, lost in sensation.

When he entered her, she gasped. "I love you," she murmured incoherently as she stroked his back and tightened herself against him, her hips moving rhythmically against his. All the past came flowing back in her memory, and suddenly she was back with Harry. She poured herself into loving him, of giving him all she had wanted to give Harry for so long, of making up for the lost years and the pain of losing Harry.

Chapter 42

She awakened the next morning, her head aching. The smell of roses and candle wax wafted around her. She realized that she was not in her own bed. She sat up suddenly, naked and alone. The previous night came rushing back to her. Sunlight was filtering around the heavy drapes pulled across the windows.

She remembered. She had experienced the dream, and had awakened in the early morning hours screaming. Gerry was there when she opened her eyes, and had held her and soothed her, until she asked for more champagne, and they made love again. She screamed as he brought her to the brink over and over. She remembered nothing else.

She shakily stood and made her way to the bathroom, where she located her tote bag. She brushed her teeth, showered and toweled dry, finding a plush robe hanging on the peg behind the bathroom door. It swallowed her small form. She found some aspirin tablets in the medicine cabinet and swallowed a couple.

She walked into the bedroom and sat on the edge of the bed, her mind reeling. Gerard walked in, dressed in a dark suit, carrying a breakfast tray.

"Good morning," he announced, his voice neutral. "Amy has already called this morning. Melanie is fit to be tied, looking for you. Amy told her you had an early appointment at the newspaper this morning. I brought you some toast and orange juice. And some buttermilk."

She looked at him gratefully, but he did not meet her eyes. Confused, she murmured her thanks as he set the tray beside her on the bed, then looked at his watch. "Charl, I've got to go. There's a directors' meeting at the bank this morning, and we have some business to thrash out."

She nodded silently, wondering at his coolness. He looked at her briefly, his eyes suddenly tender. "Will you be OK?"

"Yes, I'm just fine, just a little hangover," she assured him, reaching out and squeezing his hand. He responded a moment, his pressure matching hers before he pulled away. As he strode away, she found her voice.

"Gerry?" she called timidly.

"Yes, dear?" he replied, turning back to her.

"I don't—know how to thank you for—" she managed to say.

"Don't mention it. Drink your buttermilk," he said softly, as he left, shutting the door emphatically.

After Gerard left, Charlotte called Amy to let her know that she was fine and would see them later that evening. She knew she could not face Melanie, and she was still unsure of Gerard's demeanor that morning. *What have I done?* she thought confusedly. *Maybe he doesn't want me after all.*

She made it to work and threw herself into the bustle of the newspaper office, greeting the reporters, shuffling through her phone messages, and trying to focus on the work before her. Mainly she wanted to shut out the words of Kreiser to her the night before. *He loves me,* she kept thinking. *Surely there is a way for us to be together. No, I am crazy. It's over with him. He's ruined me and stripped me of all dignity.* She was so torn between her plans to follow through with marriage to Gerard and her muddled feelings for Kreiser that she found it hard to concentrate on her work.

She returned some calls and hammered a draft of a concert review for Ed. She knew he wouldn't like it, but kept pecking at it, fleshing out the points until the time she expected him to storm into her office, at which time she provided an amended draft for him.

Suddenly the cell phone by her elbow rang. Guiltily, she jumped, before answering it. "Charlotte Lawson speaking. May I help you?"

"Hi, Charl," Gerard's voice greeted her. "You're still at the office?"

Looking out the window, she suddenly realized that it was rapidly growing dark. "I didn't realize the time," she laughed, as she Xed out the web sites she had been perusing for research. "What are you doing?"

"I'm on the jet—have to be in Tucson early in the morning."

"Oh." She didn't know why she felt disappointed. "I'm sorry, Gerry."

"I couldn't get out of it, but hope to be back tomorrow or Sunday." He paused, apparently wanting to say more.

"I'll miss you." Charlotte suddenly felt alone without him.

"Will you?" he asked, his voice sounding odd.

"Yes, I will," Charlotte insisted, suddenly frustrated. "What's wrong, Gerry? What have I done? Have you changed your mind about me? Please tell me."

"It's nothing," he said shortly. "Charl, I gotta go. I'll call you tomorrow."

"OK," she agreed reluctantly.

She suddenly realized that she had no diversion, no reason to prevent her from going home and facing Melanie. The thought filled her with dread, but she had prolonged the moment long enough.

She drove through the back streets of the city, cutting around the thoroughfares lined with post-rush hour traffic, and made her way home. As she entered the front door, she met Amy and Dr. Amason, the family internist, at the door.

"What's wrong?" she cried, her facing flushing guiltily.

"Nothing to be alarmed about," Dr. Amason soothed her. "Melanie was just feeling a touch overtired after her soiree. I've checked her out, and she'll be better in a day or two." Patting Amy's hand, he said, "Just call me if you need me."

After the doctor left, Charlotte looked at the stairs. "Maybe I should go up," she said reluctantly.

"No need," Amy stated softly. "He gave her a sedative, and she's probably asleep by now. She worked herself into a lather wanting to talk to you earlier today, and was complaining of chest pains this afternoon. I called Dr. Amason."

"What does she want to talk to me about?" Charlotte asked.

"God only knows," Amy replied tiredly. "Don't worry about it tonight—you dodged the bullet."

"Where are the boys?" Charlotte wanted to know.

"Off at some bowling party for one of Stefan's friends."

She paused, hands on hips, staring at Charlotte as Charlotte looked away. "Well, are you going to tell me?"

"Tell you what?" Charlotte demanded.

"About last night," Amy answered angrily. "After all I've gone through for you last night and today, you could at least tell me what happened."

"I need a drink," Charlotte sighed.

Amy led the way to the library, where she poured them both a vodka and tonic, Amy's favorite. Charlotte and Amy seated themselves on opposite ends of the sofa, kicked their shoes off and intertwined their legs as they stretched out.

Charlotte without preamble plunged in. "Harry told me he loved me last night."

"No!" exclaimed Amy. "The nerve of him, after all this time. Surely you don't buy that?"

Charlotte was silent. Amy prodded her. "What, Charlotte?"

"He told me he has nothing to offer me—no future, no children. He wants me to be with Gerry. But I love him, Amy. I realized it last night."

Amy looked at her sister in horror. "You're crazy. He's right, Charl. You cannot tie yourself to Harry. What about your future with Gerry, children? Don't forget the hell you went through before because of Harry. If he loved you, he would not have put you in that position, would not have let you suffer alone."

Charlotte nodded wordlessly, the pain evident on her face. Amy insisted, "And what about Gerry? Did you sleep with him?"

Charlotte nodded, her face pained. "I want to make him happy. But I'm not sure if I can do this, Amy," Charlotte's voice broke.

"You took his ring, you slept with him, and you don't know if you want to go through with marriage?" Amy was incredulous.

"It's what everyone wants, and I want to do the right thing. Gerry is so good to me."

"God, Charl, what a mess," Amy muttered, gulping her drink. "What kind of role model are you for Stefan, when you can't keep your own life straight?"

"I'm doing my best," Charlotte retorted angrily. "Not everyone falls into the perfect life with the perfect man like you did."

Amy snapped, "It's not always perfect—we have our moments too." But, looking over at her sister, she softened. "But you're right. I have had it easy with Mike. I knew from the moment I met him he was the one, and I have been so lucky. Even having to wrest him from Kat wasn't all that bad."

"No, he is the lucky one," Charlotte murmured, rubbing her sister's foot gently. "I envy what the two of you have, and you have given me the best brother I could have wished for. And Stefan—"

"—is a blessing from heaven. I know," Amy laughed, and Charlotte joined her.

Amy sobered. "Stefan worships you, Charlotte, and he worries so much about you. Sometimes I wonder if he's not too old for his years."

"I would never do anything to harm Stefan, and I try to be honest with him," Charlotte responded soberly. "Gerry has been so good to him. He adores his godson, and spends a lot of his free time with him."

Charlotte rose slowly. "Amy, I'm beat. I drank too much champagne last night, and I need some sleep."

She hugged her sister before walking out, bounding up the stairs. She stopped beside her aunt's door, debating whether to go in. She quietly opened the door, and saw her aunt's regular breathing. Satisfied, she closed the door and went to her own room.

Early the next morning after her rowing Charlotte was sitting in the kitchen helping herself to toast and juice, when she was surprised by the sight of Melanie in the doorway. She looked older, weaker.

"Are you sure you should be up?" Charlotte stood, stunned. "I'll be glad to bring you some breakfast upstairs."

"Don't bother, I feel fine," her aunt protested regally. She sat down at the table as Daisy scurried around, tutting around the older woman.

"Oh, Daisy, don't carry on so," Melanie replied irritably. "Just bring me whatever Charlotte here is having."

Momentarily, Melanie was provided toast, coffee and orange juice. She waved Daisy away. "Leave us. We have business to discuss."

Charlotte, inwardly unnerved but determined to appear nonchalant, continued staring unseeingly at the local section of the paper as Melanie pored over the front page.

"You know, you and Gerard made a great-looking couple the other night," Melanie said, looking through her glasses at the newspaper in front of her.

Charlotte paused mid-bite into her toast. She was used to Melanie's abrupt bouts of speaking her mind. But nothing prepared her for Melanie's next words.

"Did you sleep with him?"

Charlotte gasped. Melanie sighed. "I'm not a fool, girl. I knew where you were. I knew Amy was covering for you.

"I think it's high time you got yourself married. You've been the subject of too much talk in this town. I'm not in favor of a long engagement, like the one you had with his fancy-pants brother. That time you ended up taking a powder and ran away. There was scuttlebutt about you and Harry then too. I had to clean up that mess."

Charlotte opened her mouth, but Melanie continued, holding her hand up to silence the girl. "Yes, my dear, I know what happened then, the clandestine meetings. Don't you think I can read it in your eyes every time I see you looking at Harry?"

Charlotte paled visibly, her breakfast forgotten. She stared unseeingly at her clenched hand gripping her napkin in her lap. "I don't know what you're talking about," she said quietly, her voice unsteady.

"It's plain. You found out Sammy was a fairy. I didn't want that engagement, but knew if I opposed it, you would become even more determined. Thankfully, you discovered the worst before it was too late.

"Then you lost your head and fancied yourself in love with Harry. When he finally rebuffed you, you realized what a botch you made and ran away."

Charlotte made no reply, but realized she was shaking. She suspected that Melanie had known about her and Kreiser, but the confirmation still unnerved her.

"But that is all water under the bridge. You still fancy you're in love with him, that he loves you. You are so intelligent, yet so naïve. Charlotte, you realize what a foolish idea that is? Even if Harry returned your attentions, I would never allow the match. I would banish him. I told him so."

Charlotte's head swung up to meet her aunt's eyes upon her. "Why?" she asked, startled.

"Charlotte, you can be so infantile. Harry's quite charming, but he's too old for you, he has no resources for supporting a wife of your station, and his reputation is too risqué. But most importantly, darling, he knows nothing of commitment. Everything is a grand passion of which he soon tires before moving on. He's a great addition to a dinner party, can play the pants off the organ, and is a fabulous asset to the art community here, but—oh, God, Charlotte, surely you have figured this out? He came to me himself and confessed about your little affair. I forbade his seeing you. Then you got pregnant."

"What?" Charlotte fairly shouted. "You knew?"

"Yes, dear, there's nothing you girls have ever done that has escaped me. I have paid a fortune just in keeping up with the details of your lives and escapades, and in protecting you from yourselves and others. You don't realize that a life of privilege such as yours is fraught with perils."

Charlotte stared, tears in her eyes. "You were the reason Harry and I aren't together?"

"I guess you could say that," Melanie pursed her lips. "I'm sure the handsome annual income he receives at my hands to keep his hands off you doesn't enter into the equation at all," she added dryly.

Charlotte stared at her woodenly. Melanie sighed, suddenly looking very pale and tired. "You are still such a child in many ways, my dear. What are you going to do when I'm gone? My dear one, you need Gerard. He will provide for you and take care of you. You know, it's not too late for you to consider children, carrying on the family line."

Charlotte stood, her voice icy. "You never wanted Harry and me to be together because you always considered him yours. If you couldn't have him, no one else would."

Melanie's lip trembled. "Is that what you think, child?" she whispered, her face white. "My God, I've only given myself to one man." Her voice shook. "There's not a day goes by that I don't miss him and want to be with him."

Charlotte was silent, remorseful. She sat back down. Melanie spoke softly. "Harry has had about one 'grand passion' per year. You ended up at the wrong place at the wrong time. He moved on. So should you."

Melanie stood up and slowly and painfully made her way to Charlotte, placing her hand on Charlotte's head. Then she sat down beside Charlotte.

"Can I tell you a story?" she whispered. "You think I don't know what you've been through? I fancied myself in love once, with my piano teacher. I wanted to run off with him, to elope. But my parents found out, and hustled me off to Wesleyan. It was the best thing that ever happened to me. Then I met Howard, and I never regretted it."

Her eyes misted as she gazed at Charlotte. "But with you I was helpless to stop it. Even though I suspected how Harry felt about you, I trusted him, and felt you were safely deep in the throes of infatuation over Sammy. I knew all the stories about him, so thought you safe until you found out. I blame myself for not being here when that fell apart, but when I called, Harry assured me that you were with him, and he had things under control." She paused. "Obviously he didn't. But what hurt most was your running away and not confiding in me. When I finally saw you after the miscarriage, it broke my heart."

Charlotte's eyes dilated. "You knew? A-about Johann?"

"Yes. Like I said, nothing happens to you girls that I don't know. But Amy warned me to leave you alone when you showed up there, lest you run away. That hurt most of all, having to stay away while you suffered alone." She took a deep breath, her hand over her chest. Charlotte gasped in concern, but Melanie waved her to silence.

"I had hoped so much that you and I could grow closer." Melanie paused, and her lower lip trembled slightly. "But you have always been so different from Amy, who always told me everything. Mike convinced me that I could not force you to come back."

Charlotte looked down at her hands. "I'm sorry."

"I once was able to reach you through music, but after Howard died, it's like the door was shut," Melanie whispered, taking Charlotte's hand in hers. "I trusted you with Harry, even knowing he was vulnerable to you, because he was able to reach past that shell. I was wrong. But you are wrong in persisting in this pipedream. Please listen to me on this matter, child. I only have your well-being at heart."

"But I love Harry," Charlotte whispered, her eyes filled with tears. "I cannot believe you did this, and that Harry went along with you."

"It really wasn't that hard for him," Melanie stated coldly. "He has always had expensive tastes. It might interest you to know that Harry is in complete agreement with my views on the matter.

"Charlotte, you don't love him. You have been obsessed with a delusion. And he cannot give you what you really need. You are fond of Gerard, and he of you. That's a lot more than many couples have."

Charlotte was devastated. Melanie stroked her hand gently, grasping it weakly. "You are so devoted to Stefan. Gerard adores him. Don't you want another child of your own? It would make me so very happy to think of you with a husband and family filling this house again with laughter." She squeezed Charlotte's hand again, speaking softly. "Let's set a date. Let me throw you a wedding you can remember long after I'm gone."

Melanie looked at her sympathetically. "You know, you're the executor of my will. I won't be around much longer, and Amy can't even balance a checkbook. It's a lot of responsibility, and I'd love if you had someone to help shoulder it, dear."

Charlotte said nothing. She felt her life crumbling around her. Melanie sighed. "You always were such a willful child. Promise me you'll think about it."

"How do I know Stefan isn't really my child?" Charlotte spat suddenly. "How do I know you didn't manage to steal my child and give him to Amy?"

"My God, girl," Melanie leaned back, stunned. "Surely you wouldn't believe me capable of so heinous a crime?" She took a deep trembling breath, her face white. "Oh, my dear." Tears filled her eyes. "I have truly failed you if you trust me so little that you would think that of me."

"What am I supposed to think?" Charlotte exclaimed, her own chest constricting painfully. She gasped, "I feel like I'm going crazy. My life is a shambles. I love Harry, I'm engaged to Gerry, and I see myself in Stefan. I've thrown my life away. I can no longer think straight. I have no idea who I am, and so I've become a monster. I understand Kat's pain, because I'm just as mentally unstable as she."

She stood and looked at her aunt. "I'm sorry for what I said, that I caused you pain, but you know that's all I'm good at—inflicting pain and embarrassment." She paused, hating herself for the look of raw hurt that passed across Melanie's face. "Yes, I will marry Gerry. I will try to make everyone happy." Charlotte quickly walked out of the room.

Later that day Charlotte was summoned to the hospital by a frantic call from Amy, to find Aunt Mellie in the throes of another stroke and comatose. Suddenly she was shouldered with the responsibilities of her aunt's business and financial matters, and overflowing with remorse at her last words to her aunt, as Melanie slowly slipped away.

Chapter 43

Charlotte sank woodenly, passively onto the bench in the foyer of the massive home. She was still in her black silk suit from the public memorial service provided for Melanie. She was too spent to cry, and was thankful for the solitude.

She had gone out with Amy afterward to see the family mausoleum, to make sure all was in order and to pay her respects. She had received another jolt when she discovered a small marker between Uncle Howard's and her father's berth identified only as 'Johann Lawson'.

"He was buried here?" she whispered, her eyes wide, her heart lurching in agony as she touched the etched letters.

"Yes. Auntie insisted that we bring him home, despite the chance that the news might leak to the press," Amy's voice was quiet as she took Charlotte's arm.

"She knew even then?"

"Yes," Amy was defensive. "I didn't tell her, honest. But Aunt Mellie always had her ways of finding out stuff."

Charlotte, sitting in the foyer, let her mind drift back to her conversation with Dr. Amason at the hospital, where she voiced her concerns about her angry words with Melanie. Amason was gentle. "Dear Charlotte, Melanie knew for several weeks that she was living on borrowed time. She told me the day after the party she was not willing to go into the hospital until she had a talk with you. Even before she slipped into a coma she was asking for you. She wanted your forgiveness."

She recalled her last conversation with her aunt at the kitchen table. *Our altercation caused her death,* Charlotte told herself. *She kept Kreiser and me apart. I killed her.* Feelings of intense anger mixed with those of remorse.

"It's Mr. Harry on the phone, Miss Charlotte," Daisy's voice interrupted her.

"I'll take it in the library," she said.

Walking into the room, she snatched up the phone, breathlessly speaking. "Hello?"

"Carl—I mean, Charlotte? This is Harry Kreiser. I just wanted to call you and tell you how sorry I am about Melanie. I meant to speak to you after the service, but I just couldn't bring myself to intrude on your grief, *cara mia*."

At the sound of his voice, her anger at him melted. The tears fell unheeded down her face. "Thank you, Harry. I appreciate your playing the memorial service today as well as the funeral last week. The music was lovely, just what Aunt Mellie would have wanted."

"I was glad I could be of some service to you, Carlota," she thrilled at the sound of his voice as he used the forbidden intimacy. "If there's anything I can do—"

She shocked herself by hearing herself say, "I would like to see you." She covered herself hastily. "Of course, at your convenience. Auntie had some specific items that she wanted you to have."

"Of course. You are too kind," she heard him reply. "Perhaps when you are up to receiving guests."

Why not tonight? God, what a fool I'm making of myself, she thought crossly. "Yes, that would be nice. Perhaps for some of Daisy's tea tomorrow afternoon. Four-ish?"

"I'll be there," he promised.

She rang off, mortified. There's nothing left between us, she told herself angrily. He took money, bribes to stay away from me. He disgusts me, she reminded herself.

Suddenly Gerard stood in the doorway, still in his dark suit, his tie loosened, a tumbler of scotch in hand as he regarded her solemnly. "Stefan went with Amy and Mike to dinner. We need to talk."

Charlotte stood, embarrassed as she wondered how much of the conversation he had heard. She turned her back to him, watching him through the gilt mirror over the fireplace. "I'll take one of those, if you don't mind," she said, suddenly uncomfortable at the thought of being alone with him.

He walked over to the table, selecting a decanter and pouring a generous measure into a glass. At her nod, he mixed some water in it, before slowly approaching her with the proffered glass.

He placed it on the mantel. She murmured her thanks. But he didn't move away. He caught her wrist lightly, pulling her back around to face him as he set his own drink on the mantel.

She was startled as he pulled her to him and kissed her roughly.

"Gerry, please don't . . .," she whispered.

"Why not? We're way past preliminaries, aren't we, Charl?" he interrupted, his voice husky as he held her. She could taste the Scotch from his lips. "Aunt Mellie had us slated for marriage. Is the courtship already over, or was this an arrangement for convenience only?"

Frightened at his mood, she looked at him anxiously. He regarded her brilliant eyes as she remained imprisoned in his arms. "Don't look at me like that. It drives me mad. Damn it, Charl, you're so beautiful—" he broke off, drowning her in embrace as his kiss deepened, smothering her protests.

She finally pulled away, tears in her eyes. "Gerry, we have so much to discuss, but now is not the time . . ."

"Now is the time," he interrupted again bitterly. "You could go along with your aunt that we were an item, that we were getting married, but it's all a lie, isn't it?" Releasing her and stalking away from her, he suddenly turned and faced her. "Would you have gone through with the charade if she was still alive?"

Her face flamed as she stood there, ashamed, feeling naked. "I'm so sorry, Gerry. Mellie wanted it all so badly, and I still want it for her, for you, for—for myself."

She found a chair behind her and sank down into it, not looking at him. "I was honest the other night. I do love you and want to make you happy. I promised Melanie I was marrying you." Her voice faltered as she saw the stricken look on his face.

"But you don't love me in that way," he finished for her, his voice flat. "It's always been Harry, hasn't it? Even when you gave yourself to me, it wasn't me you were making love to. Yes, you talk in your sleep."

Her face crimsoned. "No, darling, you don't understand. The dreams—"

"I understand perfectly," he turned away abruptly. "God, I thought I could handle it, that I could take anything if only you'd marry me. But the bastard will never go away. I could kill the son of a bitch right now. He'll always be between us."

She started shaking. "No, that's not true. It's not what you think. I do love you, Gerry. Aunt Mellie said my feelings for you would grow, and that—that having your children would make us better, stronger."

"What a noble sacrifice for you," he replied coldly. "Didn't you stop to think that your behavior the other night gave me momentary hope for something more from you?"

"Please listen to me," she whispered desperately.

Striding to the doorway, he paused and looked at her, his eyes glittering. "I never thought you could be cruel, Charl. I can't do this any more."

He pulled an envelope out of his jacket pocket. "Oh, I almost forgot. Here's your 'evidence'. I never gave this to you, because you didn't mention it again after you asked me to do this. All about Stefan's parentage—Mike already had it ready for the time Stefan would ask for it. I verified it all. And I had DNA done. Interesting reading. Hope that answers your question."

He tossed the envelope on the coffee table and strode out. She sat there in shock, hearing the front door slam, his words echoing in her ears as she stared at the unopened envelope. I've lost the best man in the world, she thought despairingly. Harry, you son of a bitch. I could kill you too.

The next day she prepared carefully for her meeting with Kreiser. She dressed herself in a sleek black pantsuit that fit her form and accentuated her curves. She informed Daisy to pull out all the stops on the dainties, and made sure that the rest of the family was otherwise occupied and away. She pulled out a box from the safe, replacing it with the unopened envelope from Gerard about Stefan's paternity.

When Kreiser arrived, she received him warmly, embracing him enticingly. He responded hesitantly, whether unsure of himself or her she didn't know. He pulled away from her and looked into her eyes.

"*Cara mia*," he spoke tenderly. "I am so sorry for your loss. Melanie was a wonderful but formidable woman. Please know that she loved you dearly."

"Yes, I'm sure she did," Charlotte concurred enigmatically. "Come sit beside me and have some tea."

She entwined her fingers in his and led him over to the sofa, indicating that he should sit. When he did, she sat down beside him. She served them tea and scones, and they drank in silence. She momentarily faltered in her resolve. I hate myself so much for still wanting him, she thought.

"How are you doing, Carlota?" he asked her, setting down his cup and saucer.

"Some days it is hard to press on," she said honestly. "I have something for you."

She walked over to Melanie's desk and brought forth the small box the size of a hard-bound book, tied with a ribbon, that she had earlier retrieved from the safe. She gave it to him solemnly.

He slowly took it. "What is it?" he wondered aloud.

He opened the box, and lined in tissue he found a stack of $100 bills.

"Five hundred of them—your quarterly allotment, I believe," Charlotte said, her voice mocking. "I did not want you to worry about losing it once Melanie was no longer here to pay the bribe."

"Bribe?" he asked, incredulous, staring at the bills. "I don't understand."

"Melanie was careful to tell me all about the payoff to you, only days before she died," Charlotte closed her eyes, the anger washing over her. "And all that time I waited for you to come to me, to rescue me, to be with me, Aunt Mellie was picking up the tab for you to stay away. It is just too rich," she finished, her voice catching in a sob. "You and your pure motives, my ass," she hissed.

Kreiser's eyes were cold. "That's what she told you? I don't believe you."

"But of course," Charlotte cried, wanting to strike him. "Her parting shot to me was to let me know just how naïve I had been to hope for you."

"Well, then," he spoke, standing, his voice flat, "there's no need for you to hear anything from me."

He strode out, the box of bills left on the table. She called after him, "Don't forget your money." But he didn't look back.

Later, when Stefan came in, he found the box with the money lying on the coffee table. Questioningly he looked at Charlotte, who was sitting in the overstuffed chair staring at the embers in the fireplace, a tumbler and empty decanter beside her on the coffee table.

"Get it out of my sight—just put it in the safe for now," she replied dully, her words slurred, refusing to look at him.

Chapter 44

Although it was only a couple of months after Melanie's death, Charlotte hosted a small party for Kreiser's students at her home in honor of Brad Reynolds, a graduating student. She had felt a special pride for the young man, who had come from humble beginnings and had taken the instrument by storm. She truly felt he was a future star, and he was unconscious of his extraordinary talent, and modest in the face of public clamor. She had anonymously provided a scholarship for him to continue his studies.

Although she was still angry at Kreiser, she saw no way to celebrate the young man's accomplishments without inviting his professor, so resolved to pretend nothing had happened between them. She managed to avoid prolonged contact with him and stayed occupied with serving her guests, as the young people took turns at the console, the piano or the harpsichord.

During the reception, agnostic as ever and well into his cups celebrating, Kreiser walked into the study, where Charlotte had finally escaped and sat on the sofa staring at the fireplace. He filled his wine glass and raised it to her sardonically, after she had declined any wine. The students were otherwise diverted in the salon, and no one was paying attention to Kreiser and Charlotte. She inwardly stiffened and wanted to flee, but did not want to give him the satisfaction of seeing her discomfort in his presence, so remained in her place on the sofa.

"The drink of unending life," he had intoned ominously in toast.

Surprised, she had broken her silence. "Harry, that is not even particularly good wine you brought. The stuff certainly has no properties constituting that height of sacrilege from you."

"No, no, no," he slurred slightly as he lowered himself to the couch beside her, surprising her at his proximity as he ran his fingers down her back. "I mean teaching talented, driven, deserving students. I am immortal, because I can perpetuate myself and my genius, imprinting on the virtuosos of tomorrow."

"You've always had an extremely high opinion of yourself," she had retorted, disconcerted at his nearness, as he slipped an arm around her and clumsily kissed her on the cheek and whispered "Carlota" gently.

She had covered her surprise and discomfort by pulling away quickly, trying to avoid a scene, and taking a deep draught of her iced tea.

"And you could have been one of them, my beautiful Carlota," he announced loudly, his words slicing through her like a knife as several of the students walked by the doorway and looked their way. "You ran away from your art."

She stared at him, impotent with fury, speechless. She stood, intending to walk out.

He also stood and took her arm, forestalling her. He drank deeply of his glass of wine, then set down the glass, his eyes meeting hers. "I know why. I thank you for bringing Stefan to me," he murmured, his voice so low that only she could catch the words. "But I'm still waiting for you to redeem us both."

She caught her breath, peering at him intently, but he turned away, making an inane comment to one of his students coming up. She made good her escape.

A little later, one of his students, Valerie, just turned eighteen, came up to Charlotte, her eyes bright with tears. Charlotte, concerned, asked, "What's wrong, Valerie?"

She looked nervously behind her. "I need to talk to someone," she confided.

"Let's go into the kitchen," Charlotte suggested, as she led the way.

Once there Valerie wiped a tear from her face. "Miss Lawson, Dr. K. came on to me just now."

"What?" Charlotte was instantly alarmed. She pulled out a chair at the kitchen nook. "Tell me."

They sat down. Valerie continued hesitantly, "He was drinking, and he put his arm around me, called me 'Carlota', and tried to kiss me." She paused, as more tears came. "Stefan saw it and intervened, pulling him away."

Charlotte shook her head. "I'm so sorry, Valerie. What are you going to do?" she was apprehensive, emotionally torn. Bastard, she thought. He ought to go down in flames for his behavior. But he is a great teacher, and this could ruin him, she thought.

"I don't know what to do," Valerie stated. "Stefan said he is drunk. He's a great teacher. If I tell my parents, they will have his head. I don't know."

Charlotte nodded in sympathy. "I cannot tell you what to do," she murmured. "You must do what is best for you, what you think is right.

However, I too believe he has had too much to drink, and has mistaken you for someone in his past. If you want to report him to Dean Jackson, that is your right," Charlotte said with a heavy heart.

Valerie looked at her. "He called you 'Carlota' earlier tonight, didn't he?"

Charlotte started. "Yes, he did," she faltered. "He has used that term for me ever since I first met him. But I don't know if it is confined to me," she said to herself.

"I've never heard him use it until tonight," Valerie spoke, as her face registered recognition. "But you are the student he always talks about, the one he always points to in his teaching."

"Me?" Charlotte was amazed. "I don't think so."

"Yes," insisted Valerie. "He never names you, but he is always talking about a former student and how wonderfully she did this or that. You were his student?"

"Yes," Charlotte croaked, "but that was a long time ago. I don't—play any more."

Valerie peered at her, her green eyes curious. "I don't want to get him in trouble. He's the best teacher ever. He thought he was talking to you."

"No, Valerie," protested Charlotte desperately.

"You are in love with him, aren't you?" Valerie whispered. "I've heard the rumors. It all makes sense now."

"Valerie, please," Charlotte desperately turned away, her face flushing. "The rumors aren't true. Please."

"Don't worry," Valerie stated confidentially. "I won't tell anyone."

She disappeared, leaving Charlotte in a state of agitation. *Damn it, Harry,* she thought. *Now because of him tongues will start wagging again.* She sat there, lost in thought, the anxiety overwhelming her.

Later that night, the crowd thinned out until just the two of them remained. Charlotte, uncomfortable that Kreiser remained behind, was tense and silent, busying herself by picking up glasses and tidying. Kreiser sat brooding, watching the licking flames of the receding fire in the marble-covered fireplace.

As she reached to pick up a serving bowl on the coffee table, he encircled her slender wrist with his strong fingers, holding it tightly in a vise.

He intoned, "I deserve your disgust. But you should not have been surprised. You knew me better than anyone else. I gave you my very best. You could have surpassed them all, even our Stefan. I've only done what I thought was best for you."

"Please let go of me, Harry," she had demanded with an iciness she had not used with him before. Surprised, he had complied. "I only came back because Stefan was insistent on studying with you."

He had muttered, "I don't believe that. I remember your lips uttering very different words to me only months ago. But you didn't tell me everything, did you? Can't you finally be honest with me after all this time, even now?"

"Why?" she retorted, confused at his meaning. "You certainly were not honest with me."

He demanded hoarsely, "You could have written your own ticket for teachers and venues in Europe and at home, even without me. You knew I'd never stop you, with your talent. I'd even have written references for you. Why didn't you?"

She just stared at him. "You know why."

Harry held up his hands in surrender, defeat written on his face. "I pay for my sins every time I see you, every day I teach Stefan."

He moved away, to stand before the fireplace. "Furthermore, I know Melanie told you about the money she gave me. I appreciate her motives for telling you what she did. But it wasn't true." He faltered, suddenly embarrassed. "The money was a gift, to help with my dialysis."

Charlotte's heart caught in her throat. "Dialysis? What—?"

Harry looked weary. "I swore Melanie to secrecy. I had a heart attack while you were living in D.C. I had triple bypass surgery. It was discovered that I had unusually high cholesterol levels." He hesitated. "The day I called you was right after I had come home from the surgery."

Charlotte's eyes filled with tears. "I didn't know," she whispered. "Could you not have told me?"

He continued as if she hadn't spoken. "The doctors tried everything, but still worried about my having a stroke. I cancelled a two-year teaching fellowship at Yale," he said, his voice bitter. "I had to suspend my dream to end up at Yale, at the top of my form.

"Melanie finally convinced me to go to her doctors, who placed me on dialysis periodically. It was enormously expensive," he said absently. He looked at her, flushed. "That's what the money was for."

He started pacing in front of the fireplace.

"I'm so sorry," Charlotte cried, standing up and going to him. She embraced him, and he held her to him, stroking her hair.

"Don't cry, Carlota. The treatments have helped, and they have developed some new drugs that have made a difference. But I'm old and tired."

"You're not old to me," her eyes met his, and without thinking, she kissed him, wrapping her arms around his neck. He responded tentatively, tenderly exploring her mouth as she reveled in his touch, wanting to lose herself in the moment for which she had waited so long. The kiss deepened, as both of them momentarily gave in to the passion and clung to each other.

"I loved you for so long," she murmured. "I cannot believe we can finally be together, Harry."

"Oh, Carlota, when I'm with you the years roll back. I still think of tasting you while hearing Liszt. I want you so badly."

"We don't ever have to be apart again," she nuzzled his neck.

He gently pushed her away from him. "We cannot do this," he admonished softly.

"What?" she froze and stared at him, all color fleeing her face.

"I refuse to let this happen again," he said softly, gazing at her.

"After all these years and all this pain?" she cried, confused. "Melanie kept us apart. She's gone. There's nothing, no one to stop us, Harry," she added wildly.

He stared at Charlotte sadly, still holding her at arm's length. "I kept us apart. Melanie liked to think she was in control of our destinies. But I know what a tragic mistake I made with you years ago."

"Mistake?" Charlotte sputtered. "Mistake?"

He looked away. "By making love to you, by stealing your heart. You were never supposed to return my love. I had hoped you would forget me. I wanted to spur you to anger, even hate, so that you could move on. Instead, I ruined your life," his anger matched hers. "I let my desire for you overcome my good judgment and everything I stood for as a teacher. I robbed the world of one of its greatest artists, and you of the glory that you richly deserved. I will never forgive myself."

She gasped in disbelief and drew back to slap him, but he caught her hand. "This isn't happening. I've wasted my life waiting for you," she spat. "You keep leading me on, just to reject me. I have lost everything, even my self-respect. You deny me now, after all this? What kind of cruel bastard are you?"

He gripped her arms as she struggled angrily. "The very worst kind, Carlota. But it must stop now. I have not been able to deter you from this crazy dream. My place in hell is assured, but I cannot let you hope one minute more. And the only way to redeem myself is to pray to God for Stefan, the one good thing that happened as a result of us. And I pray for you." He turned his eyes back on her, and she became still. "That you will carry on, find that inner strength, and return to your art. Better late than never."

He released her, turning his back. "I promised Melanie I'd stay until Stefan finished his studies. But Stefan doesn't need me anymore. I've given him everything I have to give. I realized I was only waiting for one thing."

Charlotte stepped backward, reeling as though he had struck her. She murmured, tears running unheeded down her cheeks, her heart leaping, "And what is that?"

"To hear you perform again, you, Charlotte Lawson, as yourself. Freely, no disguises," he replied softly. "And that will not happen as long as I am here." He walked to the door. "This summer I go to Yale. I'm not coming back."

He left her standing there, alone, shaking, sobbing silently.

PART FOUR

The mind is its own place, and in itself
Can make a heaven of hell, a hell of heaven.
excerpt, *Paradise Lost*, Book 1
John Milton (1608-1674)

PART FOUR

Chapter 45

Charlotte stepped out into the artificial brightness of the airport terminal Friday evening. She felt the headache already asserting itself, and hoped the mints would mask the smell of any alcohol.

Michael was there as she wheeled her carryon bag and specialized gun case behind her past the crowd surging around baggage claim. He hugged her, then looked anxiously at her face. "What is it, Charlotte?"

"I'm fine, just tired," she replied, averting her eyes. "Where's Stefan?"

"He told me he had several appointments and an errand to run, and would call in. I haven't heard back from him yet. But he is an adult. What can I do?"

Charlotte nodded unhappily, preoccupied. "I'm sorry he's not here too. But it is just as well." She stumbled a little and shook her head, rubbing her forehead.

"Are you OK?" Mike asked, taking her arm.

"Just a headache," she muttered, turning away.

"You have been drinking?" Mike whispered, shocked. "What is going on?"

"Just stress," Charlotte shot back, her voice low. "I'm OK. Let's go before someone recognizes me."

He took her bag and reached for the case, but she held on to it. "I'll carry this," she asserted.

He nodded silently, as he took her arm and steered her out of the airport and to the parking garage. Once out on the road, he glanced over at her.

"Are you ready for the meeting tomorrow?"

"Yes," she spoke, her expression fathomless. "Mike, I need my car. I have to run an errand this evening. Please just drop me off at my place. But do you think it possible I could stay with you all tonight?"

His eyes widened in surprise. "Of course you can, Charlotte. We'd love to have you. It's just you've never taken us up on the offer before."

She mumbled, "I just don't want to be alone."

"Missing Gerry?" he asked, glancing at her.

"Something like that," she looked away, out the window. She pulled out her cell phone and hit a number in her speed dial. "Jonathan? It is Charlotte. I know it's late. Can I see you this evening? It is urgent."

She listened a moment. "Thanks. We're leaving the airport. As soon as I get my car, I'll be there. I owe you."

Mike dropped her off at the townhouse, and after assuring himself that she was sober, secured a promise from her to call him if she was going to be late.

The next morning she left with Mike for the meeting, a skeet shoot with the senator-hopeful and Mike's boss Ben Loftin. On the way, Mike said gently, "Gerry called me late last night, said he was tied up and couldn't make it up. He wanted to make sure you had made here OK."

Charlotte replied, her voice flat, "I'll call him later."

After the meeting, at which she shot a near-perfect score and bullied the politician into a formal retraction of the rumor that they were engaged, she was carefully taking apart her 12-gauge and wiping down the parts to place in the case, when Mike reappeared after seeing his boss off.

"Charlotte, you need to sit down," he said softly. "I have some bad news."

He gently pushed her onto a bench and sat down beside her, taking her hand in his. "Gerry just called. Charlotte, it's about Kreiser."

"What about him?" Charlotte stared down at her hand in his.

"He was shot late yesterday."

Charlotte swallowed. A shudder ran through her, and she suddenly felt cold. So it begins, she thought.

Mike was silent, letting the news sink in. She closed her eyes. "He's dead, isn't he?" she whispered numbly.

Mike squeezed her hand. "Yes, dear."

"And I killed him," she whispered to herself. She sat there for a small eternity, before asking, "How?"

"No details are being given right now. It's a homicide—that's all we know. Gerry just called me. He said he left a message on your cell, but never heard from you. He was worried, and said he was flying up."

"No need," Charlotte croaked, her face impassive. "I'll call him now."

She picked up her phone and hit a button. After a moment she spoke. "Gerry, it is Charlotte. I got the message from Mike about Harry." She paused. "Don't come up. I'm OK. I'll see you when I get back tomorrow."

Mike looked sympathetically at her as she hung up. "Sis, we're going to have to tell Stefan."

She blinked, and he saw tears then. "Yes, I forgot," she spoke, her voice small. "Stefan will be devastated. Oh, my God."

She stood and quickly completed her task. "Let's go."

She was silent as Mike drove them to Chevy Chase. She leaned back and closed her eyes, trying not to think. At one point she thought, It's all my fault.

"What did you say?" Mike's voice broke into her thoughts. He was staring at her, his eyes wide.

"Nothing," she replied suddenly. "I didn't realize I was speaking aloud."

As they pulled into the driveway, she saw Stefan standing outside waiting, tears streaking his face.

"I think he already knows," she whispered.

As she got out of the car and walked toward him, he quickly moved to her and flung his arms around her. "I'm so sorry," he said over and over.

Charlotte was surprised and touched. He's comforting me, she thought. "Me too, baby," she murmured, hugging him back, as she slowly led him back into the house, Mike following them.

Later, Mike's cell phone rang. Looking at the caller ID, he excused himself. Walking outside, he answered the call.

"How is she?" Gerry asked.

Mike stated, "She is withdrawn. I think I'm more frightened than if she was sobbing about him."

"She left me a message not to come up," Gerry offered angrily.

"I know," Mike acknowledged. "Gerry, you ought to know. She had been drinking when I picked her up from the airport yesterday. She insisted she had an errand to run, and talked to someone named 'Jonathan' on the phone before I dropped her off to get her car. She spent the night with us last night, very unusual for her. She didn't make it home until after midnight. Amy said she had nightmares last night and woke up screaming. I'm worried."

Gerry was silent. Mike asked, "Are you there?"

"I'm sending the plane up, so that she and Stefan don't have to negotiate the commercial flights."

"That's a good idea," Mike agreed. "I told Amy she needs to go back with them. I'm going to stay behind and seal the deal from today, then join them."

Gerry asked, "How did the shoot with Loftin turn out?"

"She was brutal. She wiped the floor with Ben, both with the shotgun and her tongue. I think she was disappointed when you didn't show. He won't be spreading rumors about her again."

"Has she mentioned Kreiser at all?"

Mike frowned. "No. The only time she shed a tear was when I mentioned we were going to have to break the news to Stefan." Mike paused. "Don't give up on her, Gerry. Meet her at the airport tomorrow. She needs you."

Gerry laughed sarcastically. "Charlotte has never needed me, except to mop up after Kreiser rejects her."

"Bullshit, man," Mike swore, surprising Gerry. "You love her, and she adores you. She's all alone. What happens when Stefan leaves?"

Gerry sighed. "I can't manhandle her into loving me, Mike. I'm afraid when she gets back, it's only the 'beginning of sorrows', with the media speculation and the police investigation. They'll want to talk to her. I can't keep that from happening."

"When I told her, I could swear she whispered that she killed him. Later she said, 'It's all my fault.'" Mike paused, letting the information sink in. "You don't believe she had anything to do with Kreiser's death?" Mike demanded softly.

"Don't be silly," Gerry retorted. "She loved the sod. She couldn't do him in."

"What about you?" Mike asked. "I know you had no love for the man."

"Get a grip, Mike," Gerry was curt. "I need to go. I'll meet her at the airport."

Charlotte sat motionless, her golden tresses tamed into a severe chignon, her head propped against the headrest of the comfortable red leather of the seat, her deep green eyes scanning restlessly, unseeingly, out the window of the private jet. She was oblivious to the opulent interior of the plane, with the matching roomy leather seats and the highly polished oaken bar.

She was dressed in a pale green suit of lightweight wool with a peach silk scarf tied carelessly around her neck. She unconsciously fidgeted with the large three-diamond ring on her left hand. She did not acknowledge Amy in the seat beside her, bearing a striking resemblance to her, in black linen pants and white herringbone checkered short-sleeved sweater set.

The latter noisily closed a magazine and turned to her. "Charlotte, please talk to me," she whispered. "You've barely spoken since yesterday when you came back from your meeting with Ben and heard about Harry's death. And you woke up screaming again this morning. You're scaring Stefan. God, you're scaring me."

The former roused herself with an effort. "I'm sorry, Amy," she replied, squeezing the hand of her sister. "Just a bad dream—I'm having trouble erasing it from my mind." She paused, taking a deep tremulous breath.

"You didn't show much emotion when the news about Kreiser broke," Amy reminded her. "What is this—delayed reaction? What about Ben, and all this business about you being engaged to him? What has happened with Gerry?"

"What about Ben?" Charlotte echoed, staring out the plane window. "How did I ever get mixed up in this mess? I agreed to attend one fundraising cocktail party on his behalf, and only for Mike's sake, since he works for the man, and because I hoped to see Gerry there and clear the air between us. The next thing I know the media has me cast as the senator's fiancée. Amy, I have a fiancé, for what it's worth."

"How did your meeting go?" Amy demanded.

"I think I finally convinced Ben that I was not interested at all, I was not his ticket to the media circus, I would not make a politician's wife, and he needed to look elsewhere before I turned my 12-gauge on him. And he cannot shoot worth a damn—don't know why he wasted my time." She smiled slightly, a bitter smile. "I think the clincher was the probability that Gerry would not back him if it looked like I jilted Gerry for him. He was oblivious to the ring on my finger, and groveling once I spelled it out for him.

"He agreed to issue a public statement Monday correcting the misinformation about us, and I agreed to provide a generous contribution." She grimaced. "The rest of the time I spent nailing down the wording of his announcement, to make sure he didn't screw it up. The trip was otherwise a disaster: Gerry didn't show for the shoot Saturday, and when Mike broke the news of Harry, I left word for him not to bother coming up."

"Things don't seem to be going all that swimmingly with Gerry. You're no closer to a wedding than when Aunt Mellie died. What's going on?"

"I really can't talk about it right now," Charlotte pleaded. Her eyes grew brilliant. "I've screwed that up. Gerry is avoiding me. Now Harry is dead. I loved him, and I hated him. I'm finally rid of him." She looked out the window and whispered to herself, "What have I done?"

Amy berated her quietly, "That should have been over a long time ago. Damn, Charlotte, don't tell me you still loved him. We've been through all this before. In the process you've hurt Gerry. Gerry's too good for you. I just don't understand you."

Charlotte sighed, her face darkened with pain. "Amy, I can always count on you to rub my nose in my transgressions. Don't you realize I'm fully aware of what a fool I've been? I 'acknowledge and bewail my manifold sins,' particularly where Gerry is concerned. I'm trying to correct those wrongs, OK?"

Amy pursed her lips, deciding the better part of discretion was to change the subject. "Stefan is very upset about Harry's death, but I think he is more worried about your reaction, or lack of it," the other woman remarked, her voice confidential. "Don't shut him out. You must talk to him, reassure him." She anxiously searched her sister's face.

"Aunt Charlotte?" a young male voice cut through their whispered conversation. Looking up, Charlotte gazed into the handsome face of her nephew, barely out of his teens, his face etched with anxiety, dressed in pressed black trousers, a white oxford shirt and black leather jacket.

"Yes, dear?" Charlotte smiled at him, her heart thrilling at the sight of the cropped wavy blonde hair, the brilliant green eyes that stared back at her.

"Are you OK?" he asked somberly, taking her hand.

Amy stood up. "Here, Stefan, sit beside Aunt Charlotte. She could use the company."

"But—" started Charlotte, but Amy held up her hand.

"What you two have to talk about is way out of my league," Amy insisted. "I know nothing about organs and schools and teachers. And I never understood why Aunt Mellie entangled us with Harry Kreiser, that bastard, may he rest in peace. He's been nothing but trouble."

She disappeared across the aisle, as Stefan plopped down in the seat she vacated.

"Why doesn't she like him?" he sighed. "There's so much I don't understand. But Mom's right, you know," Stefan continued. "You're the one I depend on for advice on what to do from here. I just can't believe it." He finally paused in mid-stream of consciousness, pain flooding his face. He leaned closer, again taking her hand, his eyes full of unshed tears. "You haven't said much about Dr. K. How did you feel about him?"

Charlotte was touched at the youth's sensitivity. "We were close at one time. I thought he was a great teacher, Stefan," she decided to be honest. "And I'm sad that we parted on acrimonious terms."

"What about Gerry?" he asked, watching her closely.

She gazed at Stefan's solemn expression. "It's complicated—I can't explain. I—I don't even know myself," she stammered, not able to hold his gaze.

"But, Aunt Charlotte, you deserve to be taken care of. Gerry wants to do that," the youth declared soberly. "But I know there was something between you and Dr. K, no matter how much you pretended otherwise," he said, squeezing her hand. "Is that why you and Gerry aren't talking?"

His truthful assessment cut her like a knife. Her smile faded at his words. "Are you OK?" she asked, avoiding his question.

"I will miss him. The other kids complained about his toughness lately, but it was like he and I were on the same wavelength. I could even read when he was in one of his dark moods. He was very hard on me, but I knew it was for a good reason. He kept my nose to the grindstone." Stefan took a tremulous breath. "I loved him. The last few months I knew he was drinking too much, but I couldn't figure out what triggered that."

Stefan stopped, looking away, embarrassed, wiping the tears from his cheek. "Dr. K was still pretty steamed about your review before I left for D.C. I could tell he didn't want to ask about you, but he couldn't help himself. I think he kept hoping you'd call him. But, Auntie, that was a two-way street. He could have called you."

I did call him, she thought, momentarily angered. Quickly changing the subject, Charlotte interrupted, "You have to make some decisions now," she reminded him gently. "Your junior recital is scheduled for this week. Shouldn't we reschedule it?"

Stefan frowned, tears in his eyes. "I don't want to be disrespectful to Dr. K. But I want to go ahead as soon as possible. He always preached that one shouldn't lose one's momentum, and I feel ready for this recital. Right now everything is so unreal, and I can pretend nothing has happened, that he's still there. I'm worried about when the realization sets in that he's gone."

Charlotte nodded knowingly. "We'll have to see how the situation is once we reach Atlanta," Charlotte told him. "What about the next step? What were you and Harry considering for you after graduation next year?"

As Stefan began discussing his future education, Charlotte listened desultorily. Stefan is a man now, she thought regretfully. It will be a rocky transition to a new teacher. But soon he will be gone off into the world, chasing his dream, making his decisions alone.

"I don't know if I still want to do the summer program at Yale this year," he swallowed hard, "if Dr. K isn't going to be there. I was going to France after graduation, but I've got to do something about a teacher next year," he was saying, his voice catching in a sob. She nodded, squeezing his hand for reassurance.

"We'll deal with that. It will all be OK," she remarked sympathetically. "I'm so proud of your accomplishments. Harry was too. Maybe under the circumstances Dr. Philips will consider taking you at Yale. Any number of schools would be happy to have you, dear."

Stefan looked down at his hands. "But I don't want to leave you. Dad and I talked last night. Dad says that you will take my leaving harder than he and Mom put together. I wish you and Dr. K had gotten together and had kids of your own. You may be losing us both at the same time."

Charlotte's voice caught in her throat. "Your dad is much too smart for his own good. I don't want you to go away, Stefan. But life hands us tough choices sometimes, and you're an adult now. We'll figure out something." You're all grown up, but I still love you like a child, she thought, willing herself not to cry. She fought the urge to hug this youngster to her and shelter him, protect him from the hurt he was feeling.

The young man smiled sadly, but was not deterred. "I never understood about you and Harry," Stefan persisted. "There was always a tension between you two. I didn't understand it. Sometimes, when you argued, you sounded like you were married."

Charlotte looked out the window. "It's a very long story, Stefan. Maybe one day I can talk about it with you. Please don't ask me. Not now."

"I'd like to know," he replied solemnly. "It all started before I was born, didn't it?"

"Yes," Charlotte's voice broke, as she tried to blink back sudden tears.

"Does it have anything to do with my real parents?" he asked cautiously, looking at her fixedly.

Charlotte caught her breath, her features tightening. "No, my dear. What would give you that idea?"

"Oh, nothing," he responded casually, although Charlotte divined that his nonchalance was contrived.

Charlotte took his hand. "Darling, I don't know anything about that. All I know is that you have two wonderful parents now, who gave you all—commitment, discipline, love, and honesty. That's a good foundation. They have taught you what love is."

"I don't recall you cutting me much slack in those departments," Stefan retorted, an odd smile on his face as he stared at her intently.

"Although there are some misdemeanors of yours your parents still don't know about." She smiled slyly, trying to interject some levity into the conversation, suddenly nervous.

"And you are not without sin," he laughed. "But that's our little secret, remember?" he said, pinching her playfully. "Besides, you and Dr. K were tougher on me than they are."

She deftly changed the subject. "What do you want for your birthday present?"

Without hesitation he replied, "I want you to go to New York City with me. I have plans. Besides, your birthday is coming up soon too." He arched his eyebrows mysteriously.

She frowned. "Me? You don't need a chaperone. Besides, I'm a working woman. The boss might not be too happy about letting me off again so soon."

"Oh, give me a break," Stefan snorted derisively. "That old Kline realizes that you are a celebrity. Just think of all the enthusiastic readers buying up his paper for your Monday and Friday columns, as well as all the reviews. He's lucky to have you."

"Well, I'm glad I have one fan," Charlotte murmured as Stefan leaned over and kissed her cheek, and the pilot's voice came over the intercom informing them to secure their safety belts in preparation for landing.

Charlotte clutched Stefan's hand as they hit a pocket of turbulence. He laughed. "You're not still scared of flying after all these years?"

Charlotte smiled tightly, although her knuckles were white. "Only landing."

"Gran and Gramps?" Stefan whispered knowingly, solemnly.

Charlotte nodded, biting her lip apprehensively.

Chapter 46

The landing was smooth. As they disembarked, Charlotte heard her name called. Turning, she was astonished. "Gerry! What are you doing here?" She caught herself. "What a nice surprise," she stammered.

The handsome man approached her, dapper in pressed Ralph Lauren khakis, chambray shirt, sans tie, and loafers, his brown hair cropped but still wavy on top. "Jackson would have met you himself, but has been tied up with police and attorneys. He apparently is to be Kreiser's executor. Are you OK?" he asked unsmilingly, peering at her pale features with his deep brown eyes, as he reached forward and pecked a kiss on her cheek.

"I'm fine," she replied, coloring slightly. "Thanks so much for sending your jet for us."

"No problem. Hello, Stefan," he remarked, as he handed the latter a small package wrapped in brown paper and topped with a bow. "Happy birthday, a little early."

"Gee, thanks, Gerry," Stefan exclaimed, clutching the package and tearing off the wrapping.

"It's the newest gameware the company is releasing," Gerard explained. "I immediately thought of you. You're my best product tester."

"Cool," replied Stefan, beaming briefly. Seeing Gerard's eyes still on Charlotte, he remarked, "I'll go back and help with the bags."

Gerard took Charlotte's arm gently and steered her a few feet away just out of earshot. He pulled out a pack of cigarettes, offering one to Charlotte. She shook her head.

Lighting his cigarette, he mused lightly, "Remember our first cigarette together out behind the boathouse? We were, what, twelve?"

"Yes, but I never got the hang of it," she smiled nervously. "I didn't know you've taken it up now. When did you start?"

"I just bought this pack while waiting for your plane," he admitted sheepishly. "I felt I needed something to bolster my confidence before seeing you again, particularly after reading the tabloids."

Charlotte blushed. He continued. "How was the skeet shooting with the senator hopeful? What type—English, down-the-line, traps?"

"Does it matter? He doesn't know the difference," she muttered irritably. "No media was to be involved. I prevailed upon him to correct the misinformation that I am engaged to him. Almost perfect score—I nicked one when he rhapsodized about how pretty I'd look on his arm during his acceptance speech." She paused. "I thought you were supposed to join us. You had something better to do?" she asked meaningfully.

"I had some business that kept me," he muttered enigmatically. "It was important, Charl." He stared at her, as she stared back, her pupils dilated.

"Did you mention to the senator that you are already engaged to me?" Gerry continued, his voice light but his face grave. "Or is that over and done with?"

She looked away as Amy and Stefan debarked from the plane. "I don't know. I thought you broke it off. Are we still engaged?"

Gerry acted as if he hadn't heard her. "Oh, by the way, one of my men said he thought he saw signs of powder post beetle at the boathouse. I went myself to check it out. When you get some free time, we need to talk—it needs some attention. And it's time to consider re-tiling the roof of the main house. I know you are new to the estate maintenance business," he ended in a lame joke.

As she met his gaze, she whispered. "After what I've done to you, why do you care? You're too good to me."

"Heck, I'm just easily bored," he mumbled. "I'm a glutton for punishment, and couldn't stay away. And you've always needed a keeper anyway."

She averted her eyes. "I was surprised to see you today. I realize we've not seen each other a lot lately, and I know I'm the reason why. I mean—Gerry, I'm sorry. I wouldn't hurt you for the world."

"I know you didn't mean to, but you did. That's that," he said quietly, coolly, his eyes not leaving her. "I see you're still wearing my ring. Nice touch."

"Please don't, Gerry," Charlotte looked back at him, fear in her eyes. "The story about me and the senator was absolutely bogus. But—" her voice faltered, "there was also a rumor of you and some heiress in Tucson." She coughed, suddenly embarrassed. "I wasn't thinking. Of course. I won't wear your ring if you don't want me to."

She stepped away, her back to him. He replied, "That is just so much press speculation. There's no one else. You ruined me for anyone else, Charl."

"I've made such a mess. Oh God, Gerry, please tell me this isn't happening."

"I'm afraid so, Charlotte," he finally looked away, his face grim. "Wearing my ring is actually a good idea." He paused momentarily. "The paparazzi today are linking your name to Kreiser's again. Gilda couldn't reach you to warn you, so she called me."

"I don't care," she replied impetuously, then blanched as another thought hit her. "But what about Stefan? What if he should hear the rumors?"

Gerard responded, his voice low, "I'll do everything I can to protect you and Stefan."

"You've always been there for me," Charlotte whispered, facing him and touching his arm. "I meant what I said to you. I want us to be together, if it's not too late, and not just because of the tabloids. Tell me it's not gone too far." She paused. "The police—what do they know? You're not—?" she found she couldn't finish the question.

Gerard stared at her a long time, then turned away, stubbing out his cigarette. "Kreiser was murdered, Charl. They have no suspects yet. There will be lots of questions, and we'll be on their list. Do you have an alibi? What happens if the press causes the police to suspect you? We can't let that happen."

Charlotte shuddered, unable to say any more.

Gerry spoke so low she could barely hear him. "I never asked you. What was the purpose of the 'coin of death' you sent me after—after the memorial service? And the note saying 'Don't do it'? Don't do what? What were you telling me?"

"Does it matter now?" Charlotte whispered wearily.

He turned and took her arm, pulling her close to him. "What you do always matters to me, Charl." He suddenly kissed her, his mouth exploring hers hungrily. She did not push him away, responding fervently, desperately.

She whispered. "I'm frightened. Nothing must happen to you."

"Nothing is going to happen," he murmured reassuringly. "I will protect you. Just put on your bulldog persona like you did with Gilda that night. Remember—you were on your way to D.C., and that's that. No contact was made; you know nothing."

"I don't want you to give up on us. Is it too late?" she began. "The police—"

"The police don't know anything," he kissed her ear.

"But—" she began again.

"Shh," he kissed her again, silencing her.

They were unaware of anyone else until Amy cleared her throat. "You can break it up now," she stated sternly, although there were vestiges of a smile behind her frown.

Since Gerard's graduation from Stanford with a degree in architectural engineering, he had become interested in computer software, forming his own company that created and distributed both games and business applications. He had bought up a failing pest control company, refurbishing it into a successful franchise stretching across the region. He had turned his passion for hunting and sharpshooting competition into a national string of gun shops, providing firing ranges and hunting trips, catering to hunters, enthusiasts and law enforcement alike. He had obtained his doctorate and bought the architectural firm where Howard Cain had served as partner, restoring it to its former reputation. He had turned his family's stagnant fortunes around, diversifying his interests and investments and multiplying their millions. While his name had been linked with several eligible women over the years, he was still single.

Although Charlotte had accepted Gerard's proposal of marriage just before her Aunt Melanie's death only four months ago, no formal announcement was released, no wedding date had been scheduled, and their relationship had become strained. The social community was rife with rumors of whether Charlotte and Gerard were actually engaged or not, particularly after a recent tabloid article had linked her name romantically with the local U.S. representative running for senator, and his with a Tucson debutante.

Their conversation lulled at Amy's and Stefan's appearance. Charlotte turned around, and for the first time observed the shiny new black limousine parked just beyond them. Stefan's eyes grew wide as Tom, in black chauffeur's uniform, appeared to take their bags.

"Did you get a new limo?" Stefan asked, awed. Charlotte stared at the car, swallowing convulsively, then at Gerard, who met her gaze calmly.

Gerard replied, "Yep, just got it this weekend," as he hustled them inside, leaving the driver to load the luggage. Soon they were on their way, Stefan examining the buttons and gadgets in the interior and chatting with Gerard on one seat while Charlotte, facing them, leaned back and closed her eyes, rigid, anxiety-ridden. Amy beside her squeezed her hand, but Charlotte did not respond. Charlotte was avoiding Gerry's eyes, remembering another time, another limousine.

Before long the driver pulled through the familiar large wrought-iron gate and past the spreading manicured lawn up a paved driveway lined with crape myrtle trees and fastidiously trimmed azaleas, leading to the imposing brick Georgian structure that was the Cain residence. A distinguished-looking older gentleman was waiting at the steps, dressed in a well-cut dark suit, his white hair carefully groomed.

As Charlotte slid out, she met the man, who held out his arms. "Malcolm, thanks for being here," she whispered as he hugged her and kissed her cheek.

"I'm so sorry," he murmured, as he greeted Amy and Stefan. "Thanks, Gerry, for picking them up."

Gerard studied the bags being taken out of the trunk. He gently took a case from the driver and replaced it in the trunk. "I'll take this," he said quietly to Charlotte.

"Why?" she whispered, suddenly alert.

"Probably needs cleaning," Gerry replied, his mouth close to her ear. "They haven't given out any details about the murder, but hopefully I can get more information. I'm friends with the ballistics guy at the crime lab."

Gerard turned away as Tom carried the remaining luggage through the massive front door. "I'll check on you tomorrow. If you need anything in the meantime, just call me."

"Daisy would love it if you would stay to tea," she spoke, squeezing his hand gratefully. "So would I."

"No, later," he muttered gruffly.

Disappointment showed in her eyes. "Where are you staying?"

"Next door with Kat and Cece for a couple of days. They're both shaken up by what happened," he replied quietly, kissing her forehead, pulling away and taking his leave.

Charlotte watched him into the limo, sad about his reticence and knowing she was to blame, then followed the others into the house. Hovering just inside the door was a massive black woman in a black dress swallowed by a huge white apron.

Charlotte embraced her. "Daisy, it's good to be home."

The woman burst into tears. "Miss Charlotte, I'm so sorry about Mister Harry. I'm glad you're home. First Miss Mellie Anne, now Mister Harry."

Charlotte tried to comfort the woman, but no words came. "I know," she finally whispered.

Daisy pulled away, wiping her eyes with a tissue. "I know Master Stefan is hungry—he always is—so I'll have tea ready to serve in a few minutes. What, Mr. Gerry isn't staying for my tea? He specifically asked me to have you some buttermilk and cornbread ready." Daisy's hands went to her hips as she pursed her lips disapprovingly.

"No, he had business. Daisy, you shouldn't have troubled," murmured Charlotte concernedly, but seeing the fallen expression on the woman's face, she relented. "But you know we love you for it anyway. If you will give us a few minutes to freshen up, we'll be ready. And tell Jacob that the flower bed out front is just gorgeous."

The woman beamed, before bustling off to the kitchen.

Chapter 47

Malcolm Jackson paced in front of the marble fireplace. His only audience was Charlotte, who was sitting on the sofa, talking on the phone.

"I had to check on you," Jonathan said over the line. "Are you OK?"

"Yes," she responded.

"Are you going to see Gerry?" she could hear the concern in his voice.

"I already have. He met us at the airport."

"Don't you think it's in both your interests to distance yourself from him? Charlotte, think about our discussion."

"I don't think I can. I need him, Jonathan. However, he is the one putting space between us."

"Charlotte, this could get dangerous. You are in the middle of a homicide investigation, whether you want to be or not."

Her voice dropped to a whisper. "What, you wouldn't divulge what I told you in confidence?"

"Under the law your communications with me are privileged. But Charlotte, I only have your interests at heart. I'm worried about you. You're vulnerable right now. I don't agree with your plan. Do not go through with this. Think carefully about what I said."

"I have already," she was suddenly agitated. "I've made my decision. I need to go, Jonathan. Talk to you later."

She rang off, leaning back, her eyes staring at the elaborate ceiling. The room's lighting was subdued, provided by three lamps strategically placed.

Beside the fireplace was a large ornately carved wooden bookcase, its doors glass-paned. Inside, the shelves were filled with framed photographs, of Charlotte's aunt Melanie and husband Howard Cain with various important personages, of Charlotte's grandparents and parents, now long dead, and of Amy and Charlotte throughout childhood and adolescence. On the glass shelves interspersed among the frames were awards, trophies, ribbons, and certificates.

The wall opposite the fireplace boasted a built-in paneled bookcase full of leather-bound volumes. At the far end of the room was a large window-seat overlooking a huge lawn, now lying in dusky shadow. A massive hand-carved mahogany desk graced the space immediately in front of the window, taking center stage.

"I can't look at that desk without seeing Melanie busily wheeling and dealing," Malcolm remarked, turning to Charlotte. Charlotte nodded unsmilingly.

From somewhere in the distance came the faint strains of organ music. Malcolm looked in surprise at Charlotte.

"Is he practicing?"

"Always," she said, her voice small and tired. "Harry got so little reaction from baiting Stefan, because Stefan drives himself more than any of us ever thought to. It infuriated Harry. While I as a student used to rage and fight with Harry, Stefan just smiles his beatific smile, goes on and does it his way."

Jackson stood, his hands in his pockets, looking at Charlotte. "How did Stefan take the news of Harry's murder?"

"I think he's in shock. He wants to go ahead with the recital Tuesday—says he wants to do it while he feels ready, and before the reality of Harry's death sets in."

Jackson came over, sitting down on the sofa beside Charlotte and taking her hand in his. "And you?"

"I'm OK," she smiled, the stubborn line of her jaw showing. "I have to be. As Harry always warned, 'never let 'em see you sweat'." She paused. "Oh, God." She buried her head in her hands. "I know part of me has died. I never thought it could feel this way." She paused, suddenly uncomfortable. "What are they giving out about his death?"

Malcolm took her hand again and squeezed it comfortingly. "The police are not giving any details, but he was shot while playing in the gallery at the cathedral." Malcolm looked at her. "It happened sometime Friday afternoon," he was solemn.

"Any witnesses?" she asked anxiously.

Malcolm shook his head. "I don't know."

"He taught on Friday afternoons, and he loved 'his cathedral', as he called it, with its Ruffatti pipes." A shudder passed through her.

"What is it?" Malcolm asked concernedly.

"Oh, nothing," she spoke quickly, fear and exhaustion fleeting across her features as she struggled to compose herself. They were quiet a few minutes, Malcolm afraid to ask her more.

"Harry's will named me executor of his estate, such as it is," Jackson finally stated softly. "Charlotte, he had an armoire full of music scores, compositions. It will require someone to catalogue all of it. He wanted you to do it, to be the curator. And I need your help in planning his memorial service."

Charlotte sat there passively, her eyes restlessly roaming over the familiar room. "Harry abandoned me. He hated me. He was mad at me, remember?" she punctuated the stillness.

"No, Charlotte," Jackson demurred.

"Yes. He was furious. He called me and reamed me because I didn't laud his performance in my review. After he vented, drunk of course, and called me every name in the book, I hung up on him. Funny how the past keeps repeating itself," she smiled bitterly. And he rejected me, up until the very end, something for which I'll never forgive him, she thought but did not say aloud.

Jackson confided, "Harry stormed into my office after your review. He admitted that he was quite vociferous with you. Charlotte, he knew you were being honest. He knew he wasn't ready for that recital. He seemed lost, unsure of himself, very unlike himself. You knew Harry—he'd never admit when he was wrong, but he came as close with me that day as I've ever seen him. Charlotte, you meant a lot more to him than you know. And you brought him Stefan, his greatest achievement."

Charlotte bit her lip. When she replied, her voice seemed far away. "I tried to beg off covering that recital, but Kline insisted. There was no one else." She struggled to regain her composure. "I could see the old recurring pattern in him, the restlessness, the drinking, the lack of focus, and it showed through in his performance. He thought he could finesse his way through the recital, the very thing he railed at his students not to do. I was not going to lie for him. My God, Malcolm, he was a hypocrite."

"You were hurting," Malcolm suggested tentatively. "He informed me that he had told you he was leaving for Yale."

Charlotte turned her full gaze on him, her eyes flashing, coolly withdrawing her hand. "You think I clubbed him in my review for revenge? Because he was abandoning me yet again? Surely you know better. Malcolm, after all I went through with him, as much as he hurt me, I still could not have brought myself to do that."

"He thought that his leaving was best for you. He had packed and purchased a ticket to fly up Wednesday after Stefan's recital."

Malcolm, fearing he had said too much, broke off. Charlotte stood, taking his place pacing before the fireplace. Finally Jackson broke the silence.

"The police have talked to me. I have given them the names of Harry's present and past students. Charlotte, they are going to want to question you and Stefan."

Charlotte's eyes went wide. "Why Stefan? He has so much else to worry about right now."

"Charlotte, they have no idea who killed Harry, and they're interviewing everyone, looking for leads. You and Harry go back many years, and Stefan was his star student—it's only natural." He paused. "Charlotte, they know that you were trying to contact Harry the day of his death. Obviously they will want to know why."

"Does that make me a suspect?" Charlotte's eyes were wide. Not this quickly, she thought. I need more time.

"I'm sure you are not, but the police department is doing a thorough investigation. We both know you have nothing to worry about, because you could not have killed him." The statement hung heavily in the air, as though he expected her to respond. "Anyway, it's normal when there's a homicide," Jackson finished lamely.

Charlotte was silent several minutes, digesting this news. Finally she spoke. "Has anything been decided about Stefan's recital?"

"It's too early," Jackson reminded her. "This is Sunday evening. Tomorrow I will call the faculty in, and we'll try to make some contingency plans, figure out what to do with the remaining week of the semester. There's so much to determine—how to finish grading Harry's students, how to complete examinations, making referrals, counseling his students."

Attempting to draw her into less stressful subject matter, he asked softly, "Has Stefan told you his recital program?"

"No, he says he wants it to be some sort of surprise," she responded distractedly. "He has been doing most of his rehearsal away from home, and is very vague on details. I don't know what he is planning." It was evident that she was not relishing being in the dark. "But I know better than to interfere. He made one comment to Harry a few months ago. When Harry asked if he was going to include some pre-Bach, and he said he had paid his dues—it was time he did a French-guy program. I laughed. He sounded just like me in that moment. I felt the same way about my senior recital."

She turned to face him. "Stefan specifically asked if you and I would provide feedback after his performance. I of course cannot write a review for the paper for my own kin, but he wanted our honest evaluation. You wouldn't mind, would you?"

"No, of course not. Of course, I may be the one grading him anyway. I'm hoping to come up with a committee for evaluating the few remaining recitals." The dean of the music school paused. "You have done wonders with Stefan. He has grown up to be a fine young man."

"No, Amy and Mike have done wonders. They have just generously allowed me to share vicariously in the joy of watching him grow up," Charlotte murmured.

"Miss Melanie would be so proud if she were alive," Jackson remarked.

"Yes, the best of all possible worlds," Charlotte retorted dryly. "She got everything she wanted, and no one is the wiser. The family line goes on; the family honor is saved, at great cost, despite her dear niece's continued attempts to throw it all away and cause the scandal of the century."

"You know she loved you to distraction," Jackson was suddenly stern. "She'd have gone to hell and back for you. She cared not one whit what people thought about her, but she'd have killed to protect you and Amy. And Charlotte, she was very proud of you."

Charlotte, chastened, was silent.

Jackson cleared his throat. "The coroner has not released the body yet, so it will probably be next weekend or later before we can make plans. Harry was adamant in his instructions about cremation. You know the disdain he held for funeral services. I thought perhaps instead about a musical program, with the symphony and the chorus. Perhaps if we asked Alan Meredith to play?"

Charlotte nodded, rubbing her forehead. "That sounds good. Alan loved every tongue-lashing, every rap with the ruler, and asked for more. Perhaps the chorus could do some Brahms—he and Harry were kindred spirits, both blazing agnostics."

"Charlotte, don't be crass."

"I'm not—Harry loved the Requiem. And he studied with Durufle—incongruous how he could study with such a deeply religious, mystical man, who composed such moving music, and still turn out so ambivalent. Harry would want something of Durufle, I am sure."

Jackson looked at her intently. "I think you are serious."

"I am," she declared, her voice catching in a sob. He reached for her hand, but she withdrew, suddenly listening intently. The organ was silent.

"Malcolm, I'll help you in any way possible, but I can't do any more tonight," she whispered tremulously.

He rose. "I'll take my leave, then. I'll see you tomorrow, dear."

She stood, and kissed his cheek. "I don't know what I would have done without you," she murmured. "I'll never forget how you saved me from myself. Thank you."

His voice choked. "It wasn't supposed to end this way, Charlotte."

After he left, she wandered the halls, checking the door, turning out lights. Amy had turned in early, pleading a headache, and Stefan had abandoned his organ-playing. The huge house was silent.

She glided into the salon, next to Aunt Melanie's massive formal dining hall where she had held formal dinners for Atlanta's elite. Charlotte stared at the organ, its polished walnut panels gleaming in the light of the fussy room, with grand old hand-crafted chandeliers studded with Waterford crystal and casting patterns of light on the frescoed ceiling painted with Rubenesque figures reclining on clouds. She walked to the console, touching the beautifully hand-carved draw knobs, each with lettered names identifying the stops.

Something about this instrument called to her, had always called to her. She fell in love with the organ in this very room. Her first organ lesson was at this instrument. She had spent so many hours practicing here. This organ had seemed like her closest friend. She touched the keys lovingly.

She was transported back to that fateful day, as though reliving it again. She could still remember Kreiser standing over her shoulder, gently walking her through the Bach E-flat major, his hands over hers, his touching her cheek briefly as she begged him to take her as a student. She shook herself mentally.

Charlotte was suddenly back in the present, standing in front of the organ. Inside the bench were various items. She found a pair of her organ shoes and a score of Julius Reubke's *Sonata on the 94th Psalm*. She looked at the music, replete with Kreiser's markings and her fingerings noted, and shook her head sadly to herself. She removed the shoes, clutching them to her, caressing the black leather. Gingerly she put them on and fastened the straps. She slid onto the bench, and pulled the chorus of flutes out. I'll play just a moment or two, not loud enough for anyone to hear, she thought.

The Bach *Prelude and Fugue in E-flat major* came floating to her memory, the piece she had insisted on as her first with Kreiser as a child of twelve. She played without thinking, her photographic, aural and tactile memories locking into a place and time years before, as though it was but yesterday. She was oblivious to everything around her, and did not see the young man in the dark hallway outside the open door intently listening.

She completed the piece, hit a piston and launched into Mendelssohn's *Sonata No. 3 in A*. The music matched her mood: the more she let herself think about Harry, the darker and more agitated she seemed. Halfway through the peaceful interval at the end she suddenly broke down, the tears streaming down her face. She leaned her head against the music desk, sobbing. "Oh God," she cried out brokenly, "it's all my fault. I hated you, and I've killed you. Why don't I feel better?"

She held herself, rocking and sobbing. The figure silently slipped back up the stairs, unnoticed.

Later that night, she was awakened by Amy. "Charlotte," Amy shook her violently as Charlotte kept screaming, struggling against her. "Wake up, please."

As Charlotte opened her eyes, shaking and crying, Amy held her close and rocked her.

"The same dream?" she asked Charlotte, as Charlotte clung to her, disoriented and incoherent.

Charlotte's eyes suddenly focused on a figure in the doorway. At first stiffening, she clung to Amy desperately. Then trying to pull herself together, she nodded to her sister. "It is just so real, so frightening." She looked again, but the figure was gone.

Chapter 48

Charlotte Lawson, tall and trim in a deep navy silk pantsuit, made her way slowly past the rows of pews in the imposing church and found one close to the center of the room, following the pew down and seating herself unobtrusively near a column, her favorite spot in the room for listening to the organ. She could see Amy and Michael sitting near the front, but did not move to join them.

The room boasted lovely cream-colored walls, the perpendicular windows with geometric tracery framing scenes from the Gospels surrounding the nave like sentinels. The organ console stood front and center of the raised choir loft above the altar area, the entire area heavily paneled in warm dark wood. The two flanking chambers housing pipes, which spilled over out of the loft, framed a three-paneled stain glass window, of brilliant hue, which was backlit. The room also housed a split antiphonal division of pipes in the back gallery, and a division on each side of the room, one side boasting a small chapel, the other additional pews for seating. There were *en chamade* trumpets jutting out in V-formation from the paneled back gallery over the nave.

Charlotte lowered her head, ostensibly studying the piece of paper in her hand, but instead closing her eyes. A myriad of emotions assailed her. Not two weeks ago she was sitting across the room from this spot, reviewing another recital. And the performer Harry Kreiser is now dead at my hand, she thought.

Her mind unwittingly flew back over the years, to the time she at thirteen memorized the Mozart for him, only for him to fly into a rage with her, then to sit down beside her at the console and play the Fantasia as if imparting a sacred oracle to his beloved acolyte. She also remembered her own recitals in this church where she played the Mozart as well as her first Durufle. The memories of the hours of rehearsal in the room, many of them with Kreiser coaching her unmercifully, washed over her like a tidal wave. She had to steady her breathing and close her mind as other reminders started crowding in.

Opening her eyes back in the present, her vision blurred as she stared unseeingly at Stefan's program notes. She didn't notice the man approaching her until he was standing next to her. Startled out of her reverie, she looked up.

"Is anyone sitting here?" he indicated the space next to her. His form was solidly built but lean under a dark gray well-cut suit, his dark wavy hair neatly cut. Tall and forbidding, his face broke into a polite smile.

She frowned slightly, blinking rapidly and shaking her head in the negative. Tensing as he seated himself beside her, she turned to respond to someone in the aisle who addressed her.

He offered his hand. "Captain Mark Roberts, Atlanta City Police, Homicide Investigations. And you must be Charlotte Lawson of the *Chronicle*."

Charlotte did not smile as she took his hand, noting his firm grip while not acknowledging his surmise. "I'm afraid I'm not seeking out company or chit-chat tonight, Detective."

"This is not a social call, Miss Lawson," he rejoined coolly. "I left a couple of messages at your office. I tracked you down here. Are you too busy to respond to police inquiries?" Mark asked in a low voice, his smile not meeting the steely glint in his eyes.

"I have been out the last few days," Charlotte replied, her voice also low as she smiled and nodded a greeting to an elderly couple seating themselves several pews ahead of them. She noticed that the room was filling up. Good for Stefan, she thought. "I have not been back in the office yet. Forgive me, but I didn't realize that I was part of a police investigation," she continued smoothly, although her heart was fluttering.

"Did you think I wouldn't want to talk to one of Professor Kreiser's former students, a close friend and colleague, about his untimely death?"

"And just from where would you obtain such information, assuming it was true?" she asked, tight-lipped.

"I have my ways," he retorted, his voice low, gazing at her as a flush stole across her cheeks.

"Can't this wait?" she muttered impatiently. "This is not the time or place. I have to do this," she almost pleaded, her voice low. "I made a promise, and I intend to keep it."

"Was that promise to Wilhelm Kreiser?" Mark queried pointedly.

"No. Detective, I believe you're behind the times. Harry and I weren't exactly on speaking terms after my review of his recital here a few weeks ago."

As his eyes bored into hers, she smiled slightly, her voice lowering to a whisper. "An investigator who doesn't read the papers? If you had, you would not need to guess that. Or maybe that's why you want to talk to me."

Roberts' eyes narrowed. "Yes, I read that review," not volunteering that he had just read it that afternoon. "So where were you on the 12th while he was being murdered? Did you finally make contact with Kreiser that afternoon after all?"

Her eyes narrowed, and he thought he detected fear. She hissed, "So I am a suspect?"

"Charlotte, dear," a voice spoke behind them. Turning, she saw Malcolm Jackson standing beside the large concrete column. He was neatly dressed in gray dress slacks, starched white shirt, navy blazer and burgundy bow tie.

"How are you, Malcolm?" Charlotte tried to compose herself, and spoke warmly, standing. "Thank you so much for convincing the committee to go forward. Stefan did not want to put off his recital, even given the circumstances."

"I understand, and Harry wouldn't have had it any other way," he returned, grasping her hand warmly and kissing her cheek, concern written in his eyes.

Charlotte's eyes suddenly misted, and she felt panic closing in around her. Jackson felt her trembling and murmured to her, "Charlotte, you must let it go, my dear."

Mark looked on as Charlotte nodded and regained her composure, as though pulling a mask over her features.

Jackson squeezed her hand again, looking past her to Roberts. "Ah, Mark," he addressed the man pleasantly. "We don't see each other for so long, then we bump into each other twice in one week."

Charlotte looked confusedly at one, then the other. "You know each other?"

Mark replied, shaking Jackson's hand, "Yes, for many years. He gave me your name, Miss Lawson, as someone I should contact."

Charlotte looked warily at Jackson. As the lights blinked around them indicating that the recital was about to begin, Jackson asked gently, "May I sit with you two?"

"Please do," Charlotte murmured, as Jackson took a seat beside her, sandwiching her between him and Roberts.

A good crowd was in attendance. As people made it to their seats, the young man came on stage. Applause began, he bowed to the audience, then seated himself at the organ console placed center stage.

A hush fell as without preamble the booming of the music of Charles Tournemire charged the room. Charlotte was tense, turning all her attention to the performer, listening intently as the chorale boomed forth and filled the towering space. She closed her eyes, reliving another time, when she was thirteen years old and had first heard Wilhelm Kreiser perform the same number in recital. She had begged her aunt to let her attend the recital on a million-dollar behemoth in town sponsored by an anonymous wealthy and influential patron of the arts, and for which an internationally known artist had been consulted on the design.

The instant music intruded upon her thoughts. She suddenly came to herself, realizing that Stefan was mirroring his teacher's stunning performance of that day years ago. She opened her eyes, expecting Kreiser himself to be sitting at the console. For a moment she believed it was he, well over twenty years ago, and was jarred into reality at the sight of the familiar youth busily pouring forth over the instrument.

She made a note to herself on the program as the selection came to a thundering close, to equally resounding applause. Roberts looked over at her as she scribbled furiously. "What are you writing?" he whispered curiously.

"None of your damned business," she replied, her voice barely audible. She surprised herself at her sudden vehemence toward the man.

She tried to ignore him, but his nearness unnerved her. She could sense his eyes on her, and felt the fabric of his jacket brush her arm. But she could not withdraw, being hemmed in by the professor on her right.

The young performer launched into the next selection, a trio by Bach. Her voice caught in her throat. Each note brought back memories of how heartlessly Harry had grilled her, micromanaging every fingering choice, every nanosecond of sound and silence, spurring many a sparring match between them until she did it exactly as he demanded of her. She remembered learning all six of Bach's set of trio sonatas, and the hours he made her work out fingerings over and over.

Looking down at the blank space beside the title in her program, she realized she could not think of anything original to say. Her mind was jumbled, with scenes of the past and present colliding. Her review of Kreiser's last recital, so different from this one, kept intruding upon her thoughts, as her pen faltered over the paper.

Mesmerized by his student, she was reminded of Harry's comments to her only a few months back, when she had hosted the graduation reception for Brad Reynolds, a graduating student, the previous semester. She could still hear Harry as he drawled on about his immortality through perpetuating himself and his knowledge to his students. The night he announced he was leaving for good, she thought, momentarily angered.

She was suddenly dragged back into the present as the audience was again applauding the young performer. Get a grip, she told herself severely.

You need to concentrate on Stefan's recital in order to critique it coherently for him. This is not the time to fall apart, particularly with a cop beside you looking on.

She felt Roberts' eyes on her, and instinctively knew he was noting her preoccupation. As if to confirm it, he leaned over and whispered, "Am I making you nervous?"

"Of course not," she rejoined as lightly as she could muster. "You men have such enormous egos that it is hard to concentrate on anything else."

She immediately regretted her remark, as the corners of his mouth turned up into a sly grin. "So I am interfering with your concentration?"

She tried to ignore him as Professor Jackson muttered, "It's uncanny, isn't it?"

At first surprised that he could divine her thoughts, she dazedly met his eyes and nodded meaningfully. Of course, she chided herself, the distinguished professor emeritus and dean of the university's music department, the man who had helped his patron Melanie Lawson Cain snag Wilhelm Kreiser for the university's organ department years ago, would note the striking similarities between teacher and student.

"He thought Stefan was his best student yet," Charlotte's voice was uneven.

"That's not entirely true," Jackson replied quietly.

Taking a swift intake of breath to steady her thoughts, she turned her attention again to the recitalist as he launched into the Bach *Prelude and Fugue in E minor*, commonly called "The Wedge". This was again one of Kreiser's war horses, one he taught her, and the rendition cascading forth from the fingers of the student was uncannily like the master's. She was unconscious that she was actually holding her breath, anticipating and checking off the little stylistic nuances which Kreiser had drilled into his preferred students for playing Bach, the non-legato, non-staccato delivery, the tiniest of emphases on the beginning of every other set of sixteenth notes providing a rhythmic precision yet melodious cadence, the focus on the melody wherever it was found in the score.

She remembered how Kreiser related he disagreed with his own teacher about how Bach was to be played. Harry had told her that Durufle's and his wife's 'romanticizing' Bach was inimical to his early German training by his own father, a student from Leipzig, where Johann Sebastian Bach had spent so much of his musical life. "It was one argument we could never reconcile," Harry had concluded. "But it was the fashion at the time."

She was dumbfounded that this overgrown boy, her young Stefan, was performing music in the same manner as had caught her attention and heart the first time she heard Kreiser. It was as though she was hearing Stefan for the first time. She felt as though the past and present were merging, and was oddly excited about the maturity and control exhibited by her little boy, now an adult. She felt her heart swelling with pride.

It suddenly dawned on her what the 'surprise' was. I can't believe I didn't notice it before, she thought dazedly. She stared down at the program in her hand:

Choral-Improvisation sur le "Victimae Paschali"—Charles Tournemire
Trio on "Allein Gott in der Hoeh' sei Ehr"—J. S. Bach
Prelude and Fugue in E minor ("The Wedge")—J. S. Bach
Clair de lune—Louis Vierne
Choral No. 2 in B minor—Cesar Franck
Final from Symphony No. 1—Louis Vierne
Suite, op. 5—Maurice Durufle

Stefan was playing her senior organ recital program. She sat back in total shock. Only Harry had known her program. She was stupefied. Even in death Kreiser mocked her, through her own beloved Stefan. "Damn you, Harry," she whispered, as the audience applauded the young man. She darted her eyes toward Roberts, but he gave no indication of hearing her.

Then the opening strains of the *Clair de lune* assailed her. All color fled her face. She shut her mind to the memory it evoked. "No," she breathed, desperately gripping the pew in front of her.

Suddenly she was transported back to her nocturnal trysts with Kreiser, and the night in the dark salon with him where she played the Vierne as he caressed her before making love to her.

Before she could shut it off, her stream of consciousness assaulted her with another memory of an incident, only weeks later, of the time she was to give a fundraising recital at the nearby college in close conjunction with her senior recital. She was at the concert hall for a final rehearsal. She had spent a small eternity in the restroom, violently ill, retching. Weak and dizzy, she made her way back to the hall. There she found Harry sitting at the console. She could tell he was in a rage, and she could smell the alcohol on his breath. He was busy erasing her piston settings.

Taken aback, she had demanded angrily, "What are you doing?"

"You know these registrations will not do for the Reubke," his voice echoed through the vast space. "Why have I wasted all this effort with you?" he continued derisively, his voice carrying.

"We've been through this. I'm not performing the Reubke," she cried, her voice matching his, her rage coming to the fore. "I spent three hours setting those combinations, damn it," she spat.

"Good God, Charlotte, I held such high hopes for you. I would rather you attempt the Reubke than massacre the Durufle."

"Massacre?" she echoed, reeling. "You told me I played it better than any other student you've taught." Dizzy, she grasped the edge of the console. "What have I done to make you hate me? Despise me all you like, but don't be cruel about my performance."

Kreiser grabbed both her arms, shaking her violently and berating her unmercifully. "Don't you see you are ruining us both?"

He continued his verbal abuse, lost in a drunken rage. After his first words, she comprehended nothing else. At first afraid for him, half-glad he was acknowledging her at all, she had borne his impassioned vitriol as long as she could. Finally, tears streaming down her face, no longer able to listen to his oral barrage of her, and feeling the nausea returning, she had turned on him.

"You son of a bitch. You win."

She shook free of him and ran out.

In retaliation, he had canceled that recital and her post-graduation recital in New York City, and she had gone to Dean Jackson and arranged for her abrupt departure from town shortly thereafter, never performing her senior recital.

But that wasn't the worst of what he did, she thought. "No," she whispered. He stole my heart and turned his back on me. But he never knew the whole truth. I paid him back. She coughed involuntarily as the door of remembrance flung wide, the pain of the wrenching loss of Johann washing over her, her heart lodging in her throat, tears blinding her.

She abruptly stood. "Excuse me," she whispered to an astonished Jackson. "You'll have to do this alone. No—stay with Stefan."

Before he could answer, she slipped past him and silently fled up the aisle to the door.

Chapter 49

Charlotte flew silently out the door to the narthex, oblivious to everything around her, intent only on getting away. She stopped herself, her hand on the front door of the church, holding her aching chest, panting, knowing she could not make herself leave, no matter how painful the memories evoked by the young man's music. She was rooted to the spot.

Blindly she turned, groping for the railing of the stairwell leading to the gallery. Stumbling into someone, she almost fell, but was caught and pulled to her feet by strong arms gripping her. "Excuse me," she murmured brokenly, trying awkwardly to pull away.

"Here," a male voice spoke gruffly, and a handkerchief appeared in her hand. Looking at the recipient dazedly, she recognized Mark Roberts.

Panic seized her. "I'm so sorry; please excuse me," she whispered frantically. She struggled against him, trying to extricate herself, as his grip on her arm tightened.

"It's OK. Take a deep breath," he spoke softly, comfortingly. She slowly ceased struggling, trying to collect herself.

"I really don't want anyone to see me like this," she whispered tremulously. "Please."

"Would you like me to take you home?" his voice was gentle.

"No. I need to hear the rest. I have to be here for Stefan. I can't leave." Tears coursed down her cheeks as she pointed to the stairway leading to the gallery.

Divining her intention, Roberts led her up the stairs, his arm around her supporting her. She collapsed silently on the nearest pew.

He stood watching her, as she tremblingly breathed deeply and tried to regain her composure. He seated himself beside her, her form rigid and tense, as she wiped her eyes and clutched the handkerchief as though it was some talisman against evil.

Quietly they remained throughout the remainder of the recital, as the youth performed the music of Franck and Vierne, Charlotte intent upon every note. The young man accepted his applause gracefully, modestly. After making his bows, he walked up to a microphone.

"Thank you so much for coming to my recital. I know the timing is far from ideal. This has been a terrible week, for a great organist and teacher was killed. A man I greatly admired, who had coached the very best. I shall miss him very much. Therefore, I wish to close with music, in three movements, by my teacher's own teacher."

Roberts watched the woman's pale, rapt face as she drank in the music greedily, vicariously anticipating the young man's every move. Charlotte was heedless of him, as she clutched the pew in front of her, her knuckles white. Every now and then her eyes closed, and her fingers moved, almost involuntarily, in time with the young man's. Roberts was mesmerized as he surreptitiously observed her.

As the final strains of the Toccata drew to a close, she stood, abruptly seizing Roberts' hand. "He is so good, isn't he?" she breathed impulsively. Before Roberts could respond, she had released his hand, and groped in her small evening bag for a compact and lipstick. Feverishly powdering her nose, she tried to restore herself to normalcy.

"I'm so proud of him. This was very hard, particularly with Harry's sudden death. I must congratulate him," she whispered, almost to herself. "Thank you."

She brushed past Roberts absently, hurrying toward the stairs. He followed her automatically. As she entered the church, her eyes met Jackson's, and he came toward her, visibly relieved.

"Charlotte, are you all right?" he asked, clasping her hand, gazing at her concernedly.

She nodded mutely.

Jackson steered her toward the front where the young man was greeting enthusiastic well-wishers. "He's already been asking for you."

Roberts lagged behind, watching the events unfold. As Charlotte and Jackson made their way forward, the crowd parted for them. Stefan's eyes lit up. "Aunt Charlotte! Where have you been?"

As his arms enfolded her, he scanned her face and asked in alarm, "Are you OK?"

"I'm fine," she replied briskly. "It was a wonderful surprise, very moving. You brought me to tears. I'm so proud. You were phenomenal—better than I've ever heard you. Was it too hard for you?"

"No," he smiled, although his eyes shone with tears spilling onto his cheeks. "I just kept thinking that Dr. K would eat my lunch if I let my feelings keep me from playing my best, just the way he wanted."

"He would have found a way," Charlotte concurred, wiping a tear from his face. "I'm sure Harry would have been proud. I'm thrilled your parents got to hear this."

"Yes," he agreed, smiling broadly at his parents excitedly chatting with others not far away. All around them people were clamoring, and Stefan was busy shaking hands and greeting people.

"Aunt Charl? We're all going to Nikolai's. Dad made reservations. Mom and Dad, and Andy and Valerie, Carlyle and Miggy, are coming too." His smile faded. "I asked Russ and Cece, but he said she has a bee in her bonnet about something, so he begged off. You are coming?"

"Yes, of course she is," her brother-in-law Michael Chadwick came up behind her and put his arm around her. "Dean Jackson said he had to grade your recital, so declined to accompany us. Why don't you ask Gerry, Charlotte?"

Charlotte started at the mention of Gerry, but sobered as she turned and saw Roberts intently regarding her, as though patiently waiting. "I did not realize he had made it. I will," she resolved, looking through the groups of well-wishers and spying Gerard near the back of the church.

Making her way toward him, she was surprised by his almost malevolent expression looking past her. "What is he doing here?" Gerard asked her under his breath.

Following his gaze, she saw he was referring to Mark Roberts. "You know him?"

At Gerard's nod, she continued. "He's investigating Harry's murder, and tracked me down here. Malcolm apparently told him that Harry and I were friends."

"Have you talked to him?" Gerard's voice was anxious.

"Not yet," she tried to be nonchalant, but she knew his thoughts mirrored hers.

"Don't you think we should call Wally before you talk to any police?"

Wallace Meredith, an old classmate of Gerard's and Charlotte's, was a noted attorney in town, who handled business matters on retainer for his old friends.

"No, I mustn't appear worried, don't you agree?" she proffered quietly.

Gerard stated, his voice so low only she could hear him, "I got a voice mail from him today myself."

Taking his arm, she asked, anxiety-ridden, "Where were you Friday afternoon, Gerry?"

He started. "You know where I was." His eyes suddenly locked on hers. "I was in Tucson, and you were on your way to D.C., remember?" He moved closer, his face close to hers, his grip tightening. "That is right, isn't it? You didn't make contact with Kreiser, did you? You weren't anywhere near the church, right?"

Frightened, she nodded mutely.

"Don't talk to him without Wally or me present," Gerard growled, his voice so low that only she could hear.

Seeing Roberts moving slowly in their direction, she quickly changed the subject. "I'm sorry about the tabloid story, Gerry. I had no idea there was media at the airport Sunday. Do they never rest?"

"'Two-timing millionaire rushes back to grieving fiancee's arms'?" he quoted sardonically. "I was hoping you wouldn't see that. Good picture of you."

"Amy steals the morning papers to keep it from me, but I have my ways," she smiled grimly. "You seem to be taking it well." She paused. "Are you coming to dinner with us? Please, Gerry—I want you to be there."

"No, Charl," he seemed reluctant. "I was late getting here as it was. I didn't see you in the crowd." He looked at her searchingly. "Have you been crying?"

"I was moved by Stefan's performance," she muttered, looking away.

"I would stay if I could, but I'm flying tonight to Houston. I have to take care of some business, review some contracts for franchises. I've already put off this meeting once. It's early tomorrow morning. I'll be back tomorrow if I can, no later than Thursday. You know my cell number if you need me."

Charlotte's disappointment showed. "I know you're still angry at me, Gerry. I wish—" her voice trailed off.

His brow furrowed, and his voice was gruff. "All this work of mine is a matter of self-preservation from you." His remark was cutting. Then, at her hurt expression, he smiled self-deprecatingly. "It's just a joke, Charl. I'm preoccupied right now."

"Please call me when you get back," she told him. "I do care for you, whether you believe me or not."

Before she knew what was happening, he had suddenly pressed her to him, his face close to hers. "You haven't changed your mind?" he mocked her, his voice so low that only she could hear. "What, have you decided you are free to marry me with Kreiser gone? Maybe we can save face that way."

She recoiled as if he had slapped her. "Is that what you think this is about?" she whispered.

"Hasn't it always been about him?" Gerry said, his anger unmistakable.

She stared at him, her eyes wide with panic. "I'm to blame—for all of this. Now's your chance." She nodded toward Roberts as he moved purposefully toward them. "There's the police. Put us both out of our misery. Tell him I was there, that I did it. Turn me in. I won't deny anything you say."

He enfolded her to him, swearing under his breath. "God damn it, Charl. Don't be crazy. I'm sorry. I keep forgetting you still have the power to hurt me."

She realized she felt secure in his arms. He gently pushed her away, holding her at arm's length. "I'm sorry. I shouldn't have said what I did about Kreiser. Give my congratulations to Stefan."

As Roberts was gaining the last few feet, he whispered, "The timing of this meeting in Houston sucks. I don't want to leave you to face this alone, but it's too late to cancel. I promise I'll be back as soon as I can. Please don't do anything or say anything, at least until I get back. I'll call Wally tonight—I'll try to cut this trip short."

Shaken and reluctant, she nodded as he released her. Roberts held out his hand to Gerard. "Mr. Fellowes, I don't know if you remember me. I'm Mark Roberts with the Atlanta Police Department. It's nice to see you again."

"Likewise," Gerard responded graciously, shaking his hand. "I do remember. You're a captain now, aren't you? Congratulations. What can I do for you?"

Roberts smiled engagingly. "Thanks. I know you're busy, and this is a bad time. But I need to talk to you about Professor Wilhelm Kreiser. It's possible you could help us shed some light on the homicide investigation."

Gerard's smile faded. "I received your voice mail this evening. I'm not sure what I can do. I didn't know Kreiser all that well, just from my association with Charlotte's family and his friendship with my sister Kat. But I'll be glad to cooperate in any way possible."

"Well, you could tell me whether you saw Harry Kreiser last Friday," Mark watched for his reaction.

Gerard was wary. "I was in Tucson meeting with an investor on Friday—did not fly back to town until late Friday night."

"Could you tell me whether you made it to your 4:00 appointment scheduled with Kreiser that afternoon?"

Gerard stared at Roberts, surprise registering on his face. "I have no idea what you are talking about," he replied icily. "I had no appointment to meet with Kreiser," he continued stiffly, as Charlotte scanned his face, surprised.

"Do you know why an appointment with you would be written on Kreiser's calendar?"

"No, I don't," Gerry remarked slowly, his eyes flickering to Charlotte, who swallowed convulsively.

"Could it be possible for us to talk tomorrow?"

Gerard frowned. "I'm really sorry, Captain Roberts, but I can't even go to Stefan's celebration dinner tonight. I'm flying out to Houston for an early meeting. But I will be back later tomorrow or Thursday, if that would be soon enough for you. I will call you."

"I'd appreciate it," Roberts replied as he handed Gerry a business card. He looked on as Gerry pulled Charlotte to him, brushing her lips with his. "I don't want to leave you. Please take care of yourself," he whispered. "I'll be back. Remember."

"I'll walk you out," Roberts offered. Gerry nodded unhappily.

Charlotte reluctantly watched him moving away. Slowly returning to her family, she noted that Michael was following the men out.

Stefan asked disappointedly, "Gerry is not coming?"

"He has to fly out on urgent business tonight," she replied cautiously. "He sends his congratulations and his regrets."

"I'm sorry," Stefan gazed at her sympathetically, noting her drawn features. He hugged her impulsively. "I know all this is hard on you," he whispered to her. "First Aunt Mellie's death, then Gerry and you, then Dr. K's murder. Gerry will come around. You'll see. We'll get through this."

She caught her breath in surprise. "I love you, dear one," she murmured, kissing his cheek. "You sound just like your dad. Don't worry about me. I'm all right."

Amy came up with several of Stefan's friends, and their conversation was suspended. Charlotte stood around and pretended to listen to their banter.

Michael came up after several minutes and put his arm around her. "I'm sorry about Ben's *faux pas*. You handled him well Saturday. I was afraid you were going to use him as a target for a moment there. I told you he was not the sharpest knife in the drawer."

"Then why are you working for him?" Charlotte jabbed him in the ribs. "You should run for senator yourself."

"I have to learn the ins and outs of the system and campaigning first, Sis," Michael rejoined quietly. "That why the chief of staff stint."

"You know more about the political machine than anyone. I am tired of wasting my money backing these intellectual lightweights," Charlotte kept her voice low, noting that Roberts had returned and was regarding her. "Mike, step out on faith."

"I'm planning on it. But," he looked at her slyly, "in the meantime I found you a date for the evening."

She looked suspiciously at him, then at Roberts. "You have?" she addressed Michael.

"Your friend Mark has allowed me to twist his arm. He'll join us for dinner."

"He's—" she began, her eyes wide, the denial on her lips, but thought better of it. She did not want to do anything to upset Stefan, and to point out that Roberts was a police officer investigating Kreiser's murder would definitely spoil the evening. "That's wonderful," she finished, her words belying her feelings.

Michael pulled out a cell phone. "I want to call Vladimir to give him a head count."

Charlotte's eyes locked with Mark's, and he gave her a thin smile. She found that she could not return the smile, and her heart was hammering in her throat.

Moments later, Michael hung up with a triumphant smile. "OK—we're on our way to Nikolai's."

Amy, who had come up and was standing beside him, asked, "Can we all fit in one vehicle?"

"Don't forget I rented the limo for the night," Mike informed her, pecking her on the cheek. "We're fine."

Mark cut in smoothly, "Charlotte and I will meet you all there." Turning to her, he commanded, almost sternly, "Come."

Taking her arm, he led her away from the thinning crowd. She noted Stefan's curious stare at her, and smiled back more confidently than she felt.

Roberts steered Charlotte out of the church. He led her the short distance to his car, a late-model Volvo sedan. Holding the passenger door for her, he firmly guided her to sit, shutting her inside. Rounding the car and letting himself in, Roberts turned the ignition. The car sprang to life.

Charlotte, trying to mask her fright at being alone with him, started to direct him, but he cut her off. "I know where the restaurant is." He made no move to pull out from the parking space, watching her, inquiry in his eyes.

"Are you going to be OK?" he finally asked her. "That must have been traumatic for you tonight."

"I'll be fine," she insisted, trying not to sound defensive. "Thank you for helping me out back there."

"No problem," he replied, turning his attention to driving as he pulled out.

"Why did you tell my brother-in-law we were friends?" she demanded.

"I didn't. He assumed, and I didn't correct him," Roberts replied smoothly. "I noticed you did not correct him either."

"I did not want to spoil Stefan's night by announcing that you were a cop investigating the murder of his teacher," her lips were bloodless. "Why didn't you beg off?"

"Miss Lawson, we haven't had that talk yet, and I'm a persistent man. If I can't get you to speak to me one way, then I'll try another," he smiled enigmatically. "You have to admit—it beats hauling you into the police station, doesn't it? A nice dinner with family and friends."

"You're going to interrogate me in front of Stefan and my family?" she was disbelieving.

"No," he retorted, as he pulled behind the limousine. "I can wait until after dinner."

They were silent as he followed the limousine to the restaurant. Charlotte forced herself to take slow, deep breaths to stop her racing heartbeat. He weaved through traffic in silence. As he pulled to a stop before the restaurant, waiting for the valet, he looked at her, her expression stony. "Stefan is one of the most talented young men I have ever heard," he said softly. "I've never been so impressed."

As he had anticipated, her face softened slightly at his praise for the young man.

He alighted, and soon had assisted her from the car, tucking his hand under her elbow as he guided her into the building and to the elevators, punching the thirtieth floor. As they entered the elegant restaurant, the maitre saw Charlotte, his eyes lighting up.

"Mademoiselle Lawson, you look *magnifique*. Monsieur Chadwick has made reservations, no?"

"Yes, Vladimir," she murmured as he took her hand and pressed his lips to it. "You know that Stefan had his recital tonight?"

"*Oui, mademoiselle.* I am so happy for him. They have just arrived." Vladimir's voice dropped to a whisper. "It is unfortunate, no, about Monsieur Kreiser?"

"Yes," she murmured, her face somber. "It is sad."

"We will try to make tonight a happy one in spite of the circumstances," he looked at her compassionately, his gaze lighting on Mark momentarily, curiously. "Let me show you to your table."

Vladimir led them through the posh restaurant, to a table by a window overlooking the city as the others were seating themselves, Stefan directing them where to sit. Mark looked questioningly at Charlotte.

Stefan came up and solemnly held out his hand to Roberts.

"Hi, I'm Stefan Chadwick," he introduced himself.

"Hello, Stefan. It's very nice to meet you. I'm Mark Roberts," Mark shook his hand, as Stefan regarded him curiously.

"And this is Carlyle, Valerie, Andy, and Miguel, my classmates."

Michael came up behind him as Stefan pointed out their seats. Stefan spoke. "I want to sit in the middle so I can talk to everyone."

Amy sat at one end, with Michael and Stefan on her right, and Mark and Charlotte on her left. The other students took their places further down the table.

Immediately a waiter appeared and drink orders were taken, all requesting water or soft drinks except Michael and Charlotte. Mike raised his eyebrows as Charlotte repeated his order of a double bourbon sour for herself. "A little unusual for you, Sis," he muttered softly. "What's up?"

"I just didn't want you to drink alone," she replied quietly.

"That bad?" he searched her face, reaching over the table and squeezing her hand. "I know tonight was hard," his voice was low. "Are you OK?"

She smiled tightly and nodded.

"Don't let the tabloids get to you. All that stuff about you and Kreiser is fodder for their grist mill," Michael added, his voice low so that Stefan could not hear.

"What are they saying?" Charlotte's eyes were wide as she stared at her brother-in-law.

Amy frowned at her husband. "Nothing you need to worry about," Michael spoke quickly, huskily, his eyes meeting Amy's disapproving gaze.

He turned to Mark, changing the subject, his curiosity brimming. "Now tell me, how did the two of you meet?"

Chapter 50

Mark looked quickly at Charlotte, noting the flicker of panic across her features. "I've actually seen her from a distance for a long time. I am a season ticket subscriber to the Atlanta Symphony." He saw her questioning look. "My younger sister is principal violinist. It's sort of mandatory that I attend." He smiled at Charlotte. "And of course Charlotte is there faithfully, sometimes reviewing a guest soloist or the symphony."

Amy asked, "Are you a musician as well, Mark?" her eyes meeting Charlotte's amusedly.

"Used to be," Mark replied. "Cello lessons," he explained, the hint of a grin on his features. "But I didn't proceed as far as my sister. I busted up my fingers playing basketball one day—had to choose between the two. Now I'm just a music lover."

"So that's how you know Dean Jackson?" Charlotte asked quietly.

"Yes," he responded, turning to her. "Dean Jackson was my instructor. But then I went off to Chapel Hill to play basketball and study criminal justice."

Forestalling further questions about himself, he turned to Stefan. "Stefan, that was a phenomenal performance. How long have you been studying organ?"

Stefan looked at Charlotte fondly. "Since I was twelve. I would have done it sooner, but the powers that be," he nodded in Charlotte's direction, "vetoed that. So it was piano lessons until then. But I loved to hear Aunt Charlotte play, and then I found her collection of organ albums and listened to them."

"She used to play for you?" Mark asked quizzically.

"Well, every now and then she'd get some console time and let me tag along," Stefan smiled at his aunt. "And then there was Aunt Melanie's organ at the big house when we'd visit. I wanted to study with Dr. K and live in Atlanta. But it took some heavy negotiating with the folks for that to happen."

Charlotte, nervous at the direction the conversation was steering, interrupted. "Where did you get the idea to do the same program as my senior recital, Stefan?"

"Dr. K found it and showed it to me. I immediately liked it, and decided to adopt it as mine, as a tribute to you." He stared at her, as if seeking her approval.

Amy, alarmed, queried, "That was Charlotte's program?" She looked stricken, her eyes on Charlotte questioningly. Roberts noted the exchange.

Stefan looked at his mother and Charlotte, suddenly confused. "Did I do something wrong?"

"It's fine," Charlotte interposed quickly, soothingly. "I'm glad you did. It was a wonderful program, Stefan. I've never heard you play better. I'm so proud."

"Dr. K told me I had some big shoes to fill if I played that recital," Stefan's eyes shone. "He told me you were his best."

Charlotte said nothing, but her face flushed as the waiter appeared with drinks. She took a generous sip of her bourbon. They all studied the menu and made their selections, then Stefan and his friends started talking about the recital, performing a post-mortem of his performance.

"Tell me about yourself," Mark inquired quietly. "What about your parents?"

"They were killed in a plane crash when I was four and Amy eight," Charlotte replied gravely. "They went on a skiing trip, and the plane was trying to land in icy conditions, but went down. I don't remember a lot about them—Mom was very stern. Dad's work required him to travel a lot; he was fun-loving, but not home that much. Amy remembers much more about them than I do."

Noticing that Amy was listening to their conversation, she added, "Amy was always the prim and proper one. She aced all the lessons in etiquette and elocution. She could do no wrong, and everything was a sin to Mom. When Aunt Mellie took us in, Amy was her favorite. Amy always tattled on me."

"I did not!" Amy interjected in indignation. "But you were always into something, pushing the envelope, being bad. And Uncle Howard was always taking up for you."

"See what I mean," Charlotte retorted. "I was the black sheep, and Amy was the princess. Even got her Prince Charming," she chuckled, reaching across the table and patting Michael's hand.

"And I'm the poor bastard in the middle of these two," Mike laughed. They all smiled.

Charlotte teased him. "Amy and Mike were childhood sweethearts. But Amy had to wrestle him from Katharine Fellowes' arms. I thought the two of them were going to choose pistols at dawn over him."

Michael placed his hand over his wife's. "There was no contest there. I knew who I wanted." Amy's face glowed with pleasure as she smiled at him.

"Have you lived in Atlanta all your life?" Roberts asked Charlotte.

Her smile faded. "No. When our parents died, we moved here from Charleston, and were raised by Aunt Melanie and Uncle Howard. He died when I was ten. I still miss him. Then about the time I was finishing college, I moved to D. C., took a fellowship at Georgetown, not terribly far from where Mike and Amy live. I was up there for about ten or twelve years, until Aunt Mellie had her first mini-stroke."

"Music fellowship?" Mark asked casually.

"No, writing," she replied evenly, her eyes not meeting his.

There was a tense silence among the adults. Stefan interrupted. "Aunt Charlotte, what did you think of the *Clair de lune?*"

She paused, and her face seemed to pale. Roberts noticed that she quickly regained her equilibrium. "It was very moving. But," she smoothly changed the subject, "how did you know that I was going to do the Franck B minor? That wasn't on the program—the E major was."

"Dr. K told me you argued him into it. I like the B minor better, too," Stefan smiled his knowing smile.

"But what were you doing with the Franck? When you first added the choir reeds, it was not *legato*, and then you speeded up the tempo when you added the great reeds. Was that Dr. K's interpretation?"

"He told me you probably would not approve, that you had some strong feelings on the B minor," Stefan stared at her, he and his aunt on the same wavelength, miles away from the others at the table. "What did you think?"

Charlotte, solemn, replied, "It sounded like something Harry might do. But I'm not sure musicologists would necessarily agree on that. Franck was the *legato* king, you know. I don't recall there ever being any indication Franck wanted detachment. And there is no tempo change actually indicated."

"I know," he sighed defensively, "I read the authorities. I'm aware of what Tournemire and Durufle said. Very *legato*, and throw the metronome away. I mainly did it to see if you would notice."

Mike, noting Roberts' wondering observation of the two, laughed softly. "They do this all the time, tune into a channel all their own and leave the rest of us behind."

"Me? I'm not the one you have to impress, dear. The question is whether the ones grading your performance will notice and understand your motivation, or mark against you," Charlotte continued gently but firmly. "This was not just a recital; your grade depends upon your interpretation. Your problem is that Harry wasn't the judge tonight. Dean Jackson is a 'by the book' person. He is certainly not ignorant of that music."

"I thought about that before the recital, but I decided to stick with my game plan," he remarked, looking at her.

"And that is a valid strategy," she replied, her expression softening. "When you are under the gun, in the final analysis you have to go with your gut. There are so many things that can go wrong in a recital, and you have to be at the mindset where everything flows, where your concentration is at a big-picture level. One generally cannot make micro-management decisions at that point without increasing the danger of mistakes."

Stefan laughed. "Exactly," he agreed. "And if Marie-Claire Alain, our current living authority, got away with it . . ."

"Only the tempo change, and it does sound good that way. She probably inherited that instruction," Charlotte admitted. "You sound just like Harry now," she admonished. They both smiled. "But the ending was superb."

Suddenly it was as though they remembered that there were others at the table, and laughed, and everyone laughed with them. The rest of the meal was low-key chatter, and Charlotte began to relax. She declined another bourbon, opting for a coffee instead of dessert.

As the bourbon stole through her veins, she suddenly felt sapped, as though her energy had been sucked out of her. Amy read her expression. "You need some sleep," she chided her sister compassionately.

Mike picked up on the conversation. "What's been going on?"

"Just some bad dreams," Charlotte replied quickly. "Nothing to worry about."

Roberts noticed the weariness that had crept into her voice. "Well, this has been a lovely evening, and I thank you very much for inviting me to share in it," Roberts stated. He looked at Charlotte. "Where's your car?"

"I changed at work and took a cab," Charlotte responded, her eyes locking on his.

"Let me take you home," he suggested, a hint of command in his voice.

As Charlotte hesitated, Mike intervened. "That's a great idea, Charlotte. I'll get the check." He silenced her objection. "It's the least I can do after you've boarded Stefan throughout college. We'll get these young whipper-snappers home, and be there shortly."

She smiled uncertainly, uncomfortable at being alone again with Roberts. Roberts thanked Michael and stood, pulling out her chair and taking her arm.

In the elevator they were silent. He gave the valet the claim check and they waited in the balmy evening air for his car.

Bestowing her into the car, he took off. She started to direct him to her home, but he cut her off. "I also know where you live."

"You do?" she asked in surprise.

"You forget I'm a detective," he responded wryly, turning the corner. She was silent as he made his way out of the city and toward Lake Spivey.

"Did you find Kreiser Friday?" Roberts finally broke the silence.

"What do you mean?" she asked, trying to read his expression in the darkness.

"There was a phone message in his pocket, a call from you, that it was urgent you talk to him," Roberts remarked lightly. "In fact, you asked Harriet how to find him."

Charlotte's anxiety returned, but she was determined not to show it. "I was returning his call to Stefan. Stefan was out of town, and I was afraid it had something to do with Stefan's recital tonight. I was getting ready to fly up to D.C. to join Stefan, so I wanted to make sure there were no problems before I left town," she continued smoothly.

"And were there any problems?" Roberts queried.

"I—I don't know," she managed to reply, "because I never made contact with him. I kept trying until my flight was called."

"You're sure? Why would a receipt from the gun club for you be found at the church?"

"What?" she exploded, her eyes wide. "I—I have no idea. That can't be," she sputtered. "Are you sure it was mine?"

"And you have no idea why Gerard Fellowes' name and '4:00' would be written on Kreiser's desk calendar?" he persisted.

"None whatsoever," she responded anxiously, noting that his stare was penetrating.

He turned his attention back to the road. She tried to act calm, but her heart was hammering in her ears. Please don't let me faint, she prayed silently.

After a while he had pulled up in front of the majestic old home. He sprang out, quickly bounding around to the passenger door.

He took her hand and helped her out, walking her to the door. She nervously fumbled in her purse for her key, then unlocked the door, pushing the code on the keypad to shut off the alarm. Awkwardly she paused. "Thank you, Detective, for seeing me home."

He made no move to leave, standing beside the doorway. "Miss Lawson, do you think you're going to shake me off that easily?"

She sighed. "It's late, and I'm wrung dry. Besides, I've never been one to kiss and tell on the first date." Her jaw had a determined set. "That is, unless you should feel it necessary to cuff me and take me in?" She held her breath. He might just take me up on that, she thought faintly. I might have to call Wally tonight after all, from the police station.

They stared at each other, each willing the other to back down. He finally stood aside reluctantly. "Then perhaps you should clear some space on your calendar for tomorrow. I'll be seeing you, Miss Lawson. Thank you for a lovely evening."

She let herself in, and leaned heavily against the door. She looked down and saw her hands were shaking violently. I'm falling apart, she thought. She had been unnerved by the detective's questions.

I'm a suspect, she thought. But of course they're going to ask me questions. I can handle this, she kept telling herself. They have nothing. He is fishing for information. But just what are the tabloids saying? What proof do they have? Her mind was whirring, the synapses snapping, thoughts crowding in, colliding with each other.

Suddenly her fear overwhelmed her. Unable to overcome it, she staggered into the drawing room to the bar and poured herself a generous jigger of bourbon. Downing it in one gulp, she coughed as it burned her throat, then poured another. Sipping it, she tried to steady herself. Her mind kept settling on Kreiser, the sound of the shots that stilled his life. "Leave me be, Harry," she whispered, shuddering convulsively.

She wandered aimlessly, and found herself in the salon at the organ. Opening the organ bench, she found a peach-colored silk scarf. She held it to her, remembering the day Kreiser tied her knees together with the scarves to make her practice her pedaling technique, and the day she saw George again for the first time in years.

The memory faded, and she came to herself, still holding the scarf.

Later that evening, when Michael, Amy and Stefan returned to the old rambling house, the huge pocket doors to the salon were closed. They could hear the sound of the organ, the Franck *Choral in B-minor* faintly detected.

Stefan started to go in, but Amy stopped him, her hand on his shoulder. "Don't, Stefan," she whispered. "Leave her alone tonight."

"But why?" he demanded, his voice low.

"Because the decanter of bourbon is empty," Mike spoke from the doorway to the library.

"When she drinks she is fighting demons," Amy whispered, gently pulling him away. "She would not want you to see her like that."

Inside, Charlotte, the bourbon anesthetizing her churning thoughts, was lost in the music, in her memories. She changed a piston, muttering, "No, Harry, Franck is supposed to sound like this."

The music built up to a thundering crescendo as did her anger. She played blindly, the music emblazoned on her memory. As she reached the end, the sound suddenly swirling away into a calm eddy, she broke off the last chord. Angry and spent, hauling herself off the console, she walked away, empty

Waterford tumbler in hand. She gazed at her reflection in the huge ornate gilt mirror over the large marble fireplace.

"You still get your little digs into me, even though you're dead," she said aloud. "Having Stefan do my program was a nice touch. Too bad it's your last upper cut, Harry. Or is it? What more surprises are in store for me?"

Looking down at the empty glass in her hand, she hurled it into the fireplace savagely, listening to the heavy crystal shatter. Turning toward the heavy pocket door as it suddenly slid opened, she came face to face with Stefan, his face ashen.

Her hand flew to her flushed face. Embarrassed, she pushed past him, muttering, "Excuse me," and stumbled up the stairs to her room.

Chapter 51

The morning after Stefan's recital, Roberts' plan was to follow up on his promised interview with Charlotte Lawson. He found space in a nearby parking garage, and entered the white sprawling low-slung multi-storied concrete and glass structure housing the *Chonicle*. When he flashed his badge and asked for Charlotte, he was informed that she had called in, stating she would not be in until that afternoon.

Curiously disappointed, he asked if the newspaper housed its own archives, and was informed that there was an archive library in the basement. Taking the stairwell down to the basement, he was soon seated at a computer screen, pulling up articles and reviews, reading up on Charlotte Lawson's regular columns and about Wilhelm Kreiser.

About 10:00, he received a call on his cell phone.

Will's voice greeted him. "What are you doing?"

"I am at the *Chronicle* doing some research."

"You don't answer your phone messages anymore?"

Roberts started. "What do you mean?"

"Dispatch late last night got a phone call from our little eyewitness asking for you. Of course, maybe you made a house call."

Roberts grimaced at the phone receiver. "No, I didn't. I was at a social function, actually trying to garner information from our Ms. Lawson. My phone was off. Did she say what she wanted?"

He could tell Will was smiling. "No, but she called again this morning—didn't seem at all interested in talking to me. I told her to try back this afternoon. What's that about?"

"I have no idea," Roberts shrugged.

"Are you free right now?" Will asked.

"I've gotten what I want here. What is it?"

"Meet me at the Lawson woman's place."

"Out at Lake Spivey? What's going on?" Roberts was suddenly interested.

"I want to take a gander at this McCall kid, the eyewitness' boyfriend."

"Why are we meeting at Charlotte Lawson's place?"

"It's like this," Will put in his rambling way. "This Cecelia was apparently ga-ga over Kreiser, per a couple of the other students. According to them, she intimated that Kreiser had flirted with her, but they never saw anything that would indicate that he treated her any differently from the others. If he was a chronic companion to her older cousin, it's probable he would avoid conflict and scandal with the younger cousin. But who knows? Perhaps we have a jealous boyfriend.

"This Russell McCall is an interesting character. Has a juvenile record of a few misdemeanors, kind of a punk. But apparently he won some math competition and got a scholarship to the state college. He seems to be into all sorts of audio and visual gadgets, computers, software."

"Interesting," Roberts drawled, patiently waiting for the point.

"Guess where he lives?"

"I give," Roberts shrugged again.

"An apartment over Charlotte Lawson's boathouse," Will replied. "And next door to girlfriend Cece Rhodes, as they call her."

Roberts' mind was whirring. "So you're saying Fellowes and Lawson are next door neighbors as well as engaged?"

Will grunted. "Not so fast. Best we have pieced together, they grew up next door, but he now has a fancy penthouse midtown. Fellowes' dad died several years ago, and his mother just last year. She left Fellowes' cousin Cecelia a trust fund. The girl lives next door to Lawson at the family estate with Fellowes' older sister Katharine, a spinster as they would call her in the old days. Katharine and Gerard are joint heirs of the Fellowes' estate. He's in and out, but has his own place, like I said.

"Anyway," Will abruptly concluded, "I'm going over to talk with this Russell McCall, jealous boyfriend."

"Small world. Sure, I'm game. I'll meet you there."

A little while later he had pulled up to the gate of the Lawson mansion. Will was waiting for him, sitting on the hood of his blue older-model Volkswagen Jetta. Climbing in to Roberts' Volvo, he directed Roberts down a lane just inside the gate which trailed down to a rustic but charming two-story structure with small widow's walk, sitting on the bank and stretching out over the water of a large canal.

Getting out, Will whistled. "My dream home," he muttered. "Damn, some people have all the luck."

They walked into the spacious boathouse. There were two boat slips with a narrow wooden deck between them. A handsome highly polished wooden motor launch was berthed in one of the slips. A staircase hugged the edge of the wall, ostensibly leading upstairs to the living quarters.

A young man, his hair curling down around his ears, dressed in dark jeans and black Harley Davidson t-shirt, was perched on a stepladder, apparently doing some electrical wiring. Roberts peered up. "Are you Russell McCall?"

"Yes, sir," the young man replied, not looking down. "And you are—?"

Will flashed a badge. "Atlanta Police Department. I'm Detective Will Hamilton, and this is Captain Mark Roberts. Could we talk to you a minute?"

"Guess so," he said, screwing a cap on some wires, and climbing down the ladder.

"What are you doing?" Roberts asked him.

"I've been hearing rustling noises around here at night. I'm experimenting with a new security system for the boathouse."

"Could be rats," Will offered.

"Don't think so," he smiled enigmatically. "Mr. Fellowes sends the exterminator around regularly. But I'll put out some traps just in case. What can I do for you? What's this about?"

"We're just doing some preliminary information gathering relating to Professor Kreiser."

"Don't know how I can help you there," Russ was curt.

Will replied, "Nice place you got here. Are you related to Miss Lawson?"

"No," McCall was wary. "I am staying here while going to school."

"Oh, a tenant," Will supplied.

"Sort of," he assented. "I do odd jobs for her, keep the boat maintained, trim the shrubs, mow the grass and stuff like that."

"How did you know Miss Lawson?"

"My mom and Miss Charlotte went to school together, but we moved away. When she found out I got a scholarship at the state college here, Miss Charlotte offered me this so I could afford to go." He grinned. "It's a lot fancier than a dorm."

Will queried, "And Cecelia Rhodes is your girlfriend?"

"I guess you could call it that," the young man was vague. "She lives just over there," he pointed through a large window overlooking the expansive lawn, down past the water to another boathouse and deck just visible. "We pal around together."

"You get along with Miss Lawson?" Will wanted to know.

"She's good to me, invites me over to supper, asks about my grades. Yeah, she's nice," the guy looked quizzically at the two men.

"What about her relationship with Professor Kreiser?"

"I don't know," he was suddenly noncommittal. "What about it?"

"What can you tell us?" Roberts asked, his tone low and confiding, his eyes intent on the McCall's face.

"They seemed to be civil most of the time. Why?" he looked down at his hands.

"Most of the time?" Will pressed. "What about when they weren't?"

McCall glared at him sullenly.

"We're investigating Kreiser's murder," Roberts explained patiently. "We just trying to obtain as much information about him, what he did, who he knew, who had motive, things like that. We'd appreciate any information you could give us."

"The guy was a jerk," McCall volunteered.

"Yeah, I think the term you used yesterday was 'queen asshole'," Will interjected. "What does that mean?"

"I don't know," the kid was evasive. "If he liked you, great. But if he didn't, you weren't even on the radar screen. But he had this certain charm for the ladies. Cece thought he walked on water. Even Miss Charlotte seemed different around him."

"In what way?" Roberts asked, his eyes warning Will to back off.

"She seemed cool, distant, sometimes argumentative, but it was like an act. I don't know—they were like two cats circling, hissing and warning that they were about to fight each other, but it was all just talk."

"Do you know why?"

"Not really. I'm not much for repeating gossip," he replied.

"Like what?" Will wanted to know, but Roberts cut him off.

"Did you ever seen any evidence that any of the gossip was true?"

"I don't know," McCall was abrupt. "Listen, Stefan is a great guy, a friend of mine. And Miss Charlotte has been good to me. She wouldn't hurt anyone, if that is what you're asking."

Will and Roberts looked at each other. "We're not suggesting anything," Roberts stated gently. "Russ, did you ever think they were closer than friends?"

Russ' jaw clenched. "He was over here a lot when Miss Melanie was alive. He was scarce after that. He was at the house a while back when Miss Charlotte had a party for one of the students." He stopped abruptly.

"And?" Roberts prompted him gently.

"That was the night Stefan showed Cece and me the safe and the old coins and told us the story. We were some of the last to leave." He paused. "The professor was still there in the other room with Miss Charlotte when we left. Cece wanted to hang around, but I dragged her away. That was also the night of the break-in."

"What can you tell us about that?" Roberts watched his face.

Russ flushed and looked down at his shoes. Will persisted, "Where were you?"

Russ finally looked at Roberts. "I was with Cece. At the Fellowes'. I didn't tell the police; I said I was asleep here. But she wanted me to slip up to her room, and well . . ."

"You slept with her?" Roberts supplied.

Russ was silent. Roberts prompted him. "Tell us."

"First time she came on to me. Yeah, we made out."

"What can you tell us about the break-in?" Will was interested.

"Nothing," he was shamefaced. "If I hadn't been—busy at the Fellowes' house, perhaps it wouldn't have happened. I had been telling Miss Charlotte she needed to update the alarm system at the house." He swallowed. "I'm a light sleeper, and feel it's the least I can do to keep an eye on things. And I let her down."

"Would Cece back up your story?" Will asked.

"I doubt it," Russ flushed. "Do you think she is going to let her cousin find out she slept with me?"

Roberts nodded sympathetically. "I see your point."

"Tell us about your girlfriend. You call her 'Cece'?" Will prompted.

"Nice kid," he muttered. "She's really competitive. She likes the university and Kreiser. She is always busy trying to one-up someone, mainly Stefan. But she can be a lot of fun. Stefan introduced her to me. She used to have a crush on him."

"She would have no reason to make up any of her story, would she?" Will asked, watching the young man.

"Why do you ask that?" the youth stared at Will questioningly.

"Just wondering," Will gazed around the boathouse admiringly. "She wasn't sweet on Dr. Kreiser?"

"Well if you call it 'sweet' her always wanting to impress him and his seeming to be her favorite topic of conversation, then yes," replied McCall. "She dwelt on every little thing he did and said, taking it apart and analyzing it. It was nauseating. I never saw him treat her differently than the others."

"Did you see them together?" Roberts inquired softly.

Russell flushed. "I—I sometimes sneaked into the lessons, just waiting for her to finish," he confessed. "They didn't know I was there. Afterward, she'd brag to me about all sorts of stuff that happened, but I knew better. I finally confronted her one day, and she cried and admitted she made it up. She said she just wanted to make me jealous."

"Did it work?" Will asked.

"Not really," Russ smiled slightly. "She has a vivid imagination."

"Could she have developed a reason to want to see him dead?" suggested Will.

"I don't think so," Russ replied, a smile on his face. "Too much hero worship there. And she can't shoot worth a crap, if you're suspecting her of offing the professor," he volunteered suddenly.

"How do you know?" Roberts asked.

"'Cause I took her biking one day last month to an old clay pit, and we did some shooting. She wanted to go to her cousin's gun club, but I vetoed that. Glad I did. She doesn't need that gun. She couldn't shoot an elephant if it was about to squash her. She'd have hurt someone at the firing range."

"What about you? Can you shoot?" Will posited.

"Better than she can," McCall countered gruffly.

"Can you tell us your whereabouts Friday?"

"I was here all day except for a class at ten. I had to catch a ride with Miss Charlotte, and a friend dropped me off after class."

"Oh," Mark broke in. "Was she home that day?"

"She was at home earlier that morning," Russ offered. "She came back a little after noon."

"Do you know where she went?"

"Well, no," Russ rolled his eyes sarcastically. "She wasn't with me in class."

Roberts was calmly persistent. "Did Miss Lawson say where she was going?"

"She was going to the gun club," Russ was sulky.

"Did she say why?" Mark prodded.

"She told me she had to see if she could still hit skeet. She was going to D.C. for the weekend, and going shooting Saturday with the guy running for senator. She said it had been awhile, and she didn't want to embarrass herself."

"Where were you Friday afternoon?"

"I was here tinkering with my bike, trying to get it to run," McCall looked at Will. "I was here when Miss Charlotte left for the airport."

"What time did she leave?"

"I don't know," he was evasive. "Three o'clock, five o'clock. I wasn't really paying attention to the time."

"It's important," Roberts prompted him.

McCall was silent for a few minutes. Then he looked up at Roberts. "The cuckoo clock struck three."

"And you didn't sneak into the church last Friday?" Will wanted to know.

"No, sir," Russell's eyes bored into Roberts'. "My bike was dead, so I didn't have a ride into the city. I expected Cece to come here after her lesson. When she didn't show up, I walked over to her place."

Roberts nodded, his face impassive. "Thanks, Russell. We might have some follow-up questions later. You've been a lot of help."

The boy made no reply, sullenly watching them walk out.

Mark dropped Will off at his car. "What do you think?" he asked, grinning.

Will sniffed. "Well, one can't rightly accuse the kid of monopolizing the conversation. I just don't know."

"He says he didn't have transportation, unless he hired a cab or caught a ride. But Charlotte Lawson had time. She left home at 3:00, and the plane didn't leave until almost 6:00. She didn't check in until just after 5:15."

"And she apparently had the chance to practice her shooting beforehand," Will grinned. "But is she that good a shot?"

"Guess I need to find out," Roberts remarked. "I'll check out the gun club. I'll ask about that receipt we found at the scene."

As Will clambered out, Roberts asked him, "What's next?"

"I have to hurry back. Interviews are scheduled at the office. The exes are to come in. What about you?"

"I'll be there shortly." Mark looked toward the big house. "I'm going to take a chance on seeing if the lovely Miss Lawson is home. I think it's time to hear what she might have to say."

"Good luck," Will said in parting, smirking.

Mark made his way back down the main driveway, parking near the large overhang and covered porch area. Getting out, he noticed a gray BMW sedan parked nearby the front door. Wonder if it is hers, he thought. He took down the tag number.

As he walked to the front door, he could hear the faint sounds of organ music. About to ring the doorbell, he was startled by a voice behind him. "May I help you, sir?"

Looking around, he noticed an elderly black gentleman in overalls, who had just set down a flat of lush coleus. "I'm here to see Miss Lawson," he replied, flashing his badge. "Is she home?"

"Yes, sir, but she doesn't like to be disturbed when she's playing." He pulled off a pair of gardener's gloves and wiped his hands. "I'm Jacob, sir."

Mark nodded pleasantly. "I don't mind waiting until she's through. But it is important that I talk to her."

Mark spent a few minutes in small talk with Jacob, and was able to confirm Russell's story as to the times of Charlotte's comings and goings on Friday. While Jacob excused himself a minute and disappeared inside the house, Roberts did a cursory examination of the exterior of her BMW, and called a forensics tech to come check the car for evidence.

"Come with me," Jacob appeared again and said pleasantly, pushing open the door and gesturing for Roberts to follow. Roberts entered the spacious and airy foyer, at the other end of which a massive curved staircase followed up the wall to the floor above. On either side of the hall a few feet from the front door were doorways. The first one on the left was open, and apparently was a formal parlor or drawing room. The doorway on the right was closed, and from inside came the sounds of the organ.

"Feel free to wait here in the hallway or the drawing room," Jacob was gracious. "She has been in there a while, and she'll be breaking for lunch any minute now before going to the office. Can I offer you anything while you wait?"

Roberts murmured in the negative, and was left alone. He paced outside, before doing a brief once-over of the rooms opening up into the foyer.

The sound of the organ was muffled, and ebbed and flowed. Curious, he noiselessly slid open the pocket door and let himself in. He took in the massive room with paneled wood walls and pale green French jabots framing the large windows. Near him was a massive marble fireplace, a large ornate mirror with gilded frame over the mantel. A concert grand piano and a double French harpsichord flanked the fireplace.

At the other end was the organ. Between the instruments were tasteful groupings of comfortable chairs, settees, a couple of tables, and sofas in coordinating colors, some stripes, some Jacobean prints, some solids. The room was reverberant, and the sound of the organ began building.

He took a seat in the center of the room, facing the organ and listening as the golden haired woman, her back to him, was causing thunder and rage to pour forth from the bowels of the organ. He was hypnotized as she effortlessly plied the keys and pedals, and the music crashed around him.

Before he knew it, it was all over. As the sound died slowly away, she sat there, motionless. After a moment, she swung herself around and off the organ bench, bending down to remove her shoes. She was dressed in a gray pantsuit with tailored swing jacket, a colorful blue scarf peeking out from the collar. Straightening up, she saw him and froze, her eyes wide in fear, dropping the music score in her hand to the floor.

"What was that?" he inquired, pointing at the music she just dropped.

"A composition by Julius Reubke, his *Sonata on the 94th Psalm*, one of the few pieces he composed before dying in his twenties," she stared at him balefully.

"Sounds a little like Liszt," he remarked casually.

"Very perceptive. Reubke was Liszt's student. What are you doing here?" she asked curtly, her discomfort apparent. "Do you generally enter homes without permission? How long have you been here?" She stepped into low-heeled matching gray pumps.

He made no move, watching her standing there as if poised for flight. "I told you I would see you today. Here I am."

She sighed resignedly, reaching down and picking up the score nervously, placing it on the bench. "You are persistent. Can I offer you a cup of coffee? Some lunch?" she heard herself asking.

"Both would be nice," he smiled slyly.

"I'll need to inform Daisy," she muttered. "Do you mind being served in the kitchen? I wasn't expecting guests."

"That will be fine," he replied, following her out of the room and down the foyer to a large sunnily-painted hallway.

"Daisy," she called as they passed a cozy dining nook overlooking a rose garden, "would it be too much trouble to add a guest? I'm going to set up in here."

"Sure, honey," came the reply. "Just give me a minute."

"Where are today's papers?" Charlotte called, looking around the nook.

"Miss Amy took them with her," Daisy's voice was heard.

"Damn," Charlotte muttered. "I wanted to see them," she continued under her breath.

Going to a built-in mahogany china closet, Charlotte pulled out linens and plates. She proceeded to set the table as Roberts looked on.

A large black woman came bustling through the doorway from the kitchen. "Goodness, Miss Charlotte, what do you pay me for?" she remonstrated.

"Daisy, you've already worked so hard today," Charlotte replied gently. "Just put everything on the tea table and we'll serve ourselves—there are only two of us. Stefan won't be back until after his calculus exam, and this is not a social call, after all."

Turning to Roberts who was regarding her amusedly, she asked, "What to drink?"

"Anything is fine," he replied, his eyes not leaving her.

As Daisy bustled forth with food, Charlotte rubbed her temple abstractedly. "Do you want me to give you permission to search the place while we're at it?"

"Not right now, perhaps after we eat," he rejoined lightly, as he followed her lead and sat down across from her.

Chapter 52

"Please thank your family for including me on the wonderful dinner last night," he remarked.

Daisy had left them alone. Charlotte disappeared momentarily, soon returning with glasses filled with ice. Pouring iced tea for herself, she looked skeptically at Roberts. "It's unsweetened, but I have sweetened as well," she explained.

"Unsweetened is fine," he nodded.

She pointed to a set of old decanters on a lower shelf of the trolley.

"In case your tea is not strong enough," she explained. "Aunt Mellie always kept them there for male visitors to 'sweeten' their tea. Please serve yourself."

"No, thanks," he laughed shortly. "I'm on duty."

On the tray were some tempting small soufflé cups of steaming pot pie with a flaky crust, some delectable chicken salad molded and lightly dusted with slivered almonds, a plate of various fruits, asparagus spears with hollandaise on the side, a fragrant and inviting green salad, and some homemade French rolls with butter.

His expression showed his amazement. It was Charlotte's turn to laugh. "You've just made Daisy's day. She does this on a smaller scale most days, overkill for only me. Stefan and Russ generally come in the afternoons and inhale what is left. There's enough for an army today because she was counting on Amy and Mike being here for lunch. But they left for Callaway Gardens this morning, and declined a picnic basket. So for once there is an appreciative audience."

Suddenly Daisy was hovering nearby. "Do you need anything else, Miss Charlotte?"

"No, again you've outdone yourself, Daisy," Charlotte spoke warmly. "Have you served Jacob and yourself?"

"Yes, ma'am," the woman looked lovingly back at Charlotte.

"Well, don't keep him waiting. Take a rest. Officer Roberts and I have business to discuss, and we'll take care of ourselves."

The woman disappeared.

"You have no other servants?" he inquired, his eyebrows lifted in surprise.

"There's just Daisy and Jacob, Aunt Melanie's help. She had Uncle Howard build them their own wing to live in. They have been with her since she and Uncle Howard married. They are both getting on in years, but refuse to retire, and are happy to remain with us. They are members of our family, and I can't bear the thought of life without them. I try to keep anything heavy and taxing off them. I hire a bonded service to do the heavy cleaning, and Russ and a landscaping service help Jacob with the outside. We serve ourselves after 7:00 at night. If there's company, we cater out. There's no reason, since Aunt Mellie's death, for more servants when there are only Stefan, Russ and me."

They ate in silence, Charlotte again reticent and Mark observing her. She picked at her food, finished before him, and sat tensely, sipping her tea, waiting for him. Feeling his eyes on her, nervously she broke the silence. "Forgive me for not exuding more Southern hospitality. What do you want to know? Let's get it over with."

"Why did you run away during the recital last night?" Roberts was direct.

She caught her breath. "Isn't it obvious? I've just lost a friend and former teacher, and sitting there brought it all back. I feel guilty because I cannot take back my scathing review, and he left this world on bad terms with me. I sat there listening to his best and brightest student, and it was like Harry himself was playing."

"I think there's more to it than that," Roberts mused, his eyes boring through her uncomfortably. "The music brought back very painful memories. Memories of what? Were you and Kreiser lovers?"

She looked at him aghast, her throat dry. *Am I that obvious?* she wondered. She sipped her tea before responding. "Detective, I have no idea what the tabloids are saying. My family seems determined to keep me from seeing the papers." She stuttered, "I—I assumed you knew the real story by now. Harry was my organ instructor, until I changed majors and left here for the writing fellowship at Georgetown and an internship with the *Post*."

"You know the scandal sheets say otherwise? That you and he have been lovers for some time? That he is the reason you left town?" Mark sipped his tea, his eyes never leaving her face. "Were you aware that he had a shrine to you in his bedroom, with photos and clippings detailing your accomplishments? You were more than teacher and student."

Charlotte paled but responded coldly, "You can either believe me or not. I've told you. Harry and my Aunt Mellie were close. She was instrumental in getting the university to hire him. I've known Harry since I was twelve and started lessons with him. He was always around, like one of the family. I came back home after several years away, and because of Stefan and Melanie we were thrown together in social situations regularly. That's it."

"Because Stefan studied with Kreiser?"

She averted her eyes. "Yes, partly. Stefan is very stubborn when he sets his mind on what he wants. He has been in my charge since he moved to Atlanta and began studies at the university."

"What did Jackson mean last night when he said it was not exactly true that Stefan was Kreiser's best student?"

"I—I don't know," she stammered, her face aflame, surprised he had heard the dean's comment.

"Jackson was speaking of you," Roberts answered his own question. "You were Kreiser's star student, weren't you? What happened?"

"Stop it!" she cried. "What has this to do with your investigation? How dare you!"

She stood, intending to escape, but he caught her wrist and imprisoned her. "I will find out, one way or another," he said quietly. "Would it form a motive for murder, I wonder?" His voice remained low. "I noticed that you left town just before you were to receive your organ degree. Why did you quit your organ studies with Kreiser? It became personal, too personal, didn't it?"

Her eyes went wide with fear. She tried to pull away, but he held her wrist in a vise. She stared at his hand on her wrist, refusing to meet his eyes.

Charlotte finally slumped back into her seat, her cool reserve crumbling. Tears formed as she muttered, "I couldn't handle the pressure—I lost my nerve. I developed severe performance anxiety, you know, like Van Cliburn. I was useless, a wreck. I couldn't even go through with my senior recital."

Roberts, stunned, released her. She did not move, her voice reduced to a whisper. "My engagement to my fiancé was broken. The tabloids were right on that. I did find out the hard way that George was gay. Everything I touched seemed to crumble. I was crushed. I was to the point I couldn't function at the console. I was physically sick. I was an embarrassment, to myself and to my teacher. He told me so. I finally walked into Dean Jackson's office and begged him to help me. I changed majors. I had minored in English as well as my double majors in organ and piano, so I didn't have too much to make up. And I transferred out, landing a fellowship at Georgetown."

"What caused it?" Roberts asked quietly.

"Who knows?" she exclaimed bitterly. "There were so many things happening. My self-esteem curled up and died. I just choked up—I never regained my edge."

"Why did you leave the university?" Mark gazed at her suspiciously.

"Why would I stay?" she replied angrily. "Everything here reminded me that I was a failure. My life's dream was over."

"So Kreiser had nothing to do with your leaving?" Mark persisted.

She swallowed convulsively and stood, refusing to meet his eyes. "You can ask Dean Jackson if what I have told you was true. I'll serve the coffee in the library—right through that door and to the right."

Her stance brooked no further discussion. As she watched him leave she thought, What you don't know, Mark Roberts, won't hurt you.

She tried to still the shaking of her hands, and absently picked up items from the table, placing them on a tray and carrying them to the kitchen sink. She soon had the coffee ready and carefully balanced the tray as she followed him into the living room. He was standing by the mantel, looking at the bookcase of photographs, noting several pictures of her with various organists or sitting at consoles. There was one of her as a teenager, arm in arm with Wilhelm Kreiser after a recital, and one of her with a ribbon at a skeet-shooting tournament.

"Do you still play?" he asked gently, taking the tray from her and setting it on the coffee table. He pointed to a picture of a younger Charlotte sitting at a four-manual console and smiling at the camera.

"I book time at various organs when I'm pretty sure I won't run into anyone to hear me. It's sort of an addiction," she rushed on, lamely. "Once you've done it, it's hard to leave it alone."

"But never for an audience?" he queried.

"No recitals, if that is what you mean," she insisted, looking at him.

"You are truly amazing to hear. I'm sorry, Charlotte," he spoke, his eyes bathing her in a warm glow.

"Yeah, well, so am I," she responded curtly. "But my training came in handy with this job. So everything works out in the end."

"How did you land the job at the cultural desk of the paper?" he asked, as she poured steaming coffee into the cups.

She struggled to keep her tone conversational, casual. "I was drafted. I was submitting odd stuff in D.C. with the *Post* and doing a little adjunct teaching, completing my degree in English and obtaining my certificate to teach. I wrote a couple of children's stories that sold, and a novel happened to get published, which helped open a few doors. I did some ghost-writing on the side. I got an internship at the *Post*, and then an old acquaintance that knew the boss talked him into giving me a chance doing a few snippets in the arts section. I did some contract teaching. The editor started requesting more submissions, which was gratifying.

"Then I received an offer back home with the *Chronicle*, and after some soul searching decided to move back home. I was determined not to use family connections to make my way, but I suspected Aunt Mellie was behind the offer. Then she had a stroke, and that clinched the matter.

"She would have preferred that Amy and Mike come back home, but Mike is on the fast track in Washington, and they both prefer it there. So I was the default dutiful niece. I came home to take care of her. Stefan followed us after a couple years. She tried to groom me to succeed her, but I'm not a very good student." Charlotte smiled thinly. "And for some reason I'm a favorite target for the scandal sheets, more exciting than the latest UFO sighting, a grave embarrassment to Aunt Mellie and her set.

"But not long after I started with the paper there was this huge recital in town, and because I was the only one on staff with organ background I was drafted to review it."

"Is that when you renewed your acquaintance with Kreiser?"

She paused, tucking a lock of her golden hair behind her ear as she poured cream into her cup. She looked at him mutely, and he shook his head in the negative.

"Sort of. Actually, it was pretty much unavoidable. Aunt Mellie had been instrumental in getting him to come to Atlanta, and he was a fixture, always around, always on her guest list for dinner, always on everyone's guest list, very popular. He was Stefan's teacher. And he procured that first recital I reviewed. He got me in to interview Fred Swann, the soloist, and got my foot in the door. After that he asked me from time to time to assist in juries and to critique his students' recitals, I would help sponsor competitions and attendance at conventions for his students, things like that."

Her mind went back to the small dinner gathering when she had first returned to Atlanta, and her encounter with Kreiser. She dragged herself back to the present. Roberts was asking her, "Dean Jackson told me you were Kreiser's friend. When was the last time you had contact with him?"

Charlotte's mind flew back. "It was about two weeks ago. We had a row over the telephone."

"What about?"

"It started over my review of his recital, and then he became angry that I would not authorize Stefan to accompany him to New York City."

"Why not?"

Charlotte looked away. "Stefan had a paper due for his French class. He was having trouble in French, and I would not allow him to miss class for the trip." She looked up and saw Roberts' eyes intent upon her. She shifted uncomfortably.

"Is that the only reason?" he wanted to know.

"Yes," she affirmed emphatically.

"And you had no further contact with him?"

"I hung up on him. No, I had no more contact."

"Charlotte, did you see Kreiser the day of his death?"

"No," she held his gaze unwaveringly.

"But you tried to reach him. Did you talk to him?"

"No," she repeated.

"And why were you trying to reach him? What was urgent?"

"I—I told you," she stammered. "I had received word that there was a problem with Stefan's recital. I wanted to confirm that it was still on."

Roberts looked at her disbelievingly. She met his gaze with a defiant tilt of her chin.

"Do you have any idea who would want to kill him and why?"

I did, her mind screamed. Sipping her coffee slowly, Charlotte closed her eyes, willing herself to remain calm. "This question has run through my head ever since I got Dean Jackson's call last Saturday about the murder. Although he could be charming when he chose, Harry was far from a teddy bear—he rubbed many people the wrong way. Would someone go so far as to kill him? I guess someone did, but I cannot for the life of me figure out why."

"How about this Reverend Wolverly?"

"Men of the cloth come and go. The problem is that many of them have the same temperament as the church musicians. There will always be turf battles. I find it highly improbable that the good reverend bent his iron pacifist standards and picked up a gun to Harry."

"Anyone at the church? Any of his students?"

"No, sorry," she said quickly, finishing her coffee. "The ladies of the church and his students had nothing but hero-worship for him. He could ask them all for blank checks, to tie cement blocks to their feet and jump in the pond, and they would do so unquestioningly."

As she set the coffee cup down, Mark covered her hand with his, surprising her. "Charlotte, you're my great white hope for leads here. No one saw the murderer. You probably knew Dr. Kreiser better than anyone. Do you want to see his murderer walk away?"

Yes, I do, she wanted to scream. "No," she whispered, staring at his hand as she carefully pulled her hand away. "I just have trouble coming up with possible suspects. This is all so unreal."

"What about either of his ex-wives?" Mark demanded.

Charlotte gave a short laugh. "Always a possibility, but somehow I don't think so."

"Why not?"

"After a hotly contested divorce rife with rumors, first wife Tina and he ended up in a divorce settlement. They were both volatile and pushed each other's buttons. If she was going to kill him, she'd have done it back when they were married. I think she got more enjoyment out of his being alive and having to suffer her as the thorn in his side. Second wife Christy was someone he picked up, and it was apparently over and done within a month."

"Why did neither marriage work?" Mark asked her.

Charlotte's voice was even. "I wasn't married to him, so I wouldn't really know. I think these questions would be better answered by the exes themselves, don't you?"

"Agreed," Mark watched her face intently. "Where were you on Friday the 12th?"

Charlotte met his eyes calmly. "I was running errands around town, packing for the trip to D.C. In fact, I flew out about 6:00 p.m., and only heard about the shooting the next day. Dr. Jackson and Gerry both left messages on my cell phone, but I wasn't expecting any calls, and left my phone off."

"But I thought you were wanting to make contact with Kreiser?" he asked her.

Charlotte stuttered. "Y-yes, but once the pilot requested the phones be turned off, I forgot to turn mine back on once I made it to Dulles. It was late by that time."

"You had no messages from Kreiser?"

"No," she shook her head.

"Dulles? Isn't National closer?"

Charlotte looked down at her hands. "Detective, I'm not a good flyer. My parents were killed in a plane crash. Ever since the 1990s when a plane ended up in the Potomac during an ice storm, I have, when I have the choice, flown into Dulles."

Roberts nodded. "OK, I can understand that. The murder occurred sometime around 4:00 that afternoon. Do you remember where you were?" Mark leaned forward, his face earnest.

"I'm sure I was at home finishing my packing so that I could get to the airport in time to check in," she answered warily. "And no, I don't have anyone who can vouch for my whereabouts. I was alone. Stefan had left earlier in the week to spend some time with his folks in D.C., and he had a couple of appointments there. I tried to call Harry up until my flight was called," she ended lamely, knowing she was repeating herself.

"And your fiancé?" Mark's tone was casual.

"Gerry?" Charlotte's unconsciously fidgeted with the engagement ring on her finger. A trickle of fear ran down her spine. "He had business in Tucson all week. I didn't see him until he met us at the airport Sunday."

"Did you talk to him during that weekend?" Mark was direct.

"Not really; we exchanged voice mails," she admitted slowly. "We were both busy," she prevaricated.

"But you're engaged, aren't you? Lovers generally talk to each other," Mark insisted. "Or was he busy courting the Tucson heiress?"

"We're grown-ups, Detective Roberts," she laughed shortly. "Gerry's a busy man. We can handle a little time away from each other," she glanced at him warily. "And I trust Gerry. You cannot believe what the tabloids print.

"No, he called my brother-in-law Michael when he heard the news, to check on me and to offer his plane to fly us home Sunday morning." She hesitated. "He offered to fly up to D.C. Saturday, but I left a message that there was no need."

"You didn't need comforting?" Roberts watched her closely for her reaction.

Charlotte said nothing, her face a mask.

"Do you own a handgun?"

"No," she answered, her eyes flickering away from him.

"But you were at the gun club Friday morning, weren't you?"

Charlotte paled. "Y-yes," she stammered.

"And what did you do while there?" Mark asked casually.

"You can always check the gun club," Charlotte offered petulantly. "I did some skeet shooting. I was practicing for a shoot with Ben Loftin on Saturday." She stammered, "I do own a 12-gauge. I took it in to be checked out and cleaned before my trip."

"Where is it now?" he asked.

"Uh—I believe I sent it to the club for cleaning," she stammered.

"Thanks, I will confirm that," Roberts smiled at her discomfiture. "And did you acquit yourself well? Beat the senator-elect?"

"Yes, I did," Charlotte responded stiffly. "Actually, I had business with Mr. Loftin."

"What—procuring his retraction of the headline that you were engaged to him? I'm sure Mr. Fellowes was not happy about that story. Of course, everyone is wondering whether you and Gerard Fellowes are really engaged."

"I'm still wearing his ring," Charlotte countered, her smile forced.

"Charlotte, a crumpled receipt from the gun club was found in the bushes beside the side church doors Friday. That receipt belonged to you."

She turned white. Oh, my God, she thought. "I have no idea why it would be there. I—I threw it away at the club. I never keep them." She swallowed convulsively, her hand at her throat. "Detective, I did not go to the church Friday. I admit I thought about it, and even left a little early with the idea of seeing Harry because I could not reach him by phone. However, after making a couple stops, I looked at my watch, and decided I didn't have time, and went directly to the airport."

"How did you get to the airport that Friday?"

"I drove my car," she snapped irritably.

"The car parked outside? The gray BMW?"

"Yes," she was short.

"How did you make it home that Sunday afternoon?"

"Gerry picked us up in his limo," she answered sullenly.

"Who drove your car home?" Roberts asked.

Charlotte stared at him. "Jacob and Russ generally go out to the airport and retrieve my car, so that it doesn't sit at the airport while I'm gone. Why? Do you need to search it too?"

"That's not a bad idea, Miss Lawson. Thanks for volunteering. I've already called a tech. I'm sure he's outside taking care of that detail."

They stared at each other, Mark derisively and Charlotte angrily.

Marks drained his cup and stood. Charlotte stood also, feeling faint.

"Thank you for your time, Charlotte," he said politely. "We've got several leads to follow up on. I'm assuming you won't mind if I get back with you should any questions arise?"

"Do I have a choice?" she was unsmiling by then.

She followed him to the door. He held out his hand. "Thank you for the lunch and the information."

She shook his hand gravely. "Good day, Detective."

After he left, she leaned against the front door heavily, her heart pounding. She walked to the salon, staring at the organ. "Damn you, Harry," she muttered out loud. "You just don't die."

She suddenly recalled the receipt crumpled in her hand and stuffed carelessly into her jacket pocket, and of her standing at the side narthex door of the church, her hand reaching for the handle. She remembered her anxiety over seeing the long black shiny new limousine parked beside the church's side door.

Another wave of fear washed over her. Oh no, she thought. Can the police put us both at the scene?

Chapter 53

Mark Roberts strode into the police headquarters, heading for his desk next to Will's in the investigations office. Randy was lounging in Roberts' chair, his feet on the desk, listening to Will read off a list of interviewees.

Roberts shook his head good-naturedly at Randy, handing him a list of names. "Instead of keeping my chair warm, why don't you ask ATF to run a search on whether any of these people in pending cases possesses registered guns or gun permits?"

"Ahead of you on most of these," Randy yawned, glancing at the list. "Wait a minute—Charlotte Lawson?"

"I don't know," Roberts shrugged. "I just have this feeling there's something she's not telling."

Randy stood up. "Right on it."

"And Randy? I want you to check back over the last six months to find any information about a reported break-in at the Lawson residence. I want everything you can get on that."

"Sure thing." Randy grinned as he exited.

"What did she say?" Will asked, not looking up as he pecked away at a computer keyboard.

Roberts, drawing up the chair Randy had vacated, summarized his luncheon meeting with Charlotte. "And I stopped by the gun club and got chummy with one of the assistant managers there. Last Friday Ms. Lawson not only did a couple rounds of skeet with more than respectable marks—damn near perfect, so make that championship marks—but she also had a go at the firing range. The gun club confirmed that the receipt we found outside the church was hers."

"That puts her at the church, doesn't it?" Will asked.

"Well, she is adamant she did not go to the church, of course. And per the assistant manager, she does throw away the receipts as a habit. So I guess anyone could have picked up her receipt and planted it. But why?"

"Next question: did she carry her own artillery?" Will raised his eyebrows.

"She has her own shotgun, apparently, a Browning 12-gauge double-barrel over-and-under, and had it professionally cleaned and serviced. It was duly returned for servicing by Fellowes himself after her trip. She apparently regularly borrows one of Gerard Fellowes' firearms for the target practice."

"Were you able to find out what type?"

Roberts smiled. "A 9 millimeter, but not just any one—a Sig Sauer P226 X-Six Scandic with 6-inch barrel. A real beauty, with carved birch handle. However, I know your next question. The club personnel swear the gun was left there at the club afterward and can be accounted for. However, the assistant manager said he is certain that she owns or used to own a matching firearm, but hasn't appeared at the club with it in a very long time."

He paused, his face grim. "The assistant manager, one Greg Frazier, knows Charlotte Lawson well—says she and Gerry shoot fairly often. She's a 'damn fine shot', he states. He also says she is a regular, coming in quite a bit the last few weeks. He said he thought maybe she was there looking for her fiancé, but she always stayed and did a few rounds, and regularly borrowed Gerry's handguns for target practice. She favored the 9 millimeter, used it almost exclusively."

"The plot thickens."

"She states she has no gun, but did admit to the shotgun after I confronted her about the gun club."

"Well, we know Kreiser was done in by a 9 millimeter, not by birdshot," Will grinned. "You have circumstantial evidence the lovely Miss Lawson may have been at the scene, but you have no gun in her hand yet."

"I have a crime scene operative checking out her car. It's a little late, but there could be gunpowder residue. Who knows, maybe she has a Sig hidden in the trunk."

"You really want to rile her up, don't you?" Will whistled. "Get anything out of Fellowes?"

"Actually, I saw him last night after Stefan Chadwick's recital at Grace Methodist. He was not overly forthcoming with information, but did agree to cooperate with all police requests. He agreed to hand over any firearms for testing. He was actually surprised when I asked about an appointment with Kreiser.

"Once out of the hearing of his fiancée he was a little more conversational. He informed me that Kreiser had called looking for him, asking to meet with him Friday. Fellowes called him back on his cell from Tucson and told him he anticipated being back in town around 4:00 Friday afternoon, and would try to make contact with him once he landed. He said Kreiser never said why, and he had no idea.

"However, Fellowes said his plans got changed, because his chauffeur/pilot contracted some type of food poisoning and ended up at the emergency room. The doctors finally cleared the guy to return to Atlanta, because he refused to remain at a hospital so far from home. Fellowes apparently made arrangements for mediflight back to Atlanta for his pilot, notified the family, and flew himself back late Friday night. He said he went straight to the hospital to check on his man, was there until early morning Saturday."

Will noted, "That should be easily verified by the hospitals and air traffic control."

"Make it so," Roberts ordered. "Fellowes was also very protective of his fiancée, and informed me she had legal counsel. He seemed defensive when the topic switched to her whereabouts. He said he was worried about her reaction and the impact on her nephew, Kreiser's student, so he had called and left her a voice mail after he found out about Kreiser."

"Did he describe her reaction?" Will queried.

"I asked. He said he had to leave a message, because he didn't get her. So he didn't know. He finally reached her brother-in-law to make sure she was OK."

"So did he confirm they are engaged?" Will laughed.

"Yes, but in the aftermath of her aunt's death they have held off on a formal announcement. He stated there was an informal announcement at a party given for Stefan only a few weeks before Mrs. Cain's death."

Will nodded. Roberts demanded, "What else do you have?"

"Well, I interviewed Kreiser's student Andy again today. I wondered maybe if he didn't have a motive to off his teacher to get the job at the church. But that's not much of a reason apparently."

"Why?" Roberts inquired.

"Kreiser is the one who got the young man a job as his assistant. Kreiser actually signed over his church stipends to the young man to subsidize his income so he could study in America. And the dean of the cathedral has already been making noises about having a series of itinerant church musicians rather than one, thereby diluting the church music program. So, without Kreiser and his champions at the cathedral, that actually hurts this Andy's chances of scoring a full-time job at the cathedral. The young man stood only to lose, not to gain, from his teacher's untimely death. And he idolized the man."

Roberts sighed, leaning back in his chair. "How did the interviews with the ex-Mrs. Kreisers go?"

Will grinned. "Randy and I have gleaned all sorts of interesting tidbits since I saw you yesterday. Ex No. 2 is one Christy Wetherall, a little heavy on the makeup, a little too sure of herself, and a little light on the intelligence scale. She claimed she had the marriage annulled before a year out—Kreiser apparently wasn't all she had hoped. He was supposed to do a two-year teaching fellowship at Yale, and backed out at the last minute. She moved on to some hot-shot real estate developer in Savannah. That was pretty much a dead end.

"However, local gossip is that Kreiser found her in the sack with someone else before the honeymoon was over, and after the air cleared between them, he agreed not to fight her on the annulment, to keep her Catholic grandmother happy. She says she has not seen Harry since last year's New Year's annual party at the High Museum."

"And Ex No. 1?" Roberts leaned forward.

"You're just in time to sit in on that one. In fact, unless I miss my guess, there she is," Will nodded toward the glass door, outside of which a striking tall suntanned woman in a flowing fuchsia silk dress, matching heels, and lots of diamonds adorning her manicured fingers replete with long matching polished nails, and dark curly hair that ended at the nape of her neck, had stopped to ask directions. It was hard to fathom her age, but Roberts' guess was that she was in her late forties. The officer pointed in their direction. Will stood just as the door opened.

"Ms. Caldwell?" he asked.

"Yes," she replied with a cool nod toward him, her eyes appraising Roberts with interest.

"I'm Will Hamilton, and this is Mark Roberts. Thank you so much for coming by the station to talk to us today. If you will come this way."

Will led the way to a small interrogation room, holding a seat for the former Mrs. Kreiser, who was seated and crossed her shapely legs. Will took the seat across the desk from her, and Robert the one beside her. She glanced at both of them.

"OK, I'm here," she drawled. "What do you want to know?"

Will began. "Firstly, let me offer my condolences on the untimely death of your ex-husband. We are investigating the homicide, and are just trying to gather as much information as possible."

"Firstly," she began, parroting Will, "no condolences are necessary. And secondly, I take it you are without a major suspect, and on a fishing expedition."

Will and Roberts glanced at each other, Roberts barely concealing a grin.

"No matter," she replied breezily. "Who didn't like Harry? Well, that would make a pretty long list. This Rev. Wolverly at the church, anyone who made the mistake of trying to stand between him and something he wanted. Even me." At their stunned expression, she continued. "Sure. Of course, Harry did such a good job of doing himself in, he needed no help from me."

"What do you mean?" Will asked.

"Oh, nothing really," she replied cryptically. "Harry was a terrible liar. Mind if I smoke?"

Roberts shook his head slightly at Will, who ignored him, saying, "Go ahead." Roberts grimaced at Will as the woman lit up and Will pushed an ash tray toward her.

"OK, then—where were you on the 12th at about 4:00 p.m.?"

"I was at the 17th green at the club with my Friday foursome," she smiled broadly. "We finished our round, then of course tucked away some margaritas as we do each week. Feel free to check up on me."

"Thanks," replied Will dryly. "Do you own a firearm, Ms. Caldwell?"

"But of course, in a round-about way," Tina smiled broadly. "I'm married now to a self-respecting native Southern male. But no, I have never shot a gun—I find the whole concept of guns somewhat revolting. It's so much more diverting to torture a man rather than just shoot him, don't you think?"

"Can you give us any particular suspects or motives for Harry's murder?"

"Not really, although it looks as though Charlotte Lawson could fit on that list, judging from her review a few weeks back, and from the tabloids."

"Were you aware of any other reason why she might 'fit on the list', as you say?" Roberts queried.

"Not really," Tina frowned, readjusting her skirt as she uncrossed and re-crossed her legs. "I always got the impression she and Harry were rather chummy until she ran away. Even after her return there seemed to be no news that they were on the outs until that review. The girl apparently grew some claws."

"What was the reason your marriage with Harry didn't work out?" Roberts asked.

"Good question," she looked beguilingly at him. "Harry had a tough time being true to one woman, or one man it is rumored, for that matter," she postulated, watching for his reaction.

"You mean—" Will began, but she finished for him.

"He was a randy cuss. I got tired of not knowing who all I was sleeping with vicariously. He was the talk of the town, particularly the arts crowd. There was always some 'grand passion', as he called it."

She paused dramatically. "It's funny to me now. I thought Charlotte Lawson was his grand passion, but he apparently couldn't compete with the Fellowes' brothers. Although Harry could have written his own ticket with their sister Katharine."

"The Fellowes?" Will echoed excitedly.

"The very same," Tina nodded, blowing out smoke. "Mega bucks. The family was one of the early Coca-Cola investors, then on to various real property ventures, some silicon and microchip technology, what you would call some diversified interests that paid off big time. Katharine never did much other than her social flitting, her horseback riding and skeet shooting competition. They say she can be a crazy bitch, really loco, a great one to cause scenes. She followed Harry around from time to time like a puppy dog. That is, after Mike Chadwick married Amy Lawson, and she couldn't chase him around any more."

"I had not heard that before," Will interjected.

"Katharine made herself a nuisance all through their school years, and tried to break up the two young lovers. But I think Melanie Cain finally intervened in some way to ensure that match. In fact, there were once vicious rumors of a deal made, Mike for Amy in exchange for an arrangement between Charlotte and Sammy, a/k/a George Fellowes. I don't know the truth of that, but Katharine had some sort of nervous breakdown when Amy and Mike married, then apparently recovered. She and Gerry actually both ended up at national skeet and sharpshooting championships right after that. She met some guy, and was actually engaged, but for some reason she broke it off. And she was perennially an ornament on Harry's arm at social functions, but no one took them too seriously, because they dated so many other people. They were the two voted least likely to ever settle down.

"And of course brother Gerry is nothing short of a genius, worth his weight in millions. He is the real catch, but never married. He's apparently fond of the opposite sex, because he has been seen with more than one debutante and celebrity on his arm. There's constant speculation about who will snag him, and whether it will be his old buddy Charlotte Lawson.

"Brother Sammy was a playboy, and it was rumored he wasn't too choosy about his bedfellows—either sex would do. But he wasn't exactly slumming back when he was slated to marry Charlotte Lawson."

"Engaged to Charlotte Lawson? What do you mean?" Roberts inquired curiously.

"Her aunt was Melanie Elizabeth Lawson Cain—yes, of those Lawsons and those Cains. Major players in the highest economic and social strata of our fair city. Miss Melanie had no children of her own, and doted on her younger brother's girls, her wards Charlotte and Amy.

"Anyway, next thing we all know invitations were sent out for a big shin-dig, and the rumor was that Sammy and Charlotte would be announcing their engagement. Harry was fit to be tied. He considered Charlotte his star, and kept her on a short leash. I don't think he approved of Sammy as a match for his protégée."

She leaned forward, her voice dropping, her tone conspiratorial. "Then Charlotte broke it off with Sammy—seems she caught him with his pants down, and found out the hard way that she was to be a trophy wife, the little proper deb to cover his indiscretions on both sides of the fence, stop the tongues from wagging, at least for a while. She disappeared pretty soon afterward. Poor Harry, who always tried to keep her under his thumb. It was pretty sad. She really was a sweet girl, driven, talented—had debuted with the Atlanta Symphony as a child, was Peter Conrad's star also. I kind of felt sorry for her; she seems to have been regularly hounded by the tabloids all her life. You know—pretty young heiress, catch of the century, does she have a seamy side, is she a closet Paris Hilton? That sort of thing."

"What happened?" Mark was fascinated with the woman's story.

"Charlotte left these parts until a few years ago. There were catty rumors about her and Harry, but everyone really believed she left over Sammy Fellowes. The local paparazzi left her alone mostly—only a few resurrected allegations of her and Kreiser from time to time, when she might be seen at home during holidays. Then she brought her nephew home to study with Harry just a few years ago, and they seemed civil to each other, at least until this review a few weeks ago."

"And Sammy Fellowes?"

"I can answer that," Will interjected. "He died about ten years or so back."

"Why?" Mark wanted to know.

"Lingering illness, but word from my good sources is that the death was AIDS related," the woman volunteered, smiling slyly. "His sexual escapades and general debauchery were the reasons his mamma wanted the marriage with Charlotte Lawson. Mrs. Fellowes was hoping to squelch the rumors and buy a veneer of respectability for poor George. She had such high hopes, and he turned out to be a huge disappointment to her."

"You don't say," Roberts whistled softly.

"What about Harry's Ex No. 2?" Will changed the subject.

"That bubble-headed bleached blonde? She couldn't spell Harry's name, much less plan and commit murder. She got what she wanted—an introduction to the fast crowd," Tina continued. "One rumor is that Melanie Cain forced Kreiser to marry her to belie rumors that there was something going on between him and dear Charlotte. I don't know—guess it could be true. But Melanie and Harry were tight, and I don't think she would tolerate his messing with Charlotte."

The woman consulted her jeweled wristwatch. "Hey, this has been fun, but I have a bridge club date. Is that all you need for now?"

"Yes, ma'am," Will murmured, a little awed.

"It's Tina," she smiled at him. "And call me any time." Her smile broadened to include Roberts, as she uncrossed her legs, put out her cigarette, and stood.

The men stood too, Will opening the door for her and following her out. Roberts looked after them, trying to check the grin on his face as he watched Will solicitously show her out before returning to the room.

Chapter 54

"Well, this Kreiser fellow had an eye for women," Will said gruffly.

Roberts pursed his lips to keep from laughing. "What else do you have?"

"Randy has interviews with the other students later this evening, including this prodigy Stefan Chadwick. In the meantime I managed to get that organ tech and an officer small enough to go inside the organ chambers. Some great shooting—no damage inside the chambers. One of the slugs that took out the lights lodged in the ceiling, and the other nicked the stone wall in the back. Guess what the crime scene guys combing the downstairs of the church found?"

"What?" Roberts was anticipating.

"Three casings, 9 millimeter, found beside one of the columns. Ballistics guy thinks the projectiles came from the same source, but one was pretty loused up. He's studying the lands and grooves, or what's left of them. And it's his best guess, and mine too, that the shooter hit all three targets from the same vantage, both from the trajectory and where we found the casings. The shooter didn't seem afraid of getting caught, was pretty brazen, in fact."

"That's interesting," Roberts mused.

Randy walked in, piece of paper in hand. "Charlotte Lawson just happens to possess a concealed weapons permit in the state of Virginia, per the databank. And about three months ago she reported a burglary—claimed a 9-millimeter was stolen from her safe. Really nice gun—a Sig Sauer top-of-the line. A P226 X-Six Scandic with 6-inch barrel, to be exact."

"Shit! That's awfully coincidental," Will offered, as Roberts frowned.

"That's the exact same type gun she uses at the gun club. She claimed she owned no handgun," he remarked.

Randy continued, reading from a copy of a police report in hand. "Just a few months ago, she made the complaint. She also stated there were some documents, some old rare Roman coins missing, and about $50,000 in cash, all from a safe in the house. Nothing else taken."

"Wow!" exclaimed Will.

Randy scanned the report before laying it before Roberts. "How did you know about this?"

"The little conversation with the Russell fellow," Roberts' face was enigmatic.

"No other references found, no leads—property was never recovered. But..."

"But what?" Roberts saw him hesitate.

"Remember the unusual coin found in Kreiser's jacket pocket?" Will excitedly finished for him.

"That's right—the coin!" Roberts exclaimed, looking at both of them.

"Yep. I sent it to the lab," Will stated, his face brightening at the prospect of a lead.

"Can you get them to process it quickly and send it back?" Roberts asked, his eyes mirroring Will's animation.

"Sure thing," Will replied, picking up the phone. "What are you thinking?"

"We need to get a coin expert to take a look at it and determine its provenance, and from inquiries in the collector's community we can determine whether the coins have resurfaced anywhere since the burglary. That could help."

"She wouldn't have called the police in on a false report, you think?" Randy looked at him quizzically. "Besides, that was three months ago."

"I don't know," Roberts met the detective's eyes. "It would be awfully convenient for the murder weapon used on Kreiser to be missing, ostensibly stolen. And if this coin is one of those reported missing, why has it suddenly appeared, and why on our murder victim?"

Turning back to Will, he continued, "It could be a red herring, but she has been shooting the same type gun in practice. Will, ask Ballistics if they can tell anything about the make of the gun from the projectiles. And get word to that investigating officer on the alleged robbery. I want to talk to him."

The phone rang. Will picked it up. "Preliminary done? I'm impressed. No shit—you can't tell me now? You guys are too mysterious for me. OK, I'm sitting on pins and needles. Be right over."

Will replaced the receiver. "That was the coroner. He has a preliminary report for us. Doesn't know if there are any surprises or not. He won't ever tell me over the phone. I'm going over there now to pick up the report."

Roberts stood up, his curiosity aroused. "Mind if I come along?"

They walked out of the office together. As they approached the door, he heard a timid voice calling, "Detective Roberts?"

He turned. Cecelia Rhodes was standing at the front desk, encased in a short fitted black sheath dress, clutching a handkerchief. Will shot him a look as he frowned.

"Yes, Miss Rhodes?" he walked up to her, trying to appear solicitous as Will swallowed a sardonic expression.

"Did you get my message?" she drawled softly, sniffing into her handkerchief. She clutched his proffered hand, as she gazed at him with soulful eyes. "I have some information, and was hoping that you might see me a minute, Officer Roberts." Seeing his hesitation, she added, "I saw you at the recital last night with Miss Lawson. It has to do with her."

Roberts, surprised, nodded at Will. "You go on. I'll take Miss Rhodes' statement. Randy, care to sit in on this?"

Cecelia blushed, her voice low as she almost whispered, "Couldn't I speak to you alone?"

Roberts looked at her sternly. "Miss Rhodes, I don't want to break protocol. On a homicide investigation we try to have two officers present for interviews when possible." At her embarrassed look, he added, more gently, "It's for your protection as well as our own."

She nodded unhappily, as Will gave Roberts a grin and walked out. He and Randy led the young woman into a nearby interview room. As Randy sat down and started to turn on the tape recorder, she shook her head vigorously. "This is not evidence-type stuff," she said nervously, "just some things I thought you should know."

"How old are you again?" Roberts asked.

"Eighteen," she replied, sitting up straight.

"OK," said Roberts, nodding at Randy to dispense with the machine. "However, I must remind you that anything you say could be used against you, and that you have a right to seek counsel from an attorney before talking to us."

She nodded. "Yeah, he told me that already."

"What is it you wish to tell us?"

Cecelia cleared her throat, looking down at her hands. "My cousin said I should tell you what I know."

"Your cousin did not accompany you?"

"Aunt Kat has been under a doctor's care, taking a lot of sedatives since Doctor K's murder," Cecelia spoke, her voice low and confidential. "She and the professor were good friends. This has been hard for her." She cleared her throat. "I don't know if you've heard the rumors about Miss Lawson and Professor Kreiser."

"What rumors?" Roberts prompted her, his voice noncommittal.

"There are those that say he and her have had—well, you know—an affair," she finished lamely. "He spent a lot of time at her place, and he doted on Stefan." Her features hardened. "Stefan was his favorite pupil. No one else stood a chance when Stefan was around."

Roberts felt the green-eyed monster of jealousy rearing its ugly head. "Do you have any evidence that there was actually anything going on between the two, other than friendship?" he asked her gently.

"He was drunk the night of a graduation reception Miss Lawson gave for one of the students last semester. He tried to kiss one of the other students and called her 'Carlota'. Valerie went to Miss Lawson, who confirmed that it was the name he used for her. Professor K stayed on a long time after everyone went home," she added, her eyes gleaming predatorily. "He was the last one to leave."

"How do you know that?" Roberts asked simply.

"Because I watched him," she replied, then flushed as she realized the implications of what she said. "I mean—I wasn't following him or anything, but I—I was curious, that's all. They talked, and they kissed. When he left, she was crying."

Roberts looked at her dubiously, but she continued on. "That's not all. Did you know that Professor K had a life insurance policy on himself, with her listed as trustee for Stefan as beneficiary? I mean, why would he do something like that?" her voice trailed off as she looked at Roberts timidly.

"And what is the source of this information?"

"I saw the policy open on Dean Jackson's desk this morning, along with a large sealed envelope with Miss Lawson's name written on it in Dr. K's handwriting," she mumbled. "I was there to discuss continuing my studies, and the dean had stepped out." She averted her eyes from Roberts' accusatory stare.

"Where were you later that night after the party?"

She flushed again. "I—I was at home all night," she blustered.

"You're sure of that?" Roberts watched for her reaction.

"Of course," she was nonplussed. "Russ took me home after the party," she stammered.

"Were you alone?"

"Yes, except for Aunt Kat," she squirmed.

"Have you told anyone else all this?" Roberts demanded.

"Just my Aunt Kat," she stammered. "Why shouldn't I?"

"For several reasons," Roberts replied, leaning across the desk to face her. "If your conjectures and information have been construed wrongly, you could be the cause of all sorts of vicious speculation, the type that ruins innocent lives. Secondly, whoever killed Dr. Kreiser is still out there. Because we don't know the reason behind his death, we cannot rule out that the murderer might not strike again."

Cecelia stared blankly. "Do you think I might be in danger?" she asked, her eyes wide. "That I might need police protection?"

Roberts resisted a smile. "Not necessarily, if we can avoid publicizing this information until we have a chance to check it out."

"I won't tell another soul," she breathed dramatically. "But do you think Miss Lawson would kill Professor K?" she added, her eyes eager as she leaned forward.

Roberts, with a glance to Randy, who was sitting stone-faced watching the two, said quietly, "Ms. Rhodes, we are keeping our minds open to all the possibilities, but I must admit that it is something we must explore."

Her face became solemn. He added, "Let's keep this our secret for now. This is very valuable information, Miss Rhodes, and we will follow up on it. Thanks so much for your help. We'll be in touch."

He stood and opened the door as the young woman exited reluctantly, gazing timidly around her at the other officers. Watching her out of sight, Roberts was deep in thought, the gears of his mind whirring. He finally turned to Randy.

Randy whistled. "That was some great stuff about the protocol, not to mention the one about the murderer might strike again."

Roberts shrugged. "Randy, in this business, you must protect yourself sometimes from your own witnesses."

Looking at his watch irritably, Roberts continued. "I can't wait for Will. The autopsy info will have to wait. I need to see Dean Jackson. I want to find out about this new information, particularly an insurance policy."

Roberts waited until he was on his way to the university to call Dean Jackson's office. Identifying himself to the secretary, he told her it was urgent that he see Jackson.

"But Mark, he just left about thirty minutes ago. He said he had to see Miss Lawson."

"Harriet, do you know where he was going?" Roberts asked her.

"To her house, I believe," Harriet said doubtfully.

Thanking her, he rang off, making a U-turn and accelerating toward Charlotte Lawson's home.

Chapter 55

Charlotte was sitting at Melanie's desk, her face white, clutching the document handed her by Jackson, who hovered nearby as she scanned it.

"My God!" she cried agitatedly. "Why did Harry do this?"

"Where is everyone? Is Stefan here?" Jackson asked quickly, his eyes darting around anxiously.

Charlotte, understanding his concern, shook her head. "Amy and Mike left this morning to drive to Callaway Gardens for a couple days of golf. I couldn't stand them hanging over me, and told them to go enjoy themselves. Stefan had an exam, came in for a late lunch, and is gone again, practicing, as usual. He won't be back for another couple of hours at least." She reviewed the document, her face tense.

Jackson answered, "Harry confronted me a year or so ago, said he knew it was crazy, but was convinced Stefan was his son. He was beside himself, Charlotte—said he had suspected ever since you came back, but you never let on. He was upset that you would not trust him with the information that he was a father, yet he acknowledged he had no right to confront you, that you had paid dearly for his indiscretion. I denied it, tried to make him see reason, and I thought he believed me. He dropped it; I thought it was over. That's why I didn't bother you with it."

"My God, Malcolm. I didn't need this," Charlotte mumbled, her head in her hands.

She stood suddenly and began pacing in front of the desk. "What am I to do? Stefan will be devastated. He mustn't know anything about this."

She looked over at the mantel, at a picture of Stefan as a child with Amy and Mike. She said absently, "Amy and Michael have been such wonderful parents, and what he is is due to them. My past mistakes must not be visited on him."

"He is a great kid. You had a large part in his raising," Jackson laid a hand on her arm, stilling her.

"No, I'm the prodigal child who made a mess of her life, 'poor little Charlotte'. God, I tried to steer him away from music, from the organ," she lamented softly. "Anything but that. But from the first time he saw an organ he was determined to play it. Then he found Harry's old recordings, and he clamored to have them. He insisted he wanted to study with him. Stefan was always so willful, so headstrong. I dragged him all over the country trying to interest him in anywhere but here."

"He's a lot like you. How could Harry not look at him and see you?"

Jackson took her hand, and placed the large envelope in it. She stared at it, her blood running cold. "Kreiser's attorney sent this to me this morning along with the policy."

She hesitated, before tearing open the envelope and seating herself at the desk again. Inside were a letter and a large musical score, both in Kreiser's hand. Jackson took a chair next to the sofa, watching her as she read the words, the color fleeing from her face:

My dearest Carlota,

Although I am deeply hurt that you could not confide in me about our son, even after all this time, every time I look in your eyes I see what you have suffered, what you have sacrificed, and know the awful part I played. That night so long ago you came to me, so crushed, needy and trusting, your heart broken because of Sammy's infidelity, I could not say no to you. I was afraid what another rejection would do to you. And I realized suddenly how much I wanted you. God, how I wanted you, more than anything in my whole life.

Although I should have taken precautions to protect you during our time together, I was heedless, caught up in the moment, drunk on you. I thoughtlessly took something very precious from you. That week of surreptitious meetings with you was heady wine—I was so alive, and could feel, taste and smell only you. I have never thought of Melanie's dining table the same way again.

Charlotte, I think I have always loved you. From the time you first came running up to me begging for lessons, I was hooked. You were bewitching, and such an endless fountain of raw talent. I know as a teacher I drove you hard, but you drank it up and begged for more. You were the first student who challenged me, who spat back at me, who made me stop and think. I thought there was no breaking you, but I was wrong.

And I was so very wrong. There's not a day goes by that I do not berate myself for crushing that spirit in you, for driving you away. But when I told Melanie about us, she reminded me of my ephemeral infatuations of the past, and threatened to have me ruined if I did not cease and desist. I selfishly saw my life crashing about my feet. I knew then that she was right, that I had nothing to offer you and could not ask you to risk your bright future for me. I pushed you away.

Then when I called to find you, and Amy let slip you were pregnant, I was so ecstatic. I thought perhaps Melanie would relent. But she was livid, and talked me into marriage with Christy to squelch the rumor mill about you and me.

And to think that you carried our child alone, kept the secret of his conception, suffering in silence, not knowing that I longed to be with you. I so wanted to come to you, to find you, but you were deserving of so much more. I saw Melanie's hand in the adoption by Amy and Mike, and I was convinced that again she was right. And then I was laid low by my heart attack, and dependent upon Melanie's good graces for my recovery.

I couldn't believe you could still love me after all that, even after that wonderful night when my Laura appeared to me again. Your pronouncement to me the night of your engagement party destroyed me. Melanie had convinced me that you and Gerard Fellowes were right for each other, and that I should not stand in your way.

It would have been so easy to rekindle our affair the night of Brad's reception, but I knew I had to protect you from yourself and not let the past repeat itself. And I realized I had to leave—that my continued presence was a continuing and crippling hindrance to your future.

I can never make up to you for my part in this. But I wanted you to know that I knew, that I guessed. I have no right to demand anything from you. I know you have done the very best for our son.

You must no longer sacrifice your talent. You have done so for much too long. You were my very best, and must share that talent with the world, for your sake. I beg you to do this.

This policy is only a small token. I know you don't need nor want the money. But I want in some way to acknowledge, if only to you, my responsibility.

Charlotte, you have been my grand passion. I have loved you more than life. I never meant for you to love me back. My feelings for you were to be unrequited. Although I cannot undo the past, I strive to be kinder to my students, realizing that we never know the damage we may do to others. And I wronged you most of all.

I'm very proud of our Stefan. Thank you again for allowing me the opportunity to teach him and to see him grow into the fine young man he is.

Yours always,

Harry

She looked at the musical score, written for organ and orchestra. There was a note from Kreiser:

I could not resolve in my mind the final edition. I kept playing our lives out in the different movements. I decided the night of Brad's reception to bind it up and give it to you. Only you can decide the ending. I want you to have it to do with as you will. Keep it, burn it, whatever. It's all I can give you, my Carlota.

Please consider my request to take charge of my musical scores. They are yours, to dispose of as you wish.

All my love,

Harry

At the top of the score was scrawled the title "Carlota in Four Movements" in Harry's handwriting.

Jackson, watching her, disclosed, "I knew it couldn't wait, so I came out as soon as I could get away."

Charlotte was in turmoil, her face ashen, her chest heaving, distraught. "Oh, damn it all. Amy let it slip to Harry that I was with child. Oh, Harry, no, no. It's all my fault. I should have told him the truth long ago."

She was oblivious to the sound of the doorbell, or the appearance of Daisy with Mark Roberts at her heels, who stopped short in the doorway when he heard her last words.

"Miss Charlotte, he insisted on coming in," Daisy began hurriedly, as Charlotte looked up dully and saw him, suddenly faint with anxiety, not sure how much he might have heard.

Jackson, standing, moved toward Roberts purposefully. Taking his arm, he murmured, "Mark, this is not a good time," as the telephone rang shrilly next to Charlotte.

Automatically, she picked it up. "Hello? Yes, dear. Where are you? Andy and Valerie? How did you do on the French exam? Good. Remember you promised to help Jacob and me in the greenhouse tomorrow. Don't be too late—you know I'm not one to let you sleep in."

She paused. "I'm fine. Don't worry about me. I'm just tired. Later, dude. You know the drill about being careful, safe and all that jazz."

She replaced the phone, then rose, her voice unsteady. "Detective, what may I do for you? Please have a seat. Daisy, could you please brew some of your wonderful tea for our guests?"

As Daisy bustled off, Charlotte swept the desk clear of the documents she had been reviewing, depositing them in the center drawer. She glided over to the sofa and took a seat, gesturing for the two men to seat themselves.

She smiled wanly at Roberts, but he remained standing and his next words shredded away her veneer of composure. "Why did Wilhelm Kreiser leave an insurance policy with you as beneficiary in trust for Stefan?"

Her heart caught in her throat, as she weakly managed to croak, "How did you know? I just found out myself. Malcolm?" she looked helplessly at Jackson.

"I suspect Cecelia Rhodes imparted that information," Jackson replied evenly, his eyes boring into Roberts. "I knew she was snooping around my office this morning. I caught her red-handed going through papers on my desk. Yes, Mark, Harry had a policy, and entrusted it to me. But Charlotte just found out about it before you walked in."

"But why? Teachers don't leave life insurance policies for their students. Was Stefan his child?" Roberts demanded, his eyes on Charlotte. "You lied to me. You were lovers," he spat accusingly.

She was vehement. "It was all a terrible mistake. One for which I thought I had paid long ago." She stared angrily at Roberts.

Marks crossed the room and sat beside her, taking her arm roughly and turning her to face him. "That's not all," he replied, his voice low, controlled. "You do own a handgun, a 9 millimeter Sig Sauer, to be exact. Kreiser was killed with a 9 millimeter."

Charlotte reeled in panic. "I had one from back in my D.C. days. A—a friend thought it was a good idea. Some time back, some things went missing, and the gun was one of them. I swear to you. You can search the place."

At his penetrating look, she continued, stammering. "I reported it stolen. All this occurred, oh, late last year or the first of this year. I never felt comfortable having it in the house, so I didn't replace it, and the police never recovered it."

"Tell me—did you kill Kreiser?"

"Why would I do that?" she whispered shakily.

"You tell me. Perhaps he found out Stefan was his son, and threatened to tell him or expose you." Mark looked at her intently.

"No. Harry was mistaken about Stefan, but he wouldn't have done anything to hurt him. It was all my fault," Charlotte insisted, tears running down her cheeks.

"Tell me what happened between you and Kreiser, Charlotte, and this time, I'd like the truth," Roberts replied quietly, his fingers still cutting into her flesh.

"Charlotte, you don't have to say anything," Jackson intervened, alarmed, stonily regarding Roberts. "I can call your attorney."

"No," she cried tremulously. "I cannot take the chance of Stefan finding out and being hurt. The fewer people who know about this, the better." She turned to Roberts. "I'll tell you. But leave Stefan out of this. This has nothing to do with him, I assure you."

Looking into her eyes, he wanted to believe her. "I cannot promise," Roberts' voice was strangely comforting, as he released her.

They were silent as Daisy brought in tea things, looking at the group curiously, and leaving them. Charlotte served tea and scones, taking nothing for herself.

"I was about to be engaged to George Fellowes and finishing up my final year in college," she began, her eyes glued to the lush rug. "I was turning nineteen. Everything was going swimmingly. I had my senior recital scheduled, we were about to announce our engagement, and we were talking of a wedding date after my summer abroad studying in France, with the additional opportunity to apply to the Conservatoire if the summer worked out well. Thanks to Harry I had my pick of schools for graduate work.

"But ever since he came back from law school George had been strangely cold to me, except the night of my recital when he proposed. I didn't understand it. He was friendly enough in a group, but there was no intimacy. Aunt Mellie always taught us that good girls don't do it until they're married. But I thought people in love showed some affection or passion in some manner. And he had been fresh enough with me before when we were younger.

"Then I got back from the Yale audition early. It was my third—I had already done Juilliard and Curtis, all in a row. Melanie actually let me go alone this time. She had to be out of town, and Harry could not get out of classes with it being so close to final exams. I decided to surprise George. I went over to his place. I was the one surprised. He was in bed." She took a deep breath. "With someone else. A man." She was clearly embarrassed, as she relived that moment, her eyes closed.

"Did you know the man?"

"No. But I was so crushed, devastated. George said I had no business spying on him. Spying? At the time, I thought nothing could be worse—my fiancé preferred guys to me."

She paused, her eyes closed tightly, trying to exorcise the images from the past.

"I didn't know what to do. Aunt Mellie was out of town. I went to Harry's. His divorce to Tina had just become final, even though they had been separated for over a year. He was between places, so Aunt Melanie let him stay at the boathouse again. When I arrived, he wasn't there. He had a recital that night. I let myself in, found a bottle of wine, and got sloshed.

"He came home late that night, and found me there, naked in his bed, waiting for him." Again she paused, her face suffused with color. "I threw myself at him. I needed so badly to be wanted by someone. My ego was in shreds. He could be such a flirt when he wanted something, and I thought perhaps . . ."

She studied the pattern of the carpet, refusing to look at the men. "I had heard that Harry was quite a Casanova. He enjoyed being the center of attention in any crowd, and was always in the throes of some affair. I didn't care. I didn't care about anything that night."

She swallowed convulsively, looking at her hands. "I was so inexperienced. He was very gentle, very passionate. He told me everything I wanted to hear. He held me afterward and rocked me to sleep. The next morning he made me breakfast.

"That week—every night he came to me or I went to him. I was consumed with him. I forgot everything else. I didn't eat, I didn't practice, I didn't go to class. I avoided seeing other people. I was out of control. We were spending every free moment together. It was wild, passionate, something new for me."

Roberts asked softly, "You were a virgin?"

She stopped, her face red with shame, nodding.

Chapter 56

She shut off the memory of her week of liaison with Kreiser, as her mind jolted back to the present. She felt as though she was drowning. Roberts said nothing, waiting for her, watching her as she hid her face in her hands.

Charlotte choked back a sob. "It was an unreal week, a dream. I was crazy for him. I thought he felt the same.

"Then Aunt Mellie returned home. He didn't come. He was avoiding me. I walked over to the boathouse. He had been drinking, was sitting there brooding. He wouldn't look at me. He told me I had to stop coming to see him, that it was over, that he would find me a new teacher. I didn't understand. It was as though a faucet had been turned off. I demanded to know why, what had happened. He grabbed me by the arms and shook me, then pushed me out the door and locked me out.

"I was crushed. I really didn't know where to turn. After two days of crying, I finally went back to class. Aunt Melanie was beginning to notice, asking questions, waiting for me when I came in. When I saw Harry, he was more and more distant—you could cut the tension with a knife. He couldn't look me in the eye, and there always seemed to be someone else around. I could tell he was drinking.

"I was struggling to understand, while getting ready for my senior recital and a benefit and yet another recital I had been invited to give in New York City. I finally felt I had to clear the air with Harry.

"I went to the boathouse to demand that he talk to me. But he wasn't alone. I heard him and—and a female voice."

Roberts looked at her compassionately. She continued quickly, as though afraid she would break down. "I couldn't face him. My playing was suffering. He was drinking even more, and became nasty, vile. I knew I had destroyed the teacher-student relationship.

"Then we had a scene just before my senior recital, and he unilaterally cancelled my other two recitals. He was drunk. He said horrible things to me, about us, about my performance. I had worked so hard to be the best, his best. I gave him my all. It destroyed me."

She fell silent. Jackson took over. "Charlotte came to me and told me she had developed severe performance anxiety and could not fulfil her degree requirements. I was shocked. She looked terrible, so pale and emaciated—she was physically shaking. Charlotte begged me to help her get away. She was adamant she was giving up the organ. It broke my heart. She refused to go to a doctor, was afraid it would get out."

Jackson's eyes were brilliant with unshed tears. "I helped her apply for the writing fellowship at Georgetown, close to where her sister lived. She swore me to secrecy. She didn't even want her Aunt Melanie to know what she had done. When I threatened to confront Harry and go to Melanie, Charlotte finally told me about Harry's involvement. Melanie worshipped Harry, and Charlotte said she couldn't face her wrath, and did not want to ruin Harry's career. She took the entire blame upon herself."

Charlotte gripped Jackson's hand warningly as she resumed the narrative. "I packed and left without a word. Aunt Mellie was livid. And I started a new life," Charlotte added. "I tried to play again, but I just couldn't do it. The spark was gone, and I would start shaking so badly I could not play. My ego was in shreds. But I found some solace in writing and adjunct teaching, and was pretty good at it. I had started writing as a child, and kept journals, so had developed some discipline that served me well. And then Amy and Mike found the baby they had so much wanted. Seeing them so happy gave me a new lease on life."

"Well, you've established you had ample reason to hate Harry Kreiser," Roberts supplied, his face a mask.

Yes, I wanted him to suffer and die, she wanted to scream. "But I didn't hate him. I was to blame," Charlotte answered him stoically, swallowing her fear at his words. "Harry had a fling; I had ascribed more to it than it was. Harry had his own demons to battle. I didn't realize why he was pushing me away until later." She fell silent, unwilling to say more.

"That's awfully charitable of you," Roberts remarked dryly.

"I was in love with love. I was young, and the world was my oyster. I had a brilliant future ahead of me. I was so thrilled when George chose me. I always had a crush on him. He dressed well, was a great conversationalist, knew everyone, made a good dance partner, and turned everyone's head. Then he asked me to marry him. I was totally naïve. It never occurred to me to look past the surface, to wonder why me, why he never made passes at me any more. I just thought he was being the consummate Southern gentleman.

And then, it came crashing down around me. I was vulnerable, and Harry was just there. I transferred all those repressed feelings to him. I had always loved Harry; he opened the door to a musical world for me. What I did was wrong, but I was not a child. I was solely responsible," she submitted solemnly, wanting to believe her words.

"Did you get over him?" Roberts found himself asking.

"One writing instructor once told me that one never gets over one's 'first love'. He was certainly clear that there was no future for us together, although I hoped for a time that he would relent. Later I dated a few times in D.C., friends or colleagues of Mike's. He even tried to fix me up with one of his brothers." She thought back sadly to Matt and their time together.

"And Gerry?" Mark watched closely for her reaction.

"Gerry and I grew up together. He's been my best friend always. I—I love him and want to marry him," her voice trailed off.

"But you haven't," Roberts reminded her. "Why? Because you still loved Kreiser?"

She just shook her head vehemently. At his penetrating gaze, she supplied tremulously, "You're wrong. The timing has never been right. We announced our engagement at a dinner, but Melanie—" tears filled her eyes at the memory, "Melanie had a series of strokes right after that, and d-died." Yes, I let her down again, she wanted to shout. I killed her too. Don't you want to take me in? But Charlotte controlled herself.

"And the policy?" Roberts asked softly, bringing her back to the subject of the document.

"It never occurred to me that Harry would do such a thing," Charlotte responded, looking at Jackson, her face forbidding. "The policy came as a complete shock."

"May I see the policy?" Roberts asked.

Charlotte paused momentarily, but stood up and went over to the desk. She retrieved the policy, leaving the letter stuffed in the drawer, and wordlessly handed the policy to Roberts.

She gave Jackson another warning look as Roberts reviewed the document carefully, then handed it back. There's no reason this man needs to know about my pregnancy, she thought. It cannot help his investigation, but it could hurt others, including Stefan, if the truth was revealed.

"And you didn't talk about this with him?" Roberts asked. "He must have suspected that Stefan was his child. Where would he get that idea?"

"I don't know, except that Stefan came into our lives right about that time," Charlotte answered, her eyes darting to Jackson, willing him to be silent.

"And he never confronted you, never asked? No letters, no calls?" Roberts persisted.

"This is the first indication I had that Harry was laboring under the impression that we had a son," Charlotte gazed at him steadily, stubbornly. "Stefan is not Harry's son."

"Is he George's?"

She laughed shortly, mirthlessly. "There was no chance in hell of that possibility. No, Detective, Stefan is not my child. I would give anything if it was true. Stefan's mother died in childbirth and his father in a freak accident during the Gulf War. Amy and Mike had been on a waiting list for a baby to adopt, and got the call. He was a godsend to all of us. There was proof of Stefan's paternity in the safe, but it disappeared the night of the burglary."

Charlotte smiled as she remembered back to the infant's homecoming from the hospital. The baby had become the catalyst for reconciliation between Charlotte and her aunt.

She was again brought back to the present, feeling Roberts' eyes on her. "What were you thinking?" he wanted to know, his gaze softening.

"About how Stefan's addition to the family restored peace between me and Aunt Mellie," Charlotte confessed. "I had upset her by my rebellion and running away. My greatest fear was her disappointment in me. I couldn't face her knowing how I had yet again broken her rules, failed her standards. I never told her about Harry and me. But she knew anyway. Just before her last stroke she told me."

She added, more to herself, "I always felt like I had to do something to earn someone's love, and it wasn't until after Stefan came that I found out Melanie loved me despite it all. But I was never sure if it was just family loyalty, or protecting the family name."

"I'm sorry," she exclaimed suddenly. "I didn't mean to digress." She colored as Mark regarded her, his features inscrutable. "But I don't want Stefan to know about that past. Our relationship means so much to me. I want him to think highly of me. I just don't want to take that risk."

There was the noise of the door opening. Startled, she listened, and stood, aghast as Stefan appeared in the doorway, breathless. "Aunt Charlotte? I decided to come on home. I have some reading I need to do," he added, looking at the two men curiously.

Mark, noting Charlotte's panic, also stood. "I really should be going. Thank you for your help, Charlotte, Dean Jackson," he said. "I'll see myself out. I'll be in touch," he added, his mouth curving into a tight smile.

Jackson also stood. "I'll leave you two alone. Get some sleep, Charlotte. Later, Stefan."

"I'll see you out," Charlotte countered.

At the doorway she pulled Malcolm to her. As she hugged him, she whispered, "Neither the police nor Stefan have any need to know about my miscarriage. It's none of their business. I purposely didn't tell the detective, and I appreciate your discretion in the matter."

Jackson held her away from him and searched her impassive face. He nodded, pressed her hand, and took his leave.

She closed and locked the front door, and turned back to the drawing room. Stefan was standing in the doorway watching her. "This Mark guy. He's hanging around you a lot. Is he a new boyfriend or something?"

Charlotte, deciding to come clean, responded, "He is a detective with the Atlanta Police Department, investigating Harry's murder," Charlotte replied, her voice sounding far away to her ears.

"Why was he here?" Stefan demanded, his eyes wide. Charlotte detected fear and a sudden wariness. "You've been crying—what is wrong?"

Hastening to reassure him, she smiled abstractedly. "Oh, nothing. He has just been asking questions about Harry. It's all part of their job. Nothing to worry about."

"Do they have any suspects?" he wanted to know anxiously.

"I don't really know." She was suddenly very tired. She realized that the information she had given Roberts made her his prime suspect. *I'm surprised he didn't arrest me just now. It was bound to happen,* she thought despairingly. *I just never realized it might occur this quickly. I have so little time left with Stefan.*

Changing the subject she asked, "Are you hungry? What would you like to do?"

He turned away, distracted and distant. "I really do have something I must do. I'm sorry, Auntie, but I can't help you tomorrow. Something's come up. Did Mom and Dad get away OK?"

"Yes." Charlotte was disappointed. Tears sprang to her eyes. He was growing up, and had his own life. The time had come, and she had promised herself she would not hold him back. She felt all alone and vulnerable; she knew her time with Stefan was slipping away. In light of the last few days' events, she felt a blanket of despair settle around her.

"Well, I'm going up," he remarked. He turned and impulsively embraced her, holding her hard and close, kissing her cheek. "I love you, Aunt Charlotte," he whispered.

Charlotte's eyes burned with tears. "I love you too, Stefan. Is something wrong?" She clung to him instinctively, a shiver of fear going through her.

"Nothing," he laughed shortly. "You coming up? Dean Jackson was right. You need some rest. I worry about you."

"I'll be up in a few minutes," she assured him. He pushed her away, as though embarrassed for his display, and bounded up the stairs.

Watching him disappear, Charlotte felt such turmoil. She turned back to the desk, sitting down at it and opening the drawer. Pulling out Harry's letter, she read it again slowly, before putting it away carefully.

She mechanically went around turning off lights, then stopped at the door of the salon, staring at the organ. Walking to it, she sat down and turned on the blower. Pulling some stops, she began playing the *Sicilienne* from Durufle's *Suite*, Harry's favorite piece. At first tentative, she finally relaxed, giving vent to the melancholy and pathos. As the movement ended, she suddenly felt uncontrollably angry, angry at the wasted time, angry at her mistakes and the consequences that kept assailing all those she loved. And she was angry at Harry, for not being her knight in shining armor and coming to her rescue, for yet again protesting his love and then abandoning her.

And most importantly, she was resentful that Fate had placed on her one more burden of responsibility, the ultimate price she must pay to protect those she loved. Would my suicide solve the problem? she wondered momentarily. But I would still not be assured that the murder investigation would be concluded by my death. I'm just not sure I can handle much more, but I must protect them.

She pushed a combination piston, checked the registration, and launched into the final movement, the toccata, seething and churning, heedless, oblivious to her surroundings, aware of nothing but the pit of her gut from where the music seemed to emanate. Completing the piece, she stared in front of her wildly, breathing heavily, before beating the music desk with her clenched fists.

"Damn it, Harry," she cried. "I hate you. Death was too good for you."

That night she had the dream again. She and Harry were on the banquet table making love, and suddenly he shouted to her, "Why didn't you tell me about the baby?" He was choking her and she couldn't breathe. Then three shots rang out. She was holding her firearm and standing over Kreiser, dead, his eyes staring at her accusingly.

This time the dream ended differently. Suddenly Mark Roberts was standing beside her, and he was putting handcuffs on her. "Gotta take you in," he smiled engagingly at her.

She awoke, bathed in a cold sweat. She was alone. Terrified, she sat up in her bed, crying, hugging herself. "Oh, my God," she cried. "My punishment is more than I can bear."

Chapter 57

Roberts strode into the office the next morning, ill-tempered and out of sorts. As he caught Randy's eye, he ordered, "I want to see that officer who investigated the Lawson break-in now."

"Done," Randy smothered a grin.

"What do you mean?" Roberts sputtered.

"Officer Bassett is sitting in your office right now," Randy pointed. "He is now working for the PD here instead of for Clayton County. He's waiting for you."

Will smirked. "You're spending way too much time with that Lawson woman. It must be interfering with your beauty sleep."

Roberts snapped, "I'm not in the mood this morning, Will. Can't you find some investigating to do?"

He walked into the room as the officer stood and put out his hand. "Officer Greg Bassett, sir," he introduced himself.

"Thanks for coming by," Mark shook his hand. "Have a seat. What can you tell me?"

"I remember this case very well," Bassett responded as they both sat. "I've known Charlotte—Miss Lawson—for a number of years. I patrolled that area faithfully. She was instrumental in helping find a music teacher for my daughter, and was on the committee that auditioned when my Sophie got into the youth orchestra. She's a nice lady."

Roberts swallowed his irritation. "So what happened?"

"There had been a small party for a young graduate student of the university at Charlotte's house. She said everyone had left, and she locked up afterward, didn't notice anything amiss. Alarm went off about three in the morning, and I was notified as the closest unit to her.

"Safe was open. No sign of forced entry, but she was shook up." He paused.

"And?" Roberts prompted him.

"Well, she didn't seem quite herself. I noticed an almost empty decanter in the study, with only one glass, on the table beside her. She seemed a little out of it, but definitely frightened. Her nephew was there also, and seemed very protective of her.

"She said only he and she were the ones there knowing the alarm codes and the combination for the safe, or so she thought. Gerard Fellowes, her fiancé, has the house code, and her sister who lives in Maryland knows the codes, but no one else."

"What did she report stolen?"

Barnett replied, "She said there were some documents in the safe, a 9-millimeter handgun, very nice one—top of the line Sig nine-millimeter, if I remember correctly, and about $50,000 in cash."

"Why did she keep that kind of cash in the safe?" Mark mused.

"She said it was there when her aunt died, and she just had not taken the time to deposit it. And there was a framed collection of ancient Roman coins in the safe as well."

"Anything else missing?" Mark probed.

Bassett hesitated. "Well, yes, but she later said she didn't want it reported. Apparently she had two wigs and a professional makeup case in her bedroom closet that were missing."

Roberts leaned forward. "Wigs, makeup case? Why?"

Bassett looked down. "She said they were part of a costume. But then she admitted she used them when she was trying to evade the gossipmongers. She seemed really embarrassed, and begged me not to report them, for fear the press would get wind of them."

Mark paused. "Any other valuables missing?"

"No," Bassett replied. "What was weird was she had jewelry unlocked in a chest in the bedroom right next to where she said the wigs were kept. Some of her aunt's jewelry was in a jewelry chest in a bedroom instead of in the safety deposit box at the bank. There were valuables unsecured all over the place, but nothing else missing."

"Did she describe the wigs—what color?"

"Black and red, I think," Bassett replied, coloring. "I mean, what she said sounded plausible, and she seemed very upset. She could have kept it from me, I had no reason to doubt her, and she was more worried about the coins and the gun, even more so than the cash. So I didn't include the wigs in my report. She said she only told me in case it helped with the investigation and recovery."

"Did you talk to anyone else about the missing items?" Mark wanted to know.

"Her nephew Stefan was there. He also seemed shaken up by the fact that someone had come in on them unawares. He named off the people who were at the party, and he felt pretty sure none of them would have been capable of doing it."

"Did you get a list of names?"

"Yes, and I had the sergeant fax me a copy out of the file," Bassett provided a sheet to Roberts.

He scanned the sheet. "So Wilhelm Kreiser was at this party?"

"Yes, sir."

"I recognize several other names, students of his," Roberts thought aloud. "Thank you, Officer Bassett. You've been a big help."

"You know, you cannot believe the tabloids. She really is a nice lady, and I don't think she is capable of murdering anyone."

Roberts looked at him. "Is that the current story?"

"Yes, that and today's edition of the *Atlanta Watch* spouts that the nephew is actually the love child of Miss Lawson and Professor Kreiser."

"Jesus," Mark ran his fingers through his hair in frustration. "They actually make our job harder, because we have to comb through all the rumor-mongering to find the actual truth."

He saw the officer out, then turned to Randy again on his way back to his office. "Did you ever find out who 'C. C. Langley' is? I want information."

"I read the book a couple nights ago. It is about an organ professor who was killed in a cathedral gallery," Randy offered.

Mark stopped in his tracks. "What?" he thundered.

Will pulled him into his office, as Randy followed them. "It is a novel about a murder of an organ professor, very similar to our case," Randy repeated.

"And?" Roberts asked.

"One of his former students was the culprit, a female with whom he had a sexual liaison and threw her over," Randy smirked. "Sound familiar?"

"Too damned familiar," Will chimed in. "That is not even funny. Maybe that's where the tabloids get their stuff."

"Have you found this author?"

"No," Randy admitted. "There is nothing online about the author that is terribly helpful. It is probably a pseudonym. I contacted the publisher—they will not disclose identifying or contact information without a warrant." He held up his hand to silence Roberts' next question. "I have already talked to the prosecutor's office about serving a warrant and obtaining the information. I told them it was critical."

"What about the tabloid's latest revelation? Do we have any clue where that is coming from?" Roberts looked at Will.

"No go there," Will shrugged. "You know *Atlanta Watch* is not going to provide a source. They make it up as they go, and are proud to go to jail for their First Amendment rights. And the rich are lumped with the celebs, and have a hard time busting out of the 'public figure' category to win a libel suit against the tabloids, and they know it."

"What about ballistics? Have they been able to give us anything else?"

Will smiled. "As a matter of fact, David, head of that illustrious department, has opined that the markings could be a Sig Sauer. It could be some other nine millimeter. He does think to a reasonable degree of scientific certainty that the three shots came from the same gun. Now if we can only find the weapon so he could do actual comparisons."

Mark started to speak, but Will interrupted. "And Gerard Fellowes pledged to cooperate and provide any of his firearms and expertise at our disposal, as long as we don't disrupt his business. So I asked for and had ballistics test the Sig from the gun shop favored by our Miss Lawson. Close, but no match there. I've asked for all sales records on Sigs sold in the last ten years. It's a long shot. And without the actual weapon we're shooting in the dark."

"Damn," Roberts swore. "Guys, you are not helping me get a search warrant or a suspect. Let's go back to this wig business. Why would Charlotte have wigs to escape the paparazzi? It apparently doesn't work too well, because she is still a perennial favorite in the mullet wrappers."

"I have a theory," Randy offered. Both men looked at him expectantly. "Well, I've been combing Lawson's credit card bills going back for the last year. Every so often she makes these quick trips, generally to D.C., but sometimes to other big cities."

"OK, what does that prove?" Will demanded.

"I'm getting there," Randy was defensive. "You know I follow the classical music scene. It just so happens that these trips have coincided with the public appearances of this particular piano quartet, very good, much in demand. And the pianist for the group is a woman with a European accent and jet-black hair. Nothing much is known about her, and she does not do interviews and shuns pictures."

"Are you telling me you think Charlotte Lawson is posing as some European music star?" Will jabbed Randy in the ribs.

"Wait a minute," Roberts mused aloud. "She told me she suffered from performance anxiety, and could not play in public. But," he paused, "I wonder . . . Someone has to know if this is happening. The other members of the quartet for sure. Maybe Gerard Fellowes."

"Maybe even her family. Stefan Chadwick, who we have yet to interview, may know," Will added.

"Pull him in," Mark ordered. "Of course, he is Lawson's nephew, and you know we won't get much, because there will be a lawyer in tow. And I get the impression from my interview last night that Miss Lawson is very protective of him, so she would keep anything seamy about herself, such as dressing up or secret identities, from Stefan. But if we ask the right questions, we may surprise him enough to get our foot in the door.

"And I want to get up with Gerard Fellowes again. What about his alibi?"

"Hospital personnel here confirm his pilot was lifeflighted from Arizona that Friday evening. Fellowes was at the hospital there when they left, and he showed up at the hospital here about 10:00 that night. ATC has him landing at 9:07 p.m. He was listed as flying the Gulfstream himself. I'm still trying to get confirmation from ATC in Tucson," Randy proffered. "But that's a tight schedule."

"Randy, check your buddies in D.C. and see if they might interview the other members of this quartet about their pianist. Will, let's get this Stefan in. It may be a waste of time, but we won't know until we try. I'll try to find Gerard Fellowes."

Will handed him a piece of paper. "Gerry Fellowes left his personal cell number for you, in case you needed to reach him." Will put his hand on Roberts' shoulder, stopping Roberts' forward movement. "One more piece to the puzzle. I checked with the airline attendants regarding Charlotte Lawson's departure the Friday afternoon Kreiser was murdered. She showed up out of breath just as the last passengers were being seated, right around 5:30. She has connections, so is a VIP. Apparently her aunt owned quite a bit of stock in the airline, so when Lawson's name shows up on the passenger roster, which is not uncommon, they pay attention.

"The attendant thought he smelled alcohol on Lawson's breath, which surprised him. He was concerned enough about her to personally walk her to her seat. She was the last passenger on board, seemed preoccupied, agitated, and immediately requested a double bourbon as soon as she was seated. The flight attendant said that the guy sitting beside her was trying to flirt with her, and she was very curt. She seemed nervous, anxious for the plane to take off."

"So her whereabouts are unaccounted for between three and a little after five," Roberts mused. "She had time to off Kreiser and rid herself of the weapon, and was certainly acting unusually. Good work, Will."

Chapter 58

Roberts stood in the anteroom of Gerard Fellowes' understatedly elegant office suite. The room was designed with an eclectic blend of styles, bounded by smooth polished wooden panels and austere but comfortable leather furnishings and muted lighting. A large Joan Miro graced one wall, and examples of Klee and de Kooning the other two walls.

Fellowes' assistant looked apologetically at Roberts. "He tries to be punctual," she smiled. "But he was in a head-knocking mood before this meeting."

As the words left her mouth, the double doors to the conference room opened, and Gerry came striding out, a gaggle of suits in his wake. He strode up to Roberts, offering his hand.

"Good morning, Captain," he smiled, although Roberts could tell his smile was forced. He looked back at the people streaming out of the conference room. "Miriam," he addressed the assistant, "I'm taking Captain Roberts upstairs so we can be undisturbed. Hold my calls except you-know-who."

Miriam smiled knowingly, as Gerry led the way to the elevator. They entered, and Gerry inserted a key into the elevator and punched '20'.

"Bad day at the office?" Mark queried.

"I had a 'come to Jesus' meeting with the staff," Gerry smiled, more congenial. "I don't suffer fools gladly, and there were some screwups while I was gone. I don't want this deal to go south.

"But that's not why you're here," he continued. "I knew it would be a day from hell here, so thanks for coming here to meet with me. What can I do for you?"

"I wanted to follow up with you after our short conversation Tuesday night. Thanks for your cooperation thus far," Roberts replied.

The elevator opened onto a foyer, and Roberts and Fellowes stepped out. Gerry led the way into the spacious and comfortable living room/salon.

"Please make yourself at home," he remarked, moving over to the bar. "Drink?" he indicated the decanters. "Soft drink? Juice?"

Roberts shook his head. Gerry opened a small refrigerator and pulled out an orange juice for himself. Moving fluidly back over to Roberts, he seated himself across from Roberts on one of the two sofas facing each other over a carved wooden coffee table.

"It's been a while, Mark," Gerry stated conversationally. "Long time since we did pick-up games at Tech. Do you still do a lot of shooting?"

"Not as much," Mark allowed himself a small smile. "I try to get to the gun club every now and then, to stay in practice and not embarrass myself during the police certifications."

"You are good," Gerry remarked. "Shouldn't let that go to waste."

"Not as good as you," Mark responded.

"So you're a captain now? Moving up the ladder. Do you really like law enforcement work? You know I can still use good executive material."

"No, thanks. I really like it, particularly investigations. Homicide is particularly fun."

Gerry laughed. "If you say so. So what is it? Surely you don't think I made up my alibi?" Gerry smiled. "Tom was so ill. He said he had never been sicker in his life. I admit I was worried about him, and he was one miserable puppy for several hours at the hospital. He insisted he wanted to fly me home. But when the hospital said he was stable enough to move, I had him life-flighted home."

Gerry grinned. "That left me in a dilemma. I was not leaving the Gulfstream there and flying commercial."

"You're licensed to fly?" Roberts asked, although he knew the answer.

"Yep. I don't buy a horse I can't handle myself," Gerry laughed. "So I had to get certified too."

"So you didn't see Kreiser, even before this trip?" Mark's question was to the point.

"No," Gerry was direct. "I guess I won't ever know why he wanted to see me. The call took me by surprise. I really have had no contact with Harry except in social situations."

"But he was a regular companion of your sister?" Roberts watched for his reaction.

Gerry snorted. "Katharine hasn't really had a 'regular' companion. I guess Kreiser and she have been each other's default dates. I once thought about trying to arrange a marriage there, but Kat told me to back off."

"A marriage between your sister and Harry Kreiser?" Mark's eyebrows arched. "Why? To make him unavailable for your fiancée?"

Gerry flushed. "I don't try to manage Charlotte's life. She is her own person. But if there was some mutual affections between Harry and Kat..."

"You know a limousine matching the description of yours was seen outside the church about the time of the shooting?"

Gerry frowned. "It couldn't have been mine. I made arrangements for the new limo to be delivered to the house Friday afternoon. I hoped to be there when it arrived, but of course wasn't. There was no one to drive it, because Tom and I were still out west. What, do you think I got a double to pose as me there so I could slip back to Atlanta, drive my own limo and off Kreiser? That does not make sense."

"Did you have reason to kill Kreiser?"

Gerry was silent, sipping his orange juice. "We certainly weren't friends," he finally conceded.

Mark prodded him. "Charlotte Lawson revealed to me about her affair with Kreiser."

Gerry blanched. "She what?" he croaked. "I told you you have no business talking to her. She has an attorney. She has rights."

Mark was stern. "She has to invoke her right to an attorney. You can't do it for her. What are you afraid she will say?"

Gerry's face became a mask. "What did she tell you?"

"She told me about their time together, and how he broke it off. She ran away to D.C., something about performance anxiety." Mark watched for his reaction. "Did she have his child? Is it Stefan?"

Gerry's eyes narrowed. "What was her answer? Or has she negated your theory, and you just don't believe her so you're asking me?"

Mark regarded him. "Just answer my question, Gerry."

Gerry stared at Roberts. "Stefan is not her child. The resemblance is uncanny, and takes my breath away. But he is not the child of Charlotte and Kreiser. Charlotte would give anything if he was. She loves him dearly. Stefan is her life."

"And Kreiser wasn't blackmailing you or her about Stefan?"

Gerry smiled saccharinely. "No. Kreiser enjoyed the good life already. Melanie Cain provided for his needs and wants. He had no reason to resort to blackmail."

Gerry's cell phone buzzed. Gerry looked at the number. "Excuse me a minute. This is important."

He stood, answering the phone. "Hi, Wally, what is it?" Gerry walked off toward the bar, his voice loud. "Mark Roberts is here. I've given him strict instructions he is not to interview Charlotte any further without you present.

I want you to make that clear to the police commissioner." He looked back at Mark, and his meaning was clear, as Mark stared at him stonily.

"No, it's OK. Sunday? Sure. The club at 7:00? I can make it. What's up?" He paused. "Charlotte?" His voice lowered. "No, she didn't say anything to me. What the hell? I can come over there now."

He again paused, listening. "OK. Did she say why?"

Again a pause. "I don't want to wait, but if you insist. See you Sunday."

He hung up, turning back to Roberts. "OK, where were we?" Gerry asked, a frown on his face as he rubbed his forehead distractedly.

"Charlotte doesn't have an alibi," Roberts proceeded unperturbed. "What has she told you about her whereabouts?"

"She was catching a flight to D.C.," Gerry was suddenly defensive. "I was supposed to join her up there for a meeting. But in the advent of Tom's plight I didn't make it."

"Were you supposed to meet her at the cathedral that afternoon?"

Gerry laughed mirthlessly, as he reseated himself across from Roberts. "No, Mark, neither of us had plans to off Kreiser that day. Sorry, no conspiracy theory."

"How do you know what she did from the time she left home until she caught the plane?"

Gerry leaned back and closed his eyes. "I just know. I have known Charlotte since she was four and I know Charlotte couldn't kill Harry Kreiser."

"Why?" Roberts leaned forward, intent upon his subject.

Gerry opened his eyes and stared at Roberts. "Because she adored Kreiser," his voice was husky. "She has always loved Harry. She has taken his crap for years in the hopes of one day living happily ever after with him. He stole her dream, destroyed her. He continued to lead her on, then dumped her. Fortunately, I was always around to pick up the pieces afterward."

"So you really love her?"

Gerry remained silent, fingering the juice bottle.

"That's a great motive for murder, for both you and her," Roberts supplied grimly.

"Yes, but we've established I wasn't here," Gerry reminded him. "Don't get me wrong. If Charlotte wanted him dead, I'd have moved heaven and earth to make it happen. But you don't know Charlotte." Gerry looked away. "She could never pull the trigger on him, no matter what. His death has devastated her."

It suddenly dawned on Roberts. "You keep tabs on her, don't you? You know where she was because you've had someone trailing her?"

Gerry's eyes met his coldly. "I trust my fiancée. I don't need to keep private investigators on the payroll tailing her every move."

Mark said softly, "You did have her under surveillance, didn't you?" He paused. "You would volunteer to share that information if it didn't happen to implicate her, wouldn't you?"

Gerry clenched his jaw, making no response, staring through Mark.

Mark pointed over to the piano. "Nice instrument. You don't play, do you?"

"No," Gerry was curt.

"Does Charlotte practice here?"

"I wouldn't know," he was sullen. "She has the run of the place, can come and go as she wants. I bought the instrument for her. I encourage her to keep at her art."

"Does she keep her disguises here?" Mark asked casually.

Gerry's head jerked up. "What the hell are you talking about?"

"The disguises she uses to perform," Mark replied nonchalantly. "Isn't she Tabitha Auberge? Making quite a reputation, but why can't she appear in public under her own name?"

Gerry looked at him through steely eyes. "Are you trying to bait me? Where do you get this stuff, Mark?"

"It's true, isn't it?" Mark was direct. "She couldn't perform as herself, but could if she posed as someone else. Did she pose as someone else to kill Kreiser? Or maybe it's as simple as you or she hiring someone to bump him off?"

"I cannot believe you," Gerry remonstrated, shaking his head in disbelief.

"You know I wouldn't be discussing this with you if I didn't think I will be able to prove it," Mark challenged him.

"You are on one hell of a fishing expedition now," Gerry's voice lowered, although Roberts could tell he was livid. "And if you think I'm going to sit here and help you weave some fantastic story about my fiancée as the perpetrator of Harry Kreiser's murder, then you're wasting your time and mine."

Gerry stood, and Mark followed suit. "If I can be of serious help to you, you have my numbers. But, Captain Roberts," his voice became icy, "if you confront my fiancée one more time without benefit of the presence of Wallace Meredith or myself, I'll be personally calling the commissioner, and not to invite him to tea. Now, if you will excuse me, I must get back to work. I'll accompany you downstairs."

They were silent in the elevator going down, Gerry silently and thoughtfully watching Roberts head toward the glass front doors.

Chapter 59

Charlotte paused at the doors of the church. She took a deep breath, trying to steady her trembling limbs. I should not have agreed to do this, she thought. I cannot go through with it. "You have to," she whispered to herself. "There's no one else."

In view of Kreiser's untimely death, his student Andy Kutuzov was to fill in for Sunday services at the cathedral until an arrangement could be made for an organist. But Charlotte received a call Sunday morning.

"Charlotte? This is Paul Brown."

Charlotte had smiled. "How are you, Dr. Brown? It's been a while."

"Yes, my dear," he replied. "I'm looking for Stefan. I have somewhat of an emergency."

"Stefan is gone with his parents this weekend," Charlotte frowned. "Is there something I can do?"

"Yes, Charlotte. I need your help desperately. You see, Andrei played the early services, but has collapsed with bronchitis. I am on my way with him across to Piedmont Hospital. There is no one to play the principal service, with Kreiser and Andy gone."

Charlotte caught her breath. "I don't know anyone to call," she murmured.

"My dear, please don't say no. I know you can handle this. I wouldn't ask you otherwise. You know this organ, and have played it many times."

Charlotte hesitated. Brown added, "There's no one else. I was told by the choir that they are scheduled to sing *a capella*, and that you therefore only have to concern yourself with prelude, postlude, hymns and communion music. There's not much time before the service starts."

Therefore, Charlotte with great trepidation entered the door into the hall leading between the cathedral to the offices and educational building. The choir director saw her and beckoned, coming toward her. "Thank you, my dear," he said, heaving a large sigh of relief. "When Poppy said you agreed, I was so afraid you might back out. You are such a wonderful musician—you really should not cloister yourself behind that old frumpy newspaper."

He took her by the arm and steered her through the doors to the church and down the aisle, up the stairwell to the gallery and to the organ, chattering all the while. Charlotte smiled, but was inwardly hanging back, apprehensive about facing the console where Kreiser had been killed.

"You see," Frankie whispered confidentially as they rounded the bend and were suddenly standing in the gallery in front of the organ, "nothing has changed since you last played here. It all looks the same. No blood, no bullet holes. There are makeshift lights—they have to replace the others. Now I'll leave you. You have only a few minutes to do your thing before the choir arrives. Here is the service music and the psalm, all familiar stuff."

Frankie left before Charlotte could ask any questions, and suddenly all was silent. Charlotte made her way to the console, touching the wood as if to assure herself it was real. Repressing a shudder, she pulled out music and her shoes from the small bag under her arm, and quickly changed shoes.

She checked the memory levels, going to the number she knew Kreiser kept always set at certain registrations for hymns and service music. Pushing each piston, she watched the stops as they stepped forward and retired like soldiers called to attention. "Harry, it's like you are still here," she said aloud.

She had chosen conservatively, knowing that she would need all her strength to make it through the service without the added complication of difficult music. She warmed up with the selected hymns for the day, her fingers faltering over the keys before plunging in, closing her eyes and hand-registering between verses. She knew the locations of the stops from memory, and found herself easily finding the voices she needed as she weaved through the hymns and created her own final harmonization for the last verse.

"OK, that wasn't so bad," she thought. She pulled out a score and placed it before her. Instinctively reaching for a pencil, she pulled it out, knowing exactly where Kreiser kept one. She looked at the pencil, and tears filled her eyes.

She finished her practicing quickly, anxiously, and leaned against the balustrade looking into the nave as she waited for the choir. Watching the altar guild at work setting up the altar for the service, she thought back to the last time she had attended a service at this church. It was George's funeral, and she recalled the encounter with Kreiser at the visitation afterward, and his meeting Stefan.

She came back to the present, heard behind her the noise of choir members coming up the stairs, and realized that time was near. Oh God, she prayed again, don't let me screw up. I know I'm not up to it. I cannot wear a disguise today.

Leaving while the choir warmed up, she fled to the restroom, letting cold water sluice over her wrists and staring at herself in the mirror. You've played this organ a million times, she told herself. You know the music, the organ, the stops, the registrations. There's nothing you can't handle. She found herself wondering what Harry's last thoughts were, where the shots ended up. "Stop it!" she said aloud to her image in the mirror.

Somehow she made it back to the console, greeting the choir members as they left. She was alone again. It was time. She sat down on the organ bench, shaking. Charlotte, you have to start, she kept thinking. You have to do this.

She finally pushed a piston and started, tentatively at first. Once she made it through the first few bars, she felt a slight relaxing of her stiffness. She forced herself to focus on the notes in front of her, trying not to think about how badly she must sound in the nave below, trying not to think of Kreiser, about the shots that took his life. She recalled her visit years ago as a child with Uncle Howard, her first view of the organ in the gallery, and her playing for Peter Conrad. She smiled at the memory, and it helped.

She somehow made it through the service, although everything was a blur to her. She watched the clergy and director carefully, and there were no major mistakes, although she felt shaky several times, and was afraid of losing control. She didn't; however, she realized that she had no memory of what she had just done. Her mind was frozen, thinking about Harry sitting there, playing, and his life being stilled in an instant. She could see his body slumped over the console.

She played the postlude in an empty gallery, as the choir processed out and left her alone. She finished the number, then hit the 'cancel' button and swung off the bench. She bent down and unlaced her organ shoes, then straightened up. There stood Gerard.

"Oh," she said weakly. "Hi, Gerry."

He was dressed in a dark suit. He walked over to the balustrade and looked down. "It's been a long time since I've been up here," he remarked.

"Me, too," Charlotte replied.

"You were superb," he turned, smiling at her. "You should never have given it up. You have a true gift."

Caught unaware, she caught her breath. "Thanks," was all she could say.

"Was it hard? I mean, playing again, sitting there where Kreiser—" he didn't finish.

"Yes," she slipped out of her shoes and shakily stepped into her pumps.

"Do you know any more about how he—?" she couldn't finish the sentence.

"No," he shook his head sadly, his eyes scanning the gallery closely. "The department is keeping the info close to its chest. I'm still trying."

Stuffing her music and shoes into the bag, she approached Gerry.

"My God, you're shaking like a leaf," he exclaimed, as he took her arm.

She felt her legs slipping from under her, and he scooped her up. "Here, sit down a minute, Charl," he steered her to a choir chair and gingerly set her down, sitting down beside her.

"How did you know I was here?" she asked, still trying to stop the trembling.

"I called, and Daisy was just leaving the house for church. She told me," he spoke. "I was instantly worried." He paused. "Coming back here was not a good idea, Charl," she heard him saying, as though from a distance.

She felt the room whirl. "Charl, are you OK?" he asked, putting his arm around her.

"I know," she said foggily, blinking back fresh tears. "I need to get out of here, Gerry."

"Can you walk?"

"I think so," she stood shakily.

"Where are you parked?"

"Across the street."

"Let's go."

He supported her as they went down the stairs and out the front door, down the steps, and to the parking garage.

Making it to her car, he asked for her keys, and ensconced her in the passenger seat.

Springing around, he slipped in and the car sprang to life.

"Do you drive?" Charlotte asked distractedly.

"Damn it, Charl, I don't always sit in the back of a limo," he retorted. "I only do that so that I can work while someone else does the driving."

"Sorry," she closed her eyes and leaned back. "Where are we going?"

"I'm taking you home," he replied, his eyes on the road.

She looked at him apprehensively, but did not reply.

Gerry spoke smoothly, casually. "I met Wally at the club early this morning for some racquetball. He told me that you wanted him to ask me to be the executor of your will, and trustee for a fund for Stefan. He said you were discussing an *inter vivos* pourover trust in case something happened to you. What's that about, Charl?"

She swallowed. "I'm just trying to get my affairs in order, just—just in case so-something should happen," she stammered. "I wasn't sure whether you were talking to me, so asked Wally to contact you."

"You've got me worried now," Gerry muttered. "Once Wally spilled the beans, I called looking for you, and Daisy told me about your call from the cathedral." He looked over at her wan face.

"There was no one else," she whispered.

"Charl, you have got to keep that outer shell tough. The police know nothing. They are on a fishing expedition. Don't give them any reason to suspect you."

"They know about Harry and me," she mumbled, staring ahead of her.

"So does everyone who reads the gossip columns. Keep your cool, dear."

"Roberts knows so much already."

Gerry reached over and took her hand, squeezing it. "I've told you. Don't talk to him alone. Call Wally or me. Insist on it. You don't need to handle this alone."

She nodded, saying nothing.

He paused. "Charl, I've been gone a lot lately for a reason. I'm trying to consolidate some of my business holdings so that I can be home more, particularly when there are others who need me here." He looked meaningfully at her.

"I need you, Gerry," she smiled wanly. "I need you here." She squeezed his hand.

They were silent for most of the drive. He pulled in through the gate and to the front door. Getting out, he scooped her up and carried her, hitting the alarm code and letting them in, kicking the door shut behind him. He looked at her, his jaw set.

"You just made it through a couple of hours down memory lane with Harry's ghost," he said quietly but angrily. "I think you can handle my making love to you."

She gazed back at him. "I guess so."

"Do you need to get drunk first?" he asked mockingly.

"No, I want to be stone sober this time."

He marched up the stairs with her.

Afterward she clung to him and he held her close.

"Do you realize you just played in public without a disguise?" he whispered to her.

"So I did," she mumbled. "I didn't sleep at all last night," she confided. "I was all alone, and I knew if I had the dream again there was no one to wake me. And then the call came this morning from Dr. Brown asking me to play, me knowing that Harry . . ." she shuddered.

"I wish you had called me," he murmured against her hair.

"I started to, but then I realized I didn't know where you were," she nestled closer to him. "I was scared that I would get my hopes up, just to find that you were too far away."

"It's my fault. I should have called you," he stroked her hair and kissed her.

She snuggled next to him. "Gerry, I'm the prime suspect. The police know about Harry and me. I'm scared. They can put me at the church, Gerry. They found a receipt from the gun club that morning at the church."

He froze, still holding her tightly "Shit, Charl. How do you know this?"

"Roberts told me. But," she continued quickly, fearfully, "I told him I never kept the receipts. I always threw them away at the club." She buried her head against his shoulder. "What is going to happen?"

"It's all in your head. They have nothing. They are only trolling for information. I'm here, Charl," he kissed her. "I won't let anything happen to you. Sleep."

"What if you can't stop it?"

"Sh-h," he said against her ear.

"I love you," she whispered.

"Say it again," he kissed her again tenderly, her face cradled in his hands.

"I do love you, Gerry," she insisted against his mouth. "Gerry, I have something to tell you," she began, pulling away.

"It's not important," he whispered, his lips trailing down her throat.

"It is important," she stared at him. "It's critical that you know."

"If it is about Kreiser, I don't want to know," he murmured against her throat. "Please don't." He stopped and stared at her. "It's over. Let it go."

She bit her lip, her eyes brilliant. "Gerry, please promise me you will protect Stefan. He's your godson. He's eighteen, but still a child in many ways. He will need your guidance."

He gazed at her. "Stop it, Charl," he spoke sternly, shaking her gently. "Do you think for one moment I would let you go down for this? I will take care of everything." He kissed her again. She responded, and the kiss deepened as he pulled her closer. They melted into each other.

They made love again, quietly, urgently, clinging to each other fiercely. He brought them both to the brink of climax, before slowing, inserting his fingers and slowly stimulating her to the point where she bit her lip to keep from screaming. She reciprocated, manually stimulating him until, his breathing labored, he drove them both to a satisfying denouement.

Afterward he held her until she relaxed against him and fell asleep.

Later she awakened, and he was gone. She was lying under the covers naked, a tray of food on the other side of the bed. "Was it all a dream?" she wondered aloud.

She noticed a note on the tray. "Stefan called and is on his way back. He heard about your playing today, and was worried. Mike and Amy are on their way back to D.C. I thought you might not want him to find us in an 'adult situation'. I'll check on you later. G."

She smiled at Gerry's joke, but she dressed quickly and was ready, looking forward to Stefan's return.

Stefan didn't arrive until late evening. She was sitting in the library, staring at the fireplace, when she heard the door. A moment later Stefan appeared in the doorway. "Are you still up?" he asked, surprised.

"Yes," she stood. "I couldn't wait to see you, dear." She came forward.

He hugged her quickly, then relinquished her. "How was the service today? I heard you played."

"It was very hard," she confessed, her eyes downcast, concerned about his reticence. "Stefan, have I done something wrong?"

Stefan stared at her solemnly. "Of course, not, Aunt Charl. I just have a lot on my mind. I'm sorry."

She smiled tentatively. "It's all right. I guess you should get some rest."

He took her hand and pulled her along to the stairwell, then gently pushed her. "You go on up. I will lock up and turn off the lights for you. You need to rest. I know Harry's death has been too much for you. I'm glad Gerry was here for you."

She nodded dumbly, gratefully, as she ascended the stairs to her room. She poured herself a stiff drink from the decanter she had brought upstairs the night before. She was afraid to succumb to sleep any more, afraid of the dreams, of her memories. But the exhaustion was overwhelming.

In the early hours she had the dream, and awoke screaming. As she sat up in the bed, she saw a shadowy figure approaching her. "Please don't arrest me," she sobbed, putting up her hands to defend herself. "Oh, someone, help me," she cried, her voice hoarse and small.

The person sat on the edge of the bed. It was Stefan. He engulfed her in a hug. "It's OK, Auntie. It's just me," he whispered.

She tried to control her shaking, as he held her. "I worry about you if something should happen to me," she sobbed, out of control. "I love you so much, Stefan."

"Please, Aunt Charl," he crooned to her. "I'm not going to let anything happen to you. I will take care of everything. You are going to be OK."

She felt the situation surreal, reminding her of Gerry's assurances just earlier that afternoon. She murmured, "Stefan, I'm supposed to be the one taking care of you, not the other way around."

"You'll see. They won't touch you."

He finally persuaded her to lie back. He lay down beside her on top of the covers, facing her and holding her hand.

She laughed through her tears. "It's been a long time since you crawled into bed with me, my little boy."

"You sleep. It's my turn to chase the monsters away," he whispered, squeezing her hand.

Chapter 60

When Roberts walked into the police department the next morning, he looked around for Will. Not finding him in their office, he looked through the glass window of the interrogation room door. Will was facing him, scowling at someone whose back was to him.

Will, seeing him, gestured for him to enter.

Roberts, opening the door, was brought up short by the sight of Stefan Chadwick sitting there, dressed in oxford shirt and denims, his face white, his eyes wide. Covering his surprise, Roberts turned to Will. "Yes?" he asked.

"Mr. Chadwick didn't make it to his appointment with us the other day. He was just trying to explain himself," Will looked sternly at the young man.

"You were at Aunt Charlotte's the other night," the youth accused, staring at Roberts warily.

"Yes. Why didn't you show up for your scheduled interview?" Roberts was direct.

"Something came up," he replied defensively. "I'm here today. I'm sorry, but it couldn't be helped."

"Want to sit in?" Will asked Roberts.

"Sure," Mark answered, his eyes on Stefan, who was looking quite miserable.

Pulling up a chair and stradding it backward, he was surprised further by Stefan's interruption. "I'm ready to confess."

"Confess?" smiled Roberts involuntarily. "To what?"

"I murdered Dr. K," Stefan was regarding him seriously.

Will's head jerked up abruptly. "Whoa, just a minute," he said. "How old are you?"

"I'm eighteen, will be nineteen next week," replied Stefan.

"What attorney do you want me to call for you?" Roberts managed to say. "We can't talk to you without counsel present, or your family will have the entire police department out on the street before nightfall." He looked hard at Stefan. "I need to call your parents or Aunt Charlotte to let her know you are here." He stood up.

Stefan retorted angrily, "Leave her out of this. I'm an adult. And I know I have a right to remain silent, and a right to an attorney. I give all that up. Don't you want to turn on the tape recorder like they do on TV?"

Roberts, as startled as Will, reached over and turned the recorder on. He stated some preliminary information into the microphone, and sank back into his chair.

"Stefan, you have just stated that you understand you have a right to remain silent and a right to an attorney. Did we just offer to call the attorney of your choice and your family?"

"Yes, sir, and I said no," the young man stated.

"Do you realize that anything said here can be used against you?"

"Yes, sir," replied Stefan quietly and clearly.

"And you're prepared to waive those rights?" Roberts stared at the young man.

"Yes, sir," Stefan echoed.

"Now then," Will was clearly uncomfortable. "Where were you on the afternoon of Friday, April 12?"

"Aunt Charlotte thought I was in D.C. with my folks. But I had come back here. I knew Dr. Kreiser had a lesson at the cathedral with Cece—I mean Cecelia Rhodes—on Fridays. So I slipped in and—blew him away."

"Just like that?" Roberts asked.

"Pretty much," Stefan looked at him questioningly.

"What with?"

"Aunt Charlotte's gun."

"What kind of gun?"

He paused as if searching. "A semi-automatic."

Will looked up suddenly from his note-taking. "Where did you get the gun?"

Stefan spoke carefully, "Aunt Charlotte kept the gun locked up in the safe. I knew the combination. I took the gun a few months ago."

"So were you planning this for some time?" Roberts asked, his eyes intent on the young man, who was fidgeting nervously.

"Yes, sir," he replied uncertainly.

"Why? Why did you want to kill your teacher?"

"I found Aunt Charlotte's journals from when she was a student of Kreiser's," Stefan began, suddenly white with rage. "I found out what he did to her. I hated him, wanted to kill him for hurting her, putting her through what he did. He ruined her life. And here I was, by insisting on coming back to Atlanta, making her live through it all again."

"Journals?"

"Yes. They were—in the attic. I found them and read them all."

"Just what did he do to her?" Will asked curiously.

"He had sex with her, made her fall in love with him, got her pregnant, and drove her away. She quit a brilliant performance career because of him," Stefan's voice rose suddenly, and he flushed. "He ruined her."

"Do you understand what you are saying?" Will asked dazedly.

"Yeah, I know all about sex education—aced it in school," he replied flippantly.

"Don't be a smart-ass," Will retorted shortly. The boy paled and was silent, unclenching and looking at his hands.

"How did you kill him?" Will asked.

"I slipped in through the back, took aim from the upstairs entry to the gallery, and popped him."

"How many times?"

"Twice through the heart."

"Did you hit him both times?" Will's face was a mask.

"Yes, sir, I think so," Stefan faltered.

Roberts and Will looked at each other. "How did you learn to shoot like that?"

"Gerry taught me," the boy replied. "Every now and then when Aunt Charlotte thought he was taking me to his office to show me some computer games, we went over to the firing range. He thought I needed to know how to handle a gun."

"Gerry?" echoed Roberts.

"Gerard Fellowes, Aunt Charlotte's ex-fiancé," Stefan replied. "He's one of the best shooters I've ever seen."

Will nodded. "Yeah, I know. I've seen him at some competitions."

Roberts asked, "You said 'ex-fiancé. Why is that?"

Stefan started guiltily. "Well, she's still wearing his ring. But something happened after Aunt Mellie died. Gerry is gone a lot. He has his own jet, so he comes and goes at will. They still talk, but he has avoided her a lot since the funeral. They act funny around each other. But he has been there for her the last few days."

Roberts' eyes narrowed thoughtfully.

Will suddenly leaned forward, dangling an object in a clear plastic evidence bag. "Do you recognize this?"

Stefan leaned forward, examining the object held by Will. "That looks like one of Aunt Mellie's 'coins of death'," he remarked, a quizzical expression on his face. "Where did you get it?"

"'Coins of death'?" Roberts repeated.

"Aunt Mellie's collection of old Roman coins. Uncle Howard used to use them for treasure hunts for Mom and Aunt Charlotte when they were kids. Aunt Mellie told me the story about the coins, something about their being bad luck—sent by members of the Mafia to people that were slated for execution. I remember telling Cece and Russ about them. What about them?" Stefan's brow furrowed.

"Where are the other coins?" Will asked blandly.

"I don't know," he admitted, his confusion evident. "I haven't seen them since—" he paused, his mind searching his memory, "oh, a while. What does this have to do with the murder?"

"How many coins were there?" Roberts asked him.

"I don't know—ten or twelve. I think they were in a display case in the safe," Stefan replied, staring at Roberts quizzically.

"They weren't in the safe when you stole the gun?" Roberts asked.

Stefan started dazedly, his eyes searching Roberts' face. "No—yes, maybe they were. I don't remember. I wasn't thinking about them."

"Tell me what happened to your aunt's wigs."

"The wigs? They were—I—I don't know," he asked, his eyes darting from one to the other.

"The wigs she used as disguises to hide her identity. What happened to them?"

He looked flustered. "They were stolen—I don't know," he said, before realizing what he said. "I don't know what you are talking about," he quickly corrected himself, his eyes narrowing.

"Tell us about her disguises. Did she use them so that she could play recitals, move around without detection?"

"Yes, I mean, I don't know."

"You're lying," Roberts said quietly.

"I don't know what happened to the wigs. Yes, she wore disguises to perform. She said she could play when she was someone else."

He looked at first Will then Roberts, his eyes darting. A bead of perspiration appeared on his forehead.

"Tell me, Stefan, what was Kreiser doing when you shot him?"

"Nothing. He was playing the organ."

"What was he playing?" Roberts suddenly asked.

"I—I don't remember, man," Stefan put his hand over his eyes, rubbing his forehead.

"Was anyone else there?" Will asked.

"No, the place was empty," Stefan's reply was rapid. He was nodding, whether to assure them or himself Roberts didn't know.

"Where's the weapon now?" Roberts asked.

"I slipped out late the night you were at Aunt Mellie's and went to the river. I threw it in. I was worried when I saw you and found out who you were. I was afraid you might be there to search. I was scared I wouldn't get rid of the gun before you found it."

"Where are the journals?" Will asked.

"I threw them in too," Stefan replied quickly, fearfully.

An officer knocked on the door, and quickly entered and handed Roberts a note. Roberts glanced at it. "Your aunt is calling me looking for you. Don't you think we should call her?"

"Damn it, leave her alone," Stefan stood suddenly, tears in his eyes.

"Sit back down," Will ordered the youth. He complied, fidgeting nervously.

Roberts stared at the youth a long time. "Why are you here? Why are you telling us this?" Roberts leaned forward, his hand resting on the young man's shoulder.

Stefan slumped, desperation on his face. "I know you've been questioning Aunt Charlotte, that you think she killed him. I couldn't take it anymore. My conscience wouldn't let me be silent. You gotta leave her alone. She can't take any more. She was hysterical last night, most nights." His voice caught in a sob, as he covered his face with his hands, his elbows resting on the desk.

"Why would you think we suspect her?" Will's voice was gruff, but his face showed concern.

Stefan glanced at Roberts. "I—I don't know. You've been hanging around her, asking lots of questions. She was angry at Harry. She's been crying a lot. She's not sleeping, and she screams his name in her sleep. She loved him, even after . . .," he paused, frightened.

"Even after what, Stefan?" Roberts leaned forward.

Stefan stuttered, "She's scared. I can see it. I hear her talking to herself, saying things—" he stopped himself, staring at Will, his eyes wide again, fearful. He fell silent.

"What has she been saying?" Will queried.

Stefan remained mute.

"Anything else you want to tell us, Stefan?" Roberts' voice was gentle.

Stefan shook his head dumbly. His phone clipped to his belt vibrated, and he quickly looked at the number.

"Who is it?" Roberts asked.

"Aunt Charl," he swallowed convulsively.

"Shouldn't you call her back?" Roberts queried.

"No, I don't want her involved in this," Stefan insisted. "Don't you think it's gonna be bad enough when she finds out I—I did it? She can't take any more."

"OK. Thanks for coming by," Roberts smiled, nodding at Will.

"What?" Stefan exclaimed. "Aren't you going to arrest me now?"

"I'd rather wait for the real killer," Roberts replied quietly.

"But Aunt Charlotte didn't do it!" Stefan's eyes were wild as he shouted. "I killed him. I've just told you. Why don't you believe me?"

Roberts regarded him solemnly. "I tell you what. You produce the gun and those journals, and we'll talk some more."

Stefan paled. "I can't do that. I told you—I—I threw them in the river," he stammered fiercely.

Roberts looked at Will and pointed his head toward the door. "Excuse us a minute," he told the boy, perched on his chair like a gazelle about to bolt.

Just outside the door, Will laid a hand on Roberts' shoulder. "You're not going to let him go?"

"Why not?" Roberts frowned.

"What if he is telling the truth?"

"Can't you tell? He's doing this because he is afraid we are going to pin this on Charlotte Lawson," Roberts said stonily.

"I have a contact or two in the D.C. area. Charlotte Lawson had a miscarriage about seven months after she left here. So she was pregnant with Kreiser's kid, but it isn't this Stefan."

"Damn! She lied to me again." Roberts was livid. Lowering his voice, he half-whispered, "And Kreiser found out about her pregnancy, and jumped to the wrong conclusion." Roberts started pacing. "What do you think about the kid's story about dropping the gun and these journals in the river?"

"I just don't know," Will said. "He's definitely off about how Kreiser was shot. He knew nothing about the coin's being on Kreiser. He was genuinely surprised. Of course, we don't have anything to link the coin to the crime other than it was found on the victim. But if the coins went missing at the same time as the gun . . ."

"But the kid didn't know the Rhodes girl was at the scene when the shots were fired. What if he suspects his aunt, or has found evidence she did it, and is trying to cover for her?"

Roberts saw Randy and a uniformed officer walking in the door, and motioned them over. Roberts turned to the officer. "Please stand guard and watch the young man in there. Don't let him pull anything funny."

Motioning Randy and Will to follow him, Roberts walked into their office. Quickly recounting what they knew to Randy, Roberts concluded. "I want to know where this kid was on Friday, whether in D.C. or here. Check his story. Check the airlines—how would he have gotten back to Atlanta? Did he ever leave? I want confirmation.

"Will, I want you to take Stefan with you. Get him to point out where he supposedly threw away the weapon and journals."

"If they're in the river, we'll never recover them," Will snorted glumly.

"You may be right. But for some crazy reason I just don't believe him, particularly about the gun. Not enough detail in his story. I don't even think he knows the calibre of the weapon. Will, every time a gap occurs in his story, park a Jeep in it. I don't care. Get his permission to search the house. He lives at the place, damn it."

Will turned to Randy. "In the meantime I need for you to take the tape of his statement and what we know already and prepare a search warrant for the house and grounds for the gun, coins and these journals. See if we can get some eyes on the place until we can get it signed and executed. I have no idea whether a judge will sign it, so make it good."

Roberts turned to Randy. "What about Fellowes' alibi?"

"What I have so far from the hospital in Tucson checks out," Randy answered. "But guess what? I found out he had a brand new made-to-order limousine delivered that Friday, and one matching its description was seen in the vicinity of the cathedral Friday afternoon. That's just way too coincidental."

"But he couldn't have been at the hospital in Tucson and here too at the same time," Roberts objected.

Will broke in. "We need to interview Gerard Fellowes again—find out what he knows. If his fiancée was having an affair with Kreiser and had his child, if there was further involvement and Gerard found out—" he let the sentence hang. "And Mark, Fellowes is rich as sin. He could hire anyone to off the professor, and we'd never be able to prove it."

"Although he appears to be one to take care of his own dirty business," Roberts nodded. "He told me he had some quick business out of town, but should be back in the area by now. I don't care if you get the state attorney to issue an investigative subpoena. He has motive out the ying-yang too. And with his own private jet, he'd better be pretty specific regarding those times. I'm going to try to find him. I'll call his number."

Roberts turned to leave. Will stopped him. "Where are you going now?"

"I'm hunting down Charlotte Lawson, if I have to shake the truth out of her," Roberts replied, his voice betraying his emotion.

"She's our prime suspect now," Will reminded him. "Are you sure? Let's get the uniformed guys to haul her in here for questioning. That will shake her up, maybe get the juices flowing."

"I don't want to wait for that. I'll bring her in myself," Roberts was grim as he let himself out.

Chapter 61

Charlotte awoke before dawn. Stefan was gone. She lay in bed, her mind racing, unable to sleep. She had a sense of foreboding she could not shake. She knew that she was on Roberts' short list of suspects, and the most likely.

But more troubling to her was Stefan's perceived change in demeanor before last night. What was going on? Why his change toward her? She tried to tell herself that she was imagining things, but she knew in her heart she could not bear to lose Stefan's love and approval. Although it's not likely I will hold on to that if I am charged with murder, she thought despairingly. She momentarily recalled Gerry's promise to protect her, but realized that if Roberts' net closed around her there was little that anyone, even Gerry, could do.

As the dark grew progressively lighter, she gave up on sleep and got up. She at first thought started her morning routine and dressed in shorts, intending to go sculling, but she remembered that she had a deadline to meet. Kline needed a column. She couldn't write about Stefan's recital, and it would be unseemly to say nothing about Kreiser's death. She knew the time was past due to write a eulogy for him. He was an institution of the music community, and her readers and his fans would be looking to her to mark his passing with the respect it deserved.

But when she struggled with what to say, she felt empty, bereft. Had Harry really loved her as he claimed? If so, why didn't he move heaven and earth to find her when she needed him? If he thought Stefan was his son, why hadn't he confronted her, demanded the truth? Why all these years did he proclaim his love for her, only to continue to push her away? That was the ultimate cruelty, for his words had kept fueling her fruitless hopes for a future with him, and she had spent her life in a holding pattern, waiting for someone who would never be hers, a dream, a chimera.

She had always shouldered the sole responsibility for their brief affair. She never once acknowledged aloud that she deserved anything other than what she had received. But now the secret wounds, ever festering, had reopened. She was livid at him, angry at the long years of silence, even after she reluctantly returned to his world with Stefan in tow.

And he thinks he can constantly insinuate himself into my life once he's gone, she seethed. Harry still plays his mind games from beyond the grave. I hate him. If it was all to do over, I would kill him. I lost so much at his hands. Now that he's dead, why don't I feel better? Why can't he leave me alone? What a fool I was. Still am, her heart corrected her thoughts.

"I need to get to work," she said aloud. "I need to at least pretend everything is normal."

About forty minutes later she was freshly showered and dressed. She trotted down the stairs. There on the foyer table was a note.

> I have an errand to run. Something I couldn't get out of. No matter what happens, remember I love you, Auntie. Please don't worry. I'll take care of everything. Stefan

Suddenly worried, she reached for her cell phone and hit the speed dial. All she got was Stefan's voice mail. "It's Charlotte. I got your note. Please call me."

She was agitated, but did not know what else she could do. She stalked into the breakfast room, but found only the morning *Chronicle*, no *Atlanta Watch*. Smothering an oath, she grabbed her purse and walked outside, looking to see if the periodical had been cast in the bushes or driveway, but found no evidence of it.

"Two days in a row," she muttered. She jumped into her car and ground the gears, spinning off.

Some time later she arrived at the parking garage for the *Chronicle*. She walked out front to a newsstand looking for the issue of the *Atlanta Watch*. The operator recognized her.

"Hi, Charlotte," he spoke familiarly and jovially. "How are you?"

"I've been better, Buddy. How about you?"

"I'm sure sorry for all the stuff happening to you," he replied, sobering. "What can I do you for?"

"I need the *Atlanta Watch* for today. You don't happen to have yesterday's too, do you?"

"I thought you had a subscription," he laughed nervously.

"They've disappeared the last couple days. I just have a bad feeling," Charlotte peered at him. "Why?"

"So you haven't seen this?" he pulled out a copy of the previous day's issue, with the headline "Harry and Charlotte's Love Child" and a picture of Stefan.

She choked, shock registering on her face. "It's not true," she coughed, transfixed at the picture.

Buddy, sympathetic, mumbled, "It's even worse," as he placed the current issue over that one. "Love Child Fingered in Dad's Murder?"

"Oh, my God," she felt faint. She threw some bills blindly at Buddy and grabbed the two issues. Buddy called after her, "Charlotte it's all bullshit. Don't let it get you down," but she was oblivious to her surroundings, blindly stepping out into the street. The screeching of tires brought her back to the present, as a car stopped just inches from her, and the driver angrily blasted his horn.

Charlotte made it across the street, pulling out her cell phone. She again tried Stefan's phone, but got only an outgoing message. In desperation she called information and got the number for the Atlanta Police Department. Dialing it, she asked for Roberts.

"I'm afraid he is not available right now," the receptionist stated.

She was suddenly frozen with fear. "Give him a message. I'm looking for my nephew Stefan. If he shows up, they are not to interview him. If they interview him without our attorney present, I'll sue them. Have him call me immediately." She rattled off her cell and work numbers, then hung up.

Once inside the building, she called Mike. "Hi, Sis," she heard his voice.

"Have you heard from Stefan?" she asked breathlessly.

"He told me early this morning that he had a busy day ahead and would talk to us later."

"Have you seen the *Atlanta Watch* yesterday and today?" she grilled him.

"No," he was instantly concerned. "Why?"

She read the headlines to him, and the note Stefan left her. "Oh, no, Charlotte," he groaned.

"And I can't get Stefan to answer his phone. Mike, I'm scared what he might do."

"This is bad. We'll make arrangements to head back to Atlanta immediately. I'll keep trying Stefan's phone."

She took the stairs up, and dialed information again, asking for the number of John Mitchem. Calling, she gave her name and asked to speak to him right away.

"John Mitchem. How may I help you, Miss Lawson?"

"I'm Melanie Cain's niece," she began breathlessly, but he interrupted her.

"I know who you are. I was retained by Mrs. Cain to keep tabs on you and your sister for most of my career."

"Me?" she asked.

"Yes, Miss Lawson. Your aunt was very concerned about you girls."

"Are you the one leaking information to the *Atlanta Watch*?" she demanded agitatedly.

"Miss Lawson, you don't know me, or you wouldn't even consider asking that question. Once a client, always a client. However, we are talking on an unsecured line, and confidentiality cannot be assured."

Charlotte closed her eyes, her back against a wall, contrite. "I'm sorry. I know that, but I don't have the luxury of meeting with you in person right now. My nephew is missing."

"The one named in the tabloids right now?"

"Yes. Stefan Chadwick."

"And you are trying to counter the allegations that he is your love child?"

"No," she was firm. "I have evidence to refute that. But he disappeared this morning. I need to find him. I'm afraid for him." She outlined briefly about the note, and her call to the police.

"Same terms?"

"I don't know Melanie's terms, but yes. Send me a bill."

Out of breath, she made her floor and walked down the hallway to her office. Ed Kline met her at the door. "What can I do?" he asked gruffly, putting his hand on her shoulder.

"I'm sorry, Ed, but I haven't done anything on the article. I need to eulogize Harry, but I just haven't found the words, and there's been so much," Charlotte's voice broke, her eyes were wild, and he could sense the hysteria near the surface.

"Don't worry. We can handle that." Ed stared at her. "What can I do for you, Charlotte?"

Even through her agitation, she was touched. "I don't know what to do, Ed. I have an investigator looking for Stefan. He disappeared this morning, and I'm afraid for him, particularly with these articles out there."

"I'll get our people to put out feelers with the usual sources. We'll find him. It will be OK," he clumsily hugged her. "Go home, Charlotte."

"I can't go back there. I'm afraid to be alone doing nothing. I'm so worried about him."

He pushed her into her office. "Have a seat and I'll send you some coffee. Let me get some people hopping."

He motioned to his chief assistant to follow him, as Charlotte moved to her desk, trying Gerry on her phone. All she got was his voice mail. She left a short message asking him to call her. She wrung her hands nervously.

Someone brought her a cup of coffee, and she thanked him absently. She reviewed the articles before her carefully. She picked up the office phone and called the police department again. She again asked to speak to Captain Roberts, but was told he was out.

She turned on her computer, letting it boot up, and stared at it. The phone rang.

"Charlotte?" Ed's voice came on. "One of the reporters on the beat has heard a rumor that Stefan was at police headquarters this morning. We're trying to confirm that."

She hung up, even more frightened. The cell phone rang insistently. She picked it up. "Ms. Lawson, this is John Mitchem. Stefan Chadwick was at the police station earlier today. However, an investigator left with him. I don't know his current whereabouts, but am working on it. I'll let you know."

"Thanks," she whispered shakily. She stood, her purse in hand. That bastard Roberts, she thought. They have Stefan. What would he have said?

Suddenly her blood froze. She remembered his words last night and his note this morning: "I'll take care of everything." Oh, my God, Stefan, she thought. What are you doing?

Chapter 62

Charlotte's reverie was interrupted as she suddenly heard voices outside her office door, and a familiar voice asking for her. Her door opened, and Mark Roberts stood there. He strode in, slamming the door behind him, leaving the protesting copy editor outside.

"Yes, Officer Roberts?" she asked in a clipped voice. "I'm busy here, and you keep intruding on my life. What can I do for you?"

He gazed at the empty screen on the computer monitor before her, as she stood, poised like a deer about to flee. "Yes, I can tell you're busy. Can you tell me why your—nephew—" he emphasized the word derisively, "would show up this morning confessing to the murder of Wilhelm Kreiser?"

All color fled from her face. "Stefan?" she gasped. "That cannot be. Where is he? Where do you have him?"

She moved quickly from behind her desk. "I must go to him. I left word you were not to interview him without a lawyer present. I'll have your badge for this."

Roberts stepped between her and the door. "You're not going anywhere, Charlotte Lawson. Please answer my question."

She tried to make her way past him, but he grabbed her arm, turned a chair in front of her desk around and pushed her into it. Placing one hand on each arm of the chair, he imprisoned her. "It is time we quit playing these games. Stefan waived counsel, refused to let us call you, and confessed to murder one this morning, how he stole your gun several months ago and planned the entire thing."

"That can't be," she gasped. "You interviewed him without contacting me, without counsel?"

"He is an adult, and waived all that. He insisted that we not call you."

"It's not true," she rasped as Mark's face came close to hers.

"How do you know?" he regarded her broodingly. She could feel the anger radiating from his body.

"Take me to him," she begged, grasping his arm and pushing against him, trying unsuccessfully to break free. "This is false imprisonment, Detective." She stopped, her eyes pleading. "Please, Mark," she said with great effort.

"You have lied. Either you're covering for him or for yourself."

She looked at him, her panic rising. She fought to keep it in check.

"It's ridiculous," she choked. "Stefan was in D.C. on Friday."

"He says he sneaked back to town just for this," Roberts said, his voice hoarse.

"That's impossible. He had an audition Friday morning at Washington Cathedral for a recital, and a meeting that afternoon with an agent interested in representing him. I know—I confirmed with the agent that weekend that Stefan was there. I can give you his number."

"Why would he be lying?" Roberts whispered, still invading her space, so close that she could feel his breath against her hot cheek.

"I—I don't know," she breathed, swallowing, faint with fear.

"You've lied to me the whole time. You didn't tell me about your pregnancy and miscarriage," he continued relentlessly.

"No," she cried. "How—?"

"Tell me about your disguises, Charlotte. Why would you feel the need to conceal your identity?"

She whitened. "It's the only way I could play. If no one knew who I was I found I could perform again."

"So you dressed up in one of your disguises to go shoot Kreiser down?"

"No," she whispered tremulously.

"What else haven't you told me, Charlotte?" he took her chin in his hand momentarily.

They stared at each other for a small lifetime, both willing the other to back down. He finally released her with a muttered oath, turning his back to her as she shivered. He leaned against the door, facing her, blocking the exit.

"A hell of a case," he cursed. "I have a confessed murderer, and the woman he's protecting with motive out the wazoo, as well as her fiancé, if the tabloids are correct. What's more, you can't verify your whereabouts at the time of the murder. You had ample time and motive to do the deed. You tell me what I should do," he finished bitterly.

"Stefan could not have done it," she found her voice, tears pooling in her eyes, blinding her. She blinked. "I know—because I am the one. I killed Harry."

He stared at her. She continued haltingly. "I have wanted to for a long time, but the time was never right. Stefan must have guessed the truth and wanted to protect me."

Roberts laughed mirthlessly. "Oh, this ought to be good."

She stood, looking at him. "What? I've been your prime suspect. You've been hanging around waiting for me to break all this time. Now that I'm ready to tell all, you're laughing? Take me to the station, read me my rights, and let's get it over with," she proclaimed fiercely. "I can't take it anymore."

"No, let's not go to all that trouble," he replied scathingly. "Let me hear it from your lips first."

"But Stefan?" she cried.

"Stefan is safe for now," he said curtly. "I've got Will chauffeuring him around trying to prove to us he's telling the truth. I didn't believe a word he said."

Charlotte sank into the chair, the room whirling around her. Roberts, seeing her turn white, went over to the nearby water dispenser and brought her a cup of cool water. Handing it to her, he took out his handkerchief, wet it in the cool water from the dispenser, and gently pressed it to the back of her neck, taking her hand and placing it over the handkerchief. Looking at him oddly, she thanked him.

He sat down in the chair beside her, waiting patiently. She sipped the water, then clutching the paper cup and his handkerchief in her hands, she began.

"I had always hoped that Harry secretly loved me, that he would come to find me. After I found out I was pregnant, I couldn't stay in Atlanta. I left for D.C., determined to make my own way. Amy and Mike were good to me. I swore her to secrecy about my pregnancy. Not even Aunt Mellie was to know. But Amy slipped and told Harry when he called."

At Roberts' questioning look, she nodded. "Yes, he called to finally check on me, to tell me he was getting married. I called him back. He spilled the whole sorry story about him and Wife Number Two. I hung up on him. Later he called Amy, and she apparently slipped and told him that I 'and the baby' were fine."

"He didn't call or come to check on you?" Roberts wanted to know.

"No," she said sadly. "I refused to ever divulge to him about Johann, particularly after—after—" she found she couldn't say the words. After a moment she continued quaveringly, "I never realized he knew anything about our baby until the policy and his letter were delivered yesterday."

"Letter?"

"With the policy was a letter to me," she admitted. "He told me how much he loved me, how sad he was that I carried the secret and the pain alone.

After I miscarried, and Aunt Mellie found me and pulled me back together, I saw no need to ever share with him about my pregnancy and miscarriage. It never occurred to me that he would mistake Stefan for our son."

"Why did you come back?" Roberts asked gently.

"Stefan was so insistent. He was hell-bent to study with Harry, despite all our efforts to dissuade him. I was not going to let him go into that situation alone. I knew from bitter personal experience what Harry could be like. Then Melanie had a stroke, and my fate was decided. I came back to care for her, and she died just a few months ago."

"It must have been hard to face him again."

"Not as bad as I feared, at least after the initial shock of seeing him again. I wove myself a coat of armor against him, and I took great pains to make sure our meetings were few and public. And I had the greatest of all motives to get along with him—Stefan. For all Harry's faults, he is the best instructor when he's on top of his game. He demands driven, perfectionist students, but he's awe-inspiring. We called a truce."

She had unconsciously slipped into the present tense talking about Kreiser. Roberts noted dryly, "This doesn't sound much like a confession to murder."

"I'm sorry," she started. "It was just that Stefan was so tied to Harry that I had to bide my time."

"So this was planned well in advance?" Roberts asked wryly.

"Not—not really," she faltered, not meeting his eyes. "It wasn't until I started worrying about Harry's interest in Stefan."

"What do you mean?"

"His demeanor around Stefan began to change. At first, I thought I was imagining things. But then more and more Harry was spending time alone with Stefan, trying to include him on recital trips. I vetoed many of these excursions, but couldn't very well tell Stefan why."

"You thought Harry was developing a sexual interest in Stefan?"

"I didn't know," she faltered again, clearly uncomfortable. She fell into an uneasy silence. He waited. Slowly she replied, "Dean Jackson tried to warn me about Harry's suspicions about Stefan being his son, but I got the signals crossed."

"When did you decide to kill Harry?" Roberts asked quietly.

"The night of the reception I held after Brad graduated last semester," Charlotte shifted uncomfortably in her chair. "Harry made a nasty comment about the past in front of the students, about how I could have been a star. He had started making digs at me, more and more in public. At first I tried to shrug them off, but they stuck like a burr, bothering me."

She relayed the story, haltingly at first. Her mind was suddenly back to that night, to her conversation with Kreiser after everyone else had left, his revelation about his illness, and his announcement that he was leaving for good.

Charlotte was brought back to the present by Roberts' question. "The night of the graduation reception? That was the night you reported the burglary," Mark broke into her thoughts.

"Yes. That happened later that night," Charlotte slowly responded. She could see his mind whirring. "I wanted to kill Harry after that night. I had loved him, carried and lost his child, had come back to Atlanta, had waited for him. I lost everything, even my self-respect. I gave up so much of my life, made a fool of myself. I had hurt Gerry—that was the worst thing of all." She took a deep breath. "The night of the graduation party for Brad, when Harry told me he was leaving for good, it was the last straw, his last rejection. That night I saw my chance and took my gun, hiding it away and reporting it stolen," she added quickly, breathlessly.

"Tell me how you killed him."

Charlotte looked down at her hands, flexing them and exhaling. "I was going to wait until Stefan had graduated and taken his trip to France. But Harry was drinking heavily again. I saw Harry flirting with one of his female students, and then we had the argument over the telephone. Something inside snapped. Stefan was out of town, and I decided I couldn't wait any longer. I retrieved my Sig Sauer and slipped into the church."

"How?" Mark cut into her narrative.

"The side door. It's unlocked during the day—easy to park, run in, and leave quickly." Charlotte faltered, closing her eyes.

"Where were you when you shot him?"

"I stood in the center of the nave and shot him while he was practicing," she whispered.

"He was alone?"

"Yes."

"No one saw you?"

"No," she was trembling. "I know my way around that church. I took lessons there myself, and subbed for him from time to time."

"Where's the gun now?"

She was silent, her eyes down, not looking at him.

"The pistol, Charlotte?" Mark repeated.

"I threw it in the river on my way to the airport."

"What about the coins you reported stolen at the same time?"

"Oh, those," she looked confused. "I—I sold them to a private collector."

"You sold them and made a false report?" his eyebrows shot up. "Who?" he persisted.

"I don't remember his name. I'll have to look it up for you," she said tremulously.

"I will need that information," Roberts looked at her intently. "Generally the police would notify dealers about rare items reported stolen."

Charlotte whitened but said nothing.

"And you shot Kreiser how many times?"

She looked at him then, mustering as much bravado as she could. "You know the answer. Why not tell me?"

"Humor me," he brought his face close to hers.

She swallowed, her back against the chair, biting her lip nervously. "Three times," she said, her eyes closed to shut out his gaze. "Once in the head, and twice in the heart. I was taking no chances."

"Damn it," muttered Roberts disgustedly, standing.

"What is it?" she stuttered, opening her eyes, frightened.

"Why are you lying to me?" he growled angrily, turning on her.

"I'm not," she was hysterical, her voice almost a scream. "I heard the shots, and I heard when he slumped over the console. I will never be able to erase those sounds from my mind as long as I live, and to know that Harry was dead by my hand."

"You heard the shots?" Mark asked, gazing at her, a peculiar expression on his face. "That's an unusual way of putting it."

"What do you mean?" she looked at him, her eyes darting past him to the door.

"Because you're lying to me," he repeated. "Stefan lies to protect you because he has read your journals and is convinced you killed Kreiser. Now you lie to protect him, because he has confessed. I'm not any closer to solving this damned murder," Roberts swore. "But if you heard the shots, you know who killed him. Who else are you protecting, Charlotte?" He turned and grabbed her by her arms, shaking her. "Tell me. Is it Gerry Fellowes?"

"No one," she insisted, her eyes wide as she shook her head violently.

"Journals?" she echoed suddenly, as her mind locked onto his words. "What journals?"

"Stefan said he found the journals you kept during college in the attic and read them. He claims he hated Kreiser for hurting you, and stole the gun and killed him."

"He couldn't have found my journals," she looked wildly at Roberts. "No one knew where they were."

There was suddenly a knock at the door. A man stuck his head through the door. "Sorry to interrupt, Charlotte. There's a special delivery just arrived for you. The kid said it was urgent."

The man looked at the two curiously. Roberts released her and rubbed his temples wearily as Charlotte silently accepted the package. His mind was whirring with questions as to why he had just obtained a second confession to murder, as she shakily opened the envelope. He glanced up through the glass frontispiece of the door and saw Russell McCall hurriedly leaving.

As the silence grew, he looked over at Charlotte. She was staring white-faced at the contents.

"What is it?" he asked curiously.

She stood up. "I've got to go," she spoke, stuffing the envelope in her purse and moving toward the door.

"Oh, no, you don't," he grabbed her arm and restrained her, forcing her back into the chair.

"You don't understand," she pleaded, her breath coming in quiet pants. "It's an emergency."

"Do you know an author named C. C. Langley?" he asked her, standing over her, again imprisoning her in the chair.

"Of course," she looked at him uncomprehendingly. "Why?"

"Who is he, and how do I find him?" Mark insisted.

She stared at him. "I am C. C. Langley," she admitted.

"You wrote the book *One Organist Less*?" he was incredulous.

She paled. "Yes, it was a novel, Detective, fiction. Why are you asking me about this?"

"So you sent an autographed copy of this book to Kreiser? Was it a threat? A calling card?" he watched her closely.

"I don't understand," she squirmed in her chair. "No, I never sent Harry a copy. I wrote the book back when I was pregnant. I was upset, and it made me feel better. Please, Mark, I need to go."

"Why would a copy of your novel be found at the murder site with an inscription 'To H-K from C.L.'?" he asked her intently, not releasing the arms of the chair.

"I don't know," she cried, clearly agitated. "H-K? H—Oh, no. That can't be," she whispered, again trying to escape.

He was too strong for her, and she stared at him wild-eyed. She desperately wrapped her arms around his neck and kissed him full on the mouth. Caught completely off-guard, Roberts released the arms of the chair and tried to pull away. As he did, she stood, clinging to him, her arms still around him. His mouth parted involuntarily, and he found himself kissing her back, one arm reaching for her waist to pull her to him, and the other entangling her hair at the nape of her neck as his mouth claimed hers. For a brief moment they were as one.

Suddenly she pushed him violently away, took one step and snatched the door open, running out of the room. Stunned, he looked after her bewildered, before running after her, cursing under his breath. Making it to the reception area, he looked around him dazedly.

"Delivery for Charlotte Lawson," a delivery boy held up an envelope. Mark flashed his badge and snatched the envelope away.

Ripping it open and looking inside, he saw a Roman coin. With it was a note, stating simply, "Meet me. You know where."

Chapter 63

Charlotte ran breathlessly to the elevator, catching it just as the doors were closing. Slipping inside, she hit the button for the service floor.

Within seconds she was in the parking garage. She ran to her car, cranking it and pulling out. Looking behind her, she saw no sign of Roberts, and breathed a sigh of relief. She knew that the coin was a summons, and what she had to do.

While speeding along, she was oblivious to traffic, suddenly back reliving the day of her aunt's memorial service, Gerry's encounter after the service, and her confrontation with Kreiser. She thought that the chapter was closed on Kreiser, but then his disclosures the night of the graduation party had momentarily reignited her hopes yet again, until he dashed them once again with his announcement that he was leaving permanently.

She thought about Stefan's confessing to murder. Oh, my dear child, she thought, that I've unwittingly pulled you into this mess is unforgiveable.

She was brought back to the present by the sight of the familiar wrought-iron gate. Moments later, she screeched to a halt in front of the house. She noted a black Mercedes sedan parked in front.

Unlocking the door, she ran pell-mell through the empty house, checking the rooms, racing up the stairs to Stefan's room. There was no one there. She rummaged through his drawers, looked in his closets, peered under the bed, but found no journals.

"He must have made it up," Charlotte tried to reassure herself. "Amy must have mentioned something to him about my keeping journals."

As she straightened up, she saw a piece of paper on the floor. Picking it up, she noted it was a torn ticket stub, one from an organ recital she had attended just days before her miscarriage, the stub she had stuck in the journal when she wrote her impressions of the recital afterward. "No. It can't be," she cried disbelievingly.

She stared at the stub, fascinated for a moment, then disappeared.

Racing down the back stairs, she ran through the empty kitchen. Pausing a moment, she reached toward the counter and withdrew a sharp butcher knife from the wooden block, then quickly made her way out the back door, sprinting across the lawn to the boathouse.

Silently she slipped into the boathouse. Standing in the shadows a minute, she let her eyes adjust to the dimness. Then she made her way down beside a wooden narrow deck alongside the motor launch. She stopped short, staring at the man sitting on the step.

It was Gerry, and he was staring back at her. She looked down at his feet, at the old rusty lockbox, already open. Inside were a number of ancient coins and a bound stack of $100 bills.

Heedless of the rust and dirt, she picked her way around the lockbox and made her way to sit beside Gerry, laying the knife on the step beside her.

"It's already open. You sent me the coin?" she asked softly.

He nodded. "I knew you'd come when you saw it." He looked down at the contents of the lockbox. "Russ discovered this mess. I saw you had tried to call me this morning, and had come looking for you. Russ was upset. I sent him to your office with the coin to summon you."

He stared at the lockbox. "So this is where the contents of the safe disappeared. Why? And where's the gun, Charl? They mustn't find it. We have to get rid of it," she heard him say.

Roberts cursed as he took off after Charlotte, only to lose her at the elevator. He ran down the four flights of stairs onto the front, but saw no sign of her.

He breathlessly took out his cell phone, and punched the speed-dialer. "Will? Where are you?"

"I got the kid with me, and we are on the way to the house. What's up?"

"She has given me the slip," Roberts said, jumping into his car. "But she got two deliveries as I was here—the last one a Roman coin."

It suddenly came to him. "Will, meet me at the Cain residence."

Ringing off, he dialed Randy.

"Some news. The Sig Sauer favored by Miss Lawson at the gun shop was reported stolen this morning. Nothing else was taken."

"That cannot be good," Roberts remarked. "I need backup at the Cain residence right away."

Randy remarked, "I just got a warrant based on the kid's statement, and Will had said he had talked Stefan into allowing us to search the place."

"I need you and backup to meet me there. Lights, no sirens. Get the local county S.O.'s cooperation. Tell them to meet us there."

Stefan cried excitedly, "There's a cab by the gate."

Will stopped and flagged the driver down. Showing his badge, he asked, "Did you just let someone off here?"

"Yes, a high-tipping lady. I was sticking around to see if she might need another cab."

Will thanked him, then scrambled back in his car. They pulled up to the house, where Charlotte's BMW and a black Mercedes were parked. Stefan jumped out and ran toward the door. Will took off after him.

Stefan bounded up the stairs, calling, "Aunt Charlotte? Aunt Charlotte? Where are you?"

He burst into her room, Will puffing up the stairs behind him. Stefan looked out the window. He said, "I just saw someone going into the boathouse."

Surprised at Gerard's question, Charlotte echoed, "What did I do with it? What do you mean?"

Gerry acted as surprised as she. "If I had found it I would have gotten rid of it already." He shook her gently. "We need to throw it away, Charl. The cops could be crawling this area at any time."

"Just a damn minute," she interrupted irritably, standing to face him. "I'm trying to protect you. You claim you want to protect me, and then you frame me. Why would you plant evidence?"

"I AM trying to protect you. What are you talking about? God, Charl, I'm not going to sit by and let them prosecute you for murder," Gerard whispered. She noticed that his voice trembled. "I know you were there."

"Don't pretend to me, Gerry, not now," her lip trembled. "You killed him, and left my book on the altar for them to find. Why?"

"Me? I thought of killing Kreiser several times, but I wasn't here," he said slowly.

"I saw your new limousine at the church that day. I heard the shots. But it didn't matter if you pulled the trigger," she grabbed his arm. "I was to blame. I—I love you, Gerry. I can't lose you, and I am willing to go to hell for you. I'm taking the rap. I just told Roberts I killed Harry. They're on their way to find me now."

"Limousine?" Gerard echoed confusedly. He stood and grabbed her by the arms. "I didn't kill Harry, Charl. I didn't get back to Atlanta until late Friday night, and I went straight to the hospital to check on Tom."

He stopped as it dawned on him. "You didn't kill him?"

"No, Gerry. I stopped at the church on my way to the airport. I was just outside the door when I heard the shots. I did not go in. I saw the limo and was afraid that I would see you. I knew I drove you to it, and I couldn't bear it. I ran away."

He pulled her to him and hugged her with relief, and she clung to him. "Darling, it wasn't me. I swear it. Good heavens, Charl, I was so scared. The thought of their arresting you was killing me. I had to cancel my trip." He stopped short. "You saw my new limo at the church that day? My God, that means—"

"Gerry," Charlotte interrupted him, "the police have Stefan. Mark Roberts told me Stefan confessed to them. He told them he read my journals."

She pulled away from him and looked in horror at the box. "Where are my journals?" she screamed. "You didn't give them to Stefan, did you?" she demanded, aghast.

"No," Gerry was confused, taking her arm. "I don't understand. Journals?"

"When I moved back to Atlanta, I threw my journals in our lockbox. I assumed they were safe there."

"They were until I found them," a voice said. Gerry grabbed her, a shot rang out, and suddenly she and Gerard tumbled backward onto the deck.

Charlotte, stunned from the fall, looked at Gerard beside her and saw blood coming from his left shoulder, his eyes closed. He lay still. She screamed in terror, throwing her arms around him. "God, no," she cried. "Please, Gerry, I love you. Oh, Jesus, no."

She looked toward where the shot had been fired. She recoiled as a tall woman came out from out of the shadows. "But—why? Why did you shoot him?" she whispered.

"I always hated Gerry for being everything George wasn't, for surviving when George died. And then he committed the ultimate sin by getting engaged to you.

"It has always been so hard being in your shadow," Katharine Fellowes' face came into full view. "Why you could hold such fascination for my two brothers and Harry Kreiser too is just amazing. But you and your sister always had some kind of charm for the men in my life. By the way, this is a fine gun Gerry bought you."

"My gun? But how did you get it?" Charlotte asked tremulously, standing and placing her body between Katharine and Gerry.

"Did you know this gun was to be a birthday present for me? I knew all about it. Gerry ordered twin Sigs, one for me. But when I got mine, it was not a Sig but a Beretta. I later found out Gerry had given you the gun.

"How did I get it, you ask? Little Cece tells me everything. When she talked about the safe and described the contents Stefan had showed her and Russ, and relayed the story about the coins, my mind starting hatching the plan. She had memorized the combination from watching Stefan open the safe. She' a lot smarter than people give her credit.

"The night of that boy's reception was perfect. I saw you throwing yourself at Harry. You are such a slut. So I took your gun, the coins, and the money. I had Cece seduce her boyfriend back at our place, so he would be otherwise detained. I accidentally tripped the alarm on the way out. I almost didn't get away in time."

"And the journals?" Charlotte was only half-listening, her eyes on Gerry. She moved forward slightly.

"I knew all about your hiding place from years ago. I caught you two hiding stuff in it as kids. I broke into it and found the journals. What a fascinating read. I thought it'd shake Stefan up a little to read about his true parentage."

"Stefan does know his true parentage," Charlotte replied quietly. "You didn't find the DNA evidence in the safe?"

"You are lying," Katharine laughed, a brittle sound.

"What did you do to Harry?"

"Your gun worked perfectly for knocking off Harry," the woman replied, a malevolent smile on her face. "Gerry wasn't the only champion sharpshooter in the family. I knew when Harry's lessons with Cece were. Who better, and who would ever suspect me?"

"Why the coins?" Charlotte asked tentatively, taking another step forward.

"Just liked the story about them. I sent one to Harry before I offed him. And I left your book as a clue pointing to you. Even wore your wig. Yes, when I went through your room during the party, I found your disguises."

Charlotte looked up into the wild eyes of Katharine as the latter came toward her, stopping only a few feet from her, the gun pointed at her. "I don't understand. Why Harry?"

"Harry was drunk at my place the night before the reception, and spilled about Stefan being his son. I thought, that's just rich. Here I have been busting my ass to promote Cece, and dear little Stefan just falls into the greener pastures. And I tried to do everything to get Harry to notice me, but he only had eyes for you and ears for dearest Stefan. I finally thought that enough was enough. I was tired of the nepotism, never able to win."

Katharine continued, only a few feet away, her eyes dilated. "You know, Harry had earlier invited me to move to New York with him. Of course, when he sobered up, he changed his mind. That was the final blow."

Charlotte looked steadily at her, although inside she was shaking. "You're wrong, you know. Stefan is not Harry's son."

"Don't lie to me," Katharine warned, her voice ominously raised, the gun pointed at Charlotte.

"It's true," Charlotte pleaded. "I swear to you that I am telling the truth."

"And Gerry's limo was delivered that very day," Katharine continued, as if not hearing Charlotte. "It was a sign, so convenient. I drove it myself to the church."

Charlotte stumbled slightly against the edge of the steps, unobtrusively picking up the knife beside her on the steps and holding it hidden in the folds of her dress. "Please put the gun down, Kat."

"No," she replied. "We don't have much time."

"Before what?" Charlotte turned slowly toward her.

"Before the police show up to find your body," Katharine replied. "I really didn't mean to go this far. I thought it was enough to pin the murder on you, and didn't count on all this collateral mess. But Gerry was still in love with you, and was messing everything up."

Charlotte noted that Katharine's hands were encased in latex gloves. "Of course, what with your body, Gerry's here, Stefan's involvement, the gun and the journals, they'll be so confused with their number of suspects and theories the police will be busy for months. I'm betting on some murder-suicide theory. I can't wait to find out. And since I heard you say Stefan confessed, that would be just wonderful. I've eliminated all the riff-raff. And everyone thinks I'm in my own bed with Prince Valium, too wasted to be suspected."

"You don't think they'll finally figure out that you're the 'H-K' on the novel inscription?"

"They think you sent it to Harry," Kat laughed wildly.

"You're sick, Hell-Kat. You need help," Charlotte whispered.

"Don't say that," Katharine yelled, and Charlotte saw her click off the safety.

Charlotte screamed and swung out with the knife with all her might, slashing across Katharine's abdomen and striking her right hand holding the gun. The gun went off, and the bullet whizzed dangerously close to Charlotte's ear. The momentum of the knife did its job, slicing Katharine's hand open. Katharine cried out in surprise and pain, dropping the gun, which clattered on the floor and bounced past Charlotte beside Gerard's inert form.

Charlotte turned to grab for the gun, but Katharine lunged and snatched her by the neck of her dress with her left hand, dragging Charlotte bodily backwards up the wooden steps toward her and away from the gun.

Charlotte jerked away, turned and stumbled, finding her feet, and was suddenly free. Off-balance, she fell forward against the steps heavily, bruised and winded. Katharine fell backward, then staggered up from the floor, and turned. Reaching up under her skirt, she produced a second gun, the matching Sig Sauer, with her left hand. As Charlotte tried to get up and slipped, tumbling forward again, Katharine took aim.

A shot rang out.

A voice cried, "Police! Freeze! Put your hands in the air!"

Surely I am dead, Charlotte thought. She lay there, face down, winded, numb, until she felt someone roll her over, and was smothered in a great hug. Dazed, she opened her eyes and saw Stefan's tear-streaked face as he called her name again and again, holding her face in his hands. The boathouse seemed full of voices and figures, all swarming around her.

"Stefan?" she croaked. Suddenly galvanized, she turned to look at Gerard. "Gerry—is he—?"

She caught sight of Gerard. He was propped up sideways, her gun in his right hand lying on the floor beside him. Looking around painfully, she saw the fallen figure of Katharine, surrounded by police, guns drawn.

Mark Roberts was suddenly standing over her. Leaning down, he said to Stefan, "Here, give me a hand," as he helped lift her up. She staggered as her feet found the floor, but she murmured, "Excuse me," and pushed her way to Gerard.

"I thought she had killed you," she sobbed as she knelt beside him.

Gerard smiled wanly as medics came swarming up. "I'm sorry, Officer," he said weakly to Roberts, "I couldn't let Katherine kill Charlotte, so I winged her." He dropped the gun gently on the deck beside him.

The medic said, "I'm sorry, miss, but we need to ask you to move so that we can treat him."

Roberts gently led her away to a bench not far away. Again she was smothered by Stefan, who asked, "Aunt Charlotte, are you OK?"

"I think so," she was shaking uncontrollably.

"We almost didn't make it in time," Roberts told her solemnly. "A second later would have been too late."

"I thought Gerry was dead," she heard herself say. Suddenly the realization of how close they had both come to death hit her, and the room started spinning.

She woke up later, finding herself on a gurney beside an ambulance. Stefan was standing by her, wiping her forehead with a cool cloth. She smiled.

"You fainted," he smiled at her.

"Thank God you are safe," she breathed, squeezing his hand. He grasped her hand tightly.

The medic said, "I don't think anything is broken, but she's lacerated and bruised all over. She'll hurt like hell tomorrow. She'll need X-rays for us to be sure."

"Are you feeling better?" Mark Roberts' face came into view.

"Much better," she whispered.

"Why did you run away from me at the office?" Roberts asked her.

"I didn't know where Stefan was, but you mentioned the journals, and the coin appeared. I knew it was from Gerry, and I was trying to get away to meet him. I was convinced he must have killed Harry and was trying to get word to me to meet him. I was convinced no one else but Gerry could have found my journals. When I came back to Atlanta, I buried them in our secret hiding place. It seemed fitting."

Stefan looked at her with tears in his eyes. "When we got home from the recital Tuesday night and I went to my room, the journals were on my bed. I at first thought maybe you left them for me to read, but there was a note: 'From a friend. Don't tell anyone.' I read them over several nights, and became so angry.

"Every night I sneaked downstairs to hear you playing. I heard you crying, the comments about hating Harry, that death was too good for him. I was scared then that perhaps you had snapped and killed him. And when I found out that he," Stefan indicated Roberts," was hanging around, I knew he suspected you. I had to protect you. So I told them I did it."

Charlotte reached up and touched Stefan's cheek. "And I was convinced Gerry had killed him. I went to the church that day, but saw the limo there. I was hoping to stop something terrible. Then I heard the shots. I knew I was to blame. I was determined to protect Gerry, even if I had to take the fall.

"When Detective Roberts told me you confessed, I was frightened out of my mind. I was worried perhaps you had taken the gun. I then said I killed Harry because I was so afraid that perhaps it was true—maybe you did sneak back and kill him."

Stefan looked her with tears in his eyes. "I'm sorry."

"Me too," Charlotte touched his cheek. Turning to Roberts, she continued, "I was afraid for Stefan. I saw the coin and knew Gerry was sending me a message to meet him at the boathouse. I was sure Gerry must have killed Harry, because of me. At that point I didn't care what happened to me—I just had to protect both of them. But when you told me about the inscription in the book, I thought Gerry was actually framing me for the murder. It didn't matter. If it wasn't for me, he wouldn't be in trouble, or so I thought.

"It never crossed my mind to suspect that Katharine, who we called Hell-Kat, was the murderer. I had forgotten about the autographed book I gave her."

Roberts nodded. "And she sent you a coin to meet her, but you had already run out on me."

He peered at her closely. "Why did you kiss me?" he asked quietly.

Charlotte blushed. "I knew precious time was ticking, and I couldn't think of any other way to escape." She smiled shamefacedly.

As men came by pulling a gurney with Gerry, Stefan stood aside. Charlotte sat up. "Will he be OK?"

"Hell, I'm not dead," Gerry smiled at her. "I have good ears and reflexes. I heard the noise behind us, and tried to pull you out of the way. Thankfully, Kat missed, hitting me in the shoulder."

"I'm so glad," she breathed, her eyes shining, as she held out her hand and he took it. Stefan looked on at them, beaming.

As the EMTs loaded Gerry into the ambulance, Stefan turned to his aunt, hugging her again. "I'm sorry—I threw your journals in the river," he said, tears in his eyes. "I thought the police would find them and think you killed Harry."

"That's the best place to bury the past," she tousled his hair. Suddenly she asked, "You know you're not Harry's son, don't you?"

"I wondered a few times," Stefan confessed, "and he started acting a little strangely the last few months too. The evening you had me put the money in the safe, I found the envelope with the information about my real parents. I kept it. I asked Dad point-blank about it. He set me straight, and he told me about your being pregnant with Dr. K's baby and losing him. So I knew about that when we talked on the plane, but waited to see if you were going to say anything about it."

"I never wanted you to know my sordid past, and what a failure your Aunt Charlotte was."

"You didn't fail," he said to her solemnly. "I'm so proud of you, Auntie."

She felt a glow inside, as Roberts pointed. Will was over at the other side of the boathouse talking excitedly to a young man Stefan's age.

"That's Russ," Charlotte whispered.

Will and Russell walked over to them. "Great news—Russell has all the activities in the boathouse on videotape," Will announced.

They were astounded. Russ was modest. "Well, I was experimenting on a security system of my own, so installed some devices around here. I kept hearing noises around here, and set up some cameras and listening devices. I caught Miss Fellowes on tape breaking into this box. I was too surprised to know what to do about it.

"Then I found the mess today. Gerry had just pulled up, looking for Miss Charlotte. I showed him the lockbox, but didn't have time to tell him about Miss Fellowes' being here earlier. He asked me to run the errand to your office. But the cameras were rolling."

Stefan looked at his aunt with shining eyes. "I don't know what I would have done if something happened to you," he told her.

Charlotte closed her eyes. She had always told herself that Aunt Melanie and Amy loved her because they had to—she was family, if the black sheep of the fold. She never knew for sure. Furthermore, she had spent many fruitless years trying to win Kreiser's love.

Now she learned that Stefan knew her past, all of it, and still loved her. And Gerry had been willing to destroy evidence to protect her, even though he suspected her of killing Kreiser. She suddenly felt secure and loved unconditionally—what she had waited a lifetime to experience.

Chapter 64

Gerry awoke the next morning, finding himself in a hospital bed. As he stretched, he was rudely reminded of his injured shoulder. He grimaced. As he gingerly tried to readjust his position, his eyes fell on Charlotte, sitting in a chair beside his bed.

"Hey," he smiled drowsily. "What are you doing here?"

"The doctor released me this morning. He said I'd probably look like hell until the bruises faded," she smiled shyly at him. "The doctor said if you behaved you might be released as well."

"That's good news," he yawned. "I have lots of work to do."

"No, you need someone to take care of you for once," Charlotte stood. "I'd like to go home with you and take on that task."

He hesitated, but she took his hand. "I really mean it, Gerry," she whispered. "I want to be with you, to take care of you for a change. What would it take for me to prove it to you?"

He gripped her hand, but she could see the doubt in his eyes. She continued, "I wanted to tell you the other day, but you wouldn't let me. The night I went home with you, I chose you. You were the one I wanted to spend the rest of my life with."

He started to speak, but she laid a finger over his lips. "You misunderstood me all this time. I did hate Harry. I wanted to kill him, but I didn't.

"You thought that night I was dreaming of Harry. I was. But the recurring nightmares were of Kreiser finding out about our baby, choking me, my killing him and being handcuffed and taken away." Tears shone in her eyes. "You thought I was grieving over Harry and his rejection, but I was being haunted by Harry."

"Oh, Charl," he murmured, taking her hand and kissing it.

"I went to the cathedral to give Harry a head's up that day, that I was going to complete my organ degree and continue my studies. When I was at the doors of the cathedral that afternoon, I heard the shots. I was just outside the door about to go in. I had seen the limo and was convinced it was you. I knew I was at fault, that I led you to it. I couldn't face you, and ran away.

"All the way to the airport I thought of nothing but what was going to happen to you, and what would I do without you. I stopped at the airport bar for a drink, because I was shaking so badly I knew others would notice. I ended up drinking several in quick succession. I made the decision then that if it was necessary I would take the rap, because I couldn't face the thought of your going to jail for me."

"Charl, you don't have to do this," Gerry whispered. "It's over."

She continued. "No, please listen to me. When you were lying on the floor of the boathouse, it almost killed me. I thought you were dead. I no longer cared if Kat killed me, but I had to live long enough to make sure you and Stefan didn't take the fall for Harry's murder."

She gazed at him. "I love you, Gerry. All those years I was chasing a feeling, something that never was. I had convinced myself that the feeling was love, against all evidence to the contrary. And you were always there when Harry pushed me away. I can't believe you stuck with me all that time. I was so foolish."

Gerry smiled. "You are so bewitching. If only I could believe this wasn't a dream."

She pinched him playfully, and he cried, "Ouch! Why did you do that?"

"It's not a dream," she was suddenly serious. "I can only hope that you still want me."

"I'll have to think about it," he said slowly, his eyes intent upon her. "After all, I took a bullet for you. I've gone through hell for you. Our relationship has so far been fraught with peril."

She looked away, embarrassed. "Is there someone else you'd prefer?"

He laughed. "No one holds a candle to you for finding adventure."

He pulled her down to him, and she kissed him fervently.

"Are you sure about this?" he whispered the familiar line. "You know, once I start . . ."

"Will you feel differently about me after this?" she shared the joke.

"Where were you? I worried that you had backed out on me," Stefan grabbed his aunt by the arm.

"I had something I had to do first," Charlotte informed him. "I went by the cathedral, played the Debussy and lit a candle for Harry. It was what he wanted." She faltered. "I knew I could not handle playing that in public today, even for him, especially for him."

Stefan stared at her. "After all that has happened?"

"I had to forgive Harry in order to let go," she ruffled his hair and reached out to straighten his tie. "I couldn't do this otherwise."

"How do you feel?" Stefan asked her as they stood in the wings, listening to the orchestra tuning in the hall.

"Nervous," she replied. "But more like I used to feel before performance. The adrenaline is there, but I'm not frozen. And I always loved playing in this room. Bless Emilie Spivey for her dream."

Andrei Kutuzov came up to Charlotte. "Thanks so much for your help," he beamed.

"It was my pleasure. I wish you the best," she held out her hand, but he threw his arms around her neck and kissed her cheek.

After he left, Stefan asked, "What was that all about?"

"Andy is now the organist and choirmaster at the cathedral," she said quietly. "Only as an interim. He has the opportunity to apply and become permanent if they like him, and in any event he'll end up with an associate position if he wants it."

"How did you manage that?" Stefan whistled low.

"I wrote him a letter of reference. Rev. Wolverly and Peter Conrad had a heart-to-heart talk about what it takes to keep the music and liturgy moving smoothly. It seems Wolverly ended up missing Harry more than he ever thought possible. And then the memorials started pouring in for all sorts of church projects, not just the music program.

"The Pastor came to see me a few days ago, and asked me to take Harry's position. I told him I couldn't do it; there were too many ghosts for me there. But I persuaded him that Andy would provide a young, fresh perspective on the music program, while preserving the traditions already in place."

She frowned. "I knew the AGO chapter might be mad at me for not recommending the application process be opened up right away, but Wolverly had been on the verge of hamstringing the program with his plans, and I couldn't bear to see Harry's legacy die with him."

Stefan looked at her in wonder. She laughed. "Rev. Wolverly and I have become friends, surprisingly. He hasn't converted me to Romanism yet, but I see a big gap in my life where I never gave God a lot of thought except as someone to pray to just before performing. Yet God has pulled me from the edge of the abyss more than once. So I'm giving more time and attention to the Church, trying to catch up on what I've missed."

She stared out pensively at the organ console. Stefan followed her look. "Don't think twice about it," he said confidently. "There's no one but you and the organ—remember that. Everyone else is irrelevant."

Charlotte smiled at him. "How did you get to be so smart?"

"I had some good mentors," he quipped. His face suddenly solemn, he asked, "Are you over—Harry?"

"Yes," she nodded soberly. "And when I thought I had lost him, I realized how much I love Gerry, and how my foolish obsessive self-destructive tendencies had almost destroyed both of us." Taking his hand, she asked, "What about you, Stefan?"

"I could hate Harry for what you went through, Auntie."

"Please don't. I lost too many years wrapped up in those feelings, chasing a dream that never was. If I can forgive, so can you. Don't make my mistake. And don't forget my responsibility in bringing it all on myself. Remember the gift of himself Harry gave you. You are the next generation—you have so much to share."

Stefan nodded solemnly. "Maybe I'll go by and light a candle for him after this." Suddenly changing subject, he asked her, "Did Dean Jackson tell you his news about your degree?"

Charlotte nodded.

"Dr. K had approached him about conferring your degree at graduation ceremony. You had completed everything but your senior recital. It's about time."

"No," Charlotte demurred. "Senior recital was a large part of the grade."

"Auntie, it wasn't your fault. You earned your degree, and Dr. K himself acknowledged it. He even had the paperwork and degree ready to present. So even he was willing to concede after all this time. Accept it as your due."

"I have a confession," she smiled. "I had made a decision. The Friday of Harry's murder I was trying to contact him. I was going to complete my organ studies anyway. I was going to take the plunge and talk to Alan Meredith over the weekend while in D.C. I wanted to elicit Alan's help in applying again, and wanted to give Harry a head's up in case Alan called him. Harry had once promised to give me a reference, and I know that was what he most wanted."

She paused, her tone wistful. "Performance may not be the primary goal now. But I've always had an interest in performance practice and music history. What a waste I made of my life." The last words she whispered. Tears stung her eyes.

Stefan laughed. "Don't cry, Auntie. All this is supposed to be good news. And you're still as good as ever. Don't give up on performance yet. I have a surprise for you."

"What?" she smiled, blinking.

"After graduation, for your birthday, we're going to New York City," he announced. "I have us console time reserved at Riverside. That's where you were going to play your post-graduation recital, wasn't it?"

She looked at him, her shock evident. "How—how did you know?"

"Dr. K let it slip when he disclosed your senior program. It was as though he had forgotten I was there. He told how he had cancelled your recital, and how much he regretted it."

Stefan's face flushed momentarily with anger. Charlotte laid her hand on his shoulder. "Let it go, Stefan."

It had finally been decided that a recital in Harry's memory would be presented by his students, with some additional selections by the symphony and chorus. Spivey Hall had been selected. It had taken a month to finalize the arrangements. Jackson had insisted that Charlotte play something. She had demurred, still nervous about performing in public. But it was Stefan who overcame her objections and chose the selections for her.

"The Bach E-flat major—so that the Dean can explain in his eulogy about its being your first piece you studied with Dr. K at the age of 12—and the Durufle *Sicilienne*—because it was his favorite, and no one is better qualified to play it than his favorite student," Stefan had stated confidently.

"Oh, so I am not good enough to do the Toccata?" she had demanded impishly.

"You can't have that one—it's mine," he smiled his roguish smile.

They had reversed roles; Stefan was now the mentor. He coached her, making her rehearse in front of Dean Jackson, having her record herself with a sequencer and play it back while she walked around the room and critiqued herself, her touch, her registration, her volumes. She was amazed at Stefan's maturity and leadership role as he planned the recital, coordinated with the various performers, worked up the program, and consulted with others on all the details. He had a natural easy-going demeanor that amicably resolved differences and built consensus.

He glanced at the program, satisfied. "We start with Durufle, and we end with Durufle. The chorus, organ and symphony will do the *Introit* and *Offertoire* from the Requiem, and you and I will finish off with the Suite."

"Harry would like that," she murmured.

"Dean Jackson said the Brahms was your idea."

"Yes," she acknowledged.

"I'm glad Gerry made it," Stefan observed with a big smile. "How is he?"

"It's hard for him. He feels guilty about Katharine's illness, and has retained the best counsel for her. But it doesn't look good for the defense. He's torn, and she is his sister. The state is fighting any insanity defense, but I don't know that she is competent to stand trial. The police have been investigating Cecelia's involvement as an accessory. That has been difficult for Gerry to bear as well. There's also a lot of publicity. But he's Gerry, and he'll make it. He realizes now that he can't save Kat from herself.

"Gerry had his own case of unrequited love: he always wanted his sister Katharine to love and acknowledge him as her brother, even if she loved George more. I had always known that, and tried to make friends with her too. We both failed, him with Kat, and me with Harry."

She looked down at her hands. "Stefan, I want you to be the first to know. Gerry and I are about to set a date. Just a private ceremony. He's even offered to set me up in Paris to study." She paused. "Maybe you and I could room together," she teased him.

"That's great news!" Stefan kissed her on the cheek, beaming. "But are you sure? I mean, there are other possible suitors out there." Pointing, he teased her, "Looks like you have a fan in the crowd."

Stefan gestured toward the stage door in the back of the auditorium, where Charlotte spied Mark Roberts speaking with Dean Jackson. She blushed. She turned to Stefan accusatorily. "You put him up to come, didn't you?"

He just smiled. They stood waiting together as the program began, listening to the chorus. Then he kissed her cheek and pushed her forward.

Now the time had come, and she stepped toward the console. A hush fell over the room as she took her place and checked her registration. She smiled just before her attack.

Playing was just like telling a story. She felt as though part of her life was rolling as waves of music out into the corners of the room. Everyone faded away, and there was nothing but the music washing over her, exhaling from her fingers, her feet, her pores, her breath.

While she was sad at the fact that Harry was gone, that their time together was fraught with misunderstanding, and that their stars were doomed to be crossed, she was finally at peace. And she knew that somewhere, somehow, Harry Kreiser approved.